Runaway
Series

USA TODAY BESTSELLING AUTHOR

DEVNEY PERRY

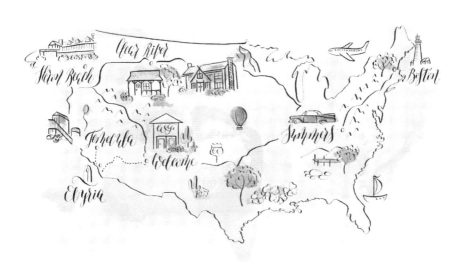

OTHER TITLES

THE EDENS SERIES

Christmas in Quincy - Prequel

Indigo Ridge

Juniper Hill

Garnet Flats

Jasper Vale

Crimson River

Sable Peak

TREASURE STATE WILDCATS SERIES

Coach

Blitz

CLIFTON FORGE SERIES

Steel King

Riven Knight

Stone Princess

Noble Prince

Fallen Jester

Tin Queen

JAMISON VALLEY SERIES

The Coppersmith Farmhouse

The Clover Chapel

The Lucky Heart

The Outpost

The Bitterroot Inn

The Candle Palace

MAYSEN JAR SERIES

The Birthday List

Letters to Molly

The Dandelion Diary

LARK COVE SERIES

Tattered

Timid

Tragic

Tinsel

Timeless

RUNAWAY SERIES

Runaway Road

Wild Highway

Quarter Miles

Forsaken Trail

Dotted Lines

CALAMITY MONTANA SERIES

The Bribe

The Bluff

The Brazen

The Bully

The Brawl

The Brood

STANDALONES

Ivy

Rifts and Refrains

A Little Too Wild

HOLIDAY BROTHERS

The Naughty, The Nice and The Nanny
Three Bells, Two Bows and One Brother's Best Friend
A Partridge and a Pregnancy

Runaway Road

1

LONDYN

"LONDYN, please. Please, don't do this."

Please, don't do this.

If I had a quarter for every time I'd heard that sentence from this man in the last eight years, I'd be a richer woman.

"Goodbye, Thomas." I ended the call. Since he usually called back five seconds after I hung up on him, I turned the damn thing off and tossed it across the bed to my best friend, who stood on the other side. "Here."

"Ack." Gemma fumbled it, she'd always been a butterfingers, and it fell unharmed onto the fluffy white down comforter. She snatched it up. "What do you mean, *here*?"

"Keep it. Smash it. I don't care. But I'm not taking it with me." I folded another T-shirt and laid it in my suitcase.

The entire thing was packed with brand-new clothes, most with the tags still attached. There wasn't a stitch of silk or satin to be found. Nothing I was taking required a press or steam and there sure as hell wasn't a pair of heels stuffed inside.

I had jeans. Normal jeans. I hadn't owned a pair in years. Now I had ten. Some had distressed patches by the knees. Some had frayed hems. Some were slouchy—or boyfriend, as the labels read.

Along with my denim, I had tees. White. Gray. Black. Navy. All the same colors as the suits I'd worn for years, but this time everything was machine-washable cotton. I might even wear them without a bra.

My wardrobe would no longer be a prison. Neither would this house. Neither would my phone.

"You have to take a phone, Londyn." Gemma planted her hands on her hips. Her cream suit was perfect—I used to have the same one. Her dark hair was styled in a tight chignon, exactly how I used to style my blond mane.

"No." I folded the last T-shirt. "No phone."

"What? That's—it's . . . insane. And stupid."

I shrugged. "We've both done it before."

"And we were both stupid before. We're lucky we didn't end up as skin suits." She threw her long arms out at her sides, huffing as she shook her head. "Take your phone."

"No."

"Londyn," she snapped. Gemma acted angry but her anxious gaze spoke otherwise. She was simply worried. If I were in her Louboutins, I would be too. "How will I find you?"

"You won't find me. That's the point." I rounded the bed and took her pink-manicured hands in my own. I'd missed our standing date at the salon for the past three weeks and my nails were wrecked. I'd ripped off my shellac and chewed them to the nub. "I'm going to be okay."

She looked at me, standing three inches taller. "Please, don't do this."

"No," I whispered. "Not you too."

"Londyn," she whispered. "At least take the phone."

I squeezed her hands tight and shook my head. "I'm going. I need to go. You of all people should understand."

"Wait just a little longer. Let things settle down here," she pleaded. "People get divorced every day."

"They do." I nodded. "But this isn't about the divorce. It's me. I'm sick of this life."

"So you're running away?"

I rolled my eyes. "You make it seem so extreme for someone who's done the same, but yes. I am running away." *Again.* "Sometimes it's for the best."

She couldn't argue. She'd run away before and look at her now. Successful. Wealthy. Stunning. No one would suspect that she'd spent her teenage years living in a junkyard outside Temecula, California.

"Ugh," she groaned. "Fine."

She didn't like this idea of mine, but she understood. My divorce had been brutal and heartbreaking. It had been the nuclear bomb to my life I'd needed. It was forcing a fresh start. Besides, I was good at starting over. I'd done it countless times in my twenty-nine years.

What was one more?

As of Thursday last week, I was single. I'd already changed my last name back to McCormack, and with my new driver's license in hand, I was not sticking around Boston any longer.

"I hate that you're doing this alone." Gemma sighed. "I'll worry."

"I'll be fine." I returned to my suitcase, folding a hoodie for the stack.

It was one of the few pieces I'd had in my closet that I'd set out to pack. It was thick and gray, the hems battered by a designer, not from use. The thing had no stretch. I'd worn it only once when Thomas had taken me sailing years ago, when we'd seemed happy.

This sweatshirt was a lot like my marriage. It looked cute but didn't quite fit.

I took the hoodie out of the suitcase and tossed it on the bed.

"What if you get hurt?" Gemma asked.

"Give me some credit." I rolled my eyes. "I have money. I have a car. I'm running away in style. It'll be a breeze."

"When are you coming back?"

Never. "I don't know."

"Will you call me? Check in periodically?"

"Yes, but you have to promise not to tell Thomas where I'm at."

She scoffed. "That son of a bitch comes anywhere near me, I'll rip his balls off."

I laughed. "There's my best friend. Glad to see some of the polish come off."

"Just with you." She smiled. "I'll miss you."

"I'll miss you too." I abandoned the suitcase and met her at the foot of the bed for a hug.

We'd been through a lot together over the last thirteen years. Gemma and I had met one night in an alley. She'd saved me from eating half a sandwich I'd dug out of a Dumpster.

There'd been times when she'd gone her way and I'd gone mine, but we'd ended up together in Boston. We'd become closer than ever, serving as each other's refuge as we'd climbed up the ranks of Boston's elite and wealthy.

I'd married into my money. Gemma had earned hers.

I finished packing, loading up my purse with the cash I'd taken out yesterday and my wallet. Then I zipped up my suitcase and hefted it down the hallway to the front door.

My keys were on the table in a dish. I took the bundle in my hand and removed only one to take along.

A car key.

"What if you don't find Karson?" Gemma asked, standing by my suitcase.

I stared at the silver key. "I'll find him."

I had to find him. I needed closure after too many years of wondering what kind of man he'd grown into from the boy I'd once known.

Past Gemma, the tile in the foyer gleamed under the crystal chandelier. The art on the wall was not my favorite, but Thomas had bought it at a charity auction, so at least it had been bought for a purpose beyond just decorating my lavish home — my former home.

I gave Gemma a sad smile. "This was the nicest place I've ever lived."

Thomas and I had a staff to take care of the mansion. A daily housekeeper cleaned and did laundry. A cook made whatever suited my fancy. A gardener kept the grass green and the flowers blooming. Here, I'd wanted for nothing.

Yet it had never felt like home.

Had Thomas and I ever been happy? I'd let myself believe we'd been content because I'd been stupid and blinded by material things. But none of this was mine.

The only thing I owned was my car. *Karson's* car.

"Will you miss it here?" Gemma asked.

I shook my head. "Not for a minute."

I'd gladly scrub my own toilets and mow my own grass for a chance to feel like a home was my own.

As a kid, I'd run away to be safe. I'd run away so I wouldn't have to watch my parents implode. Slowly, I'd ventured east. I'd been searching for work and adventure. I'd found Thomas and he'd given me both, for a time.

Now, I was running away to find peace. To find the life I needed deep in my soul. To find myself again.

I'd lost *me* these past years. When I met Thomas, I was twenty-one. He was thirty-five.

We'd married when I was twenty-two, and he'd given me a job as his assistant. Thomas ran his own company in Boston and had made a fortune through corporate investments, capital endeavors and real estate transactions.

Working for him had been the first job I'd ever had that didn't pay minimum wage. I'd learned how to use a computer. I'd learned how to analyze spreadsheets and build presentations. At first, Thomas had taught me how to speak properly on the phone. Basically, I'd learned manners.

He'd taken all my rough edges and smoothed them away.

For the most part, I'd enjoyed the transformation to a cultured society wife. Once a kid who'd grown up in a single-wide trailer, eating processed cheese slices and SpaghettiOs from the can, I'd looked in the mirror and loved the shiny version of myself. I loved showering every day. I loved my expensive makeup and my monthly hair appointments.

The truth was, I would have kept on living this life, turning a blind eye to the hole in my heart. But there were some things I refused to ignore.

Two years ago, Thomas had hired another assistant. He hadn't wanted to burn me out, even though I'd never complained about the work. I'd cut down to three days a week while she worked five.

We had different tasks, but we sat across from one another and would talk cordially as we worked. I'd take my lunch with Thomas in his office. Monday, Wednesday and Friday, he'd fuck me on his desk.

Apparently, Tuesday and Thursday were her days.

I'd walked in on them six months ago when I'd come into the office to surprise him for lunch.

This beautiful home and all the money in our checking account weren't worth the pain of a broken heart.

I grabbed my suitcase and wheeled it to the door. Gemma followed me outside, her heels clicking on the cement sidewalk as we walked to the detached garage beside the larger house. This garage wasn't where I parked normally. My BMW was in the garage, where Thomas parked his own Beemer. Maybe after I left, he'd give it to Secretary.

Fine by me. *My* car was parked here, where the gardener kept his tools.

I punched in the code to open the large door, the sun limning the space as it lifted. I walked in and ran my hand over the gray tarp that had covered the Cadillac for two years.

A rush of excitement hit as I peeled off the tarp. The chrome underneath gleamed as it caught the sun. The cherry-red paint was polished to a mirror shine.

"I still can't believe this is the same car." Gemma smiled from her position at the door.

"Remember that time when we sat in the back and smoked an entire pack of cigarettes?"

"Don't remind me." She grimaced. "I still can't stand the smell of smoke. I think I puked that entire night."

"We thought we were so tough at sixteen."

"We were."

We were. Along the years, we'd gotten soft. Maybe we'd used up all our tough to survive. Or maybe we'd forgotten how harsh the world could truly be.

"I wish I were tougher in here." I tapped my heart.

Her lip curled. "I hate him for this."

"Me too." I swallowed hard, not letting the emotions overwhelm me. Thomas had gotten all the tears he was going to get. "More than anything, I'm mad at myself. I should have known better. I should have seen him for who he truly was."

Loyalty wasn't a common theme in my life. I hadn't had it from my parents or the many strangers who'd drifted in and out over the years as temporary friends. I'd expected it from my husband.

"Fuck him."

"Fuck him." Gemma walked to the other side, helping me peel the tarp off the back and fold it into a square. Maybe the gardener could use it for something.

I opened the trunk of the car, the smell of metal and new upholstery wafting into the air. I smiled, taking in the wide space. I'd stowed a lot of things in the trunk once. I'd had it organized and sectioned to perfection. Food on the left side. Clothes and shoes on the right.

I retrieved my suitcase, wheeling it over and loading it in the trunk. "I guess I've come full circle. This was my closet once. Now it is again."

Gemma didn't laugh. "Please, be careful."

"It's only a road trip, Gemma." I slammed the trunk closed. "I'll be fine."

I walked to the driver's side, opened the door and slid into my seat. The leather scent chased away the stale air. The dash was fairly dust-free given how long this had been sitting unused. I ran my fingers over the smooth white steering wheel.

A 1964 Cadillac DeVille convertible. My pride and joy.

The passenger door opened with a pop and Gemma took her seat.

"Smells good, right?"

She smiled as she shut the door. "A lot better than when you and Karson lived here."

"Seems like a lifetime ago."

"It was." She ran her hand across the white leather seat—smooth as butter and smelling like money.

A lot of money. This car had been no more than rusted scrap when I'd paid to have it hauled from California to Boston. But I'd paid. Every dime put into this car was a dime I'd earned.

Thomas had made me sign a prenup when we'd gotten married. I'd been young and foolish. I hadn't countered a single term. What the hell had I known about contracts and legal documents?

I'd learned though. Working for his company had taught me a lot. As much as I hated how our marriage had ended, Thomas had given me something invaluable.

An education.

He'd helped me get my GED. Then he'd put me to work. And damn it, I'd worked my ass off. As his assistant, I didn't run to get his coffee or pick up dry cleaning. I proofread contracts. I built financial projections. I put together presentations for stakeholders and schmoozed potential investors with the best of them.

Thomas gave me rough ideas and projects. I added the polish.

Just like I'd done to this car.

I put the key in the ignition and turned, closing my eyes as the Cadillac rumbled to life. The smile on my face pinched my cheeks.

That glorious sound was my freedom.

I looked over at Gemma just in time to see her dab at the corner of her eye. "No tears," I said. "This isn't goodbye."

"It feels like it," she whispered. "More than any of the other times, this feels like you won't be coming back."

I wasn't.

"Want to come with me?" I knew the answer but asked anyway.

"I wish I could but . . ." Gemma didn't need a new life.

"I'll drive you to your car." It was parked in the loop in front of the house, but I wanted these last few moments together. I put the Cadillac in drive and inched out of the garage.

The sunshine hit the metal hood. The tires rolled smooth on the driveway. Damn, it felt good to drive. Why had I let this thing sit for so long? The Cadillac had been finished for two years.

The Cadillac's restoration had taken nearly a year. When it was done, I'd driven it home and parked it in the garage. Besides the rare weekend when I took it out, the weekends Thomas was gone, it had mostly sat idle for two years. Two damn years because Thomas had insisted it would get ruined if I tried to drive this *boat* in city traffic every day.

I hadn't wanted to risk an accident, so I'd continued to drive the BMW, wearing my suits and heels. I'd played my part as the refined wife he'd gotten bored with.

All while the Cadillac sat, covered and alone.

Shame on me.

I'd hidden away something important in my life. I couldn't pin the blame on Thomas either, because I'd forgotten who I was.

Too soon, I inched up to Gemma's car and put the Cadillac in park. She didn't get out. Neither did I.

"I'll call," I promised.

"You better." She twisted to me and leaned over for one last hug.

We met in the middle. She gave me a tight squeeze and then she was gone, walking with grace and elegance to her car.

Gemma had grown up in a hovel worse than mine, but she'd always had this regal nature. She'd lived on her own since the tenth grade. She had no Ivy League education or family pedigree. Yet Gemma Lane was pure class.

I hit the button to lower the convertible's top, smiling wider as the summer air filled my nostrils along with the smell of fresh-cut grass and wind. "I love you, Gem."

"Love you, Lonny." She smiled, standing next to her Porsche. Then she raised a pointed finger at my nose. "Call me."

"I will." I laughed as she got in her car, slid on sunglasses and waved one last time before racing away.

The sound of her exit faded in the distance and I took a final quiet moment to look at the house I'd called home. The brown brick façade stood tall and stately. The arched double doors were traditional and fancy. The pillars bracketing the porch were pompous.

This house wasn't me.

But my car was.

I gripped the steering wheel with both hands. It hadn't always been white, just like the seats hadn't always been leather.

Had I gone too far with the restoration? Maybe Karson would feel like I'd butchered the thing. But deep in my heart, I believed this was what the car should have looked like in its glory days. This was how it should have been before someone had forgotten its beauty and left it in a junkyard for two teenagers to squat in for a couple of years.

The modern touches, like power windows and an air-ride suspension, were purely a comfort thing. I was glad for them, given I was about to drive across the country.

I hit the gas, speeding out of the loop. When I passed through the exterior gate, I took one final glance in the rearview mirror.

No more gates.

The traffic in the suburbs wasn't awful, but as I hit the city, things slowed to a crawl. It took an hour for the congestion to break, but break it finally did.

Then I raced.

Karson had always said running away from home was the best decision of his life. I had to agree.

The wind whipped through my hair as I sped along the highway. Just me and my cherry-red Cadillac.

On a runaway road.

2

LONDYN

TWO DAYS on the road and I was free.

Boston had been slowly suffocating me, something I hadn't realized until five hundred miles separated me from my former life.

Screw daily routines. Screw schedules. Screw structure and convention. I'd been trapped in normalcy and ignorant of the heaviness in my heart. Turning a blind eye to my problems had been easy with the schedule I'd maintained. Every minute of my life had been choreographed. Sitting idle hadn't held any appeal.

Now that I had time to think about why I'd kept myself so busy, I saw that routines and structure had become a necessary distraction. When I was working, running the house or organizing a function for Thomas's company, I didn't have time to think about the last time I'd truly smiled or laughed carefree. When I was spending time at the spa or shopping, I only relaxed enough to recharge my batteries. But the downtime had never been long enough to reflect.

Sitting behind the wheel of my car forced me to take a hard look at the past eight years.

When I'd started working for Thomas, I'd enjoyed the routine, mostly because it had been an anomaly. Knowing what each day would entail had been a new concept for me. Stability had been refreshing.

And I'd been blissfully in love with my husband. I'd fit our lives together—or fit my life to his.

Thomas required structure. He thrived on a schedule. The man knew what he was doing with precision, every single day for the upcoming three months mapped out in detail. Gemma was the same way. Maybe it was a CEO thing, but the two of them had next to no flexibility. No spontaneity.

Gemma, I understood. She was desperate for surety, and after our childhood, it made sense. But Thomas's motivation wasn't born from fear of the unknown or a chaotic youth. Thomas had discipline and drive in every aspect of his life because it made him money.

Success and status were Thomas's true loves.

Why had I tried so hard to fit that mold? Because of love? I'd convinced myself I was happy, but did I even know what *happy* was?

All questions I'd been asking myself since leaving Boston. Maybe by the time I reached California, I'd have them answered.

In the meantime, I was shunning all structure. I took the road at my own pace, not worrying about the speed limit or keeping up with traffic. The clock on the dash meant nothing because I had nowhere to be.

It was peaceful, simply driving alone. When I'd made my way to Boston—and all the stops in between—it had been by bus. Trips since had been with Thomas, and if we hadn't been in an airplane, he'd been behind the wheel.

Maybe for the first time, I felt ultimate control.

No wonder Gemma had become a control freak. It was fucking awesome.

I'd plaited my hair in a tight braid, but the wind whipped a few strands free as the sun warmed my face. Occasionally, another vehicle would pass me by and the smell of gasoline would linger for a mile. Unless it was raining, I was driving with the top down.

The day I left Boston, I drove for five hours without even a bathroom break. I wanted to get the hell away from traffic and the city. Cutting through Connecticut and a sliver of New York, I didn't stop until I hit the middle of Pennsylvania.

I pulled off the interstate and found a midlevel motel. I checked in and slept for fourteen hours. The grueling months of the divorce, when Thomas had fought me hard to reconsider ending our marriage, caught up to me. So I recharged in my motel room, making up for the sleepless nights.

The next morning, I woke up tired, not ready to get on the road. So I didn't. What was the hurry? This journey had no deadlines.

I added another night to my stay and spent the day in bed with a box of pizza delivery and the television.

Thomas didn't have time for movies or binge-watching television shows. We'd had one television in the house, a flat screen in the informal dining area where we'd eat breakfast. Thomas turned it on to watch the news each morning over egg whites and turkey bacon.

I hadn't minded. Before I'd run away at sixteen, I'd spent countless hours in front of the TV. Nickelodeon and MTV had been my babysitters while my parents had been busy with their current drug of choice.

But now, when those memories weren't as sharp and TV didn't equate to loneliness, I found the mindless entertainment soothing.

I watched *John Wick* first, finally understanding the fuss about Keanu Reeves. I cried through *Beaches*, knowing I was lucky to have a similar friendship with Gemma. And I stayed up until three in the morning, laughing at a rom-com about bridesmaids.

The next morning, I slept in again, leaving before noon checkout. Then, instead of rushing for the road, I drove to a local café. For hours, somewhere in Pennsylvania, I sat at a window table watching traffic, eating lunch and eavesdropping on other conversations. I left long after the smell of the café's fresh pastries had seeped into my blond hair.

Even after driving for hours, the scent was still in my hair. I picked up a lock of it, bringing it to my nose to inhale the lingering yeast and sugar. I'd always been conscious of smells—mostly my own.

Was I spoiled? *Probably.* After sleeping in a rusted-out, junkyard Cadillac for two years, did I deserve to be a bit spoiled?

Maybe so.

One thing was for certain, running away was much easier with money, and for that, I was grateful.

I could pay for hotel rooms and café lunches. I would never fear the charge at a gas pump. I could stop for a decent meal in a sit-down restaurant instead of scraping together enough change for a dollar-menu cheeseburger.

The money I'd earned working had been considerable for a woman with a fresh GED and no higher education. A perk of being married to the boss. I'd saved it all, minus what I'd spent on the Cadillac. Everything else —our household budget, clothes, shoes, the spa, vacations—had been paid for by Thomas. I could live off my savings for years. Designer garb wasn't in my budget these days, but I'd had enough of labels to last a lifetime.

The interstate cut through the countryside and signs flew past every now and then. I reached for my purse, ready to dig for my phone and check a map.

"It's not there," I reminded myself. How long would it take to break that habit?

And I didn't need a map. I was on the East Coast and had to get to the West. How I traveled didn't need to be charted. I was driving. The road beneath my tires would take me there eventually.

A large truck roared past, its diesel exhaust leaving behind a black cloud. I scrunched up my nose and slowed, but the stink clung to the car. I'd been dealing with the same all afternoon.

"To hell with the interstate." I flipped my blinker at the next exit, seeing a sign for a gas station. I wanted to go a few miles without passing another car.

I refueled the Cadillac and washed the windshield. Then I went inside and bought a couple bottles of water and a bag of chips.

"Thanks," I said to the clerk. "I don't suppose you have a pay phone anywhere?"

"Sure do. Just go out the door and take a right. It's around the corner."

"Thanks again." I collected my things and took them to the car, dropping them in the open seat. Then I fished out some quarters from my purse and found the phone. It was old and the keys dirty. I pressed the black receiver to my ear and propped it against my shoulder as I dialed Gemma's number.

"Hello?"

"Hey, Gem." I smiled.

"Lonny?"

"Yes, it's me. See? I told you I'd call. I figured I'd get your voicemail." She laughed. "Perfect timing. I'm in between meetings and alone for once. How's it going? Where are you?"

"Still in Pennsylvania, according to my receipt from the gas station. And it's good. I'm taking it slow."

"I figured you'd be across the Mississippi by now."

"Soon enough. How are you?"

"Fine." She blew out a long breath. "I miss you already."

"Miss you too." Though I was glad she'd declined my offer to come along. As much as a road trip would have been fun with my best friend, I needed to do this alone. This trip was for me.

"Listen, I need to tell you something. I hate to do it on your first call, but I don't want you calling Thomas."

I scoffed. "I hadn't planned on it."

"Good. Because he called me yesterday."

"What?" I tensed. "Why? What did he want?"

"To find you."

I rolled my eyes. "Well, tough shit."

"There's, uh . . . something else." She paused. "It's not good. Want me to tell you? Or not?"

Not. Whatever was happening with Thomas wasn't going to change anything. I wasn't going back.

He'd stifled me, something I was coming to realize the farther I got from Boston. He didn't care about my ideas or feelings because he was the business mogul and I was only the poor girl he'd turned into a princess.

He couldn't fathom I'd leave his riches because of *a silly office affair.*

No, I didn't want to know.

Gemma knew I didn't want anything to do with him. So why even bring up his call? Was Thomas sick or something? Was he hurt? Was he in trouble?

"Tell me." *Damn you, curiosity.*

"It's, um, Secretary."

I cringed. Neither Gemma nor I would speak the woman's name. That bitch had sat across from me for months, smiling and pretending to be a friend while secretly fucking my husband. Maybe he had actually fired her.

"She's pregnant."

The phone fell from my ear, the black plastic crashing into the wall beneath the booth. The cord swung back and forth like a man hanging from a noose. *Kind of like my marriage.*

Dead.

"Londyn!" Gemma's voice yelled into the phone, forcing me to pick it back up.

"I'm here." I cleared my throat. "That's what he called to tell you? Why?" Hadn't he hurt me enough? Why couldn't he leave me alone in my ignorance?

Gemma sighed. "He wanted you to know in case you decided to come back."

"I'll never come back." Not now.

"I'm sorry," Gemma whispered. "I shouldn't have told you."

"No, I'm glad you told me. I wanted to know. It doesn't change anything. Did he say anything else?"

"Only that he's worried about you."

"Well, he's got other things to worry about now." Like dealing with the doctor who'd performed his vasectomy. "I'm going to let you go. I'm sure you're busy."

"I shouldn't have told you," she muttered. "Will you call me again soon?"

"Sure." I didn't mean it as a lie, but it felt like one. I couldn't imagine not talking to Gemma, but one call and I'd been yanked back into the life I'd just left. Maybe temporarily cutting ties with her for a while would be best. I'd call again, just not as soon as she probably assumed.

"Take care of yourself," she said.

"Bye." I set the phone in its silver cradle.

There were two more quarters in my pocket, enough for another call. I stood staring at the keypad on the phone. Should I call Thomas? The urge to scream and yell bubbled up in my chest and my fingers brushed the phone.

Since the divorce, I hadn't gotten angry. I'd gone numb and stayed quiet. My lawyer had encouraged me to stay that way so he could get me the best settlement possible. Thomas and I might have had a prenup, but Thomas had still ended up paying.

I'd hired a really good lawyer.

Aside from my own savings, I'd taken ten million dollars away from my marriage in our divorce settlement. Every cent was now being used by an organization that supported runaway kids. That money paid for clothes and shelter. It paid for education and long-term housing.

Thomas had escalated my station in life. Now his money was doing the same for other unfortunate kids who needed a helping hand. That donation had eased the sting of the divorce. It had helped me keep my temper.

Until now.

Fuck him. I stepped away from the phone, my fists clenched and my teeth gritted.

Thomas didn't deserve fifty cents.

I turned away from the phone, practically jogging for the car. I pulled onto the road and drove past the on-ramp for the interstate. Raising my hand, I gave it the finger.

Fuck interstates. Fuck Secretary. Fuck husbands who got a vasectomy at thirty because they hadn't planned on getting married five years later.

I'd been the exception to Thomas's meticulously planned-out life. I'd been a spontaneous, lead-with-your-heart decision.

This baby was because he'd led with his dick.

Fuck him.

The yellow lines in the middle of the blacktop blurred as a sheen of tears coated my eyes. I slid on my sunglasses and blinked them away.

Miles and miles streaked past as I drove along the quiet highway. The trees fencing the road were bright and tall under the June sky. Birds flew overhead. Occasionally a stream would appear, kissing the road before disappearing into the lush greenery.

It was picturesque and impossible not to appreciate.

The mental image of Thomas and Secretary holding a baby swaddled in pink was stuck in my head.

It was ironic that Thomas had impregnated the wrong woman. He'd begged and pleaded for me to stay, and if we'd had a baby, I wouldn't have left him. Betrayal or not, I would not have taken a child away from a life where he or she would have wanted for nothing.

But I didn't have a baby. I didn't have a family and probably never would.

The tears threatened again, but I refused to let them fall.

"No more," I whispered to myself. "He gets no more."

I had this adventure to give me purpose. I didn't need family when I had my freedom.

Holding tight to the steering wheel with one hand, I raised the other into the air. The moment my fingertips ascended above the windshield, they chilled. It was getting cooler now as the sun began its descent.

I'd crossed into West Virginia about an hour ago, a large, faded sign welcoming me to the state.

I stretched my hand higher, toward the fading light of the sky. Then I balanced the wheel with my knee, letting my other hand reach above. My arms stretched.

Freedom.

I was free. I was alone. I was lost.

And it was beautiful.

The air streamed through my fingers. As I stretched my arms higher, I filled my lungs, breathing deeper than I had in a long, long time.

I closed my eyes, for just a moment, until a lurch on my right tire sent the Cadillac jarring toward the centerline.

My eyes flew open, my hands snapped to the wheel. "Shit."

I yanked the wheel to get the car to my side of the road. I overcorrected. The Cadillac, the beast that she was, swayed and lurched again as the tires on the passenger side shook on the rumble strip.

Pop.

The right front corner of the car dropped. The Cadillac jerked to the side and I didn't have the strength to hold the wheel.

I hit the brake, too hard. Damn it! I was panicking and losing control. The *thwap* of my flat tire filled the air right before the screech of metal on metal. A guardrail was kind enough to stop me from dropping into a ditch.

The Cadillac came to a grinding stop. Dust billowed until the night breeze blew it away.

"Oh my God," I breathed. I was alive—if my heart didn't explode. My hands were fisted on the wheel, frozen, but the rest of my body was shaking. I couldn't seem to loosen my grip, so I left my hands white knuckled and let my head fall forward.

I closed my eyes, letting the adrenaline settle. When the shaking eased and my head stopped spinning, I let go of the steering wheel and pushed out of the car on unsteady legs.

With one hand on the car for balance, I made my way around the trunk to the other side.

"Shit." The Cadillac was smashed against the guardrail. There were streaks of red paint from where I'd dragged alongside it.

I hurried around the car again, this time to inspect the front. The tire was flat and the rim rested on the asphalt.

"No." I ran a hand through my hair. I must have hit a nail. The night was getting darker by the second, and though I could change a tire in the daylight, doing it at night was not a challenge I wanted to take on.

"This is why we have phones." I slammed my palm into my forehead. I should have bought a flip phone for emergencies. "Damn it."

And there wasn't a car in sight. I'd gotten my wish for a deserted road. How long had it been since I'd passed a town? I'd driven through a small town earlier but it had still been bright outside. It was at least an hour's drive behind me.

"Ahh!" I screamed to the sky. Not even the birds seemed to care. Which meant if I was kidnapped and murdered along this road, no one would be around to hear those screams either. "Fucking hell."

I stomped to the driver's seat and got in to put the convertible's top up. When it was secure, I collected my purse, slammed the door and popped the locks. Then I went to the trunk, digging into my suitcase for a pair of tennis shoes to trade out for my flip-flops.

"I should have stayed in Pennsylvania," I muttered as I set off down the road. I was hoping that another town or a house would appear if I kept on the path forward. There wasn't much behind me.

The farther I walked from the car, the further my stomach sank. That car was my safety blanket. Even in Boston, when it had been tucked away in the garage, I'd always known it was there, protected and safe.

Now it was on the highway, alone and vulnerable.

So was I.

I stole glances over my shoulder until it disappeared from my sight and I began counting steps to occupy my mind. When I got to five hundred, I was nervous. When I got to a thousand, I was so freaked out by the impending darkness, I stopped walking.

There was no sign of a town close. If there were homes nearby, they were hidden in the trees.

"This is crazy." I spun on a heel and ran to my car. I was sweating and out of breath when it came into view.

I ran faster.

When I reached the door, darkness had nearly descended and I could hardly make out the handle. If I had walked another five hundred steps, I wouldn't have made it back before nightfall.

I collapsed into the driver's seat, locking myself inside as my heart pounded.

What had I been thinking? Why would I leave this car? I'd sleep here tonight and flag down a passing car tomorrow. Because I wasn't leaving this car again. The only time we'd part ways was when I handed the keys to Karson in California.

If he was even in California. I'd find out when I got there.

The air was thick and humid outside my window. Sweat ran down my cleavage and soaked the hair around my temples and forehead. I turned on the car, cranking up the AC until I wasn't dripping. Then I cracked the windows and shut it off, pushing my seat back as far as it would go to stretch out my legs.

Sleeping in the Cadillac was more comfortable in the backseat, something I knew from years of practice, but sleep wouldn't come easy tonight no matter where I rested. And from here, I could see outside better and hop out quickly if a car approached.

Hours passed. Stars lit up the midnight sky. Thousands of them hovered overhead, and like I'd done as a teenager, I wished on the brightest. Lost in their random pattern, I jumped when a flash of light caught my eye from the rearview mirror.

I sat up, spinning around as blinding headlights raced my way. I flew into action, turning on the Cadillac's interior light before getting out. I hurried to stand by the hood, inching back until the guardrail brushed my calves. Then I waved my arms in the air like a lunatic as the other vehicle approached.

I squinted at their headlights, using one hand to shield my eyes as the other waved. The car didn't slow. The hum of its engine seemed to grow louder. Did they not see me? Or were they going to pass me by?

My stomach dropped as the lights got closer and closer with no sign the vehicle was slowing. My arm was still raised in the air but I'd stopped waving.

They were going to keep driving. *Asshole.*

Given my luck today, that was about par for the course. I was ready to give them the finger too when tires squealed and the engine's loud downshift filled the air.

"Thank you," I breathed, dropping my hand.

A truck came to an abrupt stop right beside me, and the window lowered. My eyes were still filled with spots from the headlights, but I squinted hard, trying to make out the driver.

"Need some help?"

It was a woman's voice. *Thank you, stars.* One of my wishes was to be rescued. Another was for my rescuer to be female.

I stepped closer to the truck. "I have a flat and am squished into the guardrail. It's dark and I didn't want to try and change it myself. And . . ." I sighed. "I don't have a phone."

"Damn." She stretched the word across two syllables. *Day-um.* "Well, Summers is about ten miles up the road. Want a lift?"

Ten miles? I was glad I'd turned around. "Is there a tow truck in Summers? I'd rather not leave my car out here."

"Cohen's got a tow. Want me to call him?"

"Yes, please. Thank you so much." My eyes were finally adjusting to the dark. As she took out her phone, the screen illuminated the cab briefly, and I was able to see her face.

The woman was likely in her late fifties, but with the dim light, it was hard to tell. The wrinkles around her eyes and mouth were slight. Her hair was either a light blond or gray. She pressed the phone to her ear and faced me, giving me a kind smile.

Of all the people in the world who might have stopped, I'd hit the jackpot. I stepped closer until I was standing right outside the open passenger window. The scent of lemon bars wafted from the truck and filled my nose.

My stomach rumbled. The chips I'd inhaled hours ago had long since burned away.

"Hey, Brooks." She didn't introduce herself to the person on the other end of the phone. "I've got a gal here who needs a tow. About ten miles north of town, a mile or so before you hit my place."

Her place? So if I'd gone the other direction, I'd have landed myself at her house? *Damn it.* From now on, I was paying better attention to my surroundings as I drove. This wouldn't have happened if I hadn't been trying to work myself out of a funk.

"Sure thing." She hung up, setting her phone in the console. "He's on his way."

"Thank you." Would it be weird to give her a hug?

"Want me to wait with you, sweetheart?"

My heart warmed. "No, you go ahead. Thank you."

"It's late. I'm on my way to the motel to deliver some lemon bars to my sister, Meggie. I bake when I can't sleep and she works the evening and night shifts. You come on over after Brooks gets you and that car to town. Stay the night in Summers."

"I think I'll do that. Thank you."

"Good. My name's Sally. And you are?"

"Londyn McCormack."

"Fine meeting you, Londyn." She lifted a hand. "See you soon."

I waved, stepping away from her truck as she put it in drive. As quickly as she'd come to a stop, she was off, racing down the highway and leaving me in the dark.

I got back in my car, swatting at the bugs that had latched on to my skin and hitchhiked their way into the car. Then I waited, watching the clock as ten minutes ticked by. Then fifteen. At twenty, I was starting to wish I'd hitched a ride with Sally after all, but then two headlights came around a bend.

I got out and waited in my same spot by the hood, only this time, my own headlights were shining too.

20

The tow truck came to a slow stop, the engine running as the driver opened the door and stepped onto the road. His dark, tall figure was shadowed as he walked through the streaming light.

"Ma'am." His hand lifted as he stepped close and his features came into view. "Heard you needed a tow."

I swallowed hard. Was I asleep? I had to be asleep. Sally was a dream and so was he. I had no experience with tow truck drivers but surely this wasn't what they all looked like. Otherwise the women of the world would be constantly popping their tires.

He shifted, blocking out more of the light with his broad shoulders. The move gave me a clearer view of his face and highlighted the line of his straight nose. Stubble dusted his strong jaw. His arms were roped with muscles so defined I wouldn't be surprised if he picked up my car with his bare hands to set it on the tow's flatbed.

"Ma'am?"

"Yes." I blinked, forcing my gaze away from his soft lips to return his handshake. "Sorry. I, uh . . . have a flat and can't change it."

"Hmm." He walked to the car, peering down the side pressed against the guardrail. "Looks like you got more than a flat."

My eyes drifted to the man's ass. *Day-um.* As he turned, I forced my eyes to his face. The last thing I needed was for him to leave me on the side of this road. "I scraped against the guardrail as I skidded to a stop. I don't even want to think about what the side of my car looks like."

"Probably not pretty. But we'll get it to the garage and take a closer look."

"Thanks." I smiled. "I appreciate you coming out here so late to help me."

He chuckled. "When Sally calls, it's best you answer, ma'am."

I cringed at the third ma'am. "It's Londyn. Spelled with a y."

"Londyn. Pleasure." Oh lord, that voice, so rich and smooth. I hoped his name was something plain like George or Frank. Something to combat the perfection. "I'm Brooks Cohen."

Not George. This was definitely a dream.

3

BROOKS

TONIGHT WASN'T the first time I'd gotten a tow call from Sally Leaf well after midnight. Normally, she needed me to tow her out of whatever ditch she'd managed to drop her old truck into. The woman drove like speed limits were a minimum and lines on the highway a suggestion.

Regardless, whenever she called, I came running. I'd hauled my ass out of my bed, then dressed in jeans and a T-shirt. I'd hurried the few blocks from my house to the garage, where I'd swapped out my silver Ford for the tow rig. As Sally had promised, almost exactly ten miles out of town, I'd spotted the car sandwiched against the guardrail.

A gorgeous car. And a goddamn knockout owner.

Londyn. *Spelled with a y.*

Her Cadillac was loaded onto the flatbed and she was riding shotgun with a purse clutched in her lap. The sweet scent of her hair drifted my way each time she made the slightest movement to shift her handbag or cross her legs.

Thank goodness it was dark and she couldn't see my wandering eyes. They'd skimmed her from head to toe, taking in that long blond hair as it draped over her shoulders and the swells of her breasts. Her loose jeans couldn't hide the rounded contours of her hips or the firm lines of her legs.

My mother would be ashamed to know I'd checked out her ass more than once.

I ducked my head, sneaking a quick sniff of my arm. *Oh, hell.* I smelled like sweat and grease. I'd showered before bed, washing away a day of grime from the garage and the stink of the five miles I'd run after work. But after loading up her car in the sticky heat, I'd melted right through my quick swipe of deodorant.

"You just passing through?" I asked as I rolled the window down a few inches. I knew the answer to that question. If she lived around here, I'd know it. Summers was my hometown and I'd lived here all my life. After

22

thirty-three years, there weren't many people I didn't know. But we'd ridden two miles in uncomfortable silence, and I was desperate to ease the tension.

"Yes. I'm on my way to California."

"From?"

"Boston."

I whistled. "That's a long trip."

And a dangerous one for a woman on her own. I didn't like to think about what might have happened had she gotten a flat somewhere other than outside Summers, West Virginia.

"I'm in no hurry." She sighed, toying with the strap on her purse.

I sat a little straighter, pretending to glance at the car in the rearview, instead checking my face. My hair was a goddamn mess. I ran a hand through it twice, taming down the dark blond sticking up on top. *Shit.* When was the last time I'd cared about my hair?

"Where are you taking my car?" she asked.

"To my garage. I'll take a closer look at it tomorrow, but when I loaded it up, I saw some damage to the wheel. The side panel's pretty banged up too."

"Damn it," she grumbled, dropping her head into her hand. "I can't believe I did this."

"Accidents happen." They were never expected and never convenient.

"This one shouldn't have," she muttered. "I don't suppose you do any custom car work? I had the entire thing restored and need to get it fixed."

"I've done some." More than some, but I wasn't going to promise I could fix her Cadillac until I got a better look at the damage. "Like I said, let's see what we're dealing with tomorrow."

"Okay." She leaned against the door, her frame slumped. She looked like she was about five minutes from falling asleep.

"Where you staying?"

"Sally mentioned something about a motel."

"I'll drop you there, then take your car to the shop."

She hummed her agreement as we reached the edge of town. I slowed as the highway turned into Main Street, then veered off to park in front of the Summers Motel.

There were fifteen rooms in total, all situated in a horseshoe around an office in the center. Guests mostly parked in the loop, but the tow truck was too large for the space so I stopped us along the sidewalk.

As expected, Sally's truck, dented and dinged, was parked beside the office. Inside, she was laughing with her twin sister, Meggie. The two were eating something, probably a dessert of sorts. Sally was always experimenting with cookies and cakes. Those two would load themselves up on sugar for a few hours and chase it down with a gallon of coffee.

No surprise that Sally was rarely seen in town before noon. Meggie owned the motel and had worked the night shift for as long as I could remember. She said it was so her employees could have the normal hours. My theory was that she and Sally were born night owls.

"Here we are."

Londyn looked over, giving me a hint of a smile. "Thank you. I'll come by the garage tomorrow."

"No rush. It'll take me some time to figure out what we're dealing with here. I can call you if you'd like. Tell you when to come down."

"Okay—no, wait," she grumbled. "I don't have a phone."

"You don't have a phone?"

"No."

My jaw dropped. "You're driving across the country without a phone? Ma'am, I know I just met you. But it's—"

"Not safe. I'm aware."

I opened my mouth, a lecture ready, but stopped myself. For now, she'd be at the motel and I could reach her here. Besides, she wasn't my concern. This woman was a stranger. She'd be out of Summers the minute her car was ready. So why did the idea of her traveling alone leave me with such an unsettled feeling in my gut?

"I'll call the motel in the morning. The garage is about three blocks away. You feel like taking a walk before I call, come on down."

"Okay." She nodded, opening her door to step down.

I unbuckled and jumped out of the rig, rounding the front to make sure she made it to the ground from the tall step. "I got the door."

"Thanks." She tucked a lock of hair behind her ear as I stepped close to slam the door behind her. "See you tomorrow."

I followed her to the sidewalk. "Have a good night."

Londyn waved but stopped midstep, gesturing to the Cadillac. "All my things are in the trunk."

"That's no problem." I walked to the flatbed and vaulted up. "Toss me your keys."

She dug them out of her purse, but instead of throwing them over, she lifted one of those long legs and hopped right up next to me. "I got it."

We shuffled to the back, where she popped the trunk. It was packed with two suitcases and a matching duffel bag. The print matched her purse too. My mom had the same luggage, something Dad had bought her for an anniversary gift last year.

That was not a cheap print. Given that her car was worth twice as much as mine, I wasn't surprised she had designer bags too.

She went to take a suitcase out, but I took it from her grip. The slight brush of her fingers against mine was like a firebolt running up my hand. Londyn froze, her eyes widening and cheeks flushing. A surge of heat ran through my blood.

Who was this beautiful woman?

Londyn broke eye contact first, dropping her gaze to the trunk. I hoisted out the backpack and strung it over a shoulder. Then I pulled out both suitcases, setting them on the flatbed as she locked up the trunk.

I hopped down first, holding out a hand to help Londyn. She took it, this second touch as electric as the first.

Goddamn. I was in trouble if it took more than a day or two to get her car on the road. I let her go and reached for the suitcases.

"I can get them," she offered.

"Sally and Meggie would have my hide if I didn't carry in your bags." Then they'd call my mother and she'd deliver her own licking.

I led the way to the motel, setting aside the luggage to open the door for her. Sally was off her stool and rushing to greet Londyn.

Sally swallowed a bite of whatever she'd been chewing. "Come on in here, sweetheart."

"I've got your room all ready," Meggie said. "Room five."

Sally winked. "It's the best one."

"You're in good hands. I'll see you tomorrow." I deposited Londyn's bags and waved goodbye. "Night, ladies."

A chorus of good nights followed me into the dark.

"Heavens, that man has an ass that won't quit."

I chuckled, rolling my eyes at Meggie's comment. She was twenty-something years my senior and had made it her personal mission in life to make sure I knew she appreciated my body.

I took one last look at the lobby as I climbed into the truck. Londyn's eyes shot up from where she'd been staring at my ass.

I grinned. I guess we were even now.

———

"MORNING, BR—" Tony looked me up and down. "There a funeral or wedding I didn't hear about?"

"No." I shrugged. "I needed a cut and shave."

"Look awful slick for a man who was up half the night towing in this car." He tapped a knuckle on the hood of Londyn's red Cadillac. "She must be prettier than Sally let on."

"I don't know what you're talking about."

"Uh-huh," he muttered, his chest shaking with a silent laugh.

Sally and Tony had been lovers for more years than I'd been alive. They weren't married. They lived in separate homes. But when she finally retired to bed, it was usually in his. That, or he was already asleep in hers. They didn't date other people. They'd been blissfully *single* for decades but were the farthest thing from it.

Sally had probably woken up early with Tony this morning—or hadn't even gone to bed yet—to give him all the details on Londyn.

She was pretty. Damn pretty. I doubted anything Sally could say would do Londyn justice. But I hadn't stopped at the barbershop *only* for Londyn. It was summer and too hot for a mop on my head and scruff on my face.

"Just needed a shave, Tony."

"Whatever you say, boss."

I ignored his smirk and walked around to the damaged side of the Cadillac, crouching down on the concrete to get a closer look.

"She did a number on this panel." My fingers skimmed the scratches that led from the passenger door to the back taillight. "The front tire's shot too."

It had to be more than a nail to blow out one of these tires. They were a custom size and practically new. Some might try to save a buck and fix this one, but it wouldn't be a solid repair.

Londyn's safety had crept up my list of priorities awfully fast.

"I'll order a new tire first thing. Get it fixed today."

"What about the panel?" Tony asked, sipping from a steaming mug of coffee. I'd never understand how he could drink it boiling hot all day long, even when it was a hundred degrees outside and the humidity was off the charts.

"I'll get ahold of Mack at the body shop. If I get this tire fixed today, maybe he can fit it into his schedule this week to fix the paint."

Which meant Londyn would be on her way in three or four days and I wouldn't feel the need to keep going to the barbershop at seven in the morning for a shave and a haircut.

"Hello?" A soft, silky voice filled the shop and made my pulse race.

"Morning, miss." Tony grinned. "How can we help you?"

I stood, catching up to him before he could shake Londyn's hand with his greasy palm. I clapped him on the shoulder. "I got this, Tony."

He looked at me, then at Londyn and back again. A slow grin spread across his cheeks, revealing the dimples that Sally praised as often as Meggie did my ass. "Then I think I'll take a wander down the road to see what kind of treats the Express Hut has today and get a refill on my coffee."

Tony bowed a bit as he passed Londyn, twisting his wrist in a wave.

I waited until he was out of earshot, then tipped my head to Londyn. "Mornin'. How was the rest of your night?"

"It was fine. Uneventful. I just fell asleep."

I did my best not to think of Londyn anywhere near the vicinity of a bed, but it was difficult given her attire. She wore a pair of shorts that molded to the perfect curve of her hips. The V-neck of her tee plunged to reveal a delicious line of cleavage.

"Brooks?"

Fuck. She'd caught me staring at her breasts. I spun away from her, running a hand through my fresh haircut. "So, uh . . . the car."

"I was anxious to see it in the light of day so I didn't wait for you to call. How bad is it?" She walked deeper into the garage, her flip-flops slapping with each step. If I'd offended her, she didn't let on. Her focus was entirely on the Cadillac.

"It's not horrible." I went to the wrecked side. "I'm going to get the wheel fixed today, but I think a patch won't last to California. It'll be best to buy a new tire."

"Okay. And the side?"

"The panel has a few minor dents but nothing that can't be popped out. The paint will have to be touched up."

"And you can do all that?"

"I'm more of an engine guy. I fix a lot of tires for folks in town. Body work isn't my specialty."

I'd make a mess of this kind of precision work, and I could tell someone had dumped a ton of money into this car. This Cadillac had all the modern touches to the interior and the engine was top of the line. When I'd unloaded it off the tow truck last night, I hadn't been able to resist a look under the hood.

The engine was almost as sexy as the woman at my side.

Almost.

"I don't know what this car looked like in the before picture, but I'm guessing it was a complete rebuild, right?"

"Yes. I had it restored a couple of years ago."

"Had to have been expensive."

"It wasn't cheap, let's just say that."

I chuckled. "Figured as much."

"What do I do? I'd really like to avoid having to go back to Boston to get it fixed. And I can't take it to California as it is. Shit." Before I could help, she started pacing, running her hands through the ponytail that hung over one shoulder. "I should have stayed on the interstate."

"Why'd you get off?"

She lifted a shoulder. "I was tired of being on that road."

I had a feeling she wasn't talking about the pavement.

"The interstate is overrated." I looked down at her, studying the color of her eyes.

They were a rich green close to the shade of a dark jade ring my sister had bought on a visit to Asia last year. Though Londyn's eyes were far more beautiful and unique than that simple stone. I suspected a lot about her story was one of a kind.

"I've got a good friend who owns a body shop in town. He's good. He can get the dents worked out and the paint redone on this side. He's usually booked out months, but he owes me a favor because I rebuilt an engine for him last year. I'll call it in."

"Thank you." She blew out a long breath. "How long?"

"Three or four days. That going to be a problem?"

"No, I guess not." She turned to the open door of the garage, looking past the large sycamore that towered over the parking lot. "I guess I'll have some time to explore Summers."

"It's a nice town. There are likely worse places to be stranded."

"Probably." She smiled. "I walked over this morning and from the bit I've seen, it does seem nice."

"The diner has the best pie in West Virginia."

"Is that right?" She raised an eyebrow. "I guess I'll have to try it out."

"Their cheeseburgers aren't bad either."

"Good to know. So you'll call me?"

I nodded, then dug into my jeans pocket to retrieve a small black flip phone. "Here."

She eyed it. "What's that?"

"A cheap phone from Walmart."

Her eyes snapped to mine and as they caught the overhead light, flecks of caramel glinted in the center starburst. Beautiful, like everything else about this mysterious woman.

"Here." I held it out.

She didn't take it. "You got me a phone?"

"I did."

"Why?"

Because last night I'd tossed and turned, thinking of her on the side of the highway, stranded and alone. "You're a single woman traveling by yourself. You should have a phone."

"Thanks, but no, thanks."

I stepped closer. "I don't want to turn on the news one night to see a story about how that gorgeous woman whose car I helped fix got butchered by some maniac at a rest stop outside California."

Her cheeks flushed. "Gorgeous?"

"You've got a mirror, Londyn." Of course she'd caught the one word I hadn't meant to say. But it was out there now and I'd own the slip. It was the damn truth.

She blushed, a smile toying at the corners of her mouth as she stared at the phone. "You don't even know me. Why do you care?"

"Just the kind of man I am, so do me a solid. Cut me a break and take the phone. My number's in the texts."

She picked it up from my palm, opening it only to close it immediately. "Three days?"

"Maybe four. Then you'll be on your way."

And I'd always wonder what had happened to the woman with the jade-green eyes and hair the color of a wheat field in fall. Had she made it to California? Had she turned back for Boston?

Maybe in five years, I'd dial the number to that phone just to see where Londyn had landed.

Maybe she'd even answer.

4

LONDYN

SUMMERS, West Virginia.

The little town surprised me. I'd awoken this morning expecting to feel restless and impatient to leave. My journey to California was in its infancy and being stranded should have made me feel twitchy. On the contrary, I was actually enjoying myself.

There was something about this place. Something different than anywhere else I'd visited or lived. Charm, maybe? Everydayness? I couldn't put a word to it, but whatever the feeling, it had wrapped around me like a warm blanket. Yet again, maybe that was just the humidity.

As I walked down a quiet road, my soul was at peace. I wasn't panicked or worried about my car's repairs. I trusted Brooks to set the Cadillac to rights—another surprise, considering I'd only just met the man.

My steps were easy and slow as I strolled, my attention on the towering trees. This town had more trees than anywhere else I'd visited. Not a lawn I passed had less than two shading the green grass. Their canopy created a pocket in the world, the towering branches shedding glitter as sunlight broke through the leaves to illuminate the pollen floating to the ground.

It was easy to think the rest of the world didn't exist in this cocoon. I'd found a long residential street on my explorations this morning. It was straight as an arrow and the trees arched over the blocks. It was like stepping into a wardrobe and finding Narnia—minus the ice queen. There was no flat tire. There was no ex-husband or pregnant mistress. Of all the places in the world to get stuck, Summers was now at the top of my list.

"Morning." A man on a porch raised a hand.

"Good morning." I smiled, replaying the words with his Appalachian accent.

I hadn't heard it before coming to Summers, and even here, not many had it. The inflections were different than a Southern drawl. Those who spoke with the accent barely seemed to move their lips as they talked.

The man nodded from his rocking chair on the porch as I passed, his newspaper in hand. He looked comfortable there, like he might sit out all day. Or maybe he'd duck inside soon to the air conditioning. It was midmorning and the heat was on the rise. Coupled with the humidity, it was like breathing air from a steam room. By the time I went to bed tonight, I'd likely be a sticky mess.

Why didn't that bother me? Another wonder. I liked the thick air. My skin felt supple and my lungs hydrated. There were days in Boston when the summer was sweltering and muggy. I'd come home from work and dive into the shower to rinse off the grime and sweat. This air, while heavy, had a sweet and earthy smell like flowers blooming and tree bark. Nature's perfume, untainted by exhaust and city waste.

My flip-flops slapped on the concrete sidewalk as I meandered past yellow homes and white homes and green homes. Not a single house on the block was the same color. Each had its own character and intricate details to set it apart from its neighbors. One owner had covered their lawn with garden gnomes. Another had painted the front door a perky teal.

This was the slowest I'd walked in years, soaking it all in.

Maybe someday I'd come back and see if this street was the same. I'd visit this place in the fall to see the leaves as they changed from green to red, orange and yellow. Maybe I'd see if Brooks Cohen was just as handsome then as he was now.

But I didn't need to revisit Summers to satisfy that curiosity. Brooks was the type of man who only grew more handsome with age. I was guessing he was in his early thirties. His body was solid and even if it softened some, he'd always be drool-worthy. With a few gray streaks in his blond hair, he'd be irresistible.

I'd always had a thing for older men.

A shrink would probably chalk it up to daddy issues. I think it was because I'd grown up fast—too fast. Men my own age always seemed to lag behind.

Brooks wore his maturity with confidence. He put on no pretense. He was simply . . . himself. He didn't seem defined by his occupation or his clothes. He was magnetic in a plain white T-shirt and a well-worn pair of jeans.

That thin cotton T-shirt had stuck to Brooks when he'd rescued me on the side of the road. It had molded to his sturdy arms and rugged chest as he'd moved around the Cadillac. The muscles on his back were so well defined, I'd fought the urge to skim my fingertips down his shoulders just to feel the dents and contours under my skin.

A shiver ran down my spine.

He was a fantasy.

I didn't let myself indulge in fantasies often. Hope was something I kept at a firm distance. Disappointment, on the other hand, was a close companion.

With Brooks, I let the fantasy play out. I was in Summers for a hot minute, not enough time for him to crush the illusion in those strong, firm hands.

God, I wanted those hands on me. My core clenched and my nipples hardened inside my bra. Was he married? I hadn't seen a ring but maybe he didn't wear one. Did he have a girlfriend?

I didn't feel right lusting after another woman's man, so in my fantasy, he was single unless and until disappointment reared its evil head and smothered this fantasy too.

Brooks had consumed my thoughts all night long. His T-shirt had been the star of my dreams, the way it would stretch as it was dragged up that sticky body. I'd slept with a pillow between my legs just for some friction to calm the ache.

"I need sex," I muttered to myself.

I needed a good, hard fuck and a long, sweaty night. I needed an orgasm that didn't come from my own fingers or the showerhead. I needed to have a man's weight on top of me as he pressed me into a bed.

When was the last time I'd had sex in a bed?

More than a year. Thomas and I hadn't had a great sex life at home. In the office, we were great, but not at home. I should have known something was up when he always wanted to fuck me on his desk. Had he been picturing Secretary in my place?

Does it matter?

The truth was, Thomas and I hadn't been in love. I'd respected him. I'd admired him. I'd adored him. But love? I wasn't sure. Did I even know how it felt to be in love?

I'd thought so, but I was questioning everything these days. Could a woman who'd grown up without affection or care really know what it was to be in love?

Maybe I'd mistaken attention for love.

I was jonesing for some physical attention. A hookup would not go unappreciated. Maybe Brooks Cohen would do me a favor before I rolled out of town. If he wasn't attached, he'd be the perfect candidate to break my dry spell.

In a goddamn bed.

My hunch was that Brooks was a considerate lover. A gentleman. He'd called me ma'am and tipped his invisible hat when he'd dropped me off at the motel. I was probably reading too much into it, but I sure would like to be with a man who knew a woman's pleasure came first.

The street came to an end before I was ready to leave my West Virginian Narnia and I paused at the stop sign, tempted to walk it again. But the temperature was rising and I could use a cold glass of water, so I took a right and carried onward.

I wasn't sure how long I'd been out walking. The phone Brooks had bought me was tucked into the pocket of my jean shorts, but on principle, I hadn't turned it on.

I didn't need a phone. I didn't want a phone. But he'd worn me down.

Just the kind of man I am.

I wasn't carrying this phone for me. I had it in my pocket for Brooks.

His simple explanation might not mean a lot for women who'd grown up with decent men in their lives. But for me, a good man was as elusive as presents on Christmas morning.

So I'd taken the phone and kept it close.

Brooks Cohen. Damn, I liked him. I liked the entire package, head to toe. Even his unique name gave me a shudder.

The one thing my parents had done right was to give me a cool name. My mother had named me Londyn after the city in England because she'd always wanted to visit there. The woman couldn't spell for shit.

Unfortunately, by the time I'd run away at sixteen, I'd picked up her spelling habits. Mom didn't write much—she didn't need to as a lifelong junkie—but when I'd been eight, I'd taken over responsibility for going to the grocery store around the block.

Wanting the escape, I went almost every day, and because my scrawny arms couldn't carry more than three bags home. Mom would send me with a tattered sticky note covered in her messy script with words spelled entirely wrong.

Melk. Bred. Sereel.

The few teachers I'd had in my early years had tried to correct my spelling. Some had succeeded. Others hadn't cared. But I'd gotten by. Who needed to spell when you worked at bars and understood your own notes?

I hadn't seen it as a flaw until I'd married Thomas.

I'd never forget the look on his face when he'd seen my GED study notes. It was one of the most humiliating moments in my life. He'd stared at me like I was a broken child, not an adult, a grown woman and his *wife.*

From then on out, I took care to double-check every single word before writing it down. I'd spent hours with a dictionary in hand. I still carried a pocket version in my purse. Math, science and world history would never be my forte, but damn it, I could spell. And my vocabulary wouldn't betray my upbringing.

After another two blocks, I changed direction for the motel, hot and ready for an iced coffee. Meggie had set up a small coffee area in the motel's office, and this morning, all of the chairs had been filled with locals. Gossip flew from one end of the reception area to the other. Some bounced to the counter, where the clerk whipped up coffee and kept watch over the covered cake stand.

Free, black coffee was available to anyone who came through the door. Fancy espressos and the treats under the glass dome were for paying customers only. The scone I'd inhaled this morning rivaled any I'd found at my favorite patisserie in Boston.

At the next intersection, I stopped and looked both ways, getting my bearings. Then I took a left, hoping I'd come up on the back side of Main Street. When the sound of an air gun filled the air, I tensed.

It was a sound often heard in a garage—a squeak and a puff of air with a compressor churning. Whenever my mechanic in Boston had called to talk about the Cadillac, that sound had been a constant in the background.

Somehow, I'd gotten turned around and ended up behind Brooks's garage.

I slowed, contemplating a retreat. I didn't want Brooks to think I was hovering. Though I did want to see my car and find out what was happening. That wasn't weird, was it? I was in the area. A brief stop in wasn't hovering, even if I'd been over yesterday.

Plus I'd get to see the mechanic himself. I wasn't going to be in Summers long. I might as well add fodder for my future fantasies while I had the chance. Maybe today, Brooks would be in a different color T-shirt.

Decision made, I walked to the large open door and peeked my head inside. This wasn't a large garage. There were only two stalls and a small office in the back corner. The tow truck was parked alongside the building in a gravel lot.

"Um . . ." I raised my hand to knock, except there was no place to knock, so I awkwardly tucked it away. "Hello?"

My car was in the same place it had been yesterday. The tire was no longer flat. Beside it in the next bay was a minivan raised in the air on a hoist. Tools were strewn on workbenches. The scent of grease hung in the air.

Not a soul was visible.

Which was probably for the best. Now that I was standing in the middle of the doorway, this seemed more like stalker than concerned customer. I spun around, hoping to make a quick escape, but a deep, sexy voice stopped my retreat.

"Londyn."

I froze. *Shit.*

"Uh, hi." I waved, turning around as Brooks came striding out of the office. "I was just walking around town. I passed by and thought I'd come to check on my car."

That didn't come across as stalking but it sure sounded a lot like I didn't trust him at all to do his job.

"Car's fine." He grinned. "Still alive."

I blushed. My hand was in the air so I pulled it down, tucking it away. Then we stood there, him staring at me while I looked around the room. Why was this awkward?

Oh, right, because he was gorgeous and somehow I'd forgotten how to speak to gorgeous men. Or because I couldn't stop thinking about stripping him of that T-shirt. Today, Brooks had traded his white T-shirt for a black one with a round crest printed on the center.

Cohen's Garage. The logo was made out of a gear. It was vintage in the way that it had once been a modern design—meaning, actually vintage. The short sleeves banded tight around his biceps, showing off the definition between shoulder and triceps. The cotton stretched across his pecs. I'd never fawned over a T-shirt so hard in my life. What I really wanted was to see it tossed on the floor of my motel room.

Another rush of desire pooled in my lower belly and the flush in my cheeks burned hotter. I was drooling. And staring.

You're staring.

"I'm going to go." I spun on a heel and marched away from the garage. The heat of desire shifted to the scorching flame of humiliation. *Jesus.* I was such a mess. His gaze burned into my backside as I scurried. There was no doubt he thought I was a lunatic.

"Got that phone?" Brooks hollered after me.

I pulled it from my pocket, holding it high in the air.

His chuckle followed me out of the parking lot.

AFTER THE DISASTROUS stop at the garage, I hid in my motel room for the remainder of the day.

I turned on the TV, doing my best to get lost in another movie, but unlike the Pennsylvania hotel where I'd struck movie rerun gold, nothing caught my attention.

Not trusting myself to inadvertently wander back to Cohen's Garage, I stayed within the confines of my room until my stomach growled and I went in search of food. My first stop was the office, hoping I'd find a restaurant or two willing to deliver.

"Hi, Londyn." Meggie smiled as I walked through the door, the bell dinging over my head.

"Hi, Meggie. Do you have any places in town that would deliver dinner? I walked all over this morning and I'm worn out."

Today's miles in bad shoes had been a harder workout than I'd anticipated. Maybe because I was so out of shape. In Boston, I'd been religious about the gym up until I'd found Thomas with Secretary. I didn't need glutes of steel or a flat stomach when the only person who saw me naked was *me*.

That, and I really liked delivery. I'd never bothered learning how to cook.

"Sure do." Meggie opened a drawer and lifted out a stack of menus.

I raised my eyebrows as she fanned them on the counter. "More options than I would have expected in Summers."

"If I could make a recommendation, how do you feel about Thai food? The place here makes the best curry you've had in your life."

"I could eat curry."

"I was hoping you'd say that." She smiled, picking up the phone. "If their delivery driver is coming, I might as well place an order myself."

Meggie got on the phone, not even introducing herself before placing the order. I guess whoever she was calling knew it was her or had seen the motel's number come up. I gave her cash for my part of the order and she took care of the rest.

As she talked, I paced around the reception area. All of the chairs were empty now, the locals who'd come in for coffee having gone home while I'd been in hiding.

The stretch in my legs was welcome after lying around all afternoon. I probably could have explored and found a dinner spot, but while I assumed Summers was a safe place, I didn't go out on foot at night.

Habits and all.

After running away from home, I'd spent a few dark nights wandering alone. I'd never felt such crippling fear as those times. Nothing had happened to me, thankfully, but the fear had been paralyzing enough. It had nearly driven me home. The fact that it hadn't, well . . . it spoke of how bad things really had been with my parents. Once I'd found the junkyard, I'd made it a point to always be inside before dark. If I was working late, Karson would escort me home.

To the Cadillac.

"Should be here in thirty," Meggie said, the phone clicking onto the receiver.

"Thanks. You must be starving." She'd ordered two plates of curry for herself and one for me. Or maybe their serving portions were small.

"The second's for my neighbor." She jerked her thumb to the wall. "I like to keep him fed."

"Ah." I nodded, then took one of the chairs.

"So you did some explorin' today?"

"I did. This is a beautiful town." I relaxed deeper into the seat. "Have you lived here long?"

"Going on thirty-five years. Me and Sally moved here together in our twenties."

Meggie took my question and ran with it, recounting story after story about life in Summers. I hardly spoke a word, happy to listen to her tales with a smile on my face.

I hated small talk, mostly because it felt forced. When I'd worked for Thomas, it had been. But this felt different, like things had this morning on my walk. Maybe it was the way her hands flew in the air as she spoke. Maybe because she didn't expect me to utter a word. But this small talk felt more like friendship.

She was in the middle of a story about how she and Sally had sunk a boat in the middle of a nearby lake when her eyes lit up and the door opened.

A teenage boy strode inside with two plastic sacks in his grip. "Hi, Miss Meggie."

"Yes, yes. Set 'em down and give me a squeeze." Meggie was off her stool, rounding the counter. She pulled the boy in for a hug, then looked him up and down. "Wyatt, you've grown an inch in a week."

The boy shrugged. "I've been hungry lately."

He was tall, standing at least six inches above Meggie's head. She was about my height, at five five, so I was guessing this kid was close to six feet tall and still growing. He was long and lean but would likely fill out that broad frame.

In a way, he reminded me of Karson at that age. He'd grown fast and long too, so much so that the Cadillac had gotten too small for him to sleep inside. He'd traded the backseat for the outdoors during the warmer months. On the few chilly nights of California winter, he would cram himself in by my side, bitching about how his legs didn't fit.

I smiled, thinking of how I'd curl into his side and fall asleep laughing.

"How's football practice going?" Meggie asked.

Wyatt shrugged again. "Hot."

"Only gonna get hotter." She pinched his cheek—he let her without a wince or fuss—then she dove into the bags he'd brought along. "Say hi to Miss Londyn."

The boy turned and gave me a nod. "Ma'am."

Oof. These West Virginians and their ma'ams.

I stood from my chair and fished out a five-dollar bill from my pocket. I hadn't carried my Louis Vuitton purse anywhere in Summers because it was snobby. I was already planning to donate it somewhere. Besides that, what the hell did I have to cart around? All I needed was some cash and the motel key on the little plastic key chain that read *Room 5*.

"Thanks for the delivery." I held out the money for Wyatt.

His eyes widened. "Oh, that's okay."

"I tipped him," Meggie said.

"Consider it a bonus." I pushed the money into his hand.

I'd survived once on tips. My hourly wage had been shit at the pizza place where I'd worked as a kid. My tips meant I got a new pair of shoes once a year and that I could afford the necessities like toothpaste and tampons.

Since I'd been able to afford it, my tips had become overly generous.

This boy didn't seem to be hurting for money. His Nikes were new and his jeans hadn't come from Goodwill—I could recognize secondhand clothes from a mile away. Wyatt probably didn't need the extra five like I had at his age, but he seemed like the type who'd appreciate it.

He stared at the bill in his hand, then carefully tucked it into his pocket. "Thank you."

"You're welcome."

Wyatt turned and walked to the door, giving Meggie and me another wave and shy grin as he left.

"That boy." She shook her head.

That boy, what? I waited for her to explain, but she only pulled out white Styrofoam containers from the plastic sacks.

"Now I know you might want to disappear into that room of yours." She clicked her tongue. "But if I could make a suggestion?"

"Sure." I collected my meal and a plastic fork.

"There's a nice place to sit behind the motel. It's a rock, so if you're not into nature, then forget it. But it overlooks the lake and you'll get a nice view of the sunset."

"I'm good with nature. Thank you."

"No problem. Technically, it's my neighbor's rock. But since I'm buyin' his dinner, I doubt he'll mind if you borrow it for a night. Now out you go before that curry gets cold."

"Thanks again, Meggie."

36

She winked, then followed me out the door. As we rounded the corner of the building, she pointed to the rock past a cluster of trees. "See you tomorrow."

I waved goodbye as she strode across the lawn to her neighbor's house. It was a two-story white home, not new but well maintained. It wasn't fancy, but it was nice. Really nice. Especially with the wide porch that stretched along its front with delicate spindles along the rail. Meggie didn't bother knocking as she marched up to the front door and let herself inside.

What a character. I laughed, turning my attention to the lake.

The rock was easy to spot once I got closer, and Meggie hadn't lied. It was enormous and nearly as long as a picnic table.

It stood about a foot off the ground and I stepped up, settling into the flat surface with my meal on my lap. I was no stranger to eating food perched on my legs. The curry spice and fresh jasmine rice filled my nose as I opened the container.

"Oh my God," I moaned with that first bite. Meggie hadn't lied. This was good curry.

I heaped another bite on my fork, brought it to my mouth, then proceeded to fling the food into the air as a voice came from behind me.

"I see Meggie gave away my favorite dinner table."

A grain of rice lodged in my windpipe. I coughed, choking and my eyes watering, as Brooks rushed over.

"Shit." He slapped me on the back, then rubbed up and down my spine.

I coughed again, managing to dislodge the rice and swallow. My eyes were blurry and my heart was racing when I finally managed to suck in a deep breath.

"Sorry. Thought you heard me walk up."

"No." I put a hand to my chest, taking in more air. "It's okay."

His hand stilled on my spine. "Good?"

"I'm okay." Convenient that Meggie hadn't mentioned Brooks was her neighbor.

I closed the lid on my dinner, setting it aside to stand, but Brooks waved me down. "Stay."

"Oh, no. I can eat in my room."

"This is a big rock. Mind if we share it?" he asked.

"Uh, no."

"Good." He grinned, creating a flutter in my chest. Who grinned like that? Only one corner of his mouth turned up, and *wow* but it was sexy.

Brooks settled on the rock about a foot away, stretching his long legs toward the water. Then I saw why I hadn't heard him approach. He was in bare feet.

Just as sexy as that grin.

He opened his dinner container, closing his eyes as he drew in the smell. When he opened his eyes, he gazed out over the rippled water. "That sure is a good view."

His blue eyes caught the fading sunlight.

Yes, it sure is.

5

BROOKS

MEGGIE DIDN'T KNOW how *not* to meddle.

I should have known she was up to something when she barged into my house, shoved a takeout container in my hands and proceeded to put away all of the fixings for a ham sandwich I'd just pulled out of the fridge.

Meggie had practically chased me out the back door, telling me to take a night off.

I hadn't argued because I was beat and I knew from the container it was my favorite curry. I'd planned to go back to the garage and catch up on paperwork in the office, but a delicious meal and an evening by the lake had sounded much more appetizing.

Toss Londyn McCormack into the mix and I couldn't help but smile.

She'd been nervous at the garage earlier. I'd never seen anyone walk that fast in flip-flops. Clearly, she'd stopped in to check on progress. I got it. There were plenty of mechanics in this world who took twice as long as they promised and charged twice as much. Many might see a beautiful woman and think they could take advantage.

That wasn't how I operated, but I didn't blame her for being wary.

"I took your car to the body shop today," I said. "I promise I'm hurrying it along. I know you want to get on the road."

"Oh, I, uh . . . sorry." She gave me an exaggerated frown. "That's not why I came. I don't mean to hover, really. I was just passing by, realized I was hovering and felt bad for interrupting you."

"No interruption at all." She could interrupt me any hour any day of the week. Her face coming through my door had been the best part of my day. Until now.

It was a gorgeous night. The breeze had picked up, softening the heat and adding coolness as the air blew across the water.

"So, Londyn"—I stabbed a piece of chicken—"tell me about yourself."

"You go first."

"But I asked the question." I chuckled. "How about this? Whatever question is asked, we both have to answer. You can ask first."

"I like that. All right." She nodded and turned her gaze out to the water.

I expected something easy. Where was I from. How long had I worked at the garage. Coming up with a personal question didn't seem all that hard, but as the seconds passed into minutes and she remained quiet, I realized why this was hard.

Shit. The reason she wasn't asking wasn't because of *my* answer.

It was because of the one she'd have to give.

"Listen, we don't have to do this. I didn't mean to pry. I'll mind my own business."

"It's not that." She blushed. "I was trying to think of an interesting question, but for the life of me, all I can think of are the boring ones. The pressure got to me."

I chuckled. "Then I'll go first. Where are you from?"

"California is the short answer."

"And the long one?"

Londyn had just taken a bite. She held up her hand as she chewed and my gaze stayed fixed on her profile. It had been a long time since I'd studied a woman's profile, and no surprise, Londyn was beautiful from any angle.

Her nose turned up at the end, just slightly. Was it strange to think someone had a beautiful forehead? Hers had an elegant curve, not too big or flat. Since I'd seen her earlier at the garage, she'd tied up her long blond hair. It was fluffed at the crown, bunched from the ponytail that draped down the center of her shoulders.

She was probably seven or eight inches shorter than my six three. She was thin, but there was strength in her body too, especially those toned legs. Damn, she had legs that didn't quit. Second to her eyes, they were my favorite feature.

She swallowed, using her napkin to wipe her soft, supple lips. "Have you heard of Temecula?"

"No."

"It's about ninety minutes southeast of LA. Great weather, which is a good thing, considering where I lived. When I was sixteen, I ran away from home."

My jaw dropped. "Sixteen?"

"Sixteen," she repeated.

"May I ask why?"

"My parents were more interested in drugs than their daughter." She sighed. "I didn't think anything of it when I was little. Isn't that crazy? I was just a kid and thought everyone's parents were stoned twenty-four seven."

That wasn't crazy but it was sad. A runaway? She didn't seem hard enough to have lived on the streets. She seemed too refined and delicate.

"I learned soon enough it wasn't normal. I learned how to take care of myself. And when things got really bad, I decided it wasn't worth staying."

At sixteen. It was unfathomable. "Where'd you go?"

"I stayed in Temecula, actually. I didn't really have a plan when I left home. I was mad and a teenager and just . . . left. Rational thought didn't really enter the mix at that point."

Yeah. Because she'd been *sixteen.* "I can understand that."

"So I left with a backpack full of clothes and some cash I'd been stealing from my parents. I was going to walk to LA."

"What made you stay?"

"I met a friend. She's my best friend to this day and was living with two other kids in a junkyard outside of town at the time."

"A junkyard?"

Londyn nodded. "Yes. That junkyard became my home for two years. Eventually, six of us lived there. That Cadillac? That's where I lived. I slept in the backseat."

All I could do was blink with my mouth hanging open.

No wonder she hovered over that car.

"Did your parents ever . . ."

"No, they never found me. I don't know if they even looked. As far as I know, they didn't report me missing or contact the police. They just let me go."

My jaw clicked shut and a rage of temper ran through my blood. *Pieces of shit.*

"Don't get angry on me there," Londyn teased, bumping my elbow with her own. "We weren't completely without adult supervision. There was a man who ran the junkyard and watched out for us. It was his property, and Lou let us live there. He let us use the bathroom and shower in his shop. If we got sick, he'd get us medicine."

I blinked at her. "He didn't report it?"

"He knew that if the cops came, we'd be gone. And we were all better off in a junkyard than going back to the hells where we'd come from. He didn't kick us out and that was more than any adult in my life had done for me before."

"Foster care?"

She huffed. "I wasn't going into foster care and no one was going to make me."

"So you lived in a car for two years."

"I did." A small smile toyed on her lips.

She spoke of that place like she'd lived a normal, happy and blessed childhood in a *junkyard.* At sixteen. It wasn't magical, but you'd think it was, looking at her face.

I shook my head. "I-I don't even know what to say."

"I know it seems crazy. But you have to understand, for the first time in my life, I had people who cared about me. The six of us kids and Lou, we were a family. We looked out for one another. We made sure we all had food to eat and clothes to wear."

"What did you do for money? What about school?"

"School was forgotten. But we all worked. We put the junkyard as our address. We used each other's names as our parents' names. I waitressed at a pizza place."

Waitressing was a typical job for a teenager. What had her bosses thought? Had her customers known she'd leave work to go home to a car? "I can't wrap my head around this life."

She laughed, the musical sound drifting out over the water. "Think of it like camping. We were a bunch of kids who camped every night of the week."

"What did you eat?"

"Easy stuff. Peanut butter and jelly sandwiches. Fast food if we had the money. Bananas. Canned green beans. I brought a lot of pizza back for us to share."

"Hmm." My mind whirled. What would that have been like? At sixteen, I'd been worried about girls and my truck. Would I have survived a runaway life at that age? Definitely not.

Londyn was one tough woman. Tougher than I ever would have guessed. She didn't have manicured nails but she took care with her appearance. Her hair was styled. She had on makeup and though her clothes were casual, they weren't cheap.

And she'd spent two years as a teenager living in a car.

"It's your turn to answer the question."

I scoffed. "Hell, I can't compete with that."

She laughed again, covering her lips with a hand to hide the food she'd just put in her mouth.

I grinned and took a bite, then set my fork aside. "I grew up here in Summers. Born and raised. My parents live here. My grandparents on both sides do too."

"You're lucky."

"Yes, ma'am."

As a kid, I'd known I had it good. But all kids took things for granted. I hadn't appreciated the necessities in my life like clean blankets, healthy food and nice clothes. Compared to her life, I'd lived like a king.

But that wasn't what she was talking about, was it? She didn't feel like she'd missed out on the material things. She knew I was lucky because I had an amazing family.

It made me feel guilty for all the shit I'd put them through.

The good thing was, we'd come out together. My dad was my best friend and my mom was a living saint.

"What happened after California?" I asked. "How'd you get from California to Boston? I'm guessing that Cadillac wasn't in driving condition if it was in a junkyard."

"No." She giggled. "It was a wreck. It came later, after we all went in separate directions. My two friends, Gemma and Katherine, and I took a bus to Montana."

"Why Montana?"

She shrugged. "Why not? We wanted to see what it was like."

"And?" I'd always wanted to visit Montana and camp in Big Sky Country. We had the Appalachians, and they were a world of their own. Once or twice a year, I'd arrange a camping trip to get away and explore. But Montana was a bucket-list trip. "How was it?"

"Beautiful. Raw."

I was jealous at the wonder in her voice. "How long were you there?"

"About four months. Gemma and Katherine stayed longer. As far as I know, Katherine is still there, but we lost touch."

"And Gemma?"

"She found me in Boston."

"Ah. Did you go straight from Montana to Boston?" I asked.

"Sort of. I made some stops along the way, but nothing lasted longer than a month or two. When I got to Boston, I hadn't planned on staying, but I met someone. We got married and I stayed. Then we got divorced and I left."

Londyn sounded as enthusiastic about her former marriage as I was about mine.

"And now you're on the road."

She nodded. "Yes."

I went back to my meal, eating quietly as she did the same, until another question came to mind. "How'd you get the car from California?"

"I called the junkyard owner and bought it. He didn't remember me at first, but I told him who I was and why I wanted the car. He wanted to give it to me for free but I insisted on paying. Then I had it hauled to Boston and had it restored."

I whistled, visualizing the price tag. It had to be at least a hundred grand. For a woman without much of an education who'd lived her life on the road, how'd she come into that kind of money? Her husband, maybe?

She tossed her fork into the nearly empty container and closed the lid. "That was amazing."

"Not bad for a small town in West Virginia."

"I'm quite impressed with this small town."

My chest swelled with pride at my home.

Londyn and I sat staring out at the water as the bottom of the sun dipped below the horizon. Night wouldn't be far off but I wasn't in a hurry to leave. Londyn didn't seem to be either, so we sat there in comfortable silence, listening to the water lap against the shoreline and the wind rustle the trees.

When was the last time I'd just sat beside a woman? The last time I'd been alone with a woman who wasn't a relative or who wasn't at the shop for an oil change had been over a year ago. A blind date from hell. The woman had talked the entire meal about money. Specifically, my money. She'd wanted to know how much I made at the garage, how much I would inherit from my parents and how much my truck and home were worth.

I'd lost her number before the waitress had delivered our meal.

Sitting with Londyn was different. There were no expectations for conversation. I asked questions not to fill the silence, but because I genuinely wanted to hear her answer. Maybe this was easy because it wasn't a date.

Londyn was leaving Summers in her rearview as soon as her car was fixed.

The lake reflected the yellow, orange and midnight-blue of twilight as tree crickets chirped and lightning bugs sparked.

"You got more than your fair share of the questions tonight," I said. "Sorry."

"That's okay." She tipped her head back to examine the stars above.

I did the same, resting on my elbows. An airplane's light blinked as it flew past.

"Do you ever wish on a star?" she asked.

"Not since I was a kid."

"I used to wish on them every night. The top in the convertible wouldn't raise or lower but the trunk was so wide that I'd lie on it every night and make a wish."

"Any come true?"

"Some." She dropped her back to the rock, lying flat. Her hair splayed over the smooth, brown surface. "I got an education. That was a wish. I didn't want to be the stupidest person in the room anymore."

"I highly doubt that was ever the case." I dropped to my back, lacing my hands behind my head.

"When I was sixteen and working alongside all these other teenagers who were reading *Great Expectations* and Shakespeare, it sure felt like I was stupid. But I worked hard in Boston and got my diploma."

"Did you go to college?"

She shook her head. "No."

"Me neither." I'd planned on college and following in my father's footsteps, but then my life had taken a different path. The good thing was, I'd had some skills to fall back on. "My grandfather started Cohen's Garage. He passed it down to me when he was ready to retire."

"Not your father?"

"No, Dad's a doctor."

"You're a car doctor instead."

"Exactly." I chuckled. "Any other wishes come true?"

"I used to wish for a home—a real home. That one came true in Boston, but then I realized a house and a husband and a paycheck didn't mean I'd be happy."

So she'd left it all behind. Was she still searching for a home? Or had she given that wish up? "Think you'll have a home in California?"

"I don't know. Maybe." She pushed up to sitting. "I might get a job. I might find somewhere new to live for a while. It's not normal, but I think that nomadic lifestyle is more my style. I like the freedom. I didn't realize it until I left Boston, but I was trapped there. I was in a cage."

I sat up too. "So it's you and your car exploring the country." She'd take her home wherever she went.

"Well, the car is going to a friend. But I'll get another. Maybe I'll drive the new one around for the next year. Maybe I'll hop on a plane and explore Europe or Australia or Asia. There's a comfort for me, knowing it's all my decision. I'm not obligated to live my life according to anyone else's plan."

"Huh." I ran a hand through my hair. The idea of travel was exciting, but not having a home to return to seemed lonely to me. But again, we'd come from different worlds. Summers would always be my home.

"Sounds crazy, right?"

"Nah. Just different. I've lived in this town my entire life. I can't imagine living anywhere else." I didn't *want* to live anywhere else, and I was still a free man.

She gave me a sad smile. "I'm glad you have deep roots."

"Me too."

She held my gaze, enchanting me with every passing second. What a life she'd lived. What a story. And now she'd give in to her wanderlust and see the world. What an adventure it would be to go along for the ride.

Her eyes glowed green in the fading light. When we'd sat up, we'd shifted closer together. All I had to do was lean over and I could take her lips in a kiss. I'd thought about those soft lips a lot the past day, wondering what she'd taste like. Would she kiss me back? Or would she dump the rest of her curry over my head? Maybe I'd misread the blushes and shy smiles.

Londyn's eyes dropped to my mouth. *Fuck it.* She was leaving and I might as well go for broke. I had just dipped low, brushing my lips against hers, when a car door slammed on the street behind us.

She jumped, breaking us apart.

Damn. The universe was telling me something. This woman, who'd be a memory before the week was out, was not for me.

"Probably better head home. It's getting late." I sighed, collecting my container and stacking hers on top. Then I stood, holding out a hand to help her up.

"Thanks." She brushed off the seat of her shorts and I didn't let myself look at her ass—much.

I stepped off the rock first, my bare feet sinking into the lush grass.

She hopped down behind me. "Thanks for not kicking me off your rock."

"Anytime."

"Good night, Brooks." She waved, then started toward the motel.

I lifted my arm to wave goodbye. I couldn't bring myself to do it.

There was something fresh about her. Maybe it was her outlook on life or her spirit. Maybe it was that she had gone through so much and she hadn't become jaded or cynical. Londyn intrigued me. She stirred my blood.

44

And damn it, I hadn't had enough time tonight. I wanted more, not just to give that kiss another go, but to talk.

I should let her go.

"Londyn?" I called.

"Yes?" She turned, flashing me those gorgeous green eyes.

"You feel like sharing the rock again tomorrow night?"

She smiled. "Yes."

6

LONDYN

"THAT'S A LOT OF MEAT. There's no way I can fit this in my mouth."

Brooks cocked an eyebrow. "The words any man wants to hear."

"Get your mind out of the gutter." I rolled my eyes, then hefted the sandwich he'd brought me to my mouth and attempted a bite.

The thing was a foot long and weighed at least a pound—a solid brick of meat and cheese with a sprinkling of shredded lettuce and tomatoes. Oil and vinegar coated it all and a thick, sturdy loaf of bread acted more like a boat than bookends.

"Yum." I hummed as I chewed, my cheeks bulging.

"Good, right?"

"So good." The words came out garbled.

He laughed, then took a bite of his own, groaning as he ate.

As with all other things Brooks Cohen, that groan of his was damn sexy. It was low and deep, more like a hum coming from his heart than a sound formed from his voice box. It was soft too—if I wasn't sitting within a foot of his side, I would have missed out.

Tonight was the third night in a row I'd eaten on the lakeside rock with Brooks. Thai that first time. Last night he'd brought pasta. And tonight, subs. Three delicious meals made more so because of the company.

We ate in silence, like the other nights, neither of us anxious to fill the quiet moments. It was like sharing a meal with an old friend, not a new acquaintance. We'd talk later. The sun had yet to drop over the horizon so there'd be time. Brooks would ask questions and I'd soak up his own answers. Last night, we'd stayed out stargazing and talking about nothing until nearly eleven.

These three meals had been three of the most relaxing I'd had in years. I didn't have a phone buzzing and demanding attention. There was no talk about work, something I realized now had been the constant theme whenever talking with Thomas.

Conversation with Brooks was a discovery. A slow, stirring journey that spanned numerous topics. He'd told me about his parents and growing up in Summers. I'd told him about my life in Boston, skirting around the details of my divorce.

The truth was, I hadn't thought much about Thomas in the past few days. I didn't miss him—hadn't for months. I didn't yearn for the early days of our marriage, when there had been more joy and thrill. Though things had taken a hard turn at the end, a part of me was glad we were over.

Would I have left otherwise? If there hadn't been Secretary and the affair, would I have ever realized how unhappy I'd become?

Money had blinded me. I wasn't in love with Thomas. My job had lost its appeal. That life was devoid of passion.

Passion, I did miss.

Which was probably another reason the last three nights had been so refreshing. Passion and anticipation coated each minute I spent with Brooks like warm chocolate on vanilla bean ice cream. It took every second to the next, delicious level.

He hadn't made a move to kiss me again. Would he try again tonight? My time in Summers was coming to a close. I wasn't sure I'd be able to drive away without at least one kiss to take with me. It would be a memory I'd tuck into my pocket to pull out and replay on the lonely days.

"I picked up your car before I came tonight," Brooks said. "It's all done. Good as new."

"Really? Okay." That was disappointing. Expected, since he'd promised three or four days, but disappointing. As a show of faith, I hadn't asked Brooks about my car. Or maybe I hadn't asked because I was content for the moment.

Brooks swallowed the last bite of his sandwich. How he could eat all that and maintain a flat stomach was borderline unfair. I'd only made it through a third of mine and was stuffed. I wrapped it in the paper and set it aside.

"You'll be back on the road tomorrow."

Did I hear a hint of disappointment in his voice? Or was I projecting my own? "That's fantastic."

Liar. Maybe I could stay longer? I didn't have a schedule. This trip was all about me and going at my own pace. Tempting, but every night spent on this rock with Brooks would only make me hold out for the next.

I *could* stay, but I wouldn't. The time had come to move along to the next stop on this adventure. Once Karson had the Cadillac and I'd satisfied my curiosity about his life, I would be free to wander and go at my own pace.

"Brooks?" A woman's voice carried across the yard behind us. We both twisted, looking past a tree trunk.

"Damn it," Brooks grumbled, pushing up to his feet. "Be back."

"Okay."

He jogged across the yard, once again in bare feet, and met the woman as she came down from his porch. She wore black sunglasses that hid most of her face. Her brown hair was pulled up into a purposefully messy knot on the top of her head. The summer dress she wore wrapped around her body, tying tight underneath her generous breasts.

She was beautiful, and clearly upset with my dinner companion. She planted her hands on her waist and screwed up her mouth in a tight line as Brooks spoke. When it was her turn to talk, she cast a scowl my way.

Shit. She'd caught me staring. Should I hide? Who was she?

I hadn't asked if Brooks had a girlfriend. Considering we sat outside his house, I was certain he wasn't married. I'd made the assumption that he was the kind of man who wouldn't be sharing dinner with a woman if he were otherwise entangled.

Maybe that was stupid on my part. My husband had just cheated on me. But, call it a gut feeling, Brooks didn't seem to be the straying kind.

He was a man who bought a woman a cell phone because he didn't like the idea of her on the road without the ability to call for help. He was a gentleman in the truest sense of the word, putting me first in everything from opening a door to taking the first bite of a meal.

Not wanting to stare as he spoke to the woman, I turned my attention to the lake. I sipped the bottle of water he'd brought me as a speedboat raced through the calm water in the distance. It traveled fast, a white fleck on the water by the time Brooks came back.

"Sorry about that." He hopped up on the rock.

"That's okay. Do you need to go?" An engine started in the distance and I glanced over my shoulder as the woman reversed a Honda out of his driveway.

"No. That was my ex-wife, Moira."

"Ah." Of course she'd be beautiful. I bet she'd made a beautiful bride in a white gown, walking to a handsome Brooks in a tux, standing at an altar. My mental picture was tinged with green.

When was the last time I'd gotten jealous? Had I been jealous of Secretary? Hurt, yes. Betrayed, absolutely. But jealous? Not really.

Had his house been Moira's home? Had she shared this rock too?

"Do you ever swim in the lake?" I blurted.

It was an odd question, given the moment, but I didn't want to talk to Brooks about his ex-wife. I sensed he didn't either. Especially on our last night.

"Sometimes." Brooks went along with my change of subject. "When it's hot."

"I only learned to swim five years ago." My parents hadn't put me in swim lessons, and I'd been busy working my summers away instead of spending them at the community pool. On my honeymoon, I'd stayed safely in a lounge chair.

It wasn't until Thomas had insisted on scuba diving on a trip to the Caribbean that I'd had to admit I didn't know how to swim. He'd insisted on lessons.

"I was supposed to take private lessons, but when I got to the pool, there had been a mix-up and they'd put me in the kids' class. They offered to switch things around, but I stayed. The kids didn't care that a grown woman couldn't swim. I wasn't quite as pathetic."

"There's a lot of folks who live around here, around this lake, and don't swim." Brooks nudged my shoulder with his. "It's not pathetic."

I smiled. "Thanks."

The inability to swim hadn't been important until Thomas had pointed out I was lacking. He seemed to find more flaws with me than I did myself. Each time he realized I'd missed something in my youth that set me apart from other cultured adults, he remedied it immediately.

Londyn hasn't ridden a horse? He bought me a horse and had it stabled with a riding instructor.

Londyn can't tell the difference between merlot and cabernet? He hired a sommelier to join us for dinner three nights a week.

Londyn doesn't like the opera? He bought season tickets because I hadn't been enough to appreciate it.

I hated the fucking opera. Red wine, no matter the grape, tasted like red wine. And horses scared the piss out of me.

Yep. I didn't miss him at all.

A bird chirped loudly from above, causing me to turn. It was perched in a tree next to Brooks's back deck. "I like your house."

"Thanks." He turned, taking in the back of his house too. "I bought it after the divorce."

That answered my earlier question about Moira. "It's nice. Very quaint."

The Victorian style was complete with tall roof peaks and curled gables in their apex. On the rear side of the home, overlooking the backyard, two dormer windows emerged from the chocolate roof. The rest of the home was white. The only thing that differentiated the various sides and sections of the exterior walls was the texture. Some of the siding was horizontal boards, other parts overlapping scallops.

"I love all the windows." The abundance of paned glass meant that most rooms were probably flooded with daylight.

"Same. That's what sold me on the place. In the summer I don't have to set an alarm. I wake up with the sun."

"I haven't set an alarm since Boston. I used to wake up at four every morning. I'd go to the gym and come home to get ready for work. In the winter, I'd be up for hours before the sunrise. Maybe I'll get up with the sun from now on too."

"Some days the alarm is unavoidable," he said. "There are days when I've got a lot happening in the shop. I've never quite mastered staying ahead on office work. It was really bad in the beginning when I took over for Granddad. I had a hell of a time keeping up. Figured it out eventually though. Tony helps keep me from drowning."

"Do you like your job?"

"Yes." His one-word answer held so much truth. Brooks *loved* his job, without a doubt. "What did you do in Boston?"

"I worked for my husband's company as his assistant." I turned to the lake again.

"Did you like it?"

"Yes, I did, actually. It was the first job where I was challenged. And Thomas was great about letting me pick and choose what I wanted to work on. I started out with the easy stuff. Phones and scheduling meetings into his calendar. But it grew."

I liked to think he'd suffered some at work after I'd quit. That was my ego talking, but no one wanted to admit they were easily replaceable.

"I've thought about getting an office manager," Brooks said. "Someone who can do the bookkeeping and order parts and keep the papers from stacking up on my desk. I sure wouldn't miss it. I'd much rather work on cars. Use my hands."

He had great hands. His fingers were long and calloused at the tips. His palms were wide and soft in the center. I was envious of my own damn car. The Cadillac had felt those hands skim across her surface.

"I wasn't sure exactly when you'd have the car done. You said a few days, but I didn't think you'd have it ready so soon."

"No faith in me?" He feigned a wince. "I'm hurt."

"You've exceeded all my expectations."

"My pleasure." His deep, soothing drawl was so comforting, it gave me the courage to ask the question on my mind.

"When I booked my room, I had it through tomorrow. I don't want to cancel on Meggie with such short notice. If I stayed one more night, would you go to dinner with me?"

I held my breath. It was the first time in my life I'd asked a man on a date. But he'd say yes. Right? He was enjoying these dinners as much as I was, wasn't he? Otherwise, why would he have invited me here each night?

"I, uh . . ." Brooks ran a hand through his hair. "I can't. Sorry."

My heart plummeted. *Ouch.* "That's okay."

A tense silence stretched between us. Brooks didn't offer any explanation as to why he couldn't meet me tomorrow. I sat perfectly still, unsure what to say. Maybe he had to work late. Maybe he didn't like eating at restaurants. Maybe he had a date. If that was the reason, I didn't want to know.

Without dinner tomorrow, this was the last time I'd spend with Brooks. I'd see him at the shop tomorrow morning when I collected my car, but it would be a brief farewell before I left Summers and Brooks Cohen behind for good.

My stomach clenched. It had to be the sandwich, not the idea of leaving. I'd simply eaten too much.

Time to go. The urge to leave hit hard, shoving me to my feet. Staying until dark wasn't going to happen tonight. I didn't have a wish to make. "I'd better get going. I need to pack."

"Londyn." Brooks stood, blocking the way off the rock. "Don't. Not yet."

"I think it's for the best." I met his blue gaze and my resolve to walk away broke. There was so much apology in those eyes. So much longing.

"I—" Without finishing, he closed his mouth and shifted, making room for me to walk past.

We both knew it was better to end this before things got complicated.

It wasn't like I didn't have some memories to take along. I'd look back on my time in Summers and remember this handsome man who'd been my dinner date three nights in a row. I'd remember this rock and how I preferred it to any table. I'd remember that almost kiss.

"Thank you," I said as he joined me on the grass. "It was lovely to know you, Brooks."

"Likewise, Londyn." He held out his hand and I slipped mine into his grip.

Neither of us let go.

He tightened his hold, pulling me closer. His gaze dropped to my lips and my breath hitched. Was he going to kiss me after all? It would certainly ease the sting of rejection. He leaned closer. My eyes drifted closed.

A whisper of a breath floated across my cheek as his mouth came down and he planted a kiss.

On. My. Cheek.

Disappointment flamed it red. My pride turned black and blue and I pulled my hand free of his grasp. "Good night, Brooks."

He took a step back. "Night, Londyn."

Then I spun around and marched for my motel room.

Time to get the hell out of Summers, West Virginia.

And far away from Brooks Cohen.

CLANK.

I jumped at the noise as it echoed from the garage. I stalled outside the door, not sure if I should get any closer. Was that normal garage noise? Because it sounded really loud. When nothing followed, I took another step.

Clank. Thud. Clank.

I jumped again, gasping at the bangs and clashes that came in a steady stream.

"Goddamn it!" Brooks roared.

Then came another crash. This one sounded like metal hitting metal, followed by the clink and clatter of tools hitting the concrete floor.

"Fuck!"

Uh . . . What the hell was going on? Was he hurt? I stepped forward, not sure what to expect, and peered around the door.

Brooks was pacing beside my car, his fists clenched in fury and his chest heaving.

I followed his gaze.

"What happened to my car?" I shrieked, stepping inside.

Long scratches ran up the length of the red paint. They were thin and narrow, angry as they cut through the smooth surface. It wasn't as bad as when I'd skidded into the guardrail, but it wasn't good either. The trunk was covered in yellow. The paint dripped to the floor, puddling next to a tire.

My hands dove into my hair. "Oh my God."

"Londyn, I can explain." Brooks held out a hand.

"Yes. Please." I nodded, unable to look away from the wreckage.

"Someone broke in last night and vandalized the place."

I tore my eyes away from the Cadillac and took in the rest of the garage. The same yellow paint on my car had been splashed on one of the cinderblock walls. Tools were scattered across the floor. Tires that had been stacked against the far wall were strewn around. There was another car in the opposite bay but it looked unharmed.

"Who would do this?"

Brooks sighed, planting his fists on his hips. "I don't know."

"Take a guess." This was a small town. He had to have some idea who would do this to me. And the narrowed look on his face said he definitely had an idea.

"Moira."

His ex-wife? "Why?" Was this because she'd seen us sitting on that rock last night? "I'm no one. I'm leaving. Or I was until this."

His lips pursed into a thin line. "She gets jealous. She knows I've got a thing for you."

"Oh." My anger flatlined. "You do?"

"Think that's pretty obvious, don't you?"

"But you didn't kiss me last night." He'd rejected my date.

"No, I didn't." He walked to the Cadillac, leaning against the scratched side panel. I couldn't see the driver's side, but I was guessing it hadn't fared well either. "That was my mistake, and I regretted it all night long."

I'd sulked for hours as I'd slowly packed up my suitcases last night, wishing things had ended differently. I guess I'd get that wish because there'd be no goodbye today.

"What about my car?"

"I'll wash off the paint, but it'll have to go back to the body shop for the scratches."

I stepped closer, running my finger over a scratch. "Is that from a key?"

"Yeah," he muttered.

"You don't sound surprised."

"No." He blew out a deep breath. "I'm sorry. I'll pay to have it fixed, but it will take a while."

"Ironic, isn't it? If your ex is jealous, she should have just left me alone. I would have been gone."

Brooks pushed off the car and strode my way. "I'm so sorry, Londyn."

"It's not your fault."

"You'd be on your way if I had stayed away from you."

Even if I could get in my car right now, I wasn't sure that was what I wanted. "Make it up to me?"

"Absolutely. How?"

"Dinner tonight."

His chin fell. "I can't tonight."

Damn. Twice? "You keep shooting me down and it's killing my ego," I muttered.

"I can't do dinner. But how about that kiss?"

My eyes whipped up as he crossed the distance between us, his hands leading the way. They came to my face, cupping my cheeks and angling my head to the side. He inched closer until his boots touched my shoes. "Well?"

I nodded.

Brooks swept down and captured my mouth, stealing all the breath from my lungs. I went up on my tiptoes as his tongue swept across my bottom lip, the gentleman seeking permission. I opened for him, letting him dive in deep.

His hands stayed on my face, pulling me to him as he let one of those low groans loose, down my throat. It sent a rush to my core. His taste exploded on my tongue, the lingering bitterness of coffee mixed with his own sweetness. His tongue dueled with mine as those soft lips pressed hard.

I would have pegged Brooks as the type to go for soft and sweet at first, but there was nothing gentle or demure about this kiss. He took what he wanted, demanding more. It was hot and I'd feel his fingertips on my face for the rest of the day.

Other than our mouths, it was the only place we touched.

I didn't dare bring my hands to his chest. I didn't dare risk wrapping my arms around his waist or sidling my hips toward his. Brooks was in charge and he was doing a damn fine job without my help.

The kiss ended too quickly. He pulled away, letting me go as he wiped his mouth, leaving a smug smirk in place.

"Th-thanks." I was off-balance. "I feel better about my car."

He chuckled. "Same."

"So, I'll, uh . . . go." I took a step backward, pointing to the exit. If I didn't get out of here, there was a good chance I'd crawl my way up his body and we'd do a lot more than kiss. I spun around as a smile spread across my face.

"Londyn?" he called.

"Yeah?"

"Sorry about the car."

I glanced over my shoulder. "I'm not."

7

BROOKS

I RAISED my fist and pounded on my ex-wife's door. We'd been divorced for a decade but it still felt strange to knock after living here for years.

Moira's heels clicked across the wood floor I'd installed the year before moving out. She had a smile on her face when she answered the door—it dropped when she spotted me.

"Hi." She was wearing a simple black dress, as she did most summer days when she worked. In the winter, she'd add a cardigan. Moira was a receptionist at a dentist's office, and to most, she looked poised and professional. But I knew a viper lurked underneath the surface.

Moira was incredible when she wanted to be. When she didn't, her claws left a nasty mark.

"Why'd you do it?" I didn't bother with a greeting. We were beyond playing nice.

She was lucky I'd waited until after five to come to her house instead of marching down to Dr. Kurt's office and having this out with her at work.

"Do what?" She crossed her arms over her chest.

"Don't play dumb." I frowned. "That's my place of business."

"What are you talking about?"

"The last time you came in and messed up the place, you set me back a week. But you crossed the line here. You fucked with a customer's car."

"Are you drunk?" She leaned forward. "I haven't been to the garage in months."

It was always the same with her. Lie, lie, lie. Even when she knew she was caught, she never admitted defeat.

"Whatever. Stay the fuck away from my garage. The next time, I'm calling the cops."

"I didn't do anything, Brooks."

"Sure." *Heard that before too.* I spun on my boot and marched down the sidewalk.

"Brooks," she snapped.

I didn't answer.

"Brooks!"

I strode to my pickup.

"Fuck you." Now the fangs were out. Was it really a wonder we hadn't made it? I was almost to my pickup when she yelled, "Wait. Please."

I sighed, pausing on the sidewalk. "Yeah?"

"Are you coming tomorrow?"

I scoffed. "No."

"You promised."

"I said I'd think about it. I have, and I'm not coming."

"Grr," she snarled, stepping inside the house and slamming the door. It echoed down the block.

Typical. That wasn't the first time she'd slammed that door on me. I'd had enough of her bullshit to last a lifetime.

Moira had come over last night and asked me over for dinner. Her parents were coming to town tomorrow and had hoped to see me. It was something we'd done over the years, even after the divorce. I wasn't a fan of my ex but her parents were good people.

I'd have to catch them the next time. Tomorrow I'd still be fuming mad at their daughter.

The key marks in the Cadillac had Moira written all over them. A year after our divorce, I'd dated the new kindergarten teacher in town. Things had been going pretty well for about a month, then she'd called me one Sunday morning and told me we were over without explanation.

I'd found out a week later it was because Moira had keyed the hell out of my girlfriend's car.

I hadn't dated for two years after that. But then I'd finally met a nice woman who'd worked with Dad at the hospital. Moira hadn't even given us a month. Six dates in and Moira had slashed her tires. All four of them.

She'd admitted to that one eventually, after the nurse had moved away from Summers. She'd gotten drunk one night and called me in tears, begging for a second chance. When I'd assured her it would never fucking happen, she'd gotten nasty and vowed no woman would ever hang around for long.

Years later, I guess she still meant it.

Moira's antics had cost me stress and money I could have used for much better things. I'd paid to have the key marks fixed and the tires replaced. But I hadn't bothered to date since. No woman I'd met had seemed worth the drama.

Until Londyn.

Even after I'd admitted it was likely my ex-wife who'd trashed her car, Londyn hadn't run away screaming. She'd asked me out. Then she'd let me kiss the hell out of her.

I grinned over the steering wheel. Londyn McCormack was one of a kind.

Traffic was light, per usual, as I drove across Summers toward my parents' place. We had a standing dinner every Monday night—had for sixteen years. Tonight was one of the few times I'd contemplated skipping.

I looked forward to Mom's cooking and shooting the breeze with Dad over a glass of scotch. But I had a limited number of nights with Londyn. More now than there had been this morning.

Moira's plan had backfired. Maybe she'd meant to chase Londyn out of town, but she didn't understand Londyn's attachment to that car. Most wouldn't unless they knew her story. That Cadillac was woven into her life. It was her childhood home brimming with fond memories.

She wouldn't leave Summers until it was in pristine condition, which gave me time. It might even take a week.

I'd called Mack at the body shop and explained the situation to him. After a string of curses, he'd agreed to fit it into their schedule again as well as cut me a break. He knew what Moira was like. But he didn't have the flexibility he'd had last week. I'd driven the Cadillac over and he'd promised to hurry.

We'd left it at that. My guess? Londyn would be on her way in a week.

One more week. Maybe she'd let me kiss her again.

Five minutes away from Mom and Dad's place, my phone buzzed with a text. They lived on fifty acres about ten miles out of town.

Mom: I didn't feel like cooking today. How about a pizza?

Pizza? I wasn't missing one of the few nights I'd have with Londyn for pizza. I pulled up Mom's number and sent the call through.

"I just texted you," she answered.

"I saw that. How mad would you be if I didn't make it for pizza?" My foot hovered over the brake.

"Hmm." A frown invaded her voice. "You never miss Monday dinner."

"Yeah, I know." I put my foot back on the gas. I *never* missed Monday dinner. The guilt was too much to live with.

"Is this about the garage?" Mom asked. "I heard what happened. I'm so sorry."

No shock Mom had heard. Tony had a big mouth. He'd come into the shop today, whistled and gotten right to work putting the place back to sorts. The two of us had had it all fixed before noon. While I'd spent my lunch hour catching up on everything I hadn't done over the morning, he'd disappeared.

Now I knew where he'd gone—to gossip with Sally.

"It's fine. No major damage." Except Londyn's car.

"Do you know who might have done it?"

Oh yeah, I knew. But Mom didn't need to know it was Moira. "Probably kids."

As far as the world was concerned, Moira and I had survived an amicable divorce. We were friendly in public. We supported one another though we lived separate lives. We smiled and played nice.

For Wyatt.

I'd been seventeen years old when my son was born. Moira and I had been high school sweethearts. Two stupid kids who thought they were invincible and that condoms were reasonable, not required.

We'd done our best as teenage parents. I hadn't spent my senior year in high school submitting college applications and making campus visits. I'd spent my free time after class at the garage working because it was the key to my son's survival.

Moira had lived with her parents until Wyatt was born, then she'd moved into my parents' place. After graduation, we'd married but lived with Mom and Dad until Wyatt was two.

The reason I didn't miss a Monday dinner was because Mom and Dad had helped us raise Wyatt those first two years. Mom had taught Moira how to feed him and rock him to sleep. She had taught me how to change a diaper and make a bottle for a midnight feeding. Dad had been Wyatt's doctor from the moment he screamed his first breath.

When my parents had needed a break, Moira's had stepped in to help.

Mom didn't ask me for much. Monday dinners weren't mandatory but I knew she looked forward to them. It was her special evening to spend with her husband, son and grandson.

Wyatt had been with Moira this past week. The great thing about us living in the same town, ten minutes from one another, was he had two rooms. He stayed with her for a week to ten days, then he'd come and stay with me for the same.

Now that he was a teenager and had his own vehicle, we didn't dictate custody schedules. Plus he was a good kid, making sure he spent time with us both.

This stretch at Moira's was going on seven days, and I missed him. We texted. I called him every day. But it was strange not to see him every night. With his summer football practice schedule and the job he'd taken running takeout around town, he was busy. It was the reason I ordered takeout most nights when he wasn't at my place. He was forced to come see me.

That, and no matter where he was staying, he came to Monday dinner.

As much as I wanted to see Londyn tonight, I needed my son more.

"Want me to go pick up pizza?" I asked Mom.

"You're coming?"

"I just pulled into the driveway."

She hung up on me and had the screen door open before I'd even shut off my truck. As long as it was light out and the temperature was above fifty degrees, Mom kept her front door open with only the screen to block the bugs.

She shooed me away as I walked to the door. "You can go."

"I'll stay." I met her by the door, bending to kiss her cheek.

"Go. Besides, your son just texted me. Apparently, no one but me and your father want pizza tonight."

My forehead furrowed, taking my phone from my pocket. "Wyatt didn't text—never mind."

Wyatt: I got offered an extra shift tonight. Can I take it?

He was desperately trying to save money for college.

Me: Sure.

Wyatt: Coming home tonight. Be there about ten.

Me: Drive safe.

"He's working," I told Mom, tucking my phone away again. But I'd get to see him tonight.

"He's a hard worker, that boy. Like his daddy." She nudged my elbow. "Go. Do what you need to do. I'll cook something fancy next Monday to make up for this week."

"Are you sure?"

She smiled. "I'm sure."

"Thanks, Mom." I kissed her cheek once more, then turned and jogged to my truck. I waved goodbye as I pulled away, then headed toward town, calling the motel as I drove.

"Hi, Meggie. Say, I need a favor."

"IS THIS SEAT TAKEN?"

Londyn's head whipped my way. "What are you doing here? I thought you were busy."

"Change of plan." I pulled out the stool by her side, leaning my elbows on the counter.

The diner was packed. Every booth was taken and all the tables in the middle of the room occupied. Besides the stool I'd just claimed, only two others were empty.

The waitress brought over a menu, but I waved it away.

"You're not eating?" Londyn asked.

"I am, but I don't need a menu. I've ordered the same thing in this diner for the past fifteen years. A cheeseburger with extra pickles and no onion. Fries. A chocolate shake. This waitress is new to town, otherwise she wouldn't have bothered with the menu."

Londyn blinked.

"What? I'm hungry." I shrugged. "It was a busy day."

"Uh-huh," she muttered. "What are you doing here?"

I spun in my stool, giving her my full attention as I leaned in close. The vanilla scent of her hair caught my notice, the sweetness beating out even the grease wafting from the kitchen. The shuffle of forks and knives, the drone of conversation in the background, all disappeared.

Our noses were practically touching. No one in the room would mistake my intention, Londyn included. "I'm here for you, honey."

A smile tugged at the corner of her luscious mouth.

The kiss in the garage had replayed in my mind on a loop today. The memory of her soft lips and the slide of her tongue had distracted me more than once as I'd worked. I didn't care that we were in a restaurant full of people. I needed another taste.

"Here you go, ma'am." The waitress broke the moment, bringing back the noise, as she slid a plate in front of Londyn.

"You ordered pie?" And not just one slice but three. The diner's famous apple—my favorite—the chocolate cream and Wyatt's favorite, cherry.

"I did." She picked up her fork. "I used to go to the grocery store as a kid and buy the pies they had on sale. You know, the day-old ones they sell cheap. When I was living with my parents, I'd hide in my bedroom and eat the whole thing myself. At the junkyard, I'd buy one if I had the money and share. But then diets and exercise became a thing and I didn't eat pie for dinner anymore. Tonight, I said fuck it."

I chuckled. "Good for you."

"When was the last time you had pie for dinner?"

"Can't say I ever have."

Her fork dove into the chocolate cream. She hummed and her eyes drifted closed when the bite passed her lips. She savored it, rolling it around in her mouth. The woman had a talented tongue—lucky pie. She moaned again, torturing me with the subtle sound.

She swallowed, then shot me a smile that was pure sex. "You're missing out."

I snapped my fingers, raising my hand in the air to flag down the waitress. When she came over, I pointed to Londyn's plate. "I'll have that."

Londyn laughed, going in for another bite.

It didn't take the waitress long to serve up my pie. I dug into the apple first. "Damn, that's good. I'll probably give myself a bellyache with this, but I'm not leaving a bite behind."

"Some mistakes are worth the consequences."

"True," I said. "What was the last mistake you made that you didn't regret?"

She tilted up her chin and cast her eyes upward, the way she did whenever she was thinking over one of my questions. When she had her answer, she looked at me with those bright green eyes sparkling. "I wasn't paying attention to the road when I got that flat tire. I was mad at myself at the time. Now, not so much."

"I'm rather fond of that flat tire, myself."

Londyn giggled, taking a stab at the cherry. "Your turn."

A mistake I didn't regret? Easy answer. *Wyatt.*

I opened my mouth to tell her about him but stopped short. He was the most important person in my life. He was my pride and joy. And though I was fond of Londyn, before I shared him with her, I'd share her with him first.

Tonight. I didn't need Moira to make an under-the-breath comment about how I was hooking up with a woman from the motel.

Wyatt had been after me to start dating again, probably because he'd had a string of girlfriends this past year. He was a star on the football and basketball teams and had inherited my tall build. After the games, the girls all flocked his direction.

Thankfully, he had more common sense than I'd had at his age, and he assured me he hadn't had sex yet. And when he did, he promised to be safe.

I shoved another bite in my mouth to stop myself from bragging about my son. The praise was begging to be set free. Instead, I found a different answer to her question.

"The shop. About three years after I took it over from Granddad, I had a guy ask if he could buy it. I got greedy and asked for twice what he'd offered. He told me to shove it and left town. After that, I regretted it for years. Until one day, I just . . . didn't. I wouldn't give that shop up for anything in the world."

Someday, I'd pass it down to Wyatt if he had any interest. At the moment, I was just glad it was me and not some other lucky bastard who had the only tow truck in town and had been sent to rescue Londyn.

"I'm glad you didn't sell your shop," she said. "We don't know each other well, but I honestly can't imagine you doing anything else."

"Same here." I'd found my dream job at eighteen. Not many could say that.

We ate the rest of our pies, talking about nothing, until both plates were clear and my stomach bulged. I paid the check, shooting Londyn a scowl when she reached for her purse. Then I followed her out of the diner, ignoring the eyes on us as I placed my hand on the small of her back.

"May I give you a ride?" I asked, waving to my truck down the block.

"How'd you know where I was? Wait." She held up her hand. "Let me guess. Meggie."

"You'd be correct." I walked to the truck.

Londyn stayed on the sidewalk. "If I get in with you, what kind of payback can I expect from your ex-wife?"

I grumbled and kicked at a stone on the sidewalk. "I don't know. I don't know what she's thinking."

She wasn't, that was the problem. Moira had likely done her worst already, but I also hadn't had a woman in my life like Londyn. Sure, the others had been nice. I'd enjoyed dating them. But Londyn was different. There was passion and urgency. She was leaving and I was determined to make the most of this while I had the chance.

We were moving at warp speed here—no choice otherwise. That wouldn't escape Moira's notice. Neither would the hole left behind when Londyn left Summers.

"It doesn't matter." She stepped off the curb, meeting me by the door. "I'm not scared of your ex-wife."

Of course she wasn't. I grinned. "Good."

"We have an audience," she whispered.

"Yep," I whispered back. "Why do people think that just because I'm standing outside and they're sitting inside behind a window, we can't see them?"

Londyn giggled. "I can feel them staring."

"I want to kiss you." I inched closer.

Londyn rose up slightly off her heels. "But you probably shouldn't."

"No." Not with half the damn town staring. And not before I had a discussion with Wyatt.

I reached past her and opened the truck's door. Londyn climbed in, letting me shut her in, before I rounded the tailgate for my own side.

I frowned at the people in the diner, still staring, then started up the engine and backed away. Hell, I hadn't kissed her, but just taking her to the motel would probably stir the rumor mill.

"Why do I have a feeling that after tonight, a lot more people will know my name?" she asked.

I chuckled. "Small-town life."

She hummed.

Was that a good hum? Or a bad? She seemed to like this small town, for the time being. But I wasn't going to get my hopes up that Londyn would stay.

"What are we doing tomorrow?" she asked as the motel's sign came into view down the street.

"You assume we'll be doing something together?" I teased.

"Yes."

I shot her a wink. "I like that."

I had ideas for tomorrow night. Wyatt had football practice twice, once in the morning and another late afternoon. Then he'd be rushing off to work until the five restaurants in town that used him and a couple other kids to deliver were closed. My ideas for Londyn involved a repeat of that kiss we'd had in the shop, this time in a place where we could make it last.

"How about we start off with dinner?" That seemed to be working well for us.

"A restaurant or the rock?"

The rock. I wanted time alone with her, not with the town of Summers watching. "Your choice."

She flashed me that sexy smile. "The rock."

8

LONDYN

"GODDAMN, YOU CAN KISS," Brooks panted as he hovered above me. His lips were flushed and swollen. His hair was disheveled from where I'd had it between my fingers. Twilight danced around us and the fading light brought out the darker blue striations in his eyes. He'd gone from gorgeous to fucking magnificent.

The most handsome man on earth wasn't a Times Square model or a Hollywood dreamboat. He was a mechanic in West Virginia.

And for the time being, he was mine.

Maybe if I had three more nights like this, I'd have his features memorized for life.

Brooks rolled away, lying flat on his back at my side. Our hands were nearly touching, but not quite.

My chest heaved as my shoulders pressed into the hard rock. I gazed up into the sky, bringing a hand to my lips. Three nights of making out like teenagers and they'd been rubbed raw.

All we'd done was kiss. Brooks always stopped us before we could go too far. So I had chapped lips and an ache in my core that hurt.

This kissing was taking a toll on Brooks too. He shifted uncomfortably, cocking a knee to hide the bulge in his jeans. An impressive bulge at that, especially when it was digging into my hip.

We'd both be going to sleep frustrated tonight. I refused to release some of the tension on my own. If and when Brooks decided to let go of the ironclad grip he had on his control, I wanted this eager desire burning hot under the surface. For once, I was letting the foreplay drive me wild.

With other men, Thomas included, kissing had become a boring preview to a boring feature title. But damn, it was fun with Brooks. I'd forgotten how fun kissing could be on its own.

Something told me that even after we had sex—if we had sex—kissing would always be an event of its own.

Well, for the days I was here.

Lying by his side, it was easy to forget this situation was temporary. Brooks erased the future with his lips. All that mattered was now. Here. My future was on this rock with nature's symphony drowning out reality.

Brooks stretched a finger to touch one of mine. "What are you thinking about?"

"I'm leaving."

"Yeah." He covered my hand with his. "But not yet."

I smiled, turning my head to look at him. His grin was waiting. "No, not yet."

My car was at the body shop and the crew there hadn't even started on it yet. They could take their time. If it was done tomorrow, I doubted I'd leave anyway.

I wasn't done with Summers yet. I wasn't done kissing Brooks.

He raised his left hand, taking a glance at his watch. "I'd better get on home soon."

Brooks had sent me on my way before ten each night. The stars were barely coming alive as I sulked to my motel room. He claimed it was because he had an early morning ahead. Really, I think he worried we'd lose control.

"Okay." I sat up, but instead of standing and collecting my trash from dinner, I came down on top of him, pressing my chest to his. My lips brushed his mouth, placing a kiss at the corner.

He groaned, bringing a hand to my hair. He threaded his fingers into the strands, then tightened his stinging grip.

"Brooks," I hissed, my core tightening. Pulling against his hold, I puckered my lips, trying to reach his. But he held me tight, keeping our mouths from touching.

"If you kiss me again, I'll fuck you on this rock."

My breath caught. "What if I want you to fuck me on this rock?"

"Not tonight."

"Tomorrow?" I cocked an eyebrow.

He laughed. "No."

"Then the day after."

"Maybe."

"I can work with maybe." I smiled and pushed up.

I took a few deep breaths, orienting myself to the real world and blinking the dizzy haze of lust away. When I went to stand, Brooks's hand was waiting.

He helped me down from the rock and then we walked across the grass. I'd followed his lead tonight and skipped shoes. The grass was a thick, soft carpet between my toes. The last time I remembered walking barefoot in grass was as a little kid, when my mom had taken me to a park on one of her rare sober days.

"Tomorrow?" I asked.

He nodded. "Tomorrow."

I stayed still, wondering if he'd kiss me good night. He never did.

When we were off the rock, there was no kissing. The only exception had been that first kiss in the garage.

Was he nervous about someone seeing us together? Unless someone was looking for us or had parked in his driveway, we were fairly well hidden and private. The rock sat far enough away from the motel that not even a guest taking a stroll on the sidewalk would notice.

Maybe he was still concerned about Moira. I'd already told him I wasn't scared of his ex-wife. But I could see why he'd want to protect me from her jealousy.

Or maybe he didn't want to be seen with a woman whose stay in Summers was as short-lived as a shooting star against the midnight sky.

"Thanks for dinner."

He tipped his invisible hat. "Night, Londyn."

My cheeks flushed. He treated me like I was a queen. Thomas had tried to do the same, showering me with gifts and luxuries. But Brooks was different. All he'd bought me was takeout. But that tip of the hat made me feel respected—admired even.

Brooks remained where I'd left him as I crossed the lawn to the motel. Every time I glanced back, he was there. His shoulders had slumped. The smile on his face had dropped. He stood like a sullen statue.

Watching me walk away.

RESTLESS ENERGY INVADED my bones the next morning. I went about my normal routine, getting ready for the day before wandering to the office for an iced coffee and whatever pastry they had for purchase. Today's were blueberry crumb muffins—I ate two.

The past few days, I'd entertained myself by reading. I'd wander to a park about six blocks away, take up a bench and disappear into a fictional world. Meggie had let me borrow her stack of tattered thrillers and I'd already devoured two. They were the perfect distraction to keep me from watching the clock, counting down the minutes until dinner with Brooks.

But today, as I stared at the words on the cream page, I couldn't make any of them connect. After reading the same paragraph three times, I tossed the book aside and flopped onto my bench. I stared at the blue sky without focusing, much like I had at my ceiling last night after leaving Brooks on the lawn.

The image of him standing stoically as I walked away had haunted my sleep.

Except he wasn't on a lawn, but a sidewalk. And I was looking at him through my rearview mirror.

Just over a week ago, I'd been more excited about this trip to California than I'd been about anything in years. I'd been energized by the open road. I'd been at peace driving the Cadillac. And I'd been happily anxious at the prospect of seeing Karson's face after all this time.

I still wanted to get to California, didn't I? *Yes*. But not with the same desperation I'd had a week ago. I was embracing my days here, holding nothing back.

A flat tire and Brooks Cohen had thwarted my plans. His long, wet kisses and the slow strokes of his tongue had taken priority over my road trip.

The dull throb in my center pulsed. This anticipation was torture. Delicious, excruciating torture. Would tonight be the night? Would either of us be able to stop at a kiss? My fingers fidgeted on my stomach. My feet tapped on the bench.

I sat up and slid on my flip-flops, hoping the walk back to the motel under the shade of the serene trees would settle some of this anxiety.

It didn't. I was still flustered, brimming with sexual tension, when my temporary home came into view.

The parking lot of the motel was busier than it had been earlier. Inside the office, most of the chairs were taken, the local crew enjoying their midmorning coffee and gossip.

The warm and humid morning air filled my lungs. I'd be begging for the air conditioning later in the day, but no matter how hot and muggy it got by dinner, I wasn't missing time on that rock with Brooks.

It hadn't been bad the past few nights, but I was considerably stickier than I had been other mornings this week. Meggie had mentioned something about a heat wave coming. If it was too hot, maybe Brooks would invite me into his house tonight. Or I could invite him into my room for a motel picnic.

Thinking about the two of us kissing on a bed wasn't helping the tightening ache in my core.

"Londyn."

That voice was an ice bucket dumped over my head. I turned slowly on the sidewalk and came face-to-face with my ex-husband.

Goddamn it. I should have known he wouldn't let our last phone call be the end.

Thomas strode over from a black sedan with tinted windows. His dark hair didn't move as he walked. It was trimmed short except for the stylish swoop on top. Only when he was close could I make out the grays threaded through his temples.

"What are you doing here?" I fisted my hands on my hips. "And how did you find me?"

He frowned, looking me up and down. I was in a pair of boyfriend jeans, the holes at the knees bigger than a baseball. "I'm glad to see you're all right."

I was more than all right. Or I had been before he'd shown up. "Answer me. How did you find me, and what are you doing here?"

Thomas narrowed his boring, betraying brown eyes. "When you didn't return my calls, I reached out to Gemma."

"I heard."

Thomas's mouth thinned into an annoying line. "You found the time to call her but couldn't let me know you were alive."

"She's my friend. You are not." What the hell did he expect? We were divorced. And there was no way I was keeping in touch to see if junior was a boy or a girl.

"She mentioned you didn't take your phone."

"Nope."

He cringed. Thomas hated the word *nope*. He hated the word *yep*. When we'd been married, I'd used *yes* or *no* in place of their more casual counterparts so as not to irritate him.

"Londyn, be reasonable." He pinched the bridge of his nose. "We need to be able to get in touch with you."

"For what? And you still haven't answered my question. How did you find me?" Even Gemma didn't know I was in West Virginia.

"You left me no choice."

Ah, yes. This was my fault. "Uh-huh."

"I hired a private investigator."

My body went rigid and I stood taller. Thomas was tall, standing just over six feet. He had inches on me and a lot of bulk. He'd always kept in shape by running and lifting weights at our home gym. But as I straightened, he went back on his heels.

"That is a gross invasion of my privacy, Thomas." I poked a finger into his chest.

"What was I supposed to do, Londyn? Let my ex-wife drive across the country?"

"Yes!" I threw up my hands.

"I'm try—"

"Everything all right here?" Brooks's deep voice sank into my bones as he stepped up to my side.

"It's fine." Thomas waved Brooks along. "We're having a private conversation."

"What are you doing here?" I looked up at Brooks. Shouldn't he be at work already?

"I had a tow call at six this morning. Once I got the car to the shop, I came home to shower and get some coffee."

The strands of his golden hair were loose and damp. My fingers itched to dive in and twist a lock around my finger.

"You know each other?" Thomas narrowed his eyes as he looked between us.

"Yep." I smiled as he cringed again.

"Here." Thomas dug into the pockets of his slacks. They were navy and the seam was perfectly creased down the center. He'd probably flown to the airport and rented that sedan this morning. From his pocket, he pulled out a phone.

My phone, to be exact.

"How did you get that? I gave it to Gemma." And she never would have given it to him.

"My PI retrieved it for me."

"What?" I shrieked. "You mean he stole it from her."

66

Thomas shrugged, shaking the phone at me. "I need to be able to reach you."

"For what?" I swiped the phone from his grip and immediately threw it on the sidewalk. The screen didn't even crack. Damn it.

"Londyn, what the fuck?" Thomas bent for the phone but it was too late.

I raised my knee above my waist and brought my heel down onto the phone. The screen cracked, but it wasn't the utter destruction I'd been after. So I tried again, still not achieving total annihilation and now my heel hurt. Flip-flops weren't exactly practical for phone obliteration.

"Grr." I stomped again, no doubt looking like a toddler having a tantrum, only to catch the edge of the phone.

"Let me." Brooks took my elbow, easing me aside. Then with one step, he shattered my phone to pieces.

"Ha!" I giggled. "Thanks. I should have done that in Boston."

"Anytime." He smiled.

Thomas stared at us both, his mouth agape.

"Was there something else you needed, Thomas? I imagine Secretary would prefer it if you scurried back to the city. Does she know you're stalking your ex-wife? Oh, and should I start referring to her as Baby Mama now?"

"She was a mistake, Londyn. I made a mistake."

"So did I," I admitted. "Somewhere along the way, I forgot who I was."

"And you've remembered?"

I'd run away from home to find a better life all those years ago. I was doing the same now. "I'm not coming back to Boston, Thomas. That part of my life is over."

He stared at me for a long moment. His silence grew and stretched until the heat surrounded us, making it uncomfortably hot. Beside me, Brooks stood perfectly still. Most men would leave me here alone with Thomas, not wanting to intrude on a personal conversation.

Not Brooks.

He was here as the protector. The man who'd already bought me a phone, not stolen the one I'd chosen to leave behind. He wouldn't leave me alone with Thomas, maybe because he sensed I didn't want him to go.

"I can't change your mind," Thomas said.

I shook my head. "No."

Thomas studied my face, his gaze drifting over my mouth and up my nose. Then across my forehead and down my cheek. What was he doing? Was he memorizing me?

Maybe he finally understood this was the end.

"Goodbye, Thomas."

"If you change your mind —"

"I won't."

He dropped his chin, then looked up with a familiar, hardened stare. That shrewd, calculating gaze I'd seen so often at his office was fixed firmly in place. Without another word, Thomas shot a glare at Brooks, then strode to his car.

I held my breath, waiting until the vehicle's red taillights flashed and sped away from the curb. Then when I blew out all the air from my lungs, the weight of our divorce lifted.

Done. It was finally done.

My foot bumped the broken phone on the concrete. I bent and picked up the shattered pieces.

"So that's the ex?" Brooks asked.

"That's him."

"I'm starting to see why you ran away."

I smiled. "We weren't a good fit. I tried to fit into his life for a while, but . . ."

"You need to be free."

How was it that a man I'd known for a week knew me better than the man I'd lived with for years? This stunning, bold man saw me for who I was, not who I'd been pretending to be.

I'd tried so hard to fit into Thomas's life. But we were from different worlds. Thomas wore his wealth like a second skin. Even today, dressed in slacks and a light blue dress shirt, he exuded a level of class that was in his blood. He'd gone to a private school and his family spent Christmas in Fiji. His first car had been a Mercedes. He had two private planes.

I didn't want to fit into that world, where I was expected to act and speak a certain way.

I needed to be free.

"Thanks." I smiled at Brooks, admiring his clean-shaven face.

"For what?"

"For getting it. Not many do."

The corner of his mouth turned up. "You're one of a kind, Londyn McCormack. I've never met another person like you."

Thomas had said something similar when we'd met. Yet he'd tried to change me anyway. And shame on me, I'd let him. But not Brooks. He said those words with so much appreciation, I had a hard time breathing.

"Still on for dinner?" he asked.

I nodded, unable to speak.

Then he bent and kissed my cheek. Right there on the sidewalk in broad daylight with the entire congregation inside the motel's office bearing witness. Had he known I'd been feeling insecure? Most likely. Brooks seemed to understand me better than anyone ever had, including Karson.

Brooks left me on the sidewalk, crossing his lawn to where his truck was parked outside his garage. I stayed put—this time I had to watch him walk away.

My shoulders slumped. My smile dropped.

I didn't like it.

9

BROOKS

I USED my forearm to wipe the sweat from my forehead, then slammed the hood on the truck I'd just finished working on. It was the Chevy I'd hauled in early yesterday morning. The owner hadn't been able to get it to start. When I'd gotten it into the shop, I'd understood why. The thing hadn't been tuned up in years. The oil was practically sludge and the battery corroded. The starter was on its last leg.

The owner was new to Summers and had recently moved into the widow Aster's place after she passed in March. He'd given me the go-ahead to fix it all, so after getting parts yesterday and clearing the shop, today it had been my project.

"Chevy's done," I told Tony, wiping my forehead again. The sweat wouldn't stop dripping. "You can go ahead and call for him to pick it up."

"Will do, Brooks." Tony unscrewed the cap on a gallon jug of water and hefted it to his lips. Most of the water went inside his mouth, but a healthy trickle dripped down his chin and onto his coveralls.

No matter the temperature, Tony wore coveralls. Today, he'd at least given up hot coffee for cold water.

"What else we got on the docket for the day?" Tony asked, catching a dribble of water with his wrist.

I blew out a long breath and stared down the shop to the office. "I need to spend some hours on paperwork."

I hadn't sent invoices in a week, and as much as I hated keeping the books, I did like getting paid. Normally, I did my billing at night. I'd stick around after the shop closed. Unless Wyatt had a night off or we had Monday dinner at Mom and Dad's house, I was here until my growling stomach forced me home.

Those three or four nights a week made it possible for me to keep up on the business side of things. But with Londyn here, I'd left every night this week as soon as the last car was out of the shop and on the road with its owner.

Last night, I'd even closed up early. I'd hoped to catch Wyatt between football practice and work so I could tell him about Londyn. But he'd had a friend over when I'd gotten home, so I'd put it off. As soon as he'd gone to work, I'd hauled ass to the diner to pick up a couple of cheeseburgers, then met Londyn on the rock.

I'd been braced for her to be in an off mood thanks to her ex's visit. But she'd been her normal self when she'd shown up to meet me. We'd talked about her life over dinner. Londyn had quickly become my favorite topic. I'd asked her more questions about the journey from California to Montana to Boston and the places she'd stopped along the way.

By the time our cheeseburgers had been devoured, the pair of us had been too full to do anything but lie on the rock and watch the sunset with our hands linked.

As much as I would have liked kissing her for an hour, my lips were chapped and my control on the brink. One taste of her and I wouldn't have had the strength to stop at a kiss.

It was killing me to send her on her way to the motel each night. Alone. I'd walked stiffly home, my cock so swollen and aching I'd been forced to take a miserably long cold shower.

At the moment, a cold shower sounded great. I was melting, and just thinking about Londyn had stirred my dick to life.

The last time I'd been this hot for a woman had been . . . never. Not even as a teenager with Moira. And I was about done waiting. I'd been patient, but there was only so much a man could take.

I glanced at the clock. It was nearly noon. Tony had come in early this morning, around six according to his punch card. I'd been in shortly after eight, having hung around the house this morning to make sure Wyatt had breakfast before leaving for practice.

He was a zombie in the mornings. During the school year, both Moira and I made sure he was out of bed because he could sleep through ten blaring alarms. I'd hoped today might be the exception to his normal dazed routine so I could tell him about Londyn. But he'd nearly fallen asleep in his eggs.

I'd kept the conversation light, talking about football and his plans for a summer Friday night. He'd woken up enough to ask if he could take a girl to the movies. I'd agreed as long as he promised to spend some much-needed time with his old man on the boat tomorrow.

"I'm ready for the weekend," I told Tony.

"Same. You got plans?" He raised an eyebrow, no doubt wondering if I had plans with Londyn. Though he hadn't outright asked about her, it was no secret that I'd had dinner with her every night this week.

Meggie knew it. Therefore, Sally knew it. Therefore, Tony and the whole town knew it.

"Wyatt and I'll probably take the boat out."

"Good plan." He fanned his face. "This heat sure came on fast."

That was no joke. Another reason all Londyn had gotten last night was a chaste kiss good night. It was too damn hot to get worked up.

The worst of the summer heat had descended on Summers and would stick around until September. The days would be sticky, the nights muggy and thick. I needed to find time to tell Wyatt about Londyn and fast, because the rock wasn't going to be enjoyable again until fall. My back porch was much more comfortable — so was my bed.

"Tony?" I glanced around the empty shop. We were done with jobs for the day. "I think I'm going to spend the rest of the day in my office. You should take the afternoon off."

"Yeah?" He swiped up his gallon of water from the tool bench. "Think I'll take you up on that."

"Good. Have a nice weekend." I waved as he headed for the door.

"You too, Brooks."

I retreated to the office, sinking down in the chair and enjoying the slightly cooler air. The ceiling vent blew air into my face.

I closed my eyes, giving myself ten minutes to cool down and work up the gumption to open my laptop. But I didn't get ten minutes. I only got three before a rap came at the door. My eyes shot open to a beautiful sight.

Londyn leaned against the doorframe with a smile. A pair of denim shorts left most of her legs bare. Her green tank top dipped dangerously low in a scoop around her neck, the color bringing out the darker greens in her eyes. "Did I interrupt nap time?"

I waved her into the room toward the chair in the corner. "It's the heat. I needed a breather."

"Seriously." She fanned her face. "Someone turned up the dial because it's miserable."

"To what do I owe the pleasure?"

She relaxed deeper into the chair. "I'm bored. It's too hot to walk around town and I couldn't stay cramped up in my motel room any longer."

Londyn was growing restless. Soon, she'd be gone. "Got a call from the body shop today. They're starting on your car first thing Monday. Should be done by Friday at the latest."

"A week." She sighed.

"Is that too long? I can ask if they can hurry it." Maybe if I asked Mack, he'd be willing to work the weekend for some extra cash.

"No." She toyed with the frayed hem of her shorts. "I was just thinking it was too soon."

"It is too soon." I grinned. If she wasn't in a hurry, maybe I could convince her to stay through next weekend too.

"Mind if I hang out here for a while?" she asked. "I promise to ask you a bunch of questions and distract you from getting any work done."

"Well, when you put it like that . . ."

"I'm kidding. Give me ten to cool down and then I'll get out of your hair."

"Nah. Stay as long as you want." Nothing I needed to do today was urgent. It could all wait until the weekend. Or next week. Or the week after that. I'd probably want the extra work after Londyn left town anyway. It would be a nice distraction.

She sank even deeper, resting her head on the back of the leather chair. "What does a sexy mechanic do on a hot Friday afternoon in West Virginia?"

"Sexy?" I raised an eyebrow.

"Definitely sexy."

I chuckled. "Well, if that mechanic has a stack of bills to pay and invoices to send, he spends it in the office. If he's not in the mood to work and doesn't have a car to fix, he's out on the lake in his boat."

Londyn sat up straight. "You have a boat?"

"I do."

"Hmm. Interesting." She tapped her chin. "I happen to like boats."

Fuck the office. I stood from my chair and took my truck keys off the hook by the door. "Let's get out of here."

"I MIGHT HAVE INSISTED on dinner here if I'd known about it." Londyn stood at the end of my dock, staring down at my boat. "What else are you hiding from me?"

I held out my hand to help her into the boat. "Not a lot."

Only my teenager.

She smiled, her eyes hidden behind dark sunglasses as she took a seat in the passenger chair. She hadn't changed from the office. We'd driven over together and while I'd run into my house to swap my jeans and boots for board shorts and sandals, she'd wandered around the back of the house and found the dock.

"This is some place." She glanced back toward the house.

"It wasn't easy to come by, but I got lucky. My dad worked with the previous owner. She was a doctor at the hospital with him. She and her husband retired to Florida. Dad knew I was looking to buy and gave me the tip."

Lakefront homes with a private dock didn't appear on the market in Summers often. This one hadn't even been listed. We'd agreed upon a price, and when they'd moved out and I'd moved in, it was the talk of the town for weeks.

Some didn't like that they'd been cheated the opportunity to bid. If they knew how much I'd paid, they wouldn't be bitching. My offer had been three times as much as a house like this in town would cost. But the location had been worth taking a loan from my parents.

"Ready?" I asked and Londyn nodded.

I started up the boat, the rumble radiating from the engine through the floor. Then I eased us away from the dock, pointing the bow toward the center of the lake. When we were clear, I lowered the throttle.

Londyn's smile widened, her eyes aimed at the shore behind us as we flew. She pointed to the rock when she spotted it and laughed.

From the rock, the shoreline of the lake jutted out about thirty feet, hiding the dock from view. But out here, in the middle of the water, you could see how each landmark bookended my property line between my neighbor on one side and the motel on the other.

"This feels so good!" Londyn yelled above the rev of the engine and the slap of water against the hull.

The air rushed around us, creating the breeze we'd been missing. Her hair flew behind and around her face as she spun forward, watching where I was going.

We cruised, making the long lap around the lake. There were a few other boats out on the water today, all fishermen bobbing along the banks at slow speeds, and we waved as we passed them by. Tomorrow the lake would be packed, everyone out to enjoy the weekend and beat the heat.

I brought us to the center of the lake, to a spot where we'd have some privacy, and shut off the boat. No one would bother us out here. The fishermen were working the edges and coves where the walleye and smallmouth bass were searching for food.

"Thank you for this." Londyn slid her sunglasses into that long, blond hair, revealing those shining jade eyes.

My mouth went dry. "Water. Need one?" I sure as hell did. My head was dizzy and my heart was beating in hard *thunks*. The heat was getting to me again — I was burning up, from the inside out.

"I was thinking of going for a swim."

Thunk. "Didn't think you had a suit."

There was no tie at the nape of her neck. She hadn't gone to the motel to change after coming to the office.

"Do I need one?"

Thunk. "Uh, no."

She gave me a sly grin, one that said she was ten steps ahead and I'd better catch up fast. Her tank top was gone in a flash of cotton, leaving nothing but skin and black lace cupping perfect breasts. Londyn looked up at me through her lashes as her fingers trailed down the flat line of her stomach to the waistband on her denim shorts.

Those slim, lithe fingers flicked open the button. The zipper clicked, one notch at a time, until her hands slid toward her hips to push the shorts down her legs. She shimmied, a gentle sway, until all that was left was black lace.

"Are you swimming with me?" She stepped out of her sandals and walked to the back of the boat, stepping up on the bench seat, then the rear deck. Her toes wiggled forward until they were gripping the edge, ready to catapult her into the water.

I managed a nod.

Then she was off, the dive graceful and smooth, like the woman herself. The stunning woman who'd swept into my life and captured my attention like no other.

Thunk.

My hand pressed against my heart. She was stealing it, little by little.

"Are you coming in here?" she hollered from the water after popping up about twenty feet away. "Or are you afraid of a woman swimming in her underwear?"

"Smart-ass." I grinned, reaching behind my head to yank off my T-shirt. My flip-flops were still under the steering wheel where I'd kicked them off during the drive. Three long strides and I was up and off the boat, stretching long as I dove into the water.

Surfacing beside her, I slicked the hair off my face. "What was that about your underwear?"

Londyn smiled, her hands coming to my shoulders as she drifted closer. Her legs tangled with mine in the cool water below as we treaded to keep afloat.

I wrapped one arm around her waist, pulling her hips flush against the ridges of my stomach. With my other hand, I cupped her ass, squeezing the wet lace in my palm. She gasped when I pressed my erection into her inner thigh.

"You're driving me crazy, honey."

She leaned in, her lips a whisper from mine. "If you kiss me today, you'd better not stop."

There'd be no stopping, not today. I'd threatened to fuck her on that rock, but the boat would work fine instead.

My lips crashed into hers, the sweet taste of her mouth consuming me as my tongue dove inside. I pulled her closer with one arm, holding tight as I plundered her mouth and my other hand stretched for the boat, using it to keep my balance as my legs propelled us.

"Brooks," she panted my name, breaking her lips away when we reached the boat's platform.

"Up." I put my hands on her hips, hoisting her out of the water. Drops fell from her tan skin, landing on me as I planted my hands on the platform and shoved myself out of the water. The moment my feet were steady, she was in my arms, our bodies crashing together and our mouths fusing.

We fumbled over the back of the boat, slipping and sliding as we made our way to the center aisle. I swiped a towel from the stack I'd brought along, shaking it out with one hand. I tore my lips away, making Londyn moan as I laid the towel on the wet carpet.

I took her hand, tugging her to her knees beside me. Then I wrapped her in my arms and eased her to the floor, hovering above her.

"This okay?"

She nodded, snaking a hand around my neck and pulling me down.

There was nothing languid or slow about our next kiss. This wasn't a kiss to explore or learn about one another. This kiss was the prelude. This kiss was the last one in a long line of kisses that had led us here, to my bare chest against her smooth skin.

My hand reached between us, cupping her breast. I pulled the cup of her bra under the curve to set her nipple free. I twisted the hard nub in my hand, rolling it to a peak as her back arched off the towel.

I needed it in my mouth. I needed to taste every inch of this incredible woman. I tore my lips away, dropping to suck on her skin.

"*Shit*," she hissed, her fingers diving into the wet strands of my hair as I rolled her nipple around my tongue. Her eyelids were closed, her wet mouth open as she breathed.

She was a picture of ecstasy and we hadn't even gotten to the good parts yet.

I grinned, giving her nipple a playful nip before leaning away and stripping the straps of her bra off her shoulders. It closed in the back so she pushed up, reaching behind to undo the clasp.

"Condom?" Her chest heaved. "Please tell me you have a condom on this boat."

"Yeah." I popped open the compartment below the steering wheel and retrieved my wallet. I'd put a condom in there earlier this week, just in case my control cracked.

With the foil packet in my hand, I tossed the wallet aside and ripped at Londyn's panties. The lace shredded as I tugged hard, and the scrap of fabric got tossed carelessly to the side.

Londyn relaxed onto her elbows, her eyes hooded as she widened her legs.

My hand went to my heart once more. "You're . . ." My heart did another *thunk*. "Beautiful."

That wasn't the right word but as a smile spread across her face, I lost the ability to think.

Her eyes darted to my shorts. "Are you going to take those off? Or would you like some help?"

"Don't. Move."

I stood and ripped the wet shorts off my legs. My erection bobbed, throbbing hard as she spread even wider. I tore into the condom, sheathing myself, and when it was in place, my eyes dropped to her bare, slick pussy.

Fuck. I wasn't going to last. My stamina was shit and she deserved more than a fifteen-minute ride.

"Brooks." She squirmed. "If you don't get down here—"

I dove on her, not letting my insecurities win out. I slammed my mouth onto hers—fuck the stamina. Today we'd scratch the itch. Tonight, the next night and the night after that, I'd worship her body until she came apart, over and over again.

Gripping my cock, I rubbed the tip through her folds. The shudder that ran through her vibrated against my skin and she arched, her hips circling as she searched for more. I positioned myself at the entrance, pausing and taking a long breath to get myself in check. Then I rocked inside an inch, Londyn's body so tight and hot I squeezed my eyes shut.

"Oh, God," she moaned. Her hands came up to my chest and her nails dug into my pecs.

My hips drove me deeper, the pulse of her inner muscles clamping down tight. I let her adjust around me and pressed forward. I inched inside, slowly and deliberately, until the base of my cock was rooted against her flesh.

"Fuck, you feel so good." I dropped my forehead to hers, giving myself another moment.

"I'm—" Her breath fluttered as her hips rolled. "More."

I obeyed, working myself in and out. The pace started slow but picked up quickly until each time I thrust inside, our bodies smacked together and her breasts shook. I held myself above her, my stomach taut as I used every ounce of strength to keep the explosion coming at bay.

My hand drifted between us, my finger finding her clit. The minute I grazed it, she about came off the floor.

"Brooks," she gasped. One more brush was all it took and her whole body shuddered, coming apart. She writhed, riding out the orgasm with a series of moans and breaths that was heaven in my ears.

She clenched around me, and the pressure at the base of my spine was too much to shove away. I came on the heels of her climax, her name on my lips.

When I recovered and the white spots in my vision cleared, I slid out and disposed of the condom in a sack I'd brought for trash. My body was damp with sweat and the water from the lake.

There was barely enough room to collapse beside her, but we both shifted onto our sides as she let me thread my arm behind her head.

I kissed her temple and wet hair. "Damn, honey."

"That was . . ." She gulped. "Wow."

"You comfortable?"

She snuggled into my bare chest and nodded.

We lay there, hot and sweaty and naked, shielded from the sun, as we looked into the open blue sky above. The boat rocked us back and forth. The water lapped against its sides.

A week. I had a week with this woman, maybe nine or ten days, to soak her in. Then I'd let her go, already knowing that watching her drive away was going to hurt like a son of a bitch.

10

LONDYN

THE MOMENT THE KNOCK SOUNDED, I leapt off the bed and rushed for the knob. I didn't bother checking the peephole — Brooks knocked with the same three short taps each night.

"Hey." Brooks grinned as I yanked the door open.

"Hi." I grabbed a fistful of his T-shirt and dragged him inside.

His mouth descended on mine as he kicked the door shut. We were a mess of hands and lips as he walked me backward to the bed, lifting me up by the ribs to lay me on the mattress.

"What took you so long?" I breathed as he kissed his way down my neck.

He broke away to glance at the clock on the nightstand, his forehead furrowing. "I'm two minutes late."

"Exactly." I pulled at the hem of his shirt, tugging it up his back. "I've been waiting forever."

He rolled his eyes as he yanked off the shirt the rest of the way. "You could have saved us some time and answered the door naked."

I giggled. "Tomorrow."

"Promise?"

I nodded, reaching between us for the button on his jeans.

This was the third night of our motel-room rendezvouses, and the dance to rid one another of clothing took less and less time each night. Practice makes progress.

I hadn't spent the day with Brooks since our boat ride on Friday. He'd been busy all weekend and unable to spend time with me during the day.

I'd done my best not to spy. The window in my room overlooked the backside of the motel, out toward the lake and not his yard. But I'd gone out of my room and wandered some. Each time, his truck had been missing from the driveway in his house. Okay, I'd spied.

But he'd come to my room each night and stayed for five or six hours, long enough that I was boneless by the time he left to walk home in the dark. Eating dinner and making out on the rock had been replaced with hot, wild and sweaty sex. A fair trade.

I worked the zipper on Brooks's jeans free, diving in to wrap my hand around his shaft.

He bit my lip as I squeezed. "Naughty woman."

That bite was just the beginning. We teased and tormented one another until I was a writhing, screaming mess, pinned to the bed with my hands above my head and his body driving me to the edge.

After we came apart, he flopped beside me, that glorious, broad chest heaving. I slid my fingers into the dusting of dark hair across it, resting my palm over his hard nipple.

"I shouldn't have worked out today," he breathed.

I turned sideways, propping my head on an elbow. "You worked out?"

He nodded. "I went for a run this morning before going to the garage."

"In this heat?" Wild horses couldn't have dragged me on a run in this humidity. He should have come here instead; I would have worked him out. "Do you normally run?"

"Hold that question." He bent and stood from the bed, giving me a moment to appreciate his firm ass and the strength in his back as he walked to the bathroom. It didn't take him long to dispose of the condom and return to the bed, the view of the front just as gorgeous as the back.

He mirrored my position, lying on a side to face me, and flicked the sheet over our legs and hips. "I need to tell you something."

My body tensed. The last time I'd heard those words, Gemma had informed me that Secretary was pregnant.

"It's not bad." He grinned, using his free hand to rub away the crease between my eyebrows.

"Okay." I relaxed a bit.

"The reason I ran this morning was because my son asked me to go with him."

"Your son?" I blinked, replaying the word. "You have a son?"

Brooks nodded. "I have a son. He's sixteen. He shares time between my house and Moira's. Last week, he was with her. This week, he's with me."

"Ah." That explained why he'd been absent all weekend. It stung that in all our conversations, I hadn't learned about his son. "Why didn't you tell me about him?"

"It wasn't because I was trying to hide him from you." Brooks took my hand and laced our fingers together. "I didn't want you to know about him and him not know about you, if that makes sense."

"It does. You put him first." A foreign concept to my own parents. Had anyone in my life ever put me first? I couldn't think of a single person, not even Thomas. Only if it served him had he made me a priority.

That Brooks put his son above anyone else endeared him to me even more.

A single dad. A *good*, single dad. This man kept getting better.

"What's his name?" I asked.

"Wyatt."

"The Thai delivery boy?"

Brooks chuckled. "Yeah. He actually does deliveries for a few restaurants in town, not just the Thai place."

"Oh. Is that where he is tonight?"

"No, he's home. We have a standing dinner date with my parents on Monday nights. Last week, I begged out of it to meet you at the diner for pie. But Wyatt and I both went tonight. Then we came home. He's at the house, texting some girl."

"And you came to me."

He tucked a lock of hair behind my ear. "I came to you."

I saw it now, the resemblance between father and son. When Wyatt had been in the motel lobby, I hadn't put it together because, well . . . why would I? But now that I could pair them together, I saw how Wyatt had Brooks's nose and the promise of the same strong build.

"Does he know about me?"

Brooks nodded. "He does."

I didn't need to ask how Wyatt felt about Brooks seeing a woman living at the motel. If his son had a problem with me, Brooks would have already said goodbye.

"When did you tell him?" I asked.

"This weekend. I told him I was enamored with one of my customers."

"Enamored?"

"Completely." He rolled across the distance between us, his bare chest pressing mine into the bed. "I'm sorry for not telling you about him sooner."

Time seemed to have slowed in Summers. It seemed like Brooks and I had been together for a long time, when in reality, it had been less than two weeks. Standing in his shoes, I wouldn't have brought Wyatt into the conversation early either. Brooks the protector had waited until it was the right time to share.

A jolt of pride hit my heart. Brooks had deemed me worth sharing. He could have kept us quiet. I'd be gone soon. But he'd shared me with his son.

"I understand."

"You do?"

I nodded, studying the smooth skin on his cheek. He must have shaved before dinner with his parents. I ran my knuckles up his jaw toward his temple. There were no grays threaded through his dark blond hair. "How old are you?"

"Thirty-three."

My eyes widened. "And you have a sixteen-year-old son?"

"Yeah. Wyatt was born when I was seventeen."

"Wow."

I'd become a parent to myself when I was sixteen. He'd become an actual parent at seventeen. There was no question that his youth had been harder. It also made sense why we connected so well when other men close to my age often seemed so immature.

Circumstances had forced us both to grow up fast.

"You had a short childhood too."

He studied my face, his eyes softening. "Yeah. But I don't regret it for a minute. Things were hard for a few years, but I had help. I had more support than you did, that's for sure. My parents. Moira's too."

Moira was Wyatt's mother. Was that why she'd acted out against my car? Because she saw me as a threat to not only her ex-husband, but her son's father too? "When did you get married?"

"As soon as we turned eighteen." Brooks dropped his head to the bed, lying close so we could look at one another. Between us, he kept his grip on my hand. "Moira and I tried, for Wyatt. But it got too hard, and I didn't want my son growing up thinking that was what a marriage should be. We didn't laugh. We didn't talk to one another. We just . . . existed."

That sounded familiar. "How long ago did you get divorced?"

"Ten years. You?"

I hesitated. It felt like longer, but in reality, it had been only six months since I'd caught Thomas with Secretary. "Officially, three weeks."

"Oh." Brooks's gaze dropped to the pillow, his grip on my hand loosening. "Three weeks. That's, uh . . . three weeks."

No time at all, unless you knew my heart. Then you'd know that those three weeks were more than enough to say goodbye to my marriage. The moment I'd found Thomas with his dick inside a moaning Secretary, I'd fallen out of love with him. I'd had months during the divorce proceedings and settlement to make peace with the end.

I'd changed my last name. I'd arranged to leave the home we'd shared. Running away hadn't been hard at all.

Brooks ran his free hand over his jaw. "This is probably a week too late, but is this a rebound thing? Or some step you have to take to get over your ex?"

"Never." I shifted up to meet his eyes. "You're not a rebound."

"You sure about that?"

I cupped his cheek. "I'm not spending time with you, having sex with you, because I'm here to prove to my ex-husband that I've moved on. I'm not having sex with you because I need to prove to myself that I've moved on. I'm having sex with you because you're an amazing kisser, your hands feel like a dream on my body and, in case you haven't noticed, I'm enamored with you too."

Brooks grinned, relief washing over us both. "Tell me something else about you."

"Like what?"

"I don't know. Anything."

I dropped to his side, stretching a leg across his as I curled into his chest. His arm wrapped around my shoulders to trap me close.

If tonight was anything like last night and the night before that, we'd lie here talking for a while before one of us would make a move. It didn't take much to ignite the simmering heat—a touch on my breast, a graze along his thigh, a whisper in my ear. But first, we'd talk.

The question game we'd started on the rock had been intended as a two-way street. Except each night, I found myself talking more about me than Brooks did about himself. Was that because he'd been trying to keep Wyatt from entering the mix? Or had I taken over our conversations, unintentionally keeping the focus on myself?

I was leaving so many stories behind but only taking a few of his with me on my journey.

"Why do we always talk about me?" I asked.

"Because I want to learn it all, and I'm running out of time."

We were running out of time. "Is my car still on track to be done Friday?"

"Far as I know."

Even if I stayed through the weekend, by this time next week, I'd be gone.

Maybe it was easier to keep talking about me. The more I learned about Brooks, the harder it was to imagine leaving him behind. I'd known everything there was to know about Thomas, and I hadn't thought twice about running from Boston.

My stomach tightened, the anxiety of that day growing. Driving away from Summers would be a hundred times more difficult than leaving Boston. Necessary, but agonizing.

"You said the car was going to a friend in California. Who?" he asked.

"His name is Karson."

"He?"

I liked the hint of jealousy in his voice, not that there was any reason to be jealous. Karson was only a fond memory. "Karson was a runaway too. He lived in the junkyard—actually, he was the one who discovered it in the first place."

Karson had been wandering around Temecula, searching for a bench or some place to sleep one night. When he hadn't found anything to his liking, he'd kept walking until he'd spotted a fire.

The old man who managed the junkyard had been burning some wood scraps in a barrel. The light had caught Karson's attention and he'd snuck in, sleeping under the stars on a foam bench seat that had once been in a truck.

"He'd been living there for a month before the owner of the yard finally came out one night with a blanket. Lou Miley was his name, the junkyard owner."

Speaking his name brought a smile to my lips. The last time I'd spoken to Lou had been when I'd called to buy the Cadillac. He'd sounded the same as ever. Gruff and grumpy. He spoke in grunts whenever possible. Lou was a naturally unhappy soul, annoyed by the mainstream world. But for us kids, he'd opened his heart. He'd been our hero.

Lou was gone now. Three months after I'd bought the Cadillac, Gemma had gotten word that he'd died in his sleep. Lou hadn't socialized much, but I knew of six people who would have mourned his passing, me included.

"So how'd you meet Karson?"

"Gemma," I said. "They lived in the same trailer park. When he stopped coming home after school, she knew he was gone. Then when she ran, she asked around until she found him. He set her up at the junkyard too. Then she found me a month later and two became three."

I'd been digging through the trash behind a restaurant for food. She'd slapped a sandwich out of my hand, rolled her eyes and ordered me to follow her. She'd taken me to the junkyard, shared some of her food stash and introduced me to Karson.

"Three." Brooks drummed the number on my lower back. "I thought you said there were six of you kids."

"It was only the three of us for about two months. Then Katherine came along. She met Karson at the car wash where he worked. Then came Aria and Clara. Those two were my recruits."

It sounded strange to say recruits. Most parents would frown at the idea of one kid talking another into running away from home. But home wasn't always a loving term. Sometimes home meant pain and fear. Home was what we'd been seeking to escape.

"Where'd you find them?" Brooks asked. There was no judgment in his voice. The shock of my life's history had faded since our first night together. He'd become more curious instead. He'd accepted that running away had been the best of a long list of shitty options.

It had been for Aria and Clara too.

"They found me. They lived two trailers down from my parents with their uncle. When they were ten, their parents died in a car accident. The uncle, he was . . . not right. You know how you can see someone from a distance and you get that shiver up your spine? That was him. Aria and Clara didn't tell me much about why they left, but they didn't need to. They walked into the junkyard one day and never looked back."

I could still picture the twins walking hand in hand into the junkyard like they owned the place. They'd heard from some kids at the pizza parlor where I'd worked that it was where I'd been *hanging out*.

We didn't tell people, even other kids, we actually lived there for fear the police would show up and take us home.

"So Karson is in California—"

"Maybe," I said. "I actually don't know if Karson is still there. Gemma got word a couple years back that he still lived in Temecula—he was at Lou's funeral—but he might have moved since."

"That's why you're going there first. To see if he's there."

"Yes. Maybe the others are too, I don't know. Katherine could be in Montana where Gemma and I left her. Aria and Clara were a year younger than me and they stayed in the junkyard when we left. As far as I know, Karson stayed with them."

"If he's not there?"

I shrugged. "I'll find him. California is just my starting point."

I'd track Karson down and give him the car. Our car.

"We lived together in the Cadillac," I told Brooks. "That's why I want to give it to him. It was as much his as mine."

"Where did everyone else live? In other cars?"

I shifted to put my chin on his chest and meet his eyes. "No. There weren't many cars still intact. Mostly it was a graveyard of rusted pieces and parts. Gemma built herself a tent. It started as this little hut she built out of sheet metal, then it grew and grew. Sort of like the empire she's built in Boston."

"What does she do?" Brooks asked, his fingers drifting into my hair as I spoke.

"She started out selling real estate. Then she took the money she made and created a cosmetics line. From there, she got into fashion. Then she bought into a car dealership. She's a silent partner in three of Boston's finest restaurants. She has this gift. She takes one dollar and turns it into ten."

Thomas didn't like Gemma, mostly because he was jealous. At her rate, she'd surpass him in wealth within the next five years. I only hoped she found some happiness outside of work. I didn't want a work-driven life for my friend.

I wished to see her laugh more, like we had in those early days together.

But whatever she was searching for, she hadn't found it yet.

Neither had I.

"Her tent was the common area for us." I smiled, remembering us all sitting cross-legged in the center of her tent as we played poker, bidding with toothpicks instead of chips. "She found these tarps and created different spaces. Katherine stayed in the tent with Gemma. Aria and Clara made their home in the shell of a broken delivery truck."

It had been bigger than the Cadillac, but Karson and I had teased them relentlessly that our car had style while theirs was a white box.

"Were you and Karson . . ."

"A couple?" I asked and Brooks nodded. "Yes. For a short time."

Besides Gemma, Karson was the first person I'd truly loved. He was the first person who'd shown me what it felt like to *be* loved. The memory of that childhood crush was everlasting.

"We ended it when I left with Gemma and Katherine for Montana. We both knew a long-distance relationship at our age wasn't going to last. I lost touch with him, but I've always been curious how his life turned out."

Brooks hummed. "I guess you'll find out soon enough."

"I just hope I find him well." It would break my heart if Karson had lost the spark of the boy I'd loved. The boy who'd walked through life with charisma and confidence. He'd never looked at our situation with anything but excitement. Maybe that was why I considered those years an adventure. Karson had made that time magical.

He had for us all. He'd been the protector. The joke maker. The shoulder to cry on. Karson was the rock and the reason we'd all survived running away from home relatively unscathed.

"What if you don't find him?" Brooks asked.

"I'll find him." Somehow, I'd track him down. "I really want him to have the Cadillac."

"Why? You love that car."

"I do love that car. But I just feel like I've had it long enough. That it should belong to him too. Yes, I paid for it. But it doesn't feel . . . mine. Does that make any sense?"

Brooks was quiet for a long moment, then leaned up and kissed my forehead. "Yeah, honey. It does."

I pressed my cheek to his heart. It never took much explaining with Brooks. He knew how I felt even if I couldn't articulate it.

"So you'll go and find Karson and give him the car. Will you search for the others too?" he asked.

"Maybe."

I hadn't really thought that far ahead, my focus so much on first finding Karson.

It would be nice to see what had happened with their lives. When I found Karson, he might know where the others had gone. I'd thought about Katherine and Aria and Clara over the years. Were they happy? Had they battled their own demons and come out as victors?

"Yes," I whispered. "I think I would like to see them all again."

"Then I'm sure you will." Brooks rolled me off his shoulder and onto my back. He came up on top of me, brushing my hair off my face. "Stay. Just a little longer. Before you set off to find these people and I never see you again, stay. Give me two more weeks, not one."

Yes.

The word was right there. I opened my mouth to say it. But as I gazed into those bright blue eyes, it wouldn't come. What if I stayed and never left Summers? What if I regretted giving up my shot at freedom? What if I stayed and he broke my heart?

I couldn't stand to think of Brooks as another mistake. Not him.

Boston had never been my long-term plan. I'd gone there knowing I'd leave. But then I'd met Thomas. He'd asked me to stay too. Look where that had gotten me.

I wanted to say yes. *Damn it, I want to say yes.* Especially to Brooks. Which was exactly why the answer had to be —

"No."

11

BROOKS

I HUNG UP THE PHONE, setting it on the boat's dashboard. "That was the body shop. Your car's done."

"Okay." Londyn kept her gaze on the water. "Do we have to go get it now? Or can we stay out here for a while?"

"We can stay."

We'd stay long enough for me to memorize how she looked today. Her hair was up, twisted in a knot, still wet from our swim. Sunglasses covered her eyes. The only thing she wore was a simple black bikini she'd bought at a local shop today when I'd invited her to spend the afternoon with me on the boat.

She was breathtaking. This was how I'd picture her in the years to come. I'd remember her sitting in that seat, soaking up the sun and stealing my heart with every passing second.

The week had gone by too fast.

That always seemed to be the case when the end drew near.

Mack had texted me earlier in the week, estimating he'd have Londyn's car done by Friday. Well, Friday was here, and true to his word, it was done. She'd be gone soon, which made my decision to take the day off work even smarter.

I'd called Tony this morning and asked if he could cover the garage. Fridays were typically busy but he'd assured me he'd take care of all the oil changes that rolled in. Worst-case scenario, he'd turn folks away for Monday. One Friday away wasn't going to sink my business. One missed day with Londyn would eat at me for years.

I'd gone over to her room first thing, before she disappeared on one of her walks around town, and asked her to spend the day with me. We'd gone to breakfast at the diner. We'd found her a swimming suit at Walmart. We'd loaded up on groceries for a picnic lunch. Then we'd headed for the water.

Much like the first time, I'd cruised us around the lake before coming to the middle to float. Then I'd stripped her out of that bikini and made love to her on the floor. We'd cooled off afterward with a swim. I'd just finished toweling off when my phone rang and Mack put a damper on my day.

She was leaving.

Fuck. Was I destined to be alone? Before Moira, there hadn't been many girls. Just a few high-school flings, forgotten before they'd even begun. Once Moira and I had hooked up, she'd made it known around Summers High that I was off-limits.

Our marriage had been doomed from the start. Moira and I had been opposites in every sense of the word—that old adage was bullshit. Opposites didn't attract. They annoyed.

After the divorce, after my failed attempts at dating, I'd decided I'd rather be single than with a woman more interested in my parents' money than me and my simple garage. Sure, I had a nice house and a new boat. I'd earned those things. I'd paid for them by working my ass off.

I had Wyatt. I had my family. I didn't feel alone.

Until Londyn.

She'd blown into town and made me realize the hole in my life. The hole in the exact shape of a five-foot-five blond woman with jade-green eyes.

Goddamn, I would miss her.

"It's really beautiful here." She smiled, casting her gaze at the trees that surrounded the lake. "I don't know if I'll ever find another lake as pretty as this one."

My heart. Replace *lake* with *woman* and she'd voiced the thoughts in my mind.

She'd been making comments like that all week, reminding us both she was leaving. How could I forget? The minutes were ticking by too quickly. The nights I spent in her motel room weren't enough. We still had the weekend, but I needed more.

I wouldn't get more. I'd asked once.

I wouldn't ask again.

One *no* from this woman was enough to crush my hopes for good.

Londyn was leaving. I had no choice but to accept it, appreciate it even.

The longer she stayed, the more I'd keep begging for another day. I'd push for a week, then a month, then a year.

I was hungry for her in a way I'd never be full.

"Want to cruise around?" I asked.

"No." She turned away from the view and slid her sunglasses off her face. The emerald flecks in her eyes danced bright in the sunlight as she reached for the bikini tie behind her neck.

I grinned. *Hungry.*

WE SPENT the rest of the afternoon on the lake, exploring the water in between breaks from exploring each other. By late afternoon, the lake was teaming with boats, people out on the water for a few hours before dark to kick off the weekend. Neither Londyn nor I felt like being one in a crowd, so we called it a day.

The boat was tied to the dock and we were in my truck, driving to the garage to check out her car. Mack had done me a favor and brought it over so I didn't have to pick it up. Tony had texted that it was safely locked inside.

"Feel like dinner on the rock tonight?" Londyn asked.

"Or . . . we could eat at my place. With Wyatt."

She looked over, her eyebrows rising above her large sunglasses. "You want me to meet your son?"

"Haven't you already?"

"Well, yes. This is a bit different though, don't you think?"

"Not really. It's just you and me eating dinner with a kid who will probably be on his phone the whole time."

She pushed her sunglasses into her hair and shifted to face me. "Is that smart? I'm leaving on Monday."

"I know. But Wyatt knows about you. He knows you're leaving. He's my favorite person in the world. You're quickly climbing that list. For once, I've got two favorites in the same place. I'm trying to capitalize while I can."

She gave me a small smile. "I get that. How would you introduce me?"

"As a friend." Or a girlfriend. My son was no idiot. He knew where I'd been going each night.

Londyn thought it over for a minute, then nodded. "All right. As a friend."

Girlfriend.

"Pizza?" I steered us into the rear parking lot of the garage where Tony and I normally parked. "Wyatt should be done with football by now. I can text him to pick one up for us."

"I never say no to pizza."

I grinned. "Neither do I."

This thing with us was good—damn good. If Londyn had moved to Summers, this might have become a real thing. She'd only been here for a couple of weeks and it was more real than anything I'd had in a decade.

I needed a woman like her, who loved pizza more than the number on her bathroom scale. A woman who spent time on my boat happy with long periods of time when not a word was spoken. A woman who preferred eating dinner on a rock to a fancy restaurant.

Londyn would be perfect if she weren't so hell-bent on leaving.

Then again, maybe the reason we clicked so well was because there was a time limit.

Leaving that thought untouched, I got out of the truck, rounding the back to open Londyn's door. Then I took her hand and walked her into the shop. I inserted my key into the lock, meeting no resistance as I turned.

Fuck. My stomach clenched. This door should have been locked, something Tony would have done before going home. I took a few steps back, glancing around the corner of the building to see if Tony's truck was still here. Maybe he'd parked alongside the tow rig today, but that space was empty.

"What?" Londyn asked.

"The door's unlocked." I went back to the handle, turning it slowly as I poked my head inside. "Hello?"

The shop was pitch black. My voice bounced off the walls but otherwise, the garage was silent. I flicked on a row of lights, stepping inside.

Behind me, Londyn put a hand on my back, the pressure gentle as she followed me down the hallway and into the main room. I flipped on a row of lights, scanning the place.

Nothing seemed out of the ordinary until Londyn gasped.

"Wha—" I followed her gaze to the Cadillac's tires.

They were slashed.

I rushed to the car, walking all around it as I inspected it from roof to wheel and bumper to fender. There wasn't a thing wrong with it except all four tires had been cut, the rubber dangling from the rims.

"Fuck." I raked a hand through my hair. I should have taken that key from Moira when I'd gone to her house. I'd been impatient to leave. I thought she'd done her worst and I could have Wyatt get it from her later. That mistake was on me.

"Was this—"

"Moira? Yeah," I clipped. "I'm calling the cops."

I dug my phone from my pocket, ready to dial the sheriff, but Londyn stopped me with a hand on my arm.

"What if it wasn't her?"

"Who else could it be?"

She frowned. "*My* ex."

"You think?"

"Well, the first time, I would have said no. But Thomas knows I'm here and he's been trying for months to get me to listen to him. What he wants more than anything is for me to come back to Boston."

"But wouldn't we have seen him around town? He doesn't strike me as the kind of guy who'd lurk corners." Thomas was an arrogant, rich asshole. He'd driven to Summers and found Londyn immediately. He was bold, not a coward who trashed a woman's car in secret.

"Maybe that investigator he hired did it for him? I don't know." Her eyes dropped to the tires and she pressed her fingertips to her temples. "I can't believe this."

"Me neither." I hung my head. "It's just tires."

"This is crazy. Totally insane. I feel . . . violated. This is my car. My beautiful car. It doesn't deserve this."

"I'm sorry. I'm so sorry." I pulled her into my side. "I can fix it. All I have to do is get the tires ordered. It's past time for a Friday, but I can place the order and they'll be here on Monday. You just might not be able to leave first thing in the morning."

"That's fine," she muttered, her eyes still locked on the gashes in the rubber. "If your ex is so desperate to get rid of me, why do this? I don't think it was her. If she had left them alone, I would have been gone already."

My stomach tightened at the idea of having lost her a week ago. I hated the shit with her car, but I'd gotten time with Londyn we otherwise would have missed.

But it had to be her. This was so damn familiar, it made me sick. When the fuck would Moira grow up?

"She's got to be worried that you might stay," I said. "This is her way of trying to run you out of town."

"Or it's not her." Londyn dug the phone from her purse, the one I'd given her. "This feels slimy and devious. A year ago, I wouldn't have said that was Thomas, but it turns out I didn't know my husband all that well. I'm going to make a call."

"Okay." I kissed her hair. "I'll leave you alone and go order your tires."

"Thanks." Her shoulders fell as she dialed the number.

I disappeared into the office, collapsing into my chair. "Fuck."

Why was this happening? I could hear Londyn talking, but I didn't need to know what her ex was going to say. He hadn't slashed her tires.

This had Moira written all over it.

Why couldn't she just let me move on? I didn't wish her to live a lonely life. She didn't date but I wouldn't stand in the way if she wanted to. I swiped up the handset of the phone on the desk and punched in her number.

She answered on the first ring. "Hey."

"Why'd you do it?"

"Hello to you too."

"She's leaving, Moira. She's not a threat. But this whole *if I can't have you, no one can* attitude is getting old. Leave her alone. Leave her car alone."

Silence. One moment later, I got the dial tone.

It wasn't the first time Moira had hung up on me and it wouldn't be the last. I set the handset in the cradle and sighed.

Londyn's voice drifted into the office from the shop, and though I knew I shouldn't listen in, I did anyway.

"I'm sorry, Thomas."

That caught my attention. Why was she apologizing? For calling? I sat motionless, my ears searching for more.

"Goodbye." Londyn let out a groan, then her footsteps shuffled toward the office.

"Not him?" I asked as she leaned against the doorframe.

"Nope. He's in Boston with Secretary . . . his girlfriend. Or mistress. Whatever she is. Her name is Raylene."

"He cheated on you?"

She nodded. "With the woman who sat across from my desk. Raylene was his *other* assistant."

That hadn't come up in all our conversations. If I hadn't asked her earlier this week about being a rebound, I might have doubted her motivation for being with me had I known Thomas was a cheat. But I believed Londyn. Nothing about this felt shallow or distant. She was in this, all in this, just like me.

"Damn." Now I was really curious why she'd apologized to the asshole.

"She's pregnant."

"What?" My jaw fell open. So this guy had cheated on her and gotten her coworker pregnant? I should have hit him when I'd had the chance. "Wow."

"Pretty much." She closed her eyes. "Well, she *was* pregnant. She had a miscarriage. When I called, he was at the hospital with her."

"Shit." I leaned my elbows on my knees. "That's awful."

"I feel horrible. I don't like either of them, but I wouldn't wish that on anyone." She came into the office and sank into the guest chair. "I guess we know that Thomas didn't have anything to do with my tires. I doubt he would have lied to me, not today."

"I get why you called to ask, but Londyn, it's Moira. I called her when I got in here and she didn't even deny it."

"Maybe dinner with Wyatt isn't a good idea." She gave me a sad smile. "You eat with him tonight. Spend time with your son. Come over to the motel if you want later. And by Monday, Moira will have nothing to be worried about."

Yeah, she was leaving, but she wasn't gone yet.

"She doesn't get to win." I stood and waved her out of the office. I hadn't ordered her tires, but I'd call them in later. We were going to eat pizza with my son and hang out at my house. Her motel room was just another reminder that she was leaving, and I'd be damned if I spent another night there when I had a perfectly good bed at my own place. "Come on."

"Where are we going?" she asked as I turned off the light behind her. "Brooks, we don't need to make this a thing with your ex. She's crazy. You're pissed. I'm pissed. But they're only tires."

"Tires are expensive. What she did isn't okay." I took Londyn's hand, trapping it in my grip as we walked through the shop to the back door.

She tugged on my arm, slowing my pace. "Normally, I'd say go after her. But not today. I'm leaving Monday and I don't want this to be a thing. She gets away with it this time."

I frowned. "I'm calling the cops."

"And what will they do? Arrest her? Fine her? While we stand here for hours getting questioned for a report? I don't want to spend my last days in Summers with the cops."

I didn't either. But I was done with shit from Moira. She didn't get to act like a brat and cost me time and money. If she wouldn't listen to me, maybe the sheriff would have more influence.

"Let's call it a day." Londyn squeezed my hand.

No fucking way. "What kind of pizza do you like?"

"Uh . . . I'm not picky but—"

"Wyatt likes pepperoni, sausage, bacon and ham."

"That's a lot of meat."

"He's a growing boy." I looked down at her. "You good with that or do you need some veggies on there too?"

"I wouldn't say no to onion, green pepper and olives. But I don't need them if he's picky."

I was glad to see she was done objecting, not that I was taking no for an answer. "Wyatt will eat anything with cheese and meat on it."

I pushed through the door, holding it open for Londyn. Then I locked it up, not that it mattered now. Moira had done her damage.

The tires sucked. But I'd deal, like always. I'd make it right. And for tonight, I wasn't going to let it take away from my time with Londyn. She seemed to be letting it go too. Either she was the most easy-going woman in the world, or she was cherishing this time together too.

We climbed in my truck and I called Wyatt with instructions for pizza. He agreed to pick it up on his way home.

"Should we get something for dessert?" Londyn asked as we pulled away from the shop.

"I'll make brownies."

She raised an eyebrow. "You can make brownies? I feel like I've been cheated this past week."

I chuckled. "I'll make it up to you in my bedroom."

"Your bedroom? I'm spending the night?"

"Let's give the motel a rest. What do you say?"

"Is that appropriate if Wyatt is at home?"

I liked that she cared about my son. "He's sixteen. He knows what I've been doing every night this week."

"Me. You've been doing me."

"That's right." I grinned. "Every chance I get."

12

LONDYN

"MORNING," I said as I came into the kitchen.

Brooks stood by the stove, stirring scrambled eggs in a frying pan. The smell of fresh coffee and bacon drifted around the room, making my mouth water. As did the chef. He was dressed in olive cargo shorts and a black T-shirt, the logo on the front for the garage. His hair was still damp from his shower.

I had fully intended to go to the motel after pizza last night, but Brooks was stubborn and tricky. He hadn't asked me to stay, he'd just made it happen. He'd worn me out in his bed until I'd passed out, blissfully sated. I'd woken up alone in his massive bed this morning as the sun streamed through his bedroom windows.

Waking up by sunshine was now a must for all future days.

Brooks looked fresh and clean and delicious. I was in yesterday's tank top and shorts, using my swimsuit as underwear.

I walked up behind him, rising on my toes for a kiss. "I'm going to get out of here before Wy—"

"Morning, Dad. Miss Londyn." Wyatt came into the kitchen wearing nearly the same thing as his father, except his Cohen's Garage T-shirt was gray and his shorts tan.

"Hey, kid. You hungry?" Brooks asked over his shoulder.

"Starving." Wyatt took a seat at the kitchen island, his eyes foggy with sleep. He blushed when he met my gaze, then dropped his eyes to the plate Brooks had set out already.

Oh, shit. Had he heard us last night? I looked up at Brooks, mortified that his son might have heard me moaning into a pillow, but he was no help. He shrugged.

"I'm gonna go," I mouthed.

"Coffee or orange juice?"

"Orange juice. But—"

"Wyatt, will you get Londyn a glass of orange juice? And pour one for me and you too, please."

"Sure, Dad." He yawned, sliding off his stool.

"Brooks, I'm a wreck. I'm wearing a swimsuit and yesterday's clothes," I whispered.

He leaned in close as Wyatt shuffled around the kitchen, getting our drinks. "You can change after breakfast."

"I can't stay and eat with you guys. It's bad enough I'm doing the walk of shame in front of your son."

"He's sixteen, not six. Besides, it's your turn. I've been doing the walk of shame past Meggie for a week."

"This is totally different."

A grin tugged at his lips. "Wyatt, do you care if Londyn is wearing the same clothes she was yesterday?"

"Brooks," I hissed, swatting him in the chest at the same time Wyatt said, "No."

"See?" Brooks smiled. "Go sit down. This is ready."

"Fine," I muttered, going to the island. I took the stool on the right, leaving the one between me and Wyatt for Brooks. He came over with the pan, plated our eggs and returned with a heaping plate of bacon. "That's a lot of pork."

Brooks nodded at Wyatt. "Remember what I told you yesterday? Growing boy."

"I don't think I'll ever forget seeing one person consume an entire extra-large pizza."

Wyatt stayed quiet—*was he sleepwalking?*—then piled a fistful of bacon strips on top of his eggs.

"Wyatt takes a while to wake up," Brooks said.

But he had no problem eating. The teenager dove into his plate with the same gusto as he had the pizza last night. By the time he'd shoveled half his eggs and two strips into his mouth, he seemed coherent. "What time are we leaving today, Dad?"

"I don't know," Brooks said, taking bacon for his own plate and putting one piece on mine. "How long will it take you to get ready?"

When Wyatt didn't answer, I looked up to find Brooks had asked me the question. "Me? Get ready for what?"

"We're spending the day at my parents' place."

"No." The son was one thing, but his parents? Never happening.

"Why not? They're the best and it'll be fun. We're taking their boat out."

"Granddad's boat is twice as big as Dad's," Wyatt said with his head bent over his plate between inhaled bites.

"That's nice." I leaned forward to smile at Wyatt, then leaned back to frown at his father. "No."

"You should come." Wyatt crunched a bite of bacon.

"She's coming." Brooks pointed his fork at my plate. "Eat."

I rolled my eyes and focused on my meal. I'd eat and disappear before the Cohen men cornered me into attending a family event.

When my plate was clear, I took it to the sink, rinsing it before putting it in the dishwasher. Then I was gone, practically running through the kitchen for the hallway that led to the front door. "Bye, Wyatt!"

"Bye, Londyn," he called back.

I was three feet away from the door when a beefy arm wrapped around my waist and hauled me into an equally beefy chest. For a man this large, he sure could sneak up on a person. "Damn it."

"An hour," Brooks said into my ear.

"Brooks, I don't—"

"One hour."

I squirmed out of his hold to face him. "I don't belong at a Saturday family event. You guys go. Have fun. I'll see you tonight."

"It's a low-key thing. Come with us."

"Why? I'm a stranger. In two days, I'll be gone and a memory. Your parents will forget me before summer's over."

That earned me a scowl. "You won't be forgotten."

"Yes, I will."

"Not by me. And someday, I might want to talk about you. The only people who know you are Meggie and Wyatt. Love Meggie, but I don't see her much even though I live next door. And Wyatt will be gone to college before I blink. My parents, they rank right up there as my favorite people. So one day when I want to talk about the woman who came into my life and turned it upside down for a couple weeks, it sure would make that conversation easier if they knew what you looked like."

"Oh." How could I argue with that? I liked that he wanted to talk about me. I liked that he would remember me, even though I was sure his parents wouldn't.

I'd remember him too.

For the rest of my life.

"Okay." I nodded. "I'll go shower and be ready in an hour."

"Thank you." He took my face in his palms, bending as he pulled me up to his mouth. The kiss was soft but short. They were all too short, even the kisses that lasted all night. Brooks let me go and opened the door for me, sending me on my way.

The heat soaked into my skin as I crossed the lawn from his house to the motel. As I walked, I tallied up the days I'd been here in Summers.

Sixteen. In a way, they'd been the longest sixteen days of my life. Each had been so full and enjoyable. Two weeks with another person had never felt so important as the sixteen days I'd been in Summers with Brooks.

This weekend was the end. Monday, I'd wake up knowing I wouldn't see him again. Would I really be able to drive away? I'd left countless people behind in my life. My parents. My teachers. My friends.

I'd known, walking away from them, it was unlikely we'd meet again. But I'd gone with a sense of adventure fueling my footsteps. I'd gone with excitement and anticipation of what was out there in this great big world.

And I hadn't looked back.

When I left Monday, I'd look back. I'd wonder.

How was Brooks doing at the garage? How was Wyatt? After he went to college, would Brooks get lonely? When would he find someone new?

Those questions would haunt me, especially the last.

But I had to leave. I wasn't going to stick around a town for a man, not again. How many experiences had I sacrificed for Thomas? How many opportunities had I missed because I'd been stuck in Boston?

This time in Summers was temporary. It was a gift.

I wasn't even that upset about the Cadillac. Normally, I'd have flown off the handle at two vandalisms. Police would have been called. Heads would have rolled. And though a part of me did feel violated, that vulnerability was easily overshadowed by the thrill of being with Brooks.

I didn't like that my most prized possession had been tarnished, but it was just an object. I'd learned a long time ago that possessions weren't important. You could walk away from belongings, homes and people and survive.

Sometimes, you thrived.

The extra time with Brooks was worth the Cadillac's weight in gold.

The heaviest thing on my mind wasn't my tires, but that phone call to Thomas. My heart went out to him and Secretary—Raylene. Knowing she was in pain had made her human again.

Did Gemma know about the miscarriage? Should I call? No, not yet. There wasn't time today. When I talked to her, I wanted to tell her about Brooks. I'd call once I was back on the road. There was no doubt I'd need a friend my first night away from Summers.

I'd call to tell her about the man who had become one of my favorite people in only sixteen days.

My motel room was quiet—lonely—and I rushed through my shower. My suit got a thorough rinse even though it would be wet when I put it on. But since it was the only one I had, I'd deal with a damp suit.

When I was ready, dressed in the one and only dress I had in my possession, a sleeveless dusty-blue shift with a tie around the waist, I packed up my purse with my swimsuit wrapped in a white motel towel.

"Sunglasses." I looked around the room, remembering they were somewhere in Brooks's truck. I opened the door to find Wyatt, his knuckles raised to knock. "Oh, hi."

"Hi." He nodded, a gesture that seemed more like a bow. Such gentlemen, these Cohen boys. "Dad sent me over to get you."

"He was afraid I'd change my mind, wasn't he? And he thought I'd have a harder time saying no to you."

Wyatt gave me a sheepish nod.

I laughed, stepping outside and pulling the door closed. "Is this weird? Sorry if it's weird."

"No, ma'am."

"Londyn."

"Yes, ma'am—Londyn." Wyatt's natural stride was double mine, but he slowed as we walked toward his home. Brooks did the same thing when we walked together.

Though father and son had similar features, it was the way they acted that made their resemblance so uncanny. They held their forks the same way. They ate their pizza the same way, chewing with the same circular motion. They talked the same way. When Wyatt's voice got deeper, I suspected it would be nearly impossible to tell them apart on a phone call.

"So, you're uh . . . leaving?" Wyatt kept his hands in his pockets and his eyes on the grass as he attempted to make conversation.

"Yes, on Monday."

"Will you keep in touch with Dad?"

"Maybe." *Maybe not.* Quitting Brooks cold turkey would probably be best for us both. I didn't want to string this out until the phone calls spanned more time. Until one or both held some resentment that we'd drifted apart.

"You should," Wyatt said. "Dad doesn't have many close friends. Especially women. He's kind of wary about them."

Because his mom was crazy and the women in town were terrified Moira would hack out a kidney with a car key. Suffice it to say, I wasn't a fan of his mother.

"Oh really?" I feigned surprise.

"A lot of women in town only want Dad because of his money."

"Huh." Brooks had money?

I studied the house as we approached, not seeing anything that screamed big money. It was nice—classic and warm—but it didn't scream wealth. He had a boat. He had a nice truck. Maybe Brooks was rich for Summers's standards.

I gave myself a mental eye roll. Once, as a teenager, I would have thought Brooks's house was a palace. Being married to Thomas had skewed my perspective too far. He had more money than I'd be able to spend in two lifetimes.

Brooks came out the front door, carrying a small blue cooler in one hand and my sunglasses in the other. "Here, honey."

"Thanks." I smiled. I always did when he called me honey.

His endearment came so naturally. He said it with such ease, I'd wondered at first if maybe he called all women honey. But as time went on, I realized it was mine. It was another gift.

I hadn't owned an endearment before. My parents hadn't bothered because they weren't endearing people. Thomas had called me Londyn and only Londyn. Even Karson had stuck to my name or Lonny, like Gemma still used.

Honey. I tucked the word into my pocket for later.

I glanced at Wyatt as I put my sunglasses on. He was trying to hide a smile.

"You can sit up front." He opened my door for me, then helped me inside. Then he climbed in the truck, sitting behind me as Brooks got behind the wheel.

Brooks asked Wyatt questions about football as we drove across town, taking inventory of the plays Wyatt needed to memorize before the weekend was over. As we neared the edge of town, the homes became larger and more spread apart. I wasn't sure how far we were going until Brooks eased off the gas to turn toward the lake. An iron gate greeted us at the end of a private drive.

He rolled down his window and punched a code into the keypad, then steered us on the tree-lined drive until a sprawling cream house came into view.

Ahh. Now I understood Wyatt's comment about money. Brooks Cohen, or rather his parents, must have it in spades. This was the nicest home I'd seen in Summers, and though it was tasteful for this town and not arrogant in size or style, it stood apart. It was probably six thousand square feet with a looped driveway, much like the one I'd left behind in Boston. A barn with a gable roof sat in the distance. Two dogs lazed beside a koi pond. And like Brooks's home, this home's windows were the focal point. They gleamed, reflecting the shine bouncing off the lake.

"Your dad is a doctor, right?" I asked.

"He is. Still works at the hospital because he says he's too young to retire. Mom stayed home and looked after me and my sister. You'll meet her today." He dropped his voice. "And a few others."

Behind me, Wyatt let out a snort.

I looked between him and Brooks. Both were avoiding eye contact and holding back grins. "Okay, what am I missing?"

They bolted from the truck before answering.

I shot Brooks a glare as he rounded the hood to open my door. When my foot hit the concrete, I opened my mouth to demand details about this *low-key thing*—and a crowd of people rushed out of the house.

Wyatt got swallowed up first. Then the swarm descended on us.

"Hi, Londyn." Brooks's mom enveloped me in a hug. "We're so glad you could come today."

"Thanks for having me . . ." I looked at Brooks in panic. What was her name? He hadn't told me their names.

"Ava," he mouthed.

"It's lovely to meet you, Ava."

"My, you are pretty." She winked at me, then pulled Brooks into a hug. "Hello, son."

"Hi, Mom." He tucked her into his side just as I was wrapped up again, this time by Brooks's father.

"Carter Cohen. Great to meet you." He slapped a hand to my back.

Whoa. He was as strong as Brooks. "You too."

He released me, grinning from ear to ear as the rest of the people around us started tossing out names I had no hope of remembering. I got lost in the handshakes and hugs.

I met Brooks's sister and her husband while their two small children chased around Wyatt's legs. There was an aunt and a great aunt. There were five or six uncles, or was one of them a cousin?

It took me the entire day to get it all straight, but by the time dinner was over and I was sitting on the back deck, I'd finally put names and relations to each face. I'd even managed to figure out which twin uncle was Henry and which was Harry.

Brooks and I were sharing a lounge chair. When I'd moved to take my own, he'd hauled me down on his lap. His fingers idly caressed my bare knee.

"So?" Brooks raised an eyebrow as he spoke low so only I'd hear. "What'd I tell you?"

"It was fun." I smiled. "You have a wonderful family."

"Sure do."

He was fortunate. He *knew* he was blessed. These people were genuine and kind. They'd pulled me into their family today like I'd been here for years. Like I'd *be* here for years.

Brooks, Wyatt and I were the only three guests left at Carter and Ava's house. Everyone else had gone home about an hour after dinner, but we'd been in no rush to leave. I wasn't ready to end this day yet.

We'd spent most of the morning and afternoon on the lake, alternating groups on the boat to go skiing or surfing or tubing. Once the boat was docked, we'd played lawn games, holding competitions in bocce ball and cornhole. I'd laughed more today than I had all year. I'd also discovered I had a competitive streak when it came to lawn darts.

After games, we'd congregated on the sprawling deck, eating a feast that Ava had prepared, forgoing some of the outdoor fun. Brooks had promised me that feeding us was her kind of fun.

Ava was an authentic mother, nurturing and kind. Today was the first time I'd seen one in real life.

This entire experience was a first. This family laughed and teased one another. When they asked about each other's jobs or homes or cars, it was with genuine interest. They knew what was happening in each other's lives because they weren't only blood relatives, they were friends.

I hadn't had that since the junkyard.

Thomas was an only child and his parents lived in Boston for a third of the year, at most. I'd missed feeling like I belonged to more than just one person. That if I needed help, I'd have an entire posse at my back.

I wouldn't forget these people. I wouldn't forget this day.

Maybe this remarkable family wouldn't soon forget me either.

"I'm hungry," Wyatt announced from the seat beside us.

"Seriously?" I asked. "You just ate a full rack of ribs, two ears of corn and half a dozen rolls."

Yes, I was keeping track of Wyatt's food consumption. It was fascinating, seeing a boy with not an ounce of fat eat more than I did in a week.

He shrugged. "But I didn't get dessert."

"Pie." Brooks sat up, taking me with him as he stood from the chair. "Wyatt's hungry and I want pie."

"The diner?" Carter stood too, holding out a hand to help Ava from her seat.

"I hope they have a slice of pecan left," she said, smiling as she led the way into her house.

The kitchen was state of the art, but there were magnets on the fridge, holding up art made by Carter and Ava's grandchildren. Pictures adorned the walls instead of expensive paintings. The house had beautiful furniture, each piece top of the line, but comfortable. I wouldn't be afraid to sit on a couch and tuck my feet up.

It was a home and the heart of this family.

And I don't belong.

The realization slammed into me as I walked down the hallway and passed a collage of framed Christmas cards. An overpowering urge to get in my car and drive far away hit. This life wasn't mine. I'd pretended today, but this wasn't my family. It never would be.

It was time to go.

The urge to leave settled deep in my bones. I'd had the same feeling at sixteen years old. Again, at eighteen. Again, at twenty and twenty-one. And again, weeks ago, when I'd packed up and left Boston.

It was time to go.

I followed Brooks to his truck, hopping in and buckling my seat belt. Then I wrapped my arms around myself. Maybe if I squeezed hard enough, the feeling would go away. Though my mind knew it was time, my heart wasn't ready to leave, not yet.

One more day.

"You okay?" Brooks asked as he got in the truck. "Cold?"

"Just a little." I forced a smile. "Nothing some pie won't fix."

He turned the heat on for me, even though it was still sweltering outside.

I focused on the drive to town, on the homes and the trees and the quiet neighborhoods. The unsettling churn in my gut was still there when we reached the diner, but it wasn't nearly as potent. It faded to ignorable as we crammed into a booth.

"I'm squishing Londyn." Ava shifted in the seat. "Should we get a table instead?"

"No." I touched her arm before she could stand. "I don't mind the squish."

I was sandwiched between her and Brooks on one side of the booth while Carter and Wyatt were in the opposite. I didn't have a ton of room, but Brooks tossed his arm over the back of the seat so I could burrow into his side.

The waiter came over and we all placed our pie orders. He'd just collected our menus and disappeared to the kitchen when another figure appeared at the end of the table.

Brooks's spine went rigid as we all stared up at his red-faced ex-wife.

"Mom?" Wyatt's forehead furrowed. "What are you doing here?"

"You called the cops on me?" she hissed at Brooks.

Oh, shit. When? I thought he'd decided to leave it alone yesterday when we'd left the garage.

"I told you I would," he said. "You crossed the line."

"No, you did." Moira pointed at him. "I didn't do anything to her car."

"Mom." Wyatt stood, placing his hand on her arm.

She turned her eyes up to her son. They softened, pleading for him to believe her. "I didn't do anything to her car."

Uh... I didn't know Moira, but that sounded a lot like the truth.

Wyatt gave her a sad smile, then pulled her in for a hug.

She held him tight, then let him go and was out the door as quickly as she'd appeared.

"What was that about?" Carter asked Brooks as Wyatt took his seat.

"Someone's been vandalizing Londyn's car," Brooks answered. "Keyed it last week. Poured paint all over it. Yesterday, we found all four tires slashed."

Ava sucked in a sharp breath, covering my hand with hers.

Carter hung his head. "When's that girl gonna learn?"

"It's okay," I told the table, my eyes aimed at Wyatt, whose shoulders were hunched forward. "It's just a car and I'm only passing through. On Monday, this won't be a problem."

Brooks's arm tightened around my shoulder.

"Are you sure it's Mom?" Wyatt asked his dad.

"I don't know, kid. I wish I could say it wasn't, but your mom's done stuff like this before."

"I know she flies off the handle, but she's been different lately. Happier, I guess. She's been seeing this guy and he's . . . nice."

"She has?" Brooks leaned forward. "Who?"

It wasn't a jealous question, more concern that another man was hanging out with his kid and he was just learning about it.

"A guy from Oak Hill. They mostly go out when I'm with you, but I've met him a couple of times. He seems like a good guy. He mellows Mom."

"Hmm." Brooks's forehead furrowed.

"Did you consider it might not be her?" Ava asked. "I know you two have had a rocky relationship, but Brooks, I know that girl. And while I wouldn't put it past Moira to do something foolish in the heat of the moment, that didn't sound like a lie."

"No, it didn't." Brooks ran a hand over his face. "Damn it. I'll call her tonight," he promised Wyatt. "I'll make it right."

Wyatt sighed, picking up his fork. "Thanks, Dad."

"So . . ." Carter met Brooks's gaze, then they both turned to me. "If it wasn't Moira, who is vandalizing your car?"

13

LONDYN

"WHAT'S ALL THIS?" I asked Brooks. His kitchen island was piled with plastic food containers, each with the lid securely shut.

"A picnic."

"Really?" I smiled. I'd never gone on a picnic before, not a proper one. The days at the junkyard when we'd eat on our laps in Gemma's tent didn't count.

Brooks walked to the large pantry off the kitchen and came back with a basket. It was a rich, tawny cedar with a red, white and blue plaid lining. The lids flipped up from the middle, one side at a time.

He owned an actual picnic basket. Why did that make me want to cry?

I looked away, blinking and swallowing away the emotion. I'd been on the verge of tears for hours. Tomorrow was Monday and I'd been letting my upcoming departure stain our day.

Brooks and I had spent the day together doing normal things any person did on a Sunday to prepare for a workweek.

We'd gone to the grocery store. I'd had to hide my quivering chin in the checkout line for no good reason other than we'd piled our stuff together on the conveyor belt. My bottle of body wash and toothpaste had been sandwiched between a bag of baby carrots and jug of cranberry juice. The cashier had rung it all up and Brooks had helped pack everything into his reusable grocery bags. I'd stood by, not listening as he'd chatted with her because I'd been trying to figure out why I'd been so close to crying. Was it the baby carrots or the blue grocery bags?

I'd analyze it later when I was on the road.

Just like I'd analyze why I'd gotten choked up in the laundry room earlier. I'd washed all of my clothes in Brooks's machine today, preparing to pack them into my suitcases. When I'd poured the detergent into the machine, the scent of his clothing and bedsheets had brought out a miserable sting in my nose. One tear had actually escaped before I'd shut the others down.

It was definitely time to go.

Hopefully tomorrow my car would be ready too, and I could escape Summers before it became another cage.

"How did your call with Moira go?" I asked Brooks.

A crease formed between his eyebrows. "As good as expected. She's pissed and has a right to be pissed. But she won't stay mad at me forever."

"That's good." I looked around the kitchen as he finished up. The smell of bacon hung in the air from this morning's breakfast. "Where's Wyatt?"

"He went to Moira's."

"Oh." A sting laced my heart. Was he coming back? Or had I missed my chance to say goodbye? While Brooks and I had run errands today, Wyatt had been at home. He'd been on the couch in the living room, his eyes glued to his phone. He'd been in the exact same spot when we'd returned.

Then I'd left for thirty minutes to take my clean clothes to the motel. I hadn't noticed his truck was gone when I'd walked back. "I guess . . . will you tell him goodbye for me?"

Brooks abandoned the basket and came around the island, wrapping me in his arms. "He'll be back in the morning before football practice. He just went to stay at Moira's so we could have some privacy."

"Oh, good." I relaxed into his arms.

"Come on." He kissed me on my hair and let me go to collect the picnic basket.

As I followed Brooks through the house, my eyes zoomed around, soaking in a final farewell. There were two bedrooms on the main floor. One was Wyatt's and the other Brooks had turned into an office, while the master and another bedroom were upstairs.

It wasn't the pieces or the layout of this house I'd remember. It was the sense of peace and comfort. Nothing matched and there was no theme. The artwork was random, some photographs and some prints scattered throughout. The furniture was leather in varying shades.

Nothing here had been styled or decorated. When I thought of the interior designer Thomas had hired to *incorporate my tastes* into his home, I let loose a wicked smile. She'd hate that Brooks's toss pillows were actually used to support heads while watching football games on Sundays. She'd hate that the coffee table didn't have a single coaster.

Brooks opened the back door that led to the outside deck. The instant he passed the table covered with a white umbrella, I knew exactly where we were headed.

"The rock?"

He grinned down at me as we crossed the grass, both of us in bare feet. "Thought it would be appropriate for our last dinner. Have it where we had our first."

"That sounds wonderful."

I'd been waiting all week for Brooks to ask me to stay again. But he

102

hadn't, not once, since I'd turned him down, probably because we both knew the answer wouldn't change. My tires would show up at the garage tomorrow. He'd work on them as soon as they arrived, then I'd be on the road. My goal was to make it to Kentucky and stay in Lexington or Louisville tomorrow night.

For the foreseeable future, I'd stick to the interstate. No off-road detour would ever compare to this stop in Summers. California was waiting and I was anxious to see what—and who—I'd find.

"I've been thinking about something," I said as we reached the rock and situated ourselves in our normal spots. We'd gotten lucky for the night and the heat had given us a break. The humidity was thick but it was bearable for dinner.

"What's that?" Brooks set the basket aside, giving me his full attention.

"I'm going to Temecula. I figure that's the best place to start my search for Karson."

"Agreed."

"Maybe . . ." I mustered up the courage to voice a thought that had been plaguing me since leaving his parents' house yesterday. "Maybe I should find out what happened to my parents."

He blinked. Twice. "Why?"

"I've thought more about them these past couple of weeks than I have in years. And being around your parents made me wonder about my own. Maybe it's a crazy idea and bound to be a disaster."

"I'd say it's normal for a child to want to know about their parents."

"They never tried to find me." My gaze drifted across the water. "If they did, they didn't try hard, but I'm still curious. I left them as an angry, neglected teenager. Maybe seeing them as an adult will give me some closure."

What if they'd turned their lives around? What if they hadn't? I wasn't sure how I'd feel if I found them in the same dirty trailer—or the cemetery. Had I become an orphan while traveling the country? Did I want to know badly enough? Did I have the courage to show up at my former home and knock on the door alone?

"What would you do?" I asked.

"The truth?" He raised an eyebrow and I nodded. "Fuck 'em. They don't deserve you."

That's what Gemma always said. None of our parents had deserved us as kids.

"You're probably right. I'll think on it longer." Maybe by the time I hit Arizona, I'd have my feelings about them in order. "Let's eat."

"This isn't fancy." Brooks opened up the basket and took out a green container for me, then another for himself.

"I don't need fancy." My favorite sandwich was still peanut butter and grape jelly. I'd eaten countless numbers of them. In Boston, I'd sneak into the kitchen on late nights when I couldn't sleep and make one for myself. The chef kept the supplies in the pantry for me, despite Thomas's insistence that we could afford *decent* sandwich ingredients.

My heart craved simplicity, like a picnic on a rock.

I popped the top off the plastic container and the smell of bacon and tomato and bread wafted into the air. I inhaled the scent of my second-favorite sandwich. "So that's why you hid some bacon from Wyatt this morning."

Brooks chuckled. "I knew it would be safe in the vegetable drawer, tucked under the lettuce."

He finished taking out the containers from the basket. When it was all laid out, he'd packed us a feast, including some of the potato salad Ava had made yesterday. Brooks must have noticed I'd gone back for seconds. We ate without fanfare, enjoying the food and a Sunday evening with the lake glittering under the descending sun.

We didn't fill the hours on the rock with conversation or questions — there wasn't much more to say. The light faded and my eyelids drooped, but I couldn't find the strength to leave. Brooks didn't seem to want to leave our spot either. *Our spot.* God, I hoped he never let another woman kiss him on this rock.

We sat there until the blue sky darkened and the white crescent moon peeked out from behind the trees on the horizon.

"There's a star." He pointed above us. "Make a wish."

I closed my eyes, sending my wish to the galaxy, knowing this one wouldn't come true. "Done."

"Did you make it a good one?"

I found his hand between us. "I wished you would come with me. I can tell you that because I know it won't come true. But I wished it anyway."

His other hand came to his heart, his eyes clouded with sadness. "In a different life, I'd drive around the world with you in that Cadillac."

But he had a son. He had a business and a life in Summers. And the reality was, I needed to take this trip alone. The only person who could guide *me* back to *me* was myself.

"This has been the best week of my life," I whispered. "Thank you. I'll never forget you."

"Same, honey." He cupped my cheek. "Same."

A tear dripped free and he caught it with his thumb. I sucked in a deep breath and began putting the containers into the basket, busying my hands and mind before I gave into the damn cry that wouldn't stay buried.

I was sniffling, snapping the lid on a container, when Brooks took it from my hands and dropped it in the basket. Then he took my face in his hands and brought his lips to mine, kissing away the sadness.

My arms snaked around his shoulders as his arms banded around my back, pulling me into his chest as we clutched one another.

The picnic basket was forgotten on the rock as Brooks and I fumbled our way to his house. We left a trail of clothes on the way to his room upstairs, breaking the kiss only to shed our shirts. When we reached his bed, my heart was racing and my body aching.

Brooks laid me down, covering me with his weight. His arms bracketed my face and his hips rested against my own. His cock was hard and thick between us as it nestled against my core.

We stilled. Our eyes locked. Our breaths mixed. His heartbeat drummed in the same thundering rhythm as my own.

"Don't forget me," I whispered. I'd been forgotten by too many people. I couldn't bear the idea of Brooks forgetting me too.

"I'll remember you until the end, Londyn." Brooks ran his knuckles along my cheek, leaving a trail of sparks on my skin. "Until the end."

I rose up and fused our mouths, giving him everything I had and trusting him with all my broken pieces.

Maybe he would forget me. Maybe time would dull his memories or disease would steal them away. But I hoped this kiss would remain.

I was falling for Brooks. I poured it into the kiss. If we had a month more or a year, he'd own my heart.

Brooks, this home and his family were enticing. What if I stayed? I'd have a home, a conventional, warm home, for the first time.

Not even Thomas had given me a home. We'd been two single pieces paired together for a while, but it hadn't made either of us whole. Brooks had the entire package. He was the corner to a thousand-piece jigsaw puzzle that created one stunning picture.

Staying was enticing. But the nagging feeling in my gut wouldn't go away, no matter how many times I kissed Brooks. No matter how many times I closed my eyes and pictured myself living here.

The puzzle was built. There weren't any spaces for me to fill.

So I kept my eyes closed and savored the feel of his hands roaming across my skin, pretending this wasn't the last night. I pretended this was every night.

His kiss drifted down my neck and to the swell of my breast. Brooks tickled a nipple with his stubble before covering it with his mouth, rolling it over his tongue until he moved to do the same with the other.

My fingers wove through the golden strands of his hair, pulling him up to my lips once more. I let go with one hand and stretched for the end table drawer where he kept his stash of condoms.

He grinned when I handed it to him. "In a rush?"

"For you? Always." I smiled, waiting as he covered and positioned himself at my entrance. With a swift thrust, he stole my breath, filling me completely.

"So good," he groaned.

I nodded, tipping my hips to send him deeper. *So good.*

Brooks was the best lover of my life. He took control when we were together. His gaze raked over my body, appreciating every inch and banishing all insecurities. The man had a direct line to my brain. If I wasn't feeling something or he thought he could take me higher, he'd change direction, because it wasn't about him when we were together. It wasn't about me either.

It was about us.

He rocked us together, slowly at first until the pounding of our hearts

105

matched the rhythm of his hips. The orgasm that built seemed to shroud us both, taking us racing toward the peak at equal speeds, until we came together, sweaty and breathless.

He left me for only a minute to take care of the condom, then he wrapped me in his arms and held me tight as we drifted off to sleep.

We woke twice more in the night, not wanting sleep to keep us apart, until morning finally forced us into the new day.

The dreaded Monday had dawned.

"What time should I come to the garage?"

Brooks stood in the bathroom, drying his wet hair with a towel. We'd showered together. I sat on his bed, wrapped in a fluffy gray towel.

He swallowed hard. "How about I drive the car to you? Then you don't need to worry about your suitcases."

"Okay."

I stayed on the bed—even as my hair grew cold on my bare skin—to listen as Brooks shaved his face and brushed his teeth. The weight of the day sank in and made my limbs nearly as heavy as my heart.

Don't let this be awkward. I closed my eyes, sending up a wish to the unseen stars. Brooks had been the best, most unexpected person to cross my path. We needed to end on a happy note—a kiss and a smile.

Brooks kissed me on the forehead as he walked to his closet.

Did he even realize how much he'd given me in our short time together? He'd shown me that leaving Boston had been the right decision. He'd shown me that there were kind, generous and loving men in the world.

Had I left him with anything good? Or after today, would I just be the woman who'd left?

Please, don't resent me.

I studied him as he dressed. When I pictured him in years to come, it would be in this room and in this moment.

He was barefoot in a pair of unbuttoned and faded jeans. His chest was bare and droplets of water clung to his shoulders. And his eyes were as blue as the sky on a West Virginia summer morning.

"Wyatt's coming over?" I asked.

He nodded as he tugged a green T-shirt off its hanger. He pulled it over his head just as the front door slammed downstairs. "Sounds like he's here."

"I'll get dressed and come down to say goodbye." I took a deep breath and stood from the bed.

Brooks nodded. "What would you like for breakfast?"

I gave him a sad smile. "I think I'll get a pastry from the motel today. You and Wyatt should get back to your normal routine anyway."

"Oh." His jaw tensed. "All right."

This wasn't all right but I feared no matter what I said, nothing would fix it. The awkwardness was coming.

I tied up my wet hair and rushed to pull on my clothes. Brooks was the one to sit on the bed now, watching as I scurried around his room.

"See you at four?"

He nodded, his eyes aimed at the floor.

I forced my feet through the bedroom door. I held my neck stiff, not letting myself twist and look back.

Wyatt was in the living room, standing beside the couch with his phone in his hands and his thumbs flying. I walked into his space and wrapped him up, trapping his arms at his sides. "Take care of him."

His stiff frame relaxed. "I will."

"It was nice meeting you." I let him go, unable to meet his eyes. Then I was out the door, jogging to the motel.

When I was locked inside my room, I leaned against the door, taking a moment for my heart to settle. I swiped away one tear and gritted my teeth to stop the others.

One goodbye down.

One more to go.

14

LONDYN

"Thanks for everything, Meggie." I tucked my credit card into my wallet, then stowed it in my purse.

"You're welcome." She leaned her elbows on the counter. "He didn't talk you into staying, huh?"

"No." I gave her a sad smile. "Have a great summer."

"You too." She sighed, then waved as I wheeled my suitcases to the door.

It was hot outside and I'd much rather wait in the air conditioning for Brooks to show with my car, but Meggie was itching for some gossip. I didn't have it in me to deflect her questions about my relationship with Brooks, not when all my energy was being used to fight the anxiety of the upcoming goodbye.

I pulled my luggage down the sidewalk to the corner of the motel, leaving it standing on the concrete while I took one last look at Brooks's house.

When I'd run away from home, I hadn't looked back at the trailer where I'd grown up. No matter how many years went by, that pile of filth was burned into my brain. The details lingered with perfect clarity.

My parents had been passed out in their bedroom that day, the same place they'd been for the three days prior. They did that, holed themselves up as they rode out their high. I used to peek in on them occasionally. Sometimes, I'd stand at the door and listen for any sound. The doors were so thin, if I listened close enough, I could hear them breathe.

It had taken me months to work up the courage to run. For nearly a year, I'd had a backpack stuffed with clothes and canned food. The final straw had been on the third day of a drug-induced disappearance. Mom and Dad had stayed quiet, too quiet, in their end of the trailer. No sound had even come from the TV. I'd gone to see if they were alive. When I'd cracked the door, Dad had been sitting up in bed, a rubber band tied tight around his bicep and a syringe poised at a vein. Mom had been asleep or passed out on her stomach at his side. Her nightstand had been crowded with half-empty bottles of brown liquor.

Dad's eyes had been glassy when they'd met mine. He'd stared at me for a long minute, tilting his head to the side. Was it regret I'd seen in his gaze that day? Or confusion? I'd never know. For a moment, I'd thought maybe he'd put the needle down. Instead, he'd muttered, "Shut the door, Londyn."

I'd shut the door. Then I'd gone to my room and collected my backpack.

Running had seemed like the best choice. No home at all was better than waiting around in a dirty trailer to open that door again, only to find the pair of them dead.

When would the image of that place fade? If I stared at Brooks's house long enough, would it become permanently ingrained too?

His home was so clean. The white siding was pristine. There was no cracking paint or water stains. The windows gleamed in the sunlight, and at the right angle, it was almost as if the glass didn't exist.

I squeezed my eyes shut, picturing the house in my head. When I opened them, a car coming down the street caught my eye.

My car.

Brooks rode handsomely behind the wheel. He was not going to make this easy on me, was he? The top was down and his eyes were covered with a pair of sunglasses. He drove with one hand while the other raked the hair away that had blown onto his forehead.

I didn't need to close my eyes to commit that image to memory for good.

Brooks pulled up to the curb and shut off the rumbling engine. "Well, it's about two weeks too late, but I can finally give you back your car."

I smiled, walking over to the Cadillac. I dropped my purse in the passenger seat just as Brooks popped the trunk. I turned for my suitcases, but he stopped me.

"I'll get them." He swung those long legs out of the car, got out and loaded up my bags. Then he met me on the sidewalk beside the Cadillac. No one would have ever known it had been scraped on a guardrail, then gouged with a key. "Anything else?"

"No, that's it." I walked up close, placing my palm on his heart to feel the heat of him against my skin one last time. "Thank you."

"My pleasure." He shifted his sunglasses into his hair. "Promise me something."

"Okay." I nodded, tense as I waited for his demand. Would he ask me to stay? Or would he ask me to come back? If he asked me to return to Summers, I wouldn't be able to say no.

"Promise me if you ever need anything—a friend, a place to crash for a week, a piece of pie—you'll use that phone and call me."

I smiled, releasing the breath I'd been holding. "Promise."

My hand fell from his heart. My forehead took its place as I snaked my arms around his waist.

He wrapped me up tight, whispering into my hair. "Goodbye, Londyn McCormack."

I squeezed my eyes shut. "Goodbye, Brooks Cohen."

His hands came to my face, lifting my cheek off his chest to brush his lips against mine. He broke the kiss too soon, and I took a step back.

I opened my mouth, but there was nothing more to say, so I walked around the hood of the car and settled into the driver's seat. I moved it up from where Brooks had adjusted it for his long legs. I shifted the mirrors. Then I gripped the steering wheel.

"All good?" Brooks leaned his elbows on the passenger door.

I nodded. "All good."

Except wasn't it supposed to feel like home? When I'd climbed behind the wheel in Boston, I'd been hit with such a sense of . . . rightness. That feeling was missing today. Maybe after a few miles I'd feel more comfortable in the seat.

A pained look crossed Brooks's gaze before he covered it with an easy, lopsided grin. He stood, tapped the side of the car with his knuckles and stepped back.

I twisted the key, igniting the engine to life. Then I gave him one last look before shifting the car into drive and easing away from the curb.

He lifted a hand to wave. I saw it from the corner of my eye but refused to turn. My eyes stayed fixed on the road ahead.

I made it twenty feet before my resolve shattered and I cast my gaze to the rearview mirror.

There he was, tall and strong, standing where the car had been with his hand held in the air.

"Damn it." Tears flooded my eyes but I kept my foot on the gas pedal. I only glanced at the road to make sure I wouldn't crash into the motel. Otherwise, my eyes were in the mirror.

Brooks stayed there, in that spot with his arm held high, until I rounded a bend in the highway and he was gone.

"Shit." I swiped at the tears as they dripped down my face. I sucked in a few deep breaths, trying to get my heart to sink down from my throat.

This would get easier, right? Maybe not today, maybe not tomorrow, but by the time I made it to California, I wouldn't feel so heartbroken.

I blew out a breath, rubbed the sting from my nose, then reached for the sunglasses I'd tucked into my purse. With them hiding my watery eyes, I focused on the road ahead.

Summers disappeared behind me quickly, but the first five miles past town were excruciating. So were the five after that.

It should feel better, shouldn't it? This is what I'd wanted, right? I was free to follow my own impulses. I wasn't trapped in the idea of someone else's conventional life.

I hauled my purse onto my lap, driving with one hand as I dug for the phone in the bottom. I pulled it out, needing to talk to someone who might understand why I was doing this.

"Hello?" Gemma answered my call on the second ring.

"Hey."

"Londyn? Where have you been? You promised you'd call." She sighed. "Are you okay?"

"I'm okay." A total fucking lie.

"Liar."

I huffed. "I'm not okay."

"Is this about . . ."

"No, this isn't about Thomas." I blew out a long breath, so long, she thought she'd lost me.

"Londyn?"

"I'm here." I looked in my rearview mirror, hoping to see Brooks and knowing I wouldn't. "I think I fell in love with someone."

"Already?" She laughed. "That doesn't sound like a problem to me."

"I just left him."

"Ah." The line went quiet.

"What do you mean, *ah*?"

"Nothing."

"Gem. Tell me."

She sighed. "It's just . . . this is what you do, Lonny. You get scared and run."

"What?" I switched my grip on the wheel so I could put the phone to the other ear. Clearly, I wasn't hearing her correctly. "I didn't run away from Boston because I was scared."

"Are you sure about that?"

Ouch. Okay, maybe calling my friend wasn't the right decision today. Gemma and I were always brutally honest with one another, but I wasn't emotionally stable enough for brutal today. Maybe I should have delayed this call a week or two.

"I left Boston to start over," I said. "It's time to simplify my life. I don't have this overwhelming desire to prove myself, Gem. I'm not like you. I don't need the money and the status."

"I don't need—ugh." She paused. "This isn't about me, and I don't want to fight."

I unclenched my jaw. "Me neither."

"I'm trying to help. You sound miserable. If you truly love this guy, whoever he is, then why are you leaving?"

"I don't know," I confessed.

"Are you afraid you'll find something real there?"

"Maybe I'm afraid I won't."

"Oh, Londyn." There was a smile in her voice. "It sounds like you already have. So why are you leaving?"

"I need to give this car to Karson. I need to see that he's okay."

"Do you have to do it today? Or tomorrow? Why not stay with this guy for a little while longer?"

"Brooks. His name is Brooks."

"Why not stay with Brooks?"

"Because." My heart hurt. The fears were working themselves free, the feelings I'd buried for so, so long. "Because what if he leaves me before I can leave him?"

That was the reason I ran, wasn't it? To get away from the big hurt. Maybe the reason I'd been able to stay with Thomas all these years was because I hadn't expected the end to hurt. It hadn't much.

Maybe the reason I'd felt trapped in Boston wasn't because I'd stayed in one place, but because that *one* place hadn't been the *right* place.

That goddamn Pottery Barn picnic basket flashed in my mind. Another woman didn't get to use that basket. It was mine.

So was Brooks.

"Turn the car around, Londyn," she said. "I'd give it all up—the company, the money, the power—to just feel *something*."

Feelings for other people wasn't my problem. Sure, I ran from those feelings, but they were there, right on the surface. Not Gemma. As far as I knew, she'd never been in love.

"Don't waste it," she whispered.

I was throwing it away. I was driving away from a man who just might turn out to be the love of my life. I was driving away from a home.

"I kept having this feeling when I was walking around Summers—that's the town where I was. I felt . . . settled. Like things were calm in my soul. Do you think that's what it feels like to be home?"

"I don't know. I don't know if I've ever felt at home. But if I had to guess, I'd say yes."

Yes. Summers was home.

Brooks was home.

"I need to go."

Gemma laughed. "Is this a real number now? Can I call you?"

"Yeah." I smiled. "This is my number."

"Bye."

"Wait," I called before she could hang up. "Thanks."

"I miss you. Maybe I'll come visit you in—where are you?"

"West Virginia."

"West Virginia," she repeated. "Call me later."

"I will." I tossed the phone aside, sitting straighter in my seat. With both hands on the wheel, I eased off the gas pedal, searching the road ahead for a place to turn around. Of course, when I needed to flip a U-turn, there was nothing but a steep ditch and trees lining the road.

My eyes were on the shoulder when the car lurched. I gasped, snapping my gaze to the road. What the hell? Had I hit something?

I looked in the rearview mirror, jerking when my eyes landed on a large truck riding my bumper.

While I'd been on the phone with Gemma, I hadn't noticed it creep up on me.

112

"What the hell?" I muttered to the mirror, alternating my eyes on the road and the truck behind me.

Had he bumped me? Why would he hit my car? I was going ten miles an hour under the speed limit. Ten. Was contact necessary? Why not just pass me and be done with it?

I lifted my arm, waving him around, but as I watched through the mirror, the grill of the truck inched closer. My arms tensed and my grip on the wheel hardened. I braced for another bump.

It was no bump.

"Ah!" I screamed as he rammed me. The Cadillac lurched again, twice as hard as the first time.

The wheels veered on their own, from one edge of the lane to the other.

"Leave me alone!" I screamed.

He hit me again.

The Cadillac's tires screeched on the road, swerving from one white line to the next. Had there been an oncoming car, I would have crashed head-on.

I touched the brake.

The second I did, the truck's engine revved and he sped into the opposite lane.

I held my breath, thinking he'd race past me and probably give me the finger. Instead, he hovered in my blind spot.

"What?!" I glanced over my shoulder. I waved him around once more. The moment I lifted my hand off the wheel, he zoomed forward until he was right next to me. Still he didn't pass. He stayed in that lane, his passenger door so close I could have reached up and touched the handle.

The truck was too tall for me to see the driver this close. I pressed the brake to slow. The truck stayed in place, hovering at my same speed. My eyes scanned the edges of the road, hoping for a place where I could turn off and get away from this crazy asshole. There was nothing.

An oncoming car appeared.

"You crazy son of a bitch." I slowed more. The oncoming car's horn filled the air. "Go around!"

The truck didn't move.

Was this some kind of sick West Virginia version of chicken?

I slammed on the brake, my tires squealing on the blacktop, just as the truck sped up and swerved into my lane. I shimmied between the center lane and the ditch, the car heavy and sluggish to respond.

The oncoming car's horn blared as it flew past and I yanked the wheel to the safe side.

The correction was too much. Instead of staying between the lines, my front forward tire sank into the soft shoulder. When the front corner of the Cadillac dipped, I knew there was no saving me from a wreck.

The Cadillac dove off the side of the road. The vehicle rattled and bounced as it came to a punishing stop. My side of the car was tipped up at least three feet above the passenger side.

"Oh my God." I shook as I looked around, my entire body trembling.

The truck was gone. From the ditch, I couldn't see it race away, but the engine's roar faded in the distance.

I pushed the hair away from my face, taking stock of my body. I wasn't hurt, or if I was, I couldn't feel it yet. My fingers barely had the strength to turn the key and shut off the engine. I fumbled with the seat belt.

My purse was on the floor on the other side. I shoved myself out of the driver's seat, the angle requiring me to stand on the passenger-side door to keep my balance. Clutching the handle of my purse, I crawled out of the car into the ditch and took stock of the situation.

"No." My heart broke. My poor car. It was so much worse than it had looked from the seat. The front corner was crumpled. The whole thing was propped sideways against the ditch. The driver's-side tires were still digging into the loose asphalt of the road. Had the ditch been any steeper or the car's center any higher, I would have rolled.

My head spun and my hands shook. I fisted them, forcing the fear away for a moment to deal with this. I fought the urge to cry, focusing on the anger instead. "That fucking asshole!"

I climbed my way up the ditch on my hands and knees, wiping the dirt from my palms as I stood on the side of the road. I looked both ways.

I was alone.

But unlike my first flat tire, I wasn't helpless. I took the phone from my purse and called the one and only number saved in the contacts.

"Londyn?" Brooks answered. "You okay?"

"No." My voice shook. "I need you to come and get me."

"Where are you?" The sound of his boots echoed in the distance. "What the hell's going on? I'm worried."

"Don't worry." I blew out a breath and collected myself. "Just head out of town on the highway and you'll see me. And Brooks?"

"Yeah?"

I looked at my car. "Bring the tow truck."

15

BROOKS

"Are you okay?" Londyn asked, leaning into my side.

"Me?" I gaped at her. "Someone tried to run you off the fucking road. Are *you* okay?"

"I'm fine." She blew out a long breath, resting her cheek against my arm. "I won't be later, but at the moment, I'm okay and that's all that matters."

I clutched her hand, holding it tight like I had over the past hour. She was keeping it together at the moment, a credit to her incredible strength. But every five or ten minutes, a tremor would run through her body. Her grip on my fingers would tighten. If and when she fell apart later, it would be in the safety of my arms.

Whoever had done this to her would pay dearly.

We were standing on the side of the highway, waiting for the sheriff's deputy on the scene to finish taking photos of her car. He'd already taken her statement.

I'd listened with silent fury as Londyn had recapped the details of the accident. I should have thrown her keys in the damn lake and refused to let her leave town.

It seemed like days since she'd left me standing on the sidewalk outside the motel, not hours. For a moment, when I'd caught her looking at me in the rearview mirror, I'd thought maybe she'd turn back.

Maybe she'd prove us both wrong—maybe she'd make my life—and stay.

But she'd kept on driving. When her car had disappeared around a bend in the highway, it had been over. I sure hadn't expected her name to flash on my phone's screen so soon after she'd left—if ever.

The fear in her voice had had me racing through town in the tow truck. I'd been a goddamn scared mess when I'd shown up to find her car toppled sideways in the ditch. I'd pulled her in for a hug and hadn't let go, even when the cop had shown up. But the time to worry had passed and now I was fucking pissed.

This was attempted murder in my book and that meant years in prison. It didn't seem like enough.

"Brooks." The deputy waved me over. I refused to let go of Londyn's hand, so together, we met him by the hood of his cruiser, the lights still flashing on top. "I'm done here. You can load it up and take it back to town."

"Can I get going on repairs? Or do we need to leave it as is?"

"Hold for now. Let me confirm we don't need anything else for the investigation."

"There's no hurry," Londyn said. "Thanks for your help."

"Ma'am." He tipped his hat, then walked to his car, his notepad in hand. He stayed parked, slowing traffic, until I had the Cadillac winched out of the ditch and loaded on the flatbed.

It took me over an hour and I hated leaving Londyn alone in the truck, but I didn't want her standing on the road. Finally, as the afternoon faded to evening, I waved goodbye to the deputy and drove us down the road to Summers.

The time outside hadn't cooled my anger in the slightest. While I snarled over the steering wheel, Londyn kept her eerie calm in the passenger seat.

"I'm going to drop you off, then take the Cadillac to the shop."

"Okay." She sagged against the door. "Feels like we've been here before."

"Yeah." I barked a dry laugh as the motel came into view.

Londyn could sit at the motel with Meggie for an hour while I dropped off her car. There was no way in hell I was leaving her anywhere alone until we found the sick bastard who could have killed her today.

"I'm going to leave you with Meggie while I take the car to the shop. You can get settled at the motel. She'll be glad to have you back." We'd all be glad to have her back in Summers.

"The motel?" She sat up straight, then slapped a hand over her forehead. "Oh. Oh my God. I'm an idiot."

"Huh?"

"Nothing." She turned to the window. "Never mind."

I wasn't in the mood for never minds. "What did you mean, you're an idiot?"

"It's nothing." She waved it off.

"Londyn." My jaw clenched tight. "I'm hanging on by a thread here. Talk to me."

She hesitated, then looked my way. "You asked me to stay."

"And you said no." I remembered that word quite clearly from our conversation.

"You didn't ask again, and I thought you were just being understanding. I'm an idiot because I didn't even consider you might want me to go.

116

That you were just in this for the short-term." Her voice cracked and she dropped her gaze to her lap.

"What the fuck are you talking about? How hard did you hit your head?" I studied her face. It was too pale. "I'm taking you to the hospital."

How could she think I didn't want her to stay? Watching her drive away had been ten times harder than I'd expected.

"I don't need to go to the hospital."

"If you think I *wanted* you to leave, then you're not thinking straight."

"You want me to stay?"

I nodded. "Very much so."

"Then why didn't you ask me again?"

"Because you said no." I tossed a hand into the air, the hold on my temper nearly a thread. "I got the message. Over and over. You're leaving Summers and not looking back. I'm not the type of guy who asks a question when I already know the answer."

"Oh." She lifted a hand to cover a smile.

I reached across the truck and pulled that hand away. "You're not leaving?"

"I'm not leaving. I was looking for a place to turn around when that truck tried to run me off the road."

But she'd been so set on going. "For how long?"

"I haven't really put a time limit on this. Would you mind if I stayed?" She paused. "With you?"

Would I mind? Fuck no, I wouldn't mind. She could stay with me for as long as she wanted. Forever, if that suited her fancy. With Londyn, each day was brighter. I didn't want to live the rest of my life alone. But I didn't want just any woman to share my life.

I wanted Londyn.

Something I wanted to talk about, but not while I was driving a goddamn tow truck.

"Hold that question for me, honey. I need to see your face."

She nodded, folding her hands in her lap. Damn it. Had that come out as a rejection? Because that's not what I'd meant.

Son of a bitch. I was pissed about the asshole who'd run her off the road and things weren't coming out right. I hit the edge of Summers and pulled the rig to the side of the road. Then I hopped out, jogging around to the other side to open Londyn's door. "Climb down."

She nodded, undoing her seat belt. Then she stepped on the running board before jumping to the road.

"Start over for me. You're staying?" I needed to hear it again.

Londyn nodded. "I'd like to stay."

"And I'd like you to stay. With me."

"Yes, please." She giggled.

I wrapped her up, pulling her into my chest. Then I laughed with her, long and loud.

She was staying.

"What made you change your mind?" I asked, dropping my cheek to the top of her head.

"The truth? I'm scared."

I let her go, taking her chin under my finger to tip up her face. "Why?"

"I've always been the one to leave."

One sentence, and it all made sense. Running away was how Londyn stayed in control. It was her protection mechanism. "I get it."

"What if you leave me?" Sheer vulnerability washed over her face. She stripped away all the guards, making her even more beautiful. "I've never stuck around to see the pieces fall apart. I don't know if I'm strong enough to take it."

"I'm not going anywhere, honey. If you stay, we're going to make a real thing out of this. Mark my words."

"How do you know?"

I took her hand and placed it over my heart, then I covered it with my own. "I feel it. Deep."

Londyn wasn't in the place to hear three little words, not yet. Hell, I wasn't ready to say them. But there wasn't a rush. We had time.

Because she was staying.

I took her mouth in a kiss, sweeping my tongue against hers for the taste I'd crave for the rest of my life. This was a big risk on her part, and I'd make sure she never regretted it. She'd never second-guess a life in Summers.

I broke the kiss and dropped my forehead to hers. "This is a better end to the day than I'd expected."

"Me too. Except for the whacko who ran me off the road."

I muttered a curse. "Let's get home."

She nodded and let me help her up into the truck.

"Want to come along with me to the shop?" I asked, easing onto the road. "Or sit at the motel with Meggie? I don't care either way, I just don't want you alone."

"I'd like to stay with you." She shivered, reaching over for my hand. The fear she'd been hiding was leeching through her calm exterior.

"This has gone too far. The vandalism was one thing, but you could have been hurt."

"Who would do this to me?" she whispered. "I don't know anyone in Summers."

"I don't think this is about you. It's got to be about me."

"Well, it's not Moira. So what other enemies do you have in town?"

"Hell if I know." Up until today, I would have said I was a fairly well-liked guy. I got along with most folks in town. My entire family was well liked too. I couldn't think of the last time I'd had an unhappy customer at the shop.

It didn't take us long to get to the shop, but unloading the car took some time. When it was in its regular stall, we both walked around the Cadillac, taking in all the damage. It wasn't horrible, but it wasn't a quick fix either.

"Mack's going to be able to send his kids to college on all the money he's making to fix this Cadillac."

Londyn laughed, leaning against me. "It's only seven o'clock but I'm so ready for bed."

"Dinner first. What would you like?"

"Pizza."

"Pizza it is." I nodded. "I'll call Wyatt and have him bring one over for us."

"He's not at Moira's tonight?"

"He is, but if I tell him you're staying indefinitely, he'll come with an extra-large meat supreme."

She smiled up at me. "With the veggies."

"With the veggies."

"It looks so sad." Her eyes raked over the car, the scratches and the dents. It would take considerably longer at the body shop to repair this wreck. It might even require some new parts.

"I'll fix it," I vowed. "Then . . ." I'd gotten so used to saying that she'd be on her way.

"Then I'll drive it around Summers."

"What about returning it to Karson? What about taking it to California?"

She lifted a shoulder. "Someday, I'd like to track him down. I'd like to give him this car and let him have it for a while. But maybe when that time comes, you'll come with me."

"I'd like that."

"We could wait until Wyatt is in college. If we pick a time when you can be away from the garage, maybe that wish I made might actually come true."

"You're sure?" I put my hands on her shoulders. "You'll wait? You'll stay in Summers until then?"

"I'm staying. Would you come with me to California?"

"Yes." Without a doubt. Londyn would have a hard time taking a trip across the country without me. "That's a lot of long-term thinking for a woman who just wanted to roam America."

Londyn laughed. "I want to roam, just not alone."

"Turns out I haven't had a decent vacation in sixteen years. Think I'm overdue."

"California first. Then where?"

I let out a long breath. "Are we really talking about this? You and me?"

"I feel it." She put her hand over her own heart this time. "Deep."

"Then California first. We'll decide where to go from there."

She crashed into my arms, winding her arms around my waist. I breathed in her scent, grateful I wouldn't have to search for it on the sheets tonight because she was here. I could hold her. Touch her.

Keep her.

We stood there, holding on to one another, until her stomach rumbled and forced us apart. "Let's get home. We'll eat and then call it a day."

The police would likely have a ton of questions tomorrow. All I cared about was that they found the person who did this.

Londyn unwrapped herself from around me and stepped away, taking another crushing look at her car.

I turned too, inspecting it once more. It was a fucking mess. The paint was scratched to hell. A couple of the panels were dented. The mirror on the passenger side was barely hanging on. The bumper was loose.

"What color was the truck again?" I asked. She'd told the deputy, but I'd been so fucking furious and scared, I hadn't absorbed the details.

"Blue."

"What kind of blue?"

She shrugged. "I don't know. Bright. Electric blue, maybe?"

Electric blue. "And what kind of truck? Do you remember any details?"

"No, not really. I just remember it was really tall. When it was beside me, I couldn't see inside."

An electric blue truck with a lift kit.

I'd seen a truck like that parked in my own driveway more than once.

"What the hell?" I stood, fisting my hands on my hips. No way.

"What?" Londyn came to my side, staring at the spot where I was looking. "What am I looking at?"

"You're sure it was bright blue?"

"Yes." She nodded.

I snatched up her hand and marched for the back door. I hit the button to close the overhead door and locked up as soon as we were outside. Then I put us both in my truck, not uttering a word.

My mind was stuck on a possibility I didn't even want to consider.

"Okay, what am I missing?" Londyn asked as I backed away from the garage.

"A hunch," I answered through gritted teeth. And if that hunch was right, I was about to lose my shit.

I sped down the streets toward home, skidding to a stop when I hit my driveway. The second Londyn and I were out of the car, I whipped out my phone and dialed my son's number.

"Hey, Dad," he answered.

"Get home. Now." I ended the call without explanation.

"What's going on, Brooks?" Londyn touched my forearm as I paced on the grass beyond the front door.

"Describe it all to me again. Start at the beginning."

"Okay." She took a deep breath. "The truck came up behind me while I was on the phone with Gemma. I didn't even see it until it was right behind me, and only then all I could really see was the grill. I was trying to watch the road. It bumped me a couple of times, then drove up beside me. I thought it would pass, but it stayed close. There was a car coming the other way so I hit the brakes. I swerved, overcorrected and veered into the ditch."

"When the truck was beside you, what did it look like?"

120

She shrugged. "I don't know. Tall, mostly. Blue. It wasn't shiny though, not like the Cadillac."

Matte electric blue. I was seconds away from nuclear, but I kept it together because I didn't want to scare Londyn. "Okay. What else? Did you see the driver?"

"No. I was just trying to stay on the road."

"Understandable. Was there someone else? A passenger? Or was it only the driver?"

Her forehead furrowed as she thought it over. "I-I don't know."

We'd find out soon enough.

I stayed in the front yard, my arms crossed over my chest, until Wyatt drove up in his white Ford F-150. We'd bought the truck about six months ago on his birthday. He'd chipped in a third from his savings, and I'd covered the rest.

If I was right, that truck was about to become a lawn ornament.

"Hey." He stepped out and waved to Londyn. "You're back."

She opened her mouth to answer, but before she could speak, I held up a hand. "Truth, son. I expect the truth."

That's all I had to say. His frame crumpled. "It wasn't my idea."

"Fuck." I ran a hand through my hair. "What the fuck were you thinking?"

"It was Joe's idea."

Fucking Joe. An idiot of a kid who, at best, had two brain cells to rub together. The kid came from absentee parents who thought restoring an old Chevy truck, complete with a monster lift kit and custom paint job, was the way to their son's heart.

"Joe's idea. That's not a reason!" I roared. "You could have hurt her. You could have killed her."

Wyatt's face paled. "We were just trying to scare her. Joe wasn't supposed to run her off the road, just tap her bumper a couple of times. Scare her into turning around."

"Oh, Wyatt." Londyn touched her hand to her heart. "It was you?"

My son's frame sank even lower as he hung his head. "I'm sorry."

"Why?" I demanded, my fury barely in check. How could my son do this to me? How could he put the woman I loved—absolutely fucking loved after only weeks—in danger like that?

"You seemed happy," Wyatt whispered. "I saw you on the rock together. That night I delivered Thai to Meggie. I forgot her extra carton of rice, so I brought it over. You were laughing. I thought, if she stayed longer, you might . . . I don't know."

He thought I'd stay happy.

So he'd vandalized the garage. He'd slashed her tires. He'd done it all to get Londyn to stay.

My anger dulled from a raging boil to a hot simmer. "Son, this was not the way."

"I know." He hung his head. "I just . . . I was trying to help."

Christ. I cast a glance at Londyn. She wasn't even mad. She stared at

Wyatt with a soft smile on her face. "You might have hurt her. Things could have ended much differently."

"I told him not to hit her car. I told him over and over to back off. But he didn't listen." He lifted his head to Londyn. "I'm so sorry. I saw you swerve into the ditch and I've never been more scared. I begged Joe to go back for you, but he said the cops would arrest us. Are you okay?"

"I'm okay." Londyn sighed. "Scared, but otherwise unharmed."

Goddamn it. I rubbed my temples. What was I supposed to do now? I pulled out my phone from my pocket and handed it to Wyatt.

"Call the sheriff's station. You can explain what happened."

Wyatt's face twisted in agony, but he nodded. "Okay, Dad."

Then I stood there and watched my son make probably the hardest phone call of his life.

The deputy who'd been on the road with us came over and took our statements along with Wyatt's confession. Londyn refused to press charges. An hour later, Wyatt had been issued a warning and the deputy was on his way to Joe's house to deliver a reckless driving ticket.

It was a slap on the wrist, but one I knew would sink deep for my son.

"I'm sorry, Dad," Wyatt said as we sat in the living room. We still hadn't eaten, but I'd lost my appetite. I'd offered to get a pizza delivered, but Londyn hadn't been hungry anymore either.

"You're grounded. Until . . . college." Maybe longer. "I'm assuming the keying and the tires and wrecking the garage was you too?"

He gave me a solemn nod.

Wyatt was the other person with a key to the garage and the thought that he'd do that to me or a customer hadn't even crossed my mind. "You're paying me back for everything. With interest."

He hung his head. "Yes, sir."

Londyn's hand came over mine as she shifted closer on the couch. She looked up at me, her eyes begging me to take it easy.

Maybe I would, but I certainly wouldn't tonight. Vehicles were weapons. I'd taught that lesson to Wyatt many times, so why hadn't he learned? And the vandalism? That was petty bullshit. I'd raised him better than that.

And as far as I was concerned, Wyatt wasn't hanging out with Joe for the rest of his life.

"Go to bed," I ordered. I'd already texted Moira what was going on. Thankfully, she'd always been in sync with me as a parent. We supported one another when it came to punishments for Wyatt.

She'd promised that while he was grounded at my house, he'd be grounded at hers too.

Wyatt stood from the chair, turning for his room, but before he walked away, he came over to Londyn, bending low to give her a hug. "Sorry."

She patted his shoulder. "Good night, Wyatt."

He sulked to his bedroom.

When his door was closed, I let my head fall back into the couch. "Shit. He did it for the right reasons, but damn. I don't even know what to say."

Londyn stayed quiet for a minute, then her hand flew to her mouth. I sat up, expecting tears. Instead, she had a fit of giggles. Her hand muffled the laughter, but her eyes watered.

"Is this really funny?"

She pulled herself together, swiping her eyes dry. "Do you think we should tell him I was turning around anyway?"

"Yes," I muttered. "He needs to suffer for his stupidity."

"But not too much." She curled into my side. "His heart was in the right place."

"Yeah." He'd been thinking of his dad. He'd seen right from the start, before even knowing her, that Londyn was someone special. "I didn't get your suitcases from the Cadillac."

"I don't think I need any clothes tonight, do you?"

Tonight. Tomorrow night. All the nights after that. "No, you don't."

We'd get her suitcases tomorrow, she'd unload them into my closet, and she'd stay. She might not realize it yet, but she was home. In Summers. In this house.

The next time she wanted to leave and find a new adventure, she'd have company.

We'd drive that runaway road together.

EPILOGUE
LONDYN

ONE YEAR LATER . . .

"I'm going to the store. Need anything?"

"No," Brooks said from beneath a gray Chevy Silverado, where he was changing the oil. "Wait. Yeah, I need shaving cream."

"Anything else?" I gave him a minute to think it over. I knew there was more. There was always more. The man never seemed to remember what he needed when I was making my list, but five minutes before I left for the store, he'd rattle off four or five items.

"Flossers."

"And?" I swung the car seat at my side, glancing down at our daughter. Ellie Cohen was fast asleep, a binky dangling from her pink lips.

"Orange juice."

I already had that one on my list. "And?"

"Uh . . ."

I sighed and looked at Tony. He stood against a tool box, his chest shaking in silent laughter. Brooks and I didn't just have this standoff for the grocery store. He'd always tack on a handful of parts right before I was ready to hit send on the order.

"I'm leaving in four, three, two—"

"Pickles."

My face soured. Thanks to my unexpected pregnancy and a horrible bout of morning sickness, pickles were no longer on my favorite foods list. But I'd buy them for Brooks because he loved them on his ham sandwiches. "Okay, we're taking off. I'll meet you at home."

"Drive careful."

"I will," I promised like I did each time he sent me off with the same warning. "Don't be late. You have one hour to get home and get showered before we need to leave."

Wyatt had his first football game of the season tonight and he was

124

starting as linebacker. He was nervous—something I found exceptionally endearing—because the girl he'd been crushing on was going to be in the stands watching.

Wyatt was still grounded, both at Brooks's house and at Moira's, but it was coming to an end. One year of near angelic behavior and his parents were struggling to punish him any longer. If it had been my decision, he would have been forgiven months ago.

"Don't worry, honey. I'll be there."

Okay, maybe I was just as nervous for tonight's game as Wyatt. "Love you," I called.

Brooks, lying on his back on a wheeled cart, pushed out from under the Chevy and grinned. "Love you too."

I blew him a kiss, waved goodbye to Tony, then headed out the back door, where my Cadillac waited. She gleamed in the September sunshine, her color coordinating with autumn's turning leaves. But I wasn't driving her around Summers today. Brooks would bring home the Cadillac and I was taking his truck—it was safer for Ellie and her car seat.

It had taken a month to get the Cadillac fixed after the crash into the ditch. It hadn't mattered much to me, considering anywhere I needed to go, Brooks was more than willing to drive me.

My first month as an official resident of Summers was spent waking up with the sunshine each morning and falling asleep beside Brooks each night. More often than not, I found myself at the garage during the day, where I stayed in the office while Brooks and Tony worked on cars.

The stack of paperwork in Brooks's office called my name. I asked for the password to his computer and figured out the rest myself, only asking questions when necessary.

Though I was already doing the work, when Brooks offered me the job as office manager, I hesitated to accept. Was I repeating the same pattern from Boston? It took me a week to work past those fears and realize they were unfounded.

Life in Summers was nothing like Boston. Brooks was nothing like Thomas.

He hadn't offered me a job with *his* company. He hadn't given me a home in *his* house.

Everything about our life was *ours*.

Brooks added my name to the title on the house. I bought into the garage as his partner.

Summers was home, but Brooks and I talked often about where we'd go exploring. We had a few years between Wyatt's graduation from high school and the time Ellie would start kindergarten.

Our plan was to take as many vacations as we could afford until it was time to put her in school. Then we'd limit travel to summers. Maybe Wyatt would come too, depending on his college schedule, and we'd make it a family trip.

Ellie was a beautiful surprise.

She was one month old and the anchor of my heart.

Brooks and I hadn't planned on getting pregnant. We hadn't even talked about marriage until that fateful day when I'd held a positive pregnancy test in my hand as joyous tears streamed down my face. But somewhere along the way, a condom hadn't worked, and like all things with our relationship, we'd moved into the future at warp speed.

The two of us had married in his parents' yard beside the lake two weeks later. Then we'd waited for Ellie to arrive. The day she was born was the day I'd learned true peace.

I'd learned unconditional love.

I vowed never to fail her the way my parents had failed me.

After a lot of thought, I'd decided to investigate my parents in the hopes it would mend those dark, open wounds. They'd died days after I'd run away—a dual heroin overdose. My parents had been found together in their bed. Maybe if they had survived, they would have come looking for me.

Maybe not.

For now, I took comfort in knowing their tortured souls were at rest. And that running away had put me on a path that ultimately led home.

I felt it. Deep.

The trip to the grocery store was uneventful. Ellie stayed asleep even as the cashier fawned over her precious face. And she slept until we were home, unloading groceries into the kitchen.

"Hi, baby," I cooed as she woke with a yawn. I hauled her out of the car seat just as the doorbell rang. "Should we go see who's here?"

Ellie tooted.

I laughed, walking to the door. I opened it up, expecting Meggie or a neighbor, but my jaw dropped at the woman on my porch. "Gemma?"

"Hi." She tugged off her sunglasses. "Surprise."

"Yes, it sure is." I smiled, waving her inside. "What are you doing here?"

Her eyes flooded. "I ran away."

———

"She's beautiful. Truly." Gemma touched her finger to the top of Ellie's nose.

"I think so." I smiled, watching my friend cuddle my daughter as we sat on the back deck.

Last night after Gemma had arrived, she'd given me the quick and dirty details of leaving Boston, but we hadn't had time to talk. Brooks had shown up twenty minutes after Gemma and we'd all rushed to the football game.

When we'd gotten home, I'd nursed Ellie, then Brooks had put her to bed while Gemma and I had spent a solid three hours on the couch, talking. We'd picked right back up again this morning.

"You're right. This is amazing iced coffee."

I took a sip of my own. "Told you so."

"If Meggie had a spa, I might just stay in Summers forever." Gemma had opted for the motel instead of our guest bedroom, wanting to give us privacy. Meggie had put her in my old room, number five.

It was good to see her in a pair of faded jeans and a loose green sweater. Her feet were in flimsy sandals. I hadn't seen her relaxed like this in years.

Since I'd moved to Summers, Gemma and I had spoken on the phone every few weeks. She'd traveled to West Virginia for my wedding but hadn't been back since Ellie was born.

"You found it," Gemma said, staring out at the lake.

"Found what?"

"A real life."

I followed her gaze to the water. "Yes, I did."

Brooks and Wyatt were on the dock, tinkering with something on the boat. Brooks must have felt my stare because he looked up and waved. The smile tugging at his lips was likely the same one that had gotten me pregnant.

"I want a real life, Lonny."

I put my hand on her forearm. "You're sure leaving Boston is the right call?"

"I'm sure." She tipped her head to the sky. "But I still can't believe I did it. That I left it all behind."

Last night, she'd told me that she'd sold her company, her house and her car. She'd kept her investments in other ventures that required little to no work, but as of yesterday, she was unemployed and homeless.

Wealthy, but homeless nonetheless.

"I don't know where I belong," she confessed. "I think when you were in Boston and I was working so much, it was easy to pretend I was where I needed to be. But I'm alone. I've been alone since we were kids."

I'd had a miserable childhood, but Gemma's made mine seem like a fairy tale.

"I figured I'd give West Virginia a try for a few days until I decide where to go next," she said, turning her attention again to Ellie. "Worked for you."

"True." I kept my gaze on my husband.

Brooks and Wyatt had the fishing poles out now. The two of them had been spending more and more time together as of late. Wyatt still went to spend every other week with Moira, but every weekend, he was here with Brooks. They were putting in time together while they still had it. Wyatt was being scouted by four different college teams, and before we blinked, he'd be gone.

Brooks looked to the house again, once more catching my eye. This time, I waved. His handsome face was rough with stubble, his hair wind-blown and unruly. My heart skipped.

"Ugh," Gemma groaned. "You're almost impossible to be around right now. You two are worse than you and Karson as kids."

"I'm not even sorry." I giggled. "He's the best thing that ever happened to me."

"I'm happy for you."

I smiled. "Me too. What will you do?"

"I don't have the faintest damn idea."

Maybe I did. I held up a hand. "Wait here."

I hurried through the house for the kitchen, finding Brooks's keys. I twisted off the two I needed and when I returned to the porch, I found Brooks at the table next to Gemma. He'd stolen Ellie from her.

"Here." I tossed Gemma the keys to the Cadillac.

She caught them. "What are these?"

"The keys to the Cadillac. Take it. When you find him, tell Karson thanks."

Gemma studied the keys, then closed them in her grip. "Thanks for what?"

I took in Brooks, who was smiling at our daughter.

"For leading me home."

Wild Highway

1

GEMMA

"I'm sorry, what did you say? Where are you? Kansas? As in Dorothy and Toto? That Kansas?" Benjamin's string of questions came in his signature style—rapid-fire. "What happened to West Virginia?"

"I was in West Virginia," I said into the phone. "Now I'm in Kansas."

"B-but *why*?"

I didn't need to see his face to know it was agape with shock. For too long, Benjamin had tracked my every move. He'd stood by my side as I'd created my empire and had executed my directives with precision. The rigidity of my schedule wasn't just for my benefit. He'd managed it flawlessly for the past six years.

This trip of mine was going to freak him way the hell out.

"I have something important to tell you."

"No." He groaned. "I'm still dealing with the mess you left me the last time you had something important to tell me."

"Sorry." I hadn't meant to shake up his world. But since I'd completely torpedoed mine, changes to his were inevitable.

Three weeks ago, I'd called Benjamin into my office and told him that I was no longer the CEO of Gemma Lane. That I'd sold my beloved cosmetics company and namesake to Procter & Gamble. The monster corporation had purchased my brand and skin care formulas for the bargain price of twelve million dollars.

The sale had been a spur-of-the-moment decision. I didn't make those, not anymore. And ever since, I'd been waiting for a ping of regret. It hadn't hit me yet.

Instead, I'd felt free.

Selling Gemma Lane had been the first spontaneous decision I'd made in years. The floodgates were open now and these past three weeks had seen countless decisions made entirely with personal motivations.

For eleven years, I'd given every shred of my concentration and energy to my businesses. I'd worked my ass off to make sure I'd never be poor or homeless or hungry again. I'd lived my life with extreme control, shutting out any added emotion that wouldn't increase my bottom line.

Then I'd just . . . walked away.

All because of a pasta and breadsticks lunch with a former colleague.

I'd gotten a random phone call from my friend Julie. She'd worked with me selling real estate years before and we'd loosely kept in touch over the years. Neither of us had stayed in real estate, and while I'd chosen to create my own company, she'd worked her way up the executive ranks at Procter & Gamble.

We'd met for lunch to celebrate her recent promotion. And she'd asked me, point-blank, if I'd ever sell Gemma Lane. The word *yes* came from nowhere, shocking us both. We'd negotiated over the meal and Julie had taken my bottom-line number to her superiors.

Five hours later, I had the legal agreement in my inbox.

My life had flown out the window, like a ream of paper being tossed from my fourteenth-floor office on a windy day. Benjamin had been trying to catch the pages and stack them neatly again, except I just kept tossing more.

"I'm taking some time away," I told him.

"In West Virginia. You're supposed to be in West Virginia visiting Londyn. Wait, what's that noise? Are you driving?"

"Yes. About that . . ." My best friend Londyn was the reason I was in this car. "I was in West Virginia visiting Londyn. But remember last year when I told you she was taking her Cadillac and driving it to California?"

"I do. Except she met Brooks in West Virginia and married him. What does this—" Benjamin stopped. He was a brilliant man and normally our conversations went this way—I'd start explaining and he'd jump to the end before I could finish my story. "No. Tell me you're not taking this car to California yourself."

"I'm taking the car to California myself."

"Are you serious? You're driving from West Virginia to California? Alone?"

"Yes, yes and yes." I held my breath as the line went silent.

"You really have lost your goddamn mind."

I laughed. "You're not wrong."

"Gemma, what is going on with you?" The concern in his voice tugged at my heart. "Is this a you-turned-thirty-this-year crisis? Should I call Dr. Brewer?"

"No." I didn't need my therapist getting involved. Dr. Brewer would dredge up the past, and my childhood was the last thing I wanted to discuss at the moment. "It was just time for a change."

"A change? This is not a change. This is a nuclear explosion. You sold the company. Your baby. Gemma Lane was your *life*. You were there from five in the morning until eight at night every single day. Now it's gone."

I nodded, waiting for him to continue. This wasn't the first time he'd reminded me of exactly what I'd done. Yet, I still didn't feel like I'd made a huge mistake.

"Two weeks ago, you handed me an entirely new list of job duties, including managing all your assets and capital ventures while you disappeared to West Virginia. Now you're driving to California? This isn't you."

"But it used to be," I said.

I used to be impulsive and adventurous. Money and success were to blame for the caution that had invaded my life. A month ago, I'd had hundreds of employees counting on me to make the right decisions. They'd needed me to take care with my actions to ensure they had jobs. In worrying about them—for hours, days, years—I'd lost myself.

Now those employees would be working for Procter & Gamble. It had been part of my agreement that every one of my employees had future employment. Except for Benjamin. He'd always worked for me personally.

"I need this," I confessed. "I used to be fun. I used to be daring and reckless. You wouldn't even recognize that version of me."

Benjamin had only known the Gemma consumed by work. He didn't recognize me without the meetings, conference calls and galas. He didn't see that the charity balls I used to love—the ones where I'd smile as I sipped champagne because Boston's elite had let a lowly, runaway kid into their midst—were now suffocating and dull.

"Where is this coming from?" Benjamin asked. "I'm not buying this 'I needed a change' explanation. Something happened and you haven't told me."

Yes, something had happened, and I hadn't told anyone, not even Londyn. "Remember Jason Jensen?"

"The guy who used to work in marketing?"

"Yes. He asked me to marry him."

"What?" he shouted, the volume making me wince. "When? How long were you dating? How did I not know about this?"

"We dated for a few months. Obviously, we didn't tell anyone because I was his boss's boss. We agreed to keep it quiet, and I didn't think we were serious. But then one night about a month ago, he took me to this fancy restaurant, got down on one knee and proposed."

"Oh, Gemma. I'm sorry." As always, Benjamin jumped to the end of my story.

"Don't pity me. Pity Jason. He was sweet and handsome and kind. But I just . . . I couldn't say yes. I didn't love him."

So in a restaurant full of people watching, I'd broken a good man's heart.

"That's why he quit," Benjamin said.

"Yeah."

The day Jason had left, I'd sat in my office alone, giving him space to pack his things and say goodbye to his coworkers. I'd stared out my wall of windows and wished I'd loved him.

He was gracious and caring. Jason hadn't hated me for turning him down, he just couldn't work for me any longer. I didn't fault him for that. He'd loved unselfishly, not complaining that I'd been in the spotlight.

And I'd felt nothing but guilt.

"He just wasn't the right guy," Benjamin said. "That doesn't mean you had to sell your company, your car and your brownstone. You gave up your life."

"Was it really that good of a life?"

He sighed. "So what now?"

"I'm taking a road trip in this incredible car. Then . . . I don't know." Most of my belongings had either been donated to charity or put into storage. My house I'd sold furnished. What I had fit into the trunk of this car, and for today, it was enough.

I'd deal with tomorrow, well . . . tomorrow.

"What can I do?"

I smiled. Maybe Benjamin didn't understand what I was doing, but he'd support me, nonetheless. "Exactly what you are doing."

He was managing my assets, paying my bills and dealing with any questions that came up with my other business ventures. It was all work I'd done myself before the sale. It had been the second job I hadn't needed but something to fill the lonely nights. Work had always been my forte.

Now I'd handed it over to Benjamin.

Since he no longer had to manage my hectic calendar and activities at Gemma Lane, he'd watch over my numerous real estate holdings, acting as the liaison to the property management company I'd hired years ago. Benjamin would step in and be the go-between with my financial managers.

The restaurants that had needed my influx of cash to get up and running were now some of Boston's finest. They ran on autopilot. I owned an interest in a car dealership, one that peddled foreign luxury as opposed to the classic Americana I was currently driving. And I was also a partner in a fashion design company, the one that had designed the black sweater I was currently wearing along with a handful of others packed in my suitcase.

Benjamin would ensure we received regular profit and loss reports from my investments along with my annual dividends, then alert me to any red flags.

"Okay," he said. "It will be in good hands until you get back."

I bit my tongue, because as the open road stretched before me, there was a good chance I wouldn't be back. I was on a new path now. Where it was going, I wasn't sure. But the excitement, the freedom, was something I hadn't felt in a long, long time.

"Call if you need anything. And, Benjamin?"

"Yeah?"

"Thank you."

"Drive safely."

I tossed my phone aside and put both hands on the white steering wheel.

Londyn's cherry-red, 1964 Cadillac DeVille convertible was a dream to drive. The car sailed down the interstate, the wheels skimming over the asphalt as the body sliced through the air.

She'd paid a small fortune to restore this car from the rusted heap it had once been. Gone were the torn, flat seats. They'd been replaced with thick cushions covered with buttery, white leather that matched the wheel. The air-conditioning kept the cab from getting too hot, and when I felt like blasting music, the sound system was deafening.

This car's look was different but the inside would always feel like Londyn's home. As an old, abandoned wreck destined for the scrap pile, Londyn had chosen this Cadillac as her shelter in a junkyard we'd called home.

The junkyard in Temecula, California, where Londyn, four other kids and I had lived after running away from our respective homes.

The six of us had made our own family in that junkyard. I hadn't lived in a car, instead choosing to build myself a makeshift tent. I'd tried to talk Londyn into a tent or structure too so she'd have more space, but she'd fallen in love with the car.

And with Karson.

He'd lived in this car with her while they'd been together. Londyn hadn't seen him since we'd moved away from California, but he was the reason she'd set out to take this car to California in the first place.

Karson would always hold a special place in her heart. He'd been her first love. He'd been our friend. He'd always hold a special place in mine too. Londyn had wanted him to have this car and see it restored to its former glory. That, and I think she wanted to know that he was all right.

If delivering the Cadillac to him would make her happy, I'd gladly drive the miles.

And I could use the time to figure out my next move.

Figure out who I wanted to be.

I glanced at myself in the rearview mirror. My chocolate-brown hair was piled in a messy knot on top of my head. I hadn't bothered with makeup in my hotel room this morning. I looked a far cry from the corporate tycoon I'd been last month.

Gone were the posh and polish. They were somewhere in the miles behind me, strewn across the interstate.

I'd left West Virginia two days ago, heeding Londyn's advice not to rush the trip. The first day, I'd driven for six hours before stopping in Louisville, Kentucky, for the night. I'd eaten dinner alone, not unusual for me, then went to bed. The next day, I'd crossed into Missouri for a stop in Kansas City. Then this morning, I'd awoken refreshed and ready to hit the road.

So here I was, hours later, in the middle of Kansas on a warm September day.

Flat fields spread like a golden ocean in every direction, only disturbed by the occasional barn or building. The road stretched in an endless line in front of me and rarely did I have to turn the steering wheel. Traffic on the interstate was crowded with semitrucks hauling loads across the country.

As the day wore on, I found myself relaxing to the whir of the tires on the pavement. I studied the landscape and its subtle changes as I approached the border to Colorado. And I breathed.

Truly breathed.

There were no emails to return. No calls to answer. No decisions to make. Benjamin would deal with any emergency that came up. As of now, I was the blissfully silent partner.

Walking away from my life had been relatively easy.

What did that mean? What did it mean that the only person who'd called me since leaving Boston was my paid employee?

Lost in my head, it took me a moment to notice the flash of red and blue lights racing up behind me. When their flicker caught my eye, my heart jumped to my throat and my foot instantly came off the gas. My hands gripped the wheel at ten and two as I glanced at the speedometer.

"Shit. Don't pull me over. Please, please, please." The last thing I needed was another speeding ticket.

The police car zoomed into the passing lane and streaked by. The air rushed from my lungs and I watched him disappear down the road ahead.

Thank God. I set the cruise control to exactly the speed limit.

Why did I always speed? When the limit was seventy-five, why did I push it to eighty-nine? When was I going to learn to slow down?

I'd never excelled at going slow or taking my time. I'd always put in twenty times the effort as others because I hadn't had an Ivy League education or family pedigree to rely on. But give me a dollar and I'd turn it into ten through sheer will and determination. I worked hard and fast, something I'd been doing since running away from home at sixteen.

If you wanted to survive on the streets, you didn't act slow. I'd figured out quickly how to care for myself. Granted, I'd had help. In the beginning, Karson had been my lifeline.

He and I had lived in the same shitty neighborhood. As kids, he'd walked with me to school and had played with me at the neighborhood park. It was a miracle neither of us had contracted tetanus from the swing set. Whenever I ran from my home crying, I'd often find him at that park, avoiding his own home.

Karson had been my closest friend. The day he hadn't showed up at school, I'd gone to check on him. When I'd peeked through his window and saw his backpack was missing, I'd known he'd finally had enough.

When I'd hit the same breaking point, I'd sought him out. There hadn't been a lot of other options. Karson had already made the junkyard his home. Then he'd helped make it mine.

A month later, Londyn came along. I'd found her digging through a Dumpster behind a restaurant, picking off a piece of wilted lettuce from a sandwich and actually opening her mouth to eat the damn thing. I gagged remembering that stench.

I'd ripped that sandwich out of her hand and tossed it back in the trash where it had belonged.

We'd been best friends ever since.

After saving her from the sandwich, I'd hauled her to the junkyard, made her a peanut butter and jelly, and introduced her to Karson. It had taken them three months to finally admit they liked each other. And another three months before Karson began spending his nights in her Cadillac.

A lot had changed since then. Life had split us all apart, though Londyn and I had always stayed friends. We'd both spent years living in Boston, meeting for drinks and manicures on a weekly basis. But Boston hadn't been right, for either of us.

I was happy she'd found Brooks and a home in West Virginia. Had the others found happiness too? A few years ago—driven by curiosity or nostalgia or both—I'd hired a private investigator to look everyone up. It had taken him a few months since I hadn't given him much to start with besides names, but he'd found them. Karson had still been in California, Clara in Arizona, and Aria in Oregon.

And Katherine was in Montana, where I'd left her behind.

The sound of my ringing phone startled me and I stretched to grab it from the passenger seat, seeing Londyn's name on the screen.

"I was just thinking about you," I answered.

"Good things?"

"I was thinking about how we met."

"You mean how you saved me from food poisoning and ultimate starvation?"

I laughed. "Yep."

"Ah, good times." She giggled. "How's the trip?"

In the background, I heard her husband, Brooks. "Ask her if the car is running okay."

"Did you hear him?" she asked.

"Yeah. Tell him it's running fine."

"She says there's a strange knocking sound every few minutes. And if she gives it too much gas at once, the whole car lurches."

"What?" His voice echoed to my ear. "I just tuned it up. Give me that phone."

I laughed at the sound of her swatting him away.

"I'm kidding," she told him. "The car is fine. Now go away so we can talk. Ellie needs her diaper changed. I saved it just for you."

"Gee, thanks," he muttered. Through the phone, I recognized the sound of a soft kiss.

Jealousy would be easy if I wasn't so happy for her.

"Where are you?" she asked.

"I crossed into Colorado about twenty miles ago. I'm hoping to get to Denver tonight. Then maybe tomorrow, I'll put in a long stretch and see if I can get to Las Vegas."

Londyn sighed. "There's no hurry, Gem. Why don't you stay in Colorado for a week? Explore and relax."

"Maybe." Did I even know how to relax?

"When was the last time you took a weekend off?"

"Um . . ." It hadn't been in recent years. "Montana, I guess."

"That was—what?—eleven years ago? I'd say you're overdue," she said. "So you were thinking about the junkyard days, huh? Why?"

"I don't know. Reminiscing, I guess. Wondering where do I go after this trip. Things were hard, but life seemed easier back at Lou's."

Lou Miley had owned the junkyard where the six of us kids had lived. He'd been a loner and a gruff old man. Unfriendly and irritable. But he'd let us stay without question.

"Are you okay?" Londyn asked. "Should I be worried?"

"No," I promised. "I was just thinking about how we all scattered. Everyone but Karson. I wonder how everyone is doing."

"You're still upset about the Katherine thing, aren't you?"

"I screwed up."

Londyn sighed. "You were nineteen years old and jumped at an opportunity to make some money. I highly doubt she holds it against you. Considering where we all came from, Katherine, above all people, couldn't fault you for wanting to better your life."

"I don't know," I mumbled.

I'd broken a promise to a close friend. I'd ditched her, choosing money over that promise and the decision had haunted me since.

This was a fresh start for me. There was nothing holding me back. Londyn wanted me to take an overdue vacation. Maybe what I really needed before I could concentrate on the future, was to make an overdue apology for a past mistake.

An idea stirred in my mind, calling and demanding some attention. It was like a flashing light, one that would keep blinking until I gave it my focus. This feeling was familiar, and usually, it meant another successful business venture.

But not this time.

This idea had nothing to do with money.

"Would you care if it took me longer than planned to get the Cadillac to Karson?" Because my intuition was screaming at me to take a massive detour.

"Nope," she said. "It's your trip. Make the most of it."

"Okay." I smiled. "Thanks, Lonny."

"Of course. Call me soon."

"Bye." The moment I ended the call, I pulled up my digital map and punched in a new destination.

These spontaneous decisions of the past few weeks suddenly made sense. They had purpose. They had meaning. They were to get me here, in this moment.

I was setting out to right a wrong. To find myself again.

On the wild highway.

140

2

GEMMA

I'D FORGOTTEN the majesty of Montana. I'd forgotten how vast the state was. How the landscapes changed from savage prairie to rugged forest as you traveled from one side to the other.

The last time I'd traveled through Montana, it had been on a bus destined for Boston. Back then, I'd cursed the driver for taking the trip at such a lazy pace. This time, I'd let myself find excuses to slow down.

In the past five days, I'd made a conscious effort to drive unhurried. Mostly, it was to avoid a ticket. But there was also a part of me nervous about seeing Katherine again, and that anxiety had given me plenty of excuses to stop along the way.

My journey had taken me north, through Colorado and Wyoming. I'd spent last night in Missoula, not wanting to arrive at the ranch at dinnertime. Really, I was a coward and had needed one more night to work up the courage for what I was about to do.

So I'd stayed in town and found a cheap nail salon for a last-minute mani-pedi. This morning, I'd taken care with my appearance, going for the makeup treatment and adding loose waves to my long hair.

The tattered boyfriend jeans I'd been wearing on repeat were traded for a pair of dark wash skinnies. My green sweater brought out the caramel flecks in my hazel eyes and my tan booties had enough of a heel that they took my outfit from casual to chic.

Still, I'd wished for one of my designer suits.

I'd worn blazers, pencil skirts and six-inch heels, almost exclusively, over the past decade. Since leaving West Virginia, my laid-back attire of jeans, oversized sweaters and sandals had been an adjustment. I didn't feel prepared. Powerful.

My wardrobe in Boston had become an armor of sorts. When I'd walked into the office in a suit, my hair twisted into a tight chignon, no one had questioned who was in charge. I needed that armor today—a bit of the old Gemma to help me get through this.

But the suits were all in storage. Today, I had to face this without airs. I'd be vulnerable. Humble. Sincere. Because today wasn't about conquering the world or turning a profit. Today was about making things right with a friend.

The trees along the road were changing. Stark yellow and orange leaves popped against an evergreen backdrop. The fall air was crisp and, if I hadn't spent time on my hair this morning, I would have driven with the convertible's top down.

The miles disappeared too quickly and when the first sign for the Greer Ranch and Mountain Resort came into view, my stomach somersaulted.

I could do this. I had to do this. I hadn't made many apologies, lately. Arrogant as it was, I did my best not to screw up, and for the most part, I had a good track record.

This would bruise my ego but would be worth it.

I turned off the highway, my heart pounding, and traversed the gravel road that led from the highway toward the lodge. Being here, on this road, took me back to another lifetime. I struggled to keep my eyes on the road as I took it all in. The mountains. The meadows. The buildings coming into view past a grove of trees.

It was exactly as I'd remembered. In the past decade, the Greer Ranch hadn't seemed to change.

The lodge was a rustic log building and the focal point for guests—or it had been when I'd worked here. Behind it was an enormous barn beside a doubly enormous stable.

All three were the same, rich brown color. The windows of the lodge gleamed in the morning Montana sunshine. Maroon and golden mums spilled from a toppled whiskey barrel beside the front steps. Three wooden rocking chairs were positioned to the left of the hand-carved front door.

I'd once cleaned those windows. I'd planted flowers in that barrel. I'd rocked in one of those chairs and walked through that front door.

Katherine had been the one to pick Montana. She'd found us jobs at this guest ranch when Londyn and I had agreed to come along. The three of us had packed our meager belongings, bought bus tickets and waited for her to turn eighteen. Then we'd said goodbye to Karson, Clara, Aria and our beloved junkyard, setting out from California to Montana on a Greyhound bus because we'd craved adventure. Not for money or power or fame, but for an experience worth retelling.

We'd been so excited. So eager. We'd been so free.

No, not we. Me. I'd been excited and eager and free.

Somewhere along the way, that eighteen-year-old girl had gotten lost.

I parked the Cadillac in one of the guest spaces, not designated by a curb, but by an old-fashioned hitching post. My hands were suddenly like Jell-O and it took all my strength to shove the car in park.

Was it too late to turn around?

Yes.

I was here and damn it, I was doing this. With my eyes closed, I sucked in a calming breath and blew it out with an audible whoosh. When was the last time I'd been this nervous?

Leaning heavily into the door, I shoved it open. My purse stayed in the passenger seat because there was no such thing as petty theft at the Greer Ranch. The guests here didn't need to steal and I doubted any employee would dare cross the Greers—they were too well respected and that likely hadn't changed.

I swallowed down the lump in my throat and began the trek to the porch. My fingers gripped the wooden railing as my unsteady legs climbed the five stairs. Then with another shaky breath, I turned the knob on the door and walked inside.

The smell of cedar and cinnamon filled my nostrils. Someone had started a wood fire in the hearth. The couches surrounding the fireplace and rock chimney were the same chocolate leather. The plaid toss pillows looked new.

I tipped my chin to take in the vaulted ceiling's wooden beams. A wide, sweeping staircase ran to my right and another to my left, both the same wood color as the floor. Directly in front of me was the reception desk, currently unoccupied. And behind me, above the door, was a mounted, eight-point bull elk bust.

Clive.

Londyn, Katherine and I had affectionately named the elk Clive the month after we'd arrived. None of us had ever seen a taxidermic animal before Clive, and we'd thought he'd deserved a name.

I smiled, happy he was still here. Happy that, besides minor changes, this place hadn't changed.

It was like stepping back in time, to the days when my younger self had two best friends and ambitions bigger than the sky.

This room hadn't changed.

But the woman standing in it sure had.

I walked to the counter, spying a silver service bell that hadn't been there before. I touched my finger to the plunger and the ding chorused through the room.

"One minute!" a voice called from the hallway that ran behind the staircase on my left. One minute was actually ten seconds. A flash of white hair caught my eye first as a woman emerged, drying her hands on a white towel.

"Morning." She smiled and my heart melted.

I'd missed that smile.

"Good morning," I said, praying she'd recognize me. Though I wouldn't fault her if she didn't. I'd only worked here for eight months, eleven years ago. The Greers had likely met a hundred seasonal workers since.

"What can I do for"—her head cocked to the side and her eyes widened —"Gemma?"

Thank God. She hadn't forgotten me. "Hi, Carol."

"Oh my word, Gemma!" She threw the towel on the reception desk and came right into my space, pulling me into a tight embrace. "My God, girl. How long has it been?"

"About eleven years." I laughed. "It's good to see you, Carol."

"Honey, you are just . . ." She let me go to look me up and down. "Stunning. Though you always were."

"And you are as beautiful as always."

"Please." She rolled her eyes. "I'm old."

The lines around Carol's eyes and mouth had deepened over the years but her hair was the same bright white, braided in a long, thick rope that draped over one shoulder. Her eyes were the same welcoming brown.

"What are you doing here?" she asked. "Where have you been all these years? Can you stay for dinner?"

I laughed, thinking that Benjamin would love Carol and her endless string of questions. "I've been living in Boston, but I'm on a vacation of sorts."

Permanently.

"Great." Carol's hands flew into the air, then she rushed around the side of the counter and began shaking a mouse to wake up a computer. "Do you want a king-size bed facing the valley? Or a queen with the mountain view?"

"Oh, no. That's okay. I've got a room in Missoula." It was forty miles away and the perfect excuse to leave before I wore out my welcome.

She ignored me. "King or queen?"

"Really, I don't need a room. I just wanted to swing by and see the place. If Katherine is still here, I'd, um . . . I'd love to say hello."

Understanding filled Carol's gaze and she nodded. The look wasn't harsh, and it didn't hold judgment, but she knew what I'd done to Katherine. She just wasn't holding it against me.

Carol might be the only one here who didn't.

"Yes, Katherine's here," she said. "She's in her office working. I'll take you up there after you tell me what room you want so I can have one of the boys haul up your luggage."

Maybe I'd known or hoped this would happen, because my luggage was packed in the Cadillac and I hadn't extended my reservation in Missoula. I'd just asked the clerk this morning if they had vacancies in case I returned.

"Queen, please." I wanted the mountain view. "My credit card is in my car."

"You're not paying," she said as she clicked and scrolled, eyes glued to the screen.

"I insist."

"Honey, I know it's been a lot of years but a smart girl like you, I'm sure you remember who's in charge around here."

I laughed. "Yes, ma'am."

"Better." She clicked one last time, then shoved the mouse aside.

Carol was in charge. She and her husband, Jake Sr., had started the Greer Ranch nearly fifty years ago. After their livestock operation had become successful, they'd expanded to start the resort, eventually passing it all down to their son, JR.

JR had been the manager of the entire operation when I'd worked here. Maybe he still was.

Or maybe Easton had taken over.

Regardless, Carol was in charge. She told the men exactly what she expected and heaven help them if they didn't follow orders.

Carol came around the counter and looped her arm through mine. "How did Boston treat you?"

"Quite well for a time."

"I can see that." She gave me another appraisal. "You always were classy. Even without a penny to pinch between your fingers, you had that air of sophistication about you. That air is still there, but I see you've got the pennies now too."

"I've saved a couple." My net worth was close to twenty million dollars. Yet standing beside Carol, I was the poor person in the room.

The land they owned in this gorgeous valley in Western Montana was worth hundreds of millions of dollars. Not that she'd flaunt it. That wasn't Carol's style. No, she was the woman with money in the bank and horse shit on her boots because a good day to her was working on this land.

I smiled and leaned in closer. "How is Jake?"

"Ornery." She shook her head. "That man hates being retired but he's so damn stubborn he won't admit it. So he putzes around, driving the rest of us who are trying to work crazy. Especially Easton. It's not a weekday if those two aren't fighting."

My heart skipped at the mention of his name. It had crossed my mind countless times on the drive here.

Easton Greer was another reason I'd stayed away. Another mistake. Someone I doubted would welcome me with open arms.

But this trip wasn't about him. I was going to find the courage to make things right with Katherine.

Any amends with Easton would be a bonus.

Maybe he'd forgotten all about me. In a way, I hoped he had.

Carol led me up the staircase, keeping a firm hold on my arm, as we made it to the first landing, rounded the corner and started up flight two. If she noticed my shaking fingers, she didn't show it.

"Katherine runs the resort side of things these days. We kept promoting her from job to job, and when we finally ran out of rungs on the ladder for her to climb, we just made her the boss."

"That doesn't surprise me in the least."

Katherine might not have had my bold ambition, but she'd always been smart and incredibly hardworking. Like me, she'd stopped going to school once she'd come to live in the junkyard. Instead, she'd worked. During the day, she'd had a job with a landscaping company. And at night, she'd washed dishes for a restaurant. Both had paid cash under the table.

The two of us had been more than friends. We'd been roommates. She'd shared my tent—though tent had never been the right word. It had started as a tent, with a tarp strung between two piles of junk to keep the rain away. Then I'd added sheet-metal walls and eventually separate bedrooms, one for me and another for Katherine. Our makeshift living room had become the common area for meals and games.

That tent had been my pride and joy, much like the empire I'd built in Boston.

An empire I'd built by leaving Katherine behind.

My shoes and Carol's boots echoed on the floor's wooden planks as we reached the second story and started down a long hallway, lined with doors.

I hadn't spent much time in this wing of the lodge since it was where the offices were located. The other wing was much larger and held all the guest rooms. I'd spent plenty of time in that wing as a housekeeper.

The Greer Ranch and Mountain Resort had become one of Montana's premier guest ranches, offering a *traditional western experience*. I'd done some googling in my hotel room last night and had been impressed by the website. The resort had always been nice, but over the past decade, they'd built five different chalets for guests to rent. They'd added more guest experiences and the meals were five-star. Prices weren't listed on the website because this place catered to celebrities and the uber-rich.

"Is she happy here?" I asked Carol.

She reached a door, rapped on it once with her knuckles.

"Come in," a voice I hadn't heard in years called from the other side.

My palms began to sweat.

Carol nodded for me to go on in. "Ask her yourself. I'll be downstairs in the kitchen. Come find me when you're ready to haul in your luggage."

"Okay," I breathed and turned the knob. *Here goes.* With my shoulders squared, I pushed the door open and took one step inside.

Katherine, beautiful as ever, sat behind a wide oak desk. She looked up from her computer screen and her entire body stiffened. "Gemma?"

"Hi." I lifted my hand for an awkward wave and braved another step.

Her eyebrows came together. "W-what are you doing here?"

"I came to see you." I sucked in some oxygen. *Breathe.* "May I?" I asked, coming into the room and motioning to one of the leather club chairs positioned in front of her desk.

She nodded but otherwise sat perfectly still in her high-backed chair.

Her corner office was enormous, as big as the one I'd had in Boston. The interior walls had floor-to-ceiling bookshelves and the others were lined with windows. A couch and two loveseats angled toward the view occupied half of the room.

It was classy yet comfortable. Inviting and clean. The entire setup suited her completely.

Though Katherine had always fit here.

From the day we'd stepped off the bus, it had seemed like she'd found the place where she'd fit. Today, she looked even more at home, sitting at a fancy desk, wearing jeans and boots, with a picture window at her back and the mountains in the distance.

Her dark hair hung straight and sleek past her shoulders. Its natural shine was something I'd envied as a teenager—adult too. And I had yet to meet a person on earth with bluer eyes than Katherine Gates. They were almost exactly the color of the cloudless sky through the window.

She folded her hands together, leaning on the papers scattered on her desk. Her expression was neutral but there was a wariness in her gaze.

Katherine was six inches shorter than my five seven. She had a petite frame and trim figure. But sitting behind that desk, she was a force of her own. She was the boss and this was her throne.

It was a good look for her.

"How are you?" I asked.

"Good, thanks." Her tone was polite. Cautious. "You?"

"I'm good." I crossed my legs, trying to appear relaxed when I was the furthest thing from it. "Carol told me you're running the resort. Congratulations."

"Thank you."

The silence that followed was excruciating.

What felt like an hour was likely seconds, but the message was clear. Katherine didn't want me here, so I gave myself a mental shove to get this over with.

Sorry. That was all I had to say. I'm sorry.

So what the hell are you waiting for, Gemma?

"I wanted to—"

The phone on Katherine's desk rang. She pushed a button to shut it off, but not one second after it quieted, her cell phone began to vibrate. She silenced it too. "What were you saying?"

The confidence I'd summoned evaporated. The last thing I wanted was to fumble through this and risk coming across as hurried and insincere.

"I'm interrupting." I stood from the chair. "I'll let you get back to work. Maybe we could meet for coffee later."

"Today's crazy. I, um . . . maybe I could take a late lunch around one. But I'd only have thirty minutes."

I'd dodged many people with the late, short lunch before.

Which meant this was my chance to say my peace and then get the hell off the Greer Ranch.

I recognized when I wasn't welcome.

"It's okay." I gave her a sad smile. "Mostly, I just wanted to say that I'm sorry. You were my friend and how I left, what I did, it wasn't okay."

"Is that why you're here?"

"Yes."

Katherine stared at me, her expression unreadable. Then slowly, it softened. Warmth spread into her eyes and her hands unclasped. "Are you staying?"

"If you don't mind." No matter what Carol said, if Katherine had a problem with me being here, I'd leave.

"No, I don't mind. I do have a crazy day. I was going to eat lunch at my desk. But maybe we could meet for dinner. In the dining room around six?"

"That would be wonderful." I let myself out, holding my smile until I was in the hallway. Then I let it stretch as years of regret and guilt vanished.

She doesn't hate me.

I could leave right this minute and feel like this trip had been valuable. But I wasn't going to leave. I was going to have dinner with my friend and hopefully rekindle a relationship I'd once held dear. My feet were practically floating as I descended the stairs.

Carol wasn't at the front desk, so I opted to head outside and collect my suitcase. I opened the door, a smile still on my face, and collided, headfirst, with a wall of muscle.

"Oh, sorry." I looked up and my heart stopped.

The smell of leather and aftershave filled my nose. I looked up to see a pair of dark brown eyes hooded by long, onyx lashes. I took in the straight nose, the sharp jaw and strong chin. My gaze dropped to the full lips I'd tasted once, on a night eleven years ago.

I'd never seen a face as symmetrical and so beautifully masculine as Easton Greer's.

Even when he scowled, like he was now, it was a wonder.

He'd gotten even more handsome. How was that possible? He'd transformed from a young man to just a man, man. Rugged and rough and sexy.

"Gemma." My name came out as a growl in his deep voice and I tore my gaze away from his mouth, taking a step back.

"Hi," I breathed, the air heavy and thick.

He took a step away, then another, his glare unwavering.

Easton cast his scowl over his shoulder and spotted the Cadillac. "That yours?"

"Yes."

"You're staying here." Not a question. An accusation. If he had it his way, I'd be uninvited.

I lifted my chin. "Yes, I came to see Katherine."

His jaw ticked. "I thought we'd gotten rid of you years ago."

Ouch. I guess he was still pissed about that whole sex in his room and waking up to find me gone.

But, good or bad, he hadn't forgotten me.

3

EASTON

WHAT THE FUCK was she doing here?

I stormed through the wide, open barn door and kicked a clump of dirt. "And who the fuck is bringing dirt into my barn?"

I looked around, spotting a four-wheeler parked in the middle of the space that hadn't been there ten minutes ago. Its wheels were caked with mud. Someone—my grandfather—had probably been driving it around the lower meadow. We'd had a good rain last night and the ground was soggy.

Sure enough, Granddad emerged from behind the tractor at the far end of the building. He had a travel mug in one hand and a wrench in the other. "What's crawled up your ass this morning?"

"We just swept out this floor." I pointed to the four-wheeler. "Maybe next time you could park it outside. Save my crew from doing cleanup twice."

"It's a barn, Easton." He frowned. "And in my day, the crews didn't have much time to sweep."

My day. For fuck's sake. The last thing I needed this morning was a lecture about how this ranch had been run in his day.

I clenched my fists and kept my mouth shut before we got into a fight that would have my father playing mediator, my mother reminding me to have patience and Grandma lecturing me about respect.

The bottom line? I'd been put in charge of this ranch but Granddad hadn't read the memo.

He reminded me daily of how he'd done things in *my day.* He'd done the same to Dad when Dad had been running the show, though it had never bothered my father the way it irked me. Maybe because Dad and Granddad usually were of the same mind.

They both questioned my decisions. Yet we were thriving because I'd pushed and pushed and pushed to do things differently.

Neither of them had cared if the barn was clean. Granddad was right, he hadn't had staff to tidy up because both he and Dad had run with a skeleton crew for so damn long that we'd gotten the reputation for burning out ranch hands faster than we could hire their replacements.

According to Granddad, I'd overstaffed the ranch. But I liked to keep my guys for longer than one season. And I liked to have a clean barn, clean horses and clean equipment.

The tractor he'd been tinkering with had lasted seven years longer than any he'd had in his day. Maybe it was because he was a good mechanic. Or maybe it was because I had insisted on both servicing it *before* it broke down and keeping it inside, out of the elements.

"What are you doing?" I asked, looking over his shoulder to the John Deere.

"I'm checking the hydraulics on the tractor. If that's *all right* with you."

"Fine," I gritted out, turned and walked away.

I loved my grandfather, but damn it, working with the man was exhausting.

I couldn't assign him work. I couldn't hold him responsible for doing something on a regular basis because he was *retired*. And because Jake Greer Sr. reported to no one but his wife.

The problem was Granddad didn't want to be retired. He'd pop in and take over jobs while I was in the middle of them. He'd take work from one of my hands without letting me know. He'd give orders to my staff, sending them in the wrong direction, all because he was bored—something he'd never admit.

Like the hydraulics. I'd already planned on checking them this afternoon. He knew I was going to do it myself because I'd told him yesterday. But did he ask if there was something else I could use his help on? No.

I walked out of the barn and stalked to the stables, my sanctuary. It was twice as big as the barn, and everyone, even Granddad, knew this was my domain. The floors were swept out regularly and every horse's stall was mucked daily. We kept this place spotless, not only for the animals and my mental state, but because unlike the barn, guests roamed in here often.

As I made my way down the long center aisle, I counted the empty stalls. Most of the animals were out on guest excursions except for three young mares that had been left behind. They didn't spare me so much as a glance, too busy munching on the grain they'd been given this morning.

Above me, the lofts were full of bales and the florescent lights were shining bright. It smelled like all stables should in my opinion, of horses, hay and hard work.

My gelding Jigsaw popped his head out of his stall the moment he heard my boots on the cement floor. I walked to him, putting my hand on his cheek. "How do you feel about doing some work today?"

He nuzzled my shoulder, anxious to get outside.

Jigsaw had been my horse since I was eleven. He stood nearly sixteen hands and was a beast of an animal. He was fast and not afraid to work. He'd gotten his name from the puzzle-piece-shaped spot on his right shoulder. Besides that white mark, he was as black as the midnight sky.

I could always count on Jigsaw. He'd never let me down. He never meddled with my schedule. He never talked back.

He never disappeared, only to return out of the blue eleven years later.

"What the fuck is she doing here?" I asked my horse.

He flicked up his nose, butting against my head.

"Yeah, we'll get going soon." I stroked the bridge of his nose and left him to get myself ready.

My office was located in the stables, beside the tack room. Dad had suggested I use the corner office in the lodge, the one opposite Katherine's, because more and more, I found myself behind a desk.

It would make things more efficient if I was sitting inside where I could talk to Katherine in person rather than call her twelve times a day. But I liked my cramped office in the stables. I liked that I could watch the trainers and the hands interact with the horses and the guests. I could witness who had the patience to take groups out on trail rides and who would be better suited for ranch maintenance.

And I liked working with the smell of horses and leather and dirt in the air.

But it meant when I needed to talk to Katherine, I had to call. When she didn't answer, I'd trek to the lodge for a cup of coffee and pop by her office.

Running into Gemma Lane had nearly knocked me on my ass.

I swiped my phone from my desk and shoved it into a jeans pocket. Then I grabbed a pair of leather gloves from the top of a file cabinet and took my Stetson off the set of deer antlers I used as a hat hook. I needed to get out of here and get some air. Think this over.

"Hey, boss." Rory appeared in the doorway, bouncing from foot to foot.

"Hey." I put the hat on my head. "What's up?"

"I'm all done with the stalls for the day, and I'm ready to help on the tractor."

Rory was the son of one of our longtime housekeepers. As a single mom, she'd worked hard to provide for her son. He'd just turned eighteen and had graduated from high school this past spring. His mom's dream was for him to go to college. Rory's was to work on this ranch.

So I'd hired him. The kid soaked up everything we could teach him. He didn't bitch about the shit—literal—jobs. And if there was a chance for him to do something with the equipment, he was all over it.

I'd promised him yesterday he could shadow me as I worked on the tractor.

"Change of plan. Jake is working on the tractor today. He said he'd love to have your help."

"Okay, cool. Thanks."

"When you're done, take lunch. Then we'll wait for the trail rides to get back in. I'm going to check the fence on the south side. Just hang out and help the guys with the horses when they get back."

"Will do." He jogged out the door.

Rory jogged everywhere. His energy was impossible to contain and he always had a slew of questions.

Those questions would drive Granddad, a guy who preferred to work in silence, nuts.

I chuckled.

"What are you laughing about?" My brother, Cash, strode into the office.

"I sent Rory to help Granddad service the tractor."

He laughed too. "You'll pay for that later."

"Worth it." I grinned. "I thought Katherine had you out with the guests this morning."

"The folks staying in the Beartooth Chalet canceled their ride. They decided to hike up the ridge and take some pictures since the weather's good. We'll ride tomorrow."

I swiped another pair of gloves from the pile of my spares. "Good. Then you can help me."

"What are we doing?" he asked as I slapped the gloves into his chest and eased past him out the door.

"Fencing."

"I knew I should have gone to see Grandma instead of coming out here."

I walked to the wall where my saddle was draped over a thick wooden post. I pulled off a saddle blanket and grabbed a currycomb, then went to Jigsaw's stall. I'd planned on just taking a survey and noting damage today, but if Cash was free, we'd tackle the repairs too.

"Do you want to ride or take the truck?" I asked.

"I'll take the truck," he grumbled. "Since obviously you're going to ride."

I didn't feel bad for making Cash drive. He spent three times as long as I did on horseback, and he could be behind the wheel for a change.

It didn't take me long to get Jigsaw saddled and outside. The crisp fall air filled my lungs and he pranced on his feet, anxious to get out in the open. My horse loved to run, but he'd been trained to wait. When I left him standing in a spot, his reins not secured, he stood and waited.

Because he was a damn good horse.

Cash pulled up with the fencing truck, the blue Ford we kept stocked with a pile of steel fence posts and a roll of barbed wire. On a thirteen-thousand-acre ranch there was always fencing to do.

"Lead the way." He waved toward the two-wheel path that would take us to the south part of the ranch.

I mounted Jigsaw and clicked my tongue to walk away from the stables. When we hit grass, I gave him his head and let him go, our pace starting as an easy lope until he was galloping through the meadow.

My heart raced as the air whipped in my face. As he picked up speed, my muscles contracted, my core engaging and my thighs warming. I gave Jigsaw another nudge, letting him break to full throttle.

We were both panting when we hit the tree line. I slowed him down and turned, seeing Cash a way back, the truck bouncing through the middle of the field.

"Good boy." I patted Jigsaw's neck, his hide sweating. Then I wiped my own sweaty brow with my shirtsleeve.

The lodge stood tall and proud in the distance. I didn't spend much time there during the day—it had never felt as much like *my place* as the barn or stables—but it was mine.

I'd be avoiding that building like the damn plague since Gemma was somewhere inside.

Her face, shocked and beautiful, was burned into my brain. Those pink lips looked as soft as I remembered. Her hair was longer now, hanging in artful waves to the middle of her back. Her eyes were that same mesmerizing hazel.

She'd grown into a stunning woman.

Exactly what I didn't need on this ranch. I wasn't sure how long she'd planned to stay, but I had enough to deal with on a good day, with the regular ranch and resort workload. We were gearing up to begin winter prep. There was firewood to cut. The cows would need to be brought down to the meadows from where they'd spent their summer grazing in the mountains.

It was not the time to have an old fling show up at my damn front door.

I'd done a fine job of forgetting Gemma Lane.

At least, I thought I'd forgotten her. The knee-jerk reaction and the fact that now I couldn't *stop* thinking about her said otherwise.

She needed to go back to wherever she'd come from and remember that she didn't belong here. Just like she hadn't belonged here years ago. With any luck, her visit would end before sundown.

Cash pulled up with the truck and rolled down his window. "You okay?"

"Yeah. Why?"

"You shot out of there like your heels were on fire."

"Just wanted to give Jigsaw a chance to run."

"Sure," he deadpanned. "You know, before I came to the stables, I helped this hot brunette with a kickass car haul her suitcase into the lodge. She looked awfully familiar, and you're in a lousier than normal mood today. She wouldn't have anything to do with it, would she?"

I gritted my teeth. "No."

He chuckled. "Whatever you say, brother."

Luggage. *Fuck.* She was staying.

How did Cash even remember Gemma? When she'd worked here before, he'd been away at college in Idaho. He must have remembered her from a trip home for spring break.

Meanwhile, I'd been here when Gemma, Kat and their other friend had arrived, having just graduated from Montana State. I'd been twenty-two, educated and energized with ideas for taking this ranch to the next level.

It had taken me over a decade to implement some of those ideas. Others had died along the way.

"I want to get through this pasture today if we can," I told Cash, needing to concentrate on work for a few hours. "Hopefully it's not too bad."

"Sounds good. I rode out here last week with Kat so she could try out that mare. I didn't notice any wires down but we didn't ride down the line."

"Fingers crossed this won't take more than a day. I'd like to get the yearlings in here next week."

Cash's forehead furrowed. "Dad said we were going to use this as the calving pasture this year and the yearlings were going north of the highway."

"What? When?"

"Yesterday. Day before. I don't know. I assumed he told you."

"No," I snapped. "He didn't."

And goddamn it, that wasn't Dad's decision to make. Not anymore.

He'd agreed to let me handle the land. I had a degree in rangeland management and another in animal science. This pasture didn't have enough grass for all the pregnant cows, and we'd end up hauling hay. But it would be the perfect pasture to let the yearlings graze before we sold them in a few weeks.

"Son of a bitch."

"Don't shoot the messenger." Cash held up his hands. "I thought it was your idea."

No, it was not. Which meant I'd have to have another lengthy discussion—argument—with Dad this week. "Let's get to work."

Jigsaw didn't need any prompting to walk easily along the barbed wire fence. He sauntered slowly so I could inspect each of the five wires and make sure none were too loose or broken. When we reached a section where a post had begun to lean and tug the wires out of alignment, I dismounted and set it to rights before continuing down the line.

Damn it to hell.

I was pissed at Granddad for being himself. I was frustrated that Dad would never let go, like his father. And I was angry that ten seconds with Gemma had me so twisted up that when I passed a downed wire, Cash had to holler at me to stop.

"What's up with you?" he asked, getting out of the truck.

"Just got some shit on my mind."

"Let's hear it."

I looked at my brother as he crossed his arms and leaned on the grill of the truck. He wasn't going anywhere until I unloaded.

"I'm tired." I sighed. "Tired of not being heard." Tired of not feeling like I had some control over my own destiny.

"It's just habit, East. They aren't doing it to run you off, they just don't know any better. I mean, look how long it took Granddad to let Dad run the show. You were—what?—a senior when he retired? I was a sophomore."

"Maybe I should have taken over the resort when Grandma asked me to."

"Dealing with guests all day? Pampering them? You would have hated that job. Besides, Katherine is perfect for it."

She was exactly the right person for that job and everyone knew it, including me. Which was why no one challenged Katherine. When she had an idea, everyone was all ears.

Maybe that was because the resort side of the business had always been Grandma's passion. When she had announced that she wanted to start a resort and was using five million dollars to build the lodge, Granddad had stayed quiet and smiled as she'd written the first check.

That was when the resort had been a hobby. A side gig. I always thought Granddad had believed in Grandma, but he hadn't expected it to take off. He certainly hadn't imagined it would ever be as successful as it was today.

The resort was pulling in more and more income each year, and Katherine had more freedom to run the business than I'd ever had managing the ranch. And I'd lived here my entire life.

"They listen to her," I said. "Completely. It's hard not to get jealous."

"And it's hard not to get jealous when you weren't even in the running to take over the resort or the ranch."

Ah, hell. "Sorry."

I didn't mean to make Cash feel like a lesser contributor. I was tired of fighting with Dad and Granddad and I clearly forgot to keep my brother's feelings in check, especially with how much I valued his opinions.

"It's okay." Cash shrugged. "Things are better this way. I love my job and what I'm doing here. As long as I have my horses, I'm a happy man."

Soon he'd have more than just horses.

I hadn't told him or anyone yet, but I'd put in an offer to buy a patch of land bordering us on the west. If it came together, I was going to build another stable and ask Cash to take over as manager for a top-of-the-line equine breeding and training facility.

Cash had a gift when it came to horses and assessing their nature. It was time to put it to use. His talents were wasted catering to guests.

I prayed the purchase didn't fall through.

Or that my family found out and put a stop to something before I'd even gotten it started.

"Let's get this fixed." I jerked my chin to the fence.

Thirty minutes later, the section was fixed and we were moving down the line. As the hours passed, the tension in my shoulders eased. There was something comforting about physical labor that soothed my soul. Something relaxing about being on a horse.

It was in my blood. Working here called to my soul.

Cash was right about Dad and Granddad. They loved this work too. They didn't challenge me to be malicious, but they acted out of habit and because they were stubborn.

So was I.

It was a trait famously passed through the Greer bloodline. And while I could rationalize it in my head, it still annoyed me on the day-to-day.

By lunch, we'd finished checking the pasture's fence and my stomach was growling. I gave Cash a nod to head on back to the barn while Jigsaw and I made the return trip at an easier pace.

Most of my frustration from my family had worked its way out. Now it was mostly Gemma plaguing my mind.

Why was she here? How long was she staying? No matter the duration, I'd make sure to keep myself busy. There was no reason to see her except . . .

Shit. My family had loved Gemma, especially Grandma.

When she'd worked here, they'd been some of our first employees. Grandma had hired them after a phone interview with Katherine because she'd *liked the girl's spirit.*

Grandma didn't hire much anymore, but she'd always been a good judge of character.

And when three young women had arrived at the lodge, fresh faced and excited, Grandma had taken them under her wing. To this day, Grandma believed that was the best hiring decision she'd ever made.

Those three had cleaned, washed laundry, gardened and waitressed. Any job they were given, they did without question while wearing real smiles.

The first time I'd seen Gemma, she'd been polishing silverware in the kitchen. I'd walked in, expecting it to be empty, but there she was, sitting on the stainless-steel table, rubbing a rag over a knife until she could see her reflection in the metal.

She'd flashed me a smile, hopped down and stuck out her hand.

I'd almost fallen over at that smile.

Then I'd done what all arrogant and stupid twenty-two-year-old guys did when faced with a gorgeous woman. I'd played it cool and ignored her. I'd pretended like I hadn't had the biggest crush of my life.

That had backfired spectacularly.

Because Gemma hadn't craved my attention. She'd been a force of her own, so tied up in her own life that others were forgotten.

What she'd done to Katherine was the perfect example.

And what she'd done to me.

Things were different now. I wasn't a young man driven by hormones and lust who wanted a young woman. Ignoring Gemma wouldn't be some tactic to woo her into my bed. I'd ignore her because sooner than later, she'd be gone anyway. I just had to bide my time for a week, maybe two.

Then Gemma Lane would disappear.

And I'd go back to forgetting the breathtaking woman with the sparkling hazel eyes who, turns out, I hadn't forgotten about, after all.

4

GEMMA

"So basically, you quit your life?"

"Well, when you say it like that it makes me sound crazy."

"Wow." Katherine grabbed the bottle of wine from the middle of the table and topped off my glass. "How many days ago was this?"

"I left Londyn's a week ago. I left Boston a couple days before that."

"And here you are."

"Here I am."

I was sitting across from Katherine in the dining room at the lodge. We were sharing a piece of chocolate cheesecake, polishing off a bottle of wine, after we'd eaten a delicious dinner of roasted chicken and mashed potatoes. Their website had not exaggerated the quality of the food. Or the wine selection.

"How is Londyn?" Katherine asked.

"She's wonderful." I smiled. "She's married and has a baby girl. She's happy."

"I'm glad. I think about her, about everyone, from time to time."

"Even me?"

"Yes. But I was hurt when you left."

"I'm sorry." I'd keep apologizing until she forgave me. Or maybe until I forgave myself.

"Don't be." She gave me a sad smile. "It was about a year after you left, I was out riding with Carol one day, and I realized that this was where I'm supposed to be. I'm happy here. I love my job and the ranch and the Greers. They've kind of made me an honorary member of the family, and I couldn't have asked for better."

"I'm glad. And I'm still sorry."

"You're forgiven."

"Really? You're not going to make me work harder for it?"

She shrugged. "It's not my style."

No, it wasn't. Katherine was too honest and real to punish me for something she'd already let go. Even after all the shit she'd been dragged through, she had never turned bitter.

"It worked out how it should have," she said. "I would have gone with you to Boston and resented every second. At the time, the promise of all that money sounded so good. But the city isn't me. Real estate isn't me. I helped with one of the deals when the Greers were buying some acreage a few years ago and I hated every second. Talk about stress. And paperwork."

I laughed. "It's not without challenges."

"Did you enjoy it?"

"I did for a time. Mostly, it was the springboard." I'd used the money I'd made to invest in other venues.

Four months after we'd come to work at the Greer Ranch, Londyn had decided to try something new. She'd enjoyed Montana but it hadn't been her landing spot. She'd asked me to come with her, to head east, but I'd stayed behind with Katherine.

I'd liked working here and being one of those honorary Greer family members.

Then about four months later, Katherine and I had been working in this very dining room. She waitressed while I'd tended bar, filling in for one of the seasonal workers who'd quit to return home. A couple had come in for a nightcap and like all other guests here, they'd oozed money.

It had been an oddly quiet night and the room had cleared out earlier than normal. But the couple had stayed and visited with Katherine and me. Three hours later, we'd confided in them—something we *never* did—telling them the story of our childhood.

They'd found it tragically fascinating.

And that night, Sandra and Eric Sheldon had changed my life.

They owned a real estate company in Boston, brokering some of the finest homes in the city. Before they'd checked out of the resort, they'd offered both Katherine and me jobs. They'd offered to hire us at their firm and give us a shot.

Sandra had given us her business card and had asked that we consider the offer. That if we were interested, Boston was waiting and so was she.

It had been a once-in-a-lifetime opportunity.

I'd been ready to hop on the bus the next morning. Katherine had been more hesitant, not wanting to abandon the Greers until they'd had replacements hired.

The more she'd hesitated, the more anxious I'd been that the Sheldons would forget about us. That this chance to make it rich would evaporate.

As an ambitious nineteen-year-old, patience had not been a strength.

I'd craved adventure. I'd craved the promise of money, to become a woman like Sandra who wore jewels dripping from her ears and nails that would never be caked with dirt.

Katherine had begged me to wait and give our notice to the Greers together.

158

Two days later, without telling Katherine, I'd taken the Sheldons' card, packed up my things while she was cleaning a guest room and left. When I'd arrived in Boston and called Sandra, I'd lied and said that Katherine hadn't been interested.

When really, I'd left her behind.

I hadn't even written a note.

Because Katherine had known exactly where I'd gone. It was truly a miracle that she didn't hate me.

Over dinner tonight, I told her all about my life in Boston. How I'd worked as Sandra's assistant for six months until I had my license. How within two years, I'd become their highest grossing agent, specializing in elite Boston properties.

When real estate had become tedious, I'd started investing. Until one day, I hadn't needed to sell properties to survive. I'd laid the foundation of my empire and kept adding bricks.

I'd spent years trying to fill the hole in my chest with money and business. But even with all the power, the prestige, the fortune, that hole was still there.

The numbness remained.

I was still just a runaway kid, numb to the world, searching for anything to make her *feel*.

"Do you talk to anyone else?" Katherine asked. "From Lou's?"

"No, just Londyn. Do you?"

"No." She shook her head. "How did you know I was here?"

"A while back, I was curious where everyone had landed, so I hired an investigator to find out. You made his job easy since your picture was all over the resort's website."

"Ah. That makes sense."

"Did you hear that Lou died?"

"He did?" Her hand pressed against her heart. "How? When?"

"Years ago. He died in his sleep."

Tears shone in her blue eyes. "I'll never forget that man."

Lou Miley had owned the junkyard when Karson had discovered it after running away from home. Karson had snuck in and out for a month, sleeping there and hiding out, until one night, Lou had come out with a blanket.

Lou hadn't tossed Karson out. He hadn't brought him inside, either. He'd simply let Karson stay.

When I'd found Karson after leaving my own home, Lou hadn't even batted an eyelash the first time he'd spotted me in his junkyard. He'd given me a grunt and a glare and disappeared into the shack he'd called home.

"He was so grumpy." I smiled. "So wonderfully gruff and grumpy."

Lou had shunned the mainstream world, living alone at the junkyard. None of us had ever asked why he'd let six kids squat on his property, but I believed it was because when we'd moved in, Lou hadn't been so alone.

None of us, not even Karson, had ever been invited into Lou's home. But he'd allowed us to use the bathroom and the shower in the junkyard's shop. Once, Karson and I had been sick with a cold and Lou had left us a bottle of cold medicine by the sink.

Lou hadn't reported us as runaways. Most adults would have called the cops and ushered us into the foster care system. But I think Lou had liked having us there. And maybe he'd known that if he kicked us out or called the authorities, we would have just run away again, probably to a place not nearly as safe.

Returning home had not been an option for any of us.

"He saved us," Katherine whispered. "No one around here understands that, but Lou saved our lives."

"Yes, he did. I wish I would have gone to his funeral. The timing . . . it didn't work out." More like I hadn't made the time. "Do the Greers know? About our childhood?"

"Have you met Carol? She got me to blurt the whole thing one night about a month after you left. I was feeling alone and angry, so I told her everything. And there's no such thing as a secret on this ranch. The next night, I went to the family dinner and you should have seen all the pitiful looks. I was so pissed."

Which meant Easton knew too.

I'd kept my past to myself when I'd worked here. We all had. The Sheldons were the only people we'd told. At the time, I wasn't sure what had caused Katherine and me to spill our tale, to guests, no less. But after working with Sandra and Eric for a few years, I'd learned that it was their nature. They had this magnetic pull, a way of drawing people out of their shells.

Even after I'd stopped working for their firm, I'd kept in touch with my former mentors. Sandra was my constant companion at Fashion Week in Paris.

There were others who knew my story—I'd spent years telling Dr. Brewer the horrid details—but the list was small. Not even Benjamin knew about my past. Because, as Katherine had said, the fastest way to earn someone's pity was to tell them about our youth.

I didn't want pity from the Greers. I certainly didn't want pity from Easton.

All I'd ever wanted from him was affection.

Which I'd gotten one glorious night.

Hours before I'd boarded a Greyhound bus and left Montana behind.

"Do you ever miss the tent?" Katherine asked, pouring us both more wine.

I laughed. "I don't miss sleeping on the ground, but I do miss the nights when we'd have everyone crowded inside because it was raining. I miss the days when we were all bored and would play cards for hours and talk and laugh."

"Me too. It's sad that we've all lost touch. But for me, it's easier this way. To just go on with my life and not look back. I mean, we were happy in the junkyard. As happy as homeless kids could be, but it was hard."

"So hard," I agreed. "My God, we were tough."

160

"And lucky."

There were countless other stories of runaway kids whose lives had been cut short. Whose lives had no happy ending. Kids who'd gotten addicted to drugs and alcohol. Girls who'd disappeared into a trafficking ring, never to be seen again.

Lucky was an understatement.

"I'm glad you came back," Katherine said. "It's good to see you."

"I'm glad I came too." There was a sense of peace here. A calm weight to the air. "It's relaxing."

"Tonight's a quiet night. You came at exactly the right time. Normally, the dining room is full until eight or nine. But this is a slow week."

Which explained why we were the only two in the room except some staffers wandering in and out, checking to see if Katherine needed anything.

After I'd settled into my guest room earlier, I'd called to check in with Benjamin. As expected, he had everything handled and no emergencies to report. But with nothing else to do—something that hadn't bothered me while I'd been driving *because* I'd been driving—I'd pulled out my laptop and spent an hour going through emails.

It had felt good to reconnect with that familiar part of me. The person who worked efficiently and effectively, checking boxes off lists and moving things forward.

Except there hadn't been much to move along. Mostly, it had been correspondence from my financial management team who were still processing the details from my sale of Gemma Lane. Then there'd been a few notes from acquaintances around Boston wondering if the rumors of my hastened exit from the city were true.

Those emails I'd simply deleted. There'd be buzz about my departure for weeks. People would speculate that I'd lost my mind or burned out. They'd gossip about my shortcomings or that the pressure had become too much.

It didn't matter.

Boston was history and I had no plans to return.

The rest of my afternoon had been spent reading. I couldn't remember the last time I'd read a book for sheer pleasure. I hadn't even owned a book, but my room had compensated for my shortcomings. It had come stocked with three different paperbacks in the dresser drawer.

I'd lost myself in a thriller until Katherine had knocked on my door around six for dinner. We'd been talking for hours. I'd told Katherine about my life and she'd told me about hers here at the resort.

My gaze traveled around the room in a slow, appraising circle. The tables were arranged much like a restaurant, in varying sizes, around the space. Katherine had explained that they employed a full-time chef and served both breakfast and dinner here. Sack lunches were available by request, mostly because keeping regular hours with the resort activities was difficult.

A few guests had come down for dinner but had since retired to their rooms. Others must have opted for room service. The guests who rented the chalets—at four thousand dollars per night—had access to a different chef who'd go to their chalets and prepare a private meal.

"This place looks fantastic," I told Katherine. "When I came in this morning, my first thought was how nothing here had changed. But that's not true, is it?"

"About four years ago, we started doing some renovations," she said. "Mostly cosmetic. Paint. Curtains. Art. Bedding. It's made a difference."

"It was your idea, wasn't it?"

She hid her smile in her wine.

The differences had Katherine's gentle and classic touch written all over them. She'd transformed the resort from lovely to magical.

The subtle differences had escaped my quick inspection earlier. The walls were a brighter shade of white, something that complemented the rich wood ceilings and floors. The chairs in the dining room had once been wooden, but they'd been replaced with cream upholstered pieces that softened the room and brightened the crystal chandelier's golden light.

It was still rustic, but now there was a chic edge to the decor. It was fancy without being pretentious but would appeal to the wealthy who could afford a vacation here.

"We actually did updates all over the ranch. The stables are a dream these days. You could eat off the floor because Easton insists on keeping them spotless."

Easton.

I'd seen him earlier from the window in my room. He'd been riding a huge black horse through a meadow in the distance. I'd spied on him until he and his horse had become nothing but a fleck in the green pasture.

But I'd known it was him. I'd recognize Easton's broad shoulders and black cowboy hat anywhere. I remembered how his dark hair looked when the ends curled at the nape of his neck, and how his strong arms filled out the sleeves of his plaid, pearl-snap shirts.

The thud of boots echoed through the room, drawing me from my musings.

Katherine's attention darted over my shoulder. "Hey."

"Hey."

Tingles ran up my spine at the familiar deep rumble.

But I refused to turn and pay Easton any mind. He'd been cold and unfriendly to me for as long as I could remember. Well, except that one night. But after today's collision by the front door, it seemed nothing had changed.

"What's up?" Katherine asked him.

"Came to grab some dinner before I go home."

Home? It was almost nine o'clock at night. Didn't he have a wife or a girlfriend waiting?

"You remember Gemma, don't you?" Katherine gestured to me with her wineglass.

I looked over my shoulder and gave him a tight smile.

Easton was standing at my side, his arms crossed over his chest. His jaw was granite and his eyes didn't so much as flicker my direction.

He ignored Katherine's reintroduction entirely.

Asshole. "Nice to see you again, Easton. You look . . . older."

Older. Sexy as hell. *Same thing.*

He harrumphed, but didn't bother with any other acknowledgement, addressing only Katherine as he spoke. "I need an hour tomorrow when you have one to go over some schedules. I need to steal a couple of the hands from guest services to help move some steers."

"Okay." She nodded. "I'll check my calendar and shoot you a text with the time."

"Fine."

"Would you like to join us?" She gestured to the empty seat beside me.

Easton answered by walking out of the room, not sparing me another glance before he disappeared through the door that led to the kitchen.

Wow.

"I see you two still hate each other."

It had never been hatred. More like two kids who hadn't realized that hate was actually foreplay.

Katherine stood from her chair and walked over to the bar along the rear wall. She swiped a wine bottle off the shelf, opened it with the corkscrew and brought it to the table. "I'll probably regret this bottle in the morning."

"Me too." I held up my glass.

"How long are you staying?"

"I don't know. A day or two. Is that okay? If you have an incoming reservation, I can take off tomorrow."

"No, stay. I'll need the room back next week. It's hunting season and we're booked solid through Christmas. But if you want to stay longer, you can stay at my place. We have a guest bedroom that's always empty."

"We?" My eyes darted to her naked ring finger. "I didn't know you were living with someone."

"I live with Cash."

"Oh. I didn't realize you were together."

"No, no, no." She waved it off. "We're not together. We're just room-mates. And coworkers. And friends."

Friends. With the way she stressed the word, either he wanted more, and she wasn't interested, or it was the other way around.

Cash had been at college when I'd worked here, and I'd only spoken to him once when he'd come home for spring break. But I'd recognized him instantly when he'd helped me bring my luggage into the lodge earlier. He had the same good looks as his older brother, though Easton carried a rougher edge. The biggest difference between the Greer men was that Cash was nice.

Easton, not so much. Though he was nice to look at.

"Carol and Jake built a house in the foothills about five years ago," Katherine said. "Cash and Easton were living in their old place, but a few years ago, Easton decided to build too. So rather than stay in one of the staff apartments, it made sense for me to move into the house. It was getting weird for the staffers to have the boss living next door."

The staff quarters were what I'd imagined a college dorm was like. Fun for a younger crowd but totally impractical for adults who'd outgrown their communal living days.

I'd loved living in the quarters. I'd loved having a decent shower and soft mattress. The accommodations weren't spacious, but for Katherine, Londyn and me, they'd been sublime. A giant step up from the junkyard.

The door to the kitchen opened and Easton came striding out carrying a plate covered with aluminum foil in his hand. He kept his brown eyes aimed forward, not oblivious to the way Katherine and I watched him walk, just uncaring.

Was he heading to his house alone? Even with the foil, I could tell his plate was heaped with food. It was enough for two people.

There was no chance Easton was still single. He was an extremely sexy man with a steady job and an ass that looked delicious in a pair of Wranglers.

And without.

Too bad he was a jerk and probably married. A night with Easton Greer was exactly the thing my newly spontaneous self would have applauded.

"Goodnight," Katherine called to his back as he walked past the threshold that connected the dining room to the lobby.

Easton's steps didn't slow. "Night, Kat."

Rejected again. *Damn.* Eleven years later and it stung. But there was no use dwelling on the actions of a man I'd leave behind in a day or two. I'd done that enough. I'd wished for his warm smile when all I'd ever received was the cold shoulder.

That hadn't changed. The only time he'd taken notice was the night I'd let him take me to his bed.

A night I hoped had remained a secret.

"He calls you Kat?" I asked.

"It's something Cash started." She shrugged. "I'm the little sister, so I got a nickname."

A nickname and status she didn't want. At least, not with Cash. Her *friends* comment was beginning to make sense.

"Would you like to go on a few excursions while you're here? Maybe a ride or a hike while the weather's good?" she asked, changing the subject.

I hummed, sipping my wine and thinking it over. Without work, I had nothing to do but sit in my room. "I haven't ridden a horse since I was here last. That might be fun."

"Great. I'll arrange a private lesson for you tomorrow."

"Perfect." When she raised her glass, I clinked mine to hers. "There's something else I wanted to talk to you about. Carol wouldn't let me pay when I checked in, but I'd like to. Can you make that happen? Please? She did so much for me, and the least I can do is pay for my room."

"If she finds out, I'm dead meat."

I zipped my lips shut.

"Okay." She laughed. "You can pay."

"Thanks." I smiled. "And thanks for hearing me out. I know I've said it about a hundred times tonight, but I am sorry. Truly."

"It's okay, Gemma."

"Are you sure?"

Katherine nodded. "I swear. It's forgotten."

The two of us stayed in the dining room until midnight, chatting and drinking more wine before saying our goodnights. When I fell asleep, it was with a smile and a light heart.

Katherine didn't hate me. She'd accepted my apology. And I'd reunited with my friend.

But the next morning when I showed up at the stables for my riding lesson, I realized I'd assumed too much. Maybe she was out to punish me for my mistake, after all.

Because Katherine, *my friend*, had paired me with the worst riding instructor on earth.

Easton.

"Forgotten, my ass," I muttered. "She hates me."

5

EASTON

"WHAT THE FUCK? *You're* my ten o'clock?"

"Hey, don't look at me like that." Gemma fisted her hands on her hips. "This wasn't my idea."

"Goddamn it." I pulled my phone from my pocket and called Kat's cell. She didn't answer. So I called her office. It went straight to voicemail. *Shit.* "I don't have time for this. We have paying customers who need lessons. And I have work to do."

"I am paying," Gemma shot back. "But forget it. I don't need to ride a horse this bad."

As she spun on a boot heel and marched away, my phone dinged with a text from Katherine.

EVERYONE ELSE WAS BOOKED. You were the only instructor available.

A MISTAKE I'd fix on next month's schedule.

Every month, Katherine and I sat down and outlined lesson blocks and paired them with instructors. We always made sure there was one private lesson slot available for one-on-one rides throughout the day because guests often had last-minute requests. So one instructor stayed behind, while the rest were sent out on the scheduled rides and lessons.

Personally, I hated the group shit. It was tedious and slow. I did better one-on-one when I could go wherever I wanted and the pace was faster. So when we were shorthanded, like we were this week because one of the guys was on vacation, I was the backup for private lessons.

Starting tomorrow, I'd start training Rory so I'd never be on the damn schedule again.

My phone dinged again with another text from Kat.

• • •

She's my friend. And a guest. Be nice. For me? Please?

Yeah, that's a no.

I loved Katherine. She'd melded into our family seamlessly and was the closest thing to a younger sister I'd ever have. She was hardworking, smart and kind. But adopted sister or not, there was no way in hell I was spending two hours alone with Gemma.

My phone buzzed again.

Do this lesson and I'll make sure Jake is too busy to bother you for two weeks.

Katherine would probably beg Granddad with those blue eyes for a special task. Something that would flatter him and make him brag at family dinners. I could hear him already.

I can't help with the equipment next week. Katherine needs me.

Goddamn it. Younger sisters were overrated.

"Fine," I muttered, not bothering to respond. Kat knew she was dangling a carrot and I wouldn't resist.

"Wait," I called to Gemma's back as she neared the door.

She kept walking.

I tucked my phone away and chased after her, my long strides eating up the distance between us. "Gemma."

She didn't slow.

"Gemma!" I bellowed as she stepped out the door and into the sunshine. "Would you stop?"

"Why?" She spun around and threw her arms in the air. Her long ponytail whipped over her shoulder. "What now?"

I wasn't going to apologize or beg her to come back. Even two weeks without Granddad bothering me wasn't worth my pride. "Have you been on a horse in the past decade?"

"No. Hence the lesson."

My gaze traveled up and down her body. She was wearing an oatmeal sweater with a V-neck that dipped low enough to show the swell of her breasts and a pair of jeans that encased her toned thighs. They were cuffed at the ankle, above the line of her tan, suede boots. Her legs looked a mile long and behind my zipper, my dick stirred.

Christ. This lesson would be impossible if I couldn't keep my eyes off her.

"We're riding horses, not walking the runway," I snapped. "Do you have boots?"

"These are boots." Her eyes dropped to her feet. "What's wrong with them?"

"Those are *not* boots."

"They'll work for today." She crossed her arms over her chest.

"Don't come crying to me if you step in horse shit."

Her eyes narrowed. "I'll be fine."

Maybe if I pissed her off enough, she'd quit. Then I could tell Kat I'd held up my end of the bargain.

I turned and walked back inside, heading straight for Jigsaw's stall. I'd saddled him when Katherine had texted me about this *last-minute lesson*. She hadn't bothered to give me the client's name. Another mistake. If I couldn't avoid the schedule, I'd ask for specifics from now on.

"Come on, boy." I hadn't bridled him yet, so I took his halter and led him into the arena beside the stables. When I went back to get Gemma's horse ready, I'd hoped she might have changed her mind.

But no. She was standing beside Sprite's stall, stroking the mare's cheek. I'd planned on taking Pepsi, one of our other mares and Sprite's sister, but when a rider took a shine to a horse and that affection seemed to go both ways, sometimes it was best to go with it.

"That's Sprite."

"Hi, Sprite." She smiled at the horse's gray-speckled nose, her voice dropping to a sweet caress.

There'd been a time once when she'd given me that smile and talked to me with that same voice. The combination was a gut-puncher. But I refused to be jealous of a horse.

I yanked a currycomb off a peg beside the stall and nudged Gemma out of the way with my shoulder. The right thing to do would be to make her saddle Sprite, but that would involve a lot of close contact.

One of the other instructors could teach the woman how to strap on a saddle.

Not that I expected her to be here much longer anyway.

"When are you leaving?" I asked, sliding into the stall.

"Please tell me you're nicer to other guests."

I grunted and ran the comb over Sprite's back as she hovered by the horse's nose.

Actually, I was great with guests, not that I owed her an explanation. I wasn't charming like Katherine or charismatic like Cash, but I had my own appeal. Guests loved that I was authentic. I was a Montana rancher who loved the land, my family and a marbled, medium-rare steak.

They liked me because I loved my roots. Something Gemma wouldn't understand.

Gemma Lane was too wild for roots.

She'd run from here sooner than later, and this time, I wouldn't let it wreck me.

I wasn't sure where she'd been these past eleven years and I wasn't asking. Clearly, she'd run into some money. One look at her clothes and that Cadillac and you knew she had cash. If she was a paying guest, she'd come here to spend it.

168

"I don't know when I'm leaving," she said. "I don't really have a schedule."

"What about your job? Don't you need to get back to it?"

"I'm unemployed at the moment."

"I thought you left here to be some hotshot real estate agent."

"I was in real estate for a while. Then I invested in some other companies around Boston. Eventually I started a cosmetics company. I sold it three weeks ago so . . . unemployed."

"You made a couple bucks and decided to quit on payday." I scoffed. "Typical."

That was exactly what she'd done here. Gemma had earned a good wage, but when the promise of something more came along, she'd bailed, leaving her best friend behind in tears. And showing me exactly what she'd wanted from me—a roll between the sheets and a couple orgasms—nothing more.

Gemma's glare was waiting when I came out of the stall. "If you call twelve million dollars a couple of bucks, then yes. I quit on payday."

My feet faltered a step at the number.

She saw it. The corner of her mouth turned up as I marched past her to put the comb away and grab a saddle blanket.

Twelve million dollars was quite an accomplishment for a kid who'd lived in a junkyard, not that I'd give her anything resembling a compliment.

Katherine had told us about her homelife as a kid. How she'd run away from home, scared and hopeless, until some other kids had pulled her into their fold—Gemma being one of them.

They'd lived in a junkyard, for fuck's sake. Gemma and Katherine had built a tent out of sheet metal, tarps and whatever else they could find and had slept on the ground for years.

My horse lived better than that.

But looking at Gemma, you'd never know it. She held her shoulders straight. She kept her chin up. She was as shiny as my Sunday boots, and as refined as any of the wealthy people who shelled out thousands of dollars to go glamping here each summer.

And damn it, there was a swell of pride in my chest. *Twelve million dollars.* She'd made it. She'd set herself up to never sleep on the ground again.

"Why does it bother you that I'm here?" she asked as I came back with the saddle blanket.

"Because," I muttered.

Because she was a distraction. Because when she was here, I couldn't think straight. Because those hazel eyes were so enchanting, and if I let myself, I'd get swept up in her all over again.

She'd be gone soon, chasing the next dollar or wild adventure, leaving me behind, wondering what kind of man could compel her to stay.

It sure as fuck wasn't me.

We didn't speak as I finished saddling Sprite. She followed close behind when I led the horse out of her stall and to the arena, stopping inside the gate.

"Walk her in a circle to get her blood flowing."

"Okay." Gemma nodded, taking the leather straps in her dainty hands. Her glossy nails caught the morning sun and they gleamed, clean and pale pink.

Mine were permanently stained with dirt.

As she walked Sprite, I hurried to my office and grabbed my hat. Then I scribbled a note for Rory to oil Mom's saddle before lunch. He was over at the barn, cleaning up the mess Granddad had brought in with the four-wheeler yesterday and the tools he hadn't put away.

If I made it through this lesson with Gemma, I'd have two weeks without Granddad screwing with my plans.

Theoretically.

Katherine was good at managing Granddad but she wasn't infallible. And he was unpredictable. But Sprite was saddled and so was Jigsaw, so I was committed to see this through.

With a deep breath, I returned to the arena. Private lessons were typically two hours, but this was going to be ninety minutes, max.

Gemma didn't hear me as I walked up. Sprite's hooves thudded in the soft dirt as Gemma led her in a circle, the noise drowning out the sound of my own footsteps.

"Okay, Sprite," Gemma said. "Help me out today. Don't make me look like a total fool in front of him. Please."

I froze. The way she'd pleaded with the animal, the vulnerability in her voice . . . *fuck*. She did a hell of a job making sure to keep her confidence in place, but to hear her beg a horse. Maybe it wasn't as steely as she pretended.

And maybe I was being a dickhead, punishing her for a decade-old mistake.

Jigsaw, the bastard, chose that moment to snort and caught Gemma's attention. When she spotted me listening in, the gentle expression she'd had with Sprite hardened.

"That's good enough." I closed the gap and tightened Sprite's cinch. Then I jerked my chin for Gemma to follow me to the horse's left side where I held the stirrup for her. "Foot in. Hand on the horn. Then up you go."

With one graceful swing, she was in the saddle. A small smile toyed on her pink lips.

I adjusted her stirrups, then handed her the reins. "Wait here."

Jigsaw jittered as I approached, the excitement radiating off his large body. "It's not that kind of trip today."

He nudged me in the shoulder with his nose, leaving a snot mark. "Thanks."

After a couple of walking laps, I cinched him up, pulled on his bridle and climbed on. I clicked my tongue and led the way out of the arena, heading toward the two-lane road that created a large loop in one of the pastures.

Sprite had been trained well. She followed behind Jigsaw without Gemma having to do a thing but stay seated.

I looked over my shoulder occasionally to check that Gemma was sitting correctly and wasn't choking up on the reins. Every time, I expected to make a correction but she looked good there. Natural.

"Come on up here." I pointed to the other lane. Having her behind me wasn't going to teach her anything about leading a horse if she was only following.

She nodded, her eyes fixed on Sprite's white mane, then gave a gentle nudge with her heels and steered to the right. When we were walking side by side, she glanced over.

Normally, this would be the time in a lesson when I'd shower a student with praise. *Good job, you steered the horse three feet to the right.* I'd prattle on about horses and gauge the student's comfort. I'd talk about the ranch and answer questions, making small talk and ensuring the student had a nice time.

Except this was Gemma. My normal approach had flown out the window when I'd snapped at her in the stables. And as much as I'd like a quiet, no-conversation ride, it actually made the tension worse.

"So you drove here?" I asked at the same time she said, "Katherine said you built a house."

"Uh . . . yeah," I answered. "A few years ago."

"I bet it's nice to have your own space. And yes, I drove here."

"Nice car."

"It's not mine. Do you remember Londyn?"

I nodded, recalling the blonde who'd arrived with Gemma and Kat. She'd left not long after the first snowstorm. "The other friend."

"The Cadillac is hers. When we lived in the junkyard, it was her home, for lack of a better term. A while ago, she had it hauled from California to Boston and completely restored."

"How'd you end up with it?" Maybe she'd bought it with some of her millions.

"Londyn was driving it back to California a little over a year ago. She got a flat tire and ended up stuck in West Virginia. The mechanic who rescued her is now her husband. After I sold the company, I went to visit, and she got this crazy idea for me to take the car to California in her place."

Like I'd suspected, this was only just a temporary stop. "Why California?"

"To find an old friend from the junkyard. It was their car, Londyn and Karson's. She wants him to have it."

"That's quite the gift." Restoring a junkyard car would not have been cheap. "But if she's got money to burn."

"Londyn saved for a long time to restore that car," Gemma fired back. "It was important to her and she worked hard for it."

I shrugged. I didn't care. This was just conversation and a way to pass the time. I wasn't all that interested in Gemma's life story and how she'd come here. I was interested in when she'd be leaving.

"Why are you in Montana if you're headed to California?"

"For Katherine." She glared. "I wanted to see her and to apologize."

"You two looked fairly chummy last night, drinking all the expensive wine."

"Is that what this is about? The profit margin? I'll pay for the wine, okay?"

Of course, she would. She was loaded. "We don't need your money."

"God, you're something else. First, I need to pay my way. Then, you're too good for my money. You haven't changed at all, have you? In eleven years, you still only know how to send one type of message: mixed."

"Mixed? I think my intentions the last time you were here were pretty fucking clear."

I'd wanted her. I'd told her I'd wanted her. Lying in my arms, I'd told her I'd thought we had something real.

And she'd left anyway.

"I didn't . . ." She blew out a deep breath. "I'm sorry."

It was too late for an apology. I didn't trust her, not after she'd snuck out of my bed and disappeared without so much as a word. All because she'd wanted to strike it rich.

"Keep up," I barked, pulling down the brim of my hat a fraction of an inch. Then I urged Jigsaw faster.

Today wasn't Gemma's first time on a horse. She didn't need to be coddled. She was doing just fine walking, so we'd trot for a bit and put an end to this conversation.

The asshole who'd been pissed at her for eleven years wanted her to falter. To get scared and beg to slow down. To dent her confidence as way of punishment.

But I wasn't a complete asshole and when she stayed right by my side, actually seeming to enjoy the faster clip, another surge of pride swelled.

Gemma wasn't scared of anything, least of all me or a gentle horse.

She relaxed into the saddle, finding her rhythm with Sprite's, and by the time we made it through the loop and back to the stables, Gemma looked damn good on that horse.

Too good.

Her hair swung as she rode. Her thighs flexed and her breasts bounced. There was a peach flush to her cheeks and an added sparkle in her eyes. She looked beautiful. Satisfied.

Hell. What if she'd actually enjoyed herself and wanted to do this every day? I was on the lesson schedule all week.

The cool edge to the fall weather had been burned off by the bright morning sun, and the horses were panting by the time we walked them into the arena. I hopped off Jigsaw first, then took Sprite's reins from Gemma to hold them while she dismounted.

She gripped the horn, shifted in the saddle, then swung her right leg up and over. She swayed on the ground but found her balance. Her hands were shaking and there was a bead of sweat by her temple.

I really was a dickhead, pushing her so hard. She might have liked it, but I'd still gone too far.

Before I could apologize, Gemma took Sprite's reins from my hand and forced a too-wide smile. "That was fun. I forgot how much I liked it here. Maybe I'll take Katherine up on her offer to stay a while."

My eyes narrowed, the apology forgotten. "What offer?"

"To stay in the guest bedroom at Cash and Katherine's place. I'm in no hurry to get to California. So maybe I'll stay."

I scoffed. "You'll make it a week, maybe two before you get bored."

"You're so sure you know me. That you have me pegged." Her eyes blazed defiance. "But you don't know shit."

"Oh, I know you. Intimately." I inched closer, the smell of her perfume hitting my nose. She held my gaze by raising her chin higher. Those luscious lips right there, positioned and ready for the taking.

If I kissed her, would she kiss me back? Or would I see the Cadillac's taillights racing toward the highway by supper?

"What do you want from me, Easton?"

For you to get the hell out of my head. "I want you to leave. You don't fit here."

I'd expected a snarky comeback. More of that stubborn, infuriating attitude that clearly hadn't changed in the years she'd been away. But something flashed in her eyes that looked a lot like sorrow.

She dropped her chin and unlocked her gaze, turning to stare off into the distance. "Maybe you're right. I'm not sure where I fit."

Her words were no more than a whisper, but they sent me rocking on my heels.

Gemma brushed past me, leading Sprite to the stables.

Son of a bitch. This wasn't my problem. If this road trip was Gemma's way to find herself, more power to her. *She. Is. Not. My. Problem.* So why wouldn't my heart climb down from my throat?

I gripped Jigsaw's reins and he followed me without hesitation into his stall.

Gemma was standing in Sprite's stall, pointing to the saddle. "What should I do?"

"I'll take care of it."

"Okay." She patted Sprite's cheek. "You did good. It was nice to meet you."

I took a step back, giving Gemma a wide berth to exit the stall. She gave me a small nod, then turned and walked down the center aisle. Lesson complete.

She wasn't the same girl who'd left here. I was man enough to admit she'd changed—not to her face, not today. Gemma had grown into a mature, breathtaking woman. Even with the sadness in her eyes, the longing, she was close to irresistible.

But if I let myself worry about Gemma, I'd turn myself in knots.

"She's a good girl."

"Shit." I jumped at Grandma's voice, slapping a hand over my heart. "Give a guy a warning."

She laughed, watching as Gemma disappeared around the corner and into the sunshine. "How was the lesson?"

"Fine."

"She's lost, that girl. Always has been. She's running from anything that makes her feel."

I frowned. "She screwed Kat over. You remember how upset Kat was when Gemma ditched her."

"She was nineteen years old, Easton. I recall a few mistakes you made at that age. There was the time you stole your dad's car and drove into town to get drunk at the bar. There was the time you—"

"All right, all right." I held up a hand. "You've made your point."

"Katherine has chosen to forgive her and welcome her here. We can all do the same. For however long she wants to stay."

I swallowed a groan. "She'll leave."

"I'm not so sure. Not this time."

I wouldn't argue with Grandma, but her soft spot for Gemma had made her blind. There was nothing for Gemma to do here. She wasn't cut out for ranch work. She'd be bored working for Kat in one of the trivial jobs at the lodge. And where was she going to live? Cash and Kat's guest bedroom?

She'd stay and this vacation of hers would run its course, then she'd be gone.

I just had to wait it out. Stay away from Gemma so that the second time around, I didn't fall into her trap.

And make the same mistake twice.

6

GEMMA

"KNOCK. KNOCK." I inched Katherine's office door open and peeked inside.

"Hey." She waved me in. "What's up?"

"I need to ask you a question and I need the answer to be yes."

"Okay," she drawled. "Should I be nervous?"

"Probably." I plopped down in a chair across from her desk.

Katherine's hair was pulled into a ponytail and she was wearing a long-sleeved zip-up with the resort's name embroidered on the chest. She looked comfortable yet authoritative.

I had the comfort with my jeans and black sweater, but I lacked authority.

I *missed* authority.

"I'm bored," I admitted. "Like, going-out-of-my-mind bored. Can I have a job? Please?"

It had been three days since I'd gone on my ride with Easton, and I'd spent those days largely in my room. It was easier to avoid him while locked inside. I'd passed the days by reading and pestering Benjamin. After my seventh call in seventy-two hours, he'd threatened to block my number. There were zero emails in my inbox and I'd poured over my financial statements with more attention to detail than I had in the past five years—total.

My life had gone from ninety miles per hour to a standstill gridlock. This morning, I'd admitted defeat.

Vacation pace was highly overrated and simply not for me.

I needed to work.

Katherine blinked. "A job?"

"Dusting. Cooking. Scrubbing toilets. I'll do anything. But I don't want to leave yet and if I spend another day in my room reading, I might die."

"But you're on vacation."

I grimaced. "I hate that word."

"Why not do the four-wheeler excursion? Or hike? Or go for another ride?"

"Thanks, but no, thanks," I muttered.

It was too risky outside. It was much safer indoors where Easton avoided me and I had more places to hide.

"You don't have to pay me," I said. "Just give me something to do so I don't sit around and dwell on the fact that last month, my life had purpose. And now the only thing I have in my future is a long trip to California in someone else's car. Please. Pleasepleaseplease. Give me toilet bowl duty."

Katherine giggled. "You're sure?"

"Positive."

She picked up the headset to her desk phone and dialed a number. "Hey, Annabeth, it's Kat."

Kat. I was still getting used to her nickname. To me, she'd always be Katherine.

"I have someone here who'll be working temporarily for the resort. Would you mind if I send her your way?" She paused, the smile growing on her face. "Great. Thanks. She'll be right over."

"Thank you," I said as she put the headset into its cradle.

"You're welcome. Annabeth is in charge of the staffers. She coordinates the housekeeping, food service and front desk crews." She pointed to a wall of bookshelves. "Her office is two doors down. She'll get you through the HR paperwork and find something for you."

"I mean it. Don't pay me." It wasn't like I needed the money, something Katherine had learned over a dinner. The two of us had spent every night in the dining room, eating decadent meals and consuming an exorbitant amount of wine.

This week, we'd pulled on our old friendship and I hadn't been surprised when it had fit like my favorite sweater. I'd forgotten how easy it was to talk to Katherine. How comfortable and effortlessly the conversation flowed. We'd talked about everything, from her time with the Greers to my experiences in Boston.

The only time I'd dodged a topic had been when Easton's name was dropped.

That man . . . grr. I wanted to strangle him and kiss him and kick him and lick him all in the same moment.

Katherine had asked me how the ride had gone and I'd lied through my teeth. It hadn't been horrible. Riding Sprite had actually been fun, but with Easton there, infuriating me with every word muttered from that delicious mouth, it had been nearly impossible to enjoy myself.

Easton was loyal and proud. He was punishing me for screwing up years ago, with him and with Katherine. It would be a lot easier to dislike him if he didn't have grounds for his attitude.

It would be a lot easier to hate him if he wasn't so damn attractive.

The way that man looked on the horse, his eyes hooded by the brim of his hat, was grossly unfair. No one in Boston would believe that Gemma

Lane, always composed and sophisticated, would be lusting after a rugged cowboy with dirt on his jeans and a smudge on his cheek.

Until they saw him, then no one would fault me.

"Dinner tonight?" I asked Katherine. If she said no, I'd probably drive into town and get a little space from the ranch. It was much too easy to think of Easton when I was here. Especially in my room, sitting on the bed. Or when I was in the shower. Or when I was breathing.

"Yes, but I was hoping you'd be up for a change of scenery. Friday nights we always eat dinner at Jake and Carol's. It's a family tradition."

"Oh, then that's okay." I wasn't part of the family and there was one family member in particular I was hoping to avoid until Montana was a smudge in the Cadillac's rearview mirror. "You go. I was thinking about driving into town anyway to see what's changed."

The Greer Ranch was located ten miles outside the small town of Clear River. From what I remembered, there wasn't much more than a gas station, post office, café and a bar in town, but it was better than nothing.

"Not happening, sweetheart." My head whipped around to the voice behind me as Carol marched into Katherine's office. Her white hair hung loose today, draped over her shoulders. "You're coming to dinner."

"But—"

She held up a hand. "Think of it as a peace offering."

"A peace offering? For what?"

"For the little arrangement you two girls made behind my back." Carol aimed her finger at Katherine. "Don't think I didn't notice Gemma's credit card on her room."

"Oh. That," I muttered.

"I told you that you weren't paying, but if it means that much to you, then I'll let it slide. But you're coming to dinner. We eat at six o'clock. Be early. You two can ride together since you haven't been to our new place."

"Sounds good." Katherine didn't bother arguing. It would be pointless.

"I'm going to go." I stood from the chair, gave Katherine a wide-eyed look, then scurried from her office before Carol could rope me into any other family functions.

Two doors down, I knocked on the half-open door and met my new boss, Annabeth, who I liked immediately. She was in her mid-fifties with warm eyes and a cute blond bob. We chatted briefly about my work history and situation here—the way I was leveraging my friendship with Katherine to score a job to keep me occupied—and she promised to be gentle with me since I hadn't had a boss in over seven years.

Annabeth hired me as an unpaid intern. I'd never been an intern before or unpaid, but when she took me to the front desk and explained my new duties, I'd accepted them with a genuine smile.

The resort hadn't had a receptionist in three weeks, not since the previous one had moved to Texas. It was the reason Carol had greeted me when I'd arrived earlier this week. So here I was, ready to greet anyone who walked through the front door.

There wasn't much walk-in traffic at a five-star mountain resort that filled its rooms with long-term, advance reservations. But when guests did come through the lobby, it was nice to have someone there to greet them — besides Clive the elk.

After signing a handful of employment papers and a brief tutorial on the computer system, Annabeth left me on my own, promising I'd be bored in minutes.

She wasn't wrong.

But being bored at the front desk was better than being bored in my room.

I spent a couple hours getting familiar with the computer system, poking around the events calendar and reservation software, both of which were relatively intuitive. Carol brought me a ham sandwich from the kitchen at noon — my agreed-upon salary with Annabeth — and ate with me at the desk.

We talked about Jake and the ranch and how she wished Cash would *open his damn eyes.*

She didn't elaborate on that one. Not that she needed to.

After lunch, she went back to work doing whatever it was Carol did and I manned my station at the desk. Few guests entered the lobby and when they did, I waved and inquired about their day. I played solitaire, partaking in the occasional staring contest with Clive — he won two out of three — until the clock neared five, my shift was over, and it was time to head to my room to freshen up before dinner.

I'd just closed down the computer when footsteps sounded beyond the door, lifting my spirits at the anticipation of another rare guest interaction. I squared my shoulders and readied my smile, but when the door opened, my expression dropped. "Oh, it's you."

Easton narrowed his eyes as he walked into the lobby. "What are you doing?"

"Working."

His jaw ticked. "What?"

"I'm working. Katherine hired me this morning."

"Like hell she did."

I rolled my eyes. "I'm here, Easton. Deal with it."

He gave me his famous silent, brooding stare.

"I'm not leaving." Yet.

"Because you have nowhere else to go, so you'll just leach off us here until you're ready."

"I'm not leaching." *What a jerk.* "But no, I don't have anywhere else to go at the moment, so it looks like you're stuck with me."

He arched an eyebrow and headed straight for the stairs. Conversation over. I'd been dismissed.

I didn't let myself watch him walk away.

Grr. No one had ever climbed under my skin as quickly as Easton. One of these days, I was going to do something to shock that hard, unwavering scowl off his handsome face.

I'd once been so desperate for eye contact from that man. I'd been the nineteen-year-old girl trying not to be affected when he walked into the room. The one trying not to look at him because it stung deep when he'd never looked back. Easton had always had better things to do than bother with me.

Not much had changed.

Except me.

I no longer had anything to prove. I'd shown the world I was more than where I'd come from. I'd made my mark, my fortune and fame.

And I'd learned the hard way it was just as hollow as the home where I'd been born.

This journey was about searching for a real life. The life money couldn't buy.

I wanted the things I'd never had.

Family. Love. Peace.

Chasing down riches was easy. I could do that—I *had* done that.

There was no easy way to find the safety and security that came with love and family. People were either born with it, or they weren't. For those of us who weren't, letting others in meant exposing your weaknesses. It meant trusting others not to break your heart.

The concept was easy enough to grasp. Dr. Brewer and I had talked for years about my talent for maintaining emotional distance from others, even my friends. The problem *was* me. The solution was me too.

But letting someone share your life . . . they could turn it all upside down.

Because trust was something often betrayed, and innocence could be taken when the person you trusted didn't protect you.

Like a mother.

A mother who allowed a man to drag her fifteen-year-old daughter out of her bedroom simply because the guy wanted an audience while he got a blow job.

The chains wrapped around my heart were courtesy of her betrayals.

I blinked the memory away, refusing to think of my mother's face. It greeted me in the mirror each morning, and that was bad enough without letting myself revisit the past.

Hurrying upstairs to my room, I refreshed my makeup and brushed my hair. I touched up my lip gloss—three times—and changed my clothes twice. It was the fact that Easton would be at dinner that had me pacing my room, waiting for Katherine's knock. It came at precisely fifteen minutes to six.

"Ready?" she asked.

"Sure," I lied. I'd tamed cutthroat attorneys and ruthless fashion designers, so why was I so nervous about a family dinner?

"Easton just stopped by," she said as we walked down the hallway. "He told me to fire you."

"Stubborn ass," I muttered.

"Don't worry. I told him to mind his own side of the business."

I frowned and followed her downstairs, making our way through the rear exit where she'd parked her truck. "So who's going to be at dinner?"

"The usual suspects. Carol and Jake. JR and Liddy."

I nodded, remembering Easton's parents. "I always liked Liddy."

"She's a sweetheart. And then the guys. Just family tonight. That's the rule."

The Greers and Katherine. *Just family*. I was happy that she'd found one. But where did that put me? "Should I be going? I feel like I'm intruding."

"You're not. And besides, it's too late now." She laughed as she drove. "If you don't show up with me, Carol will just come and collect you herself."

We bounced along the gravel road, driving toward the mountains that had greeted me each morning this week. When a house came into view beside a grove of aspen trees, my mouth fell open. "Wow."

"Pretty, right? Carol wanted to coordinate the house with the lodge, so they went with the same look."

The dark wooden siding along with the stonework out front was rustic yet classy. The house was warm and inviting but too big to be considered cozy. It was the castle for a Montana working couple who'd earned their retirement.

A line of dirty vehicles crowded the long gravel driveway, and before we were even parked, the front door opened. Carol's white hair caught the fading sunset's light, tinting the soft strands pink.

"I only have five bottles of wine," she said, waving us inside. "Save two for the rest of us, will you?"

Katherine and I both laughed as we stepped across the threshold. Then we were mobbed.

"Welcome back." Jake hugged me first, then pulled Katherine into his side, pinning her there.

Next came JR who clapped me on the back. "I'm Jake Junior. Or JR. Not sure if you remember me or not."

I smiled. "Of course, I do."

"Heard you're our newest employee."

"That's right," I said. Easton was standing in the living room, close enough to overhear. I shot him a smug grin. "Today was the first day of many."

He scowled and took a long drink from the beer bottle in his grip.

"Hi, Gemma." Liddy took her husband's place for a hug. "It's so nice seeing you again. Welcome back."

"Thank you for having me."

"Hey, again." Cash extended a hand from where he stood beside his mother.

"Hi, Cash." I shook his hand, taking in the similarities of the Greer men now that they were in the same room.

Easton had inherited his father's and grandfather's black-coffee eyes, while Cash had gotten Liddy's hazel irises. But that seemed to be the only thing she'd passed to her sons. Otherwise, with their strong jaws and dark hair, Easton and Cash were younger versions of Jake and JR.

"Come on in and sit." Carol escorted us all to the long dining room off the kitchen.

Above the table, a bright glass chandelier illuminated the room. The table was a deep stained walnut, the top satiny smooth and each place set with a glossy cream plate.

"Liddy. JR. Cash. Katherine." Carol pointed to the assigned chairs as she fired names.

I held back a smile that she'd paired Cash and Katherine together. Then my heart dropped. Because there were two seats left beside each other.

One for me.

One for Easton.

Damn it, Carol.

"Wine?" JR offered, lifting a bottle after we'd taken our seats.

"Please." I held out my glass. *And keep it coming.*

Easton ripped his chair out, sitting down with a loud huff. The clank of his beer bottle hitting the table sent the message loud and clear. He was pissed I was here, and he was pissed he had to sit beside me.

I gave him a saccharine smile and held out my glass. "Cheers."

His lip curled.

"Cheers." Cash chuckled and came to my rescue, extending his beer bottle across the table to clink with mine. Then he tipped his bottle to Katherine's glass before taking a long pull.

I took a sip of mine as Liddy, seated to my left, held out her hand. She smiled sweetly.

What was she . . . *oh. Right.* The prayer. The entire table joined hands as Jake Sr. bowed from his seat at the head of the table.

I took Liddy's hand, then kept my eyes glued to my plate as I lifted my right into the air. It was up to Easton if he was going to touch me or not.

His hesitation was obvious.

The entire table waited. And waited.

Jake cleared his throat, and finally, Easton grabbed my hand, jerking my arm in the process as he lowered his chin.

The smell of his soap wafted to my nose. His face was clean shaven, and he must have showered between the time he'd seen me in the lobby and the time he'd come here because his hair was damp at the ends.

Easton's grip was rough, his callouses pressing into the tender skin of my palm as Jake prayed. Tingles shot up my arm and that scent of his was dizzying. But I'd held up under more extreme situations than this. I would not let myself drool.

"Amen."

The second the word echoed around the table, my hand was dropped like a hot coal.

Liddy gave my other hand a light squeeze, then let me go to drape a napkin in her lap.

I reached for my wine, sharing a look with Katherine across the table. She lifted her glass in a sign of solidarity.

"So, Gemma." Jake scooped a heap of mashed potatoes onto his plate as the rest of the food began the circle around the table. "Katherine told me you drove here from Boston. That's quite a trip."

"Technically, I drove from West Virginia, but yes, it was a long trip. I have to say, the best part was through Montana. I'd forgotten how beautiful it was here."

"We sure are having a nice fall," Liddy said, passing me a bowl of green beans. "How long are you planning to stay?"

"Not long," Easton answered, before he drained the last swallow of his beer.

I shoved the bowl in his face. "Beans?"

He wrenched the dish from my grasp, grumbling something under his breath that earned him a scowl from Carol on his other side.

"How'd Rory do on the trail ride today?" JR asked Cash after the food had been passed around.

"Good. He's a quick learner and the guests like him."

"Maybe you should put him on the schedule," JR told Easton.

Beside me, his teeth ground together audibly. "I know how to delegate my staff. It was my idea to send him along with Cash in the first place."

The tension in the room grew thick. The plates and the food were of sudden interest as all eyes dropped except for Easton's and JR's.

My plate was overloaded with mashed potatoes, roast beef, gravy, beans and a roll. It seemed like the perfect time to shove a huge bite into my mouth and occupy myself with chewing.

Was something happening on the ranch? Were Easton and JR fighting? If I wasn't sitting here, how would this conversation really have gone?

"Jake, I was hoping you could help me for a couple of weeks." Katherine was brave enough to break the silence. "I've got a project and need your expertise."

"I can probably do that." He nodded, aiming his eyes to Easton. "That means you'll need to handle the equipment and prepping the snowmobiles for winter."

"I know." He sighed. "I've got it covered."

Why was I suddenly feeling bad for the guy who'd been a jackass to me this week? His shoulders were bunched and his back stiff. The frustration radiating off Easton's body was palpable.

Part of me wanted to put my hand on his forearm and give him a reassuring smile. The other part remembered . . . jackass. Besides, whatever this family dynamic was, it was not my business.

"Gemma, we never did hear *your* answer to Mom's question." Cash sent his brother a smirk. "How long are you staying?"

"I'm not sure exactly. Maybe for a few weeks. Katherine said something about an empty guest bedroom at your place."

Easton scoffed.

I ignored him.

But Carol wasn't having it. "What is your problem tonight?"

"She's not staying, Grandma."

"That's not really up to you, is it?" she snapped.

Easton put down his fork. "I'm not saying she *can't* stay. I'm just saying she won't."

Really? Because to me, it sounded a lot like him telling me I couldn't stay.

"And why not?" Katherine asked.

"She's like the guests here, Kat. They love Montana for a week. But soon, she'll be ready to get back to the city. Back to her manicures and massages and Starbucks. This isn't the place for her."

"And who the hell are you to dictate the place for me?" I twisted in my chair, meeting his glare with one of my own.

"I'm calling it like I see it."

"Well, you're wrong."

"Yeah? You won't last a month. Hell, you only made it a few days before you went running to Kat because you were bored."

I guess Katherine had told him the reason for my sudden employment. When I glanced her way, she mouthed, "Sorry."

"I like to be busy."

"Sure," he deadpanned.

I leaned in closer, sitting taller in my chair. "You truly are an asshole."

The table snickered around us but I kept my eyes locked on Easton's.

He leaned closer, his breath caressing my cheek as he taunted, "But am I wrong?"

"Yes."

"Prove it."

"By staying? No problem. That was already my plan."

"Like I said. You won't make it a month."

"I bet she makes it past Christmas." JR chuckled. "Just to prove you wrong, son."

Easton gave his dad a scowl, then turned to the meal, shoveling a bite of potatoes in his mouth.

"I think it will be wonderful to have you here through the holidays," Liddy said.

Wait. What? When had I agreed to stay for Christmas? That was over three months away.

"I appreciate the offer, but I don't think Katherine and Cash want me living with them for three months. I'd love to stay for a few weeks, but months? I, uh . . ."

A slow, evil grin spread across Easton's face as he chewed.

Bastard.

Katherine had offered me a guest room, but for three months? That wasn't a guest. That was a roommate.

"Gemma will stay at the cabin," Carol announced.

"Huh?" I was getting whiplash. "What cabin?"

"The one Jake and I built when we first moved here. It's a little old and outdated but it's all yours."

Fantastic. Easton had all but dared me to stay, and now there were no excuses to why I couldn't.

"The cabin it is." My cheery voice betrayed my terror.

Easton's smug grin dropped.

Good.

He'd baited me. He'd flustered me and now I was in Montana for three months because there was no way I was letting him win. Even if that meant crashing in an old cabin.

I'd show him.

Ugh.

What the hell had I just gotten myself into?

7

GEMMA

"ARE you sure you want to do this?" Katherine asked.

I shrugged and looked around the room. The place had running water and electricity, luxuries I didn't take for granted. "It's not that bad. I mean, it's not my posh room at the lodge, but it's a thousand times nicer than our tent at the junkyard."

"True."

"This will be great," I promised. "It's a nice cabin."

"If you change your mind, you're always welcome to our guest room."

"Thanks." I'd been living alone for a long time and actually preferred having this older cabin to myself than sharing someone's space.

The last roommate I'd had was Katherine. We'd stayed together in the tent, then here when we'd been in the staff quarters.

Whenever the two of us had been bored, we'd practiced our poker skills. Karson had taught us in the junkyard. We never had money to bet, but we'd play and practice with toothpicks.

"Do you still remember how to play poker?" I asked, setting down my suitcase in the middle of the cabin's living room.

"Absolutely." Katherine walked over to the kitchen, running a finger through the dust on the countertop. "About a year after you left, Cash was home for spring break or something and he came over to the staff quarters. Some of the guys were having a poker tournament. I asked if I could play too. They all teased me that they didn't have time to teach a girl how to play."

"Did you win?"

"Hell, yes, I won." She laughed. "Every once in a while, Cash and I go into town to play at the bar. They have games on Friday and Saturday nights. You should come with us next time."

"Maybe." Though I hadn't played in years. "So what's the story with you and Cash?"

"No story." She shook her head. "We're roommates. Coworkers. Friends."

Lies. She was in love with him. And Cash was oblivious.

But I wasn't one to lecture on matters of men. I was staying in an old cabin that needed a deep clean because I'd let a man bait me into a foolish challenge two days ago.

Thankfully, Londyn didn't care how long it took me to get to California. I'd called her after the family dinner and told her everything. Once she'd finished laughing her ass off, she'd told me I had no choice but to show Easton up.

So here I was, in a Montana cabin for the next three months.

"It's a good thing we raided a cleaning cart." Katherine opened the refrigerator and cringed at the smell, shutting it quickly. "No one would think less of you if you said screw this and left."

"Easton would."

"Does his opinion really matter?"

Yes. "No, but I like it here. So why not shut him up?"

"If you're sure."

I nodded. "I'm sure."

The truth was, I'd contemplated leaving. After the dinner, I'd thought about getting in the Cadillac and abandoning this ridiculous notion. I'd considered it a lot in the past forty-eight hours. It was Sunday and if I left tomorrow morning, I'd be in sunny California before the end of the week.

But I wasn't ready to go.

Besides the benefit of proving Easton wrong, I was enjoying my time here. Katherine and I were bonding. The Greer family was incredibly welcoming and my simple job at the front desk was refreshing.

Every time I heard Easton's voice in the back of my mind, telling me I didn't belong, I shut it up by finding something about this situation that appealed.

This cabin was one. It was two miles from the lodge, nestled in a clearing of evergreens. There wasn't a sprawling mountain view or an on-call masseuse. But it was my own space, peaceful and secluded. I had room to think. To start deciding what I would do with my life once these three months were over and my trip to California was complete.

Because at the moment, I didn't have a damn clue. I needed this time to reflect. To plan.

Besides, I could survive anything for three months.

And I'd lived in far, far worse places.

"What's your plan for today?" Katherine asked.

"Clean."

"Want some help?"

"Nah. I don't mind. You go and enjoy your day off."

"Day off?" She gave me a quizzical look. "What's that? I'm going to the office to catch up on emails. Maybe, if I'm lucky, I can squeeze in a ride this afternoon. Want to join me?"

"Maybe. Shoot me a text."

"Okay." She took another look around the open room and her eyes widened. "Good luck."

I laughed and walked her outside, leaning on one of the porch's log posts as she got into her truck parked beside the Cadillac. "Bye."

She waved. "Bye."

As her truck disappeared around the curve in the road, I took a long breath of the clean, mountain air, then made my way inside the cabin.

The smell was musty. Dust floated everywhere, catching the glint of sunlight attempting to stream through the filmy windows. Carol had offered to clean the cabin because no one had stayed here in over three years—she'd come out to tidy up and check for mice a few times each year but otherwise the place had been empty—but I'd declined her offer, insisting on doing the work myself.

In a way, cleaning would make it my own.

I whipped off my sweater, folding it and setting it on my suitcase, then I got to work.

The bulk of the cabin was one large room. The living area was no more than a rawhide couch, a matching chair and a coffee table. Opposite it was a two-seat table and a small kitchen. The rear half of the cabin had the single bedroom. It was cramped with a queen-sized bed and a set of dresser drawers. The adjoining bathroom was designed for function with only a standing shower crammed beside the sink and toilet. The square laundry room by the back door doubled as the pantry and storage room.

I tackled the bedroom first, wanting to get my things put away. There was a canvas tarp over the bed to keep it from getting dusty, but I still stripped the quilt and sheets and tossed them into the washing machine. Then I dusted every surface and wiped out the dresser's drawers before sweeping and mopping.

Sweat beaded on my brow after I was done with the kitchen, having washed all the dishes, then scrubbed the floor on my hands and knees.

Even with the lack of care, it didn't take me long to make my way through the cabin, because it was just that small.

I opened the door to let in the fresh air and did the same to the windows once they were clean. The smile on my face felt earned. Carefree. I'd worked my ass off since the day I'd run away from home at sixteen, first to simply stay alive, then to make something of myself. Accomplishment gave me satisfaction.

Or at least, it had. The past year in Boston had lacked fulfillment.

What I'd needed was a hard day of cleaning where I could see my work unfold before my eyes.

Three months here? Piece of cake.

I was one laundry room away from a sparkling cabin when I heard a truck approach. My mood tanked when I saw its driver.

"What is he doing here," I muttered from the cabin's porch.

Easton parked beside the Cadillac and hopped out, not sparing me a glance as he walked to the back and hefted out a huge cooler. "Where do you want this?"

"Uh, what is it?"

"Food. Mom didn't want you running to the store, so she spent yesterday in the kitchen."

Liddy had cooked.

For me.

My own mother hadn't cooked for me. But his had. My heart squeezed as he walked up the porch stairs carrying the cooler.

Easton scanned me from head to toe, and like always, he frowned.

I glanced down at my jeans and the gray tank top I'd had underneath my sweater. "What?"

"Nothing." He brushed past me and stomped inside.

"Take off your boots. I just cleaned." I bit the inside of my cheeks to keep from laughing as he spun around and gaped. "Kidding."

Easton didn't find me funny.

I followed him to the kitchen, leaving the front door open, as he set the cooler beside the fridge. He bent and flipped open the lid to start unloading, but I waved him away. "I'll take care of it."

"'Kay." He stood and walked outside.

"Goodbye," I called after him, then turned my attention to the cooler. "Nice to see you too. And thanks. I *did* do a great job cleaning. How kind of you to notice."

"Talking to yourself?"

I jumped at Easton's voice. "I thought you left."

He hefted a tote in the air. "Wine. From my grandma."

"Carol gets me." I stood and took the tote from him, setting it on the counter. Then I waited, assuming he'd actually leave this time unless there were more gifts in his truck.

But he didn't leave. Easton walked into the living room and ran a hand through that thick, soft hair as he glanced around. He'd traded his normal, long-sleeved plaid shirt for a fitted thermal. The textured cotton stretched across his biceps, showcasing the strength of his arms. It molded to his torso and that flat stomach.

If he'd just smile, a little, he'd be so incredibly handsome. Gruff and stoic worked for Easton. The man was a challenge and an enigma. His serious composure gave nothing away and that was a turn-on for a woman like me who enjoyed the uphill battle.

I'd learned in my week here that he didn't have a wife or girlfriend, but I had no doubt the local ladies swooned over his rugged, somber exterior. But a smile . . . damn, I wanted to see a smile.

I'd seen it once—eleven years ago when he'd taken me to his bed, and I hadn't forgotten it in all this time.

Easton's smile was unmatched. It was rare. Maybe the reason it was so special was because he gave it to so few people.

"Looks good in here."

My hand flew to my heart and I feigned surprise. "Was that . . . a compliment? Did you actually say something nice to me?"

His lips pursed into a thin line.

"Oh, relax." I turned to the cupboards and opened the one where I'd found glasses earlier. "Would you like to stay for a glass of wine? Or has five minutes in my presence irritated you enough to leave me alone for a week?"

"I don't drink wine."

"Of course, you don't." It probably went against the cowboy code to drink anything but milk, water, black coffee, beer and whiskey neat.

"But I'll take a glass of water."

Seriously? I'd been joking in the invite. Why would he take it? What was he up to? I didn't ask as I filled his glass from the tap, but I kept an eye on him as I uncorked a bottle of Cabernet. I'd thank Carol later for including the opener in my tote bag.

"Here you go." I handed him his water as I joined him in the living room.

Easton took it and sat on the couch, tossing one long arm over the back. Then he lifted an ankle, crossing it over a knee.

"What do you want?" I sat in the chair and cut right to the chase. Easton wasn't here to be friendly.

"You. Gone."

"You'll get your wish in three months."

He studied me, his gaze full of scrutiny.

"What? No reminders that I won't make it?" I asked.

"No. You know how I feel."

"Yes, you've made it crystal clear. So I'd say we're at a stalemate."

"Guess so." He drained his water with three long gulps. The bob of his Adam's apple was mesmerizing.

I expected him to leave with the glass empty, but once again, he stayed seated, settling deeper into the couch. "Don't you have somewhere to be?"

"No." He looked around the room, his eyes taking it all in. "When Cash and I were little, Dad would take us camping here. Boys only. We'd go fishing at the creek. He'd build a fire and we'd have a cookout outside. I haven't been inside in ages. Every time I come back, it seems smaller."

Why was he telling me this? Again, I didn't verbalize my question. Because when Easton wasn't snapping at me or barking something condescending, I soaked up his every word. Especially if it had a thing to do with his youth.

Because his childhood was my dream.

"Do you know how to use that?" He pointed a finger at the wood stove in the corner.

"Uh . . ." I glanced around, searching the walls for a thermostat. There wasn't one. "No. I don't."

"I'll show you."

"I can figure it out."

"And burn down a Greer family legacy? I'm not taking that chance." He stood and walked to the stove. "Come here."

"Ask me nicely."

He shot a look over his shoulder that wasn't exactly a glare, but it wasn't polite.

I enjoyed a warm house too much to annoy him, so I set my wine on the coffee table and joined him in a crouch by the stove. There was a small stack of wood and a basketful of newspaper beside it, along with a long-handled lighter.

Easton showed me how to use the paper and kindling to get it going, then gave me instruction on how to set the airflow. Within minutes, the fire was roaring, chasing away any of the chill in the air.

"Thanks." I stood and went to close the windows.

I left the door open, assuming he'd leave at any minute. Then I went to unpack the cooler, stacked full of plastic containers. "She made all this in a day? It's more food than I'll eat alone in a month."

Easton crossed the room, closing the front door, and joined me at the fridge. "Want some help?"

"Unpacking? No, I've got it."

"No, not unpacking. Eating."

I blinked up at him as he leaned a shoulder against the fridge. "You want to stay for dinner?"

"Mom made my favorite ham and potato casserole. She only makes it for special occasions and because you're our guest, you got it."

Ah. So that was why he was here. "Jealous?"

"If you're not going to eat all this food, I'll take that casserole off your hands."

"Too bad. It's mine." And I was going to eat it first. Any meal that made Easton act remotely civil must be outstanding.

He shoved off the fridge. "Come on. Give it to me so someone who will actually appreciate it will eat it."

"Excuse me?" I surged to my feet. "I don't think you get to tell me what I appreciate. For a guy who has never gone hungry a day in his life, I can assure you, I appreciate each and every meal I eat."

Easton winced and the annoyed look on his face vanished. "Sorry."

I crossed my arms over my chest.

"That casserole is important." He sighed. "To my family."

"A casserole."

"Yes. It was my grandmother's recipe. My mom's mom. She died before I was born in a house fire. Not much survived the blaze except some of her jewelry that was in a fire-safe box and a few recipe cards she kept in a metal tin. That casserole was Mom's favorite too. The reason she only makes it for special occasions is because it's hard for her to see my grandma's handwriting."

My anger vanished. "And she made it for me."

"She made it for you. So if you're not going to eat it and fuss over it and make sure Mom knows exactly how much you appreciate the heartache it took for her to make you that meal, then give it to me so I can."

"Okay."

190

"Okay." He went to grab it from the cooler, but I slapped his hand away.

"I'm not giving it to you. But you can stay for dinner. And we can both make sure she knows how much it was appreciated."

Not his first choice, but he kept his mouth shut and nodded.

Most of the time, I wanted to strangle Easton. But then there were moments like this one where he showed me a glimpse of the good man lurking inside that solid body. The man who would come here and suffer through a meal with a woman he couldn't stand, just so the next day he could make sure his mother felt appreciated and that her grief had not gone unnoticed.

I glanced at the clock on the microwave and saw it was nearly five. "Are you hungry now?"

He shrugged. "I could eat."

"Then I'll get it started." I went about preparing our meal, following the instruction card Liddy had taped to the casserole's aluminum dish. While it was in the oven, I set the small table while Easton went outside to bring in some more chopped wood to set beside the stove.

"Is that always here?" I asked as he stacked the split logs. "The firewood."

"No, I, uh . . . I brought it over yesterday."

"You?" My jaw dropped.

"As tempting as it is to let the snow and cold chase you away, the last thing we need is a city girl freezing to death on ranch property. Goes against the sales brochure for the resort."

I snorted. "Was that a joke? Who knew Easton Greer has a sense of humor buried beneath the snide remarks and muttered censure?"

He frowned.

Predictable, this man. "Ah, there's the face I recognize. I was worried for a moment."

The timer dinged on the oven before he could deliver a snarky come-back. I smiled to myself as I took dinner from the oven. Tonight's banter felt different than our normal bickering. It was almost fun. Charged.

It felt a lot like foreplay.

Not that Easton had any notions of taking me to bed. At least, not again.

With our plates served, we sat and began the meal in silence, neither one of us doing more than shovel those first few bites.

"Wow. This is amazing." The casserole was the definition of comfort food. It was warm and cheesy with just the right amount of salt and those blessed starchy potatoes.

"Told you," he said, dishing his plate with seconds. "You and Kat seem to be getting along."

"We always did. Before I left."

"You lived together, right? In California?"

I wasn't sure where this curiosity was coming from, but I'd take conversation over a quiet meal. I'd eaten alone enough times in my life to prefer company, even if it was grouchy. "In a junkyard outside of Temecula."

"When Kat told us about that, I didn't believe her at first. Not because I thought she was dishonest. It just didn't seem . . . I couldn't wrap my head around it."

"That's because you grew up with a family in a loving home." I'd told my story to enough people to know the reason Easton struggled to understand—he had good parents.

"There were six of you?"

"Yes. One of the kids lived in the neighborhood where I grew up. Karson. He ran away when he was sixteen, and since it seemed like a damn good idea, I left too." After a particularly bad night at home, I'd finally had enough. "It was impulsive," I told Easton. "I didn't have a bag packed. There was no preparation. No stack of cash hidden underneath my mattress or a stash of extra clothes and food. One day I lived with my mother. The next day, I lived with Karson in a junkyard and slept on the dirt."

"Jesus." His fork was frozen midair. His eyes were filled with pity.

"Don't do that," I whispered. "Don't pity me. Just believe me when I tell you that the junkyard was the better place. Running away was the best decision I've ever made."

If Easton asked for more details, I wasn't sure I had the strength to talk about it tonight. I didn't talk about that time with anyone but Dr. Brewer, and even then, I'd stopped seeing her four years ago.

Some memories were better left in the murky corners of our minds where, if we were lucky, they'd eventually fade.

"Londyn came along after me." I forced a smile as I ate another bite. "Her parents were drug addicts."

"Katherine's were too, right?"

I nodded. "Her mom. I don't think she ever knew her dad. Karson was working at a car wash and met her. She was begging for change, so he brought her to the junkyard that day. Introduced us. She actually went home after that, then showed up two weeks later with a garbage bag full of clothes and a black eye."

Easton's hand gripped his fork so hard I worried the metal would snap. "She didn't tell us that."

"We don't like to talk about it."

"That's fucked up," he said. "Not that you don't like to talk about it. The black eye."

You have no idea. "After Katherine came two other girls. Twins. Aria and Clara lived in Londyn's trailer park with their uncle after their parents died in a car crash. The uncle was mentally off. Creeped the hell out of me the one and only time I saw him." The image of his beady eyes still gave me the shivers. "They came to the junkyard one day, holding hands and wearing backpacks, and that made six."

"You were just kids. Living in the dirt." He shook his head, his lashes lifting. When his eyes met mine, they weren't full of pity this time. They were soft. Kind. He almost looked . . . proud. "And you just sold your company for twelve million dollars. Good for you, Gemma. Good for you."

Whether it was his expression or the sincerity of his words, I wasn't sure. But I wanted so badly in that moment to cry. To let Easton be nice to me and stop holding up that arm that kept everyone at a distance.

But I didn't cry.

I didn't lower my arm.

Instead I lifted my glass and gulped the last swallow of my wine.

Then I picked a fight.

"Do you like your job as assistant manager of the ranch?"

8

EASTON

ASSISTANT MANAGER.

That woman knew exactly where my hot buttons were and just how hard to poke them.

It had been two weeks since I'd stormed out of the cabin, irritated and angry that she'd known damn well I was in charge of the ranch but had purposefully pissed me off.

If Gemma wasn't running from people, she was shoving them away.

For the past two weeks, we'd stayed clear of one another. At least, as well as we could considering we worked together and my family had pulled Gemma into the fold.

My family loved her, especially Grandma and Mom.

After Mom's casserole, Gemma had sent her a bouquet of two dozen roses, delivered all the way from Missoula, as a thank-you for the meals. Grandma had received a case of expensive wine the next day.

Whenever I'd come to the lodge, she'd be at the front desk with a smile waiting. Though never for me. Those smiles would vanish the second I walked through the door. But it was nice to have a cheerful face behind that desk.

For the guests.

The only reason I wasn't using the rear entrance was because the parking lot behind the lodge was always crowded with staff rigs. My trips to the lodge had nothing to do with Gemma or her smile.

And this trip to the cabin was out of necessity, not because I hadn't seen her in three days.

My truck bounced on the rough road. There seemed to be more bumps than normal. I made a mental note to have Granddad find Gemma an old truck to drive around since this wouldn't be good for the Cadillac.

If that car got ruined, well, it would be a travesty to the American classic.

194

And Gemma was staying.

My plan had backfired—something I wouldn't admit no matter how many times Cash had razzed me about it this week.

If she was staying, we'd have to make sure she had the right tools to survive on the ranch and in the cabin through the winter.

The leaves on the trees had mostly fallen over the past two weeks, the orange and yellow littering the ground and fading to brown. This fall had been short thanks to the cold patch that had swooped in over the past week. Every night had dropped below freezing and we weren't even ten days into October.

Next week's forecast was calling for snow.

I was simply glad we'd moved the cattle out of the mountains, even if Dad had gotten his way and they'd been put in the exact opposite pastures where I'd planned to have them.

We'd argued. He'd won.

Yesterday, I'd been so frustrated I'd spent my day working alone.

A plume of smoke rose above the patch of pine trees, and as I rounded the last corner of the road, the cabin came into view and I saw Gemma outside, her arms loaded with wood. The sound of my diesel caught her ears and she stopped, watching me pull into the space beside her Cadillac.

"Hey," I said as I hopped out.

"Hi." She gave me a small smile and disappeared inside. When she came back out to the porch, she brushed at the flecks of bark that had stuck to her sweater.

This one was olive, the same as the first day she'd arrived nearly a month ago. She looked pretty and relaxed, standing there in the doorway to the cabin. Her hair was up in a ponytail that flowed over her shoulder in loose waves.

Breathe, East. She's just a beautiful woman.

"What's up?" she asked.

I cleared my throat and jerked my chin to the bed of the truck. "I've got a load of wood for you."

"Thanks. I was starting to run low." She rubbed her hands up and down her arms, shivering at a gust of wind. "It's been cold."

"This should last you a couple of weeks."

"Let me grab my coat and I'll help."

"All right." Maybe the chivalrous thing to do would be unload the half cord myself. But I'd grown up with grandparents who'd worked side by side their entire lives. My parents too. And Gemma wasn't the type who'd sit by and idly watch someone else work.

I dug another pair of leather gloves from the jockey box of my truck and laid them on the tailgate for her. Then I started hauling loads to the metal rack Granddad had welded together fifty-some years ago.

Gemma joined right in, not saying much as we crossed paths. Every time I walked to the truck, she walked away from it with wood in her arms. Then I'd load up and we'd do the reverse.

It meant with every trip, we'd share an awkward glance, so I pushed harder, trying to change the timing. But the faster I pushed, she pushed. No matter how quickly I walked or loaded, she was keeping pace.

No one could accuse Gemma of slacking.

When the split logs we could reach from the ground were stacked, I nodded for Gemma to climb in. "Why don't you hop in the back and push the wood toward the tailgate."

"Okay." One of those long legs lifted and in a swift motion she was up.

That should not have been a sexy move but my dick jerked. Her legs, encased in faded jeans, were at eye level. When she bent, I had the perfect view of her ass and my palms twitched, wanting to squeeze her curves and mold them to mine. *Fuck*. This was the reason I'd been avoiding her for two weeks. Because every night when I went home, I had to jack off in the shower to the image of her legs wrapped around my hips and my greedy hands on her body.

Gemma and I argued. We were at each other's throats, and it was because if we didn't fight this attraction, if we gave in . . . we'd be doomed.

I dropped my gaze and focused on the job at hand, refusing to look at her until the work was done.

When the last log was stacked, she hopped down and I slammed the tailgate closed.

"Thanks." She removed the gloves I'd lent her and handed them over.

"No problem."

"How long did it take to cut and split all that?"

I shrugged. "A few hours."

This was what I'd done yesterday when I'd escaped to work alone.

"I appreciate it," she said.

"I know." Gemma, unlike a lot of people with her substantial wealth, appreciated effort from others. I waved and walked to my truck door, opening it up and was about to get in when she stopped me.

"Easton?"

"Yeah?"

"Want to stay for dinner?"

If I stayed, we'd probably get in a fight. It would be smarter to decline —I had work to do, and I'd already planned to stop by the lodge and grab dinner. Instead, I tossed the gloves into the truck and slammed the door. "Yeah."

It wasn't about the food.

It was Gemma.

She dropped her chin, hiding her smile as she walked past me and into the cabin.

I followed, toeing off my boots beside her shoes inside the door, then went to the fireplace to add another log. "Is it staying warm enough in here at night?"

"It's been great. Very cozy." She went to the fridge. "Beer, water or chocolate milk?"

Chocolate milk was a staple in my diet but I saw she had a glass of wine poured. "Beer, please."

She took out an amber bottle and twisted off the top, bringing it over for me in the living room. Then she returned to the kitchen where she'd been in the middle of chopping when I'd arrived. "We're having spaghetti."

"Want some help?"

"No, I'm good. This is easy."

I took a seat on the couch and looked around the room. It was the same cabin I'd known my whole life, the same furniture, but there was something different about it. It was cozier and more . . . intimate. Maybe that was because the wind was blowing outside, rustling the trees, and in here, there was the crackle of a fire, the scent of garlic and onions, and a beautiful woman standing in the kitchen, sipping wine and making us a meal.

It was impossible not to watch her as she moved. To appreciate the sway of her hips and the way her ponytail swished across the middle of her back. A lock of hair kept falling from where she'd tucked it behind her ear, and anytime she'd glance my way, there was a rosy flush to her cheeks.

She was bewitching. She pulled me into an alternate universe where there was just us.

"So you went from here to Boston, right?" I asked, needing to make some conversation before I did something hasty like get off this couch to kiss her in the kitchen. I didn't need to taste Gemma's lips. I had once and they'd been sweet and destructive, like a poisoned apple. So I'd keep my ass on this couch until it was time to leave.

"That's right." She nodded. "I assume you've been here since I left."

"Besides the occasional vacation, this is it for me." I'd work here, live here and, God willing, die here too.

"Ever get married?" I asked, for no other reason than I wanted to know.

Maybe most women would take offense to the blunt question, but not Gemma. She faced me and leaned a hip against the counter. "No. You?"

I shook my head. "No."

"Girlfriend?"

"Not presently." I took a sip of my beer, drinking in the liquid and her gorgeous hazel eyes. "I don't have time for a girlfriend."

"Because you're so busy with work."

"Yeah. As the assistant manager," I muttered.

She threw her head back and laughed, the musical sound stirring something in my chest. Making the urge to stand even stronger.

Gemma set her wine aside to snap some pasta in half and put them in a pot of boiling water. Then she crossed the room, floating with an easy grace, to curl up in the chair beside the couch. "What's happening with the ranch these days?"

"Same old. We're always wishing for rain and good cattle prices. The resort has grown these past few years—Kat gets a lot of credit for that—which adds a level of complexity. More staff, more guests, more problems. But we're getting into a good groove. Mostly, my headaches come from men with the last name Greer."

"Jake and JR."

"Yeah." It wasn't something I'd confided to anyone but Cash in so many words. But talking with Gemma, despite how she frustrated and baited me, was surprisingly easy. She listened. She wouldn't play mediator like my family members and try to fix the problem.

Sometimes, all I really wanted was a person who listened.

"They don't want to let go," I said. "And I wish I could say I didn't understand, but when a place is your whole life, when you've given it everything year after year, I get it. It's just . . ."

"It's your turn."

"I want to build upon their legacy. I want to take the ranch and the resort a step further and be able to give that to the next generation. It's hard when they don't want to let go. When no one bothers to ask your opinion and when you make a decision, it's under a microscope."

"Makes sense. When I sold my company, the new owners asked me if I'd stay on for a year and act as interim CEO. But I knew I'd hate it. I wasn't going to answer to someone else's rules when I'd been making them for so long."

"So what would you do if you were me?"

She ran a finger around the rim of her glass. "I don't think you want my answer."

No, I was pretty sure I did. "Tell me."

"If this was my home, if this was my family, I'd thank my lucky stars that I had a grandfather and a father who were still trying to give what they have to offer because they'd rather die than see me fail."

"Well, fuck."

Gemma laughed. "I told you that you didn't want my answer."

"No, you're right." I sighed. "You're completely right and I hate it." Because I wasn't going to fail. And if I did, they'd be there to pick me up.

"I can empathize where you're coming from," she said. "And in your shoes, I'd feel the same. But you're talking to someone whose mother thought the next generation was there to service her boyfriends when they'd grown bored with her."

The beer bottle nearly slipped from my fingers. "What?"

"I don't know why I said that." Gemma flew out of the chair and returned to the kitchen.

She left me speechless while she ran.

But this time, Boston wasn't an option. And in a cabin of this size, there just wasn't far for her to go.

Was this her coping mechanism? She shut down and shut people out. She shoved them away. Was that why she'd left eleven years ago? Because I'd made her feel? Because here, she'd have a family who wouldn't have let her brush the past under a rug. Had she been hiding in her work ever since?

I set my bottle aside and walked to the kitchen as she furiously stirred the simmering sauce. "Gemma."

"Please forget I said that."

I crowded in close and tucked that lock of hair behind her ear. "Can't do that, darlin'."

She set the spoon down and looked at me with pleading eyes. "I don't like to talk about my mother or that part of my life. I spent years in therapy, and on my last session, I swore I didn't need to talk about it again. I really don't know why that slipped out."

"We don't have to talk about it." My hand fit perfectly around the nape of her neck. "But I'm here if you change your mind."

"Thanks." The tension eased from her shoulders as I skimmed my thumb over the skin beneath her ear.

I'd only meant to touch her for a second. To show her I was here and nothing more. But there was no such thing as a touch when it came to this woman. A zing raced beneath my skin. Electricity crackled between us and that pull, the gravity that surrounded her, sucked me right in. My hand trailed down her spine and her lips were so close that all I had to do was take them.

Gemma shivered, leaning in to my touch, as her gaze dropped to my mouth. Her tongue darted out and wet her bottom lip.

Then the pot of noodles boiled over. The hiss of the water hitting the burner broke us apart.

I dropped my hand and took a step back as Gemma fumbled for the dial to shut off the gas.

"This is probably about ready," she said.

"I'll set the table." And take a minute to get my head on straight.

Christ, I should have stayed on the couch.

The plates weren't in the same cupboard where Grandma had always kept them, and the silverware was in a different drawer. Admitting that Gemma's layout of the kitchen was more functional would only confirm out loud that she was fitting in, making this place her home, so I kept it to myself.

I heaped a pile of noodles onto my plate and smothered them in sauce and dug in. "This is great."

"It's actually your mother's recipe."

"Sauce from a jar with some embellishments? She tried to teach me but I never get the embellishments right and end up with just sauce from the jar."

Gemma smiled, twirling a string of noodles around her fork. "When I was here before, your mom was covering for the cook one day. There was this nasty cold running around, so there weren't many of us to feed. Londyn, Katherine and I were healthy—I always thought the junkyard gave us immune systems of steel—so we went to the kitchen to help her."

I leaned back in my chair, taking her in as she spoke because she captivated that kind of attention.

You set your silverware down for a woman like Gemma Lane.

"She taught us how to make her spaghetti," she said. "It was the first time anyone had ever taught me to cook."

"It's delicious. As good as hers. Do you cook often?"

"No." She shook her head. "I worked. And it's sort of depressing to cook for one person every night."

"I can relate." I went back to my meal, the two of us eating without much conversation.

When my plate was clear, I leaned deeper into my chair, making no move to leave. There wasn't anywhere else I wanted to be at the moment. The only thing waiting for me at home was the television and a massive pile of laundry. And Gemma's company was addictive.

"Want to know the real reason I left Boston?" she asked.

She'd told me it was because she'd sold her company and had wanted a change of scenery, but I'd wondered lately if that was only a half-truth.

"Yeah."

"I didn't feel anything about my life." She lifted a shoulder, like she was just as confused as I was why she was telling me these things. Then she dropped her gaze, hiding the emotion in her eyes by toying with the uneaten spaghetti on her plate.

I didn't blink. I didn't breathe. I didn't move for fear that she'd stop talking.

"I don't know when I went numb. I used to feel things." She looked up and forced a too-bright smile. "Anger or annoyance or excitement. On the day I was approached about selling Gemma Lane, that idea hadn't even crossed my mind. I don't even know why I entertained it, but I was eating lunch with an old colleague and she asked me if I was sick."

"Were you?"

"I don't get sick." She shook her head. "It took me a minute to figure out what she was talking about. But then I realized she thought I was tired. And I wasn't. I really wasn't. I was just . . . empty."

"Maybe you were ready for a career change."

She shook her head. "A life change. It wasn't just work. I was dating this guy and he'd asked me to marry him."

A flare of jealousy raced through my veins, but I set it aside.

"Obviously, I said no." She wiggled the bare fingers on her left hand. "So I had this friend who thought I was sick. A man who wanted to share his life with me, but instead I broke his heart. And it all came together and made me pause. I looked over the past year and realized that I was going day after day and I didn't feel . . . anything."

Her eyes turned glassy, but she held tight, not letting a tear fall.

I stretched my hand across the table and covered hers. "Gem."

"I don't want to live like that." She flipped her hand over so our palms were pressed together and stared at them, my wide hand nearly covering her long fingers.

"And since you got here? Feel anything?"

Her eyes flashed to mine. "Some days."

"Besides frustration with me?"

A smile spread across her stunning face. "Maybe."

"Good." A surge of pride swelled in my chest because I'd done that. Me. I'd put that smile there and it was mine. "Glad I could piss you off."

"Among other things." She laughed and slipped her hand free, then collected our plates and took them to the sink.

"Want some help washing up?"

"I've got it. Want another beer?"

"Better not."

If I stayed, I wouldn't leave. We'd put the fighting aside tonight, and we both knew this was heading toward dangerous territory. She was in a strange emotional place and I knew nothing would change.

Gemma would stay until Christmas, mostly because I'd dared her. Partly because she wanted to. Then she'd head to California, leaving me behind.

I'd spend another eleven years wondering what had become of Gemma. I stood from the table. "Thanks for dinner."

"Thanks for staying. And for the firewood."

"See ya." I went to the door to tug on my boots. Then I opened the door before I decided kissing her was worth another eleven-year wait.

9

GEMMA

THE MOMENT he opened the door, I chased after him. "Easton, wait."

"Yeah?"

I crossed the room, not caring that the cold night air was chasing away the fire's warmth and stepped into his space.

Standing before him in my bare feet, his tall, strong body shrouded mine. He made me feel small—safe and protected. He made me feel free to be myself.

Easton made me feel. Period.

I wasn't ready for him to go and take the feeling with him. Not yet. Not when I'd been numb for so long and with him here, I was alive.

"I'm sorry."

His forehead furrowed. "For what?"

"For leaving like I did. After that night, I shouldn't have snuck away without a goodbye."

"It's fine." His gaze was unreadable. "We were young. It was just a hookup."

Except it hadn't been a hookup.

Easton had been my first.

Not that I'd been a virgin, but he'd been the one *I'd* chosen. Me.

When I was fourteen and still living at home, I'd lost my virginity to a guy who'd worked as a clerk at the gas station close to my neighborhood. I'd ridden my bike over to get away from my mother for a few hours. I'd gone in to use the bathroom and he'd stopped me on the way out. He'd asked if I wanted a case of beer, offering to sell it to me even though he'd known I hadn't been twenty-one.

I'd picked wine instead because my mother served her boyfriends beer. And they were trash. I was going to be classy and that meant drinking wine—or it had to my fourteen-year-old brain. The boy had sold it to me, and I'd stayed at the gas station drinking while he'd finished his Saturday shift.

Then, in a dark alley that had smelled like garbage, I'd let him take my virginity in the backseat of his car.

That boy hadn't been my choice. Yes, I'd picked him, but not because I'd been attracted to him or liked him or could remember his name. I'd picked him simply so I could *give* my virginity, not have it taken. I'd been terrified that eventually one of the men Mom had brought around would take me against my will.

I knew that eventually, one of them wouldn't be satisfied when she made me watch or when she made me touch.

But Easton, he'd been mine.

He'd been the first man I'd desired.

There'd been countless nights since when I'd remember the feel of being in his arms and how he'd held me. How he'd kissed me with tenderness and how he'd cherished my body.

The morning I'd left his bed, before the sun had risen, my footsteps had never been heavier.

Easton had been so good to me. He'd set the standard for future men in my life and not one had measured up.

No, it hadn't been a hookup.

That night had been my everything.

"Hookup or not, thank you." I placed a hand over his heart. "That night meant a lot to me."

Easton studied me, trying to figure out where this was coming from. Maybe he'd eventually figure me out, as it seemed like he was trying.

Maybe if he did, he could clue me in because I was as fucked up now as I'd been at sixteen.

My hand rose and fell with the rise of his chest. My fingers looked tiny compared to the breadth of his shoulders. Through the cotton of his shirt, his heart pulsed in steady beats and the heat of his skin warmed mine. I let the spark between us sink deep into my veins.

Easton covered my hand with one of his, trapping me to him. "What do you want, Gem?"

A place.

A safe place. A forever place.

Maybe that place didn't exist for women like me, so I stood on my toes, threw my free arm around his shoulders and brushed my lips against his before I gave him my second choice. "You."

He didn't hesitate. Easton crushed his lips to mine, letting my hand go so both arms could snake around me. The heat from his body spread like fire, racing through my body and stealing my breath.

I gasped as he lifted me off my toes and took one long stride into the cabin, kicking the door closed behind us with his boot.

His tongue swept inside my mouth, twisting and tangling with mine, as a rush of desire pooled in my core. The erection beneath his jeans dug into my hip and his hard length only increased the frenzy.

I was needy. Aching. Melting into his strong body. I latched on to his bottom lip, sucking it into my mouth as my arms clung to him.

"Stop." He broke his mouth away, panting. "Are you sure?"

"If you walk out that door without fucking me, I'll never speak to you again."

The corner of his mouth turned up. "Promise?"

I laughed and leaned in to take his earlobe between my teeth. "Easton. Fuck me."

"Whatever you say, darlin'." His mouth latched on to the skin of my neck and he spun us toward the living room but stopped after two steps. "Wait. Damn it. I don't have a condom."

I pointed over his shoulder to the coat rack. "Purse."

Easton spun us again, growling against my skin as he walked. His hands dropped to my ass, palming it with those large hands before setting me down so I could yank my purse off the hook and dig.

His chest hit my back and his lips found the sensitive spot beneath my ear. The caress of his breath and the wet warmth of his tongue dizzied my brain and I swayed on my feet. His arms banded around me, and one hand cupped my breast as the other went for the button on my jeans.

"Hustle up," he commanded.

I was struggling to keep a grip on my purse, let alone search through it in the hopes that I'd find the condom I carried for emergency purposes.

When I couldn't feel it in the interior pocket, I started throwing things onto the floor. Lip glosses. Pens. A packet of gum. I ripped items out in a flurry, just wanting to find my goddamn wallet as Easton tortured me with his lips and hands.

My nipples were pebbled inside my bra and when he slipped a hand underneath my sweater, raking those calloused fingers up my ribs, I began to quiver.

"Gemma. Condom."

I snapped back to reality, clinging to the last thread of my focus to search for my wallet. When I had it in my hand, I threw my twelve-thousand-dollar handbag on the floor and ripped open the flap of the matching wallet.

My finger hit the foil packet at the exact moment Easton's slid into my panties and found my clit.

"Oh my God." I sagged against him, letting him hold me up as my eyes fell closed. "East, I . . . ." My ability to speak and form coherent sentences disappeared as he toyed with me, playing me with those expert fingers.

"Come." His gravelly voice tickled my skin as two of his fingers slid inside. "Come on my fingers."

I managed a nod before a surge of heat spread through my limbs. Ecstasy consumed every nerve ending until I bucked against his hand and detonated. My orgasm was hard and fast and so fucking satisfying. I was still riding the high when he slid both his hands free and spun me around, catching me before I could topple to the floor.

Easton shuffled me backward until my back hit the wall. He took my chin in a hand and tipped it up, holding me exactly where he wanted me as his mouth crashed onto mine.

My palm flattened against his zipper, rubbing his arousal through the denim. He groaned down my throat, pressing deeper into my touch. Then his hand released my jaw so he could use both hands to strip the jeans off my hips.

I kicked them off as he took a fistful of my lace panties and shredded them off my body.

"Open it." He nodded to the condom I'd managed to keep in my fingers. Then the sound of metal scraping metal filled my ears as he flicked the clasp on his oval belt buckle. The sound of his zipper opening came next.

"Holy fuck." My eyes bulged as his thick length bobbed free. He'd been wearing nothing under those jeans the entire time. No boxers or briefs. Just Easton Greer going commando as he'd sat at my small table eating spaghetti.

Too distracted by the sight of his cock, I nearly dropped the condom. He snatched it from me before it fell from my fingers and put the foil between his teeth to rip it open and sheath himself.

Then I was up, his hands lifting me in the air with a swift bounce before he spread my legs wide and thrust inside.

"Ah," I gasped, stretching around him as he fell forward, cursing and groaning into my neck. "Move."

He shook his head.

"East, move." I dug my nails into his back, clawing through his shirt. That earned me a nip on my jaw as he slid out only to push inside again, this time going even deeper.

My entire body shivered.

"Fuck, that feels good."

I hummed my agreement as he slid in and out once more.

We moved in tandem, his hips rolling forward as I leveraged the wall to meet his strokes. The sound of slapping skin and labored breathing filled the room. He kept his eyes locked on mine, that intense gaze boring into mine with every move. Easton held me captive, pinned and at his mercy.

The build of my second orgasm was slower than the first, but it didn't take Easton long to bring me to the breaking point. Sparks pooled and I felt—I felt everything—as I toppled over the edge. The explosion was devastating. He shattered me completely, leaving me in tiny pieces that would never fit together in the same way again.

"Christ, Gem," he whispered, leaning into me as I clenched around him, pulse after endless pulse, until he moaned into my ear and shuddered with his own release.

I collapsed into him as we both came down, my arms limp and boneless as I gave him my weight. My ponytail had come loose and my hair was draped around us. My ankles were locked around his back and my cashmere sweater was likely ruined from this encounter with a log wall.

Much like with my French lace panties, I couldn't find the energy to care.

With a kiss to my temple, Easton eased me to my feet, holding my elbow as I found my balance. "Good?"

I nodded and shoved my hair out of my face. "I'm good."

"Be back." He pulled his jeans up to cover his ass, the zipper and the belt hanging loose, as he disappeared down the hallway to the bathroom.

I blinked away the fog and searched for my jeans. I stepped into them and had them buttoned as he emerged.

Jeans zipped. Belt fastened. Shirt tucked.

His eyes flickered between me and the door.

"So . . ." I picked up the scrap of fabric formerly known as my underwear.

"I'm not good at this," he admitted, raking a hand through the hair I'd tousled at some point. "The after."

The after? Oh. After a hookup. *Right.*

"Then let's skip it. Goodnight, Easton."

He sighed and walked toward the door, hesitating for a moment like he was going to come over and kiss me. But he didn't. He twisted the knob, tipped his chin and said, "Goodnight, Gemma."

"HEY." I knocked on Katherine's open office door.

"Hey. Are you done for today?"

"Yep." I took my usual chair, the one I sat in every afternoon at this time. "My relief has arrived."

Annabeth had hired a local high school girl to work the desk after school each evening. It was a great hire for the long-term resort staff. For me, it meant that after four o'clock, I had nothing to do but go to the cabin. Alone.

"Want to have dinner?" I asked.

"I can't tonight." Katherine rolled her eyes. "I have a town council meeting."

"Well, look at you. You're on the town council."

She shrugged. "I took a seat after Liddy stepped down last year. Rain check?"

"Sure." I smiled, wishing I had her jam-packed schedule like the one I used to have in Boston.

Because if I had meetings and appointments each night, I wouldn't go home and dwell on the fact that I'd had sex with Easton last night. I'd already spent the day overthinking it.

What had I been thinking? How was I supposed to be around him now? How was I supposed to act during family dinner or when he came into the lodge or when I ran into him outside?

Had that just been another one of his hookups? Did he do that with other people at the resort? There were some pretty girls who worked here.

I'd seen them coming and going as they worked. In a way, they reminded me of Katherine, Londyn and me at that stage. Had any of them caught Easton's eye? Had any of them begged him for a riding lesson?

Bitches.

"Okay, what's wrong?" Katherine asked.

I blinked. "Huh?"

"I don't know where you were right then, but the look on your face was murderous."

I groaned and folded forward, dropping my face into my hands. "I had sex with Easton."

"What?" Katherine shrieked. "When?"

"Last night." I cringed. "And . . . eleven years ago."

"Sit up and spill."

I obeyed. "He came over last night to deliver firewood. I asked him to stay for dinner and . . . sex." Incredible. Unforgettable. Wild sex.

"You're blushing, Gemma," she teased.

I covered my cheeks with my hands. "He's . . . well, you've seen him. He's gorgeous and infuriating and overwhelming."

"So last night. What about eleven years ago?"

"It was the night before I left. He was living in one of the apartments beside the staff quarters, remember?"

"Yeah. I took his apartment when he moved out." She scrunched up her nose. "Eww. You had sex in my bed."

I giggled. "Sorry."

She waved it off. "Continue."

"I was outside watching the sunset. And he found me."

Easton hadn't known it at the time, but I'd been outside watching the sunset and memorizing the line of the mountains since I'd been ready to leave. And for the first time, he hadn't given me a chin jerk and kept on walking. He'd stopped, leaned against the same fence rail, and stared at the horizon.

We hadn't talked much. He'd asked me if I liked it here.

I'd told him the truth.

Yes.

I'd always loved the Greer Ranch.

But that hadn't stopped me from leaving.

"We stayed outside until after sunset. When he escorted me inside, he had this look. Like he wanted to invite me into his room, but he wasn't sure I'd say yes. It was the first time I'd seen just a tiny crack in that confidence of his. So I kissed him."

I'd spent the night in his bed until he'd fallen asleep, and then I'd snuck out. Before the sunrise, I'd walked the miles to the highway and had hitchhiked my way to Missoula. Then I'd hopped on a bus and left for Boston.

"That explains why he was such a grumpy bastard those months after you left," Katherine said. "I always thought it was because he was mad at you on my behalf. Which was sort of sweet, in a big brother way."

"Oh, I'm sure that was part of it too. He loves you."

"Like a sister. They all love me like a sister." The light dimmed in her eyes for a split second before a smile spread across her pretty face. "Is this a bad time to remind you that we have a no-fraternization policy for employees?"

I picked up a paperclip from her desk and threw it at her head. "You're not helping!"

She laughed. "Sorry. What are you going to do about him?"

"I have no idea. He's . . . complicated."

The attraction between us was this steady charge, this undercurrent impossible to ignore. If we weren't at each other's throats, fighting, it was futile and well . . . that had led to us fucking against the cabin wall.

"What would you do?" I asked.

"Talk to him. He's dealing with a lot right now and he's supposed to be in charge, but people forget to *talk* to him. They forget to ask what he thinks or how he feels."

I loved my friend. And I loved her even more for seeing Easton's struggles when everyone else around here seemed oblivious.

It wasn't my place to decide how to proceed after last night—Katherine was right. I'd made that decision last time by leaving and had taken Easton's choice away.

I wouldn't make the same mistake twice.

So three hours later, I drove the Cadillac to his house.

It was dark outside because I'd waited until after dinner before getting in my car. I hadn't wanted to get here and have him still be working somewhere on the ranch. Katherine had written down directions to his place, and I'd held the sticky note in one hand while I drove with the other.

I'd had to drive away from the lodge and across the highway, to a section of the Greers' property that wasn't used for the resort. This was pure ranch country with open meadows bordered by groves of trees and barbed wire fences. The gravel road to his home followed a wandering stream, and when his house came into view, it stole my breath.

The house was centered in the field with the mountains rising up in the distance. The roofline matched almost exactly to the highest peak on the horizon. Golden light flooded through the abundant windows, beckoning me closer. The umber wood siding matched the other buildings on the ranch.

The home, commanding in size and stature, made a bold statement yet fit absolutely in its natural surroundings. It was exactly what I'd expected from Easton, yet surprising at the same time because of its sheer elegance.

The garage door was open as I pulled into the driveway and Easton came outside with a red rag in his grip.

My heart fluttered, seeing him in a pair of jeans and simple white T-shirt. Stubble dusted his jaw and his hair was mussed from a long day's work. A dull throb pulsed between my legs at the sight of him. Damn, he was hot.

Was he wearing boxers today? Or was he going commando again?

208

I'd come here with the intention of talking and talking only, but if he showed even the slightest interest, I was going to break that plan.

I sat in my car, parked, but unable to shut it off and get out. I simply stared at him through the windshield.

And he stared back.

Easton broke first, a frown crossing his handsome face as he planted his fists on his hips in a silent ultimatum. Was I coming or going?

Coming.

I sucked in a deep breath and shut off the car, stepping outside into the cold and hurrying toward the garage. "Hey."

He looked me up and down. "Where's your coat?"

"I need to buy one. I was supposed to be in California in October, not Montana."

He stomped into the garage and hit the button to close the door behind us. "What are you doing here?"

"I thought we'd better talk about last night."

"Why?"

Why? Seriously? "Because I thought you might have an opinion about what happened and you're the one who said he wished other people would consider his opinions. But hey, if I'm wrong and you just want to forget it ever happened and go back to treating me like shit beneath your boot, I'll stay out of your way until Christmas."

I wanted to turn and march to my car, but he'd trapped me inside. The only way out of the garage was through the button at his back, so I crossed my arms and shot him my best glare.

He ran a hand through that thick hair, then stalked my way.

I'd worn a scarf over the only coat I'd packed—a black leather jacket. Easton unwrapped the scarf from my neck. "Sorry."

"I'm not here to fight with you."

Easton tossed the scarf on the cement floor. It was as clean as the floor in the cabin. His hands skimmed my arms, sliding over the buttery Italian leather, until they came to my face. "I don't want to fight either."

His mouth dropped to mine, erasing the trace of irritation and replacing it with a burning lust that had me pushing the hem of his shirt above his ribs.

"Inside," I panted against his lips, tugging his belt buckle free. I wanted him in a bed and the chance to do this all night long.

Easton shook his head and walked me to the workbench that ran the length of the garage. I opened my mouth to protest, but then I was lost in an oblivion of Easton's mouth and hands and body. When I walked out of the garage an hour later on wobbly legs, I had a smile on my face, his scent on my skin and his taste on my tongue.

I was sated. For the first time in years, I didn't feel the urge to move on to the next thing. I didn't have work or a task to tackle. I could just enjoy the moment.

And I did, for the first five minutes of my drive home. Then I replayed the night. And last night.

Easton and I had fucked twice. Hard. Both times, he'd screwed me on the closest available surface. Maybe he'd been as desperate for me as I'd been for him.

Or maybe my mother had been right from the start.

Maybe I would always be just another cheap thrill.

10

GEMMA

AVOIDING a man who worked and lived in the same place you did wasn't an easy feat, but somehow, I'd managed to dodge Easton for three days.

Or maybe he'd been dodging me.

Other than a glimpse of him riding Jigsaw away from the stables yesterday, I hadn't seen hide nor hair of him since the night I'd driven away from his house. He'd looked incredible on that horse. His breath had billowed in a cloud around him—so had Jigsaw's—and he'd been wearing a heavy canvas coat, cowboy hat with the brim tipped low and leather chaps laced up his long legs.

Easton had perfected sexy, mysterious cowboy. The man belonged on the cover of a romance novel—shirtless, of course.

His mouthwatering appeal was the reason avoidance had become necessary.

When he was around, I couldn't think clearly and I was in need of some unmuddied thinking.

Either I could lean into this, soak him up until it was time to move on, or I ended it now.

My brain was lobbying for option two. It would be easy to retreat to the robot I'd been in Boston. But my heart was struggling to get on board. Because damn it, here I was, living, breathing and feeling for the first time in a long time, and it was a rush.

Then again, a numb heart didn't hurt when it was broken.

It was Friday and the Greers were expecting me for family dinner, but the idea of sitting beside Easton, pretending that I hadn't had him inside me twice this week . . . well, that wasn't an option.

So I'd begged Katherine to make my excuses and because Carol was the type to come track me down at the cabin, I'd done what all grown-ups would do.

I got the hell off Greer property.

The moment my shift at the lodge had ended, I climbed in the Cadillac and drove into Clear River. Shopping at the small, local grocery store hadn't taken me as long as I'd hoped. When there were only seven aisles, it didn't take a long time to go up and down each. Twice.

So after loading up my foodstuffs, I'd decided to stop for a drink at the Clear River Bar.

I wasn't the only one in need of a cocktail, judging by the crowded parking lot.

Trucks of varying makes and models had taken all but three open spaces. I eased the Cadillac in between a white Ford and a filthy black Chevy, then got out and hit the locks. A chocolate lab sitting shotgun in the Chevy stared me down as country music filled the air. The bar's windows were crowded with neon beer signs, and the red tin siding had faded under years of brutal sunshine. A plastic, camo banner had been tied to the front of the building, advertising HUNTERS WELCOME in bright orange letters.

The smell of beer and stale cigarettes assaulted my nostrils when I opened the door and my eyes took a few moments to adjust to the dim light. Conversation seemed to halt as the whole room turned in their stools and chairs.

The bar was situated along one side of the room, and as I crossed the scuffed tile floor, heading for one of the only empty stools, most faces followed my path. I'd never felt so many eyes on my ass in my life.

Maybe a drink was a mistake.

It was only when I was on a stool, ass hidden, that the dull drum of conversation resumed, merging with the jukebox's music from the corner.

"What can I get you?" the bartender asked, setting out a paper coaster. Besides me, she was the only female in the room.

"Do you have wine?"

She looked me up and down, leaning in to lower her voice. "Were you looking for the resort? Because I think you might be lost."

"Nope, not headed for the resort."

"Then you'll be disappointed. All I have is a box of Franzia, vintage last month."

I laughed. "Then how about a vodka soda with lemon?"

"That I can handle." She smiled, then went to the other end of the bar, talking to a few other patrons while she mixed my drink. When she brought it back, she snagged a menu off the stack. "Cheeseburgers are on special tonight if you're hungry."

"Sold."

"Fries?"

I nodded. "Please."

"You got it." She returned to her end of the bar, leaving me alone.

The two guys next to me were wrapped up in their conversation about politics and paid me no attention as I twirled the red straw in my glass, clinking the ice cubes and poking the lemon wedge. I sipped my drink slowly as I took in the room.

A lot of eyes flickered my way but none lingered too long. The man on the stool exactly opposite mine finished his beer, shook hands with the guy at his side, then waved goodbye to the bartender. As he opened the door to leave, another figure appeared beyond him.

His cowboy hat dipped as he exchanged greetings, then my stomach dropped.

Because I knew that hat.

Son of a bitch. How was I supposed to avoid Easton in a bar this size? Wasn't he supposed to be at dinner?

He walked inside, scanning the room and lifting a hand to wave at a few tables. Then he walked to the bar, taking off his hat as he pulled out the stool that had just been vacated. He greeted the guy directly on his left, then grinned at the bartender as she approached.

Easton's gaze drifted past her and when he spotted me, the grin dropped.

Ouch.

I lifted my glass, giving him a silent salute.

Easton acknowledged me with a single nod.

My heart was in my throat as I took another drink, wishing I hadn't ordered that cheeseburger. Wishing I was in any other seat than this where I had no choice but see him when I faced forward.

How was I supposed to avoid that strong jaw and those dark, dreamy eyes when they were *right there*?

"Here you go." The bartender emerged from the kitchen with a plastic basket lined with parchment paper. At least I wouldn't have to wait long for my meal. The cheeseburger was bigger than my face and the heap of fries was the equivalent of three extra-large potatoes. "Hope you're hungry."

I had been. "Thanks."

I cut the burger in half as she returned to her post, leaning a hip against the bar as she focused all her attention on one man.

Easton.

I kept my eyes on my meal, but the claw of jealousy scraped deeper every time I heard her laugh carry over the music. Or when I'd catch his smile from the corner of my eye. I was chewing with rabid fury when she leaned in closer to whisper something in his ear.

He laughed. She laughed.

She smiled. He smiled.

I was most definitely not laughing or smiling.

No, I was his latest conquest, and he'd waited a whole three days before moving on to someone else. Or maybe go back for another round with a former lover.

She was gorgeous and fresh faced. Her blond hair brushed the tops of her shoulders in effortless, beach waves. Her tee dipped low enough to show a hint of cleavage and she had the perfect hourglass figure, curves I'd only dreamt of having.

But it was her smile that I envied most. It was carefree and effortless. A pretty smile. One that made Easton smile too, wider than I'd seen since arriving in Montana.

He didn't smile around me, not like that. And as I'd suspected, it was devastating.

"Hey, sweetheart."

I jerked, forcing my eyes away from Easton and the bartender as a man leaned against the bar at my side.

"How's it going?" he asked.

"Fantastic," I deadpanned, not in the mood to deal with stranger small talk and a guy who likely saw me as fresh meat.

He'd brought a beer along from wherever he'd emerged and tipped it to his lips as he grinned. "New in town or just visiting."

"Visiting." I ate another bite, busying my mouth so I didn't have to talk, and cast a glance toward Easton.

His gaze was waiting, the tension in his jaw visible as he squeezed his own beer bottle to death.

For a moment, I thought he might come over, but then the bartender stood in front of him, giving Easton an eye-level shot of her generous breasts.

My appetite vanished and I tossed the uneaten portion of my burger into the tray, wiping my hands and lips with a napkin. Then I dove for my wallet, ripping out a hundred-dollar bill and slapping it on the bar.

I wasn't sure how much a burger and a cocktail cost in Clear River, Montana, but that should cover it.

"Leaving already?" the man asked.

Not bothering with the obvious answer, I slipped the strap of my purse over my shoulder and—eyes forward—I walked out of the bar and into the fading evening light.

In a way, I should be happy he'd come to the bar. That he'd flirted with another woman in front of me. I'd been conflicted over what to do with Easton, but tonight had been eye-opening.

This was not the place for me.

Easton was not the man for me. As much as I liked my little cabin, I didn't fit here. He'd been right all along.

I didn't fit.

Spending three months here wouldn't change that fact. Bet or not, I was leaving. He could gloat to his family while I was a thousand miles south, enjoying some California sunshine.

I'd stick around long enough to spend a few more nights with Katherine. But as soon as the groceries in my trunk were gone, so was I.

The light was nearly gone by the time I made it home to the cabin. The stars were out in full force and the temperature was dropping fast. Before unloading the Cadillac, I made a fire to warm up the cabin, then I busied myself with putting groceries away.

There was enough food here for a week. I'd invite Katherine over as often as possible and the two of us would have a bit more time together before I hit the road. If I was lucky, the weather would hold out and I wouldn't get snowed in.

By the time the groceries were unloaded, the cabin was toasty warm and I poured myself a hearty glass of wine, lifting my glass to the empty room. "Cheers to another week. And a lonely Friday night."

Tears flooded my eyes, and before I could pull them in, I was crying off my makeup.

This wasn't why I'd come to Montana. This wasn't why I'd started this journey.

I wanted to feel, but this? *No, thank you.*

But the dam had broken and there was no holding back the flood. Drops of ugly poured from my body in a stream of uncontrollable tears and broken sobs.

I stood there, in the middle of the room with my wine sloshing over the rim of my glass and cried.

I cried for the life I'd worked so hard to build. The life that had meant so fucking much to me three months ago. The life I'd left behind.

Selling the company and leaving Boston hadn't been a mistake, but for the first time, I mourned. Because twelve million dollars in the bank hadn't made me any less alone.

The tears came faster. The sobs wracked harder. My knees were seconds from giving way, collapsing me into a pathetic puddle, when two arms wrapped around me and kept me from falling.

Easton pinned me to his chest, holding me with one arm as he took the wine from my hand and set it on the table beside us. Then he let me soak the front of his green shirt with my tears.

I held tight, letting him keep me standing, because I couldn't seem to pull it together. No matter how many deep breaths I sucked in through my nose, they exhaled in a mess. Until finally, minutes later, one of them stuck. Then another. And the tears just . . . ran out.

Even when I stopped crying, Easton didn't let me go.

"I'm okay." I pushed him away and wiped my face dry, turning my back to him because he'd witnessed rock bottom. "Sorry."

"What was that, Gem?"

"Nothing." I waved him off. "What are you doing here?"

"You left the bar upset."

Honestly, I was surprised he'd noticed. And that he'd come to check on me. Or maybe he was here for a hookup. Regardless, I was such a train wreck that I hadn't even heard him drive up. "It's nothing. Sometimes women cry."

"Bullshit. What the hell is going on?"

"Nothing. It's been a long week."

"Gemma." He took my elbow and spun me to face him.

"What!" I batted his hand away. "It's nothing."

He stood there, unwavering, and leveled me with a look that said he had no intention of leaving until he got his answer.

The stubborn ass. "You were flirting with the bartender."

"Liz?" He barked a laugh. "I don't flirt with Liz. She's been my friend since we were in diapers."

"That was flirting. You smiled at her. You were laughing and whispering."

"Yeah, she told me the guy three seats down smelled like cheese. I laughed because she's funny and easy to hang out with."

Long-time friend or not, I didn't want to hear about how much he enjoyed another woman's company. "You don't laugh with me."

"You're not funny."

I poked him in the pec. "I'm being serious."

He scowled and rubbed the spot where I'd jabbed him. "So am I. Say something funny and I'll laugh."

"But I'm not funny." The tears came again and this time, they just made me angry. "Goddamn it!"

He shook his head, coming closer as I furiously wiped my eyes dry. "You were jealous."

"Yes," I admitted. "I have some issues when it comes to men."

"Let's get one thing straight." He clasped my shoulders, looming and waiting until he had my undivided attention. "There are no *men*. There's one man. Me. And if you have an issue with me, we'll sure as fuck talk it through."

I dropped my head into my hands, the shame no doubt showing on my face. "Sorry."

Easton took my wrists and pulled them away. "Should we talk about why you've been avoiding me this week?"

"You wouldn't take me to your bed." Apparently, there was no stopping the truth flood tonight.

"Huh?"

"You screwed me against the wall." I flicked my wrist, motioning to said wall. "And made me come on that bench in your garage."

"Three times."

"Three times." I rolled my eyes. "But you wouldn't take me to your bedroom."

He shook his head, blinking as he tried to make heads or tails of my nonsense. I didn't blame him for the confused look on his face.

"Ugh. Never mind." I threw my hands in the air. "I'm losing my fucking mind. Welcome to the mixed-up world of Gemma Lane. This actually feels like your fault. What are you doing to me?"

"The same thing you're doing to me," he grumbled. "Driving me fucking insane."

I laughed.

It wasn't funny but it was funny.

"I worked so hard to not be crazy. To not be my mother. I left her house and decided I would never be out of control again. I'd prove that I was better. So I worked hard and showed the world—myself—that I would never be her. I succeeded. I am a millionaire. I am in control of my destiny, and I am not the person she tried to make me. I am not *her*."

"You're not her."

I shook my head. "No."

There was a comfort in saying it out loud. And for the moment, that was enough to soothe some of my jagged edges.

Mortifying as it was, I was glad the person here to witness it was Easton.

"I'm sorry," I said again. "Forget about all of this. Please."

"I can't do that." He lifted his hand and cupped my cheek. "You said you don't want to talk about it. I get that. But this is the second time you've cracked the door to your past, darlin'. I think it's time to open up and let me in."

"It doesn't matter. The whole point of this rant is that I might be having a crazy moment, but my mother was certifiably insane. No one rescued me from her. So I rescued myself. And part of that meant shutting out the world. But here things are so . . . different. I can't hide from you in my work. I don't have work. I wanted to feel things and here I am, feeling again. It's an adjustment."

He studied my face, his eyes softening. "That goes both ways. You're all I've thought about for three days and I know the smartest thing for me to do would be to walk out that door. But . . ."

"But what?" I whispered as his thumb traced a line of tingles on my skin.

"But I'm going to take you into the bedroom and make sure you know that the reason I fucked you against that wall and in my garage was not because you don't deserve the bedroom." He bent and brushed his lips against mine. "But because when it comes to you, I have no control."

11

EASTON

"Morning, boss," Rory called from the hayloft before tossing a bale down. "You're here early."

"Rory, what are you doing here?"

"Oh, uh, Johnson called to see if I'd cover his shift today. He's sick or something."

Sick, my ass. Johnson didn't like Saturday mornings because he was usually at the bar too late on Friday nights. He'd probably shown up not long after I'd left to chase Gemma last night, then stayed until Liz kicked him out at two. This was the second time in a month I'd come to the stables on a Saturday expecting to see him and finding Rory instead.

If Johnson wasn't careful, I was going to fire him and give Rory a hefty raise.

Rory was due one anyway. He showed up on time and worked hard. His attitude was unmatched. Hell, it was better than mine.

"When you're done up there, come on into my office."

"All right." He nodded and tossed down another bale.

I left him to his work and retreated to my office. The room was cold, so I turned up the baseboard heaters before shrugging off my coat. Then I eased the door closed to keep the warmth inside and settled in behind my desk.

Doing paperwork and checking emails was not my favorite task, let alone on a Saturday morning before seven, but after slipping out of Gemma's bed this morning, I hadn't wanted to go home.

She'd been out cold, her hair spread across the pillow and her face burrowed under the covers. I'd lit a fire to warm up the cabin, then driven away with the image of her sleeping peacefully in my mind.

Last night had been intense. Finding her sobbing, breaking down, had destroyed me. I knew she'd been embarrassed, not that there was anything to be ashamed of. And as much as I'd wanted to dive deeper into her past, the moment I'd kissed her, the chance to talk had flown out the window.

The two of us had spent the night exploring each other's bodies and the sex had been just as intense. She met my desire with a raging passion of her own.

That woman had me twisted as tight as the braid on a bullwhip.

So this morning, I escaped to the stables because the distraction of work might be my only hope of getting my head on straight.

After the night Gemma had driven out to my house, I'd given her some space, not wanting to come on too strong. Last night, I'd begged out of family dinner because I hadn't wanted to make her uncomfortable in front of my family.

Maybe giving her that space had been a mistake.

But I was glad I'd found her at the bar.

Had I been flirting with Liz? I'd known her since we were kids. Her family was as local to this valley as mine. She was my friend. We'd shared a fumbling kiss sometime during middle school, but besides that, our relationship had always been platonic.

Liz touched my arm a lot, and she always hung out near my end of the bar when I was in, but did she have feelings for me?

No. No way. Liz didn't act anything like a woman who wanted me in her bed. She was a friend. Nothing more.

Gemma was the only woman who'd be tangled in my sheets.

She put on such a strong façade. She was fearless and wild. But beneath it all, she was scared. Of me. Of her future. She hid her fears well, but last night, I'd been given a glimpse. Would she run from those fears? Or would she stay here and face them?

Would she let me in?

Rory appeared in the door's window and I waved him inside. He shrugged off the Carhartt coat he'd been wearing and hung it on the hook beside my own.

"Thanks for coming in today," I said.

"No problem. I like the hours."

I steepled my fingers in front of my chin and took a long look at the boy. Though he wasn't really a boy anymore. Maybe because I'd seen him grow up, I still saw him as the kid who'd chased Mom's border collie, Max, around the yard. But Rory stood nearly as tall as me at six three and if he kept working like he did, he'd fill out his lanky frame.

"I'm giving you a raise."

His jaw dropped. "You are?"

"An extra two dollars an hour." There was no need to wait on his raise. He'd earned it. And it was time to give him more responsibilities too. "I want you to start shadowing Cash in the afternoons when he's not on a ride. You're a natural with horses but I want you to get more experience with breaking the younger animals."

If this new horse facility worked out, Rory would be a good asset for Cash. It would suck to lose him here, but I wasn't going to cost the kid an opportunity at a better job because hiring stable hands was a pain in my ass.

"Okay." A grin stretched across his face. "You got it."

"Good. Focus on the stables this morning. Then I'd like you to take Oreo out for a long ride. Work him hard. Cash said he was a real shit the other day for one of the guests. Maybe he just needs to burn some energy and get a reminder about who's in charge."

"Will do." Rory stood from the chair and grabbed his coat but paused as he opened the door. "Thanks, Easton. I sure do appreciate the raise. And the opportunity."

"You've earned it."

He nodded, closing the door behind him and leaving me to my emails. There wasn't much for me to do on a regular basis in the office. Thankfully, our bookkeeper made sure the bills and employees were paid. It allowed me to be out where I needed to be, on the land with the animals and with the staff.

But there were days when desk work was unavoidable. The schedule needed to be drafted for next month so I could send it to Katherine. We'd have a three-hour meeting to pair my staff with her resort activities and guest needs. Then I'd fill in gaps to make sure all the ranch work was covered.

I rolled up my sleeves and dove in, putting in the couple of hours necessary to work it through, while I ate a few granola bars I kept stashed in my desk. After the schedule was penciled into the calendar, I fired up my computer and scrolled through the emails I'd been ignoring for the last week.

Most were deleted and I'd almost cleared through everything when the ding of an incoming message filled the room.

It was an email from my Realtor and I clicked it immediately to read the message.

"Yes." I fist-pumped and double-clicked the attachment. It was the same moment my phone rang. "Hey," I answered. "I just opened your email."

"Good," she said. "I wanted to call and make sure it came through and you didn't have any questions on the buy-sell."

"Seems straightforward." The sellers had accepted my offer with a few reasonable contingencies. Which meant it was time to tell my family what I'd been doing and hope they didn't freak the hell out that I'd done it behind their backs. "I'll get it signed today and sent back."

"Sounds good. Thanks, Easton. And congratulations."

"Thanks." I hung up and read the agreement in detail.

The door to my office opened and I glanced up, expecting Rory.

But it was Gemma leaning against the frame. "So this is where you're hiding?"

I frowned. "Where is your coat?"

"This is my coat." She gestured to the black leather jacket she'd worn to my house. It wasn't thick enough or warm enough for the weather.

"Here." I stood up and took a flannel off the hooks. It would be too big for her, but at least it would add another layer of warmth.

"Is this your way of telling me to get out?" She arched an eyebrow as I handed her the flannel.

"No." My head was still a mess when it came to her and work hadn't helped, but I wouldn't chase her away. She looked too beautiful, her cheeks rosy from the chill outside, and her lips a darker shade of natural pink from my kisses last night.

She came into the office, closing the door behind her and took the chair opposite my desk. "You left without waking me this morning."

"Is that why you're here?"

"Yes." She took a deep breath. "I owe you another apology for last night. I unloaded a lot on you and I'm sorry. I hate that you saw me cry."

This woman. She pretended to have it all together. Except no one did. When would she realize she didn't need to pretend for me?

"It's fine, Gemma."

"It's really not. I apologize for the drama." She folded her hands in her lap, keeping her expression neutral and her posture poised. Her hair was styled, curled in loose waves that fell over her shoulders and down her back. Her eyes were lined with black and shaded with a soft glimmer.

She looked gorgeous this morning. Chic.

Guarded.

Goddamn it. She really was driving me fucking insane. I shook my head, annoyed and frustrated. "Don't. Just . . . stop."

"Stop what?"

"Stop apologizing," I barked. "I don't want a fucking apology."

"Never mind." She held up her hands and stood from the chair, leaving the flannel draped over the arm. "I'll let you get back to work. Clearly, I'm bothering you."

She was two steps out the door when I shot out of my chair and chased her down.

"Oh no, you don't." I gripped her elbow and spun her to face me. "You don't get to run away from me."

"You just snapped at me." She threw an arm toward the office. "I'm not running away. I'm letting you cool off."

"Well, I don't want to cool off. I don't give a damn about the drama. For once, it was nice to see *you*. The real you without all of"—I flung my wrist, motioning up and down her body—"this."

"Clothes? Pretty sure you saw me without all my clothes last night."

"No." I frowned. "With the armor."

"Oh."

"Be real with me." I inched closer, bringing my hands to her shoulders. "If no one else, be real with me."

She dropped her gaze. "I don't know how."

"Yes, you do." I hooked a finger under her chin, tipping it up. "You were last night."

"That was me having a breakdown, then practically begging you to take me to bed. And this morning, I woke up alone. Not that I blame you for sneaking out. If I were you, I wouldn't want to deal with my mess either."

"Now hold up. Me leaving this morning had nothing to do with you crying last night." She'd been all too tempting naked in that bed. The reason I'd left was definitely not because she'd let her guard down.

"Sure," she said, dryly.

"It's the truth. I left this morning because I'm doing my best to keep some distance from you, Gemma."

Another woman might have gotten pissed at me for that comment. But not Gemma. Her eyes softened and the tension in her shoulders fell away. "Can I make another confession?"

I nodded.

"You make me feel things."

"You told me last night. Isn't that what you wanted?"

"Yes," she whispered. "But that doesn't make it any less terrifying."

She had nothing to fear when it came to me. There wasn't a thing she could do that would make me think less of her, make me judge her or make me dislike her.

Except leave again without a goodbye.

"Can I make a confession?"

She nodded. "Yes."

"I'm scared to get too close to you because I know you're eventually going to leave." It was only a matter of time.

"Where does that leave us?" she asked, not denying what we both knew was the inevitable.

I shrugged. "I don't have a damn clue. I wish I could say I'd steer clear of you and that cabin and we could call this thing quits. But I won't."

"I don't want you to steer clear of me and the cabin, and I don't want to call this quits. What if we kept things casual?"

"Great theory. But you have to know that the minute my mother or my grandmother sees us paired together, casual is out the window."

I wouldn't put it past Grandma to move Gemma into my house, making up some bullshit excuse that the cabin was too cold or too isolated or too small for a single woman in the winter.

"Then let's keep it between us," she said. "Except I already told Katherine."

"She's the only person on this ranch who can keep a secret."

"Then it's settled." Gemma winked, then took a step away. "See you around."

"What?" I tried to catch her but she was already moving backward. "You're leaving?"

"Aren't you working?"

"Yeah." But I didn't want her to go. It was Saturday and instead of sitting behind my desk, I wanted to spend some time with her. "Come with me. I want to show you something."

She gave me a curious glance, but when I turned and marched to the office to get my truck keys, coat and her flannel, she followed.

Gemma played along, not peppering me with questions as I escorted her to my truck. She sat quietly in the passenger seat, her expression relaxed as we drove away from the stables and to the soon-to-be site of the Greer Ranch's latest expansion.

When I pulled over to the edge of the gravel road that ran the length of the new property, she looked around and asked, "What am I looking at?"

"See that right there?" I pointed to the open field out her window and the large barn in the distance. "I just bought it."

"Nice. This is a pretty spot."

Pretty and the setup for the facility was perfect with the flat, wide fields. "My Realtor called me right before you came into the office and told me the buyers accepted my offer. You're the first person I've told."

"Lucky timing on my part."

"No, not just today," I corrected. "At all. I didn't tell anyone I was putting in an offer."

Her eyes widened. "No one?"

"Nope."

The magnitude of what I'd done settled on my shoulders. I'd been so desperate to make a decision without debate or counsel that I'd bought land in secret. My plan was to use the ranch's capital reserves to pay the three-point-one-million-dollar price tag. The money was there and at my discretion. But I should have told my family before making this big a commitment.

Shit. What did that say about my trust in them? Maybe the reason they questioned my decisions and stayed so in the loop was because they feared I'd shut them out.

Which, ironically, I had.

"Was that stupid?" I asked Gemma.

"What will you use it for?"

"I want to expand the horse operation. We're known around the area for our stock. We have some of the best genetics but mostly, we have skill. Cash is one of the best horse trainers around. He's wasted on guest activities."

A smile tugged at her mouth. "So you bought this place for your brother?"

"Partly. And because my gut says it will be a success. Worst case, we use the land for more pasture and expand our cattle operation."

"You did your homework?"

"I did." I had profit and loss projections at my home office and every worst-case scenario plotted out.

"Then no. I don't think this was stupid." She turned to the window again, surveying the frozen ground.

The ice crystals clung to the flaxen grass, reflecting the bright morning sun. The sky stretched powder blue above us, wrapping around the snow-capped mountains rising up around us.

And Gemma seemed to soak it all in. She seemed at ease this morning. She looked comfortable in that seat, wearing my flannel and not minding the smell of dirt and hay that, no matter how many times I cleaned this truck, was permanent.

I'd seen plenty of people come and go from the ranch. It was easy to pick out the guests who'd return on another vacation. Because Montana's rugged and raw landscape called to something deeper in their soul.

They'd found peace here.

It wasn't for everyone but it was in Gemma. How could she not know that she fit here?

Maybe she needed more time. Maybe she needed to see more than the lodge and the cabin.

"What are you doing today?" I asked.

"Nothing much. Why?"

I grinned. "Because I'm going to put you to work."

"OH, SWEET JESUS, THAT STINKS." Gemma gagged and plugged her nose. "I'm never eating eggs again."

I chuckled and placed another two eggs in the bucket she was carrying. "When I was a kid, Mom's favorite punishment was to make us clean out the chicken coop. I always made sure I was on my best behavior when it had been a couple of months between cleanings."

"I don't think I like chickens." She gave one of the hens perched a sideways glance. "How do I get the eggs from under her butt?"

"Just reach in there and take them."

"You do it."

"Don't be scared. Just brush her aside. She'll move."

"I can't. Please don't make me." Gemma turned her eyes up to me, those hazel orbs melting me into oblivion. How was I supposed to say no to that face?

"Fine." I moved the hen aside, sending her fluttering to the floor and took the eggs.

"Is that it?" Before I had a chance to agree, Gemma ducked out the door.

I shook my head, a smile on my face, and walked out to catch her.

The two of us had spent the morning working together. First, we'd driven to one of the pastures where we'd recently moved a group of about two hundred cows. We drove through, checking on them and looking for any that might be injured. Then we'd circled through an empty meadow that would be next on the rotation, making sure the fence was in good shape.

From there, I'd taken her to one of my favorite places on the ranch—the thousand acres situated directly behind my house.

I'd told her we were checking another section of fence when really, I'd just wanted to spend more time with her peaceful smile as we drove. To listen as she talked to me about nothing. To smell her perfume in my truck.

We'd returned to the lodge to grab a sandwich from the kitchen for lunch and had been halfway through eating when Mom had called to ask if I could gather the eggs from her chickens. She and Grandma had taken a spur-of-the-moment trip to Missoula to spend the day shopping. So Gemma and I had driven to Mom and Dad's place and I'd introduced Gemma to Mom's favorite animals.

"What's next?" Gemma asked after we put the egg basket inside the house where Mom would wash the eggs later.

A warmth spread through my chest that she hadn't asked for me to take her to the Cadillac at the stables. With every job we finished, she was eager for the next. "I was—"

A vehicle door slammed, and I turned away from Gemma, seeing Dad and Granddad climbing out of the truck parked next to mine.

"Hey, guys." Dad waved. "What are you up to?"

"Mom called and asked if we'd gather the eggs. She and Grandma went shopping in Missoula."

"Uh-oh." Dad fished his phone from his pocket and glanced at the screen. "Three missed calls. Guess that means I'd better buzz into the grocery store and have flowers waiting when she gets home."

Mom didn't need flowers. She wasn't the type to get spun up about him not answering his phone. He'd buy her flowers simply because it would make her smile.

"Coffee first." Granddad started up the steps to the front door, his silver travel mug in hand. "I need a refill. Later on, Easton, we need to talk about calving. Time to get a plan together."

"I have a plan." A detailed plan that outlined staff who'd take the daytime and night rotations to ensure we didn't lose any animals.

"Since when?" He paused on the step. "News to me."

"Me too." Dad nodded.

"Because you're retired. You're both retired." I blew out a long breath and fought to keep my cool. A fight would only ruin the good mood I'd had from a day with Gemma. "I respect you both and your opinions, you know that. I'm grateful that I have a chance to build on your success. Seven years ago, you put me in charge of this ranch. Please, trust me to do my job."

Granddad's face hardened and he opened his mouth, but Dad held up a hand and shot him a look to keep quiet. "You're doing a fine job, son. But it's hard to let go. You'll learn that one day."

"Understandable."

Dad nodded and followed as Granddad continued up the steps.

"Wait," I called. "If you have a minute, there's something I'd like to talk to you both about."

"We've got time. Come on in." Dad motioned me inside as he and Granddad disappeared inside.

"I'll wait in the truck," Gemma said. "Take your time."

225

"No. You should come in. I want you there when I tell them about the property." Maybe with her there, they wouldn't disown me. Yet.

"Are you sure? This seems like family business."

She fit into the family, something else I doubted she realized. Besides, it had been her advice to cut them both some slack. And I needed to do a better job of expressing my frustration. I needed to explain in a way they'd hear how I was feeling. Not exactly easy for a guy like me.

Arguing with Dad and Granddad had always been easier than the heart-to-hearts.

"I'm sure. Unless it would make you uncomfortable."

"Not at all." She gave me a reassuring smile and followed me inside. Then she sat at Mom and Dad's kitchen island, pride gleaming in her eyes, as I told my father and grandfather about the land I'd bought and explained my vision for the ranch.

I shocked the hell out of them.

Then they'd shocked the hell out of me.

They'd agreed it was the right opportunity for Cash and that the price for that chunk of land was too good to pass up. By the time we all walked outside—Gemma and me to drive to the stables to get her car while Dad took Granddad home, then went to buy Mom flowers—they were as excited about the expansion as I was.

And tonight, all three of us would tell Cash together.

I opened Gemma's door, holding it for her as she climbed inside, then waved to Dad and reversed my truck out of his driveway.

Gemma pulled her lips together, unsuccessfully hiding a smile as we drove toward the stables.

"Just say it."

She let loose that smile, stealing my breath and the last piece of my heart. "That wasn't so hard, was it?"

12

EASTON

"Oof," Gemma grunted.

I popped my head out the stall door to see what was happening. She had a bale lifted by the twine and was attempting to heft it toward Sprite's feeder. "Want some help?"

"No." She shot me a warning glare. "I can do this myself."

I held up my hands, chuckling as she shuffled across the floor.

A month ago, she could barely lift the bales an inch. Those square bales were little compared to the ones we used for the cattle. These we kept stocked in the loft for the horses when they weren't out to pasture. They weighed about seventy-five pounds and moving them around by the thin, red baling twine wasn't easy. But she'd been working with me every weekend in the stables and was becoming quite the hand.

Gemma's arms had grown stronger, so had her legs and her core. I knew because I'd seen the definition in her muscles sharpen on the nights I'd spent in her bed at the cabin.

When she had the bale in place, a proud smile stretched across her face as she took the Leatherman I'd lent her this morning from her pocket and cut the twine. Then she went about putting the hay in Sprite's feeder before taking a chunk to Pepsi's empty stall.

I'd let her do the feeding while I'd mucked out a few stalls, a job that I hadn't done in years because I'd hired hands to do it instead. But I'd let Rory go with some of the guys this morning instead of working in the stables. He was out helping prep for the afternoon wagon ride.

Over the past month, he'd spent a lot of Saturdays out with the other staffers. Not only because it gave him more exposure to other tasks, but because it allowed me the chance to work alone with Gemma.

If time with her meant mucking stalls, I'd called it a win.

Thanksgiving was approaching and the resort was at maximum occupancy. Mostly, we catered to hunting parties, but we had some guests who'd come here for a week getaway. We offered wagon rides where they could get a look at the Montana scenery while drinking cocoa or spiked cider. We had families flying in soon who'd stay here through the holiday, enjoying the lodge and the chalets and the renowned chef's food spread.

Meanwhile, my family would all eat together at Grandma and Grand-dad's place, as was tradition.

And Gemma and I would pretend, like we had been all month, that we were coworkers and friends at best.

If my family had any clue that I drove to Gemma's cabin a few nights a week, no one had mentioned it—which meant they didn't know. Besides my mother, the Greers weren't known for subtlety.

So Gemma and I were keeping up appearances when we crossed paths at the lodge during the week. I didn't stop to talk to her at the front desk. And on Saturdays, when everyone else was at home, this had become our routine. We'd eat Friday night family dinner, limiting conversation and pretending to ignore the other. Then I'd leave first but instead of going home, I'd go to the cabin. By the time Gemma arrived, I'd have a fire roaring and was usually naked in bed, waiting for her to join me. Saturday mornings we'd share a pot of coffee, then I'd come up with a handful of jobs for us to tackle together.

"Okay, I'm done." Gemma appeared at the stall door, brushing her gloves on her jeans.

It was cold outside, the air frozen and the ground covered in a fluffy layer of fresh snow. But there was a light sheen to her brow from working hard and her cheeks were flushed.

She'd shed her navy winter coat—one she'd ordered weeks ago after I'd lectured her relentlessly for an hour about Montana winters. Over her long-sleeved black tee, she'd shrugged on one of my flannels to keep her clothes from getting too dirty.

Her hair was up in a messy knot because she hadn't washed it this morning when we'd showered together. She wasn't wearing a lick of makeup and a few pieces of straw clung to her boots—another purchase I'd *encouraged* her to make.

Standing there, fresh and relaxed, Gemma stopped my heart. Damn, but she was beautiful.

"Have you ever thought about swapping the storage stall at the end of the stables to one in the middle?" she asked. "It would save foot traffic."

"Um . . . no." That stall at the end of the stables had always been used for storage. I couldn't think of a reason why—that's where it had always been. "But I will."

"Just an idea."

Gemma had been tossing out ideas all month. The way she did it was always more curious than intrusive. But she saw things in a way the rest of us didn't. And so far, I'd taken every single idea she'd pitched.

"What's next?" she asked.

"This." I fisted a handful of her flannel and dragged her into the empty stall, smashing my lips on hers as I pressed her against the wall.

She moaned, her gloved hands sliding up and around my neck as she opened her mouth to let me inside.

My tongue swept against hers and licked in long, smooth strokes. I leaned into her, my cock swelling as she gripped my ass and pulled me closer.

"Easton." My mother's voice resonated in the cavernous space.

I broke away from Gemma instantly, sucking in some air and wiping my lips clean.

Gemma pulled her lips in to hide a smile as she brought one finger to her lips and sunk down against the wall. Hiding.

I was sick of the fucking secrets.

"Easton?"

"Yeah," I called back, scowling at Gemma as I walked out of the stall. "Hey, Mom."

"Hi." She smiled brightly. "How are you today?"

"Fine." I'd been better a second ago. "What's going on?"

"Oh, nothing. I was dropping some extra eggs off at the kitchen and saw your truck, so I wanted to come say good morning."

"Glad you did. Good morning." I held out my elbow so she could loop her arm through mine. Then I walked her down the center aisle. "What are you up to?"

"Not much. I'm—"

"Hello!"

Mom and I turned at Kat's voice, seeing her come inside with a wave.

Since when were the stables such a popular Saturday spot? Normally, I was the only one who worked on the weekends, besides Katherine. But she usually stayed in the office. Everyone else who'd *retired* worked Monday through Friday.

Mom immediately let my arm go to give Katherine a hug. "Morning, sweetheart."

Katherine kissed Mom's cheek. "I was just on my way to your place but I saw your Jeep. When I went to town yesterday, they had a special on flowers, so I grabbed you a couple of bundles. They're your favorite peach roses."

"Ha." Mom laughed. "Great minds. I went to the store first thing this morning and bought this beautiful pink bouquet I thought you'd like."

As the two of them laughed and talked about flowers, I glanced over to the stall where Gemma was hiding. She could come out. She could pretend to have been working. But she stayed hidden.

"It's been ages since we took a ride together," Mom told Kat. "Let's plan one for this week."

"I'd love to."

"Can you come over for a little while?" Mom asked her, earning a nod as they walked together toward the door.

If I knew them, which I did, they'd spend the rest of the day at Mom's house. She'd lure Kat over with the promise of coffee and cookies, then she'd talk her into staying and helping bake a pie or working on some craft project. It would become a mother-daughter day, Mom having adopted Kat as the daughter she'd always wanted.

I stood and watched until they disappeared outside. "Coast is clear."

Gemma emerged from the stall and her bright smile had dulled. Her eyes went to the door where the sound of Katherine and Mom's slamming vehicle doors echoed. As she stared outside, her expression went blank.

Except I'd spent a month studying Gemma's face. She was doing her best to block out her thoughts and maybe others wouldn't notice, but I saw the hurt she was burying.

"You okay?"

She nodded and forced a smile. "Great."

That was a total lie. But if I pushed, she'd shut me out completely, so I'd wait until she was ready to talk.

"Jigsaw needs a workout. Let's go for a ride."

"Actually, I think I'm going to go—"

"For a ride. With me." I jerked my chin toward Sprite's stall. "Get her curried off. Then I want you to saddle her today."

"What if I don't want to go for a ride?" She fisted her hands on her hips.

"Too bad." I stepped close and took her chin in my grip, holding her gaze for a moment.

There were so many incredible things about this woman. She was smart and driven. She was beautiful and loving. But damn if she wasn't blind.

Would she ever see what was in front of her?

Everything she wanted, everything she needed, was right here. A home. A family.

Me.

I'd stopped lying to myself over the past month. My heart was hers—it had been since the moment she'd nearly knocked me down on the lodge's front porch. I'd stopped pretending that my feelings for her weren't as real as the breath in my lungs or the pulse in my veins.

I'd stopped kidding myself that it wouldn't destroy me when she left.

Because I believed she'd leave.

And I wasn't going to beg her to stay.

"Holler after you get Sprite combed." I leaned in and dropped a kiss on her forehead.

"Okay." She didn't argue because, deep down, I think she needed some air and a ride as much as I did.

It didn't take us long to get the horses ready. Gemma was able to saddle Sprite without much help, remembering most of the steps from our first lesson. I usually only had to show her something once, then she'd tackle it on her own the next time. She remembered the details that most dismissed.

No wonder she'd been so successful in Boston.

The woman was brilliant and her determination to succeed was unmatched.

As we started across the snowy meadow, the horses antsy and happy to be out, Gemma kept her eyes aimed forward. Her coat was bundled up to her neck and she'd pulled on a slouchy beanie.

"Loosen up on the reins," I said. "Sprite's not going to buck you off. Just relax."

Gemma blew out a long breath, doing as I'd instructed.

"Good. Now let's talk. What's wrong, darlin'?"

She didn't say anything for a full two minutes—I counted the seconds tick by—but then she looked at me and shrugged. "I'm jealous."

"Jealous. Of?"

"Katherine. She found a mother. Yours. And I'm so, so happy for her. But I'm jealous too. And I'm angry at myself for being jealous."

She didn't have to be jealous. She could have that same relationship. Gemma had no clue how much love my mother had to give. It was endless. She'd pull Gemma into her life and never let go.

I opened my mouth, unsure what to say, but Gemma spoke first.

"My mother was crazy."

I closed my mouth, watching her profile as she kept her gaze locked on the path ahead. This wasn't the first time she'd hinted at her mother's issues, and unlike her other mentions, I hoped her story wouldn't end here. I hoped she'd keep talking and finally get some of this shit out in the open. To set it free and let the wind carry it away.

"Not like wild and crazy," she clarified. "Crazy, crazy. It took me a long time after leaving to understand that there was something fundamentally wrong with her. Her mind, it wasn't right."

"What happened? Why'd you run?"

"To stay sane. Things were . . . unlivable. As I got older, it kept deteriorating. Until I knew if I stayed, I'd go mad. I'd end it before I became like her."

The air vanished from my lungs. The pain in my chest was crippling. Gemma was fierce and strong. For her to consider taking her own life . . . things were far worse than I'd ever imagined.

I shifted Jigsaw closer and held out a hand, palm open.

Gemma laid hers on mine and I held it so tight that she'd have to rip it free.

"My mom was beautiful," she said. "I look in the mirror each morning and she's staring right back. I hate that I look like her."

"I'm sorry."

"I almost got a nose job in Boston so I wouldn't be the same. But then I found this great therapist and he helped me see that my looks were my own. Some days though, I still want the plastic surgery. Maybe that's me being weak."

"There's not a damn thing weak about you. I get it." And if she wanted to change her nose or her chin or her cheeks, I'd drive her to the surgeon.

"I want to hate her," Gemma whispered, the words barely audible above the horses' steps and the breeze rolling across the meadow. "It would make everything so much easier, except I don't. I pity her. Her father, my grandfather, raped her from the time she was twelve. It broke her mind."

I gritted my teeth, holding my breath so I wouldn't explode as my temper surged. *Fuck. Fuck. Fuck.* Raped . . . by a parent? It was the unthinkable.

"As you can imagine, she was never right with men." Gemma shook her head. "And thankfully, the bastard had a heart attack when she was six months pregnant with me."

My heart stopped. Gemma had never mentioned her father. Was she—

"No," she answered the question I hadn't been able to think, let alone say aloud. "Once my mom turned eighteen, my grandfather never touched her again. She wasn't interesting enough for him. My father was some guy Mom met at a bar and screwed in a bathroom. She was quite . . . forthcoming about her sexual escapades. She always told me every little detail. Other girls got fairy tales as their bedtime stories. I got detailed comparisons of Mom's lovers."

Gemma truly had lived in a hell.

"Mom worked at a grocery store," she said. "I had a roof over my head and never went hungry. She'd buy me cute clothes from Kmart. I remember her laughing and tickling me when I was little. It's hard for me to pinpoint exactly when I realized she was crazy, and I'd been too young to notice early on. We were poor, but we weren't unhappy. Then everything changed."

"What changed?" I asked.

"Me. I got older. I wasn't as naïve to the boyfriends Mom had always invited to our house. She'd parade me in front of them and say things like, 'Isn't she pretty?' or 'You can touch her hair.'"

My stomach rolled. I wasn't sure I could keep listening to this, but I held her hand and let her talk because this wasn't for me. This was for Gemma. Maybe she'd told a therapist about this, but she needed to air it out here too.

She tightened her grip on my hand. "Most men who came over never came back. They either got what they'd been after from her or they saw Mom's crazy and left."

"Fucking cowards," I spat. "*They* left. But they left you there too."

Hadn't anyone called the cops? Hadn't one of those bastards seen a girl in danger?

"Everything would have been fine if they all would have left," she said. "Some were worse than cowards."

"Gem, did you . . . did they . . ." *Christ.* I couldn't get the words out of my mouth.

"I was never raped. But there are things that happened that I won't ever talk about again."

And I wouldn't put her through reliving that time, especially now when the grip I had on my self-control was slipping. "Okay."

"My mother didn't deserve me."

"That's a damn understatement," I muttered.

"The house that I grew up in was my mother's childhood home. She lived there, even after what my grandfather had done, and after he died."

"That's insane."

"Like I said, she's crazy. And I want to hate her," Gemma repeated. "I very much want to hate her."

I took a few breaths as Gemma stayed quiet, her eyes forward. Jigsaw let out a snort and their footsteps thudded loud against the frozen ground. She tugged her hand free and I let it go, but I stayed close.

Around us, the world seemed so at peace. The snow blanketed everything and the scent of a warm wood fire clung to the air. It seemed so simple. My life seemed so simple. Easy. Blessed.

Gemma was a warrior. She'd fought every day to survive, and I was so proud of her. I was proud that she'd broken the cycle.

"After you ran away, did you ever see her again? Your mother?"

Gemma nodded. "She always knew where I was. I never told anyone, but I went home and checked on her about once a month."

My jaw dropped. "She knew you were living in a junkyard and didn't do anything about it?"

Gemma gave me a sad smile. "She did do something about it. She didn't make me come home."

Maybe there'd been a shred of sanity in her mother after all.

"I don't know what to say."

"There's nothing to say. But now you know. When I see your mother hug Katherine and buy her flowers because she knows how much Katherine loves pink, I get jealous. And Katherine deserves that. She deserves a mother."

"And what about you? Don't you?"

"I have a mother. She lives in the same house she's lived in her entire life. And I bought it five years ago so she doesn't have to work and will never have to move."

"What?" My eyes bulged. "You still . . . you what?"

She'd kept in touch with her mother all these years. She'd provided for her. She'd funded her life.

She wanted to hate her mother. She wanted to change her own looks to escape her mother.

But she'd chained herself to the woman.

God, she was strong. I'd never known anyone with Gemma's strength and resilience.

"I moved out," Gemma said. "I didn't turn my back on her."

"Does Kat know?"

"No one does." There was a warning in her tone.

Gemma had made up her mind about caring for her mother a long, long time ago. And not a soul on earth would make her change her mind, even me.

She tightened her grip on Sprite's reins and clicked her tongue, picking up the pace and ending the conversation.

I urged Jigsaw forward and caught up, staying silent as I let her choose the path of the ride. Her story ran over and over through my mind, and though I had questions, I kept them to myself.

Where did Gemma and I go from there? Would this confession bring us closer together? Or now that I knew the truth, would it give Gemma the excuse she'd been searching for to run?

Or would she realize that she'd just opened up to me, because she'd finally found the place where she belonged?

13

GEMMA

"Happy Thanksgiving." I smiled into the phone, hearing the baby coo in the background.

"Happy Thanksgiving," Londyn said. "How are you?"

"Cold. It's freezing here. How are things with you?"

"Um . . . interesting."

My smile fell. "Everything okay?"

"I'm pregnant."

"What?" My hand came to my heart. "Really? Congratulations."

"Thanks." Londyn laughed. "This wasn't exactly what we'd planned, but oh my God, Gem, you should see Brooks. He's so excited."

And she was too.

"I'm so happy for you, Lonny."

"Me too. So what are you doing today? Are you eating with the Greers?"

"I'm sitting outside Carol and Jake's house as we speak."

"How's the Cadillac fairing in the snow?" she asked.

"Not too bad. Though I think it'll be happy to see warm weather again." Easton had offered to get me a ranch truck to drive around, but I'd declined. For now, the Cadillac was doing fine on the roads they kept plowed. And if that changed, I'd take a truck.

"Are you still thinking you'll leave after Christmas?"

"Unless the roads are bad." The idea of leaving made my heart ache, but eventually, my time here would come to an end.

It had to end.

Dreams were only meant to last a few short hours. Already I'd had mine for weeks.

"There's no rush," Londyn said for the hundredth time since I'd left West Virginia. Every time we'd talked, she'd reminded me to take some time.

"I know, but this entire stay in Montana was just a vacation," I lied. "It's time to move on."

To where, I wasn't sure. After I delivered the Cadillac to Karson, I had no idea where to go next. But I had twelve hundred miles to figure it out.

A wail sounded in the background. "Uh-oh."

"She's exhausted." Londyn sighed. "Too much excitement today and she's fighting sleep."

"I'll let you go. Bye." I hung up the phone but didn't get out of the car.

Mine was the only one in the driveway besides Liddy's Jeep and even though Easton wasn't inside, I wanted a moment to prepare for tonight.

Things between us had been different over the past two weeks—uncomfortable and distant—and it had everything to do with my past.

I should have stayed quiet on that horseback ride. I shouldn't have told him about my mother.

Easton came over a few times a week and we'd have dinner together. We'd have sex. But there was a distance between us, even when we'd fall asleep in the same bed. I found his gaze waiting for me more often than not, and in the quiet moments, he'd look at me like he was expecting me to decide something.

Except what was there to decide? I wasn't going to cut off my mother. No matter how much I struggled with her as a parent and what she'd done to me, she had no one in the world except me. If he wanted me to disown her, he'd be disappointed.

What the hell had I been thinking telling him everything? Why couldn't I have just kept my mouth shut?

And now I had to survive another family function as the one non-family member. I'd pretend that everything was fine. I'd pretend to be happy.

And I'd pretend not to be in love with Easton.

The days were getting harder and harder to endure. Every hour I had to remind myself this was temporary. And the longer I stayed, the more painful it would be to drive away.

Easton hadn't asked me to stay. He *wouldn't* ask me to stay. This was casual. This was for fun. He certainly hadn't insisted we stop hiding our relationship from his family.

But what if we did? What if we told them we were together? What if I came back after driving the Cadillac to California?

Would he want me back?

"Are you coming inside?" Carol hollered from the front door.

I nodded and pushed open the door to the Cadillac, stepping outside and hurrying to the door. The snow was falling lightly and I brushed the stray flakes from my shoulders and my hair before stepping inside. "Happy Thanksgiving."

"You too." Carol took the gift bag from my hand, peeking inside, as I shrugged off my coat. "Oh, you are so sweet. These are gorgeous. Thank you."

"You're welcome." I smiled as she slid out the charcuterie board I'd found at a gift shop in Missoula last weekend. I'd skipped the last two

Saturdays with Easton, using holiday shopping as an excuse for two trips into Missoula.

Leaving the ranch had been good for me. It had been a reminder that there was an entire world out there for me to explore, and with my disposable income, I could go anywhere I wanted. There was more to the world than the Greer Ranch.

A month ago, that idea had excited me. Now, it made my stomach knot.

"Are you okay?" Carol asked. "You seem distracted."

"No, I'm great," I lied. "Can I help with anything?"

"Of course not. You're our guest, so you can sit down and relax."

Right. I was the guest.

The kitchen island was loaded with appetizers. There was a spinach dip and a wheel of brie. Crackers. Olives. Prawns. Three bottles of wine were open and four different bottles of whiskey were out beside a handful of tumblers.

The smell of a cooking turkey filled the air and Liddy was at the sink, peeling potatoes. "Hey, Gem."

"Hi." I loved that she called me Gem. There weren't many who did, just those I loved. "This looks amazing."

"Help yourself." Carol handed me a glass of wine. "I hope you haven't eaten anything all day. We'll never get through all this."

The doorbell rang as she popped an olive into her mouth.

"I'll get it." Before she could argue and remind me again that I was a guest, I set down my wine and hurried to the door, expecting Katherine. Besides me, she was the only one who rang the doorbell. But it wasn't my friend standing on the stoop.

It was the bartender from town. Liz—*funny* Liz.

"Hey there." She smiled, taking a step forward to cross the threshold.

"H-hi." I shook out of my stupor and moved aside, holding the door for her. Then I remembered my manners. "I'm Gemma."

She hung up her coat as I closed the door, then held out a hand. "Liz. Nice to officially meet you."

"You too." Normally, I'd make polite conversation, but my mind went blank.

Liz wore a fitted sweater dress. It was far from scandalous with its long sleeves and turtleneck, but paired with her knee-high boots, she looked beautiful and sexy. Her hair was pinned up in a pretty knot and her makeup was elegant.

I was in black jeans and a plain sweater that was far from sexy. I hadn't even worn heels.

"Liz, welcome." Carol breezed past me and pulled Liz into a hug. "What are you drinking tonight?"

"Wine, please. Thanks for having me."

"You're always welcome. I'm just glad JR ran into you at the store yesterday."

"Me too." Liz laughed. "This is much better than a chicken pot pie at home alone."

So she was here, a guest like me, who would have been alone for Thanksgiving if the Greers hadn't come to her rescue.

The door behind us opened, forcing us all deeper inside as Cash walked in with Katherine following close behind.

Hugs and greetings were exchanged as Jake and JR came in from the den where they'd been playing pool. Each carried a tumbler of whiskey in their hand.

Unless there were more guests, everyone was here except Easton. The others had barely removed their coats when the door opened and he stepped inside.

His eyes found mine immediately and hope bloomed that he'd be different tonight. But then his eyes flickered straight to Liz and a broad smile stretched across his handsome face. "Hey, Liz. Glad you could make it."

Wait, he'd known she was coming? And he hadn't mentioned it to me?

Nice.

The group shuffled toward the kitchen, everyone collecting drinks and sampling the pre-dinner smorgasbord. I stuck close to Katherine, not wasting any time as I drained my first glass of wine.

Easton was kind enough to pour Liz's glass.

I refilled my own.

"Did your parents make it to Texas?" JR asked Liz.

"They did. And they've already inundated my phone with photos of the baby." She took out her phone and pulled up one of the photos, earning a sigh from Katherine and Liddy as they took in the pink bundle.

"That's my new niece," Liz told me. "My brother lives in Austin and he and his wife just had a baby on Monday. My parents flew down to spend the week with them."

Leaving her here alone for Thanksgiving.

"She's beautiful," I said, honestly. There was something about a baby's pout that always melted my heart.

I wasn't sure if I'd get to be a mother. At the rate I was going, it was unlikely, but I'd be a good aunt. Londyn's daughter, Ellie, would be loved beyond measure.

"I wanted to go"—Liz set her phone aside—"but someone had to be around to run the bar."

"Liz's family has owned the Clear River Bar for, what?" JR asked her. "Thirty years?"

She nodded. "Started by my grandfather."

"He and I went to school together," Jake added. "A hell of a long time ago."

"Remember that time your granddad came out here and tried to steal my horse?" JR chuckled. "Swore up and down that I'd been so drunk at the poker table the night before that I'd forgotten I'd bet my horse and he'd won."

She giggled. "He was such a goof."

An hour later, I'd lost count of the number of stories the group had told about Liz's family or tales from her bar. She fit into the mix so well, that with each one, my status as guest felt more and more obvious.

Liz had been Cash's date to their senior prom. Liz had thrown Katherine's twenty-first birthday party. Liz had gone skiing with Easton a few years ago and had come home with a broken nose, courtesy of a tree branch.

Liz. Liz. Liz.

She was sweet. She was funny and charming.

And she was infatuated with the man who'd been sharing my bed.

The way she smiled at him was subtle, like a girl who'd learned to hide her long-time crush well. Unless you were looking closely—which I was— it might seem like a tight friendship. But her eyes were on him a tad too often. When he laughed, her cheeks flushed. She made to stand beside him, casually shifting whenever he moved.

And the part I hated most was that he'd be better off with someone like her.

By the time we sat at the dining room table, I'd lost my appetite. The three glasses of wine I'd consumed had given me a sharp headache.

Easton held out Liz's chair, taking the seat beside her, per Carol's seating assignments.

I was ushered to the chair directly across from them, giving me the perfect seat to watch the two reminisce.

But he didn't look at me, not once. Easton was keeping up his end of the bargain, pretending like I was nothing more than the fleeting guest.

Even if we weren't pretending, what could I contribute to this trip down memory lane? I couldn't razz him about the time in college when he'd brought his girlfriend, the vegetarian, home to a cattle ranch only to have her dump him one week later. I didn't know the name of his dog that had died in eighth grade or the truck he'd driven in high school.

I didn't know much about Easton's past because he'd never offered much up.

No, I was the headcase we normally examined. I had to give him credit. Easton listened like he cared, but really, I doubted he'd wanted to know the horrid details.

It hadn't stopped me from blathering on though, had it? God, I was so stupid.

I didn't fit here. These were nice people, but even Katherine fit in better. She knew where to get the silverware from Carol's kitchen to help set the table. She knew where the dishes went after unloading the dishwasher. She offered to fix Jake and JR a drink and knew without asking how they took their whiskey.

"You okay?" Katherine whispered at my side as we passed platters and bowls of the feast around.

"Yeah," I lied. "Just a bit of a headache."

Katherine knew Easton and I were sleeping together, but whenever we'd talked, I'd downplayed my feelings for him. She thought we were casual. She thought we were fleeting. She didn't know how much I'd grown to care for him and she definitely didn't know I'd had a jealous breakdown about Liz.

"Do you want me to get you some Advil?" She pointed toward the bathroom down the hall because she knew where they kept the medicine. That shouldn't have annoyed me, but it did.

"I'll be fine." I scooped a heaping spoonful of stuffing on my plate. "Nothing some carbs and more wine won't knock out."

"Amen." She picked up her fork and dug into her candied yams.

With any luck, we'd all be too busy eating for much more conversation. And once this meal was over, I'd explain my headache was unbearable and return to the cabin where I'd barricade myself in the bedroom, hide under the covers and *if* Easton showed up, he'd find the door locked.

"So, Gemma. You and Katherine grew up together, right?" Liz asked.

"That's right." I looked to Katherine who gave me a slight headshake, which meant she'd told the Greers about our childhood, but not the local bartender.

I doubted many others outside this family knew how we'd grown up because it wasn't easy to share.

"And you're working at the lodge?" Liz asked.

I nodded. "Just while I'm here. Katherine was nice enough to give me something to do until Christmas."

"Oh, I didn't realize you were leaving. I thought you lived here."

"No, she doesn't." Easton spoke before I could answer. He finally dared to make eye contact.

Those eyes were unreadable. The tone of his voice wasn't flat or annoyed or cold, it was just matter-of-fact.

I didn't live here.

So why stay until Christmas? This dare, his challenge, didn't matter. I had nothing to prove, not anymore.

I'd already lost.

"I'm on my way to California," I told Liz. "I just came to visit Katherine."

"Ah." She nodded and there was no mistaking the hint of relief in her gaze. She'd pegged me as competition, even though Easton excelled at making sure I looked insignificant to him. Liz nudged Easton's elbow with her own. "I'm going snowmobiling next weekend. Want to come?"

"Maybe. What day?"

"Saturday. Mom and Dad will be back to cover the bar."

I held my breath, waiting to hear his answer. Saturdays were our day. Or at least they had been until I'd opened my mouth and told him about Mom.

"Let me see how the week shakes out," he told her. "Maybe."

Maybe.

He hadn't said no.

My nose stung with the threat of tears but I kept them at bay, taking a long drink of my wine and concentrating on the meal.

Conversation around me continued, light and jovial and festive. But the

240

delicious food had lost its flavor. The wine wasn't numbing the pain. And the headache I'd lied to Katherine about began pounding in my temples.

It was only by sheer force and years of practice that I managed to hold a slight smile through dinner. But when Jake mentioned giving it an hour before eating dessert, I knew my façade wouldn't survive the rest of the night.

"Excuse me." I stood from the table and went to the powder room, closing my eyes once the door was locked and dragging in a shaky breath.

I just wanted to go home.

But where was home? Boston? California? The cabin?

None of those places were home. I was filthy rich and utterly homeless. The closest thing I had was that Cadillac outside.

Maybe it was time to get in it and get on with my life.

I washed my hands and gave myself a few minutes to compose my emotions, then I returned to the main room, finding Carol and Liddy in the kitchen clearing plates. "Thank you both for an incredible meal."

"You're welcome." Liddy smiled. "Would you like more wine?"

"Actually, I think I'm going to get going. I'm getting a nasty headache and I don't want to infect everyone with a lousy mood."

"Oh, no." Carol rushed around the island for a hug. "Do you want to rest in the guest bedroom and see if it passes?"

"My sweatpants are calling. I think I'll just sneak out."

"You go on ahead. We understand."

Liddy came over and hugged me goodbye, then without returning to the dining room, I gathered my coat from the hook beside the door and slipped into the night.

The Cadillac's tires crunched on the hard snow as I steered the car on the bumpy road to the cabin. It was quiet outside, not a breath of wind rustled through the trees. The black and soundless night only made it more obvious I was alone.

That there was only one heartbeat in the car. There were only one set of footsteps in the fresh snow outside the cabin. There was only one jacket to hang on the coat hook.

Easton's scent clung to the air and I could smell his spice. I dragged in a deep breath, wanting so much to curl into a ball on the couch and cry.

It wasn't his fault. Easton was being nice to his friend and nothing he'd done tonight had been remotely flirtatious. Like a typical man, Easton probably didn't even know Liz had feelings for him.

This urge to scream and wail was not on him. This was my issue.

Yet another to add to my growing collection.

Tears welled in my eyes, but I swiped them away and marched to the bedroom.

I knew when it was time to leave. I'd had this same feeling at sixteen. I'd had this same feeling in Boston.

My time here was over. Montana wasn't the place for me anymore.

So I dragged my empty suitcase from the closet.

And packed.

14

EASTON

"HERE, I'LL TAKE THAT." I stood from the table, collecting Liz's empty plate to take to the kitchen along with my own.

"Oh, I can help." She began to stand but I shook my head.

"Nah. You sit. I've got it." Something was wrong with Gemma and I'd been looking for a reason to leave the dining room, but I hadn't wanted to make it obvious.

Mom and Grandma were in the kitchen and I'd expected to find Gemma with them, but she was nowhere in sight. "Here you go."

"Thanks." Grandma took the dishes from my hand and put them in the sink. "I'm going to grab the ice cream from the freezer in the garage, Liddy. Just in case anyone wants dessert."

"Okay." Mom pushed the start button on the dishwasher. "I'll get out the pies."

As she buzzed around the kitchen, I walked into the living room, thinking Gemma had wanted a quiet moment alone, but the room was empty. Where was she?

"She's not here."

I turned around at Mom's voice. "Who?"

"Gemma." She rolled her eyes. "You two might be fooling everyone else, but I wasn't born yesterday."

"Oh," I muttered.

I shouldn't have been surprised. Mom had a nose for secrets.

Cash and I had only gotten away with throwing one bonfire kegger at the ranch. She'd sniffed out all the other planning attempts and had smothered them. And she'd admitted years ago that the only reason we hadn't been busted for the one successful party was because I'd been in college and it had been Cash's senior year sendoff.

"Where'd she go?" I asked.

"She wasn't feeling well."

"What?" My gaze whipped to the window, and sure enough, the Cadillac was gone. "She's sick?"

Gemma had been fine this morning when I'd left the cabin. I hadn't seen her at the lodge today, but when I'd arrived here tonight, she'd appeared okay. Not that I'd outright asked her because when we were here, I didn't talk to her. I did my best to treat her like an acquaintance. I didn't want anyone to notice the way I looked at her, so I'd decided it was better not to glance at her in the first place.

"She said she had a headache," Mom said.

"Since when?"

"I'm guessing since Liz arrived." Mom shook her head, glancing over her shoulder to make sure we were alone. "I love your father, but that man can be thick as a brick wall sometimes."

"Huh?"

Mom pursed her lips. "Like father like son."

"What did I do?" I scowled.

She reached up and flicked the shell of my ear.

"Ouch." My hand flew to rub the sting. Mom hadn't flicked my ear like that since I'd been a teenager. "Seriously?"

"Shame on you, Easton Greer. If that girl stays after the way you treated her, I'll be shocked."

"What should I have done, Mom?" I stepped closer, careful to keep my voice low. "Gemma and I agreed to keep this between us. We don't need anyone else involved when she's just going to leave in a few weeks. And I couldn't exactly ignore Liz. Dad invited her, not me. But I don't blame him. She would have been alone at Thanksgiving."

"I know." She sighed. "Don't get me wrong. I like Liz. I actually thought Cash would chase after her one of these days."

"Really?"

"Yeah. Not that he'd have any luck. She's always had a crush on you." She cast her eyes to the ceiling. "My boys are both clueless."

"I'm not—wait, what? Liz doesn't have a crush on me."

Mom flicked my ear again.

"Jesus Chr—"

"Language." She pointed a finger at my nose.

"Sorry." I rubbed my ear again. "What was that for?"

"That was for Gemma. Because you were so busy not looking at her, you missed the way Liz *was*. That's why Gemma left, fighting tears and faking a headache, because you are so worried she's going to leave that you're practically pushing her out the door."

"Because she *is* leaving. Why drag all of you into this? Why get everyone's hopes up that she's going to stay when she won't?"

After hearing Gemma's story about her mother, I didn't blame her for leaving. She deserved to find the place she wanted to stay. She deserved the life of her choosing. She'd been forced into too much.

So I wouldn't beg her to stay for me. I wouldn't guilt her into a life here simply because it would make my dreams come true.

I was in love with Gemma.

I loved her enough to set her free. This was her decision to make.

"She wants a home, son."

"I know."

Mom put her hand to my cheek. "Then give her one."

If only it were that easy.

"Oh, sorry." Behind Mom, Liz stopped at the edge of the room. "I didn't mean to interrupt."

"It's fine." There wasn't much more I could explain to Mom without delving into Gemma's past. And that was her story to tell, not mine.

"Should we have dessert?" Mom gave me a tight smile, then turned and walked for the kitchen.

"Actually, I'm going to take off."

She glanced over her shoulder and nodded, knowing exactly where I was headed. "See you tomorrow."

"Happy Thanksgiving, Mom. Thanks for cooking."

"My pleasure." Mom's expression was a mix of hope and worry— though not for me. Mom loved Gemma too. And she was counting on me to make this right.

But what if the only way to make it right was to let Gemma drive away?

She'd break my heart but I'd stand back and watch her go.

It would hurt us both far more if I had to watch her fade away simply because I'd asked her to live the life *I* wanted.

"You're leaving already?" Liz asked, following me to the door.

"Yeah." I took my coat off the hook and shrugged it on. "It's been a long day and there's always work tomorrow."

"It was nice to see you."

"You too. I'll stop by the bar one of these nights and beat you at a game of dice."

"Ha." She huffed. "You wish. When was the last time you beat me? Six? Seven years ago?"

I chuckled. "To be fair, you get more time to practice."

"True." She smiled. "Are you just going home?"

Eventually. But first, I had to make a stop at the cabin. "Yep," I lied and zipped up my coat.

Liz stepped close, too close, and traced her finger up my arm. "Want some company?"

Well, shit.

"Look, Liz, I—"

"Don't say it." She cringed and stepped away, slapping a hand to her forehead. "I'm sorry. We're friends. I shouldn't have done that. I'm stupid."

"You're not stupid. I just don't feel that way about you."

She met my gaze, her own screaming *why?*

"I'm with someone."

Her forehead furrowed, then her eyes went to the door and the space where Gemma's Cadillac had been parked. "Oh, it's Gemma, isn't it?"

"Yeah."

"Can we forget this happened? Please?" she pleaded.

I nodded. "Sure."

"Thanks, Easton." She took another step away. "See you around."

"See ya, Liz." We both knew I wouldn't be in to play dice. Even if Gemma wasn't in the picture, even if Gemma hadn't captured my heart, Liz would only ever be a friend. I wouldn't lead her on. Hell, maybe I'd been leading her on.

Once again, Mom was right.

When it came to women, I was thick as a brick wall. Someday, I'd remember that my mother was always right.

I slipped outside without saying goodbye to the others. Tomorrow, I'd run into town and get Mom and Grandma flowers for all their work, but tonight, my gut was yelling that something was wrong with Gemma and it wasn't a headache.

The cabin's lights were on and a stream of smoke trailed from the chimney. I didn't bother knocking at the door and let myself inside. "Gem?"

A drawer slammed in the bedroom before she emerged in the hallway. Her hair was up in a ponytail and her face was flushed. "So you just let yourself in?"

"So you just left without a word?"

"I didn't realize we were speaking when other people were around." She fisted her hands on her hips. "My bad."

"I didn't come here to fight." I paused in the middle of unzipping my coat. "Do you want me to go?"

For a second, I thought she'd say yes. But then the angry look on her face softened and she pinched the bridge of her nose. "No."

"Are you feeling all right? Mom said you were sick."

"I'm fine," she muttered and walked my way as I hung up my coat. "Want something to drink?"

"No, I'm good."

She passed me on her way to the kitchen, not looking at me directly, so I slipped off my boots and followed, standing behind her as she took out a glass and filled it with some water from the tap.

"Hey." I stepped into the space behind her, lifting the glass from her hand and setting it beside the sink. "There's nothing with Liz."

"I know. You're friends."

"Yes. We're friends. I've known her a long time. But that's where it ends. And after you left, I made sure she understood that."

"It's fine." She waved it off and tried to move away, but I wrapped my arm around her shoulders and pulled her back against my chest.

"What's wrong?"

Gemma hung her head. "Nothing."

"Try again."

"I don't fit here, Easton," she whispered, and my heart cracked.

Maybe I'd seen this coming. Maybe I should have expected it sooner.

245

But these past two weeks as Gemma had pulled away, I should have seen it as the beginning of a goodbye.

I let her go and took a step away.

She turned to face me. "I'm not what you need."

I scoffed. "Spare me that, okay? You walk away from here, that's your choice. But don't play the martyr."

"I'm not playing at anything. It's the truth."

"You made the decision for me. Why? Because Liz was at dinner?"

"It's not about her."

"Bullshit."

She shot me a glare, then stormed out of the kitchen for the bedroom.

My temper spiked as she disappeared down the hallway and I marched after her.

"Why—" My question fell away as I reached the doorway. There was an open suitcase on the bed with most of Gemma's clothes inside. "You're leaving."

"I'm leaving." She yanked the nightstand drawer open and took out the few things she'd stashed inside. A lip balm and a box of condoms got thrown on the suitcase pile.

It was impossible to take a full breath. My chest felt tight like someone had wrapped it in steel.

I was supposed to have until Christmas. I was supposed to have time to prepare for this.

I wasn't ready.

"Would you have even said goodbye?" I asked.

She stood from the drawer, throwing a hand lotion onto the bed, and her shoulders drooped. "No."

It was eleven years ago all over again.

Well, fuck that. I wasn't letting her slip out again. This time, she could watch me walk away when I was goddamn ready to leave.

I blew into the room, my rage a force, and took her face in my hands. I held it tight, then slammed my mouth on hers in a hard, brutal kiss.

Gemma melted against me, surrendered, as I poured my frustration into her lips. She leaned into it, taking everything I had. She let me punish her with this kiss.

Except I didn't want to punish her. I wanted to love her and keep her and . . . *fuck*. It would break her.

I tore my mouth away and dragged in a jagged breath as I dropped my forehead to hers. Her scent was everywhere, and I realized how foolish I'd been not to take her to my bed. Because I had nothing of hers to keep. When she left this cabin, she'd be gone.

"I'm sorry." Her voice cracked. "I don't—"

"It's okay." I cupped her cheek and leaned away to meet her eyes. They were full of unshed tears. When one dripped down the smooth curve of her cheek, I wiped it away with my thumb. "It's okay."

She stood on her toes, brushing her lips against mine. This time, it was my turn to melt. I wrapped her up tight, holding her close as she opened her mouth to let my tongue sweep inside.

I'd memorize her taste. I'd memorize the way she felt in my arms. I'd do all of that because I hadn't all those years ago.

This time around, I wouldn't lose her memory so quickly.

Our hands fumbled to strip clothing as we shuffled to the bed. Her sweater came first so I could mold my hands over the black satin of her bra. Her nipples pebbled beneath the fabric, digging into the flesh of my palm. My button-up came next, followed by the white T-shirt underneath.

When the backs of her knees hit the edge of the mattress, I eased her down and flicked the button open on her jeans so I could drag them off her legs. With them gone, the only thing left on the bed was Gemma in her bra and panties. And that fucking suitcase.

I shoved it to the floor.

Gemma scowled as her clothes spilled everywhere.

I shrugged and unbuckled my belt. If this was the last time, I wasn't going to be hindered by that fucking luggage.

Gemma sat up and ran her hands across my stomach, her pink nails digging into the dips between each muscle. Then she ripped the button free and tugged down the zipper. The moment I sprang free, her tongue was on me, licking the tip of my cock before taking me completely into her mouth.

"Gem." I cupped the back of her head. "Fuck."

She moaned and the vibration of her throat nearly tipped me over the edge.

I pulled her off me with her ponytail, then I shoved off my jeans, and tore at her panties while she unclasped her bra. When I covered her naked body with my own, she wound her legs around my hips. Our eyes locked. Our breaths mingled. And when I slid inside her bare, I wrapped her in my arms so she'd feel the beat of my heart.

It was hers.

And when she left here tomorrow, she'd take it on the road.

Gemma trembled beneath me, her legs cinching tighter to pull me deeper.

"I need to get a condom," I whispered in her ear.

She shook her head, her arms holding me close. "Not yet."

I loved this woman. Damn, did I love her. But if I didn't put a condom on now, there'd be no chance I'd stop again. And as much as I wanted to see her growing with our child, that would only make things worse.

So I pulled free as a groan of protest escaped her lips and riffled around the floor until I found the box of condoms. When I rejoined her on the bed, she spread her legs wide and welcomed me home.

"You feel so good." I kissed her open mouth. "So fucking good."

She hummed her agreement against my lips as I rocked us together, taking her higher, stroke after stroke. When her legs began to tremble and her breath hitched, I reached between us and found her clit.

One touch and she detonated. She pulsed around me with wave after wave of pleasure, causing her body to quake. The squeeze of her inner walls and the sheer ecstasy on her face was too much. Tingles raced down my spine and my blinding orgasm broke.

We held tight to one another, grasping for just one more second together. Our bodies were slick with sweat and her ear was against my lips. The words I wanted to whisper begged to be free. *I love you.* I wanted to say them. I wanted her to know that she meant everything to me. But I swallowed them down because I wouldn't make her deny them or repeat them. I wouldn't give her anything to feel guilty about when she left.

Before I eased away and stood from the bed, I kissed the underside of her jaw, then her collarbone, stealing little tastes while I could. Then I left her on the bed while I went to the bathroom to deal with the condom.

Maybe tonight, if I could talk to her and get her to relax, I could find out where her head was at. I could find out what had happened and see if I could delay this for a couple more weeks. If I got really lucky, we'd get five feet of snow and she'd be stuck here until spring.

It might only delay the inevitable, but it might be my only chance to give her the time to change her mind. To decide on this ranch as a home.

On me.

I washed up and expected to find her in bed when I got back to the room. Instead, she was dressed. Her hair was twisted in a messy knot and she was on her knees beside the suitcase.

She wasn't putting the clothes back in the dresser.

She was packing them to leave.

So much for one last night.

I swiped my jeans off the floor and jerked them on, leaving the belt hanging loose. Gemma held out my T-shirt and I ripped it from her hands before pulling it over my head. I couldn't see my button-up in the mess, but I wasn't going to stick around and search for it.

"When?" I barked.

"When what?" Her voice was calm and quiet.

"When are you leaving?"

"Tomorrow, I guess."

I scoffed and searched the mess on the floor for my socks. When I found them, I shoved them in my pocket and spun for the door without a word.

If she wasn't staying, neither was I. Sleeping beside her for another night, having her curled into my side, would be torture.

I stalked to the door, taking my coat from the hook and not bothering to put it on while I stepped into my boots. My anger would be enough to keep me warm all the way home.

Gemma's footsteps stomped on the floor as she came down the hallway. "So that's it? You come here, fuck me and leave?"

"Are you kidding me? Fuck, you drive me insane." I raked a hand through my hair. "You're the one who's hell-bent on racing out of here in the morning. What do you want from me?"

"You? What about me? What do you want from me?"

I want you to stay. More than anything, I wanted her to stay.

But I wasn't going to beg. If she chose this life, if she chose me, she'd have to be sure. Because the minute she said yes, I'd hold on and never let go.

I wanted her to make her own choice.

"I'm not going to beg you to stay, Gemma."

Something flashed in her eyes, but before I could make sense of it, she blinked it away. Then she reached past me to whip the door open, and with one hand pressed into my chest, she shoved me outside.

Right before she slammed the door in my face, I heard her whisper, "No one ever does."

15

GEMMA

"WHAT ELSE IS HAPPENING?" I asked Benjamin.

"That's it," he said. "Everything is under control."

"Okay. Good."

I'd called him to check in, like I did every Friday morning. And per usual, there wasn't much to report. Since I'd left Boston, Benjamin had done exactly what I'd asked. He'd taken over.

Each week, he had fewer questions for me to answer. Fewer tasks for me to complete. It should have made me feel good that I'd put such a competent and capable man in charge. Benjamin was caring for my investments and capital ventures like they were his own.

But I'd come to dread these Friday morning phone calls because they were another blunt reminder that I wasn't really needed.

Not in Boston.

And not in Montana.

I'd leave the Greer Ranch today and though Annabeth would be disappointed that once again the front-desk position would be vacant, she'd eventually find my substitute. Katherine had other friends to hang out with. And Easton . . .

For the moment, I wasn't ready to process the heartache of leaving Easton Greer. Of knowing he'd eventually find a better replacement. So I wouldn't think about Easton, not today. I'd save that for my road trip.

"How are things in Montana?" Benjamin asked.

"Coming to an end. I'm leaving today."

"O-oh. Really? I thought you were staying until Christmas."

"Change of plan." My stomach twisted. It had been in a constant knotted state since Easton had left last night.

I'd done my best to fight back tears, mostly by throwing myself into packing. Then I'd cleaned the cabin, tongue-and-groove ceiling to hardwood floor. Finally, I'd fallen asleep from sheer exhaustion—emotional and physical—and had woken up with the sunshine streaming through the cabin's bedroom window.

It hadn't taken me long to load up the Cadillac, though there was more in the trunk now than when I'd started this journey. I had the winter coat Easton had insisted upon along with the boots I'd used on our working Saturdays. And I had the plaid shirt he'd left behind last night, tucked safely inside my purse.

All that remained was to finish this call, stop by and say goodbye to Katherine, then get on the highway.

"Would you mind booking me a hotel room?" I asked.

"When and where?"

"I'll find some motel along the road tonight, but I was hoping to get to San Francisco tomorrow and stay there for a few days." I needed to build up some mental walls before venturing to Temecula. I wasn't sure if I had the strength to stop by and visit my mother, but it was something I'd been considering.

"The usual amenities?" he asked, the sound of computer keys clicking in the background. He'd probably already pulled up a travel website.

"Please." Benjamin knew I'd prefer a boutique hotel with a spa and five-star menu.

"Done. I'll email you the details. Anything else?"

"No, thank you. I'll check in later. Have a good week."

"Gemma, wait. Before you hang up."

My heart stopped. *Please, please don't quit.* I couldn't handle it right now. I couldn't deal with leaving the Greer Ranch and having Benjamin leave me all in the same day. "Yeah?"

"Are you okay?" There was genuine concern in his voice, probably because mine sounded flat and lifeless.

"Sure. I'm great."

There was a long pause on the other end of the line. No doubt he was debating whether or not it would be smart to call his boss on a blatant lie. Thankfully, he let it go. "Would you like company in San Francisco?"

"Who? *You?*"

"Yes, *me*. I've missed you."

"I've missed you too." My eyes flooded.

As much as I would like to see a familiar face, my days in San Francisco would be miserable. I had a broken heart to mend. It would be better to see Benjamin when the two of us could laugh and talk without a cloud of sorrow hanging over my head.

"How about we meet up after I deliver this Cadillac? We can spend a week or two somewhere tropical. Bring Taylor and the three of us will spend a small fortune gorging ourselves on food between spa appointments. You two can pick where we go."

He chuckled. "Taylor is going to want Bali."

Escaping to the opposite end of the world with Benjamin and his spouse seemed like a good idea at the moment. "Bali it is."

"Keep in touch, please. I don't like the idea of you driving alone."

"I'll be fine," I assured him. "Talk soon."

"Bye."

With the call over, I tucked my phone into my purse and slung it over my shoulder. Then I stood from the couch in the living room and took one last look at the cabin.

My temporary home.

It had always felt temporary. That had to mean something, right? That I'd never wanted to live here forever? I liked the cabin. It was cozy and warm. But it wasn't home.

This place wasn't home.

So I drew in another breath, savoring one last inhale of the fire I'd built this morning that had nearly burned out. Then I walked to the door, twisted the lock on the handle before closing it behind me and got in the car.

I wouldn't let myself look in my mirror as I drove away.

It was simply another fleeting stop.

And like I'd done before, it was time to search for the next.

"Stay another week," Katherine pleaded. "Or two."

"I can't."

"Please? I already have your Christmas present. Just stay until then."

She wasn't making this easy on me. Our friendship had bloomed in my time here and I'd miss her terribly. I dearly hoped our relationship wouldn't end.

"I'm going to miss you." I pulled her into a hug and squeezed tight.

We were standing in the middle of her office. I'd found her behind her desk, as always, working with a smile on her face.

I envied that and so much else. But I was so happy for her. I was glad she'd found her place.

"Call me," I said. "And I'll call you. I don't want to lose you again."

"You won't." Her arms cinched tighter. "What happened, Gemma? Why are you leaving? You seemed happy."

I was happy.

But I wasn't going to mix up Easton's life. Especially if he wasn't going to ask me to stay.

Last night, I'd felt sixteen again. When I'd left my mother's home, she'd been there. Watching. She'd sat on the living room couch and watched me walk out the door without a word.

I'd cried for ten blocks knowing she wouldn't chase after me.

That pain had been nothing compared to Easton's declaration he wouldn't beg me to stay.

But I wasn't thinking about that. Not now.

My priority was to get on the road and drive.

One of these days, maybe I wouldn't feel so lost. Maybe one day I'd set foot into the place where I was meant to be and know, in my bones, it was mine. Maybe I'd finally quiet the unsettled energy that zipped through my veins.

"I have to go." I let Katherine go and blinked away the threat of tears. "You have my number."

She nodded, swiping at her own eyes. "Are you going to come back?"

"Someday." Maybe.

But only when I could handle the notion of seeing Easton again.

Until then, I was planning on inviting Katherine along on Benjamin's trip to Bali. I'd whisk her away until I had the courage to return. Until I was strong enough to face Easton, knowing that when I left here today, he'd never forgive me.

"Take care of yourself."

She gave me a sad smile. "Same to you."

I turned away and hurried from her office before she could see my unshed tears. Then I made my way outside to the Cadillac parked in front of the lodge.

I'd tried to find Carol and Liddy earlier, but they'd gone into Missoula for Black Friday shopping, so I'd left them a note. They'd probably hate me for that note, but it was better than hanging around.

The Cadillac was warm when I slid inside, the seats soaking up the early morning sun. I cranked the heat anyway as I started the engine, feeling a cold so deep that I doubted I'd be warm for a hundred miles.

Goddamn it. Why? I wasn't even sure what *why* I was asking. Why was I like this? Why was life so hard? Why didn't he love me? Just . . . why?

My chin quivered and I sucked in a few short breaths, but it was no use. The tears flooded and the world became a glassy blur as I cried into the steering wheel.

What was wrong with me? Why was I leaving?

Because I'm terrified.

The answer came immediately. This time in Montana had woken me up. I was feeling again. I was living. I'd fallen in love.

And I was scared that it would all fall to shit.

If I decided to stay and everything here broke, it would destroy me.

Self-preservation was kicking in, and foolish or not, habits were hard to break. I'd been taking care of myself—depending on myself, protecting myself—for a long, long time.

I wiped my face dry—taking the makeup I'd put on this morning away with the tears—then I took a deep breath, sat up straight and put the Cadillac in reverse.

The road was covered with last night's dusting of snow. There was only one set of tracks to mark the path, probably from Carol and Liddy. Before I could stop myself, I glanced in the rearview mirror, seeing the lodge grow smaller in the distance. Then I rounded a turn and it disappeared behind a towering wall of evergreens.

My hand came to my chest, rubbing my sternum to try and erase the sting.

I pushed the Cadillac faster. Snowy roads or not, it was time to rip off the bandage and get the hell off Greer property.

A billow of snow rose up behind me as I picked up speed and ahead, the highway came into view. The pressure in my chest was nearly crippling, but I breathed through it with both hands locked on the wheel.

Then a black streak caught my eye.

I blinked, once, then twice, and tried to make sense of what I was seeing.

There was a man on a horse, racing along the barbed wire fence that bordered the highway. He was flying.

I gasped, a hand flying to my mouth as my foot lifted off the gas pedal.

Jigsaw was running flat-out, his legs stretching in front of him as he galloped. And on his back, Easton rode with a fluid grace that was so stunningly beautiful, I barely noticed that I'd brought the Cadillac to a full stop.

Easton turned Jigsaw as he neared the road but didn't ease off the pace. He didn't slow until he was close enough for me to see his flushed cheeks, his panted breaths, and that he wasn't wearing a coat.

He leapt off Jigsaw, the animal breathing as hard as his owner, and while the horse stood by waiting, Easton strode to the Cadillac and ripped open the door.

His face was a storm. His eyes blazing.

He was livid. *Fantastic.*

The reason he'd run me down was probably because I'd stolen his shirt.

Easton jerked his thumb over his shoulder. "Out."

Okay, not livid. Murderous.

I eased out of the car, watching as he fisted his hands on his hips and hauled in a few deep breaths.

Easton ripped the cowboy hat off his head and tossed it on the ground. There was sweat at his temples and the temperature was below zero.

"Where's your coat?"

That question earned me an icy glare. "I saw you in the parking lot. Crying."

"Oh." I should have traveled farther to hide my tears. "So?"

He raked a hand through his hair. "I've been waiting over a month for you to figure it out. And you still haven't."

"Figure what out?" That he didn't want me enough to ask me to stay?

He took a step closer and I had the perfect view of his ticking jaw. "Where do you fit, Gemma?"

"Why are you doing this?" Was he trying to hurt me? How could he ask me that question when he knew I didn't have the answer?

"Where do you fit?" he repeated.

Nowhere. I clamped my mouth shut and lifted my chin. Hadn't we done enough of this last night? Did he really need to pick a fight when I was seconds away from leaving him to his life?

Easton stepped forward, closing the distance between us and lifting a hand to my cheek. Then his voice dropped to barely a whisper. "Where do you fit, Gemma?"

The gentleness of his touch melted away my anger. "I don't know."

"Guess."

I shrugged. "On the ranch?"

Easton shook his head and *damn him*, it shattered my heart.

I tried to step away but he had me pinned. "East—"

"With. Me." He dropped his forehead to mine. "You fit right here with me."

A sob escaped, followed by another, and as the tears streamed down my face, he pulled me into his arms. "I don't want to leave."

"Then come home. Please."

"I thought you weren't going to beg me to stay."

"Let me rephrase. Come. Home. That's not me begging. That's me giving orders."

I laughed and cried, burrowing into his shirt as he held me tight.

"I don't want you to go, Gem. Stay."

"Okay," I whispered.

The tension in his frame vanished and he loosened his hold enough to catch my lips.

He licked at the seam and kissed me slow and soft. It was maybe the sweetest gesture he'd shown but my mind was whirling, and it was hard to concentrate on the taste of his tongue and the heat of his breath.

How was this happening? Had he really raced up to me on his horse—his freaking horse—and now I was kissing him? This was one of those moments I'd replay in my head for years to come and still not believe it had been real.

When he pulled away from my lips, I studied his face, trying to make sense of it all. "Why? What made you change your mind and come after me?"

"I was in the stables, pissed at you. I wasn't supposed to be there but my truck got a flat this morning and instead of calling for help, I hiked back."

"Because you were pissed at me," I muttered.

"Yep. Well, I'd just walked in and happened to look over. There you were. Crying and . . ." His eyes melted into dark chocolate pools. "Breaks me to see you cry."

So he'd ridden after me.

He must have come straight from the stables toward the highway, because as the crow flies, it was the fastest way off the ranch. Lucky for me, the road curved and wound its way, otherwise, I would have missed him.

"I don't want to trap you here," he said. "That's why I didn't ask. That's why I said what I said last night. You went through enough. After you told me about your mother, I thought on it and I just . . . I don't ever want you to live somewhere you don't want to be."

That was why he'd gotten strange after my confession? Not because of what I'd told him, but because he'd been worried for me.

He'd been willing to let me go because he'd wanted me to be happy.

"I love you," I blurted.

"I love you." He grinned. "I fucking love you, woman. I'm going to marry you. I'm going to have babies with you. I'm going to fight with you. I'm going to kiss you every morning. And show you every day that this is exactly where you belong."

I wanted it. Every word. Every promise. "Are you asking me to marry you?"

He arched an eyebrow. "Did I ask?"

I laughed and stood on my toes to brush a kiss to his lips. "Let's pretend you did and that I said yes."

Easton's smile stretched across his face. It was the most honest, real smile I'd seen from this man and instantly made me smile back. He only let me appreciate that smile for a second, then his lips were on mine again and there was nothing sweet about our kiss. It was consuming. Branding. Claiming.

I was his. I belonged with him.

The chaos I'd felt for, well . . . forever, seemed to simply uncoil.

Easton kissed me until we were both breathless, then he let me go and jerked his chin to the Cadillac. "Now get back in the car before you freeze. I need to get Jigsaw to the stables, then I'll meet you at the house."

"Okay." I nodded, hesitant to let him go, but I didn't want him outside either.

"Here." He held up a finger as his other hand dove into his jeans pocket, pulling out his keys. On a leather strap were four keys and a black fob. He twisted off the only brass key and pressed it into my hand. "That's yours."

I stared at it in my palm and the lump in my throat came back.

He'd given me the key to his home.

Most people wouldn't be stunned speechless by a key. But I wasn't most people.

Whenever I'd needed a home, I'd gone out and found or built or bought one myself.

And Easton had just given me his.

He kissed my forehead and clicked his tongue to Jigsaw, who hadn't so much as moved from the spot where he'd been left. With a fast swing up, Easton was in the saddle and loping down the road, not wasting any time as he made his way to the stables.

I climbed back in my car, Easton's key clutched in my hand, and drove toward his house.

A smile tugged at my cheeks as I pulled into the space in his driveway, parking in front of the garage. Londyn was going to love this. So was Katherine. So was Benjamin, though I was still going to send him and Taylor to Bali.

I decided to leave my suitcase in the trunk—Easton would haul it in

256

later—and walked up the steps to the porch and to the front entrance, slipping my key inside the lock. I held my breath as I turned the bronze knob, not sure what to expect on the other side of the hickory door. But when I stepped across the threshold, my jaw dropped.

Easton's home was picture perfect. The open floor plan gave me a view of the wide, expansive kitchen. It flowed seamlessly from the dining area to the living room, filled with leather furniture and walnut pieces. The bay windows in the front of the house were as impressive as those showcasing the view behind the house.

The style was rustic and woodsy, very Easton, yet not overly manly. It was warm and inviting. It was exactly what I would have designed for a home at the base of a mountain.

I took another step inside, closing the door behind me. If Easton had wanted to give me the tour, he'd have to live with the disappointment. The guest bedrooms on the main floor were down a hallway off the living room along with a sparsely decorated office. I peeked into the pantry along with both the mud and laundry rooms.

When I walked down the hallway leading to the back of the house, Easton's scent greeted me before I stepped into the enormous, master suite.

His bed was unmade. The charcoal sheets were rumpled and the suede quilt strewn on the floor. Every night he'd spent at the cabin, he'd slept like a rock, barely moving. Which meant last night, he'd probably tossed and turned.

I walked deeper into the bedroom, not bothering with the light. He'd vaulted the ceiling in the bedroom and the back wall was made almost entirely of glass. Sunbeams streamed inside, lighting the room and warming my face.

Every step felt heavy. Deep. Like with each one, my feet sank through the hardwood floor, past the concrete foundation and into the earth.

Like a tree's roots taking hold.

A wave of emotion welled in my chest and I was crying again. Damn it, I'd cried more in the past twenty-four hours than I had in the last eleven years.

Maybe that was expected when someone like me finally found it.

Home.

I hadn't cried for long when two arms banded around me and Easton pulled me into his chest. "You okay?"

I nodded, leaning into his embrace. "They're happy tears."

"Good. Welcome home, darlin'."

EPILOGUE

GEMMA

Six months later . . .

"I don't like the doctor."

Easton chuckled. "At last week's appointment, you loved her. You invited her to the wedding."

"She can forget that invitation now."

He reached across the cab of the truck and took my hand, holding it as we bumped down the road. "We'll get the car to California. It's just not going to be for a while."

"A long while." My shoulders fell. "I need to call Londyn."

"She's not going to care."

"She might."

He lifted my hand to his lips and kissed my knuckles. "She won't."

My fiancé was right. Londyn wouldn't care about the car. Hell, she'd had it in West Virginia for a year before I'd taken it on my adventure. Mostly, I was pouting because the doctor's news was not what I'd hoped to hear.

As of today, I was on activity rest. I'd be trapped inside the house for months while I finished growing this baby. And the trip that we'd planned to take to California in three weeks was on hiatus. Neither Easton nor I would risk being on the road with the warning light on this pregnancy.

"I hate this," I muttered. "I'm scared."

He looked across the cab. "It's going to be okay."

"What if we can't get my blood pressure down?"

"We will."

I found it cruelly ironic. If the doctor didn't want me stressed during the remainder of my pregnancy, she shouldn't have told me all the bad stuff that could happen.

She was definitely not invited to our wedding.

The day Easton had stopped me from leaving and given me his

258

caveman proposal, we'd spent alone at the house. He'd brought in my things and had helped me unpack, moving me into his house—our house. And that night, he'd insisted we go to family dinner.

We'd walked in the door at Carol and Jake's, and before anyone could react to the fact that I wasn't on my way to California or scold me for leaving a note, he'd announced we were engaged.

Two weeks later, he'd come home with a diamond ring.

Two weeks after that, I'd come home with pregnancy tests.

So far, this pregnancy had been a cakewalk. I hadn't had any morning sickness and my energy levels had been great. But two weeks ago, I'd gone in for a routine checkup and the doctor had worried that my blood pressure was higher than normal. This week was more of the same. If next week's checkup was a continuation, I'd have to take medication, something I'd avoided completely since my pregnancy test had shown positive.

I was eating healthy. I was getting exercise. But the anxiety of growing a human and becoming a mother was getting to me.

I hadn't exactly had a good role model during my formative years.

"I just want the baby to be okay." I stroked my belly, taking deep breaths.

"He will be." Easton clutched my hand. "You both will be."

It would be easier to believe him if his nerves weren't coming through his voice and there wasn't a worry line between his eyebrows.

Easton was over the moon that we were having a boy. Last month, he'd gone into Missoula with the trailer to pick up some specialty mineral supplements for the livestock, and while he'd been at the farm and ranch supply store, he'd found a pair of baby cowboy boots. And a baby cowboy hat. And a baby pair of felt chaps.

The getup was currently in the nursery closet, awaiting the day when he'd be old enough to wear them and I'd take a million photos.

Easton had also told Cash that the best colt born this year was ours.

Maybe I hadn't had good parents, but I was lucky that the man at my side would more than compensate for my shortcomings. And we could lean into our family.

The Greers were as excited about this baby as we were.

We pulled up to Carol and Jake's place and Easton shut off the truck. We were late for family dinner because my appointment had gone long, but it was a gorgeous evening.

The May flowers were in full bloom, the front of Carol's flower beds brimming with canary-yellow daffodils and fuchsia tulips. The ranch was as green as I'd ever seen it, the meadows lush and the trees overflowing with blossoms.

Calves danced around their mother's legs. Fawns bounded through the grass. JR and Liddy had a batch of baby chicks and there was a litter of new barn cats.

And soon, I prayed, we'd have a healthy and happy baby boy.

"Don't get out," Easton ordered. "I'll come around and help."

Normally, that would earn him an eye-roll. But tonight, I'd listen because he was worried and I knew he felt helpless.

As he opened my door, I swung my legs to the side and took his face in my hands. "I love you."

He leaned in, sliding his arms around me and tucking his head against my neck. "I love you too."

We held on to each other until the front door opened and Cash called, "Granddad wants to know if you both want cheese on your burgers."

"I'm pregnant. What kind of stupid-ass question is that?"

Easton laughed and leaned away to holler at Cash. "Yes, cheese."

"Double on mine!"

He grinned and helped me to the ground, then pinned me to his side as we walked to the house. The minute we crossed the threshold, we were bombarded with questions about my appointment. Carol ushered me to a chair at the dining room table, Liddy brought me a glass of iced water and Katherine sat down beside me.

Easton dropped a kiss to my cheek, then disappeared outside to find the guys who were hovering beside the grill, while I gave a recap of my appointment.

"So I guess this means your trip is canceled," Katherine said.

"Yes." I sighed. "I'll call Londyn later and tell her."

"She won't care."

"I know. It's just disappointing." I'd been looking forward to the trip, not only to find Karson, but because Easton would be going with me.

When—if—I decided to see my mother, I wouldn't have had to face her alone.

I shrugged. "Eventually, we'll go."

It would be after the baby was born, and after the wedding we'd planned for next June. Maybe this road trip to California could be part of our honeymoon.

Carol, Liddy and Katherine had thrown themselves into the wedding planning. The four of us met each Sunday to go through bridal magazines and talk about ideas. They were anxious to make me an official Greer, though I didn't need the last name to feel a part of this family. Every day that went by, those roots grew deeper.

I'd been dealt a miserable set of cards for the first part of my life, but now I was getting straight aces.

"Can I help with dinner?" I asked, practically begging not to have to sit here while people waited on me.

Carol scoffed. Liddy gave me a sweet smile while shaking her head. Katherine hid her laugh in a glass of wine.

"Activity restrictions," I muttered. "This sucks."

And if I knew Easton, he was outside right now talking to his grand-father, father and brother about how to cut my hours at the training facility.

The expansion was in full swing on the new property, with Cash taking the lead. We'd planned to take the trip to California in a few weeks because it would be before the construction crew broke ground on the stables at the new training facility.

Once construction started, I didn't want to miss a minute, especially after contributing a million dollars to the project. It was the first of three major investments I'd made in the past six months, though with the other two I truly was silent.

One was a women's shelter in California for women who'd escaped their nightmares. Dr. Brewer had recommended the organization to me and they'd been thrilled to welcome me aboard. The other was a national children's organization that focused on serving runaway kids. I'd been happy to give them large sums of money and let them run with the dollars.

Benjamin had been more than happy to take them under his wing so I could concentrate on activities in Montana.

The expansion would be time consuming for us all to get it off the ground, though particularly so for Cash and me. Easton thought the expansion was part of my elevated stress levels. He wasn't entirely wrong.

If they voted to have me station the lodge's front desk again, I was moving back to the cabin.

Not long after Christmas, the time spent planning the training facility had ramped up. On top of the already busy resort and ranch activities, Easton and Cash had struggled to keep up with the emails and phone calls and general office work.

Enter me.

I loved barking orders and making decisions and as it turned out, my entrepreneurial expertise came in handy, so I'd been promoted from silent investor to joint director of operations. Cash and I were working together to get the breeding and training facility open. We were having a blast, though the hours had been demanding.

Maybe too demanding.

But it was hard to slow down when everyone was so excited. When *I* was excited. This was more than just my new job. This was more than turning a profit. This was about building a legacy for my son.

"Promise you won't make me sit at the front—" Before I could get Katherine on my side in this inevitable war about what was best for Gemma, the doorbell rang.

"Who could that be?" Carol stood from the table, but before she could take a step, Cash flew inside.

"I got it. I got it. I got it." He waved us all back into our seats and rushed to the door. He swung it open and a female voice floated through the air.

My stomach dropped and I turned to Katherine, seeing all the blood drain from her face as Cash escorted a pretty blonde into the house.

Holding her hand.

No. Cash, you idiot.

Katherine's eyes were glued to their linked hands. She studied them for a long moment as Carol and Liddy greeted the guest, surprised as we were by the addition.

"You guys remember Dany?" Cash asked, getting nods.

"Hey, Kat." Dany waved.

"Hey." Katherine forced a smile but it didn't reach her eyes.

I stood, using my growing belly to block out Katherine and give her a chance to recover. "Hey, Dany. I'm Gemma. Nice to meet you."

"Nice to meet you too."

I let go of her hand just as Easton came inside carrying a platter of burgers.

He saved me from making small talk and with everyone clustered around the table, fixing their burgers and diving into the meal, it allowed Katherine time to pretend this wasn't killing her.

I loved Cash. We'd gotten to know each other these past six months and he was genuinely a good man, like his brother. But for fuck's sake, he was stupid when it came to women.

What on earth had possessed him to bring a woman tonight? Who was this Dany? And when had they started dating? The two of them sat side by side at the dinner table, whispering and canoodling and annoying the hell out of the rest of us.

I nudged Easton's elbow with my own, then shot him a silent question. Had he known about this?

He shook his head, as shocked as the rest of us.

The minute her burger was done, Katherine took her plate to the kitchen without a word. I stood to follow.

"Leave your plate," Carol said.

"It's an empty plate." I ignored her and found Katherine in the kitchen, refilling her glass of wine. "Hey."

"Hey."

"I take it this was a surprise."

She nodded and gulped her wine.

"Sorry."

"It's fine."

"Liar."

Katherine hung her head. "I'm so stupid. I mean, I knew this would happen eventually. I just hoped . . ."

That Cash would love her, like she loved him.

"I can't keep doing this," she whispered. "Waiting. I need—I don't know what I need."

"A vacation." An idea sparked.

It happened to me every so often—where something hit me with such force that I knew instantly it would be brilliant. Like the time I'd sunk an entire year's profit at Gemma Lane into development of an organic, eco-friendly skin care line. It had paid off tenfold within thirteen months.

"I don't have time for a vacation," she said.

"You need to make time. Get away from here. Get away from him. Carol and Liddy and JR will cover for you. Let your heart heal a little bit."

Her eyes tracked to the dining room where Dany had said something to make Cash burst out laughing. "Where would I go?"

262

"Drive the Cadillac to California."

"No," she said instantly. "I'm never going back there."

I didn't blame her for that. "Then how about, um . . ." I snapped my fingers. "Oregon."

"What's in Oregon?" she asked.

"Not what, but *who*." I smiled. "Aria."

"Huh?"

"Take the car to Aria. It's fitting, don't you think? I took the Cadillac from Londyn. You can take it from me. And if you don't want to go to California, I bet Aria would. Give her the car."

"How do you know? Have you talked to her?"

"Well, no. But worst case, she doesn't want to, and you return home with a car. Then once the baby is old enough, Easton and I will drive it and find Karson."

"How do you know Aria's still in Oregon?"

"Well, I don't. But it wouldn't be hard to find out." One call to my private investigator and we'd know before breakfast.

"What about Londyn?"

"You said it earlier. She's not going to care."

Katherine sipped her wine, thinking it over. Then her eyes went to the dining room once more just in time to see Cash drop a kiss to Dany's forehead. "Okay. I'll go. Give me a day to get things in order."

Oh my God, it worked. I thought it would take more convincing. "Great! We'll have the car ready to go."

She nodded and set her wine aside, then she walked out of the kitchen, not headed toward the group, but straight for the door. She paused with her hand on the knob and looked back. "Thanks."

"You're welcome."

I stayed put, watching as she slipped out.

"Damn." Easton sighed, appearing at my side. "She's upset."

"Yeah."

He put his arm around my shoulders, pulling me close. "How are you?"

"Full. Tired." I leaned into him. "Ready to go home."

"Okay." He kept hold of me as he called into the dining room, "We're taking off. Kat's headed home too."

After a round of goodbyes and a plastic container of chocolate chip cookies, we drove home with the windows down, savoring the fragrant spring air.

"Katherine's going to drive the Cadillac to Oregon," I told him.

"Alone? When?"

"Well . . ." I took a deep breath and told him my plan.

My whole plan.

What I'd told Katherine had only been a part of my grand scheme.

"You sure this is a good idea?" he asked as we walked into our house and he tossed his keys on the kitchen island.

"Positive. This will work."

"For Katherine's sake, and Cash's, I hope you're right."

"Me too." I rubbed my belly, feeling the baby kick. "Ooh. Come here."

Easton came closer and I took his hand, positioning his palm on my side. We stilled, waiting, then another kick jabbed in just the right spot.

"Did you feel that?"

His eyes softened, his palm never moving as his free arm wrapped around me and he dropped his cheek to my head. "It's going to be okay."

"Yeah. It's going to be okay." I sank into his side.

I'd work the boring front desk and let Cash handle the expansion. I'd stop spending late nights in our home office. I'd take up reading or crochet or prenatal yoga. And if needed, I'd go on the medication.

Because this baby was worth every sacrifice in the world.

"It's going to be more than okay."

———

Two and a half months later, our son was born. Jake Easton Greer joined the world in perfect health with a mat of my brown hair and his father's dark eyes.

And that real life I'd been searching for . . .

It had been in Montana the whole time.

Waiting for me to come home.

Quarter Miles

PROLOGUE

"Are you sure about this?" Aria asked. She'd buckled her seat belt but hadn't closed the passenger door.

The ocean breeze drifted inside the cab and caught the flyaway hairs by my temple. One strand tickled my nose and another stuck to the gloss on my lips.

Was I sure about this?

No.

I wasn't sure about anything anymore. But that's what happened in life. You endured the moments of excruciating pain. A death. A heartbreak. A betrayal. You made decisions that would alter the course of your life in the hopes that there was something good waiting for you at the end of the road. You survived today to get to tomorrow.

Yesterday, I'd had a home. I'd had a job. I'd had a family.

Yesterday, I'd been in love.

But a lot had changed since yesterday. Even more had changed in the past five days.

My only wish was that tomorrow, some of this crippling heartache might fade. That the urge to scream and cry would wane.

There was only one way to find out.

I jammed the key into the ignition. "Close the door."

1

KATHERINE

FIVE DAYS EARLIER . . .

Eight hundred and thirty-one miles.

My heart thumped harder as I stared at the number on the map. My breath caught in my throat. It was only a road trip but my stomach was in knots.

I hadn't left Montana since the day I'd arrived. As a fresh-faced and eager eighteen-year-old, I'd found safety here. A home. I'd rarely left the Greer Ranch and Mountain Resort, let alone the state, but I had to get out of here.

I needed every one of those eight hundred and thirty-one miles.

Excitement mixed with anxiety as I closed the GPS app on my phone with trembling fingers. Scanning my office, I racked my brain for anything I'd forgotten to do in my whirlwind attempt to prepare for this no-notice, yet overdue vacation.

The staff had my number in case of an emergency. Emails could wait until I stopped at a gas station or when I was in my hotel room each night. They'd be fine without me for a couple weeks, right? Besides a natural disaster or fire, I could handle almost any emergency remotely.

The resort ran like a well-oiled machine, at least when I was behind the wheel. I'd refined processes and procedures, training my subordinates with precision. My capable team could handle anything that came up for two weeks. As long as no one quit.

Oh God, please don't let anyone quit. My heart thumped again. Was this how parents felt when they sent their children off to college? No wonder mothers cried and fathers loitered on drop-off day. It was disquieting.

This resort was my baby. My everything. I worked ten-hour days, six days per week. I came in every other Sunday morning to approve payroll and stayed late on Tuesday nights to meet with the chef and go over his upcoming meal plan.

We were heading into the peak summer season and I actually didn't have time for a road trip across the Pacific Northwest. *Maybe I should cancel.*

Except I truly, desperately, achingly *needed* this trip.

Because if I had to see Cash today after he'd spent the past two nights away from home and in a woman's bed, I'd claw my eyes out. Since I really loved my eyes and the ability to see, I had to get some space.

Eight hundred and thirty-one miles of space, to be exact.

That was how far it was to Heron Beach, Oregon, from Clear River, Montana.

After one last scroll through my email, I shut down my computer, stuffing the laptop along with my phone in my tote. The two pens beside my planner—one red for employee-related tasks, one blue for guest activities—were put into their designated slot in my drawer. The paper clip that was attempting to escape a contract was straightened. The sticky note I'd used for this morning's checklist was crumpled and tossed in the trash. Then I ran my hand over the back of my executive chair, pushing it under the oak desk.

The clock beside my wall of bookshelves showed I had ten minutes until eight, when I was due at Gemma's to pick up the Cadillac. I'd been working since five but this nagging feeling that I was forgetting something made me wish I'd come in at four.

I took one last glance at my tidy desk and my eyes caught on the single framed picture I kept beside the phone. It was of me standing with the Greers. As an honorary member of their family, they'd invited—ordered—me to show up on picture day seven years ago. This was the family photo currently on the resort's website and in its brochures.

Now that Easton and Gemma were engaged and having a baby, I suspected we'd be taking a new photo soon. But this one would always be a favorite. Maybe because it was from so long ago.

Everyone looked the same, more or less. Jake and Carol, the ranch's founders, had a few more wrinkles these days. Their son, JR, and his wife, Liddy, had both retired. Easton smiled more since he'd fallen in love with Gemma.

But Cash looked exactly the same. Handsome with his devilish grin and bright hazel eyes that reminded me of sunshine streaming through a forest's leaves.

He had his arm around my shoulders as he smiled straight ahead at the camera. Maybe the reason I loved this picture so much was because it was easy to look at it and pretend that we were every bit the loving, happy couple we appeared to be.

Except Cash had been my friend, and only my friend, for twelve years. We'd met early on in my career at the resort, when I'd been a housekeeper and living in the staff quarters. He'd come home from college for spring break and the two of us had hit it off over our mutual love for Mountain

272

Dew. In all those years, he'd never once flirted. He'd never once asked me out or led me on.

This ridiculous and epic crush was entirely one-sided.

I put the frame down, face-first, hiding the picture from view. We weren't a couple. We wouldn't *be* a couple. And it was time to let him go.

It was time for a new picture.

"Katherine?" Carol poked her head through my office door. "Oh, good. You're still here."

"Hi." I smiled at my adopted grandmother and the woman I wanted to become. For as long as I lived, I doubted I'd meet anyone with as much fire and spirit as Carol Greer. "What's up?"

The smile on her face was warm and gentle as she crossed the room with an envelope in her hand. Her hair was braided in a long, bright-white rope that draped over her shoulder. She was in a soft flannel shirt tucked into a pair of well-worn jeans. The woman had more money than I could even contemplate amassing in my lifetime, and her boots—the ones I'd bought her as a birthday gift five years ago—were scuffed beyond recognition.

"This is for you." She extended the envelope across my desk.

"What is it?" I took it from her, giving it a sideways glance.

She smiled and the crinkles around her brown eyes deepened. "Open it."

I lifted the unsealed flap and pulled out a check she'd folded in half. A check for . . . "Oh my God. Carol."

"It's just a little something from me and Jake to you."

"This is not little." She'd written me a check for ten thousand dollars. "I can't accept this. It's too much."

"Yes, you can and yes, you will. It's a gift. I want you to enjoy this vacation. You haven't taken one in twelve years. Have fun. Spend that money recklessly. Enjoy your time away. We'll have everything here covered."

My eyes stayed glued to the amount. I earned a good living as the general manager at the Greers' multimillion-dollar resort. My truck was paid for and Cash refused to let me pay rent at the house we shared, so most of my salary went into savings. But seeing the numbers on a computer screen after my bimonthly direct deposit wasn't quite the same. I'd never held a check, *a gift*, for ten. Thousand. Dollars. I forced my gaze from the paper. "Thank you. This is . . . *thank you*."

"You're welcome." She nodded and dug into her jeans pocket, pulling out a quarter and handing it over. "And I have one more thing. It comes with a story."

"Okay." I smiled. Carol's stories were my favorite.

She perched on the edge of my desk. "When I was a kid, my daddy took me on a road trip. It was just for a weekend. We were poor and couldn't afford anything fancy. We loaded up a tent and some sleeping bags and a cooler full of food and set out. My mom was five months pregnant and Dad wanted to do something with just me before my sister was born."

"That's sweet."

"He was a sweet man." There was so much fondness in her voice. I was glad she'd loved her father and sad that she'd lost him. "We played a game. Heads left. Tails right. That's how we decided where to go."

"What a fun idea. Where'd you end up?"

"Not far. I think we spent most of one day driving in circles. But we made it almost all the way to Idaho before the time was up and we had to turn back."

The quarter, pinched between my finger and thumb, glinted as the sun streamed through the windows at my back.

"Don't feel like you need to rush back," she said. "Take two weeks. Take three. Take four. Take the time you need, and if you feel like exploring, flip the coin."

Four weeks? I swallowed a laugh. She'd be lucky if I actually made it the planned two.

I tucked the quarter into my pocket. "Thank you. For the gift. And for sharing your story."

She rounded the desk and put her hands on my shoulders. "We love you, Kat."

"I love you too." I went easily into her arms, closing my eyes and taking a long breath. She smelled of wind and earth and lilac blooms, sweet, but strong and free.

"Miss you already."

"You too." I gave her one last long squeeze, then let her go to heft my tote over a shoulder. "Call me if you need anything. Annabeth has a list of everything that needs to be done for the guests and Easton has the excursion schedule—"

"Honey, did you forget who built this resort from the ground up?" Carol laughed, taking my elbow and steering me for the door. "We'll manage."

"I know." I sighed. "Sorry. I don't mean to be disrespectful. I just feel . . . guilty."

"Because you work too hard. And I know you don't mean to be disrespectful. But this is your chance to disconnect. Trust me. We'll be fine."

"Okay." I leaned into her, taking one last glance over my shoulder at the windows and view beyond.

I loved this office. I loved the woman I was in this office. Confident. Commanding. Successful. Never in my wildest dreams would I have thought I'd grow up to be the woman in the corner office, running one of Montana's premier, luxury ranch resorts.

Green meadows blanketed the valley bordered by rolling, tree-covered hills. The mountains in the distance stood tall and blue. There was snow on their peaks, the white caps shining under the brilliant morning sky.

It was captivating and bold. Guests from all over the world came to stay here because the landscape was wholly enchanting. There was a reason why I hadn't taken a vacation in years. When you lived in paradise, why leave?

274

This trip of mine wasn't out of wanderlust. It was a necessary escape. The mental image of Cash canoodling with Dany, the surprise girlfriend, at Friday night's family dinner was enough to make me scream.

Carol escorted me out of my office, flipping off the light as we passed the threshold. She probably felt my itching desire to go back in and check my planner just one more time, so she kept her arm looped with mine, leading—dragging—me down the long hallway. Her boots echoed on the floor's wooden planks as we passed the row of empty offices.

This wing of the lodge was mostly offices, storage and two conference rooms for the occasional corporation who sent their executives away for a working retreat. Beneath us was the dining room and five-star kitchen. The guest rooms were on the other end of the lodge and we also had chalets and extravagant tents.

We sold Montana luxury. Our guests came here for a *traditional Western experience*—at least, that was the marketing pitch. Nothing about the Greer resort was traditional. We catered to the uber rich, the celebrities and urban wealthy who wanted to escape reality for a week to go hiking, horseback riding and glamping in Montana.

Our reputation and quality of experience meant we could charge four thousand dollars per night for a lavish, rustic, three-bedroom chalet.

I glanced at Annabeth's office as we passed, my heart sinking to see it dark and empty. I was late to meet Gemma but I would have felt better had I touched base with at least one employee before leaving.

Besides the kitchen staff who'd been here since six, most of my employees wouldn't arrive until eight thirty. JR's office was across from mine, and while technically retired, he liked to come in around eleven each day, giving him plenty of time for one last cup of coffee before raiding the kitchen for lunch.

"I went through the menu for the next two weeks, but when JR comes in today, will you ask him to check in regularly? Chef Wong will go off menu if someone isn't keeping tabs."

The man was a brilliant chef who we'd hired from New York, but he forgot at times that we weren't in Manhattan and our guests weren't here to try gourmet fusion.

"Yes, we'll make sure he stays on menu," Carol said as we reached the top of the wide, sweeping staircase that dropped to the lobby.

"And will you remind Annabeth that we have a guest in a wheelchair coming Thursday? It's a little boy with cerebral palsy. They're staying in the Eagle Ridge Chalet and I'd like to have her escort them personally to make sure the arrangement will work."

"Anything else?" Carol side-eyed me.

"Um . . ." Yes. About a million things. "You know what? I'll just email Annabeth from the road."

"Katherine, will you relax?"

"I'm relaxed." I forced a too-wide smile as we reached the lobby. The smell of fresh coffee, bacon, eggs and pancakes filled the air. A couple crossed the foyer, headed for the dining room. "Good morning."

They both smiled and returned my greeting before disappearing to get breakfast.

"Shoot." I slipped my arm free of Carol's and rushed to the front desk, where the receptionist's stool was empty. "I forgot to tell Chef Wong about a party coming next week. They requested a special prime rib dinner, which shouldn't be a problem, but I don't want him to forget."

"Which reservation?" Carol asked, appearing at my side.

"Boyd. They'll be in the Grizzly Chalet."

"Okay." She waved me off and grabbed a pen to scribble on a sticky note. "I'll take care of it."

"I can just buzz into the kitchen—"

"Katherine Gates." She pinned me with a stare normally reserved for her grandsons, son or husband. "I will see you in two weeks."

"Fine," I muttered. "I'm going. I'll call and check—"

"You will do no such thing." She planted her hands on her hips. "Don't call."

"But—"

"Kat, take this vacation. It's for your own good."

I fought a cringe, despising those words.

Carol's voice gentled and the pleading in her eyes made me hold my breath. "Let's not pretend I don't know the reason why you decided to take this whirlwind trip. Cash showed up at family dinner with a woman and . . . I get it. I think it's a brilliant idea for you to get away."

I had too much stubborn pride to confess that I was in love with my best friend. But I'd been a fool to think Carol hadn't noticed my feelings for her grandson. I'd loved Cash for years. Did all of the Greers know? Did they share pitiful glances behind my back?

Our poor Kat, stuck in the friend zone for life.

I swallowed a groan.

"Go." She put her hand on my arm. "When I told you to take some time, I meant it. You need to get away from here and decide if this is really the life you want."

"What are you saying?" Why wouldn't I want this life?

"We love you. You are a part of our family, whether you live and work here or not. But you need to get away from here. Breathe. Think. Let him go."

Ouch. Hadn't I thought the exact same thing myself? So why did it hurt so much to hear from someone else?

"I don't want you spending your life waiting," she said.

The lump in my throat made it impossible to speak, so I nodded and stretched a tight smile across my face.

"Go." She kissed my cheek. "Think it over. I would hate to lose you, but I would hate for you to stay here and be unhappy even more."

I walked away from the desk, my head spinning. Why did it feel like I'd just been kicked out? Why did it feel like I'd just been given an ultimatum?

Get over Cash or go somewhere he's not.

Carol had good intentions and I believed that she was looking out for me. She didn't want me to suffer here while he moved on with his life. I didn't want that for myself.

But it was a stark reminder of the truth. I wasn't a Greer. I was the guest in the family photo.

Cash was the Greer, and she wasn't losing her grandson.

My truck was waiting outside the lodge, parked in front of a hitching post we used for space markers. I climbed inside and sucked in a deep breath, fighting the urge to cry.

Part of me wanted to shove my head in the dirt and pretend like this wasn't an issue. After all, I'd been practicing that move for years. I could go about my work, enjoy my simple life and drown the feelings I'd been harboring for a decade in work and denial.

But that wasn't working out so well for me, was it? I'd arrived at a crossroads and maybe after eight hundred and thirty-one miles, I'd know which path to take.

I sucked in another deep breath, then started the truck and reversed out of my space. The gravel road that wound from the lodge to the highway was damp from last night's rain shower, and the grass along the drive glistened. My tires didn't kick up the normal cloud of dust as I drove, giving me a clear view of the imposing lodge through the rearview mirror.

Its logs had been stained a dark, reddish brown. The towering peak of the eaves was nearly as tall as the hundred-year-old evergreens that clustered around the structure.

That building was home. It was my sanctuary. And with every turn of my wheels, I felt it slipping through my grasp. As the lodge grew smaller and smaller in the distance, I was more and more certain I wouldn't see it again.

"You're being silly," I singsonged to myself, aiming my gaze straight ahead.

This was only a vacation. I'd be back in two weeks or less, my feelings for Cash under control. Plus, I had a ten-thousand-dollar check in my pocket.

The frugal girl who'd once begged for spare change demanded it go into savings. But the woman who rarely splurged on herself pictured spa treatments and monogrammed robes and a shopping spree.

A wave of excitement rushed through my veins, swirling with my nerves in a heady mix of anticipation.

Oregon, here I come.

I'd be on my way as soon as I picked up the car.

Eight hundred and thirty-one miles. And twenty-five cents in my pocket.

Maybe Carol had been onto something. I had no schedule. Though I wasn't going to spend three or four weeks on the road, maybe I needed to force myself to spend two. Fourteen days was plenty of time to get to Oregon and hop on a plane home. It was plenty of time to spend an extra day or two exploring.

The coin in my pocket begged to be flipped.

Heads left. Tails right.

I smiled, anxious to pick up the Cadillac and sit behind the wheel. One more stop, then I was gone.

One more stop, then I'd take this trip by quarter miles.

2

KATHERINE

I PULLED into Gemma and Easton's driveway just as my beautiful, pregnant friend came out the front door.

"Morning," I called as I got out of my truck.

"Hey." She waved me up the porch. "Easton should be back soon with the car."

"Where did he take it?" I was anxious to get on the road.

"To fill it up."

I frowned as I reached the top step. "I know how to get gas."

"Oh, I didn't send him away for you. He was driving me crazy, hovering over my every move, so I kicked him out."

I giggled. "How are you today?"

"Good." She smiled, leading me to the porch swing. "How are you?"

"Nervous," I admitted. "I haven't taken a trip in a long time."

"You'll love it." She stroked her belly as I sat at her side, her eyes wandering over the view ahead.

"Yeah, I think I will. It was a good idea."

"Thank you." She shimmied with pride. "I have my moments."

Like the other Greer homes on the property, Easton and Gemma's place was rustic and refined. The dark-stained exterior was broken by shiny, glimmering windows. The meadows surrounding their place were blooming with spring flowers. A deer and her fawn inched out from a copse of cottonwood trees, their noses bent to the grass and their ears raised at attention.

We sat on the swing, rocking gently in the cool, crisp morning air. I tugged the sleeves of my sweater over my chilly knuckles as Gemma shoved her sleeves above her elbows. For the past month of her pregnancy, she'd cursed often how it was *so damn hot*.

"Any word from your private investigator on Aria?"

"He emailed me last night and said she's still in Heron Beach." Gemma shifted to take a sticky note from her pocket. "Here's her address and the name of the hotel where she works."

I took the note and stuffed it into my pocket. "God, this is crazy."

"Maybe."

"What if she doesn't want to see me?"

Gemma scoffed. "Please. This is Aria we're talking about. She'll hug you so hard it'll probably crack a rib."

I smiled. "True."

It was going to be strange seeing Aria after all these years. I could still see her and her sister, Clara, standing at the bus station, waving as Gemma, Londyn and I boarded a Greyhound destined for Montana. Clara had been crying while Aria had laughed, flipping us off for leaving them behind.

"Do you think she'll take the car to California?" I asked.

Gemma shrugged. "I don't know. Maybe. But if not, that's okay. Come home and Easton and I will take it after the baby's born."

On cue, a shiny red Cadillac appeared on the gravel lane ahead.

This was it. That was my ride. Damn, I was nervous. About leaving. About driving. About everything. When had I become this cowardly recluse?

I'd grown up in Temecula, California. Though the city at large appealed, my childhood had not. I hadn't grown up in a dreamy, suburban home with a white picket fence and a goldendoodle named Rover. My youth had been a nightmare. At sixteen, I'd run away from home to live in a junkyard with five other teenagers who'd each survived nightmares of their own, Gemma included.

She'd been my roommate in the junkyard. The two of us had shared a makeshift tent, while Aria and Clara had lived in an old delivery van, and Londyn and Karson had turned a rusted 1969 Cadillac DeVille convertible into a home.

The very car that bounced and bumped our way.

"Did you call Londyn?" I asked Gemma.

"I did. And she thinks my idea is brilliant too. She loves that her car is bringing us all together."

"Me too."

As we'd grown up, I'd lost touch with my junkyard friends. Gemma, Londyn and I had come to Montana for jobs at the resort, but they hadn't lasted long. Londyn only four months, Gemma eight. They'd both landed in Boston and we'd gone years without talking until one day last fall, Gemma had shown up at the resort out of the blue, driving a Cadillac.

Londyn had rescued her Cadillac from the junkyard and she'd had it completely restored. It was a piece of classic Americana. A showstopper. She'd set out in that Cadillac on a journey of her own, to find a new life. After she had, she'd given the car to Gemma, urging her to take her own trip.

Now it was my turn behind the wheel.

"Have you, um, talked to Cash?" Gemma asked. "About the trip?"

"No. He didn't come home on Friday." Or last night.

Every Friday night, the Greers had a family dinner at Carol and Jake's home. It was a long-standing tradition, and much like the family photo, I'd been invited—expected—to attend. Maybe my last name wasn't Greer, but from the outside, you'd never know.

I'd cherished that invitation and rarely missed a Friday.

When Gemma had arrived, they'd invited her too. They'd pulled her into their family without hesitation, but besides us, the unspoken rule was that dinner was not for others.

Easton, Cash and I didn't bring dates to family dinner because unless it was serious, you came alone. None of us had ever been in a serious enough relationship to warrant a family dinner introduction.

Or so I'd thought.

Last Friday, Cash had brought Dany, a pretty blonde I'd known for years, to dinner. Her family was from this area and they had their own ranch outside of Clear River. Her father served with me on the town council and always bragged about how much Dany loved being a nurse in Missoula, the closest city, located forty miles away.

All through dinner, Cash had been enamored with Dany. Laughing. Whispering. Touching.

It had broken my heart. Just like it had broken my heart knowing he'd spent the weekend with her while I'd been home alone, crying into a pint of ice cream because the man I'd loved for years would only ever see me as Kat, his unofficial sister.

"I'm pathetic," I whispered.

"No, you're not." Gemma took my hand. "He's an idiot."

"No, he's not."

Cash Greer was a good man. He loved working with horses. He loved his family. He loved this ranch.

He just didn't love me.

Easton pulled the Cadillac into the space beside my truck and Gemma pushed herself out of the swing, leading with her belly. My hands shook as I stood, shifting weight from one foot to the other as Easton climbed out of the driver's seat. The cherry-red paint on the Cadillac's hood was polished to a shine. Its chrome fender gleamed. It was one hell of a sight.

And for the next two weeks, it was mine.

I scrambled down the porch steps, greeting Easton as I went to the truck to unload my things. The sooner I got out of here, the sooner I would relax. I went to lift my caramel suitcase and move it to the Cadillac's trunk, but Easton was there to do it for me.

"Just this?" Easton asked.

"And my purse." I grabbed it from the truck's front seat and took it to the Cadillac. "Thanks for taking care of everything. Call me if something comes up, okay?"

Easton slammed the trunk closed, my suitcase safely stowed. "I will."

While Carol had insisted on handling everything on her own, Easton wouldn't be as insistent on shutting me out. When things weren't running smoothly at the resort, it only caused him stress, and when Easton was stressed, he wasn't quiet about it.

The Greers had set up their business in two parts—the ranch and the resort. Both worked closely in tandem with one another, and while I managed the resort, Easton managed the ranch.

With thousands of acres to manage and maintain, he didn't have time to dabble in guest services, nor did he have the desire. He would rather stay in his office in the stables than in the lodge with a waiting smile for any guest.

As I focused my daily efforts on hospitality, Easton was busy overseeing all operations concerning the land itself and the livestock. He and his staff ensured pastures were fenced and free of noxious weeds. They managed the cattle herd and the horses. When my guests wanted to go on a trail ride, Easton's crew led the excursion. From hikes to wagon rides to bonfires to guided hunting experiences, his team handled anything outdoors.

If an activity involved a pillow, fork or confirmation number, it fell under my domain. When JR had retired and I'd been promoted to manager four years ago, the two of us had developed a system. We counted on each other for honesty and open lines of communication. Our relationship was built on trust.

If there was a disaster, Easton would call, and knowing that settled some nerves about this vacation.

"Have fun," Gemma said, settling into Easton's side. "Don't worry about things here."

I nodded. "I'll try."

"Got your Triple A card?" Easton asked.

"Uh, no." Why would I have Triple A? I hadn't gone anywhere in years so why would I need roadside insurance? "But I have a phone."

He frowned. "What if you get a flat?"

"Then I'll change it and finally put the hours of practice you made me endure to good use."

Jake and JR had taken shifts teaching me how to drive. They hadn't been able to believe that I'd come to Montana at eighteen and never been behind a wheel. But it was Easton I'd called when I'd gotten my first—and only—flat tire on a trip to Missoula. We'd come home and for the next week, he'd made me change one tire a day until he was sure I had it mastered.

Easton was the oldest of the Greer sons and the closest thing I had to a big brother. He was overprotective and mildly annoying, but kind. When Gemma, Londyn and I had come to the ranch from the junkyard, he'd been working on the ranch, having already finished college. He was handsome and rugged, but he was too broody and serious for my taste. Besides, his heart had been Gemma's for a long, long time.

They were the perfect pair. Her sass and steel mellowed him. He tamed her wild nature and gave her roots.

They would be difficult to be around if I didn't love them both so much.

"Do you want some cookies for the road?" Gemma asked, looking down the gravel road. "I made some last night."

"No, that's okay. I think I'll just get going."

"But are you sure? You might get hungry." Before I could protest again, she held up a finger and walked toward the house.

"Tell me these aren't an experimental batch," I said to Easton once she was out of earshot.

Gemma had been *enhancing* a standard chocolate chip cookie recipe for the past month. Every few days, she'd come to my office with a half dozen for me to sample. When she'd brought in the batch with raisins and pistachios, I'd told her I was on a new diet, no sugar allowed.

"No," Easton said. "These are actually pretty good."

Gemma emerged a minute later with a zippered plastic bag stuffed with cookies. She took each step slowly, her eyes once again searching the road as she came to my side.

I glanced over my shoulder but the lane was empty. "What?"

"Nothing." She handed me the cookies. "I thought I saw a deer."

"Ah." I nodded. "Okay. Time to get going."

The quarter in my pocket was getting heavier and I was anxious to give it a flip.

Gemma pulled me in for a hug. "I wish I could go with you."

"Me too." I held her tighter, her baby belly requiring me to stand on my tiptoes to get over the bump. "Rest, okay?"

"Yeah," she muttered.

At her prenatal checkup on Friday, the doctor had put her on activity rest, concerned with her blood pressure. Until their baby boy was born in a couple months, she was to *relax*. Gemma didn't actually know what that word meant so I suspected the next two months would be entertaining at the very least.

In all the years I'd known Gemma, she'd never stopped moving. Her ambitions were unparalleled.

Cash was that way, in a state of perpetual motion. Unless we were watching a movie together, he always had something to do, whether it be an odd job around the house or something with a horse at the stables. Then again, maybe I just saw him as busy because we shared a home.

The idea that he hadn't been home made my heart twist.

Was he still with her? Would he even notice I was gone? Or would he take this opportunity to fuck his girlfriend on our living room couch?

Five years ago, I'd moved in with Cash. At the time, I'd been living in the staff quarters—a dormitory of sorts for the single, young, seasonal employees who didn't have their own home in the area, complete with cramped rooms and communal bathrooms. Not that I was picky. I'd spent years in a dirty junkyard, and my childhood home before that hadn't been much better.

Carol and Jake had just built a new house in the foothills, their retirement home, and Cash had been living in their old home, alone with nearly three thousand square feet and two extra bedrooms.

I'd accepted his invitation immediately. Living with Cash was easy. Comfortable. We talked every morning over coffee and cereal. We ate dinner together each night. He was my best friend. My confidant. My companion.

Five years, and in that time, he'd never once disappeared to a woman's bed. Hell, he hadn't even bothered to tell me he had a girlfriend.

A trip to Oregon and back was just what I needed to erase the sting of his silence.

"Be careful," Easton said, giving me a hug goodbye.

"I will." I stepped to the door, ready to get in, when the sound of a diesel engine caught my ear. My gaze flicked to the road as a truck appeared.

Shit. That was Cash's truck.

Call it petty, but I'd hoped to give him a dose of his own by keeping this trip of mine a secret.

The urge to hop in the Cadillac tempted me toward the driver's seat. But damn my feet, they stayed rooted in place, waiting as he eased into the empty space beside my truck in the driveway.

Had Gemma been waiting for him? Was that why she'd been looking down the road?

No. No way. This trip was her idea. She'd been at dinner on Friday night when Cash had arrived with Dany. Gemma knew how hard it had been for me to see him with another woman. This trip had been her idea. She'd suggested I take the Cadillac, get some distance and give my heart a chance to heal.

Though she didn't look surprised as he shut off his truck and stepped out. No, she looked . . . guilty.

Cash sauntered over wearing the same clothes he'd had on Friday night.

Nice. That was exactly what I needed—a reminder that he'd been sleeping somewhere other than his own damn bed.

"Hey." His voice was gravelly and rough, like he'd just woken up.

It was the voice that made my knees weak every morning when he shuffled into the kitchen in search of coffee. His dark hair would be sticking out in all directions. He'd be wearing only a low-slung pair of pajama pants, his broad, naked chest and washboard abs on full display.

Was that where things had gone wrong? Maybe I shouldn't have moved in with Cash. Any hot-blooded woman would fall for a sexy cowboy with a strong, stubbled jaw and a sleepy, devilish smile.

Convincing myself that living together was the problem might have been plausible if this crush of mine hadn't started years before we'd ever shared a roof.

My feelings for Cash had grown like the evergreens, ring by ring until the trunk was so massive I couldn't wrap my arms around it.

Still, when I got back, I was moving out. If I managed to get my feelings under control, great. Even then, I didn't want to hear Cash's bedsprings squeak when he let Dany sleep over.

284

I'd never liked that girl. She was too perfect, with her satin blond hair and perpetual smile.

Dany. Ugh. My lip curled.

"What?" he asked, stopping in front of me, his gaze on my scowl.

"Nothing." I waved it off.

"How'd it go?" Easton asked Cash.

Really? Couldn't they do the play-by-play of Cash's weekend spent screwing his girlfriend *after* I left?

Cash shrugged. "Meh."

Meh? I guess Dany wasn't so perfect after all. It cheered me up a smidge to know she was mediocre in bed.

"Did you see the lion?" Easton asked.

Wait. What? "Lion? We have a lion?"

Cash nodded. "Gemma said she saw a mountain lion at the expansion property."

"When?" My eyes bugged out. "Why didn't you tell me?"

"Didn't I?" She twirled a lock of her chocolate-brown hair. "Huh. I thought I did. Pregnancy brain is no joke."

I narrowed my stare but she refused to make eye contact.

"We need to change activities," I said, instantly switching to crisis management mode. "We can't have guests out hiking if there is a lion in the area. Should we call that guy? What was his name? The one with the hound dogs?" My vacation had just taken a hiatus, but I couldn't leave guests at risk. "I'll go to the office and call the game warden."

"Hold up." Easton raised his hand, stopping me before I could race to my truck, and looked to Cash. "Did you see any signs?"

He shook his head. "Not a sign. I hiked all over, looking for paw prints or scat. Didn't see a thing."

"When?" I asked.

"Where do you think I've been for the past two nights?"

My heart stopped. He hadn't been with Dany.

"Glad you missed me at home. Did you watch our Netflix show?"

Yes, I had watched the show we'd been binging, but I hadn't felt guilty about it until now. "Uh . . ."

"I knew it." He frowned. "Watching our show without me, eating my popcorn while I was sleeping in the back of my goddamn truck, trying to find this mysterious lion."

He hadn't been with Dany. My spirits soared like a kite on the wind, flying into the open blue sky. But before I got carried away, I tugged them back in. Cash still had a girlfriend. They hadn't had a tryst this weekend, but it was only a matter of time. He had a girlfriend. And I was only his best friend.

"Gem, are you sure you saw a lion?" Cash asked.

She lifted a shoulder. "I thought so. It was big but pretty far away. Maybe it was a coyote."

A coyote. A toddler could tell the difference between a mountain lion and a coyote even at a distance. What was she up to?

I planted my hands on my hips and willed Gemma to look at me. She was six inches taller than my five one and she kept her gaze carefully lifted above my head. With Easton and Cash both standing inches above six feet, I was by far the smallest in the group.

The runt.

I hated being short. I squared my shoulders and lengthened my spine, demanding attention. Maybe I was short in stature but that didn't mean I didn't have my own force. "What's going on, Gemma?"

"What?" She feigned innocence. "I thought I saw a mountain lion."

Easton dropped his gaze to his boots, shuffling and kicking at a rock on the gravel driveway. That asshole had never been a good liar.

Regardless of their motives for this lion stunt, at the moment, I could hug them both. Cash and Dany were an inevitability that I'd have to deal with. But for today, I'd get to leave for my trip and not have mental images of them together clouding my windshield.

Gemma finally met my gaze and gave me a small smile.

I mouthed, "Thank you."

She winked.

"Are you guys taking the Cadillac out today?" Cash asked Easton, covering a yawn with his fist.

I shook my head, willing Gemma to keep her mouth shut. She did. It was Easton who I should have kicked in the knee.

"Actually, Katherine's taking a vacation," he said.

"What?" Cash asked at the same time I shot Easton a glare.

So much for disappearing. Part of the reason I hadn't wanted to tell Cash about this was to punish him. The other part was because he wasn't the only overprotective Greer in the mix.

"Where are you going? Why? When?" Cash asked, crowding me with that imposing body. It was a classic Greer intimidation tactic and once upon a time, it would have worked. But I'd become immune to the way they hovered and glowered to get their way.

I was a woman in charge. After all, I'd been taking notes from Carol for years.

I poked a finger in his chest, sending him back a step, and held up my chin. "Today. And I'm not sure exactly where I'm going yet."

"Huh?" Gemma asked at the same time Easton said, "I thought you were going to Oregon."

"Yes, eventually I'll get to Oregon. But Carol stopped by this morning and gave me an idea. So I'm going to explore before I go see Aria. I'm going to flip a coin and see where it takes me."

Easton shook his head, crossing his arms over his chest. "That's dangerous."

"But you're fine with me driving to Oregon? It's the same trip with a few more turns along the way."

"It's different."

"No, it's not." I was still going on a trip. Alone.

"Well, I love it," Gemma declared.

"Didn't Grandma do that with her dad once?" Cash rubbed the beard he'd grown over the past month.

"Yes, she did."

He hummed, his eyes darting to Easton and Gemma's house. "Mind if I use your bathroom?"

"Go for it." Easton waved him inside.

Cash squeezed my shoulder as he walked past. "Don't leave yet."

"Okay." I'd expected some sort of objection to this trip, but maybe he'd hug me goodbye and that would be the end of it. That was a good thing, right? If Cash wasn't worrying about me, thinking about me, then I could go and attempt to not think about him.

"I don't think this is a good idea," Easton said.

"I think it's great." Gemma jabbed her elbow into his ribs, hissing, "Be supportive."

Easton's shoulders fell. "Drive careful."

"I will." I gave him one last hug, then did the same with Gemma.

Easton held the driver's side door open as I slid behind the Cadillac's smooth, white steering wheel.

The matching leather seat wrapped me in a buttery hug as I inched it forward so my feet would touch the pedals. The interior was impeccable and smelled like polish and pine—Easton's doing, no doubt. When I turned the key, the engine purred. The moment the temperature was above seventy, I was lowering the convertible top and driving with the wind in my sable hair.

This Cadillac was a dream. Londyn had done the restoration right, maintaining the car's classic appearance while enriching it with modern touches. It was hard to believe this was the same car that had been parked beside Gemma's and my tent. The rust and wear were gone. The doors closed without squeaks. The windows were uncracked.

It was a masterpiece.

Easton pushed the door closed, shutting me inside.

I rolled down the window and let my palms rest on the wheel, excitement bubbling through my fingertips.

"I love this quarter flip," Gemma said, crouching as low as she could next to the window. "I wish I could go with you."

"Next time." I smiled as Cash emerged through their front door. I did a double take as he jogged down the porch stairs.

Why was he carrying a backpack?

Cash clapped Easton on the shoulder before rounding the hood toward the passenger side. He flung the door open and bent in half, sliding into the seat.

"What are you doing?" I asked.

He answered by shutting his door and buckling his seat belt.

"Cash," I warned.

"Hand over the quarter." He held out his hand. "I'll flip the coin."

3

CASH

I NEEDED A SHOWER AND A NAP, in that order, but I doubted I'd get either.

"Where are you going?" I asked as Katherine took a right on the highway. "I thought heads was left."

I had flipped heads, hadn't I? I was nearly delirious after two sleepless nights in the backseat of my truck.

Camping out had been fun in my teens and twenties, but damn it, I was thirty years old and wanted to sleep in a bed. The next time Gemma confused a mountain lion with a coyote or a grizzly bear with a Black Angus bull, I was making Easton track the animal.

"We're going home," Kat said.

"Mind if I hop in the shower before we take off?"

"There's no we." She shook her head. "I'm dropping you off."

"Didn't we just have this conversation?"

Kat had tried to kick me out of the Cadillac but I hadn't budged. We'd sat in Easton's driveway long enough that both he and Gemma had given up observing the argument and had retreated inside. When Kat had finally reversed away from Easton's place, I'd thought she'd consented. I should have known better.

Once, I'd bought her a coffee mug that read, *Though she be but little, she is fierce.*

"You're not coming with me, Cash."

"You're not going alone, Kat."

"Yes, I am." Her nostrils flared and her face was turning this violent shade of red that meant soon she'd be spewing profanities and calling me every dirty name in her arsenal. But Kat could yell and rant and curse me up one side and down the other.

There was no way I was letting her drive aimlessly around the country alone.

288

It wasn't safe. It wasn't smart. And it sure as fuck wasn't happening.

"I don't want you along," she barked.

"Tough shit, sweetheart. I'm coming."

"No, you're not." Her foot jammed the accelerator, jolting me into the seat. "Jackass."

The names would get more creative, but unless she developed super-human strength in the next five minutes, there was no way she'd be able to haul me out of this car.

I'd stolen some clothes from Easton's closet—thankfully we were the same size—and some toiletries from their guest bathroom. After Gemma had moved in with him, she'd stocked the place with the essentials. I'd taken the liberty of acquiring a toothbrush, toothpaste and bottle of shampoo.

"You're a dickhead," Kat muttered.

"I know." I relaxed deeper into the seat and closed my eyes. The Cadillac was surprisingly comfortable, and though it wasn't as good as a bed, I'd survive. Twisting and turning, I shifted until my head was propped up between the seat and the door. "Give me a couple hours, then I'll take the next shift to drive."

No response.

I waited five breaths, then cracked an eyelid.

Katherine's mouth was pursed in a hard line and if she didn't let up on the steering wheel, her fingers were going to make permanent indentations.

"Hey." I reached across the cab and brushed my knuckle over her elbow. "Don't be mad."

She jerked her arm away. "Prick."

"I don't want you taking this trip alone. Easton is right. It's dangerous." Too many things could go wrong. There were too many sick fucks in the world. "It's for your own good."

Kat gave me a sneer that would eviscerate most men. "I'm not some hopeless waif who needs your protection."

"I know." Katherine Gates was the strongest, toughest woman I'd ever met. That still didn't mean I was sending her off into the unknown alone. "Then what if I just want a vacation too?"

"Take a vacation."

"I am." I grinned. "With you."

"What about work?"

I scoffed. "Some of us are replaceable."

That got her attention. Some of the fire in her crystal-blue eyes faded. "That's not true. What about the expansion?"

My family was in the middle of expanding our operation to include a state-of-the-art equine breeding and training facility. It would be mine to run with Gemma. When Easton had announced his plans to expand the ranch, she'd invested as a partner.

"Now's the time to leave, before we get busy. Besides, if I'm not there working, Gemma might actually relax." My soon-to-be sister-in-law wasn't one to sit when other people were standing.

Kat sighed. She knew I was right. "Jerk face."

I chuckled and sat up straighter. "Why don't you want me to come along? Are you mad at me or something?"

She'd been noticeably quiet on Friday night at dinner with the family and it wasn't like her to exclude me from anything. It also wasn't like her to arrange for a spontaneous trip without so much as mentioning it to me.

"Kat?" I prompted.

No answer.

Okay, she was mad. "What? What did I do?"

"Nothing," she muttered.

"Then let me come along. Mom and Dad will check on the house. Easton already knows I'm leaving, so he'll rearrange the schedule to cover my shifts."

There were plenty of other guys on his payroll who'd be happy to lead the guided horseback tours and private lessons. I didn't do many of those these days anyway with work ramping up at the training facility.

"Please?" I begged.

"What about Dany?" Kat asked. "Won't she get the wrong idea?"

"Nah." I shifted in my seat, slumping down so far my knees jammed into the glove box. "We called it off on Friday."

The car jerked to the side.

"Whoa." I sat up and glanced behind us. "What was that?"

"Uh . . . gopher."

She swerved to miss them. I swerved to kill. The pests would be running around from now until the end of summer, digging holes in our pastures for the cattle and horses to step in.

The turnoff to our place approached and Katherine slowed the car, easing us off the highway. *Damn it.* She wasn't making this easy.

Well, she wasn't the only stubborn one in the car. She could park at home for hours and I'd just take my nap until she realized, whether she liked it or not, I was going on this trip.

She wasn't the only one who craved a spontaneous vacation. These past few months had been exhausting. Planning at the training facility was going well and the construction crew was slated to break ground within the month.

But working with family—my family in particular—was tough. Everyone had a different opinion.

We need twenty stables. No, we need thirty.

We should hire a separate staff. No, we should utilize the existing hands.

Let's only buy colts this first year. No, we should buy fillies.

There were days when I held up my hands, said fuck it and disappeared to the arena to work with the horses.

Ultimately, how we ran the facility was my decision. But I wanted to let my family feel comfortable expressing their point of view. I valued their experience and input, even when it was overwhelming.

A vacation to let it breathe for a week or two sounded damn nice.

I wasn't sure how Easton did it with the ranch. No wonder he'd been so frustrated these past few years. If not for Gemma, he might have blown a fuse.

But I didn't have a beautiful woman to come home to at night. Well, except Kat. When I needed to vent, she'd always lend an ear. She'd find a way to make me laugh.

Not that I wasn't grateful for this new opportunity. The training facility had been Easton's idea. He knew my talents with horses were wasted on guest excursions and routine ranch work. When this facility opened, if we could just get it running, it would be a dream.

But we had to get it open first.

A road trip with my best friend might save my sanity.

"So, um . . . what happened with Dany?" she asked, the car's wheels crunching on the gravel road as we rolled past a green meadow on the way home.

"We got in the stupidest damn fight." I shook my head, still unable to believe we'd gone from *I adore you, Cash* to *I fucking hate you, asshole* in a span of ten minutes.

"About what?"

"You." I blew out a deep breath. "She didn't like that we lived together."

Kat looked over, her mouth falling open. "Why? Did she, uh, say something specific?"

"No. Just that she didn't like that I had a female roommate."

"Oh."

"Whatever." She wasn't who I'd thought she was anyway. It was no loss.

I'd invited Dany over on Friday night but she'd muttered some comment about not being Kat's biggest fan. How could anyone not like Kat? She was awesome. Funny and smart. She was kind to animals and people alike and as far as I knew, she'd been nothing but polite to Dany.

But what the fuck did I know about women? Our argument had escalated quickly. I'd taken Kat's side. She'd gotten defensive. When Easton had called and told me about the mountain lion, I'd been more than happy to cut the night with Dany short. And I hadn't minded seeing her taillights drive off my ranch.

If I was being honest with myself, I hadn't liked her much. She was a bit shallow for my taste. Too soft. We would have eventually killed each other. But I hadn't dated in a while—a long while—and she was pretty, on the outside. Thankfully, I'd dodged a bullet. Hell, we hadn't even slept together.

"Sorry," Katherine whispered. "You liked her."

"Meh. We only went out twice."

A crease formed between her eyebrows. "But you brought her to family dinner."

"It was just dinner." A dinner I didn't have to cook.

"I thought . . . never mind." She waved it off.

"Thought what?"

"Just that you were more serious if you'd bring her to family dinner."

There was an unspoken rule that Friday dinners were for family members only. Why I'd thought bringing Dany would be a good idea, I wasn't sure. Maybe I'd wanted to see if she could cut it. Stick out my grandmother's scrutiny and laugh at the Greer family inside jokes.

Dany had survived that like a champ. It was my friendship with Kat that had sent her running. *Women.* My guy friends had no problem playing second fiddle to my female best friend. I wouldn't tell Kat this, but Dany hadn't been the first almost girlfriend intimidated by her position in my life.

But like I'd done before, I'd made the easy choice.

Kat.

She let me tease her and wasn't afraid to throw it back. She listened without judgment. I'd take her friendship any day over a lousy lay and relationship drama.

"Oh." Kat kept her eyes on the road, shaking her head.

"It's no loss," I said with a shrug.

Our house came into view down the road. The driveway was empty since both our trucks were at Easton's. My bed was inside that house. My shower. Both were tempting.

But not as tempting as this trip. When was the last time either of us had taken a vacation?

"Let me come with you," I said. "Please?"

She pulled into the driveway, parking in front of the garage. Then she shoved the Cadillac in park and looked over, studying my face.

Katherine's long, dark hair was curled today. Normally she left it straight and tied in a ponytail, but this morning it swirled in soft waves past her shoulders. She'd forgotten sunglasses and the sun caught the blue in her eyes, turning them into sapphire jewels.

"Go take a shower," she said. "You stink."

"Are you going to be here when I come out?"

"Depends. You have to agree, right now, not to touch the radio."

She hated music when we were driving. Something about wanting to hear the wheels on the road and enjoy the quiet. It had never bothered me because when we went on trips to Missoula or drove around the ranch, we talked. I didn't need the radio when she was there to keep me company.

I grinned. "Wouldn't dream of it."

"HERE." I handed Kat a sunglasses case I'd swiped on my way out of the house.

She kept one hand on the wheel as she pried it open with the other, revealing a pair of mirrored Oakleys. "What are these for?"

"Just because." The last time I'd been in Missoula, I'd stopped at the mall to buy myself a new pair. I'd grabbed those for Kat too, thinking she'd like them. The woman was always losing her sunglasses.

She ran her finger over the frames, staring at them for a long moment before turning to me with a smile that didn't quite reach her eyes. She looked almost sad as she said, "Thanks."

"You're welcome." I winked, hoping to cheer her up. "Should we take a bet on if you have those when we get home?"

Kat rolled her eyes and slid them on.

After my two-minute shower, I'd packed a bag of my own clothes and my own toothbrush for the trip. True to her word, Kat had been waiting for me in the car, her fingers flying over the screen of her phone, probably shooting off a string of last-minute emails.

I rolled down the window, letting the air dry my damp hair as Kat pulled onto the highway. "How's this gonna go?"

She shrugged, speeding up to seventy. "I don't know. I guess when we get to the next place we feel like flipping the coin, we'll flip it."

"But we need to end up in Oregon."

"Yep. We're taking the Cadillac to Heron Beach. To Aria."

Aria. How did I know that name? I played it over and over, trying to place it, then it came to me. "She was one of the kids in the junkyard with you and Gemma, right?"

Kat nodded. "Yes."

"There were six of you?"

"Aria and Clara, the twins. Karson, the only boy who lived there. Then Londyn and Gemma, who came here with me."

I'd been in college when Kat and her friends had arrived, but I'd met them on a trip home for spring break. Grandma had introduced them to me as *her girls*. She'd also warned me to stay away from *her girls* if I wanted to keep breathing.

Carol Greer didn't make idle threats, so I'd stayed away, and after graduation, when I'd returned to the ranch to work, Katherine had been the only *girl* left. By that point, she'd been all but adopted by Grandma and Mom. She was the daughter both of them had always wanted.

Any plans I'd had about hitting on her, asking her out, had flown out the window. And I'd definitely wanted to ask her out.

But it had been for the best. A relationship on the ranch would only lead to disaster. We saw enough of that with the staffers. There'd be flings and hookups, and inevitably, one or both of the involved parties would quit.

I'd resented my family some at first for dictating the type of relationship I had with Kat, limiting my options. Over the years, I'd become grateful. We were too good of friends to risk losing it all. My family had been right to discourage me from pursuing her.

Look how quickly things had fizzled with Dany. Or the women who'd come before. Quality boyfriend material I was not. Friend, I could manage.

And maybe without the other family members around, Kat would finally open up about her past. The two of us talked about anything to do with the ranch. The only topic of conversation Kat ever shied away from was her past.

Years ago, she'd confided in Grandma about her childhood, that she'd run away from home to live in a junkyard, of all the fucking places. The thought made my skin crawl. My Kat, tiny, beautiful, loving Kat, living in trash.

She'd never trusted me with the story and I'd only heard it secondhand.

Grandma and Mom had warned me specifically not to push, that it was Kat's business and not to pry. So I hadn't for years. We'd had plenty of other things to talk about, work and whatever drama was happening with my family or guests at the resort.

But Kat had opened up more since Gemma had returned and it had piqued my curiosity. Kat wasn't forthcoming with details about the life she'd lived before Montana, but she also wasn't running away from the topic like she used to. She must have sprinted from her childhood like a horse bolted from a rattlesnake.

Maybe on this trip she'd feel safe airing some demons.

Maybe I'd finally confess my own secret.

"What's Aria like?" I asked.

"I don't know. I haven't spoken to her since the day we left the junkyard."

"You're sure she's in Oregon?"

"According to Gemma's investigator, she works at a hotel there." Kat shifted to dig a sticky note from her pocket. "The Gallaway."

"And why exactly are we going to see Aria?"

"Because eventually, this car needs to get to Karson in California."

"Then let's go to California."

"No."

I stared at her profile, waiting for an explanation. "Just, no?"

"No, I'd like to find Aria."

"Okay." There was more behind her reasoning than reconnecting with an old friend, but I knew Kat's tones well enough to recognize when a door was about to be slammed in my face. Time to try sneaking through a window. "This was Londyn's car, right?"

"Yeah. She lived in it with Karson. He was the first one at Lou's and kind of made it our place."

"Wait. Who's Lou?"

"The owner of the junkyard. I told you about him, remember?"

No, she hadn't. Maybe she'd told Grandma but not me. "Doesn't ring a bell."

"Lou Miley. He was this grumpy old recluse who lived there. One day, Lou came out of the shack where he lived and found Karson sleeping on an old car seat. Lou brought him a blanket. Karson had been sneaking in and sleeping there for a month by that point. I'm not sure if Lou knew the whole time or what, but he didn't make Karson leave."

It baffled me that an adult wouldn't have called the authorities and rescued those kids. The few times she and Gemma had spoken about the junkyard, they'd made it seem like it was paradise. They'd preferred it to an actual home in the foster care system.

I didn't get it, but I'd stopped trying to make sense of it.

Kat had done what she'd had to do at too young an age to make the best of a shitty situation. She was good at finding the bright side. Whenever we watched a bad movie, she'd spout three things she liked about it during the credits.

Once, we'd run out of coffee in the middle of a blizzard. The roads had been too snowy to traverse so she'd set up a tea station and tried to get me to like tea. I'd sampled every flavor from a variety pack that day, then lied and told her tea wasn't so bad. It was shit compared to coffee, but she'd tried.

"Gemma was the second one to move to the junkyard. Her home was . . ." Kat shook her head. "It was awful. Has she ever talked to you about it?"

"No, and I never asked." In the past six months, I'd gotten to know Gemma fairly well. The two of us worked side by side nearly every day and I couldn't have dreamed up a better partner for Easton, not just because she adored my brother but because she was a damn riot. Feisty and sarcastic, confident and bold, Gemma hadn't been born with the last name Greer, but she would wear it well. You'd never know her childhood had been hell.

"She doesn't tell many people the story," Katherine said.

Kind of like you.

I'd earned Kat's trust in so many other areas. With horses, when I'd taught her to ride. With the stress from work, when she was the one who needed to vent. Hell, she trusted me to cook dinner every Wednesday without backup. So why wouldn't she trust me with her past?

"Anyway," Kat continued, "after Gemma moved to the junkyard, Londyn came next. Actually, Gemma hauled her there after she found Londyn trying to eat a sandwich from a garbage can."

"Did you do that?" My stomach rolled. I hated this for her. "Eat garbage?"

"No, we never ate garbage. There was always food around. We'd have peanut butter and honey sandwiches. The trunk to the Cadillac was a great pantry. But if I never eat another banana, I'll die happy. Same with green beans."

"That's why you don't like Grandma's green bean casserole at Thanksgiving or Christmas." Mom would always send us home with some leftovers but Katherine wouldn't touch it. I'd always thought she was just leaving it for me because it was my favorite holiday side dish.

Kat's face puckered. "That's a no on the green beans. It's a miracle I can stand to eat pizza. Londyn waitressed at a pizza place and she'd bring us back pizza most nights she worked."

"Heaven," I teased.

She laughed. "Even you would have gotten sick of pizza."

"Never."

We didn't get a lot of pizza at the ranch. Delivery to the boonies wasn't an option, which was probably why I insisted on it whenever we visited a town with a Domino's.

"Okay, keep going." *Please, keep going.* "Tell me more about Aria."

"She and Clara were a year younger than the rest of us. I think they might have come to Montana with us if we would have waited but . . . we had to get out of there."

"Understandable. Were they mad?"

"No, I don't think so. And it was better they stayed where it was safe until they turned eighteen. Karson promised to stay with them at the junkyard until their birthday. I assume he lived in this car until he left."

It made sense now, why the car was supposed to get to California. "Londyn wants Karson to have the Cadillac."

Katherine nodded. "Londyn and Karson dated. They lived in this car together. After she got it restored and left Boston, she wanted him to have it."

"Why didn't she take it to him?"

"That was the plan, but she got a flat tire in West Virginia, fell in love with her mechanic and never made it to California. Instead, she let Gemma take it."

"And Gemma got waylaid by Easton."

"Exactly." Katherine laughed. "This trip was Gemma's idea. Londyn passed the car to Gemma. Gemma passed it to me. And I'll, hopefully, pass it to Aria, who might take it to Karson."

This wasn't just a vacation for Kat. It was a sentimental trip. "Thanks for letting me come along."

She arched an eyebrow over the brim of her new shades. "Did I have a choice?"

"Nope."

She smiled.

"This is cool. The handoff thing. I guess the only difference is that you're coming back home when it's all done."

Kat shifted in her seat and the smile fell from her face. Her fingers flexed around the wheel. She kept her eyes aimed straight ahead and the sudden stiffness in her shoulders made me pause.

She was coming home, right? This wasn't the same type of trip her friends had taken. Kat had a life in Montana. A job. A family. With the mountains and the open range and the clean air, she'd always told me that Montana was where her heart had found home.

She was coming home. That's why she didn't answer. It was a given.

She was coming home.

"Whose idea was it to come to Montana?" I asked.

"Mine." Her smile reappeared. "I thought it sounded like an adventure. I saved up some change to buy a map, then I marked the biggest towns. Every day, I'd walk to a pay phone and call the local newspapers in Bozeman, Billings, Missoula and Great Falls, asking for any new classifieds."

"And they read them to you?"

She nodded. "The receptionists took pity on me. The paper in Great Falls only did twice so I stopped calling them. After a couple of weeks, I heard about the ad Carol had placed for housekeepers. I called her that day and inquired about it. She told me that if we could get to Montana, there'd be a job waiting. So we waited until I turned eighteen, because I was younger than Londyn and Gemma, then we left. We saved up for bus tickets and . . . you know the rest."

Yes, I knew the rest. There wasn't much I didn't know about Katherine's life since she'd come to Montana. "I'm glad you found that ad."

"Me too."

I twisted to the backseat, where I'd tossed a baseball cap, and pulled it on, trapping the strands of my mostly dry hair. Then I relaxed in my seat.

There were more questions I wanted to ask. Why was she so insistent about not returning to California? Why had she arranged this last-minute trip and not told me about it? But Kat had confided in me more today than she had in years. When I was training a young horse, I didn't push my luck. I wasn't going to with Kat either.

So I flipped Grandma's quarter a couple of times above my lap. "Oregon, here we come."

4

KATHERINE

No.

No, Cash.

No, you may not come on this trip with me.

Why was it so easy to say *no* to Cash in my head but not in person? So much for my trip alone. Damn it. When he'd told me about dumping Dany for me, my resolve to take this solo vacation had disintegrated like wet toilet paper.

Except he hadn't broken it off with her *for* me. *Because* of me. The distinction was essential.

Cash snored in the passenger seat. He'd tipped his hat over his eyes and straight nose. His beard looked soft, like a dog's fur, and I was tempted to sneak a touch.

He grew a beard every November, calling it his winter hide, much like what his horses grew. And like the animals, he'd lose it once the tulips bloomed. Cash would pick a random day to shave and waltz into the kitchen with a grin on his face, proudly displaying that razor-sharp jaw.

I'd miss that annual ritual. I'd miss seeing him every day. But over the last fifty miles, as he'd slept, I'd come to a decision. I couldn't live with Cash. It was time for me to move out.

I'd start with the staff quarters and search for a house of my own.

It would be awkward, returning to the quarters. My time there had been fun, but that had been years ago. The age gap between me and the others was noticeably wider. The younger staff needed a chance to unwind, and having their boss next door was a major buzz kill, but they'd have to deal with it for a while.

There wasn't much of a real estate market in Clear River, but I might find a fixer-upper with projects galore to keep me occupied at night. I'd find something and establish some distance from Cash.

This trip would be our last hurrah. Part of me was glad he'd turned alpha-male brute and insisted on tagging along.

We'd flipped Carol's quarter five times and fate had brought us north and east, over the narrow and quiet Montana highways. There were hours of daylight remaining but as the sun began to lower on the horizon, I wound along a river.

I turned on the radio, scanning for a local channel, then dropped the volume low, letting the twangy jingle of classic country fill the car.

Cash thought I hated the radio on road trips, probably because that's what I'd told him. Really, I hated the radio when *he* was in the car. He didn't hum along or sing the lyrics. That I could handle, even if it was off-key. No, he had this whistle—this ear-splitting, toothy whistle—that was my equivalent of nails on a chalkboard.

That whistle was nearly as annoying as his tendency to let crumbs pile up around the legs beneath his dining room chair. For days, they'd accumulate until finally I couldn't take it anymore and would vacuum them up.

The thing that had irritated me the most was when Cash had christened me Kat. God, how I'd despised that name in the beginning. Of course, I was the only one. He'd started calling me Kat the year after he'd moved home from college, and every member of the Greer family plus the ranch and resort employees had jumped on the *Kat* hay wagon. I'd stayed quiet, not wanting to alienate the family or my coworkers, despite how the name grated on me. I didn't need constant reminders that I was the short and small one of the bunch. That I was the *runt*.

But then Easton had asked Cash why Kat instead of Kate or Katie. Cash had shrugged and told him it was because he admired my claws.

That moment had been another ring around the tree, another moment my love for Cash had grown. I adored the man, piercing whistle and table crumbs included.

The evening air was cool and when I leaned my elbow on the door, the glass of the window was cold against my skin. Covering a yawn with my hand, I kept watch for a sign nestled between the trees, anything to mark an upcoming town. Hopefully one large enough for a motel with two vacancies.

It was exhilarating, not knowing exactly where we were. My entire life, I'd always known my place. I couldn't recall a time when I'd been lost. Trapped, yes, but never lost. Trapped with a mother who'd hated her daughter from the day she was born.

One would think Mom would have screamed *hallelujah* the day I'd left —or had attempted to leave. Instead, she'd slapped me across the face and dragged me to my room, confining me inside for the worst week of my life.

My hand drifted to my cheek. There were still days when I could feel the smack of her palm.

The conversation with Cash must have brought up the memory. I hadn't thought about my mother in months. I shoved her aside, into the box where I kept the past locked away. Cash had rattled the chain around it with his questions earlier.

A sign approached on the road's shoulder. The Idaho border was five miles ahead.

"Hey." Cash shifted in his seat, sitting up. "Sorry, I fell asleep."

"That's okay."

"Where are we?" His deep, husky voice sent a shiver down my spine as he blinked sleep from his eyes.

"We're crossing into Idaho."

He rubbed his jaw. "Want to stop or keep going? I can drive for a while."

"Let's stop." There was no rush. "I want dinner. Maybe we can crash here tonight and start again in the morning."

"Sounds good."

We crossed a long bridge that stretched over the river I'd been driving beside. On the other side, a small town greeted us with welcome signs and the American flag. At the first stop sign, I scanned up and down the streets, searching for a motel.

"Want me to check?" Cash dug his phone from his jeans pocket.

"No. Let's just explore." Eventually we'd have to engage the GPS, but for this first day, I wanted to simply find my way. To embrace the adventure.

"All right." Cash plucked our quarter from the cupholder, positioning it on a knuckle and flicking the edge with his thumbnail. Up it went, end over end, until it smacked in his palm. "Heads."

"Left." I cranked the wheel.

That quarter was lucky. Three blocks down, a neon-orange sign caught my eye with the word *Vacancy* illuminated. Across the street from the Imperial Inn was a restaurant, Harry's Supper Club. The letter board beneath an arrow dotted with light bulbs advertised *Daily Prime Rib Special.*

"Here?" I asked.

"Sold," Cash said. "I'm starving."

"Dinner first." I pulled into the parking lot of Harry's and twisted to grab my purse from the back. The restaurant was dim compared to the bright evening light outside. The décor, rustic and primarily wood, would have fit well at the ranch. But the smell—my God, the smell—made my stomach growl.

Juicy steak and homemade rolls and fluffy potatoes. I was practically drooling by the time the hostess escorted us to a navy booth in the corner. The light hanging over our table gave off a golden glow, enough to reflect glare off the plastic-covered menus. We ordered our drinks and as the waitress described the prime rib special, Cash and I shared the same hungry look.

"Two, please," he told her. "Medium rare. Ranch on the salads. Extra croutons on mine. No tomatoes on hers."

Someday, when—if—I decided to start dating, I hoped the man I chose to sit across from me would take as much notice as Cash so he'd be able to order exactly what I wanted too. It wasn't like I couldn't order myself, but it made me feel special, cherished, that someone knew me well enough to place my order for me.

"We should have made a note of how many miles were on the Cadillac before we started today," Cash said after the waitress delivered our waters. "Would be interesting to know exactly how far we go."

"Oh, I wrote it down in the car."

Cash chuckled. "Always one step ahead of me."

I smiled. "I try."

"So tell me more about the junkyard." He leaned back in the booth, draping one long arm across the back.

He'd worn a long-sleeved Henley today, a shirt I'd bought him two years ago for Christmas because I'd thought the grayish green would bring out the matching flecks in his eyes. The sleeves were pushed up toward his elbows and the muscles on his forearms were tight ropes, strong and defined from years of physical work. The cotton clung to his biceps and stretched across his broad chest. The buttons at the collar were open, revealing a sliver of tan skin and barely a hint of dark hair.

Damn, I'd done good with that shirt. I dropped my eyes to my water, taking a long gulp, hoping the cold liquid would squelch the fire spreading through my veins.

It would be a lot easier to fall out of love with Cash if he weren't so attractive. But how was I supposed to ignore that gorgeous face? How was I supposed to act ambivalent toward that Herculean body and how Cash wielded it with surprising grace? And the way that man looked on a horse, the way his hips glided in a saddle and his bulky thighs clenched—a dull throb bloomed in my core. Even the mental image of him on horseback was intoxicating. Ignore Cash? *Impossible*. I might as well attempt to drive the Cadillac to the moon.

"Kat."

I blinked, forcing my eyes away from my glass. "Huh?"

"The junkyard. Tell me about it. Or about growing up in California."

I scrunched up my nose. If there was a topic to take my mind off this insane attraction to my best friend, California was the winner. The state itself wasn't to blame. Many loved its temperate weather and abundance of activities and Hollywood flair. But when I thought of California, I thought of my mother.

Cash was tugging on my memory box's chain again.

"Did you decide on a name for that new foal yet?" I asked, hoping to steer the conversation away from my past. It might have worked had any other person sat opposite me.

"Daisy. And I see what you're doing here." Cash's chuckle drifted across the table, the low vibration melting into my bones. "I don't want to talk about home or work. Tell me something I don't know. Pretend it's a date and we're getting to know each other."

A date.

I gulped. This wasn't a date. Yes, we were at a nice restaurant in a secluded booth. The lack of a bustling crowd meant the room was hushed, weaving the illusion of intimacy. But this wasn't a romance.

This wasn't a date.

Except it felt like one. Not that I'd been on many lately. It was hard to go out with one man when you were in love with another.

Was it love? Could it be love when it was so exceptionally unrequited? I'd never been in love before. Maybe this was infatuation. Or a deep, respectful friendship.

Because true love was shared.

My feelings were most definitely not.

"Are you okay?" Cash asked, dropping his forearms to the table as he leaned closer.

No. I wasn't okay. "Just tired," I lied. "It was a long day of driving."

"Tomorrow, it's my turn."

"Okay." I wouldn't argue. Though the Cadillac was a powerful, sleek machine, after nine hours behind the wheel, it had lost some of its shine.

"So tell me more about the junkyard," Cash pressed again.

"You know most of it." Wasn't talking about it in the car enough for one day? Normally, I would have skimped on some of the details that I'd told him earlier, but it seemed important he understand a little more than the basics before we met Aria, if only so he didn't feel left out.

"What about school?" he asked.

"Why do you care?"

"Because this is the one part of your life that I don't know everything about. Indulge me."

No.

It was right there. One easy little word. I didn't have trouble telling Easton no. Or their mom, Liddy. Or JR. Or Jake. The only person I struggled to deny was Carol.

And Cash.

He'd inherited her tenacity and persistence. Coupled with that sexy smile, he was my ultimate weakness.

I caved.

"You already know about school," I said. "I dropped out and earned my GED the year after I moved to the ranch."

"That's right. Mom helped you study."

"Every day at lunch." Liddy would come to the lodge and I'd take a break from cleaning or laundry. We'd sit in the kitchen, eating sandwiches, and she'd help explain any concepts I was struggling with. Not that there were many. Getting my GED had been a piece of cake.

"She told me once that you didn't need her help," Cash said.

"I didn't. But I really liked eating lunch with her every day."

Liddy had been the mother who'd shown me how horrendous my own had been. Maybe when I moved out of Cash's place, she'd help me decorate. She could teach me how to cultivate a garden. Liddy would understand my need for some space, right?

"She liked eating lunch with you too. Mom always said she fell in love with you over that GED book."

"Same here," I whispered. "I owe her a lot. Carol too. All of you."

"You don't owe us anything, Kat. You're family."

Family. *The sister.* It had been harder and harder not to feel bitter lately. Being part of the Greer family, even unofficially, was a dream. For a woman who had no family, belonging to one was all I'd ever wanted. So why couldn't I get over my own selfish crush, put this attraction aside and just be *family*?

I looked up and my heart—my sadistic heart—skipped. *That's why.*

Cash's face was shadowed by the dim light. His hair was a mess from being in a hat all day. He'd taken it off when we'd sat down because he wouldn't wear it at the dinner table. It intensified his sparkling gaze. It defined that bearded jaw and accentuated the soft pout of his lower lip. He was mysterious and sexy and utterly mouthwatering.

Screw you, heart.

I don't love Cash.

From now until the end of this trip, I'd tell myself constantly.

I don't love Cash.

"Where did you work? When you lived at the junkyard?" he asked.

I really didn't feel like delving into the past once more, but the alternative wasn't an option. I couldn't sit here across from Cash with his unassuming smolder and pretend the sight of him wasn't making me wet.

Talking was the lesser of two evils. "I worked at a car wash. Karson worked there too. The owner was kind of a jerk but he paid in cash and didn't ask questions."

When I'd filled out the application, I'd put the junkyard's address as my own. Gemma had been listed as my guardian, Londyn a personal reference. Both had been listed with bogus phone numbers. If the owner had known, he hadn't cared. He'd hired me on the spot.

"Is that how you met Karson? At the car wash?"

"Um, sort of." This was why I didn't want to open that box. One question led to another, then another, and I wouldn't lie to Cash.

"Sort of?"

I sighed. "Yes, I met Karson at the car wash, but not as a coworker. I was on the sidewalk, begging for money." It felt as pathetic to admit years later as it had at the time.

The easy look on Cash's face disappeared as a crease formed between his eyebrows. "What?"

I lifted a shoulder. "I was broke."

"Kat—"

"Don't worry. It was just an experiment. That was the first and last time," I said, cutting him off before he could ask questions. Maybe if I steered this conversation in the right direction, we could just avoid anything that would lead to a conversation about the pre-junkyard days.

Not even Carol or Liddy knew that whole story.

"Did you text your dad? Will he check on the house and water my plants while we're gone?" I asked.

"Nice try, sweetheart." Cash shook his head.

Sweetheart. As if Kat weren't enough of a nickname. Why had he given me a pet name too? It was so endearing and affectionate and . . . sexless. Like I was an eight-year-old girl.

"There's nothing more to explain. I didn't have a penny to my name and I really wanted some money to buy a new pair of shoes."

"Why'd you need the shoes?"

"Does it matter?"

"Kat."

"Cash."

His gaze drilled into mine, and that stare, combined with the stubborn set of his jaw, brooked no argument. His expression mimicked Easton's more scrutinizing gaze. "Why did you need the shoes?"

"Because the only pair that fit were flip-flops," I blurted. "And I was days away from turning sixteen so I could apply for a real job. I'd already talked to the manager at a fast-food place, but she told me I needed closed-toe shoes for work."

It had always struck me as ironic that I couldn't get a job to earn the money to buy the shoes without the shoes themselves. Asking my mother for money had been out of the question since I'd been lucky to have the flip-flops in the first place.

"I sat on a street corner with a cardboard sign and a chipped, green plastic cup that I'd taken from my house. And I earned seven dollars and ten cents."

Cash sat perfectly still. Even his chest was frozen, like he'd forgotten how to breathe. But his eyes said everything he wasn't going to voice.

"Please, don't look at me like that." I'd worked so hard to prove myself. To be the strong, capable woman in charge of an award-winning Montana resort.

Cash cleared his throat. "Sorry."

"You can't pity that girl, because she's me. And without her, I wouldn't be sitting across from you right now."

"I don't pity you, Kat." His expression gentled and he blew out a deep breath. "I don't like to think of you living like that. Begging for money. It hurts."

And that was why loving Cash Greer was so damn easy. My pain was his pain. Part of the reason I didn't want him to know my story was because then it would hurt us both.

"I didn't have to beg for long," I said. "I had been sitting there for about three hours, hot and embarrassed and miserable, when Karson came over and introduced himself. He gave me twenty dollars and offered me a place to stay."

The kid living in the junkyard had given me more than money. He'd given me hope.

"Wait." Cash's face hardened. "Did he proposition you? Because you talk like Karson is this good guy but—"

"No." I laughed, realizing how it must have sounded. "Nothing like that. If it was any other person than Karson, I would have run away screaming. But he *is* a good guy. He sat down beside me. Told me that he'd run away from home and where he was living. And he told me about Gemma and Londyn."

"He could have been lying," Cash said.

"But he wasn't. I went with him to the junkyard that day to scope it out." I'd walked with Karson across town to the junkyard, curious and desperate. I'd returned home determined. The plan I'd concocted that day hadn't exactly turned out as I'd expected, but eventually, I'd found my way back. To Karson. To Gemma. To Londyn. To the start of a new life.

"Here you go." The waitress arrived at the edge of our table, carrying two overloaded platters. She slid them in front of us, refilled our waters, then left us alone with our food.

Dinner halted our conversation as we tore into the meal. I, for one, was grateful for the reprieve. We ate mostly in silence, devouring the meal, and paid the check—Cash insisted because I'd driven all day. He never let me pay for a meal out, always finding an excuse to treat me—cleaning the house, washing his towels. He wouldn't let me pay at a restaurant but didn't argue about splitting the grocery bill. Men made no sense.

But after a decade of arguing, with not only him but all the Greer men, who refused to let a woman cover the dinner bill, I'd admitted defeat. I believed in gender equality and empowering women, but I also recognized it was something Cash needed. It was his way to show gratitude.

"Thanks for dinner," I said as we climbed into the Cadillac.

"Welcome. Thanks for letting me tag along."

"Ha," I deadpanned. "Did I have a choice?"

"Nope." He grinned, reached across the cab and flicked the tip of my nose.

I swatted him away, smiling as we drove across the street to the motel.

The rooms at the Imperial Inn were all outward facing. The building was L shaped, with an office at one end that smelled like fresh coffee and vanilla air freshener. After the clerk handed over the keys to two neighboring rooms, Cash and I reparked the Cadillac closer to where we'd be staying and he hauled my suitcase inside.

"This is nice," I said, tossing my purse on the fluffy, floral bedspread. The room was modest but clean. It wasn't the Greer Resort, but nothing was.

"Do me a favor," Cash said, setting my leather suitcase beside the closet. "Don't open the door unless it's me. I've never liked places where the doors open to the outside."

"No problem." I'd seen enough horror movies and thrillers to fear the knock on the motel room door after dark. My lock would remain deadbolted until sunrise. "What time do you want to leave in the morning?"

"Seven?"

"Okay." I nodded. "Have a good night."

"You too." He crossed the room and bent low, wrapping me in a hug.

I slid my hands around his waist, burrowing into his strong shoulder and taking one long heartbeat to savor his strength. To soak up his spicy cologne and heady, masculine scent. I dragged it through my nose, holding it in.

His arms drew me closer.

I squeezed my eyes shut, pretending for a split second this was real. That this embrace was more than a friend wishing another friend good night. Then before I was ready, he was gone.

The heat from his chest disappeared, replaced by the cool night air, as he took a too-long step away.

Cash's forehead furrowed as he stared down at me, a look of shock marring his handsome face.

Oh my God, I'd sniffed him. I'd sniffed him and he'd heard and now things were weird. *Shit.* And I'd been holding on to him so tight. I'd been clinging to him. *Clinging.* What did I do? What did I say? My brain was scrambling for any way to downplay that hug, but before I could make up some lame excuse about feeling lonely or tired, Cash patted the top of my head and strode out of the room, the door swinging closed behind him.

I waited, listening to his bootsteps, as he walked down the sidewalk to his room. The door opened and shut, echoing through our adjoining wall. Then it was silent, the insulation between our rooms preventing me from hearing anything else.

I blew out the breath I'd been holding. Mortification flamed across my cheeks.

Did he know? Had that hug just given me away? There was a reason I kept a safe physical distance from Cash. Two feet at minimum. Because apparently my body couldn't be trusted.

I groaned, collapsing onto the end of the bed and burying my face in my hands.

Cash had patted my head.

I'd hugged him, sniffed him, and he'd patted my head.

What the fuck was wrong with me? Why was I doing this to myself? Why couldn't I just shut it off?

I don't love Cash.

I don't love Cash.

I don't—

A sob came out of nowhere and escaped my lips. I slapped a hand over my mouth in case there was another. This roller coaster was killing me. We were friends one minute, talking and eating and laughing, then the next I just wanted him to hold me. To say good night with a kiss instead of a childish pat on the damn head.

Why was letting him go so hard?

Why couldn't he love me back?

5

CASH

"CASH," Kat snapped as the tires buzzed on the rumble strip.

I jerked my gaze up and righted the car before drifting into the other lane. Thankfully it was empty.

Fuck. What was with me today?

"What's with you today?" she asked.

Of course she'd snatch the words from my head. The two of us had been friends for so long, it wasn't uncommon to finish each other's sentences.

"Sorry," I muttered. "Just, uh, lost in thought."

Katherine hummed and returned her gaze to the passenger window, staring out over the green fields that rolled beyond. Her attention had been fixed on the landscape all morning, which was probably why she hadn't noticed that the reason I'd been bouncing between the white line of the shoulder and yellow center divide for the past twenty miles was because my eyes hadn't exactly been on the road.

They'd been on her.

I ran a hand over my jaw, then gave it a smack, wishing I could knock some sense into my head. Since I hadn't shaved my beard yet, maybe it would cover some of the confusion on my face.

Something was not right. Things felt . . . weird. With Kat. And I couldn't put my finger on why.

Last night, we'd had a normal dinner. At least, it should have been normal. Just two friends sitting across from one another, talking. And she'd confided in me. Finally, Kat had trusted me with details from her past.

Was that why dinner had felt so . . . intimate? Maybe it was just the setting, but damn, it had felt like a date. I'd teased her about thinking of it like one but hadn't expected to actually fall for it myself. And not just a date.

A good date.

The best date.

I shook my head and gripped the steering wheel harder. *Eyes on the road. Do not look at her knees.*

They were just knees, like the shoulder I'd been glancing at a minute ago was just a shoulder. It was only bare skin, smooth and creamy. Flawless except for the one freckle that dotted the apex of her arm and the other that peeked out from the hem of her denim shorts.

When had Kat gotten freckles? Why was I noticing today?

I reached for the console and cranked up the air conditioning. Maybe if it was colder she'd cover those knees and shoulders and skin with something. Because Kat hated to be cold and if I dropped it low enough in here, she'd produce the sweater that was no doubt hiding in that suitcase she called a purse.

When had Kat begun showing so much skin? Normally she wore jeans and long sleeves, her shirts always embroidered with the resort's logo. Even on weekend workdays, she wore a T-shirt and jeans. Was that even a tank top? With its lace trim and satin sheen, it looked more like lingerie.

The temperature had spiked today and the sun was beating down on us since she'd asked to drive with the top down for a while.

"Why did you turn the air on?" she asked, looking above us to the open air.

"I'm hot." *Desperate.* What would it take for her to put on a goddamn sweater? "Are you wearing sunscreen?"

"Uh, no." She gave me a sideways glance. "Why?"

"You're going to get burned." *Get the sweater, Kat. You know you want to.*

"I'll be fine. At the next gas station, I'll grab a bottle for us."

Us. Why did that word sound so serious? It wasn't the intimate kind of us. There was no us. Not in the couple sense of the word. Did I want there to be an us?

Yes.

That lightning-fast internal response nearly had me slamming on the brakes, turning this car around and going back to Montana, where the world was normal.

Kat was my friend. My best friend. Roommate. Coworker. Pseudo sibling. There were days when I'd trade Easton for her permanently. Okay, any day. There were plenty of ways to label our relationship and *us* was not one.

I could not—would not—tear down the boundaries that nearly a decade and firm family reminders had put in place.

Yes, Kat was a beautiful woman. But like I'd told myself at the beginning, after my family had practically adopted her, Kat was off-limits. A single prime-rib dinner and a trip to Oregon weren't going to change that.

I was blaming Harry's Supper Club and the Imperial Inn. That goddamn hotel. Tonight, we were sure as fuck staying somewhere nicer. A hotel with working alarm clocks and decent towels. Big towels. Towel sheets. The scraps they'd justified in the Imperial were a goddamn joke.

Because maybe if I hadn't witnessed Kat clutching a scrap of terry cloth to her naked, dripping-wet body this morning, I wouldn't be so spellbound by her knees. It would be easier for me to remember that she was off-fucking-limits.

Fuck you, towels.

I'd woken up this morning at my normal time, around five thirty. I'd showered and done my best to shake off the non-date dinner. Then I'd dressed, packed my bag and gone to Katherine's room.

I'd knocked once and waited. Then twice. After the third time with no answer, I'd been ready to kick the door in when her footsteps had sounded, running for the deadbolt and chain.

Kat had flung the door open and my mouth had gone desert dry.

The image was printed on my mind like a brand on a steer's hide, burned there forever.

Her hair had been dripping wet, the dark strands depositing glistening drops on her skin. They'd run over her shoulders and down the line of her neck and collarbone. They'd raced over the swells of her breasts, disappearing into the towel.

Her face had been clean and her cheeks flushed, like she'd raced through the end of her shower to answer the door.

She'd rambled something about an alarm clock and her phone not being charged and sleeping late. Her words had been a jumble, delivered so fast they hadn't penetrated my haze, but I could recall with vivid clarity how her lips had moved, soft and pink and ripe. The hand not clutching the towel had flailed in the air as she'd spoken, the movement causing the terry cloth on her left breast to slip and a hint of areola to show. The hem of that towel had barely covered the supple cheeks of her ass as she'd dashed toward the closet to pull out some clothes, only to disappear into the bathroom to get dressed.

I'd forced myself to close her hotel room door, her on the inside, me on the outside, and suck in some damn air as I'd tried to get my hard-on under control.

I'd gotten hard for Kat. My Kat. Katherine Gates, my incredibly sexy, incredibly off-limits best friend.

Kat would come along with me and some buddies whenever I took the family boat to the lake on rare summer weekends off. I'd threatened many friends with death by drowning because of the way they'd ogled her in a bikini.

I'd seen her in less than that towel. I'd seen her countless times after a shower. Granted, normally she wore the lavender puff monstrosity of a robe that my mother had bought her for Christmas a few years ago. It covered her from neck to calf but it was still after-shower attire.

But damn that towel.

I'd wanted to strip it from her body and taste her lips, discover for myself if they were as sweet and pure and clean as the water droplets clinging to her skin.

This was crazy. Fuck, I was losing my mind.

And I was hard again.

Son of a bitch.

"Do you want me to drive?" she asked, shifting in the seat. She tucked one ankle under the opposite knee and the position meant there was a lot of long, lean thigh in my periphery.

My eyes zeroed in on the dotted yellow line that broke the asphalt into halves. I refused to look at her leg. "No."

"Okay." She plucked the quarter out of the metal ashtray, where we'd stashed it.

Ahead, a sign indicated we were about ten miles away from the next town and the interstate. Idaho was long gone, apparently along with my self-control. We were in Washington, headed south.

"Let's flip to see if we go straight or turn."

" 'Kay." I nodded. "Heads, we keep south. Tails, we go east or west. We'll flip again to decide."

The coin turned end over end above her lap and landed with a light thud in her palm. She slapped it on the back of her opposite hand. "Tails."

That meant we'd be getting on the interstate. East would take us toward Montana. Part of me wished for east, longing for the normalcy of home. But I knew Kat. She wasn't going to be satisfied until the Cadillac was delivered, which meant whether I liked it or not, we were headed to Oregon.

Heads. Come on, heads.

She repeated the flip. "Heads."

"West," I breathed.

At least fate was sympathetic to my pain. If the coin flips continued to go in my favor, we'd keep this up. Maybe this attraction was a temporary glitch and tomorrow morning I'd feel differently. But if not, the second that quarter began to work against me, I was tossing it out the window and punching Heron Beach into the GPS.

"Want to stop?" I asked as we neared a gas station beside the interstate's onramp.

"Yes, please."

I nodded and eased off the road, deciding to fill up too and parking beside the pump.

"Are you coming in?" Kat hopped out and slid her sunglasses into her hair. It blew in the breeze and as a few wisps tickled her forehead, she lifted an arm to brush them away.

That move wasn't anything I hadn't seen a hundred times, but I sat in the driver's seat, transfixed. She'd curled her hair again, for the second day in a row. It was as long as it had ever been, the glossy locks tumbling over the spaghetti straps of her dainty top.

"Cash."

I blinked. *Fuck. My. Life.* "Yeah, I'll be in after I gas up."

"Okay." Her long legs were impossible to ignore as she crossed the parking lot to the convenience store. I mean, they weren't long. Not at all. I could pick her up with one arm and toss her over my shoulder, she was that small. But damn they looked long. Miles of smooth, tight skin leading down from an ass that my cock wanted to kiss.

I dropped my eyes to my zipper and the bulge forming beneath. "Fuck you."

This couldn't be happening. I couldn't have the hots for Kat. She'd laugh in my damn face.

We were friends.

We'd been friends for over a decade.

I shoved my door open and went about getting gas, taking a few moments to get myself in check. It wasn't like these thoughts were completely foreign. It wasn't like today was the first time I'd noticed that Katherine Gates was a gorgeous woman.

But today, it was like my body had finally had enough of my mind games.

After twelve years, denial's ironclad grip was beginning to falter, and without my family around, there was no constant reminder that I was expected to behave a certain way where Kat was concerned. That they'd kill me if I broke her heart.

Yes, Kat and I had spent plenty of time together at home without my body getting overheated. But it was my grandparents' former house.

Last night, she'd confided in me. She'd trusted me. And how was I repaying her? By sporting a goddamn chubby all day and gawking at her body.

I was such a fucking asshole.

The nozzle on the gas pump popped and I returned it to its cradle, closing the cap on the Cadillac's tank before stuffing the keys in my pocket and walking into the store.

Katherine snared my attention instantly. She was standing in the candy aisle, her eyebrows furrowed. She was probably trying to decide between a salted nut roll or chocolate bar. Sure enough, I rounded the corner and she held one in one hand and the other in the opposite.

"Get both."

She looked at me and frowned. "You always say that."

I chuckled and walked closer, bending in front of her to pick up my own salted nut roll. On the way up, I miscalculated, moving too close. My arm brushed against hers and Kat's peach scent drew me in. I hovered, unable to step away.

Her blue eyes lifted to mine and she held my gaze. God, she was close. So damn close. My fingers itched to run up the bare skin of her arm and see if it was as velvety smooth as the fruit she smelled like.

When my gaze dropped to her lips, she gasped.

Christ. I took one long step back, then tossed her my nut roll. What was wrong with me? "I'm, uh . . . gonna use the restroom."

"Okay." She put the chocolate bar back and pointed to the row of coolers along the far wall, not looking at me. "What do you want to drink?"

"Water."

She bolted away so fast her flip-flops nearly slipped on the glossy linoleum surface.

Hell. Now I'd made her uncomfortable.

I marched to the bathroom and splashed a handful of cold water on my face. "Get your shit together, Greer."

The smell of industrial cleaner and a urinal cake chased Kat's scent from my nose but as soon as we were back in the car, it would be waiting. It was how our house smelled, sweet and fresh. It was not a new smell, yet today, there was a heady, alluring undertone. I'd noticed it last night in the hotel room when she'd hugged me good night.

When she'd come into my arms so easily that for a moment, I'd forgotten I had to let her go.

I used the bathroom, my mood growing more and more irritable with every passing second. When I stalked out of the men's room, Kat was visible through the store's plate glass window, standing beside the Cadillac, her head bent and her fingers flying over the screen of her phone. I walked to the candy aisle, grabbing the chocolate bar she hadn't bought and a pack of gum, delaying my return to the car for just another minute.

This trip was supposed to be fun. Yesterday had been fun, driving wherever the quarter directed. Hearing stories about her past from her own lips. Sharing a good dinner and her company.

Dany's jealousy hadn't been that off base, had it? Last night had stirred emotions that I hadn't wanted to acknowledge—lust, for one.

Well, lust could fuck right off. I wasn't going to sabotage my friendship with Kat just because my cock was going through a dry spell.

I paid the clerk for Kat's chocolate, then squared my shoulders and stalked outside. My steps slowed as I approached and caught the scowl on her face. "What's wrong?"

"Carol told my entire staff not to email me. Which is ironic because Annabeth just emailed me to tell me they aren't allowed to email me."

I chuckled. "Sounds like Grandma."

"Grrr." Kat tossed a hand in the air. "I'm on vacation. I'm not dead."

"She's just trying to help."

"But it's stressing me out. I love my job."

"I know."

"I want to do my job."

"And you can." I stepped closer and put a hand on her shoulder. How many times had I done this? How many times had I touched her? Hundreds. Thousands. Yet like last night when I'd given her a hug, suddenly everything felt differently. I yanked my hand away, the heat from her skin too hot and electric.

She looked at me, then her eyes dropped to the place where I'd touched her. They alternated back and forth, like she was checking to make sure I hadn't wiped a booger on her or something. Then her gaze went to the ground and her shoulders slumped.

"Here." I handed her the chocolate.

"What's this for?"

I shrugged. "Just because."

She lifted her lashes and gave me a sad smile. "Thanks. Maybe a few hundred empty calories will make me feel better."

"Grandma just wants you to take a vacation. A real vacation. Let her handle whatever happens at home."

"What if there's a crisis?"

"She'll call. Trust me. No news is good news."

"Fine," she muttered. "I feel like I got kicked out."

"No one would ever dream of kicking you out."

She sighed. "I'll take the next shift driving."

I dug the keys from my pocket and handed them over. We'd left the doors unlocked because the top was down, so I gave her some space to walk past me and around the hood before climbing in the passenger seat.

It should have been better riding shotgun, because my gaze could wander, but as we headed west on the interstate, it constantly seemed to drift toward her, like a magnet to steel. My foot bounced on the floor. My hand tapped on my knee.

Kat was stunning behind the wheel, the sun lighting her face and those floating tendrils of hair brushing her shoulders. She'd be even prettier with a smile.

"Tell me more about Aria," I said, hoping to take Kat's mind off work and mine off Kat. "How'd she come to live in the junkyard?"

"Because of Londyn," she said. "They'd lived in the same trailer park. Aria and Clara were living with their uncle. Their parents died in a car accident and the uncle was the only living relative so he got custody. I never saw the guy or met him, but Londyn knew him from their neighborhood. Gemma saw him once when she snuck to their trailer with Aria to steal Clara's bike. I guess he was a major creep. Gemma said he had these beady eyes that made you want to take a shower."

"Did he do something to Aria and Clara?"

"I don't know. It was a no-go subject. They knew that Londyn had run away from her druggie parents and started asking around, trying to find out where she'd gone. They walked into the junkyard one day, holding hands, and that was it. They lived with us." A smile tugged at the corner of her mouth. "They each had these huge backpacks stuffed so tight that when they unzipped them, everything inside just exploded. Clothes. Food. Money. Medicine. They were far more prepared to live there than any of the rest of us had been."

"Londyn and Karson had this Caddy. Gemma and you were in the tent. Where did Aria and Clara stay?"

"In a delivery van. They were smart. They picked a place off the ground and with fewer holes so they didn't have to deal with the mice."

My stomach knotted, like it had yesterday, not wanting to think about Kat sleeping with vermin. "Was it really better than home?"

"Yes." No hesitation.

"What about foster care?"

She shook her head. "That junkyard was my only option."

"And your parents—"

"Should we flip again?" She was already taking out the quarter, balancing the wheel with her knee as she tossed the coin.

At the next exit, Kat got off the interstate and turned on the radio. The music blared, and with the wind whipping over us, it would be impossible to talk.

Conversation over.

She drove with her gaze fixed on the road, never wavering. Never offering another opening to a new topic, certainly not about life before the Greer Ranch and Mountain Resort.

I should have thanked her because instead of thinking about the bare skin of Kat's legs or the slender line of her neck or the graceful drape of her wrist over the steering wheel, I spent the next few hours wondering why my best friend was so hell-bent on keeping secrets.

Maybe she kept hers for the same reason I kept mine.

Because the truth would drive us apart.

6

KATHERINE

"Want to flip or . . ." *Please say no. Please say no.*

"When are you supposed to meet Aria?" Cash asked.

"There's no schedule. She doesn't even know I'm coming, but I think sooner rather than later."

"Then let's get into Oregon today."

Thank God. I dropped the quarter onto the leather seat, not caring if it got wedged in a crack and disappeared into the Cadillac for life. Then I put the car in drive and pulled away from the motel where we'd stayed last night.

This trip was the worst idea I'd had in years. Actually, it had been Gemma's idea, so I was placing the blame at her feet.

I wanted to get to Heron Beach, give this car to Aria and hop on the nearest plane to Montana. Assuming she'd take the car. Oh God, what if she didn't take the car? What if I had to endure a return trip with Cash?

I sent up a silent prayer that Aria would buy into this whole Cadillac handoff thing because there was no way I'd go to California and I didn't know if I could survive another awkward and tense day with Cash.

So much for a last hurrah.

How had it come to this? How had two people who could finish each other's sentences have so little to say? Never in a million years would I have expected this road trip to be so miserable. I mean, I'd expected it to be hard because I secretly loved him. But no harder than any regular day.

It was my fault. He knew. That first night, Cash must have realized my feelings for him weren't entirely platonic.

Me and my sniffing and lingering hugs. I'd stared too much over dinner at the supper club. I'd been too happy that he'd dumped Dany.

He knew.

Yesterday, he'd barely made eye contact, and when he had, there had been restraint in his gaze, like he was consciously weighing every move.

He'd put his hand on my shoulder, realized he'd touched me, probably feared I'd take that gesture to heart, and snatched his hand away so fast he could have dislocated a shoulder.

I'd wanted to crawl under the front tire and let him run me over.

And he wasn't the only one measuring his words. I was terrified to speak in case he'd see just how deep this crush of mine ran.

This had to end. If we drove straight through today, we could get to the coast. We'd be one step closer to calling this trip a bust and going home.

The radio was on low and it crackled with static so I scanned for a new channel. The Cadillac had satellite radio and Bluetooth for my phone, but having to change stations every hundred miles was at least something to do. A twenty-second pardon from the stifling silence.

Cash recognized the song. Damn. I braced, waiting and . . .

The absentminded, piercing whistle hissed from between his teeth. I'd stopped hiding my cringe.

Not that he'd noticed. Cash was stoically staring down the road.

"How far is it to Heron Beach?" I asked.

Cash entered it into his phone's GPS. "About ten hours."

Stupid quarter. Yesterday, the coin had led us backward. We'd gone south, but much too far east, exactly the opposite direction of where we'd needed to head. The universe was conspiring against me.

We were in Idaho again, having recrossed over from Washington. Last night, we'd stopped before dinner and checked into a hotel on the outskirts of Boise. Rather than force us together for an uncomfortable meal, I'd told Cash I was tired from a long day of driving. We'd picked up sandwiches and eaten alone in our respective rooms.

I'd tried calling Gemma but she hadn't answered. Neither had Liddy or Carol. So I'd found a movie on TV and gone to bed early.

Why had I thought this trip would be more exciting? Sure, the countryside was pretty. There'd been one stretch of highway that had been so shrouded by trees, it was like we'd driven through a leafy, green tunnel. But besides the occasional gas station break, when we loaded up on sugar and junk food, the repetitive miles had begun to take their toll.

"How was your night?" Cash asked. His sunglasses were on, shielding his eyes.

"Fine. Yours?"

He lifted a shoulder. "Fine. Watched a game. Crashed early."

What game? Who won? Did you sleep okay? All questions I'd have normally asked before I'd made things weird. Now I was worried that if he made me laugh, if he made me smile, the wall would crack and he'd see the truth shining through.

I don't love Cash.

Even I wasn't buying my own lies.

"I've been thinking," I said, taking a deep breath. "When we get home, I'm going to start looking for my own place."

"What?" Cash shifted and slid his sunglasses into his dark hair. His hazel eyes were so colorful this morning, honey swirled with chocolate and sage. Even with the Cadillac's top up, sunlight bounced off the golden flecks.

I kept my eyes on the road and my hands glued to the wheel. There was no way I'd get through this if I was looking at those eyes. "You need your own space. So do I. The roommate thing worked for a while but it doesn't really make sense. We're adults. We can live alone."

"Is this about Dany?"

"No." Partly. When he did find a woman who'd come to his bed, I didn't want to be on the other side of the house.

Cash put his sunglasses on and his bearded jaw ticked as he stared forward. Mile after mile. Minute after minute. His lack of response made my heart sink, beat after beat. Didn't he care? Couldn't he pretend or slightly object or act like he'd enjoyed having me as a roommate for the past five years?

Finally, he said, "Okay."

Okay. Ouch. His rejection was worse than the time my mother had taken a pinch of my skin between her fingers and twisted it so hard that I'd dropped to my knees and vomited. Then she'd made me clean up my mess.

I fought the urge to cry by biting the inside of my cheek. It was a trick I'd learned early on in life. If I concentrated on my teeth, on how my flesh felt pinched tight between the molars, the tears would disappear.

Crying wouldn't get me anywhere. If I cried, Cash would take pity on me and pity was far worse than any form of heartache.

This was only a change. A shift in—hopefully—the right direction. Some space from Cash and we'd find a normal routine again. We'd go back to being friends. He'd start dating. Maybe I would too. Though the idea of any other man held no appeal but . . . someday.

I wanted a family. My *own* family. Kids who'd run around on the ranch through the green grass in spring and pick wildflowers from the meadows. A dog who'd trail behind them, keeping watch. A husband who'd let me curl into his lap on cold winter afternoons and hold me while the snow fell.

That man wasn't Cash. The sooner I stopped picturing his face in that dream, the sooner I could open my mind and heart to finding love.

"How long?" Cash asked.

"How long, what?" I glanced at him, then back at the road.

"How long have you been planning on moving out? Would you have told me?"

I frowned. "Of course I would have told you."

"Like you told me about taking this trip."

Score one, Cash. "Well, I'm telling you now."

He crossed his arms, stared out the window. "Just like Kat. Keeping the world at arm's length."

"Excuse me?"

"You don't trust any of us. You are part of our family, but there's no trust."

I shook my head. "What are you talking about? Where is this coming from?"

"How long have we known one another? You've never told me about Aria or Clara or Karson or Lou until this trip. Until I peppered you with questions and there wasn't any place for you to go and avoid them."

I sucked in a calming breath. Cash was just lashing out. I'd wanted him to be upset that I was moving out. Well, he was upset. He wasn't wrong. The past was a topic I avoided at all costs, but he also wasn't being fair. He had no idea what I'd undergone, and if I wanted to keep it locked away, that was my choice. "It's not something I like to talk about."

"That's my point."

My knuckles were nearly as white as the steering wheel. "I told you about the junkyard a long, long time ago."

"No, you told Grandma and Mom. Not the same."

Why would I want to tell him about the ugliest times in my life? Why would I want the man I'd been crushing on for years to see my dirty pieces? I'd been clinging to the hope that he'd see me as a sexy, appealing, available woman. Not a pathetic *runt* who'd once been given a stick of deodorant by Mr. Kline, her ninth-grade gym teacher, because she'd smelled and hadn't been able to afford any herself.

Maybe the reason I'd opened up on this trip was because I'd finally given up hope. Cash wouldn't see me as anything more than a friend, a sister, so why hide the truth?

"Can you blame me?" I asked. "Why would I want to talk about it?"

"Because we're *supposed* to be friends. We're supposed to confide in each other."

"We *are* friends."

Cash scoffed. "Then act like it, Katherine. Talk to me."

"I am talking to you!" I threw up a hand. "I'm telling you right now that I want to move out. I need some space."

"From me."

"No." *Yes.* "I just . . . need a change."

"Okay."

There was that word again, laced with sarcasm and disdain. I'd missed the nasty undertones the first time.

The silence returned. The radio was cutting in and out, but I didn't bother changing the channel. My molars ground together. Cash's nostrils flared.

What the hell did he have to be mad about? We were in our thirties. Wouldn't he want a place to himself? Why keep a roommate when he didn't need the financial support? And how dare he tell me that I didn't confide in him.

"You're one to talk about not confiding."

"What?" He shot me a glare. "You know everything there is to know about me."

"Do I? Then let's talk about the ranch."

"What about the ranch?"

"How do you really feel about the expansion?"

It had been Easton's idea to create a state-of-the-art horse breeding and training facility. He'd bought the land for the expansion to the ranch, all the while planning on having Cash run it, but he'd never asked. He'd done it without consulting Cash, or anyone, first.

Cash was fairly easygoing. It took a lot to fluster him, but he was a proud man. He was a leader in his own right. And no one had asked if he even *wanted* to run the training facility. They just assumed that since he loved horses, since he had a gift with the animals, he'd follow suit.

"I'm excited for it." Cash shrugged. "It'll be great once we get it going. I'll get to spend more time with the horses."

"That's not what I'm asking. How do you feel about how it all came about?"

"You mean that East bought property without telling any of us?"

"Yes."

"It's fine." Another shrug. "You know how it is with Dad and Granddad. They aren't great at letting go. This was Easton's power play. He wants to make his mark."

He'd badgered me for not sharing my feelings, but he was doing the same. "But what about you?"

"What about me?"

"Easton should have talked to you. He should have told you what he was planning."

"Maybe."

My temper flared. "Maybe? Yes. He should have talked to you."

"Okay, fine. He should have talked to me. But he didn't."

"Doesn't that make you angry?"

"What do you want me to do about it, Kat? Get into it with Easton? He's already fighting Dad and Granddad on the management stuff. I'm trying to tread lightly and just get the goddamn project done. Why does it matter when at the end of the day, I want to work with horses? This will make that happen."

"But—"

"There's no but. Yes, Easton of all people should know what it's like to feel excluded. To be talked over and brushed aside. But I've known my entire life what it feels like to be in second place. I'm the second son. Causing a fight about it isn't going to change that fact."

It wasn't fair. Cash shouldn't be talked around. He shouldn't be ignored. Didn't he realize how talented he was? How smart?

Why was I angrier about this than he was? Maybe this wasn't an issue for him. Maybe I'd misread the situation.

Or maybe I was picking a fight because moving out when we got home would be a lot easier if I was pissed at Cash first. If I was going to make him mad, I might as well go all in.

"Why do you let people decide how your life is going to go?" I regretted the question immediately.

Cash turned to stone.

My stomach plummeted. Now who wasn't being fair? Cash didn't let people dictate his life, but his family was packed full of strong personalities. They didn't walk over him per se. He just didn't battle.

I couldn't remember a time when Cash argued with his parents or grandparents or Easton. Which was a good thing, except in a family where a Friday dinner wasn't a Friday dinner without some sort of bickering. It had always struck me as off that Cash was rarely in the fray.

He sat motionless and unspeaking, his expression passive. The tension was so thick, his soundless rage so consuming, my own guilt so heavy, that I struggled to breathe.

One hour bled into two. Five to six.

As we drove out of Idaho and into Oregon, I spent the passing miles attempting not to cry. I'd bitten the inside of my cheeks so hard I'd drawn blood.

The farmland around us was a brilliant kelly green. Fences broke up fields. Snowcapped peaks rose tall above the sweeping valleys in the distance. It was a beautiful day outside, bright and clear. But the storm brewing inside the car was as black as midnight.

Hour after hour, regret ate a hole through me like acid through an apple. I wanted to apologize, to make this right, but Cash was too furious to listen. And I was too afraid that if I opened my mouth, too much truth would escape.

Maybe he suspected I had feelings for him, but I'd spent many, many years with my secrets guarded. I wouldn't confess my feelings now.

We had to stop. I had to get out of this car.

A sign along the road marked eight miles to the next town. The gas pump, restaurant and hotel icons indicated it offered services and lodging. We'd made considerable progress today and Heron Beach was only hours away. We'd be there before nightfall if I kept driving.

But I was so weary, so desperate to stop, that I pulled off the highway at the first hotel.

"You don't want to keep going?" Cash asked as I parked.

"Not tonight." My voice was hoarse as I tried to speak past the choking lump in my throat. "I'd rather get there fresh tomorrow to find Aria. Is that okay?"

"It's your trip." He opened his door and stepped out, going to the trunk.

I sucked in a deep breath. Fifteen minutes. I only had to make it fifteen minutes, then I'd be in my room and I could cry alone.

After popping the trunk, I collected my things from the car and climbed out, locking the doors as Cash carried my suitcase in one hand, his duffel in the other, into the lobby.

"Good evening," the clerk greeted, a young man wearing a tweed vest and white shirt. "Checking in?"

"We don't have a reservation," I said. "Do you have a vacancy?"

"Sure." He clicked on his computer. "I've got a standard king room on the second floor."

"Two rooms," Cash corrected, digging out his wallet to slap a credit card on the counter.

I shifted for my purse to fetch my own.

The clerk's gaze volleyed between the two of us. He was probably wondering if we'd just gotten into a lover's spat.

Nope. Definitely not lovers.

He finished checking us in and with room keys in hand, Cash and I walked to the elevator bank.

I reached for the button, he did too, and our fingers jabbed the up arrow at the same time. It was nothing more than a simple brush of the fingers, something we'd done a hundred times—going for the remote, flipping on a light, reaching for a set of keys—but Cash jerked away from me like I was leprous. Was my touch really that revolting?

The metallic taste of blood filled my mouth again as I bit at my cheek once more. But I would not cry, not over Cash. As much as I wanted to blame him for this, it was my fault. I'd gone too far in the car. And if I was honest with myself, none of this would have happened had I not gone too far with my heart.

We stepped into the elevator, taking opposite ends of the car. Two floors felt like eleven and the doors were slow to open.

Cash bolted through them the moment they were wide enough to accommodate his broad shoulders. He took the lead down the hallway, bags in hand, while I followed behind, eyes aimed at the maroon and gold paisley carpet.

He set my caramel leather suitcase beside my room and without a word disappeared to his own.

Tears flooded my eyes, blurring my vision as I slid my key card into the slot. The stupid light blinked red. I did it again. Red again. "Come on," I whispered.

Finally, on the third try, when the first tear escaped, the green light blinked and I shoved my way inside. The moment the door closed behind me, I dropped my suitcase to the floor and my face into my hands. My teeth clamped together, keeping the sobs inside, but the tears were harder to control.

Why were we fighting? We never fought. Why couldn't he have let me go on this trip alone?

I would have come home and everything would have been fine. I would have broached the topic of moving out after I actually had a place to go. Because now, we'd go home and walk around each other on eggshells while I packed to leave.

Sucking in a breath, I stood straight and closed my eyes. This was only a hiccup. Today was rough. Tomorrow would be better. I sniffled and darted into the bathroom to blow my nose and dry my eyes. Then I met my gaze in the mirror.

"You're a mess." I laughed at my reflection. My hair was in a bun because I hadn't washed it this morning. My nose was puffy and my eyes were red. Tomorrow I'd take a little extra care.

I walked out of the bathroom, planning on calling home to check in. I'd waste a couple of hours, give Cash some space to cool down, then I'd go to his room and invite him for dinner, where I'd apologize and beg for his forgiveness.

He was still my friend.

I was rifling through my purse when a knock came at the door. I froze, not sure I wanted to answer it. There was no doubt it was Cash, but if he saw me, he'd know I'd been crying.

He knocked again. He'd keep knocking, and there was no use delaying my apology.

I crossed the room, double checked the peephole, then opened the door. "I'm sor—"

Before I could finish, he took a long step into the room. His hands came to my face, his palms cupping my cheeks.

And then Cash, my best friend, kissed me.

7

CASH

WHY WASN'T THIS AWKWARD?

It should have been. Kissing Kat should have killed any delusions that there was chemistry between us. This kiss was a test. I'd marched over here from my room to prove that there was no spark. What better way to shove Kat firmly into the friend zone than to kiss her and cringe?

Except there was no cringe. There were no alarm bells that this was wrong. And there was definitely no desire to stop.

Kat's pink lips were soft and supple. Her face was the perfect shape for my hands, and when I licked the seam of her lips, she gasped and let me sweep my tongue inside.

Goddamn, she tasted good, like sweet peaches and mint.

I shuffled us backward into the room and the door slammed closed behind me, but I didn't care about anything except this kiss.

Katherine's hands slid up my chest as she rose on her toes, lifting to meet me. Why wasn't she slapping me away? Why did her tongue dart out to tangle with mine?

Who fucking cares?

I was kissing a gorgeous, incredible woman and—*holy hell*—it was hot. I angled my head, dropping my hands from her face to wrap my arms around her body, and I hauled her to my chest, lifting her off the floor.

Her toes dangled above the carpet and one of her flip-flops slid free with a thud. Kat's arms were trapped between us but she wiggled them free to loop around my neck.

So there was something here. I wasn't the only one who'd felt it. The way she kissed me back, melting into my arms, there was no denying she wanted me too.

This trip. This fucking trip.

It was going to ruin us.

As I plundered her mouth, I couldn't find the will to care.

My tongue explored every corner of her mouth, tasting and sucking, until I was dizzy. The bed beckoned, drawing me closer, and without thinking twice, I laid Kat down, giving her my weight.

Her legs parted and even though she was small, I fit there. Above her. Around her. I molded my body to hers as she gave me everything she had.

How had I not noticed her before this trip? My skin tingled and electricity shot through my veins, all from her touch. How had I missed this?

Maybe I hadn't. Maybe I'd turned a blind eye to the charge between us because this was Katherine. My Kat. We weren't supposed to be kissing.

That rational thought flittered out of my mind as I sank deeper into her embrace. Never in my life had a kiss been this intense or consuming. The spark wasn't just a flicker, it was a wildfire that might destroy us both, leaving nothing but ash and destruction in its wake.

Still, I couldn't stop. I couldn't bring myself to pull away from her delicious mouth. For every second I kissed her, the heat intensified until I was panting and desperate to feel her skin, sweaty and sticky, against my own.

Finally, when I was seconds away from tearing at her top, I tore my lips away and propped up on my arms.

Fuck, but she was beautiful. Katherine's lips were red and swollen. Her cheeks were flushed and her eyes hooded.

Beneath my jeans, my erection strained painfully against the zipper. One more kiss like that and I'd make good use of this hotel room.

"Tell me to stop," I whispered. Because I couldn't do it on my own. "Tell me to go."

She shook her head. "Don't go."

Fuck. Me.

"Kat, I . . ."

What? I wasn't even sure what I wanted to say, I just knew there had to be talking.

Her hand came to my cheek, her fingertips brushing through my beard. She arched her hips, pressing her core into my hard cock, and moaned. If she liked the beard, I was never shaving again.

"Are you sure about this?" I asked.

Her eyes locked with mine and those sky-blue orbs stole my breath. "No. Are you?"

"Yes."

Yes, I was sure. Maybe tomorrow common sense and history would muddy the waters, but right here in this moment, I was sure that I'd never wanted another woman the way I wanted Kat.

She blinked and her hand fell away from my face.

"I'll go. Tell me to go," I repeated. If she wasn't sure about this, if her brain was working better than mine, I'd leave this room instantly.

Kat answered by pushing up on an elbow, closing the space between us and smashing her lips to mine.

I circled her in my arms and didn't think twice. My tongue dueled with hers and I sent a relieved groan down her throat. The one that followed was sheer lust.

She clawed at me as I clung to her. Her hands roamed the plane of my chest as I let mine knead the slight curves of her hips.

When I moved, she moved, the two of us so in sync it was like we'd been dancing around one another for years, off beat, and finally, the rhythm was coming together. Like when a rider and a horse finally found their stride.

It was fucking perfection.

"Cash." Katherine broke away from my lips to push up, forcing me to my side.

Oh, fuck. Please don't tell me to go. I would. I'd never disrespect a woman's wishes, especially Kat's, but it would be torture to return to my own room. "What?"

"Off." Her fingers grappled with the buttons on my shirt as she did her best to strip it from my shoulders.

I sat up and her hands fell away as I worked the shirt free, wanting to rip it to shreds but I didn't have a lot of spares. I yanked it from my arms and tossed it aside, reaching behind my neck to whip the undershirt away.

Katherine watched as I came down on top of her once more. Her fingertips dug into my skin, dipping and tracing between the lines of my abs. The ferocity of her touch sent a rush of heat to my throbbing cock, and I closed my eyes, praying for the shreds of my self-control to hold together.

No matter what, I'd make this good for her. I wasn't the kind of man who chased around. I dated women and even then, I rarely jumped immediately into bed. For Kat, I'd pull out all the stops because she deserved my very best.

One knee at a time, I eased my way down the bed and away from her hungry fingers. My hand dove beneath the hem of her shirt, revealing her smooth, silky skin. I dropped my mouth to her body, letting my lips skim down the centerline of her stomach until I hit the waistband of her jeans.

I tugged the button open and slid down the zipper as my feet found their way to the floor. Her jeans stripped easily from her legs and I tossed them aside, swallowing hard at the sight of her black lace panties.

Kat's toned legs were sexy as hell. How had I not noticed them before? I skimmed my fingers up her ankles, past the underside of her knees, until I had the sides of her panties in my fists. Then I dragged them off her skin, one agonizing inch at a time.

My heart beat too hard in my chest and the tightness in my ribs was painful. My cock wept, she was so stunning.

Her gaze was waiting when I forced my eyes away from her slick and bare center. Her lower lip was worried between her teeth. Kat didn't get nervous much but biting her lip was a telltale sign.

"You're perfect. You are so fucking perfect."

A flush crept up her cheeks and a smile stretched across her face. "Oh my God." Kat laughed, slapping a hand over her face to shield her eyes. "Take your pants off."

I grinned. "Yes, ma'am."

My cock sprang free as I toed off my boots and shoved my jeans and boxers down my thighs. I gripped the shaft, giving it a tug and using my thumb to spread the bead at the tip across the head.

Soon. Soon I was going to ease my cock inside Kat's body and hear her gasp my name.

Her eyes were still covered and the blush in her cheeks was spreading. I took her unaware and wrapped my hands around her ankles, earning a squeal as I jerked her to the edge of the bed. Then I dropped to my knees. Her pussy was there, glistening pink and begging for a lick.

"Cash—"

I ran my tongue through her folds.

"Oh, Cash." She arched off the bed, her hips tilting up for my mouth.

She tasted so fucking good. Sweet and hot and wet. My cock ached but before I sank into her body, I wanted her loose and ready.

I latched on to her clit and gave it a good suck, then slid a finger inside. "Wet for me, sweetheart?"

Kat moaned and fisted the covers at her sides. Her eyes were squeezed shut and her legs trembled as I found her sensitive spot and stroked. Over and over I sucked, adding another finger until she squirmed.

When her orgasm broke, it was mesmerizing. The flush on her chest. The way her body writhed against my touch. The part of her mouth and the sheer ecstasy on her beautiful face. Kat cried out and her body shook as I stared, hypnotized.

Finally, she collapsed on the mattress, limp, and I shoved up off my knees and wiped my lips dry.

I bent to fish my wallet from the pocket of my jeans, fumbling through it for the condom I kept in case. With it rolled over my erection, I eased onto the bed.

Her eyelids were heavy as I took her under the arms and hauled her into the pillows before settling into the cradle of her hips. Kat's dark hair spread everywhere, the silky strands a beautiful contrast against the white cotton.

I brushed a hair from her eyes. "Good?"

"So. Good," she panted.

I tugged at her shirt, bringing it over her head. Then I unclasped her bra and peeled it down her arms so I could get a glimpse of her naked. God, she really was perfect. I cupped her breasts in my palms. "Ready for another one?"

The corner of her mouth turned up. "Show me what you've got, Greer."

Damn, I loved it when she challenged me. Kat had a feisty, teasing, competitive nature that she didn't often show. It was a thrill to see it in bed, to see how she'd push when I pulled.

I dragged the tip of my cock through her folds, then I positioned it at her entrance and held those blue pools as I inched inside.

She gasped and looked down to where we were joined. Her eyes widened at the sight of me stretching her, filling her.

I rocked gently, careful to give her time to adjust, and when I was as

326

deep as I could go, she moaned, taking her knees in her hands to spread them wider.

"Fuck, that is hot."

She hummed her agreement.

I eased out and thrust inside, earning a hitch of breath and a coy smile. My mental notebook of what it took to create Kat's whimpers and moans was filling up fast. Maybe today was the exception, but damn it, I hoped I'd get to experiment again.

Sunlight streamed through the windows as we moved together, bringing one another higher and higher. Kat's hands were like butterfly wings, brushing over the sensitive places on my torso and hips and shoulders and ass. They fluttered, driving me wild.

She rolled her hips with my strokes, that push and pull better than I could have imagined. Missionary with Katherine Gates was fucking erotic. She really was something special. I'd known it outside this room but add the sexy and wanton woman screwing me senseless, and she was like the rarest of diamonds, shining only for me.

The threat of reality caught the edge of my consciousness, tapping on my shoulder to remind me that this was my best friend I was fucking. Had I ruined us? Had this just destroyed the one friendship I held above all others?

I shoved those thoughts away. For today. For tomorrow. Forever. Later, I'd think about how everything between us would change.

Bending down, I sucked at the column of her throat. Her fingers threaded into the longer strands of my hair at the nape, tugging them with just enough pressure that I grinned and nipped at the underside of her jaw.

"Harder," she moaned.

I let loose, pistoning my hips faster and faster. Slamming us together until the sound of skin slapping against skin was probably audible in the hallway. My kisses on her bare skin became frantic. I pinched one of her nipples, then enveloped the hard bud in my mouth.

Kat arched, her grip on my hair as tight as ever.

We fucked, hard and so, so good, and when her second orgasm broke, I didn't try to hold back. Pleasure shot down my spine and I tightened, letting my release take over. Wave after wave, I groaned through every pulse of her inner walls squeezing and draining me dry, until I was wrecked.

My heart hammered inside my chest as I eased out of her body to collapse by her side. My legs were shaking and my arms boneless.

Kat sprawled on the bed, her breathing as ragged as my own. We were sweaty and sticky, just like I'd wanted.

And for one last, brief moment, I didn't think about what was to come. The unavoidable conversation. I took her hand in mine and held it like she was my lover.

That short moment was all I got.

Kat shot off the bed, blinking and shoving her hair out of her face. "I, um . . ."

327

Instead of finishing her sentence, she spun around and raced for the bathroom. The spray of the shower's water sounded after the door's lock clicked.

I brought my hands to my face, rubbing away the sex fog. Then I pushed up to a seat, peeling off the condom.

Fuck. What did this mean? Never in my life had I connected with a woman like that. It was . . . my mind was too hazy to come up with the right word. Phenomenal wasn't strong enough.

I stood on shaking legs and took the condom to the trash can, then sat on the end of the bed, hanging my head forward.

I wouldn't regret it. Even if Kat said it was a mistake and she wanted to just be friends again, fine. But I wouldn't regret it.

Maybe we could . . . I wasn't sure what I wanted.

To date? That sounded cheap for someone like Kat. All I knew was that I'd never be able to look at her the same way again. I'd always see her naked and wild beneath me. For a short time, she'd given me that trust.

Before bolting from the bed like she couldn't wait to rinse me from her skin.

The sound of my phone ringing jolted me from my stupor and I bent, plucking it from my jeans.

Grandma.

"What's up?" I answered, trapping the phone between my ear and my shoulder so I could pull on my boxers.

"Well, hello to you too, grandson. Yes, I'm doing well. Thanks for asking."

"Great. You're welcome."

She laughed. "Smartass."

"Learned from the best."

"I was just calling to check in. See how you are doing."

"We're fine." *Fan-fucking-tastic.* But it wasn't like I could tell Grandma that I was totally messed up over my best friend, who was currently in the shower.

"Good. With that out of the way, I have something to tell you."

My heart stopped. "What? Is everyone okay?"

"Oh, yes. Everyone is fine. Your dad is covering for you at the facility."

I rolled my eyes. There was nothing to cover. None of the questions left unanswered had to be solved immediately. We hadn't even started construction. Dad had just jumped at the chance to make some decisions without any interference.

Whatever. If I didn't like something, I'd just change it later.

"Nice of him to do that," I said. "What did you have to tell me?"

"That trip wasn't for you, Cash."

I blinked and stood tall. "What?"

"You should be at home."

"Work will wait two weeks. Besides, it's not like I'm a critical component." Yet.

328

Kat had been onto something in the car. Something I *never* spoke about. Something I rarely mentally acknowledged.

For the past decade, since I'd graduated college, I'd been treated more like an employee at the Greer ranch than the owner I was.

The only consolation was that the family dynamics were hard for Easton too. Which was why I had been pissed when he'd gone ahead and bought property for the training facility without asking.

But what was I supposed to do? Fight with him about it? I was getting my dream job. Not in the way I'd wanted it, but once the expansion happened, did it matter?

"I'm not talking about work," Grandma said. "That was Katherine's trip to get away."

"I wasn't going to let her drive off alone. It was a dangerous idea from the beginning."

She scoffed. "Katherine is tougher than any person I know."

Grandma wasn't wrong. "Then maybe I wanted a break too."

"But it's not about you."

"Okay." Where the hell was she going with this?

"You don't get it."

"Then explain it to me."

She sighed. "Just don't dictate how the trip is going to go."

"I'm not."

She scoffed again. "Yeah, right. I know you. You'll play the big brother and suddenly Kat's vacation will be yours."

I was *not* her brother. I gritted my teeth together. "Anything else?"

"Just . . . give her the chance to explore. To think."

"Think about what?" What the fuck was Grandma talking about?

"About the future."

My heart stopped. Was this about Kat moving out? Had she already told Grandma? Or was there more?

I was missing something. A big something. But what?

I'd thought this trip was for Kat to take a break from working twelve-hour days and to reconnect with an old friend, but as the days had progressed, the unease in my gut had begun to brew like an angry storm.

I was losing her.

My gut screamed that I was losing her.

The water from the shower stopped and the curtain scraped across its rod. "Bye, Grandma."

Without waiting for her response, I ended the call and tossed the phone aside. Then I wadded up my jeans and shirts and picked up my boots, taking them to the closed bathroom door. "Kat?"

"Yeah?" she called back.

"I'm going to go back to my room. Take a shower."

"O-okay."

"Do you want to meet for dinner?" I held my breath, unsure if I wanted the answer to be yes or no.

Before Grandma's call, I would have insisted, but her warning, the way this trip had been going, something had me on edge. Maybe I'd been pushing Kat too hard.

Like my grandmother had said, it wasn't about me.

I stood, waiting for her answer. The water from the shower dripped and dripped. Finally, she said, "No."

No.

What the fuck had we done?

I walked out of her room and into mine, knowing things would never be the same.

8

KATHERINE

PATHETIC. Idiotic. Reckless. Pretty much any way I studied what had happened between me and Cash yesterday, there wasn't a positive adjective to be found.

Cash had kissed me.

Cash had kissed me *everywhere*. I should have been elated. I should have been laughing and happy. For years, I'd dreamed that he'd take notice and just *kiss me*.

Wish granted.

Except now I felt like a fool.

Thank God I'd disappeared to the shower to hide my happy tears yesterday.

I'd used the five-minute shower after we'd had sex to compose myself. To have my quick, squealing fit of joy. Cash had worshiped me. There was no other way to describe it. He'd made my body come alive.

As I'd stood under the spray, I'd worked up the courage to tell Cash how I felt. To tell him I wanted more than his friendship.

I was grateful that he'd left before then. I hadn't had to witness him re-dress and leave. He'd saved me from an extravagant rejection. Part of me wanted to be furious with him. Mostly, I was ashamed.

Did he know I had feelings for him? I'd thought my hug from the first night had tipped him off, but maybe I'd guessed wrong. Maybe he'd just been in a strange mood. But if he didn't know I had feelings for him, why come to my room yesterday? Why have sex with me? Mind-numbing, toe-curling, soul-shattering sex.

The right thing to do would be to talk about it, but we hadn't spoken. Not one word since he'd left my room. There'd been no hello in the hotel lobby this morning. When I'd come down to check out, he'd been in the lounge area adjacent to the front desk—bag packed, ball cap on and ready to leave.

I was too scared to bring it up. Reliving painful experiences through conversation wasn't my favorite pastime and Cash walking out on me yesterday had been excruciating.

Yesterday's drive had been awful. Horrifically awful. It paled in comparison to today's.

We'd arrive in Heron Beach today and though I was nervous to see Aria after all this time, I could hardly wait for another person to buffer the conversation.

But first . . . the apology I'd planned to give Cash was still overdue. And the truth was, I needed Cash today.

I needed him by my side when I saw Aria.

What if she'd changed for the worse since our parting at the junkyard? What if her life was in shambles? It would break my heart. My reunion with Gemma had been different. *She'd* found *me*, and we'd been on my turf. What if Aria didn't want to see me, or worse, remember me?

I clutched the steering wheel and took a deep breath. I was the general manager of a multimillion-dollar resort. I'd earned the position without a college degree or professional training. I could mend fences with my best friend.

"I'm sorry about yesterday," I said. "For what I said in the car."

Cash looked over and gave me a small smile. "Me too."

"I don't want to fight."

"Kat." My name sounded pained and his voice hoarse. He blew out a long breath. "Yesterday. In your room. I—"

"What if we don't talk about it?" Because if he wanted to forget it, if he wanted to pretend like it hadn't happened, my heart would break. So I'd say it first. "What if we forget it ever happened?"

"No."

I blinked, glancing over at him. His jaw was tight. His hazel eyes waiting. "What do you mean?"

"It happened, Kat. I don't want to forget."

"Then what do you want?"

"Truth? I have no fucking clue."

"Me neither." I sighed, so unbelievably relieved he didn't have an answer. That he didn't want to forget about me.

"You're my best friend. The reason I was so pissed in the car yesterday was because you're right. I don't want to admit you're right. Sometimes, it's easier to shut it off."

"I understand." After all, I did the same thing. But this . . . this wasn't my mother or my childhood that I could avoid. I saw Cash every single day. "We had sex. This changes everything."

"Yeah, it does." He nodded. "But today's a big day. Let's get through it. Find Aria."

"Shut it off."

"For today."

I breathed another sigh, this one of gratitude. I could use a day or two off to let yesterday's emotions simmer.

"How's today going to go?" Cash asked.

I shrugged. "I don't know."

"Nervous?"

"Yes. I'm sneaking up on her with this car idea. We had an investigator look into her life. She might not remember me or appreciate that I've searched her out."

"I think you're worrying for nothing. It'll be good." He reached over, his finger ready to flick the tip of my nose, a gesture he'd done a thousand times, but before he touched me, he retracted his hand.

I tried not to let it hurt.

Cash rubbed his bearded jaw. "Grandma called yesterday while you were in the shower."

"Oh." Carol would call him but not me? I'd tried her, Liddy and Gemma last night and no one had answered. No one had returned a single one of my texts or voicemails. What the hell? Didn't anyone miss me? It made sense why'd they'd call Cash. He was real family. I was the employee on vacation.

"She just wanted to check in."

"That's good. Did she say anything about work?"

"No."

My heart sank. I put out metaphorical fires daily at the resort. Didn't anyone need my help? How was it that I ran myself ragged for days but no one had reached out? No one. Not even Carol.

But that meant she was handling it. I was replaceable.

It wasn't something I wanted to admit.

Work was my life and without it, who was I? The friends I had were from the resort. Everyone in my life was connected to the Greers. I hadn't dated a man in seven years because I hadn't had—or made—time.

I'd been so focused on the tiny sphere of my world that I'd forgotten there was more beyond.

And what a beautiful world.

The highway had been bordered by thick bushes, limiting the view beyond the road. But as the Cadillac crested the top of a hill, the greenery cleared and there it was.

Heron Beach. Beyond the town, the ocean stretched.

White, foamy waves broke against a smooth, sandy beach. On the horizon, blue sky met the Pacific, gray waters and the colors blurring into an ombre line.

"I've never seen the ocean," I whispered, my eyes trapped on the view. The car slowed as I pulled my foot from the accelerator, wanting more time to savor this view. I rolled down my window, wanting to feel the air on my face. The salty air filled my nostrils and I held it in my lungs.

"Really?" Cash asked. "What about California?"

"No." Temecula was an inland town and it wasn't like Mom believed in mother-daughter vacations to the beach. "It's beautiful."

And suddenly, Montana's firm hold, the grip it had caught me with at eighteen, began to loosen.

What if I didn't live and work in Montana my entire life? What if I gave Oregon a try? I could see myself living here, walking along the beach each morning with a dog who chased his own tail. I could ride a bike with a wicker basket around the quaint, small town. Maybe one of the beach condos would fit into my price range.

Before this trip, I'd never had a desire to travel the world. To smell new scents. To explore new towns. All I'd ever wanted was to carve out a place to stay.

A home.

Londyn had set out in the Cadillac to run away. She'd wanted to create a new life and she'd found one in West Virginia. Gemma had found her place in Montana.

What if I'd been thinking about this all wrong? This trip was for me to clear my head and put my feelings for Cash aside. What if this wasn't a vacation, but my own fresh start?

The idea startled me. I blinked, forcing it away.

No. No way. I couldn't leave Montana.

Except I could.

"Cool place," Cash said, sitting straighter in his seat and pulling me from the craziest idea I'd had in years—crazier even than sex with my best friend.

I hummed my agreement.

From a distance, Heron Beach was exactly as I would have pictured an ocean tourist destination. My foot pressed on the gas, ready to see it up close. As we dipped down the hill, the ocean dropped out of view, hidden by the trees towering above. Buildings sprouted along the highway.

I followed the signs into town, slowing as we hit more traffic near the coast. The downtown streets of Heron Beach teemed with people who smiled as they wandered and shopped.

Flowerpots overflowed with florescent blooms. Sun-soaked shingles covered nearly every storefront. Most businesses were retailers who probably flourished this time of year with the crush of tourists. The hotels along the way were small, likely with a capacity of ten to fifteen guests.

None were as grand as the Greer Ranch and Mountain Resort but they had a different kind of charm. I could own a hotel of that size on my own. I'd been saving for years and my nest egg would probably be enough for an oceanfront cottage. And I had that check Carol had given me for ten thousand dollars.

"Where are we going?" Cash asked, again dragging me back to reality.

I picked up Gemma's sticky note that I'd set on the dash earlier, rereading the hotel's name. "The Gallaway."

He dug his phone from his pocket and entered the hotel's name into the GPS.

I followed its directions through Heron Beach until a grand hotel, one that could compete with even the Greers' establishment, filled the view. "Wow."

Four stories of taupe siding trimmed in white. Gleaming windows that offered guests a magnificent view of the ocean roaring in the distance. The Gallaway sat on a rocky cliff—twenty feet of jagged, charcoal rock that dropped to flawless, golden sand.

The hotel's parking loop was tall and wide enough to accommodate a tour bus and two stretch limos with room in between. I pulled the Cadillac to the curb and before I could touch the handle to open the door, a valet was at my side.

"Welcome to The Gallaway."

"Thank you." I stepped out, smiling as I took in the entrance.

The front doors were open and the floor's stones were made of the palest gray. Any accent was done in white or gold to keep the ambience bright and airy.

Everything in Montana was decorated with dark tones and earthy pieces. I'd finally gotten so sick of the wood that when Carol had given me the thumbs-up to make some enhancements, I'd added light touches wherever possible. From upholstered dining room chairs to freshly painted walls to quilts and pillowcases. Any surface where I'd been able to swap a shade of brown or maroon for something cream or white, I hadn't hesitated.

Cash met the bellhop at the trunk. The poor kid tried to retrieve our sparse luggage, but Cash shot him a look of dismissal. *He carried the bags. Got it.*

I rolled my eyes and dug for Carol's quarter I'd tossed aside earlier. I found it and set it in the metal ashtray, then hooked my purse over a shoulder and handed the keys to the valet. My eyes traced over every detail from the overflowing planters that bracketed the entrance to the gold *G* embedded in the stone tile beneath the entrance's threshold.

If the entrance was this nice, I couldn't wait to see the guest rooms. I'd be taking mental notes during our stay of things we could incorporate at the lodge.

Cash glanced over his shoulder to where the valet was easing the Cadillac through the loop. "I hate valet. Always screwing something up with your vehicle. Don't be surprised if we get it back with a scratch."

"He's not going to scratch the car."

We didn't have valet at the resort because we didn't cater to mass numbers of guests. At most, we had ten to fifteen cars in the parking lot. Most guests flew into Missoula and our shuttle service brought them to the property. We offered an experience, not a luxurious hotel that turned guests over by the hundreds.

The lobby was as stunning as the entrance, with gleaming marble floors and a chandelier that hung low, its crystal facets fracturing the light everywhere into tiny rainbows.

I spun in a slow circle, taking it all in before Cash nudged me toward the front desk.

The blonde behind the counter greeted us with a wide smile. "Welcome to The Gallaway."

"Thank you."

"Name?" she asked, fingers poised above her keyboard.

I scrunched up my nose. "We don't have a reservation. Do you have any rooms available by chance?"

"Oooh." The woman cringed. "Um . . . let me see what I can find. We're at the beginning of peak season so I'm not sure if we have any openings."

Why hadn't I called ahead? Oh, that's right. Because this trip had been a whirlwind and the situation with Cash had occupied my every waking thought. I crossed my fingers, hoping as the receptionist's nails clicked on keys that she'd find us a room. I really didn't want to find another place to stay but the chance of a vacancy was slim if the activity in the lobby was any indication of occupancy.

People streamed in and out from what looked like a long deck on the back of the hotel that overlooked the ocean. Some carried coffee cups from the espresso bar located past a set of french doors. Others milled around in the gift shop.

"Ah, you're in luck." My heart soared as the blonde's smile widened. "I've got one standard king room available. It's a garden view room on the first floor."

No. Damn. I needed to start leading with the number of rooms. "We actually need two rooms so —"

"We'll take it." Cash pulled out his wallet.

I should argue and insist on a hotel with two rooms. Things were tense enough as it was without us sharing a bed, but this place was a hotel resort manager's dream.

The woman's fingers flew as she checked us in. The smile on her face never faltered, even when Cash grumbled at the price.

I leaned close to whisper. "You do realize how much we charge, don't you?"

"Garden view," he whispered back.

Staying at the Greer lodge cost thousands of dollars per night. For the chalets, we charged a premium. It was the reason we catered to the wealthy and famous. With our on-site amenities, excursions and gourmet food from Chef Wong, we offered an experience you couldn't find anywhere else.

Paying four hundred dollars for a garden view room was nothing. Besides, it wasn't like Cash was hurting for money.

With our key cards in hand, I picked up my suitcase from where Cash had rested it on the floor. I turned away from the desk only to remember why I was here and whirled back around to the clerk. "Could I trouble you for one more thing? I'm looking for Aria Saint-James. We're old friends."

"Would you like me to page her? I can have her call your room."

Gemma's private investigator had done his job well. "That would be great. Thanks."

When I turned away again, expecting to see Cash behind me, he was gone. I scanned the area and spotted him just before he stepped out onto the deck so I hurried to catch up.

The moment I stepped outside onto gray-stained boards, the smell of the sea encircled me. The scent of a fresh Montana spring morning was hard to beat, with its green grass and cold mountain mix. But this was invigorating. The breeze rushed past my face, cooling my skin. The gulls crowed above our heads.

I joined Cash at the deck's railing and soaked in the view. The ocean stretched before us and in that moment, I didn't mind feeling small.

Waves rushed to the sand, breaking and fizzling as they faded away. The shores were full of people walking in bare feet, the water erasing their footprints as it rushed to the beach.

I shielded my eyes from the sun and scoped out the deck. They'd filled the space with Adirondack chairs, chaise lounges and white benches. Between the seats were pots of blooming flowers and spilling foliage.

Someone here had a green thumb. I suspected who and had a feeling the garden view wouldn't be so bad.

The ocean's calming rush soothed away the tension from the trip. Now that Cash and I weren't cramped together in the Cadillac, it was easier to breathe. I dropped my suitcase at my feet to lean my forearms on the railing.

Cash stood with his hands shoved in his jeans pockets. He stared at the water, his eyebrows two dark slashes above narrowed eyes.

"What's wrong?"

He sniffed the air. "It stinks like fish."

I laughed. "For a man who spends most of his days around cow pies and horse apples, I didn't realize you were so sensitive to smell."

He shot me a scowl, then glanced over his shoulder to take in the hotel's backside. His chin tipped up as he scrutinized the four floors and their balconies above. "I bet the standard room is half the size of ours at the lodge."

"Probably." We lived in Big Sky Country and the resort's standard rooms were the most spacious I'd ever seen.

"Four hundred bucks." He scoffed. "What a rip-off."

"You didn't have so many complaints about the last two hotels."

Not that he would. It was no contest. His problem with The Gallaway was that this place could offer some competition and he was in a shit mood.

Cash was normally a cheerful man who wore a smile often and laughed in earnest. But he was a Greer and not only were they stubborn, they had a grouchy streak that ran deep.

"Should we go somewhere else?" I asked.

"No." He bent to pick up my suitcase. "Let's go see our *garden view*."

I shook my head, blowing out a long breath. If he wanted to sulk, I'd leave him in our room and go explore the ocean alone.

As we reentered the lobby, I noticed more of the classic details. They'd put mirrors on the walls instead of art, making the space seem larger. Every other glass door was monogramed with the same *G* as the entrance.

Cash led the way and before disappearing into the alcove with the elevators, I took one last glance at the lobby. A door behind the receptionist desk opened and a man in a charcoal suit emerged.

He was tall with broad shoulders and a trim physique. He spoke over his shoulder and when the woman he'd been addressing emerged from beyond the door, my hand slapped over my heart.

Her hair was a shade darker than I remembered but her smile was exactly the same, mischievous and daring. The man said something that made her laugh and her shining brown eyes drifted through the lobby as she followed him around the counter. Her gaze swept past me, then snapped back, just as Cash appeared at my side.

She blinked, then that infectious smile spread across her face.

"Are you coming?" Cash asked, his gaze following mine. "Wait, is that—"

"Aria."

9

CASH

"I CANNOT BELIEVE YOU'RE HERE." Aria laughed, shaking her head like Kat wasn't sitting beside her at the table. She'd said the same, done the same, after crushing Kat in a hug in the lobby earlier today. I've never seen two women hug so hard. The moment Kat had spotted Aria, the women had rushed toward one another, colliding in a fierce embrace.

They'd hugged again before Aria had returned to work, then again when we'd met this evening at the hotel's steakhouse.

"I know." Katherine smiled with her friend. "I was actually worried you wouldn't recognize me and I was going to have to introduce myself."

You're unforgettable. I swallowed the words. Three days ago, I could have said them and made Kat blush. They wouldn't have been anything but a friendly compliment. She would have teased me for being gooey and I would have slung an arm around her shoulders and flicked the tip of her nose.

But that was three days ago. Now a compliment wasn't simply a compliment. A compliment like that might make Kat think I was flirting. That it was foreplay. Maybe it was.

Maybe it had always been.

"I'd never forget you." Aria put her hand over Kat's, then let her go to pick up the menu. "I'm starved. I haven't eaten here in a while but I always leave full."

"Any recommendations?" I asked.

"The steaks are incredible," she said.

"Sold." I closed my menu and set it aside. Steak was a staple in my diet and as a co-owner of a large Montana cattle ranch, I supported the beef industry whenever possible. But I doubted The Gallaway could deliver a filet I could slice with my fork.

This place was too pretentious. Kat was fascinated with the hotel but something about the place made me uneasy. Maybe it was because I'd never seen her so awestruck. Our resort was ten times better, so why was she drooling over everything?

Kat ran her finger down the stem of her water goblet. "I love these."

Of course she did. Which meant in a month, the resort would have all new water goblets.

The scrape of silverware on plates and dull conversation filled the room. There wasn't an empty table in sight. Waiters bustled around wearing white-collared shirts and black vests. Our dining room staff was only required to wear slacks and a button-up with the resort logo on the breast pocket. If Kat made them don a vest, we'd have a riot in the staff quarters.

"Sorry I couldn't meet with you earlier," Aria said. "We're right at the beginning of peak season and I've been swamped now that the rain has finally stopped and everything is in full bloom."

"No problem," Kat said. "I should have called first."

"I'm glad you didn't." Aria folded up her menu and set it on top of mine. "I love surprises."

Katherine giggled. "You haven't changed."

"My sister says that all the time." Aria leaned her elbows on the table. "What did you do today?"

Kat glanced at me, finally remembering I was sitting at the table too. "Not much. We did some exploring around town."

After Kat and Aria's reunion, Aria had returned to work while Katherine and I had dropped off our luggage in our room. One look at the bed and Kat had tossed her suitcase aside and announced she wanted to go shopping.

I hated shopping but it was better than staying in that room alone, dwelling on yesterday.

What were we going to do?

Part of me wanted to explore this thing, see if we were as combustible in bed a second and third time. But the other part of me longed to cling to our friendship and do everything in my damn power to put us back to normal.

I didn't want to lose her.

If we tried this thing, if we failed, I'd lose Kat.

"It's a cute town, isn't it?" Aria asked.

Kat nodded. "So cute."

It was just okay. After we'd dropped off our bags and I'd surveyed the room—as I'd expected, it was nice but smaller than any of our guest rooms—we'd left the hotel to wander downtown.

The sidewalks had been crowded with visitors like us. She'd been interested in the stores but completely engrossed with every bed and breakfast that we'd passed. We'd popped into a few shops and she'd bought some souvenirs to take home.

The town's economy was clearly driven by tourism. There were knick-knack displays on every block. For fifty dollars, Kat had bought a pale blue glass jar filled with *authentic Oregon seashells* as a gift to Mom. Easton and

Gemma were getting a driftwood coaster set. She'd picked up T-shirts for Dad and Granddad, then a postcard for Grandma.

She knew that my grandma didn't love trinkets, so instead, she'd decided to send a postcard that Grandma would receive before we ever got home. She'd written a note on it when we'd arrived at the room before dinner, then had disappeared to find a stamp. The task had taken her up until the very moment she'd come back to the room to change clothes and get ready for dinner with Aria.

As she'd searched for the mysterious stamp, I'd unsuccessfully tried to nap. I hadn't gotten much sleep in last night's hotel room, not with Katherine's scent lingering on my skin and her taste on my lips. But sleep was difficult with so much unknown swirling in my mind.

Every thought was consumed with Kat.

I stared at her as she browsed the menu. It was impossible not to think of how she'd felt in my arms and how her smooth skin had felt pressed against mine. She was wearing a pair of skintight jeans and sandals. Her top was another silky piece with thin straps that I'd never seen before and its rust color made her eyes vividly blue.

I forced my eyes away to the silverware resting on a pressed white napkin. When I glanced up, looking anywhere but at Kat, Aria's eyes were waiting.

Aria was taller than Kat—most people were. Her hair was dark and her eyes warm with a slightly cunning edge. She smiled effortlessly but there was a hesitancy behind her gaze. Either she was sizing me up or she held people at bay.

Probably both.

The waiter arrived with a bottle of wine and he poured Kat the sample. She sipped it, then nodded and lifted the glass for more. After he'd made the rounds, filling our glasses, he took our order and then left us to talk.

"Tell me about your life." Aria shifted in her seat to face Kat, giving her friend her undivided attention. "How was Montana?"

"Good. I'm still there, working at the resort."

"Not just working," I corrected. "She's the manager. Kat runs the whole show."

Katherine blushed. "Not exactly."

"Yes, exactly." Why was she being modest? She'd accomplished so much, made so many improvements to the resort. I, along with every member of my family, was amazed at what she'd accomplished in the span of a few years.

Systems were streamlined. Guest satisfaction had never been higher. The staff was happy and turnover was at an all-time low. It was because of Kat and I was damn proud of her.

"And how did you two meet?" Aria asked.

Kat gave me a small smile and damn it if that quirk of her lips didn't make my heart skip. "Cash's family owns the ranch and resort."

"Ah. How long have you been together?"

I opened my mouth to answer but Kat beat me to it with a wave of her hand. "Oh, no. We're not together. We're just friends. And coworkers."

"Don't forget roommates." There was a bitter edge to my voice.

"And roommates," she added.

Why did it bug me that she was so quick to dismiss us as friends? We were friends. And coworkers. And roommates.

I gulped from my wineglass, hoping it would take the edge off. It was better with Aria here to defuse some of the tension, but she didn't erase it entirely. The undercurrents tugged and tormented. I should have stayed in the room and let this be a private reunion.

"Ah." Aria lifted her own glass, studying me over the rim as she took a drink. "Well, what brings you *roommates* to Oregon?"

Kat took a deep breath and a long drag of her wine before answering. She and Aria hadn't spoken in the lobby earlier, deciding to save the conversation for dinner, when it wouldn't be rushed. She set her wine down and smiled at her friend. "You, actually."

"Me? Why? I thought it was just a coincidence."

"No, not really." Katherine bit her bottom lip.

I shifted my leg, extending it beneath the table so my foot touched hers and when she looked up, I gave her a nod. For the first time since yesterday, neither of us stiffened from the touch. This, right here, was why I was at the table. Tonight, Kat needed me to be her friend.

"Okay, let me start at the beginning," Kat said. "You know that old Cadillac that Londyn lived in?"

"Yeah." Aria nodded.

"A while back, Londyn had it shipped to Boston, where she was living. She bought it from Lou and had it completely restored."

"Lou," Aria whispered. "Haven't heard that name in a while. Did you hear that he passed? Clara found out from someone in Temecula about a year after he died."

"Yeah," Kat said. "Gemma told me."

"You've talked to Gemma?"

"She actually lives on the ranch."

"She's getting married to my brother," I added. "And bosses us all around."

Aria laughed. "Why am I not surprised? How is she?"

"She's wonderful," Kat said. "It was actually her idea that I come out here but let me back up. Londyn had the Cadillac in Boston. She'd just gone through a nasty divorce and decided to drive the Cadillac to California and find Karson. But she got a flat tire in West Virginia and ended up meeting her husband, Brooks, so the California trip never happened."

"Is she happy?" Aria asked. "Londyn?"

"Yeah." Kat smiled. "I don't talk to her often. She's closer to Gemma than me, but she's happy. They have a little girl named Ellie and she's pregnant again. Due any day now."

"That's so good to hear," Aria breathed. "I think about them, everyone, once in a while. I'm glad she's happy. Gemma too."

It had always struck me as odd that Kat hadn't kept in touch with the kids from the junkyard. After such a harrowing childhood, why wouldn't they have bonded together for life? But then again, I lived in Clear River, Montana. My graduating class had been fifteen people, most of whom still lived around the area, working on their family's farms and ranches. Kat and her friends had scattered across the country.

"Gemma was in Boston with Londyn," Kat said. "I lost touch with both of them after they left Montana, but those two stayed connected. Last year, Gemma sold her company in Boston and kind of . . . quit her life. She went to visit Londyn in West Virginia and Londyn suggested she finish the trip to California instead."

"Did she find Karson?"

Kat shook her head. "No. She came to find me in Montana. And fell in love with Easton."

My brother had told me a few months ago that he wasn't sure how he'd gotten so lucky. The day that Gemma had rolled onto the ranch in the Cadillac was the best day of his life. Granted, at the time he hadn't realized it. But after the two of them had stopped trying to tear one another's heads off—tearing clothes off instead—they hadn't been apart.

"They're having a baby boy in a few months," I said.

"And you?" Aria asked Kat. "Are you happy?"

"Of course." Kat shifted in her chair again, reaching for her wine.

My heart sank. Maybe Aria had bought the lie but I'd heard the truth in Kat's voice.

Why wasn't she happy? Didn't she like her job? Didn't she like life on the ranch? Or was it just stress from the past three days I was hearing?

"That brings me to this visit," Kat said, continuing on. "Gemma hired a PI a while back to look us all up. She was curious and wanted to know where we'd all landed. I hope you don't mind. I—we—drove the Cadillac here to find you."

"Not Karson?"

"No." Kat shook her head. "I'm never going back to California."

Because of her mother? Because of the memories? Hell if I knew the answer. More than I wanted anything from Kat, her body or her friendship, I craved her trust.

"I can understand that." Aria gulped the rest of her wine and refilled her and Kat's glasses. "I'm not going back either."

"Oh." Kat's shoulders slumped. "Damn. We were hoping that you might take the car to Karson."

"Is he in California?"

"According to Gemma's PI, yes."

Aria hummed and twirled the wine in her glass. "You know, I've thought of doing the same, with an investigator. Except for the fact that I'm a gardener and can't really afford that sort of thing."

"You're a gardener?" I asked.

Aria touched the tip of a tulip in the vase on the table. "Everything around the hotel has been grown by me or a member of my team. I cut these flowers this morning in our offsite greenhouse after I saw you in the lobby."

"I wondered about that." Kat smiled and looked to me. "Aria was always growing things in the junkyard. She'd buy a packet of seeds and find an old egg carton. Then we'd all get a plant or a flower for our own, usually in an empty can of green beans. I was sad to leave them behind when we left."

Aria's face soured. "I hate green beans. But don't worry, I took care of your flowers. I found these industrial buckets and I made Karson help me fill them with dirt. Then I replanted everything and staged them all around the junkyard. I'll never forget the look on Lou's face when he came out of his shack one day to see all the green leaves and pink flowers I'd put beside his front door. It was this hilarious mix of shock and disgust and pride."

"Poor Lou." Kat laughed, fondness in her gaze.

Poor Lou? That man had let a bunch of kids camp out in his junkyard, living in abandoned cars and ramshackle tents. But that reverence that Katherine and Gemma had for the junkyard, for Lou, was written on Aria's face too.

"Remember that time your cat destroyed all my seedlings?" Aria asked.

"She didn't destroy them." Kat rolled her eyes. "She just knocked over a couple."

"All of them. That animal was an evil, orange beast. I still hate cats to this day."

"Did, um . . . did Lou feed her after I left?"

Aria nodded. "And all of her kittens. When I finally left the next year, there were like twenty cats living around his shack. But no mice."

"You had a cat?" I asked. Another thing I wished I had known.

"Just this stray that kept coming by." Kat shrugged. "She wasn't really mine. I fed her a few times and then she didn't leave. We didn't let her sleep in the tent with us, but she kind of gravitated toward me."

"She *only* gravitated toward you," Aria said. "That cat would hiss and scratch the rest of us if we tried to pet her."

It was strange to observe Kat with someone else from her youth. For the first time, I was the outsider. Gemma and Kat didn't talk about the junkyard. If they did, it was done at their weekly girls' night because whenever they were around the family, conversation was focused on life and happenings on the ranch.

But Aria had no connection to the Greers. I'd learned more about Kat in the past few days than I'd learned in a decade.

The waiter arrived with our dinner and conversation halted as the three of us began eating.

"Wow." Katherine's eyes widened after the first bite of her steak. "This is amazing."

I swallowed my own bite, hating to admit that it was good. I'd also cut that bite with my fork.

"Do you still paint?" Aria asked as she fluffed her baked potato.

Kat shook her head. "No, not anymore."

"You paint?" My fork froze in midair. "I didn't know that."

She shrugged and popped another bite into her mouth, chewing and avoiding eye contact.

"She's talented," Aria said. "She did this mural inside the tent of this meadow with wildflowers and birds and butterflies. It was so bright and cheerful. Whenever I had a bad day, I'd go into the tent and just lie down in the common area, close my eyes and be surrounded by the colors."

"Why'd you stop?" I asked Kat, not caring that my knowledge—or lack thereof—was showing.

"It got harder and harder to do. With work being so busy, it was one of those hobbies that fell away."

Did she have other former hobbies I didn't know about? Besides working at the resort, she didn't do much for herself. She'd go horseback riding at times. She'd hang out and watch a basketball or football game with me at home.

How had I known her all these years without knowing she'd had a cat in the junkyard or that she'd been a painter? So much for me being the all-knowing best friend.

"What happened after we left?" Katherine asked Aria.

"Nothing much. It was boring without you guys there. Karson stayed until we turned eighteen, but he wasn't around much. He worked a ton, we all did, trying to save some money. Then on our birthday, Clara and I packed up our stuff and took a bus to Las Vegas. Karson hugged us good-bye, we left a note for Lou, and that was it."

"How long were you in Vegas?"

"About a month. I hated it. Too many fake people. Too much desert. Clara liked it and stayed for a while before moving to Welcome, Arizona. But I had to get out of there. So I started calling hotels along the coast, seeing if there were any jobs open. I started as a housekeeper here at The Gallaway for about a year. Then one day, the head groundskeeper found me weeding one of the flower beds. He took me under his wing, showed me everything and taught me a lot. When he retired a few years ago, I took over."

"We both started as housekeepers then," Kat said. "That's how I started at the resort."

"What do you do, Cash?" Aria asked.

"I work with horses. I do some guide trips. Train the younger animals. Do whatever ranch work needs to be done."

"So you're a cowboy?" She leaned back to look under the table. "Boots and all."

I chuckled. "Something like that."

"Cash has a real gift with horses," Kat said. "They're building a brand-new training and breeding facility that he's going to run."

"With Gemma," I added. "She came to my rescue and saved me from the office work."

"I'll have to come and visit the resort one of these days. I'm intrigued."

"You're welcome anytime," Kat said.

Conversation turned light as the three of us focused on our meals. Aria told some funny tales about catching couples screwing on the beach when they thought no one was looking. She raved about the hotel's owner and how he was the best boss she'd ever had and the kindest rich man she'd ever met.

When her plate was clear, Aria set her napkin aside, leaning forward to focus on Kat. "I love this visit. I love the whole idea for your trip. What if I took the Cadillac?"

"To California?" Kat asked. "I thought . . ."

"No, to Clara, in Arizona. I'll be next up in the daisy chain. Once she hears about how the handoffs have worked with the car, I'm sure she'll take it to Karson."

"Really?" Kat's face split in a huge smile.

"Sure. As long as you're not in a hurry. Work is crazy right now, but as soon as I can get away, I'll do it."

"There's no rush. For either of you. If Clara doesn't want to drive to California, we can leave the car in Arizona. Gemma will come get it at some point. Or Londyn."

"Then it's settled." Aria clapped. "Though I'm not worried about my sister. Clara will love the idea even more than me."

"Thank you," I said. Not only because that would save us a long drive home, but because of the smile she'd put on Kat's face.

"You're welcome." Aria yawned and checked the time on her phone. "Okay, I'd better get home. I have to be back at five thirty. We try not to let the guests see us with our hands dirty."

I signaled the waiter for our check, having him charge it to our room. Then we stood from the table and before Kat even had her feet, Aria had pulled her into another hug. "God, it's good to see you."

"You too." Katherine squeezed her, then let go.

"What are you up to tomorrow?" Aria asked as we weaved past tables, making our way toward the exit.

"Not much," Kat answered.

"I need to get some work done first thing in the morning but come and find me whenever you get up. Just tell the front desk to page me."

"Okay." Kat hugged Aria again, then waved goodbye as her friend walked through the lobby. Katherine stared at her until she disappeared behind a door marked *Employees Only*, her shoulders sagging as it closed.

"You okay?"

"I wish I hadn't lost touch with her. With all of them."

"You found her now. And you'll always have Gemma close."

Katherine hummed. Was that a yes? A no? I used to understand her hums.

"Should we go up?" My mouth went dry as I finished the question. There would be no more escaping the bed or the fact that what I really wanted to do was kiss her again. To worship her body until we both passed out.

346

"Actually, I think I'm going to take a walk." Kat tucked a lock of hair behind her ear. "I'll be up in a while."

"Mind if I join you?"

"I was going to go to the beach. I thought you didn't like the smell."

Was that why it had taken her so long to get that stamp for Grandma's postcard earlier? Kat had probably escaped to the beach.

"The beach is fine." Not as good as Montana, but it was a sight to behold. My irritation earlier hadn't been with the smell but with how Kat had seemed to instantly fall in love with the place. "Lead the way."

She crossed the lobby and the moment we walked outside, the evening breeze picked up the loose curls of her hair. She'd spent an hour twisting it into soft waves, a style I'd seen more times on this trip than I had in the past five years combined.

My God, she was sexy. The clothes. Her hair. The dark, smoky shadow on her eyelids and the peach on her cheeks. My attention was so fixed on her that I barely registered the stairs as we descended the long staircase off the deck and I tripped over a few, catching myself on the railing before I fell. The steps led us down the cliffs to the beach below and though there was much to see, my eyes were glued to the sway of her hips and the way her hair swung across her shoulders.

Finally, when we hit the sand, I looked out and let the power of the ocean hit me square in the chest. It really was magnificent, like Kat. When I stopped fighting it, when I pulled the blinders down, it was spectacular.

Our feet dug into the beach as we made our way across the sand. Then we stood at the edge of the surf, staring out at the dark water, its waves catching the silver moonlight in diamond glitters.

"I like the beach," she whispered, so quietly I wasn't sure she was talking to me or simply telling herself.

"I didn't know you had a cat at the junkyard."

"It was only a stray but I loved it. I named her Patch. She was my companion. Londyn and Gemma were always the closest. Londyn dated Karson so the three of them were together a lot. And Aria and Clara were inseparable. I was normally the odd one out and that cat . . ."

That cat had been hers and hers alone. "Why didn't you bring Patch to Montana?"

"A wild cat on a bus?" She scoffed. "Yeah, that would have gone over well."

"Do you want to get a new cat?" We had a ton of barn cats roaming around free because they kept the mice away. There were constantly litters of kittens. Or I'd take her to a pet store and get her one from there.

"Maybe someday." She shrugged. "When I get my own place."

"You know, you don't have to move."

"Yes, I do."

"No, you don't. Look"—I turned to face her, taking her shoulders in my arms so she had to turn and face me too—"I know things are strange right now. I don't regret what happened, but I'm not going to lie and say it hasn't fucked with my head. You're my friend. My best friend."

"I know." She stepped out of my grip and wrapped her arms around herself, rubbing at the bare skin of her arms. "I'm cold. I think I'll go back inside."

Without another word, without acknowledgement that I was trying to muddle my way through this, she spun away and marched toward the staircase.

"Fuck." I let her go, watching until she was halfway up the stairs before turning to the water.

The waves crashed on the sand, then retreated into the dark depths of the ocean. If I reached down and gripped the edge, no matter how hard I pulled, the wave would slip away. It was that way when I was training a stubborn horse. The harder I tugged on the reins, the longer the fight, and inevitably, I'd lose.

Maybe I was pulling too hard on Kat. She'd asked to forget about the sex and pretend it hadn't happened. Maybe we should.

She could keep her secrets.

And I could keep mine.

I stayed on the sand until the moon was far above my head, then slowly made my way to our room. The lights were off when I eased the door open except for the lamp on my nightstand. I hurried through brushing my teeth and pulling on a pair of cotton pajama pants, then I eased under the fluffy comforter, savoring the feel of the cool cotton on my naked chest and back.

"Kat." I turned on my side, facing her. She had her back to me and had stuffed a pillow in the center of the bed. "You asleep?"

"Yes."

I grinned. "Can I ask you a question?"

"No."

I asked it anyway. "Why don't you want to go back to California?"

Tell me. Please, talk to me. I was pulling again, something I'd convinced myself on the beach I wouldn't do, but I was desperate. I craved information even more than her luscious body.

She shifted, inching farther away and burrowing deeper under the covers. We didn't need the pillow between us. She was already miles and miles away. "Good night, Cash."

10

KATHERINE

"When I said come and find me in the morning, I didn't expect you to get up this early." Aria dragged a long hose across the deck of The Gallaway, moving down the row of potted flowers.

I tugged the hose, giving it slack. "I was up."

After next to no sleep last night, I'd snuck out of the hotel room while Cash had snored quietly into his down pillow. Before dawn, his arm had crept over the divider I'd placed in the center of the mattress and when his hand had rested on my hip, I'd slid from the sheets and tiptoed my way out of that bedroom.

It was supposed to be a dream, sleeping side by side with Cash. Except in the dream, he cuddled me in his arms as I drifted off to sleep. There was no need for his and her sides of the bed. We'd wake together in the morning to share a kiss. The stark gap between the fantasy and reality had sent me scurrying to the lobby this morning after dressing in the dark bathroom and tying my hair into a knot.

I'd been on one of the cushioned benches in the lobby, waiting for the espresso bar to open, when Aria had arrived promptly at five thirty. She'd let me tag along with her as she'd worked.

We'd been watering flowers for the past hour. Before that, I'd carried a garbage bag behind her, following as she pruned flower beds and deadheaded hanging baskets.

At least someone wanted my help. I'd checked for emails and texts and missed calls from Montana and to my increasing disappointment, there'd been none.

I shouldn't be so annoyed that things were running smoothly at the resort. That was what I'd worked for, right? Maybe if this vacation hadn't gotten so tragically off course, I would have enjoyed the break. But right now, I needed to feel useful. I needed the constant of work, something familiar to focus on when everything else was upside down.

Gardening with Aria had been a salvation.

The sun was up and the sky was more white than blue. The sound of the ocean was a constant calm in the background.

"What's up with you and Cash?" she asked as we walked down the deck.

"I'm surprised you waited this long to ask."

She laughed. "It's been killing me. Spill. That man is hot. Mega hot. So why are you *best friends*?"

"And coworkers."

She clicked her tongue. "And roommates."

"It's complicated." I groaned.

"Sleeping with your best friend tends to complicate things."

I blinked. "How did you know we were sleeping together?"

"Please." She rolled her eyes. "I was at the dinner table last night. Best friends who aren't having sex don't emit that kind of sexual tension."

I groaned again, my shoulders slumping. "It just happened on this trip. It was the first time and . . . ugh."

"Please don't tell me that man is bad in bed. It'll break my heart."

"No. Definitely not bad." The memory of his hands running over my skin, the way his mouth was hot and wet and so fucking talented, made me shiver. And that beard. That goddamn beard. My cheeks heated. "Really, really *not bad*."

Cash had probably ruined me for any other man.

"Then tell me why you are down here with me this morning, schlepping around the hotel, doing gardening work, while that sexy cowboy is in a bed upstairs."

"He's my best friend." I sighed. "Or he was my best friend. Now . . . I don't know. Everything is different. It's like we don't know how to be around one another."

"Got it. You want to stay friends and he doesn't."

I twirled a finger in the air. "Other way around."

"Oh." She straightened, letting the water run on the deck boards. "You're in love with him."

"I'm in love with him," I whispered. Had I ever let those words escape my lips? "I don't think I've ever admitted that out loud."

Aria took a step closer and put her hand on my shoulder. "He doesn't feel the same."

"No. I'm firmly in the friend zone. He calls me Kat, like the cute little sister he never had."

"But you slept together."

"I don't understand it either." Because Cash had been the one to make the move. He'd come to my room and kissed me. Why? Was it because I'd been the only woman in the vicinity? Had it been an experiment? "He says he doesn't want to pretend it didn't happen, but I think that was just because he's trying to save my pride."

When we got home, I doubted he'd be forthcoming about what had really happened on this trip. I didn't want to tell his family anyway. It was far too humiliating since Carol, Gemma and, I suspected, Liddy knew I was in love with him.

If they found out we'd had sex but were definitely *not* together, all I'd earn was pity.

I hated pity.

"I can't keep doing this anymore."

"Have you told him how you feel?" Aria asked.

"No. I'm a coward."

"Or maybe you're protecting your heart. There's no shame in that."

Self-preservation was something I'd learned early on. It had taken me a long time to break the habits from my childhood. I shut down and shut people out when I didn't feel safe. There was no question that Cash cared for me and wanted to protect me. But that didn't mean I was safe with him.

It wasn't just my heart, my love life, on the line. If I lost Cash, I'd lose his family too.

He would always be a Greer.

And I was the hired help.

"Maybe if it was just us, I would have told him," I said. *Maybe not.* "But with his family involved, it gets messy. I couldn't have asked for a better home. They took me in and have taught me so much. They gave me a trade and work experience. I truly love them and I don't want to lose them."

"Do you really think they'll kick you out on the street if you and Cash aren't friends?"

"No. They'll support me no matter what happens with Cash. They're amazing people. But if I admit to Cash that I have feelings for him and he rejects them, I won't put myself through the misery of reliving that at the family dinner each week. Things will be awkward, whether we pretend or not. And he's their son."

The Greers would never kick me out on the street but Carol and the ten-thousand-dollar check in my purse sure had opened the door for me to leave on my own volition.

"Maybe he won't reject you."

I scoffed. "We had sex two nights ago. He can barely talk to me or touch me. Cash is a good man and won't admit that he regrets it. But I know him very, very well. He regrets it. The rejection is coming. He's just working through his mind how to deliver it gently."

"Ouch." Aria winced. "Sorry."

"Me too."

Maybe we'd recover from this trip. If I didn't admit out loud that I loved him, he'd never know the truth and we could move forward like this was nothing more than a slipup by two people on vacation.

I tugged on the hose, pulling it toward the next planter, ready to get back to work. There was something soothing about being productive, not dwelling on the mistakes I couldn't correct.

"Do you think you could go back to being friends?" Aria asked as we shuffled along.

"I don't know."

When I looked back over the past decade, there hadn't been a time when I hadn't loved Cash. First as friends, then more. It was that slow build, like the growth of an evergreen. Or the rising tide. One minute, you looked down and saw a huge expanse of sand. The next, the water was crashing at your feet.

I glanced over my shoulder to the view. There was nothing tropical about Heron Beach. There were no cabanas on the sand. No women in skimpy bikinis and floppy hats drinking cocktails with pink umbrellas.

Still, it was a beautiful change of scenery from the majestic and rugged Montana landscape. It was every bit as daunting, with the water stretching farther than the eye could see, but stunning nonetheless. It was impossible not to stare and count my heartbeats against the rhythm of the waves.

The Oregon coast was brutally breathtaking. Large, black rocks stood proud off the shores. Bold structures that had refused to succumb to the ocean's power. Their magnificence contrasted with the sandy shores, smooth and pristine. There was peace in the sand's submission.

Maybe it was time for me to surrender too.

Aria sprayed the last bloom of flowers and we returned to the spigot, turning off the water and coiling the hose away. She dried her hands on her jeans. I wasn't sure how she could wear a white hotel T-shirt and not get it smudged with dirt, but it was spotless, as was the monogrammed *G* on the breast pocket.

"What's next?" *Please don't tell me to go away.* If I didn't have something to do, I might be tempted to return to the room.

"I forgot this book I promised one of the girls I'd lend her so I was going to run home and grab it. Want to come?"

"Are you going to get sick of me tagging along with you all day?"

Aria surprised me by pulling me into a tight, short hug. Then she released me and nodded to the sidewalk that wrapped around the building. "Let's go."

"I don't remember you being such a hugger," I teased.

"That's Clara's fault. We always hugged goodbye and hello. Now that we don't live together, I find myself hugging everybody else to compensate."

I fell into step beside her as she walked away from the hotel. It was early so the sidewalks weren't yet crowded with people. I waited for her to stop at one of the cars parked beside us, but she kept on walking, leading us away from the beach and into a neighborhood. In a town this size, I guess walking was probably the quickest way to work.

"I feel bad for not asking more about Clara last night. How is she?" I asked.

"Good. She lives in Arizona with her son, August."

"I didn't realize she had a son."

Aria nodded. "He's four. Smartest kid I've ever met in my life. He loves his Aunt Aria almost as much as he loves his mom."

"And his dad?"

She shook her head. "Not in the picture. Clara cut him loose when Gus

352

was a baby. She knew he was never going to be a good father, so rather than try unsuccessfully to turn him into one, she had him sign over his rights and moved away from Vegas so he wouldn't be close."

"Do you see them often?"

"Every couple of months. In the summer, they come to see me because I'm so busy and Arizona is hot. In the winter, I fly down a few times. Thanksgiving. Christmas. Mostly, I try to plan my trips around Clara's boss's schedule. I hate him with the fire of a thousand suns, so I make sure he's gone when I visit."

"What's the deal with her boss?" I asked.

"He's this rich, smug guy." Her lip curled. "Clara worked for him in Vegas as his assistant. When he decided to move to Arizona, he offered to take her along. The timing worked out because it was after Gus was born and she wanted to get out of Vegas anyway. So he bought her a car and built a guest house on his property so she wouldn't have to find an apartment."

"Okay," I drawled. "That sounds . . . nice? What am I missing?"

"Ugh. Not you too. Clara defends him mercilessly. She's always telling me that he's a good man. That he's kind to August and pays her more than she'll ever make at another job. But he grates on my every nerve. He throws money around like it's meaningless. He's spoiled. He likes to remind me that I'm the lesser fraternal twin." Aria's hands balled into fists. "We've learned to avoid one another so that Clara isn't in the middle."

We changed directions, starting up a side street and making our way farther and farther from The Gallaway. Aria set a fast pace, one that made it hard for me to study the neighborhood, but that didn't stop me from trying. My eyes darted everywhere, taking in the green lawns and blooming trees. The homes were painted in light colors from baby blue to sage green.

For a woman who hadn't traveled much in her life, it was invigorating to experience something new. Heron Beach screamed casual. Welcoming. Friendly.

I loved Montana.

But I could love Oregon too.

"I like it here," I confessed as Aria made another turn on our way to her home.

"Me too. I drew the lucky straw when I found my job at The Gallaway."

"I feel the same about finding the Greers."

Regardless of the mess I'd made in my relationship with Cash, I loved the resort. But maybe my job there was done. Maybe it was time to take on a new challenge. Leaving Montana would be excruciating, especially now that Gemma was there, but soon, she'd have a baby.

Soon, her last name would be Greer.

I would always be a Gates.

Aria pointed to a row of two-story condos ahead on the street. "That's my place."

I didn't have to ask which of the four front doors was hers. The hotel had stunning flower displays and her home was no different.

A purple and pink fuchsia hung from the porch beam. I counted ten planters, all of varying sizes and colors and shapes, staged beside the front door. The sweet floral scents filled the air and I took a long inhale as Aria unlocked her door.

I should have suspected more of the same inside.

"This is beautiful." My wide eyes scanned the interior as Aria led me through the short entryway and into her living room.

She'd created a beach cottage with white sheer curtains, cozy cream furniture and lush greenery. This was a cookie cutter condominium complex but she'd turned her condo into something unique.

After the way her and Clara's parents had died, I was glad that she'd found some serenity. In a way, this reminded me of their delivery truck in the junkyard. While I'd painted the inside of my tent with bright colors, a meadow and flowers, Aria and Clara's home had always been bright. Even in what was essentially a steel truck, they'd found the light.

The delivery truck had been in an accident, hence the reason it was at a junkyard. They'd turned the jagged holes in the walls and ceiling into windows. Aria had filled the place with plants and Clara had added her own gentle touch with tidy bedrolls and shelves made out of tattered books.

Aria walked to the coffee table, something made from a piece of driftwood, and plucked up a paperback. "This is my book club's favorite reread."

"I love that you're in a book club."

Aria laughed. "This is a small town. Us locals stick together. Things get hectic during tourist season, but in the winter, when it's cold and gray, we sort of band together to keep from going crazy."

"We do the same in Montana. We still have guests in the winter so it's not like there isn't a peak season for us with skiing and snowmobiling. But it's slower than the summer months. And when we get a big snow, we'll find ourselves in someone's house, eating and playing games and reading and sitting around a fire."

"I meant what I said last night. I'm going to have to come and visit you and see this place for myself."

I smiled but stayed quiet. Would I still be there?

Aria and I didn't linger in her home. We returned on the same path that we'd taken, giving me a second taste of the allure and charisma of the locals' Heron Beach. When The Gallaway came into view and the bustle of downtown began to crowd the sidewalks, I took one last glance over my shoulder to the quieter streets behind.

The sound of the ocean in the distance filled my ears. The laughter and smiles from the guests coming and going from the hotel were contagious. When we walked into the lobby, the line at the espresso counter was ten deep but no one seemed to mind having to wait for their latte. The restaurant where we'd had dinner last night was closed, but the café next door was crowded for breakfast.

Was my crush on The Gallaway because I was on vacation? Because I was off duty? I could enjoy the bustle of the guests and not worry about their enjoyment. Customer satisfaction was the last thing on my mind.

"Aria, there you are." The same suited gentleman I'd seen her with yesterday appeared at our sides.

"Hey, Mark. What's up?"

"Whenever you're free, would you mind stopping by my office?"

"Sure. I'd like you to meet someone. Katherine Gates, this is Mark Gallaway. My boss."

"Nice to meet you." My heart did a little lurch as I held out my hand to shake his. Gallaway. As in The Gallaway?

"Katherine and I are old friends," Aria said. "We grew up in the same town. Now she runs a fancy guest ranch in Montana."

"Ah. Are you staying here at the hotel?"

"I am. It's lovely."

"We're proud of it." He grinned. "The Gallaway has been in my family for three generations."

Mark Gallaway was likely in his late forties. There were streaks of gray in his brown hair and fine lines around his eyes. But with that suit and his tall stature, he looked every bit the millionaire I suspected he was. I knew how much a hotel like this could potentially rake in, especially if run well.

"What's the name of your resort in Montana?" he asked.

"The Greer Ranch and Mountain Resort."

His eyes widened. "No kidding?"

"Have you heard of it?" Aria asked him.

"Often." He nodded. "I stayed there about five years ago. I was with a group of guys who went in the fall to go hunting. It's one of a kind. World renowned."

A blush crept into my cheeks and I fought a smile. "Like you, we're proud of it too."

"It's not easy to get a reservation there these days. My friends and I have been talking about going back, but you're booked out for the next three years."

"Hunting season is popular, but occasionally we'll get a cancelation. I can add you to the wait list if you'd like."

"I was told there isn't a wait list."

I leaned in close, Mark mirroring me, and lowered my voice. "There is if you know the general manager."

He leaned back and burst out laughing. "You've made my day, Ms. Gates. How long have you been the GM?"

"Four years."

"Well, I commend you. My visit to Montana was one I'll never forget. In the most positive way."

"Thank you." I shared a smile with Aria. "I'll let you two get back to work. Call me later?"

She nodded. "Now that you've made my boss's day, I'll be taking the afternoon off. I'll find you when I'm done."

"Wait." Mark raised his hand, stopping me before I could leave. "I have to ask. And you should know that this is very unlike me. I realize it's not exactly the polite way to do business, attempting to recruit another establishment's employee."

My jaw nearly dropped. Was he going to offer me a job? I might have been toying with the idea of moving, but I wasn't ready to decide. My pulse raced and my fingers trembled as he reached into his suit jacket and pulled out a business card.

"My general manager is retiring in three months. Aria has pitched in to help ease the transition but she wants to be in management about as badly as I want to water the plants."

Aria hummed her agreement.

"I'm having a hell of a time finding an experienced replacement." Mark handed me his card. "If you're ever interested in a location change—"

"She's not."

My head whipped to the side as a familiar, towering figure crowded into the space between me and Aria.

"Cash Greer." He held out his hand to Mark.

Mark returned Cash's handshake, looking guilty for having just been busted *poaching*. "Mr. Greer. Welcome to The Gallaway. If there's anything I can do to improve your stay, please let me know."

Cash nodded and slipped his hand around my elbow. "Katherine, may I speak with you for a moment?"

Damn. He'd called me Katherine. I was not going to like this conversation.

"Sure." There was no point arguing. Cash was not going to leave me here with Mark. "It was a pleasure meeting you, Mr. Gallaway."

"Mark. Please." He gave me a slight bow, then backed away. "The pleasure was mine."

Aria followed him toward the front desk, mouthing, "Later."

I nodded and steeled my spine, then turned to face an angry—*extremely* angry—Cash Greer.

11

KATHERINE

THE DOOR SLAMMED behind Cash as we walked into our hotel room. He strode past the unmade bed to the windows, practically ripping them apart as he flung the drapes away from the glass.

He hadn't spoken a word on the elevator ride to the second floor, but the lecture and fight were coming. Cash didn't lose his composure often, which was why our arguing on this trip was so abnormal. When angry, he'd close down and disappear to spend some time on a horse until he'd had some time to cool off.

We were a long way from his horses.

I braced when he turned from the window and planted his fists on his hips.

"What *the fuck* was that?"

"Nothing." When his hazel eyes turned hard as stone, I realized playing dumb had been the wrong decision. "I was just talking with Aria's boss."

"He offered you a job."

"Not officially," I muttered.

Mark Gallaway hadn't even seen my résumé. He might decide to find someone with broader experience when he learned that the only people I'd ever worked for were the Greers and that my education had peaked at a GED.

Cash huffed and shook his head. "You didn't turn him down."

"Please." I rolled my eyes. "He was joking, Cash."

"You didn't turn him down." He pinned me with that cold stare.

My feet were glued to the carpet and my heart raced. No, I hadn't turned Mark down. A week ago, I would have politely declined and returned the business card instead of tucking it into my jeans pocket as I walked to the elevator.

"It's flattering," I admitted. "And maybe a bit tempting."

At my confession, Cash's face turned to ice. There was no easy smirk or warm smile lurking beneath the surface. His eyes flashed with betrayal. He looked at me like I was a stranger.

I opened my mouth to say something, but what? I wouldn't apologize for speaking the truth.

His nostrils flared and the fury emitting from his broad shoulders slammed into me like a tidal wave. "Why?" he asked through gritted teeth, then pointed to the bed. "Because of this?"

Yes. No. Maybe. I struggled to articulate an answer, so I threw out some questions of my own instead. "Haven't you ever wanted something different? Haven't you ever wanted more?"

"More?" He scoffed. "We've given you everything."

"And I'm grateful but —"

"Are you? Because the fact that you didn't tell that son of a bitch no on the spot doesn't feel much like gratitude. It feels a lot like a slap in the face for everything my family has handed you."

My mouth fell open. "Excuse me? Don't you fucking dare make me out to be some charity case. I worked my ass off for your family. I *earned* what I've achieved. Me."

Through blood, sweat and tears. The last time I'd been a charity case had been in California, sitting on a hot curb, begging for spare change. I'd vowed then to take control of my life and never be a beggar again.

"But you want more," he shot back. An unspoken *selfish* hung in the air.

"I want . . . I don't know. Can't I at least explore my options?"

"For what? Are you going to move here and work for a fancy hotel that's focused on turnover, not experience?"

That had been my marketing line. When I'd taken over as the manager at the resort, I'd made sure all of the Greers knew that in order to take the place to the next level, our marketing pitch had to be in sync. We weren't selling a comfortable stay or plush hotel room. We were selling an experience.

For Cash to throw that in my face, I'd done my job well.

"I can't fucking believe this," he said before I could come up with something to say. Some of the fury vanished but the hurt in his voice intensified. "I can't believe you'd leave us. You're part of our family."

"No, I'm not."

He winced. "If you truly believe that, then I'm ashamed of us. Because you are. You are one of us."

Ouch. Cash's words were a slap across the face. But the guilt was what hurt the worst.

He wasn't wrong.

I did feel like part of their family—most of the time. Liddy brought me flowers from the grocery store when she saw a bundle I'd like. Carol always managed to find the best birthday gifts, even when I didn't know what I wanted. Jake and JR and Easton protected me. They doted on me but respected my opinion and position. They'd all treated me like a part of their family.

Was I really throwing them away? Why? So what if Cash didn't love me. So what if we'd had sex. Yes, it would be miserable to see him fall in love with another woman and get married someday. Yes, it would be painful to see him teach his children to ride a horse or throw a ball. Hard to witness, but not unlivable.

I guess I hadn't broken the habits of my childhood like I'd thought.

When the world got to be too much, when my heart and spirit were broken, I ran.

My chin quivered and I bit the inside of my cheek. But despite my best effort to thwart it, a tear dripped down my cheek.

"We never fight," he whispered. The shreds of Cash's anger vanished and he put a hand to his heart, clutching his chest like there was a wound beneath the skin. "What is happening to us?"

"I don't know," I lied.

I knew exactly what was happening to us.

We were coming to an end.

Cash and I would go home to Montana. I'd return to being an honorary member of the Greer family, working at the resort and living my life. But my friendship with Cash would never look the same.

This was the end.

"Talk to me." He crossed the room and put his hands on my shoulders.

There was nothing to say and if we only had a fraction of time left, I didn't want to spend it fighting.

I rose on my toes, letting my hands slide up his chest until my fingertips found their way into the longer strands of hair at the nape of his neck. I pulled him to me and brushed my lips against his.

Cash didn't hesitate. His arms banded around my back, crushing me against his strong body, and he fused his lips to mine. Teeth nipped. Tongues tangled. Heartbeats thundered.

I yanked and pulled at Cash's shirt, working frantically to get the buttons undone. He reached between us and loosened his belt, letting it fall free as the scrape of his zipper sounded past the blood rushing in my ears.

With his jeans open, I reached beneath the elastic of his boxers, finding his swollen shaft and wrapping it in my fist. Cash groaned into my mouth, tearing his lips away from mine as I stroked his velvety flesh.

He dove under the hem of my tee, his calloused palms rough and hungry against my skin. Cash's hands were so large that they spanned the length of my ribs. He held me, immobile and panting, as he tore his lips away and leaned back.

The lust in his eyes was heady. Lust, for me. It was a cheap substitute for love, but my foolish heart didn't care.

"I don't have any more condoms," he warned.

I gripped his shaft hard, pulling him closer. I'd been on birth control for years. "I'm safe."

"So am I."

I stroked him again, this time adding a single nod.

Cash dragged his shirt off his body, then crowded me, his lips recapturing mine. His height forced me to bend backward, so far that if not for his firm hold, I would have dropped to the floor.

I clung to him, letting go of his throbbing cock to clutch his shoulders as he swept me into his arms and walked us to the bed, not once breaking from my lips.

He set me on the mattress but before he could trap me underneath his body, I twisted, shifting to push his body into the soft sheets instead. Cash went willingly to his back, giving me a wicked grin as I straddled his waist and whipped my shirt off my torso. My fingers fumbled to unclasp my bra.

The pulse in my core ached, desperate for him to be inside. I worked the buttons of my jeans free, leaning forward to shimmy them and my lace panties off my hips while Cash shoved at his jeans and boxers. The moment the denim was on the floor, Cash's hands palmed my bare ass, kneading and working their way toward my wet center from behind.

I straddled Cash's waist, my hands sliding up the hard ridges of his stomach to the dusting of hair between his pecs.

His hands came up to cup my breasts. "Damn, you are gorgeous."

I covered his hands with mine, letting my head loll to the side and my eyes close as he squeezed, his thumbs toying with my pebbled nipples. His scent surrounded me, the cologne he'd put on this morning and his own natural, masculine spice.

Cash slipped one hand free and I let my own fingers pinch the nipple in his absence. I opened my eyes to take him in, and the hunger in his eyes, the desire, made me tremble.

He dragged a finger through my slippery folds, barely grazing my clit before bringing his finger to his mouth to lick my juices. "So sweet."

My core spasmed and I forgot about torturing my own nipple and reached between us, taking his cock in my hand at the same time I lined my entrance up with the tip and sank down.

"Oh God," I gasped, savoring the stretch and feel of his bare erection filling me. I spread my thighs wider, taking him as deeply as possible, rolling my hips to grind my clit against the hard root of his cock.

"Fuck, sweetheart, you feel so good." He arched his neck into the pillow, his Adam's apple bobbing as he swallowed and sucked in a jagged breath. Cash's hands came to my hips, picking me up like I weighed nothing, before dropping me back down, connecting us again.

I planted my hands on his chest and lifted myself and as I slammed down again, he thrust his hips upward, going so deep I gasped. The tip of his cock hit a spot inside that made me whimper. My hands went back to my breasts to tug at my nipples as we rocked into one another, up and down, until my legs trembled and I chased my release with reckless abandon.

"Ride me, Kat." His hands dug into the curves of my hips, the roped muscles in his forearms flexed tight.

Faster and faster, I rode him, just like he'd demanded. My orgasm came without warning. I shattered, my entire body clenching as stars exploded in my eyes, blinding me from reality. I cried out, reveling in the best orgasm of my life and the feel of Cash's roaming hands as I pulsed around him, over and over and over.

I was still riding out the aftershocks when Cash flipped us in a swift spin. He dropped a soft kiss to the corner of my lips, then took my hands in his, lacing our fingers together at our sides.

This man was made to pleasure women. Hovering above me, his eyes darkened to caramel and hunter-green gems, he was unabashedly seductive. His body was a work of art and strength.

The roughhewn, captivating mountains of Montana, the dynamic, awe-inspiring beaches of Oregon. No matter where I traveled in this world, nothing would ever compete with the view of Cash in this moment.

Sunshine streamed through the window like it had the first time we'd been together, illuminating his features. I memorized the sound of his hitched breath. I studied the way his tongue darted out to lick his bottom lip every few strokes and the soft hum he gave me when I flicked his nipples, the sound sweeter than any song or symphony. I took a mental picture of the way he looked when his eyes drifted closed in ecstasy, his sooty eyelashes sable crescents against his tanned skin.

I savored every second, knowing that we were racing toward the harrowing end.

Cash's eyes locked with mine, the shaking in his body the only warning he gave before coming inside me in long, hot strokes. I didn't blink for fear of missing a second of the rapture that played across his face.

Spent from his release, Cash collapsed onto me, his body as limp as my own. When he'd regained his breath, he shifted to the side, releasing my hands and circling me in his arms, my back flush against his damp chest.

This was why our friendship was over.

I'd never be able to look at him again and not think about how perfectly we fit together. I'd never get a whiff of his cologne without remembering how it smelled mingled with mine.

Cash took a long inhale of my hair, holding me closer. "We should go home."

Except home wasn't the same anymore and I wasn't in a rush to face it.

He held me until the sweat from our bodies cooled and the growling of his stomach drove us apart. "I'm going to take a quick shower, then maybe we can get something to eat."

"Okay." I nodded as he kissed my temple. Then I pressed my nose into the pillow, taking one more moment to remember how he'd felt inside me.

The water in the bathroom turned on and I slid off the bed, my legs wobbly, and hurried to dress. Before Cash could stop me, I rushed from the room, easing the door closed as quietly as possible.

Leaving him so I could find a place to cry.

Alone.

———

"YOU RAN AWAY." Cash dropped to the beach to sit beside me. The strands of his hair were damp from the shower.

"Sorry," I said, my voice raspy with unshed tears.

I'd come out to the beach to cry but the moment I'd plopped down in the sand, I hadn't had the energy. Because my tears weren't going to make this any easier and at this point, I needed to save my strength.

Cash had been right earlier. It wasn't fair to abandon the Greers and take a spur-of-the-moment job offer. But I was going to move out of his house. I was going to stay in the staff quarters for a while. And I was going to start mapping out what my future looked like.

Without him as the constant of my universe.

"Did I do something?" he asked.

"No." I looked at his profile, melting at the concern in his voice. "I just needed some air. It's been a string of emotional days."

He huffed a laugh. "It's been less than a week since we left. Feels like longer."

"Yeah," I murmured, turning to the ocean.

There were families building sandcastles. Couples taking selfies. Not a soul on the beach was without a smile, except for the two of us.

"Am I losing you?" he asked, his gaze straight ahead.

"I'll always be your friend." I leaned over, resting my head on his shoulder.

"That's not what I'm asking."

"I know," I whispered.

"Talk to me."

"I don't know what to say." *I love you?* No, thanks. My wall of self-preservation was about to double in thickness.

"Why don't you want to go to California?"

"Because there's nothing for me there but old memories. I'd rather focus on making new ones."

There was no family. No friends. I didn't want to see the junkyard, because I was worried that the reality of where we'd lived would be too much to take.

"Do you want to take a job here?" There was a twinge of pain in his voice, likely because he knew the answer.

"Maybe. I think . . . I think I'd like to stay in Heron Beach a while longer. With Aria."

Carol had been right all along. I needed to take some time, to think and decide.

Cash didn't have to be told he wasn't invited. He nodded, his jaw clamping shut. Then he stared at the water and the other tourists, the two of us sitting on the beach for hours.

"Do you remember the goat?" he asked as a dog ran by with a frisbee in its mouth.

"You meant the white devil that tried to kill me?"

He chuckled. "Dad asked me about a month ago if we should get some goats to graze."

362

I shuddered. "Tell me you told him no."

"I said, 'Over my dead body. Kat will smother me in my sleep if she finds out I agreed to raise goats.'"

I smiled. That was exactly what I would have threatened, verbatim.

Liddy was the one who'd brought a goat to the ranch. She'd seen a baby at the farm and ranch supply store in Missoula, and JR, being the loving, doting husband he was, had bought his wife a goat. Cash and Easton had built their mom a pen for the animal but somehow, that goat always managed to find its way out. Or its way over, we learned.

The damn thing could jump like Air Jordan.

It had never been a nice, sweet animal. To this day I believed the display goat that Liddy had seen was a fake. Because the goat she brought home loved nothing more than to chase unsuspecting humans and head butt them in the ass—specifically, me.

The goat hated me.

One day, I brought Liddy a pie I'd made from scratch. It had been one of my first since she'd taught me how to bake. She'd spent years teaching me little tricks and handing down her favorite recipes.

I was so damn proud of that strawberry rhubarb pie I didn't want to wait. The second it was cool enough to carry without an oven mitt, I drove it over to her house.

Except I didn't realize the demon had escaped its pen.

I parked, took my pie and got out of my car, nudging the door closed with my hip. That fucking goat came around the corner of their house and I panicked, running into a field with it chasing behind.

Cash had been out riding that day. He caught sight of me and barreled toward us, chasing the goat off with his horse and swiping the pie dish out of my hand right before I tripped.

Maybe another man would have tried to save me from falling. Not Cash. He knew the hours I'd spent with Liddy in the kitchen. That was before we'd moved in together, but he knew how important it was for me to bake her a gift.

So I'd eaten a face full of dirt. But he'd saved my pie.

That day, I'd fallen in love with Cash. That day had been the turning point from like to love. That day was also the last day a goat had lived on the Greer ranch.

"Remember the time we went dancing at the bar and you bent to flip me over and your pants split down the ass?" I asked. "I've never laughed so hard in my life."

"In my defense, those were very old pants." He chuckled. "How about that time you and Easton got into an eating contest over a plate of nachos?"

"Please don't say that word." I grimaced. Nachos were now classified with green beans.

We talked for another hour, reminiscing about old times. It was what I'd miss as we adjusted to a new normal. I'd mourn the loss of our friendship for a long, long time.

My butt had fallen asleep. My legs needed to stretch. I opened my mouth to tell Cash I was going to take a walk down the beach when suddenly his hands were cupping my face and his tongue swept past my lips.

I moaned, falling into him as we kissed on the beach. The taste of his lips, the soft caress of his hands, the tickle of his beard, it was the best kiss of my life.

He shoved off the sand, holding out a hand to help me to my feet. Then he threaded my fingers through his and led me across the beach to the stairs that led to The Gallaway. We didn't pause or linger on the way to our room. We didn't hesitate to strip one another of our clothes and fall into bed, a tangled mess of limbs.

We passed the hours of the day exploring each other's bodies. When Aria called, I told her I would just see her tomorrow. Cash and I ordered room service and ate naked in bed. And only when the sunlight had faded to moonlight through the window did we settle in to sleep. And to speak.

"I don't think we should tell anyone about this," I said. We were facing each other, our hands joined between us. "When we get home."

He stared into my eyes and kissed one of my knuckles.

I waited, wondering what was going on in his head but he didn't speak. "Cash."

Silence.

"Say something," I whispered.

"Tomorrow." He tucked a strand of hair away from my face. Then he closed his eyes and drifted to sleep.

Tomorrow.

Tomorrow, he'd say his goodbye.

The morning sun was barely above the horizon when I snuck out of the hotel the next morning. Once again, I took the coward's way out. Because I couldn't say goodbye. Not yet.

So I left him a note.

See you in Montana.

12

CASH

"COULD this elevator be any fucking slower?" I muttered. "I hate this hotel."

The couple standing beside me shared a look that I caught in the reflection from the polished silver walls.

I ignored them and growled. Was this how horses felt when you trapped them in their stalls? Itching and uncomfortable and desperate for freedom?

My molars ground together, the grating sound filling the car, until the light bar finally illuminated the number one. The doors slid open and though I wanted out, I waved a hand for the couple to exit first. They skittered away.

I marched from the elevator, scanning the lobby for Katherine. The note she'd left me this morning was crumpled so tight I could use it as a golf ball.

When my hand had stretched for hers this morning, I'd found stiff paper and cold cotton sheets instead of warm skin, and I was goddamn tired of searching for her in this place.

She didn't do this at home. She didn't disappear the moment I looked away. I found her at the office more often than not, but that was for work. She'd never avoided me so much.

Had she?

There was no sign of Kat in the lobby so I walked to the deck. She wasn't standing against the railing or sitting in one of the seats. A few people were out this morning on the beach, but none with her petite frame and dark hair.

I turned and strode through the lobby, heading for the front desk to page Aria. It was too early for shops to be open downtown and my guess was Kat was with Aria again.

"Good morning, sir," the man behind the counter greeted as I approached. "What can I help you with?"

"I'm—" A flash of a familiar smile caught the corner of my eye and I changed direction, walking away from the man and across the lobby for the hotel's café.

There she was. My beautiful, infuriating best friend and lover was seated at a small table across from the motherfucker who'd offered her a job yesterday.

My bootsteps echoed on the marble floor as I stormed into the café, bypassing the hostess, who had the good sense to give me a wide berth.

Katherine was laughing, covering her mouth with a napkin as she chewed. There was a half-eaten croissant on a plate beside a mug of black coffee.

Mark Gallaway was relaxed in his chair, his legs crossed. "I can't believe you've never seen that movie."

Katherine shook her head, dropping her napkin and opening her mouth to respond when she caught me from the corner of her eye. Her smile fell. "H-hey."

I didn't bother with pleasantries. "Let's go."

A flush crept up her cheeks as her eyes darted between Mark and me. "I'll meet you in the room soon."

"Let's. Go," I repeated, doing my best to hold my temper in check. It was rare that I got this mad, but goddamn this woman, she was pushing me to every edge on the emotional cliff this week. "Now."

Kat arched an eyebrow. "I'm busy now."

Mark stared at me with a smug grin on his face, not bothering to hide it as he sipped his own coffee.

I stood tall and crossed my arms over my chest. "We can talk in private or we can talk right here. Doesn't matter to me. But we are talking."

Katherine held my gaze, her eyes narrowing. She knew me well and she knew I sure as fuck wasn't bluffing. "Five minutes."

"I'll wait."

"Fine," she huffed, dismissing me with a glare as she put on a smile for Mark. It wasn't her real smile. It was the polite and placating one she used for guests. "I'm so sorry, Mark. Will you excuse me?"

"No problem." He smiled at her. "You have my card."

"Yes." She reached for her purse hanging from the back of her chair and retrieved her wallet.

Mark waved it off. "On me. Please. I've enjoyed talking with you this morning. I hope to hear from you again soon."

Oh, fuck this guy. I dug for my own wallet in my jeans pocket, taking a crisp one-hundred-dollar bill from the fold and slapping it on the table. Then I jerked my chin toward the door.

Kat gave Mark an awkward smile as she stood, but the second her gaze landed on me, it was full of fire and venom.

She took my elbow and shoved me away from the table. I'd worn a T-shirt today rather than my normal button-up and her fingernails dug into my skin. "You're a child."

"No, I'm fucking pissed." I ripped my arm free of her grip, then clasped her hand and marched us toward the elevator.

"It couldn't wait five minutes?"

"No."

The elevator was empty as she stepped inside, yanking her hand free from mine to punch the button for our floor. Then she crossed her arms over her chest and shook her head. "That was embarrassing, Cash."

"So was waking up alone after last night."

Hadn't that been special? Hadn't I treated her like the treasure she was? Hadn't I promised we'd talk tomorrow?

Damn it, I had a lot to say. The words clogged my throat, scratching and pleading to be set free. But this was not something I wanted to do in public.

An elevator was not the place to tell your best friend that you were in love with her.

I'd known it yesterday, sitting beside her on the beach. Maybe I'd known it the day I'd first seen her at the ranch all those years ago.

I was in love with Kat.

Any other woman and I probably would have blurted it out last night, but she wasn't any woman. This was Kat. And to say those words, to take this leap, was risking our friendship. And it was risking her happiness.

I was a Greer. I'd always be a Greer. And if this thing between us didn't work out, she'd lose more than a boyfriend. She'd lose a mother, a father. Grandparents and a brother. Her job. Her house.

If Katherine didn't want to explore this thing, I knew, deep down, that eventually she'd leave Montana.

Maybe she'd already made that decision.

Maybe she didn't feel the same way.

Maybe I was twelve years too late.

We needed to go home. We needed to get on familiar ground and talk this through. If she thought I was leaving without her, she was insane. No way I'd leave her with all the shit we'd gone through this week. No way I'd leave her with vultures like Mark Gallaway circling.

"Did he offer you a job again?" I asked.

"Yes."

Son of a bitch. "And?"

"And what? We had this conversation last night. I'm just exploring options. Not all of us are content to settle for the same old thing."

"Settle." I scoffed. Her claws were coming out. "That's what you think."

"Yes." The elevator dinged and she flew past me, stomping down the hallway in her flip-flops to the room. She slid the key into the slot and turned the handle. I planted my hand in the door, pushing it with too much force. It slammed against the rubber stop with a bang before slamming closed behind me as I followed her into the room.

She was ready for the face-off. She stood in front of the TV with her arms crossed. My heart jumped into my throat. When Kat entered a battle, she usually walked away the victor.

Not this time. I wanted us both to win.

"I love my job," I said. Before we covered anything else, I wanted to clear the air. "All I've ever wanted to do was be a cowboy. That's not me settling, that's me understanding reality. I'm the second son, Kat. My entire life, my father has been grooming Easton to take over the ranch. And I'm okay with that. I don't need to be in charge everywhere because when I am in charge, they respect that. When one of them needs help with a horse, they come to me. The rest . . . it was never meant for me."

"Doesn't that bother you?"

"No." I sighed. "Why does it bother you?"

"Because it's not fair." She threw her hands in the air. "You deserve all of it. You deserve the chance to choose the job you want."

I really did love her. She was standing here, furious on my behalf, when there wasn't anything to be furious about. I stepped closer. "I did choose. I am exactly where I want to be in my life. I don't want or need it to change."

A flash of pain crossed her gaze. "Right. Well, I don't feel the same. Mark—"

"Screw Mark." My rage returned with a vengeance at his name. I spun around and walked to the closet, yanking out her suitcase. Then I brought it back and threw it on the bed. "Pack. We're going home."

This trip was a disaster and though I wanted to talk to Kat about the future, I sure as hell wasn't doing it when we were at each other's throats.

"I'm not ready to leave." She jutted out her chin.

"We're leaving."

"I don't take orders from you, Cash."

"Yeah? That's not how it went last night." I'd ordered her to come and she'd done it on my command.

Her lip curled. "You're an asshole."

"Maybe. But I'm not the one turning away from their family without giving them a fighting chance. They deserve an explanation. If you leave like this, if you just don't come back, it will crush them. Grandma. Gemma. Mom. My mother loves you like her own."

"But I'm not her own!" Katherine's shout made me flinch. "She's not my mother. And do you know how painful it is to wish so badly it were true? To wish I could claim her?"

"No." I threw my arms in the air. "Because you don't talk to me. I've learned more about your past on this trip than I have in twelve years. Why?"

"I don't like to talk about my childhood."

"Even with me?" I pointed to my chest.

"Especially with you."

Fuck. Her words slashed me to the core. If she didn't trust me with her past, there was no way she'd trust me with the future.

"If you want to stay, then stay." I turned from her and strode for the door. I'd take a page from her playbook this morning and hit the beach to think. Get some air. Then I was finding an airport and getting the hell back to Montana where I belonged.

My hand gripped the door's handle just as a pair of dainty fingers touched my elbow.

"It's dirty," she whispered to my back. "It's grimy. And I hate the idea that you, of all people, might see me differently."

I turned and stared down at Kat. Her gaze was on the floor so I hooked my finger under her chin and tipped it up until I got those blue eyes. "No matter what you say, no matter where you came from, you'll always be my Kat."

Her eyes turned glassy.

The sight of unshed tears, the struggle in her eyes was nearly too much to take. I wrapped my arms around her. "Talk to me. Please. I want to understand."

"It hurts."

"Because you're keeping it all inside. This isn't a burden you have to carry alone." I didn't care that I already knew the truth. I just wanted her to confide in me. To trust me.

And maybe once she did, I'd tell her my secret. We'd rip the past wide open so that we actually had a chance to start fresh.

Katherine nodded against my chest, then stepped free, retreating to the bed. She plopped on the end, her short legs dangling above the carpet.

I sat by her side, taking her hand in mine and lacing our fingers together.

"My mother was tall," she said. "When I was a little girl, I used to look up at her and wonder if I'd be tall too. I was tiny, always the short kid in school. They'd put me in the front row in every class photo because the other kids stood head and shoulders above me. I hated it. I just wanted to be tall."

"Like your mom." When I was a kid, I'd wanted to be strong like my dad.

"No, not like my mom. I didn't want to be like my mom. I just wanted to be tall."

Kat sat motionless, unblinking as she stared at the floor. The air conditioner kicked on, but it did nothing to suppress the thick air.

"The tall kids didn't get picked on," Kat said finally. "Their mothers didn't call them Runt. I was five when I learned that my name was Katherine. Five. She had to enroll me in school and when she told the secretary my full name, I remember thinking, *Who is Katherine Gates?* Until then, I'd always thought my name was Runt. That's what she called me. That's how she introduced me to others."

"What the fuck?" I stared down at her, my mouth hanging open. "She didn't call you by your name?"

Kat shook her head. "No."

"Had she meant it like . . . an endearment?"

"No."

My stomach clenched. How could a mother name her child and then not use that name?

"She didn't want me. To this day, I don't know why she kept me. Maybe to be her punching bag."

My heart stopped. "She hit you?"

"Pinched. Slapped. The occasional kick. I think my life would have been easier if I bruised easily."

"But you've got the toughest skin on the planet."

How many times had I teased her about it? The woman would run her shins into the coffee table and other than a slight red mark immediately afterward, she didn't bruise. The only time I'd seen her black and blue was when we'd been playing baseball for fun and she'd caught a ball with her eye instead of her hand. Even then, it had healed in a couple of days without a trace.

"What about your father?" Kat hadn't spoken of him, though I'd known she'd run away from her mother's home.

"I don't know who he is. Probably one of my mother's meth-head friends."

"Meth."

Kat nodded. "Mom's drug of choice during my teenage years. I didn't care because when she was using, she'd disappear for days on end. It was when she'd come home that things were bad."

"I don't . . ." Christ, I wanted to hold her. "I'm sorry."

"We never had money. If not for school food, I would have starved. She spent everything. Stole whatever I managed to scrape together, no matter where I hid it."

Which had led her to the sidewalk, where she'd sat and begged for money to buy some fucking shoes. My insides twisted into a knot. I *hated* this for her. I hated that she'd had to endure so much strife.

"After I met Karson and followed him to the junkyard, I went home. There were some kids at my high school in foster care and I didn't want to go through that, bouncing from place to place. The junkyard sounded fun so I spent a week slowly packing. Trying to make it inconspicuous. Then I waited for Mom to disappear. It took a week, but she left and I was ready. I figured I'd be long gone by the time she showed up again. But she only left for an hour. She came home and caught me three steps away from the door, carrying a garbage bag and a backpack." Kat's hand drifted to her eyebrow, to the small scar barely visible between the dark hairs.

I'd asked her once how she'd gotten that scar. "You didn't get that from running into a shelf, did you?"

"It was a shelf. I didn't run into it though. She pushed me and I fell. For a woman who constantly spoke about getting rid of me, she really hadn't liked that I was leaving. She flew into a rage and locked me inside my room. The window in my bedroom had been boarded up for years. I couldn't get the door open. She locked me up and left for a week. If not for the bottles of water and the loaf of bread that I'd already put in that backpack to take with me to the junkyard, I would have probably died."

370

"Kat—"

"I had to pee in the corner of my closet." Her jaw tensed, her eyes narrowing. "I hope it smelled for years after I left. I hope she had one sober day when she realized what she put me through."

I gulped. "How'd you get out?"

"One of her drug dealers came over because she owed him money. He opened my door, thinking she was locked inside. He took one look at me and decided I'd be payment enough."

"No." My stomach pitched. "He didn't—"

"I was so weak. So hungry. I wouldn't have been able to fight him off. But he got close enough, smelled the urine and decided a punch to the face was good enough. I blacked out and when I woke up, he was gone. He'd left the door open so I cleaned myself up, grabbed my bag of clothes and left. You know the rest."

"Kat, I'm sorry." My voice was hard to use past the lump in my throat. I clutched her hand to my heart and dropped a kiss to her knuckles. "I'm so, so sorry."

"It's okay," she whispered. There was a numbness to her voice. A robotic tone that I hadn't heard before. "I found my way out."

For a lot of years, I'd felt guilty about what I'd done to her mother. Maybe Kat would hate me for keeping this secret, but knowing this, how her mother had treated her . . .

The guilt was gone.

"Thank you for telling me." I clutched her hand, binding her to me so she couldn't flee. "Now I have to tell you something."

"About what?"

I met her blue eyes. "About your mother."

13

CASH

"WHAT ABOUT MY MOTHER?" Kat slipped her hand free from my grasp.

Where did I even start? *Shit.* There was a reason I hadn't told her about this. A reason that I hadn't told anyone in my family.

Guilt.

I'd made a choice to protect Kat, and at the time, I'd been confident in my decision. I'd done it with her best interests at heart. But year after year, doubts had crept in, making me question my actions on that day. I realized now that I'd stayed quiet not to protect Kat, but to protect myself. I didn't want to lose her.

I hadn't wanted to miss this chance to love her and the chance she might love me back.

Fuck, this was going to be bad. She was going to hate me for this. Hell, I kind of hated myself.

"Cash," she warned.

"She came to the ranch," I admitted. "Your mother."

"What? When?"

"Five years ago." I remembered because it was the first weekend after Kat had moved into my place—our place. I'd wanted to give Kat the chance to settle in without feeling like I was hovering, so I'd left her alone on a Sunday and gone to work.

I was in the stables, in the arena halter-breaking a colt, when a woman appeared at the fence. One look and I knew she wasn't a guest. Her clothes were nice—jeans and a pink blouse. No-brand tennis shoes. Inexpensive clothing, not something any of our guests would have worn. And she was missing four front teeth.

Like Kat said, she was tall. I went over to the fence and she stood only a few inches shorter than my six foot two. She had Kat's hair, dark though streaked with thick strands of gray. Her eyes were blue but not as crystal clear as Kat's.

372

The resemblance didn't register until she asked to see her daughter, Katherine Gates.

"Five years?" Kat shook her head. "Why didn't you tell me?"

"She introduced herself. She told me her name was Jessica Gates and she was looking for her daughter, Katherine." Her visit had instantly put me on guard. Rightly so. "I asked what she wanted." I hadn't been nice about it. I think my exact words had been, *What the fuck do you want?* "She said that she needed to find you. To talk to you. I told her no."

"You what?" Kat shot off the bed, standing above me.

"I was trying to protect you. All I knew was that you'd run away from home. That you'd lived in a junkyard. You didn't speak of your parents but it didn't take much to put together that she wasn't a good mother. All of us had talked about it."

"You talked about me?" The color drained from her face. "Behind my back? Like a pity party."

"No, it wasn't like that. It was just . . . your story was shocking. None of us really knew what to think."

"So yes, a pity party. That's why you started inviting me to Friday night family dinners."

"No. Look, it wasn't like that. We just wanted to include you. Make sure you felt like you had a home. Is that so wrong?" And of all the staffers who'd come and gone at the ranch, none had ever fit into our circle like Kat.

"My mother." Kat crossed her arms over her chest. "What did she say?"

"When I told her no, she begged to see you." Jessica Gates had reached her bony fingers across the fence separating us as we'd spoken and grabbed my hand, squeezing it with more strength than I'd expected from a woman who looked like she'd lived hard.

"And you still turned her away. How could you?"

"Because she just wanted money." The hurt that flashed across Kat's face broke my heart. "I told her that we knew all about your childhood. That you were better off without her. And I told her that you didn't want to see her."

"You had no right."

"I was trying to protect you. I wanted to see what she'd do. How honest she was in her intentions. You know what it looks like when you roll onto the property." Like money. The lodge was enormous. The stables and barn too. The Greer Ranch and Mountain Resort was designed to impress the wealthiest people in the world.

"And?" Kat stared at me, her face twisted in rage, but the hurt was beginning to show through. Her features were beginning to crumple. Because she already knew where this was going.

"I told her I'd give her five thousand dollars, cash, to leave the ranch and leave you in peace."

She swallowed hard. "She took it?"

"Yes."

To her credit, Jessica had waged an internal debate. She'd stood across from me, her eyes cast to the dirt, and weighed my offer for a solid five minutes. As the time dragged on, I almost gave in. I almost offered to go get Kat and bring her to the lodge. But right before I could cave, Jessica held out her hand.

Maybe she thought that my five thousand dollars was more than she'd ever get from Kat. When the selfish bitch accepted my offer, I didn't waste a second before getting her off my ranch.

"She'd flown to Missoula, then paid for an Uber to drive her to the ranch. I went to the lodge. Got some money out of the safe in Dad's office. Then I gave it to her and drove her to the airport in Missoula myself."

The forty-mile trip was the longest of my life. A few times I caught Jessica catching a tear with her fingertips as she stared out the passenger window. When I pulled up to the airport's terminal, she opened the door, ready to leave without a word, but paused.

Tell her I'm sorry.

Then she was gone.

I'd wondered for the past five years if we'd see her again. If she'd come begging for more money now that she knew a trip to Montana was an easy payday. But I'd never seen Jessica again.

And for years, I'd unsuccessfully prodded Kat for information about her youth. I'd needed to know that I'd done the right thing by sending Jessica away.

"Did she ask about me?"

Damn it, this was going to hurt. "No."

Jessica hadn't once asked if her daughter was happy or safe or loved.

Kat dropped her gaze to the floor. Her hair draped in front of her face but I still saw the quiver of her chin.

"I'm sorry."

"You should have told me," she whispered.

"I know."

"How could you keep this from me? All these years?" She looked up and the pain in her expression wasn't just from her mother's visit, but because I'd betrayed her.

"It was for your own good."

"Oh, fuck you," she snapped.

I flinched. "Kat—"

"You and your family are always trying to protect me. Except what any of you don't seem to realize is that I don't need your protection. Carol forbids me from touching base with the resort staff while I'm on this trip and it's for my own good. Gemma sets up this entire trip and it's for my own good. You don't tell me about my mother coming to find me ten years after I've seen her and it's for my own good. I don't need your protection. I'm capable of judging what's *for my own fucking good.*"

"We're just looking out."

"I don't need anyone to look out for me."

"That's what family does."

"Family?" She scoffed. "You sent my only living relative away. You took away the last chance I ever had to see my mother."

"I'm sorry. If it means that much, we can go find her. I'll go with you to California. We can leave today."

"Too late." Kat's eyes turned glacial and her expression flattened. "She's dead."

The air in the room went still. My heart dropped. "What?"

"She died of an overdose. Five years ago."

No. Oh shit, no.

"I remember because it was the second weekend after I moved in with you. We were supposed to have everyone over for pizza."

But she'd canceled because of a migraine. We'd rescheduled to another weekend. Except Kat didn't get migraines, did she? That was the one and only time I recalled her having one, and at the time, I hadn't realized it was a lie.

"How?" I choked out. How had she died? How had Kat known?

"The sheriff came out that morning. I was at the lodge, weeding one of the flower beds. I'd thought he'd come to have coffee with your dad. Instead, he'd come to find me. To tell me that my mother had been found dead in her home two days prior."

I stood, ready to hold her and tell her I was sorry, but she shook her head and took a step away. My feet froze.

"When her neighbor went through her things, she told me she found four thousand dollars cash in her purse. I never understood how, but now I know. The other thousand must have gone toward a plane ticket and however much it cost to flood her system with meth."

Fuck me. My head spun and I sank down to the edge of the bed. I'd given Jessica the money she'd used to end her life. Horror coursed through my system. Despair and guilt clouded my vision. I dropped my head forward, my elbows on my knees. "Kat, I'm sorry."

"She was clean before that. She'd changed her life."

"What?" My head snapped up. "How do you know?"

"Gemma's not the only one who can hire an investigator," she said. "After I found out she'd died, I had to settle her estate. Not that there was much. And I wanted to know what her life had been like but I didn't want to visit."

So she'd hired an investigator. Meanwhile the rest of us hadn't had a clue that she'd been carrying this burden alone.

Kat barked a mocking laugh. "Turns out, all she'd needed to get clean was for her daughter to abandon her. According to her records, she went to rehab about a year after I ran away from home. She stayed sober ever since. She worked at a local women's shelter. She moved into a nicer neighborhood. One of her coworkers at the shelter told my investigator that Mom had spent years setting aside money to go to Montana. She'd just been too scared to make the trip."

And I'd chased Jessica away.

I'd chased her back into the drugs that had cost her a daughter.

I'd chased her into a grave.

"I had her cremated and spread her ashes on Hangman Peak," Kat whispered.

"You did?" Hangman Peak was one of the hardest hikes we offered to our guests, but the view at the top was worth every step. I made it a point to go up there at least twice a year.

She lifted a shoulder. "I thought she would have liked the view."

"You went alone?" Why hadn't she asked me or anyone else to go with her?

"Alone means people won't disappoint me." She leveled me with a glare. "How could you?"

"I'm sorry." I stood again but she took another step away. "I'm so, so sorry. It was a mistake."

"You stole my chance to see her."

"I didn't know you'd want to."

Her stare narrowed. "That doesn't make it right."

"I know." I held up my hands. "Tell me what I can do. Please."

Kat didn't answer. Instead, she flew past me, going to the dresser and opening the top drawer. She scooped out the clothes she'd put in there when we'd arrived and rushed to the bed, flipping open her suitcase and dropping them inside. Then she did the same with the second drawer.

"Kat."

She shook her head, disappearing into the bathroom. The clink of plastic bottles being shoved into a bag echoed in the room.

"Kat, please," I said when she came back into the room, dropping her toiletry case into her purse. "I'm sorry. I didn't know. You never told me."

"Don't you dare blame this on me."

"I'm not." I held up my hands. "I'm only trying to explain. I didn't know. You never talked about it. I made an assumption and it was the wrong one."

"Why would I talk about it?" She whirled on me, her face flushed and her eyes blazing. "Why would I talk about how my mother hated me? Why would I talk about living in the dirt for two years because sleeping in a trash heap, in a makeshift hovel with tarps and metal sheets and *mice*, was better than the alternative?"

"I'm—"

"Sorry?" She went to the suitcase, slamming it closed and zipping it tight. Then she turned to me, her hands planted on her hips. "I can't talk about that time. I don't want to relive those memories. Sure, we all pretend that living in the junkyard was this magical fairy tale. But it was scary. We were *scared*. You have no idea what it's like shivering yourself to sleep on cold nights and wishing you had just one more blanket. You don't know how it feels to wake up so hungry you can't see straight because all you had to eat the day before was half a peanut butter and honey sandwich on stale bread."

I struggled to breathe. The raw, ruthless emotion on her face cracked my heart.

"We were sixteen," she said. "So young and so foolish. But that was what life had dealt us and we made the best of it. Yes, there were some happy times. Yes, we were relatively safe. But the fear. You don't know what it's like to live in that kind of fear, so forgive me if I don't want to remember just so you and your family can talk about it over coffee."

She hefted her suitcase from the mattress and took three steps toward the door but stopped and turned again. "The reason I painted back then was because I needed something pretty. I needed to wake up to a world where I was in control. Where the flowers were pink and the sunshine was yellow because I said it was that way. It was the only control I had."

My throat was burning, but I managed a nod and a hoarse, "Okay."

"I stopped painting because I didn't need it. I wasn't scared anymore. When I came to Montana, I could wake up, look out the window and there was my magical meadow. There. In real life. For me to touch and know that tomorrow would be okay. I was safe because I'd found a home. And I was safe because I had you."

"You'll always have me."

She shook her head, blinking away a sheen of tears. "No, I won't."

"Kat, please." I closed the distance between us, putting my hands on her shoulders. "Don't go. Let's work this out."

"I'm such a fool." Her eyes filled with tears. "Pining after you for all these years. Hoping and dreaming that one day you'd love me the way I love you."

My heart dropped. She loved me? The words unknotted the twisting fear in my belly. If she loved me, then we'd figure this out. We'd be together and we'd find a way to put this behind us. We could overcome this, right?

I opened my mouth to tell her I was in love with her, to drop to my knees and plead with her to stay. But before I could, she stepped out of my hold and my hands sank like bricks in water to my sides.

"Thank you." Her voice was as icy as her glare. "You know what this trip was about? It was my chance to let you go, to stop wasting years waiting for you to love me. When you came along, I didn't think it would help. But here we are and now I have what I wanted. You're nothing to me now. Not even my friend."

"We're more than friends."

She turned and opened the door, her parting words ringing loud and clear even after the door slammed shut. "Not anymore."

14

CASH

IN LESS THAN ONE WEEK, I'd fallen in love with my best friend.

And in a single hour, I'd lost her.

I drummed my fingers on the reception desk, willing the man who'd disappeared behind the employees-only door to hurry the fuck up. My duffel bag rested at my feet. I'd tossed the clothes inside as haphazardly as Kat had done her own.

Stupid bastard that I was, her confession about loving me had sent me into a tailspin. When I should have been running after her, I'd stood frozen in the middle of our room.

It had probably only been five minutes, ten max, that I'd stood like a dumbfounded chump, but it had given her enough lead time to escape.

She loved me.

How long? How long had I been blind to the truth?

I'd realized, standing in that hotel room, there was a reason I constantly bought Kat trinkets and gifts and chocolate bars. When I saw something that would bring a smile to her face, I had to have it.

Just because.

Just because.

Just. Because.

Just because I was in love with her.

After shaking off my epiphany, I'd flown into action, packing while leaving a panicked message on her voicemail. Since then, I'd left six more and ten texts, none of which had been returned.

Damn, I was a fucking idiot, though idiot wasn't strong enough a word. Once I got Kat back—and I was getting her back—she could call me every awful thing from prick to asshole to douchebag that popped into that gorgeous head of hers and I'd agree with them all.

If she wanted to take a job in Oregon, then Heron Beach would be our home. I'd give up the ranch, the horses and that life, because she was worth it.

My mother had always told me the reason our ranch worked was because every generation had tackled it as a team. Granddad and Grandma. Mom and Dad. Easton and Gemma. They worked it together because that was what made it special. A partnership. Two halves making a whole.

And at the moment, my other half was nowhere to be found.

This time, I wasn't going to find Kat in the café or on the beach. She'd packed her bag and was either at another hotel, far away from me, or she'd hauled the Cadillac out of valet and was on her way to . . . anywhere. So I'd checked out of the room, then asked this clerk to find out if the Cadillac was still parked.

Had he gone to the parking lot or garage or wherever the hell they kept the cars to check himself? How hard was it to find out if a ticket had been claimed for a goddamn car?

Beside me, a couple laughed as they checked into their room. They couldn't keep their hands off each other. *Honeymooners.* They'd been telling anyone who'd listen.

That should be me and Kat. We should be the ones kissing and smiling and anxious to get behind a closed door to strip our clothes off.

I dragged a hand through my hair. *Come on. Come on.* What was taking so long?

My eyes were glued to the door where he'd disappeared. My foot tapped on the floor. If they'd just tell me where they parked the cars, I'd go find out if the Cadillac was there myself.

I dug my phone from my pocket and checked again for a message from Kat. *Nothing.* Where was she? Maybe this clerk would give me Aria's number. Had Kat told her where she was going? Were they together?

The door opened and I held my breath, but instead of the clerk, fucking Mark Gallaway emerged, wearing the same suit and smug grin he had in the café. Didn't that guy have a corner office to lurk in?

"Mr. Greer." He came around the desk, hand extended.

I shook it with a tad too much force. "Mr. Gallaway."

"Have you been helped?"

"Yes." *By your impossibly slow staff.* I should have been out the door ten minutes ago.

"Excellent. Enjoy your stay." He turned and took three steps away, his polished shoes clicking on the floor.

I wanted to watch that guy disappear and never see him again. I wanted to say fuck Mark Gallaway, I didn't need him to help me find Aria. But my pride was in tatters. It had been ripped to shreds by the five-foot-one woman who owned my heart. And above all else, I wanted her back.

"Wait," I called to Mark's back.

He turned and raised an eyebrow. "Yes?"

That son of a bitch knew where she was, didn't he? "I'm looking for Kat. Have you seen her?"

"I have."

I gritted my teeth. "And where was that?"

His smirk stretched as he sauntered my way, arrogance rolling over his shoulders. Swear to God, if she'd taken a job in the last hour while I'd been packing and searching for her, I'd . . .

Deal. I'd deal with it.

We'd do whatever she needed to do, even if that meant working for a man like Gallaway.

"I believe she left with Aria. Something about a road trip."

Fuck my life. "Thanks." The word tasted bitter. "If I asked, would you give me Aria's number?"

"Are you asking?"

"Yes." *Don't punch him. Don't punch him.*

He stared at me, cold and calculating. I expected the asshole to turn and walk away without another word, but I stood tall, patient, because he wasn't the only powerful man in the room. Maybe I didn't show it. I didn't need to wear an Italian suit or four-thousand-dollar watch.

But I wasn't backing down.

Kat was mine.

He could try to steal her and he'd lose.

She'd been mine for a long time, even when I hadn't wanted to admit it to myself.

Kat had said something on the trip, during our first fight. *Why do you let people decide how your life is going to go?* God, she'd pissed me off.

She was wrong about people pushing me into a certain job. I'd always gone willingly. Except maybe that statement wasn't entirely wrong, she'd just pegged the wrong target.

My family's influence over my relationship with Kat was stronger than I'd let myself recognize. They'd dictated that she be a family member. I'd followed their lead.

But Kat wasn't only my friend. She wasn't only my best friend.

She was mine.

She'd been mine since the day a young stallion had bucked me off into a fence and I'd gotten a concussion. She'd crept into my room every two hours that night, waking me as the doctor had instructed to make sure I was okay.

She'd been mine since the night she'd gotten so drunk at a bonfire party that she'd decided my bed was more comfortable than hers and had crawled in next to me, snoring so loud I'd heard it down the hallway from the living room where I'd slept on the couch.

She'd been mine since day one.

And whether Mark Gallaway gave me Aria's phone number or not, I'd find her. I'd search every highway in the country until I tracked her down.

Mark's eyes narrowed as I held his gaze. I stood steady and strong until, finally, he reached inside his jacket and pulled out a phone, scrolling through before rattling off Aria's number.

"Did you need me to write it down?" he asked.

"No." I mentally repeated it once. Twice. Then it was there. "Appreciated."

He gave me a nod, then turned again. I didn't wait for him to disappear. I went back to my spot at the desk, took out my phone and let my fingers fly across the screen as I called Aria's number.

It rang three times before it clicked to voicemail. "Aria, this is Cash Greer. I'm looking for Kat. Please have her call me."

I ended that call and dialed Kat's again. It went straight to voicemail. "Kat. Please. Let's talk about this. Please call me back." I sent the same in a text, sending it off just as the clerk returned.

"I'm sorry for the delay, sir."

"That's fine," I lied.

"It looks like that car is no longer in valet."

Son of a bitch. Where had she gone? She couldn't have gotten far, but I was without wheels and unsure of the direction to head.

"Is there anything else I can assist you with?" the clerk asked.

"No, thanks." I bent and picked up my bag, only to turn back again. "Is there a rental car place in town?"

"Yes." He took a sheet of paper from beneath the counter—a map. Staring at it upside down, he circled the destination and used a highlighter to mark directions from the hotel.

"Thanks again." I took the map and wasted no time walking the five blocks to the rental place.

It took another thirty minutes to rent a car. People in Heron Beach didn't seem to be in much of a hurry. The nervous energy I was emitting didn't inspire them to work with much urgency either. Finally, with the keys to a black SUV in my hand, I loaded up my bag and got behind the wheel.

But where was I going?

Kat and Aria hadn't returned a call or text, so I made a different call instead, bracing because I knew it was going to sting. I sucked in a deep breath as the phone rang and when my mother's voice answered, I blew it out in a shaky stream.

"Hello! I was wondering when you'd call."

"Hey, Mom."

"Uh-oh. What's wrong?"

There was no hiding anything from Liddy Greer. At least, not if you were her son. "I fucked up, Mom. I need your help."

"I'm listening."

I spewed the story in a rambled rush. Mom stayed quiet on the line as I spoke, and replaying the story, hearing my own words again, was nearly as bad as having to confess it to Kat.

"Cash." She was shaking her head at me. I didn't need to see it to know. "You fucked up."

"I know." It wasn't often that Mom said fuck, or any variation. For her to curse, I hadn't just fucked up, I'd done it royally. "I can't find her. She's not answering my calls, and I can't lose her like this."

"Maybe you should."

I flinched. "What?"

"Maybe you need to let her go. I know she's your friend and you care about her. But son—"

"I'm in love with her."

My declaration was met with a deafening hush. Wouldn't Mom want us together? Maybe I didn't deserve Kat, especially after all I'd done to hurt her, but damn it, I'd spend the rest of my life righting my years of wrongs.

"Mom," I whispered. "Please."

"You're sure you love her?"

"Took me a while to figure it out but she's the one."

Mom sniffled.

"What? Why is that wrong?"

"Oh, it's not wrong. It's just about damn time." She laughed. "What can I do?"

I sighed. "She won't take my calls and I don't know where she's at."

"Okay. Let me see what I can do," Mom said, then ended the call.

Waiting and sitting idle was not an option, so I started the rental car and pulled up my GPS app.

Kat couldn't have gone far, but if she was racing down the highway, a ten- or twenty-minute lead meant it would take me hours to catch up. That was, if I even started in the right direction. At least one thing in my favor was Kat's propensity to always drive the speed limit.

Had she started home? Kat could be miles on her way to Montana. Maybe she'd changed her mind about California after all, though I doubted it. She could have taken that quarter and let it decide.

They were all options, but I didn't punch Clear River or Temecula into the navigation. My gut said Kat was with Aria.

So I was headed toward Welcome, Arizona.

15

KATHERINE

"Damn, girl," Aria said. "I'm sorry."

"I hate him," I lied, my fingers tightening around the wheel. We both knew I'd never hate Cash.

Over the past thirty minutes, I'd told Aria everything that had happened today. Everything I hadn't when I'd found her at the hotel with my suitcase in hand to say goodbye.

Aria had known something was wrong, but rather than push me to talk or let me leave, she'd stuck close. Loyalty was my second favorite quality of hers, the first being her ability to listen. As the Cadillac flew down the highway, she sat in the passenger seat, attuned to my every word.

We were on the highway that would eventually lead us to Arizona. Maybe after twelve hundred miles I wouldn't feel quite so broken.

I'd set out on this trip to get over Cash. To put the hopes and dreams of an *us* in my rearview mirror. Maybe one day I'd stop loving him, but what hurt the worst was that I'd lost my friend.

My best friend.

He was the one I ran to on bad days. He was my safe haven. When I'd gotten food poisoning from grocery store sushi, he'd been the one holding my hair back as I puked for twelve hours. When one of our guests had sent me a scathing email about his bad experience with allergies at the resort— as if I had some control over the pollen in the air—Cash had let me cry on his shoulder and mourn the loss of my impeccable five-star Google rating.

His absence was like a gaping hole in my heart.

But at least I had Aria.

After I'd left Cash standing in the room, the truth tainting the air, I'd hurried to the front desk to page Aria. She'd come into the lobby with a smile that had brought me to tears. I'd hugged her, told her I was leaving and that I was so happy to have found her again. I'd apologized for the last-minute change of plan but I wasn't leaving her with the Cadillac.

I needed it to make my escape.

Without asking why I was seconds away from an emotional break-down, she'd grabbed my free hand and hauled me to the second floor, winding through a maze of hallways until we reached Mark's office. I'd waited in the hallway while she'd gone inside to talk to him. When she'd come out, she'd looked at me and said, "Let's go."

On the way out of town, we'd stopped by her home so she could pack a bag and ask her neighbor to water her plants.

She seemed used to taking time off. To stepping away. Maybe this trip of mine wouldn't have been such a disaster if I'd taken more vacations before this. Maybe I would have realized much sooner that I was replace-able at work and that the family I'd clung to wouldn't bother to call for days, not even Gemma.

The open road ahead did nothing to give me a sense of freedom. Instead I looked down the double yellow lines that divided the pavement and felt lost. Alone. Where was I going? Arizona was a start, but then where? What was I doing with my life?

I just wanted . . . I wanted to go home. I wanted to rewind this week and go back to the days when I wasn't so angry at Cash I could barely breathe.

"You okay?" Aria asked.

"No."

"Want me to drive?"

I clutched the wheel. Having it under my palms felt like the only thing in my control at the moment. "No, thanks."

Her phone rang in her hand and she narrowed her eyes at the number. "Um . . ."

"What?"

"Area code four-oh-six."

"It's Cash."

"Should I answer it?"

"Definitely not." He'd been calling me relentlessly and sending texts. My phone rested on the seat, tucked beneath my knee. I'd felt it vibrating and held tighter to the wheel every time, resisting any temptation to answer.

"He really didn't say anything when you said you loved him?" Aria asked.

"Nothing." To be fair, I hadn't really given him the chance.

He'd looked so shocked, like a deer in the headlights. Of all the things he'd said to me in that hotel room, his silence had by far hurt the worse.

"I hate him," I whispered. *I love him.* Even furious, my heart belonged to him.

"I'm sorry about your mom," Aria said.

"Me too."

I'd been wrestling with feelings for my mother for years. I was sorry that she'd died. I was sorry that she'd lived a life without much joy. But I didn't forgive her and I doubted I ever would. She'd hurt me too deeply, and even if I'd had the chance to see her again, even if she'd apologized, I wouldn't have wanted a relationship with her.

Did I blame Cash for her death? No. She'd given me up long, long ago. A visit to Montana wasn't enough to compensate for her actions. And I knew, bone deep, that Cash had only done what he'd thought was best.

Bone deep, I'd already forgiven him for always looking out *for my own good*.

My phone rang again, vibrating against my jeans. Temptation got the better of me and I slid it free, surprised to see Liddy's name on the screen.

"Who is it?" Aria asked.

"Cash's mom."

It rang in my hand as I alternated my gaze from the phone to the road.

"Are you going to answer?"

"He probably called her." That or she was finally returning my call. Any other person, I would have ignored it. But this was Liddy, the woman I loved more than my own mother, so I answered. "Hi."

"We love you," she said.

I blinked. "Huh?"

"We love you," she repeated. "No matter what happens with you and Cash, we *all* love you. He wants me to find out where you are. He's desperate, Kat. But I'm going to hang up before you can even tell me. Do what you need to do for you. And we'll be here whenever you're ready to come home."

I opened my mouth to speak, but Liddy had already hung up.

Just like that, she'd made me a promise. She'd erased all of my fears. No matter where I lived, no matter where I worked, she loved me. They all did.

Even Cash, in his own way.

God, this hurt. The ache in my heart twisted so hard it stole my breath and a little sob escaped my lips.

"Oh, Katherine." Aria placed her hand on my shoulder.

"I'm okay." My eyes flooded and I swiped at them, catching the tears before they could fall.

I'm okay.

This was just another bump in the road. Another unexpected turn. I'd deal with it like all the bumps that had come before. On my own.

Aria and I drove in silence, the whirl of the tires offering no comfort. The scenery was lush and green, and though we were headed away from the ocean, its salt still clung to the air.

It was nice. Different. Except I didn't want different. I wanted to breathe in the clean Montana mountain air, smelling hay and horses as I watched Cash work.

Training the younger animals was his favorite. Cash would spend hours with a foal, teaching it in slow, methodical steps how to wear a halter and follow a lead. Then as the horses got older, he'd teach them to wear a saddle on their backs and a bit in their mouths.

It was magic, watching him work, and one of my favorite pastimes. He was the definition of steady. Gentle. Patient. I'd stand at the arena's fence, unable to tear my eyes away. Every few minutes, he'd glance my direction and gift me with a smile.

That smile.

There had always been love in Cash's smile.

Liddy had said he was desperate. Desperate for what? To find me and apologize again? Or was there more?

I'd run from him so fast today that I hadn't given him the chance to explain. I'd shut him out and thrown up my guard. I claimed to love him but hadn't truly let him in.

Tears filled my eyes again and no amount of biting my cheek would make them stop. They fell in silent streams down my cheeks, dripping onto my jeans and creating dark indigo circles as they fell.

My foot came off the gas. "I'm so sorry, Aria. I can't do this."

She gave me a sad smile. "I understand."

"I just . . . I can't run from this." From my home. From my family. *From him.*

"What about Cash?" she asked.

"I don't know." I sighed. "I'm mad."

"Uh, yeah." She nodded. "I would be too."

Though with every passing minute, my anger was subsiding. He shouldn't have kept my mother's visit a secret, but I understood why he had.

We all love you. Liddy's words rang in my ears. We *all* love you. What was she getting at?

"I can't exactly avoid him forever," I said. "We'll figure it out eventually. But there's no rush. A few more hours to let things settle won't hurt."

"I wouldn't count on that if I were you."

"Huh?"

She glanced over her shoulder and through the back window. "He's been behind us for the past few minutes."

"What?" My eyes whipped to the mirror, where a black SUV was nearly clinging to my bumper. I'd been so focused on the road ahead, I hadn't noticed it approach.

The SUV's headlights flashed and a strong, sinewy arm extended out the driver's side window, waving to get my attention.

My breath hitched. I knew that arm.

I let the Cadillac drift slower, my foot barely pressing the brake as I scanned the side of the road for a place to pull over. A mailbox caught my eye ahead, marking the entrance to a private driveway. I put on my blinker, slowing down as Cash eased back to give me some space so we could both pull off the highway.

"I'll just wait here." Aria grinned as I opened the door.

I stepped onto the ground, my feet barely steady, as Cash rushed to me, sweeping me into his arms in a crushing embrace.

My hands dug into his shoulders, holding tight. I wasn't sure if I was gripping him so strongly because I was trying to punish him or because he'd come after me. But I didn't protest as he held me tightly against his chest, lifting me off my feet until they dangled by his shins.

"I'm sorry." His voice was filled with pain and regret. "God, Kat. I'm sorry."

"I forgive you."

He pulled away and his eyebrows came together. "You do?"

"I'm hurt, but I forgive you. Your heart was in the right place." And in his boots, I might have done the same. I wouldn't have wanted him to be hurt by a woman who'd take my money without even asking about her child.

"Doesn't matter." He shook his head and set me down. "I should have told you."

My shoulders sagged and I nodded. "It's done."

What was the point of staying mad at him? It wouldn't change anything. It wouldn't undo the past and it wouldn't change the relationship I'd had with my mother.

I glanced past him to the SUV. "How'd you know where I was going?"

"Lucky guess."

I looked up and met those hazel eyes. "Why'd you come?"

"Because I love you."

My heart dropped. My mouth went dry. "What?"

Cash stepped closer, taking my face in his hands. "I love you, Katherine Gates."

This wasn't actually happening. How long had I dreamed of hearing those words? How long had I hoped for them? Too long. It was impossible to believe they were real. "As a friend."

He shook his head. "Not as a friend."

"As a little sister."

That earned me another head shake. "Definitely not as a little sister."

"You love me?"

"I am *in love* with you."

Cash was in love with me. My head spun as it tried to flip the switch from fantasy to reality. I opened my mouth to say something, anything, but there were no words.

Actually, there were three.

"I love you."

Cash's entire body radiated relief. He flashed me that sexy grin, giving me a split second to enjoy it, before he slammed his mouth down on mine. His kiss was so consuming, so powerful and adoring, it felt like he was claiming me forever, branding me as his and his alone.

He loved me.

The fears, doubts and insecurities I'd clutched for years were swept away with his hot tongue. The internal box that had guarded my secrets, and my heart, was wide open.

The blare of the Cadillac's horn filled the air. "Get a room!"

I giggled at Aria as Cash broke away, holding me tight.

"I love you, Kat," he whispered.

"I love you, Cash."

"Don't go," he pleaded. "Stay with me. Lean on me. I swear, I won't let you fall."

I dropped my head to his chest. The only man in the world who could make me that promise, make me believe it, was Cash. "Okay."

The passenger door to the Cadillac popped open and Aria stepped out, rounding the trunk to join us. "Hi, Cash."

"Hi, Aria."

"How fast were you going to catch us?" she asked.

He grinned. "Fast enough."

A semitruck blazed down the highway, the noise so loud it reminded me that we were essentially on the side of the road. "Should we head back to the hotel?"

"I've got a better idea." Cash shook his head and walked past me to the Cadillac. He leaned inside and when he stood, he held up the quarter I'd left in the tray. The quarter Carol had given me. "How about we start this adventure over?"

Drive wherever the quarter intended. Explore the countryside with the man I loved. Share hotel rooms and sleep in each other's arms. "Yes, please."

"Would you take the Cadillac?" Cash asked Aria.

"Of course." She stepped closer and took me in one of her fierce hugs.

I clung to her, holding her close. "Thank you. For everything."

"Thanks for coming to find me." She let me go and leaned back. "I've missed you."

We didn't need to voice that we'd see one another again. We didn't need to say call me or text. Now that I'd found Aria again, I wasn't going to lose her.

"Nice to meet you, Cash." She held out her hand.

He shook it, then pulled her in for a hug. "Don't be a stranger. Come see us in Montana."

"Will you teach me to ride a horse?"

He chuckled and let her go. "You got it."

"Will you be okay driving to Arizona alone?" I asked Aria as Cash went to collect my suitcase and belongings from the Cadillac.

"Of course, but not today. I'm going home. I have to work on Monday."

"What?" My mouth fell open. "But the trip—"

"Oh, I figured he'd catch up with us after about an hour or two." She winked at Cash as he slammed the trunk.

"How'd you know?"

"Please." She rolled her eyes. "That man loves you too much to let you go."

I cast a glance at Cash, where he was hauling my purse from the back-seat. And I loved him too much to actually run away.

Aria and I shared one last hug, then she waved goodbye to Cash and climbed in the Cadillac, flipping it around and disappearing down the highway.

"Think we'll ever see that car again?" Cash asked, pulling me into his side.

"No."

That car had taken me on the trip that I'd needed, just like it had with Londyn and Gemma.

Cash led me to the passenger door of the SUV, closing it for me once I was inside. Then he jogged around the hood and slid behind the wheel, holding the quarter up between us.

I took it from his fingers and gave it a flip. "Heads left. Tails right."

"HEY," I answered Gemma's call.

Cash touched his invisible watch, reminding me that we were kind of in the middle of something, but I held up a finger. I wouldn't have answered except it was the first time on the trip that she'd called, and I wanted to make sure everything was okay with her and the baby.

"Hi," she whispered. "How are you?"

"Fine. Why are you whispering?"

"Because I'm breaking the rules by calling you and if Carol finds out, she's going to banish me from the lodge."

"What rules?"

"We're not allowed to interrupt your vacation. Carol's orders. She wanted you to have time to disconnect and explore and whatever. I would have broken the rule sooner but she promised to make me a fresh cherry pie and I was waiting until she delivered."

Carol. So she was the reason that my phone calls and texts had gone unanswered. I should have expected her to lay down the law with the family like she had with the resort staff.

The only contact we'd had with home over the past four days was when Cash had called Liddy, assuring her that we were together and that everything had worked out. He'd also asked that she not tell anyone that the two of us were together before we had a chance to tell them ourselves when we got home.

"So where are you? How's it going? Did you and Cash hook up yet?"

"Did Liddy tell you?"

"What?" Her voice got louder. "You hooked up? And Liddy knows? Why didn't she tell me?"

"If she didn't tell you, how did you know?"

"It was only a matter of time. You two needed to get away and do something without everyone in the family watching over your shoulders so he could realize how wonderful and beautiful you are and the idiot would finally pull his head out of his ass and fall in love with you."

"Thanks, Gem," Cash muttered at my side.

I laughed. "You're on speaker."

"Oh," she muttered. "Well, I stand by my statement. Hi, Cash."

"Hi," he said. "When you made me camp out and search for a mountain lion, there wasn't really a lion, was there?"

"Nope."

And his appearance the morning I'd been slated to leave hadn't been coincidence either. It was why she'd made me take cookies. Why she'd had Easton go fill the car with gas.

I'd hug Gemma for that later and bake her a dozen cherry pies.

"Where are you?" she asked. "When are you coming home? I'm bored. So, so bored. Carol took this activity rest restriction from the doctor to the extreme. She has me at the front desk and I'm slowly losing my mind. And you should know that things are totally falling apart around here."

"Really?" A smile spread across my face. "That's great!"

"It is?" Cash asked and I waved him off.

"What's happening?" I asked Gemma.

"Well, let's see. Annabeth got into a huge fight with one of the house-keepers and the two of them made this big scene in front of a guest. It was wildly uncomfortable and Easton had to step in. You can imagine how well he handled that."

I cringed. "Who'd he fire?"

"Both of them. But Carol rehired them ten minutes later."

"Okay." That was going to take some fixing. It had to have been bad because Annabeth wasn't one to lose her composure. My guess was the stress of my absence was taking its toll. My chest swelled with pride.

I'd feel guilty about that later, but at the moment, I was just happy that they hadn't been perfect without me.

"That's not all," Gemma said. "Chef Wong has gone rogue."

I scrunched up my nose. "He does that at times." Hence the warning I'd given Carol.

"When JR walked into the kitchen and found him making tofu instead of beef, things got dicey."

Cash chuckled, glancing over to the woman at the counter.

She nodded and said, "We're ready for you, sir."

"I'll call and check in with Annabeth tomorrow," I told Gemma. "And I'll call Chef Wong."

"Good. We need you. So when are—"

"Hey, who are you talking to?" Carol's voice carried through the phone.

"Oh, shit," Gemma hissed, then called out, "No one!" The line was silent for a long moment until she returned. "Phew. That was close."

Cash jerked his chin and reached for the red circle to end the call but I swatted him away.

"Gemma, I have to let you go."

"When are you coming home?"

"We, um . . . we'll probably need another week."

"Ten days," Cash corrected just as the wedding march rang over the speaker system. There was a large diamond ring on my finger, one Cash had given me last night on bended knee.

"Wait, what is that?" Gemma asked. "Katherine Gates, are you elop—"

Cash ended the call, took the phone from my hand and tucked it into his jeans pocket, where he'd kept our quarter. He'd taken ownership of flipping the coin over the past four days and fate—as he'd called it, though we both knew it wasn't coincidence—had brought us to Las Vegas. To the Clover Chapel.

He led me toward the aisle. "I love you, Mrs. Greer."

"I'm not Mrs. Greer yet."

"Close enough." My soon-to-be husband framed my face with his hands and dropped a kiss to my lips.

The same soft kiss he gave me after Elvis pronounced us husband and wife.

EPILOGUE
KATHERINE

FIVE MONTHS LATER . . .

"Don't touch my hair," I whispered.

Cash's hands, centimeters from a curl I'd spent two minutes perfecting, stopped beside my ears. He brought them forward, toward my cheeks.

"Don't touch my face."

He grumbled and shot me a scowl. He was midstroke, his cock buried deep inside my throbbing core. "Then where can I touch?"

"Anywhere below the waist."

Cash pulled out, grabbed me by the hips, yanking me away from the counter, and spun me around before sinking deep.

I moaned, letting my head sag to the side.

Cash's hands dug into the flesh of my hips. His lips found the sensitive skin below my ear, and even though it was dangerously close to the makeup I'd spent an hour on, the nip of his teeth was too good to pass up. "Fuck, but you feel good."

I hummed, rocking back against him as he thrust in and out.

His hand slipped beneath my shirt, his rough fingers sliding over my belly, dipping lower until his middle finger found my clit. He strummed the hard nub, bringing me closer and closer. My legs trembled, my heart raced. I was so close, I gasped, ready to detonate—

"Kat?" Jake's voice came from the hallway as he knocked on the door. "Are you in there?"

Cash froze.

My gaze whipped to the doorknob. *Locked.* I blew out a breath. "Y-yeah?"

"She's in the bathroom, Carol!" he yelled down the hallway.

"Tell her the photographer's here."

"Honey, the photographer's here," Jake repeated.

Cash began moving again, his finger swirling.

I caught his gaze in the mirror and the bastard was grinning. "Glad you find this so funny," I hissed.

He wouldn't be laughing if we got caught screwing in his grandparents' guest bathroom.

"Kat?" Jake called again. "Did you hear me?"

"I-I'm"—*oh my God*—"coming."

White spots broke across my vision and I exploded, feeling nothing but pulse after pulse of blinding pleasure as Cash continued his delicious torment.

Cash groaned, dropping his face to my shoulder right before he let go, his orgasm hard and fast like my own.

When we'd both regained our breath, I lifted my heavy lids and smiled at our reflection. "I love you."

"I love you too, sweetheart." He wrapped his arms around me, holding me tight for a long moment before sliding out and tucking himself into his jeans. Then he bent and pulled my panties up my legs and smoothed down the skirt of my dress.

The whole family was at Carol and Jake's place for Friday night dinner. Except we'd had to arrive two hours early because before our regular weekly meal, we were having photos taken before sunset. The whole crew was going to hike out behind the house to a grove of cottonwood trees brimming with gold and orange leaves. In all my years in Montana, I'd never seen a prettier fall.

The photos were for the resort website—my idea. It was time to update the family photo with all of the Greers, including the cutest addition, Gemma and Easton's two-and-a-half-month-old baby boy.

I straightened the sleeves on my green dress and looked down at the skirt to make sure there weren't any wrinkles. My knee-high boots were polished and I did a quick fluff of my hair.

Cash tucked in his starched white shirt and rebuckled his belt. Later tonight, I was stripping him down to nothing and having my way with him again. This bathroom escapade had only been a preview of later.

We had a lot to celebrate.

This morning, the two of us had spent another few minutes in a bathroom—the one we shared at home—as we'd waited for the results of three pregnancy tests.

Next year, we'd have to retake photos with our own baby Greer. I doubted anyone would mind.

"Should we tell them?" I asked as Cash leaned into the mirror to wipe the hint of gloss I'd left behind.

"Do you want to tell them?"

He looked down at me and grinned. "Yeah."

"Good. Me too."

I wasn't waiting months to tell our family we were having a baby. Besides, as soon as Carol realized I wasn't drinking the bottle of wine she'd brought for me tonight, the secret would be out.

Our family hadn't been thrilled about the fact that we'd eloped and excluded them from a momentous occasion, but they'd all been so happy to see Cash and me together, their irritation hadn't lasted long. Plus we'd thrown a huge reception so they'd at least gotten a party.

Besides Friday night dinners, that had been our only night out since returning home. Not only had Cash and I been savoring our extra time alone, merging bedrooms and closets, but he'd been consumed with work.

The training facility was up and running and for the past month, Cash had worked tirelessly to train his own staff as well as the new animals. Easton's lack of communication with his brother had rubbed me the wrong way, but Cash had confronted him about it when we'd gotten home. Easton had apologized and ever since, there had been no question about who ran the equine center. No decisions were made by anyone but Cash.

I was proud of him for how hard he'd been working. He'd already been interviewed by a major horse magazine, and breeders from all over the Pacific Northwest were clamoring for him to see their horses.

He was as happy as I'd ever seen him. Energized and excited. We both were. But work wasn't the best part of my day anymore. Coming home to Cash, sharing this life with him, was my dream come true.

"Okay." I smoothed my dress down once more. "You go out first."

Cash lifted my hand to his lips, kissing my knuckles, then gave me the sexy smirk that had brought us to the bathroom in the first place. He eased out the door and I counted to ten, hoping not to draw any notice when I joined my husband and the others downstairs.

Gemma was sitting on the couch, nursing the baby, when I reached the living room. "Your cheeks are a little flushed, Katherine. You weren't doing something naughty in the bathroom, were you?"

"Shut up." I sat beside her. "It's not like you and Easton haven't done the same thing."

"Touché." She peeked beneath her cover-up at the baby, her eyes softening at her son. "Your phone was buzzing while you were . . . indisposed."

I reached for my purse on the end table beside the couch where I'd left it when we'd come inside and pulled out my phone. "It was Aria."

"Call her back," Gemma said. "We have time and I'd like to say hi."

Aria answered on the first ring. "Hey!"

"Hey. You're on speaker. I'm here with Gemma."

"Hi, mama. What are you guys doing?"

Gemma smiled. "We're getting ready for family pictures."

"I've never done those before," Aria said.

"Me neither," Gemma said.

"What are you doing?" I asked, hearing what sounded like wind in the background.

"I'm on my way to Arizona." She whooped. "Finally. Though I'm tempted to keep this car forever and not tell Londyn. It's been so much fun to drive all summer."

Aria hadn't been able to get away from work for a while, but we'd all assured her there was no rush. One of her staff members had quit and with the busy tourist season, she'd needed to stay close to The Gallaway. Clara and her son, August, had visited Oregon and offered to drive it to California, but Aria had insisted on driving it to Arizona. She was committed to this handoff.

"Drive safely," I said.

"I will. I have two weeks off and I'm in no rush. Clara's asshole of a boss is going to be gone when I get there so that's a bonus."

Gemma and I shared a look.

Aria and I had talked often since my trip to Oregon. She'd also reconnected with Gemma and Londyn, bringing Clara into the loop too. The five of us had a weekly girls' night video chat. It had originally started as a book club but after six chats where no one had mentioned a book, we'd called it what it was—wine club. Though I'd be switching to sparkling grape juice for the next nine months.

Clara hadn't been able to make last week's chat. Her boss had needed some last-minute help preparing for a trip to Europe. But Aria had been there and she'd spent the first ten minutes of the call reminding us that Clara's boss—*Broderick "Brody" Carmichael*—was a prick. She'd even done the air quotes around his nickname.

Gemma and I suspected that Aria's hate maybe wasn't hate at all.

It was too bad Brody was going to be gone while she visited Arizona. Two weeks with the billionaire might have made for an interesting wine club chat.

"Text me when you get there," I said. "And say hi to Clara."

"Will do. Bye."

"She's got a thing for the boss," Gemma said, carefully detaching the baby as I put my phone away.

"Totally." I draped a cloth over my shoulder and reached for baby Jake. "I'll burp him so you can freshen up."

"Thanks," she said and handed him over before disappearing into the powder room.

I kissed Jake's cheek as I patted his back. His hair was thick and dark like Easton's. I suspected our baby would have the same.

"You're going to be a cousin," I whispered. "Do you think we'll have a girl or a boy?"

He answered with a juicy belch.

"Yeah, I'm thinking boy too."

Gemma returned, looking beautiful in her sage dress, and the two of us walked outside, me carrying the baby, to where everyone else was standing around the photographer on the front lawn.

Easton came over and took his son from my arms. "Hey, bud. Did you get a snack?"

The baby burped again, causing his father to chuckle.

"Okay." Carol clapped, her smile wide. "Everybody ready?"

After a chorus of nods, Jake took her hand and the two of them led the family around the corner of the house.

JR held out his elbow to escort Liddy behind his parents.

Easton tucked the baby in the crook of an arm and laced his fingers with Gemma's before the three of them set out across the lawn with the photographer.

Leaving me and Cash to trail behind.

I took one step onto the grass but he put his hand on my elbow to stop me.

"I have something for you." He reached into his pocket, pulling out a square, velvet box.

"What is this?"

He handed it to me. "Open it."

I lifted the lid, revealing a diamond bracelet, and gasped. "Cash, it's beautiful."

"There was a guest here a few years ago," he said, taking the jewelry from the box and clasping it around my wrist. "Some famous author you loved. She had a bracelet like this and you told me twice how much you loved the style. Simple and elegant—something like that."

Not something. Those had been my exact words and he'd remembered. How long had that been? Seven years? Eight?

Part of me wished we had figured it out sooner. That we'd realized there had always been more than friendship between us. And the other part of me was happy exactly the way our love story had played out. Because looking back on those moments of friendship, knowing that Cash knew me better than any person dead or alive, made these little moments precious.

I rolled my wrist, letting the diamonds catch the light, then looked into my husband's sparkling hazel eyes. They were prettier than diamonds and I hoped our baby would inherit them.

"What is this for?"

He brushed a kiss to my lips, then took my hand, leading us on the path to our family. "Just because."

Forsaken Trail

1

ARIA

"ARE YOU HERE?" August asked.

"Not yet."

"Uhh." He grunted into the phone. "When are you gonna get here?"

"Soon, buddy. I'm about an hour away."

"An hour," he groaned. "That'll take forever."

I laughed. "Go play outside and by the time you build a fairy fort for me to inspect, I'll be there. Now where's your mom?"

"She's sick."

"What?" My spine stiffened. Clara hadn't seemed sick when I'd called last night. "What kind of sick?"

"Um . . . coughing sick? When you get here, can we open my present first?"

"Yes, we can open your present first."

My nephew was five, and I'd missed his birthday. The guilt was real. My attempt to assuage it had resulted in the scooter gift wrapped in the trunk along with a Nintendo Switch game, a puzzle, three books and a remote-control car.

August's birthdays had always been a priority, but I hadn't been able to get away from work this year. Summers were a hectic time at The Gallaway for the head groundskeeper. Toss in my latest duties as fill-in general manager for the luxury hotel on the Oregon coast, and even a quick vacation to see my sister had been impossible.

Normally, Clara and Gus would take a summer trip to my home in Heron Beach for his birthday. Had this been a normal year, we would have celebrated as a family. *August, born in August.* But this year, their trip to Oregon had been moved up to June.

Clara's arrogant and demanding boss had decided that he *needed* his assistant along for his two-week hiatus in Aruba over Gus's birthday.

I couldn't blame Clara for jumping at the lavish vacation. August had turned five in an extravagant, boutique hotel with his favorite person in the world—his mother. They'd gone snorkeling in the ocean and swimming in their suite's private infinity pool. The chef had made Gus's dinner favorite —mini cheeseburgers—then baked him a three-tiered chocolate cake.

Experiencing that moment through Instagram pictures had been depressing.

Maybe we should have partied early for his birthday during their visit in June, but applauding five when you were stuck at four seemed borderline cruel.

This vacation was my chance to make up for my absence. I was as excited to get to Arizona as August was for me to arrive.

Two weeks with my sister and her son. Two weeks in sweatpants and going barefoot. Two weeks of takeout, games and fun.

"Can you take the phone to your mom?" I asked August.

"Okay. Mom!" he shouted.

I pulled the phone away from my ear and laughed. His feet pounding through their house echoed in the background. After some rustling and mutters, my sister took the phone.

"Hey," she said, her voice muffled and thick.

"Gus said you were sick."

"Ugh." She coughed and sniffled. "I woke up this morning and felt like crap."

"Sorry. I'll be there soon to entertain August so you can get some rest."

"Where are you?"

"About an hour away." I'd worked a half day yesterday to beat the weekend traffic flocking to the coast. I'd pushed hard, spending my Thursday night on the road until I'd finally found a place to stop and a motel room for the night. Then I'd woken up this morning to finish the rest of the twelve-hundred-mile journey, wanting to get to Clara's before dinner.

"Drive safe," she said. "See you when you get here."

"Bye." I ended the call and tossed my phone into my purse in the passenger seat.

Then I gripped the Cadillac's white wheel and relaxed as I floated down the highway.

I loved this car. It was going to break my heart to leave it with Clara in two weeks. But the restored 1964 Cadillac DeVille convertible was not mine to keep. She had been entrusted to me for a short time and soon, she'd continue on her journey to her rightful owner.

But for today, for this trip, she was mine.

The afternoon sun roasted the asphalt. Heat waves rolled across the road, leaving blurry ripples in the air. There were no clouds in the blue sky, nothing to offer relief from the sun's punishing rays. Yesterday I'd spent most of the day with the top down, enjoying the wind in my hair and sunshine on my face. Today I'd keep the top up and the AC cranked.

This heat was the reason I avoided the desert in the summer. By October, it should have cooled, but this year was unseasonably hot.

402

No wonder everything died here.

Why Clara loved the desert I had no clue. I'd stick with my home on the coast, where the breeze was cool, crisp and freshly salted. Plants and flowers flourished in the ocean air and under the frequent rains.

Life seemed harder here. Nature was unrelenting and only the strong survived. The plateaus in the distance had been eroded into towers and flat-topped spires on the horizon. They'd endured centuries of abuse from wind and water, leaving behind their own unique beauty.

The bushes, cacti and wildflowers that managed to thrive were tough as hell. I'd give them credit for their tenacity.

Maybe that was why Arizona appealed to Clara. She was tough as hell too.

The road stretched long and wide ahead. White marking the edges. Yellow the center.

Route 66.

The iconic highway had been mostly empty today, and the stretch ahead was mine and mine alone. I sank deeper into the buttery leather seat and leaned an elbow on the door.

This trip to Arizona wasn't just a trip to visit my twin sister. This trip had a purpose. I was the next driver in a cross-country journey that had started in Boston and would end in California.

This spring, I'd had a surprise visit from an old friend. Katherine Gates had been a welcome sight when I'd spotted her in the lobby of The Gallaway. My childhood friend had traveled from Montana to Oregon. With her and this Cadillac had come memories of the past. Memories I'd locked away for, well . . . too long.

Once upon a time, Katherine and I had lived together. Our home had been a junkyard. Our family had been a rabble of six runaway teens. We'd been friends. Companions. Protectors.

Katherine.

Londyn.

Gemma.

Karson.

Clara.

Me.

As kids, they'd been the most important people in my life. Then we'd all gone our separate ways, built separate lives, and though I doubted any of us would ever forget the junkyard, time and distance had made it easier to ignore.

When Katherine had surprised me in Oregon, the past had come rushing back. As did my love for my old friends. We were a unit again, the women at least. None of us had been in contact with Karson, not since the junkyard.

But for us girls, we'd rekindled our friendships. Our family.

We had a group text string that more often than not included pictures of wherever we were at the moment. We had video chats to talk about books, though we had yet to talk about books. We had emails and phone calls.

So why, when I had so much love and friendship in my life, was I so lonely?

I clutched the wheel tighter, wishing the hole in my heart away.

The loneliness was probably because I'd been working so much. And because I'd gone so long without my sister. It would all be better once I got to Arizona, right? Maybe this heavy heart was because I hated goodbyes and soon I'd say farewell to the Cadillac.

God, I was going to miss this car. I would miss all it represented.

The Cadillac hadn't always been a gleaming red classic. Once, it had been Londyn's home, more rust than metal and home to a few mice. Her bedroom had been the backseat. The trunk had served as a closet and pantry. The passenger seat had been the guest room slash living room slash dining room.

What a wonder it was now.

Londyn had started the Cadillac's journey on the East Coast. A flat tire had landed her in West Virginia and in the arms of a handsome mechanic. When Gemma had gone in search of her own fresh start, Londyn had insisted she take the car.

That had been the first handoff.

Gemma had gone to find Katherine at a guest ranch in Montana. Two friends reunited. And two flames. After Gemma had found love, she'd encouraged Katherine to take a trip of her own. Kat had come to find me, and when she'd headed home with her new husband, Cash, it had been my turn with the Cadillac.

Londyn wanted this car to go to Karson, who lived in California, but since I had no desire to return to the Golden State, I was giving the Cadillac's keys to my sister.

One more handoff.

One more trip.

Londyn. Gemma. Katherine. They'd each had their road trip. Mine wasn't as eventful, but it was mine. They'd all found something seated behind the Cadillac's steering wheel. I had no hopes that a car would lead me to the love of my life, but I did hope to find the piece of myself I'd been missing lately.

I'd spent months driving this gorgeous vehicle around Heron Beach. The two-day trip to Arizona was my last hurrah and I was savoring this last hour behind the wheel. Once I arrived at Clara's, there'd be no more driving. I'd fly home in two weeks and get back to work.

Work. I glanced at my phone and debated calling to check in. I dismissed that idea immediately. Before I'd left, Mark, the owner of The Gallaway, had told me to enjoy my well-earned time away. He'd finally brought on a general manager so I could relinquish my temporary command.

Some women, like Gemma and Katherine, wanted to be the boss. They thrived on it. They excelled at it. Not me. All I'd ever wanted was to tend to my plants, watch them grow, and if there was a chance to make a living doing just that, then I was happy.

Especially for The Gallaway. The hotel was a dream.

Before Oregon, Clara and I had lived in Nevada. We'd left the junk-yard for the glitz and sparkle of Las Vegas. As two eighteen-year-old girls with nothing to lose, a gamble on Sin City had seemed like a good idea.

I'd lasted a month.

The hotel where I'd worked had been teeming with fake people, both on staff and as guests. So I'd decided Vegas was not my final destination and got busy job hunting. The Oregon coast, where the world was lush and clean, had instantly appealed.

I'd started as a housekeeper at The Gallaway and worked for about a year cleaning rooms. About six months into my employment, I noticed the flowerpots were in need of some pruning. So I came to work early and tackled the blooms, shaping and cultivating them.

One day, the head groundskeeper found me weeding in my maid uniform. He took me under his wing, requesting a transfer from house-keeping to his staff. When he retired, his job became mine.

I worked so The Gallaway overflowed with pink and white flowers in the spring. Peach and purple flourished in the summer. And when the fall came, sprays of yellow and orange and red were everywhere to be seen.

That was the job I wanted. Not management.

But Mark had been good to me, and after the former GM had retired months ago, finding a replacement had been more difficult than expected. Mark had burned through two candidates, one of whom had clearly lied on his résumé and another who'd been a great fit, but her fiancé had proposed one month into her employment and she'd quit to move to Utah.

I crossed my fingers and sent up a silent prayer that this latest hire would stick. Months of doing two jobs had run me dry.

A couple weeks with Clara and August were sure to fill the well.

This drive had filled it some too.

When Clara and Gus had come to Oregon in June, she'd offered to drive the Cadillac home, but I'd insisted on taking it to Arizona myself.

Life had been too stressful. Too frantic. Too busy. This had been my chance to reset and think. I'd never wanted to be the woman who worked endless hours, the woman whose success was defined by the zeros on her paycheck and the title on her business card.

Money was not the end goal of my life.

I focused on the road, my energy spiking with every mile. Today was not the day to kick my own ass for working too hard this summer. Today was for fun and freedom and family.

It took me less than the hour I'd promised August to reach Welcome, Arizona. Rolling down the highway, I took only a brief glimpse at the small town Clara loved. Then I left it in my rearview as I sped toward her home.

A metal security gate greeted me at the driveway entrance. I punched in the code on the keypad and eased down the single lane.

The landscaper had gone for a natural look on the grounds. Mostly rocks and some native shrubs, but there were a few desert willows and velvet mesquite trees to mask the monstrosity at the end of the drive.

Two stories of gleaming glass as sterile and lifeless as the cement walls. Other than a small scrap of green no one could consider a proper front yard, the house was devoid of life, much like the barren and dry landscape that made up the estate.

The modern mansion was only five years old. It had been built around the time August had been born, yet it looked new. It was too clean. Too lonely. It wasn't a home, lived in and loved. It was a showcase. A display of wealth and arrogance.

The house fit its owner.

Broderick Carmichael was all about flash and flaunting his money.

"At least he's not here," I muttered.

It was easy for me to hate the man. Brody had been rude and pompous during our every encounter. How could Clara stand his presence? I'd been asking her that for years without an answer.

When we'd moved to Las Vegas after the junkyard, I'd gone into hospitality while Clara had scoured the classifieds for an office job after getting her GED. She'd started as a receptionist for Brody's company, Carmichael Communications, and had quickly climbed the ranks. When Brody's personal assistant had quit—probably because his boss was spoiled and needy—Clara had been offered the position.

They'd worked together for years. Besides me, Brody was her best friend. Another thing I couldn't make sense of. She was everything he wasn't. Kind. Loving. Compassionate. Clara swore he was all those things, but I wasn't buying it.

When Brody had decided to relocate from the city to this nowhere, tiny town in Arizona—something about a satellite office—he'd offered to bring Clara along. And when he'd built the museum that was his house, he'd also built a small home for Clara and August too. Thank God her house didn't look like its parent.

I turned off the main driveway and parked in front of Clara's garage.

Her home had a modern vibe, like Brody's, but on a subdued scale that rendered the look fresh and simple. The slanted roof allowed for a long bank of windows that overlooked the property. The white siding was clean and bright. The stone accents, along with the plethora of potted succulents and ornamental cacti—my doing—gave it character and color.

Most of the greenery was overgrown from the summer. During my vacation, I'd remedy that with a few hours of trimming and pruning. Clara's only requirement for me when I'd added all of the greenery had been maintenance. She'd water but that was about it.

I put the Cadillac in park, and before I could step out, the front door to Clara's house burst open and Gus came racing my way.

"Aunt Aria!"

His dark blond hair had grown some since our last FaceTime. His legs looked longer, his face fuller. I'd blinked, and my nephew had changed from a toddler to a boy. He had a dust streak on his cheek and grass stains on his bare knees. He grew too fast.

"Hey!" My heart leapt as I climbed out of the car. I bent, bracing for impact, and scooped him into my arms when he came crashing like a wave. "Oh, I missed you."

"Where's my present?" He squirmed out of my hold, taking in the car.

"August," Clara scolded, coming out the door.

"It's okay." I waved it off and took in my beautiful sister. "Hi."

"Hi." She, like her son, came rushing into my embrace. "We went too long this time."

"I know." I squeezed her tighter.

Normally, we planned five to six visits in a year. Seven if I was lucky. But going four months without seeing them was too long. Work might have kept my mind and body busy, but my heart had paid the price.

A mistake I wouldn't make again.

Clara and August were my only family. We needed each other.

Today maybe more than yesterday.

Clara's nose was red and her cheeks splotchy. Her pretty brown eyes didn't have their usual sparkle and her shoulders slumped low. She'd trapped her blond hair in a loose ponytail, the ends hanging limp over one shoulder.

"You don't look good."

"I don't feel good." She shrugged and ran a hand over the gleaming hood of the car. "Wow. Look at this thing."

"A beauty, isn't it?"

"I can't believe it's here. That it's my turn." She smiled and stroked the car again. "I love this whole handoff thing."

Clara was a romantic. As teens, she'd buy romance novels for a dime at the thrift store and stay up late reading under the glow of a flashlight. I suspected I'd find a stack of them beside her bed, or a well-stocked Kindle, when I tucked her in for a nap this afternoon.

We'd taken care of each other for the past twenty years. Longer, really. Since our parents had died. We were thirty years old, but that wasn't going to stop me from pampering her while I was here. She'd do the same for me.

"You can gush over the car later. First, we unload. Then, we do presents."

"Yes." Gus did a fist pump.

"And after that, you're taking a long, hot bath followed by a long nap."

Clara gave me a sad smile as exhaustion clouded her pretty face. She looked like she was about to cry.

"What? What is it?" I asked.

"Nothing. I'm just really tired."

I pulled her into my arms again. "Then we'll make sure you get lots of rest."

She collapsed onto my shoulder. "I'm so glad you're here."

"Me too. We both need a vacation, even if yours is at home. No work. Fun only. Just the three of us."

"About that. There's sort of been a change of plan."

I let her go and narrowed my eyes. "What change?"

The whirl of tires and the hum of an engine filled the air before she could answer. A shiny black Jaguar came down the driveway and my heart dropped.

No. That son of a bitch Brody Carmichael was going to ruin my vacation.

"He's supposed to be gone." If he dared encroach on my time with Clara, I'd sneak poison ivy into his bed.

"It's not his fault." Clara sighed, quick to defend her boss.

"Did his private plane not have enough spiced cashews for his liking? Surely he can afford jet fuel."

The second-best part of this week, besides Clara and Gus, was Brody's scheduled absence. Clara knew there was no love lost between me and her boss, so she'd suggested travel dates that coincided with his vacation.

Yet here he was, parking a car that likely cost more than all of my worldly possessions combined.

Brody parked behind the Cadillac and stepped out of his car, sliding the sunglasses off his face. He wore a navy suit tailored to perfection around his broad shoulders and long legs. In the years I'd known him, I'd never seen him in anything but a suit. Did he not own jeans?

"Brody!" August raced over, holding up a hand for a high five. "Aunt Aria is here. We're gonna open my presents."

"I see that." Brody's lips turned up in a smile. Barely.

If the man ever learned how to deliver one properly, actually show some teeth, he'd be devastating. Especially with the dark, trimmed beard he'd grown a few years ago. It gave him a sexy edge. Or it would have, if his perpetually sour mood wasn't such a major turnoff.

He definitely, definitely didn't turn me on. Oh no.

Broderick Carmichael was enemy number one.

One day I hoped to convince Clara to quit her job with Brody and join me in Oregon. The only flaw in my plan was that she loved her job. She loved her boss.

My beautiful, loyal sister had been duped by the devil.

"Hey." Clara waved at Satan incarnate. "How was the flight back?"

The flight back? From where?

"Fine." He shrugged. "Just wanted to stop by and see how you're feeling."

"I'm good," she lied.

"She's sick," I corrected. "And she'll be spending the weekend recuperating."

His jaw clenched but he didn't respond. He simply gave Clara a nod. "Call me if you need anything. See you tomorrow."

"I'll be ready," she said.

Without another word, he ruffled August's hair, then got in his car and disappeared.

I turned on my sister. "Um . . . ready for what?"

"It's nothing. Just a work thing. And I don't have the energy to get into it right now, so how about presents and that nap you mentioned?"

If not for her cold, I would have insisted on answers. But I'd gotten pretty good at ignoring Brody's existence, and Clara deserved a break.

So I did exactly what I'd promised. I hauled in my things and we both cheered as August opened his gifts. With their living room littered with wrapping paper, I put her to bed and spent the rest of the afternoon and evening entertaining Gus before it was time to put him to bed.

With him tucked in bed, I did the same for my sister, who'd roused around dinner.

"I'm glad you're here." She snuggled into her pillow. "Thanks for watching him."

"My pleasure. Now sleep." I kissed her forehead. "See you in the morning."

She was snoring by the time I eased out of her room and closed the door.

The fading evening light drew me outside to her deck for a few moments alone. I'd stolen Clara's Kindle and uncorked a bottle of wine. As I settled into a lounge chair, I tipped my head to the heavens.

Stars twinkled like diamonds in the midnight sky. There wasn't a breath of wind. In Oregon, even from my place in town, there was the constant whisper of the ocean's waves. Not here. There was nothing but the occasional screech from a hawk or the scrape of a lizard's claws on a nearby rock.

From my seat, I had the perfect view of Brody's home. It stood dark and endless. The only light came from the second-floor balcony. Maybe if I was lucky, he'd get Clara's cold and be bedridden for a couple weeks.

A girl could hope.

I'd unlocked the Kindle's screen, ready to dive into the tale of a pirate and the fair maiden he'd kidnapped at sea, when something caught my eye.

Brody emerged onto his lit balcony, wearing only a towel wrapped around his narrow hips.

Even from this distance, the definition of his hard stomach was impossible to miss. As was the plane of his wide, bare chest dusted with dark hair. Brody's arms were ropes upon ropes of muscle.

My breath hitched. My pulse quickened. Damn you, Brody Carmichael. Why couldn't he be ugly? It would be so much easier to hate him if he didn't elicit such a strong physical reaction. Undoubtedly, when I dove into my novel, Brody's face would be the pirate's.

His sixth sense must have prickled. One moment, he was leaning, arms braced, on the balcony railing. The next, he stood straight, his hands fisted at his sides, and faced my way.

I gave him a little finger wave and a glare.

I got nothing in return. As quickly as he'd come outside, he vanished inside his concrete castle.

The bastard was probably annoyed that I was here to steal Clara's attention. *Whatever*. These were my two weeks with her. Mine. I was here now, and the loneliness had begun to fade. The well wasn't bone dry.

Four months apart had been too long. Maybe it was time to push harder for a change. Maybe it was time to open my mind to a change of my own.

Clara needed help with August. I simply needed Clara and August. There was a weight on her shoulders that hadn't been there in June, and it had nothing to do with her cold. She was here, working alone. Living alone. Parenting alone.

Enduring alone.

Our lives had been harder than they should have been, harder than my parents had planned. We'd walked a rocky, rough road.

Maybe it was time to switch directions. To forge a beaten path.

And find out if there was a rainbow waiting at the end of my forsaken trail.

2

BRODY

"How long will *she* be here?" I asked Clara.

I stood at the floor-to-ceiling-window wall in my office that overlooked the property beyond the house. The office was adjacent to my bedroom, and from here I could see Clara's backyard and deck. I'd designed it that way, wanting to give her privacy but be close enough in case of an emergency. I'd wanted a line of sight.

I was regretting that decision. Just like I had last night when I'd come out for a quiet minute alone, only to realize I hadn't been the only one seeking a moment of solitude.

She had taken over Clara's deck. Last night. Today. She'd brought the old Cadillac. Wasn't it time for her to scurry on back to Oregon?

Outside, Aria was stretched on a chaise with August tucked into her side. The two of them were reading a book, the boy eating up her every word. Her toned legs stretched long to her bare feet. She'd sat in exactly the same chair this morning, painting her toenails.

"Two weeks." Clara sniffled, her voice thick and raspy. "I'm not sure why you're asking me a question when you already know the answer."

I frowned. "Because I was hoping the answer would change."

"Don't." She sighed. "Please. I don't have the energy to play referee."

"What a fucking disaster," I muttered.

Not only had my grandmother's phone call completely disrupted my plans for the next two weeks, forcing me to cancel the trip I'd planned for a year, but now I'd have to be around Aria Saint-James for the next two weeks.

"She's my sister, Brody," Clara said. "She's welcome here. And if you make her feel unwelcome, then I'm moving."

"You can't move." I spun away from the glass. That was the first time she'd ever made that threat, and I didn't like how serious it sounded. "That's your house."

"No, it's *your* house. I just live there."

"Semantics. You're not moving."

Welcome was a safe community with good schools. Selling her on the move here hadn't been difficult for those reasons. Plus a new home with state-of-the-art security. She belonged here. If that meant I had to play nice with the sister, so be it.

"I'll be on my best behavior." I feigned a bow.

"Good. This is an important trip for Aria. I haven't seen her in months, and she's going through something."

"What something?" I asked, forgetting that I didn't care.

"I don't know." Clara dug through the pocket on her hoodie, pulling out a wad of tissues. "She hasn't told me anything, but I can feel it."

Clara and Aria were fraternal twins, similar physically but each with their own unique traits, yet they had a bond like nothing I'd seen before. Their link was one I'd never understand but it existed like the walls, ceilings and floors of this house.

There were days when work was so stressful that Clara reached her wits' end—Aria would always call. There were days when Clara would excuse herself in a meeting—she just had to text Aria. It was like they had a direct tap into each other's moods and knew when the roller coaster had hit a low.

"Can we talk through the plan for tonight? The pilot will be ready to take off any time after five. What time do I need to be ready?" Clara put the tissues to her nose and blew hard. A snot bubble escaped the edge.

"Hell. You can't go tonight."

"Yes, I can."

"You're not going. You look awful."

She pulled the tissues away from her face. "Gee. Thanks. I hope you don't say that to your real dates."

"You know what I mean." I walked to the bathroom off the office and rifled through the cabinet until I found a fresh box of tissues. Then I brought them out to Clara where she'd collapsed on the couch, curled into the fetal position. "Here."

"Thanks." She clutched the box to her chest, her eyelids so droopy she couldn't keep them open.

"Go home. Get some sleep. I'll go solo tonight."

"No way." Clara pushed herself up with a grunt. "I'll be fine. I just need a nap and a shower. Then I'll be good to go."

I sat beside her. "Sorry, but you're not coming. Boss's orders."

"Ha." She laughed, which turned into a fit of coughs. "Since when do I take my boss's orders?"

"Fair point."

Clara relaxed, her body sagging toward mine. I put an arm around her shoulders and held her before she could collapse onto the floor.

It was rare for us to hug. Was this a hug? Clara hugged everyone she knew but I wasn't really the hugging type. But I considered her a friend. A best friend. Or . . . the closest thing I had to a best friend. Did it count when you paid them?

Probably not.

Such was my life. Nannies. Tutors. Chauffeurs. Chefs. All had been friendly. In the early days, I'd confused their smiles and affection for love. But they'd understood what I hadn't as a child.

When the kid was happy, you got to keep your job.

Me being the kid.

After any of the employees assigned to my care had quit or left the Carmichael estate for other opportunities, I'd never heard from them again.

The same would be true with Clara. If she quit and left here, I wouldn't hear from her again.

Finding another assistant like her would be impossible. She had years of experience on my staff. She was organized and efficient. She knew the boundaries between personal and professional. She pushed when necessary but didn't cross the line in the sand.

And she was nice. I liked Clara. She was an easy travel companion. August was a cool kid. I hadn't been around many children, not even when I'd been a child, but he was funny, bright and polite.

Clara was not moving.

I simply wouldn't allow it.

"You should go home," I said. "Get some rest."

She didn't answer.

"Clara?" I bent, taking in her face. Her eyes were closed and her mouth was hanging open. She'd fallen asleep.

"Clara." I gave her a little shake.

"What?" She jerked awake, wiping at her mouth with the back of her hand.

"Go home."

"Okay." She nodded and paused, summoning the strength to stand.

"Here." I threaded my arm under hers and hoisted us both up to our feet. "Can you make it home?"

"Yeah." She slipped free and shuffled across the room, then stopped beside the door. "What time did we decide?"

"No time. You're not going."

"Brody, you shouldn't go alone."

"I can handle this." My family's functions were like swimming with sharks, but it wouldn't be the first time I'd jumped in the water alone. Yes, a date would have been a nice buffer. But it wasn't worth making her miserable.

"You need—" She sneezed, which made her cough. The cough led to a fresh glob of snot shooting out of one nostril. She dove for a tissue, blowing and wiping.

My God, she looked awful.

"You need a date," she said.

"I'll go alone."

"Brody, I'll be fine. I can go. I have the dress and everything. It's the least I can do."

"You're miserable."

"I've survived worse."

She'd survived too much. Occupational hazard of working so closely with each other. Clara knew about my life. I knew the vague details of hers. She was more tight-lipped about her childhood, but I'd been in the front row during the struggles she'd overcome in Las Vegas. Namely, August's father.

If I couldn't be spared from tonight's spectacle, I could at least save Clara from the same fate. "It's a wedding. I've gone to weddings alone before."

"And you hated every minute. This isn't just any wedding."

No, it wasn't. Tonight, my ex-fiancée was marrying another man. The woman I'd once cared for was marrying my younger brother.

"Please, don't go alone. Otherwise . . . oh, never mind."

"Otherwise I'll look sad and alone and pathetic."

She blew her nose. The honk was a resounding yes.

I'd planned to be blissfully absent from the wedding festivities, lounging on my favorite beach in Fiji. Except one phone call from Grandmother and I'd been summoned to attend. No exceptions.

Or she'd sell the company.

"One more year." I sighed. "One more year and she won't be able to pull my strings."

Clara gave me a sad smile. "It will be worth it."

"God, I hope so."

In another year, I'd be thirty-five and the stipulations on my trust would expire. My grandfather had left me a large inheritance after he'd died unexpectedly of a heart attack. Upon my thirty-fifth birthday, the funds would be completely at my disposal. The money would be nice, though I already had plenty, but what I really wanted was full control of the company.

The shares Grandmother controlled on my trust's behalf would also be released on my birthday.

Coreen Carmichael was about to lose her grip on my leash, much to her dismay because Grandmother loved nothing more than to manipulate her grandsons. Especially me.

My attendance at this wedding had been *requested*, according to the email her assistant had sent Clara. Requested meaning required. So though I'd been halfway across the world, I'd informed the pilot that there'd been a change of plan and we'd turned around to head home.

"Let's think of alternatives." Clara pushed away from the door and returned to the couch, plopping down on its edge. Her sweats bagged on her frame, the hems pooling at her ankles and the slippers she'd worn over here this morning. "What about Marie? The girl you dated a few months ago."

"No." I crossed my arms and perched on the edge of my desk. Clara didn't know the details, but Marie was more likely to cut my throat than agree to a date. She'd been angry, to say the least, when I'd dumped her after she'd told me she was in love with me. Maybe another man would have let her down gently, but I'd only been seeing her for three weeks. We'd gone on four dates.

Marie had loved my billions. Not me.

"I could call some friends from my yoga class," Clara said. "There are a few single women who'd probably go."

"I'm not taking a blind date." That sounded more torturous than the wedding itself.

Clara chewed on her bottom lip. "Yeah, you're right. You need someone who knows this is only supposed to *look* like a date."

"This is business."

She nodded. "Then that only leaves us one choice."

"You're not go—"

"You have to take Aria." We spoke in unison.

I blinked. "Pardon?"

"Aria. You have to take Aria. We can explain to her what's going on. She'll be able to act as a buffer and keep the vultures at bay. You won't look sad and alone and pathetic. It's actually better than if I were to go with you. She'll look like an actual date, not your assistant."

Was she serious? This had to be the cold medicine talking. She was delusional if she thought I'd actually take her sister. "No."

"This is perfect." Her face lit up and some of the weight came off her shoulders.

"No."

"She's my size, so she can wear my dress."

"No."

"You need to leave here around five. The flight to Vegas is less than an hour but there might be traffic. I don't want you to be late."

"No."

"The wedding starts at seven, right?"

"No."

Her forehead furrowed. "It doesn't? I could have sworn the invite said seven. I have it on my desk. I'll double-check when I get home."

"Yes, it starts at seven. But no, I'm not taking Aria."

"Why not?"

"Because . . . I don't like Aria."

Her mouth pursed into a thin line.

"She doesn't like me either."

Clara huffed. She knew I was right.

There had never been a minute, a second or a fraction of a second that Aria and I had gotten along. The first time we'd met had been in Vegas, not long after I'd hired Clara as my new assistant. Aria had come to visit and Clara had wanted to show off her new office, so she'd brought Aria in for a tour.

At first, I mistook her for the weekend cleaning crew. I didn't notice the similarities in her features to Clara's. After Aria corrected me, I took maybe ten minutes out of their precious visit, ten fucking minutes, to run through a to-do list with Clara. Apparently, my business annoyed Aria. I'd infringed on *her* time. She had the gall to snap at me. In my own goddamn office. She had the nerve to tell me that Clara was off the clock and my precious demands would have to wait.

No one told me what to do, certainly not in my own building.

So I told her that if she didn't like it, I could arrange for her to be flown home. Immediately.

That was one of the tamest exchanges we'd had over the years.

During one visit here, she'd walked through Clara's new house and made a list of improvements. The deck—three inches off the ground—needed a railing. The front door—of a house guarded by motion sensors and a gate—didn't have a deadbolt. The staircase should have a baby gate and the cupboards needed safety latches—for a baby who couldn't so much as roll over.

The list went on for two pages. Not wanting to burden Clara with the task, Aria marched it over, threw it in my face and told me that if I had enough money to build my monstrosity of a house, I could at least make sure Clara's cottage was safe for an infant.

Just thinking about it made my nostrils flare.

Last year, Clara had gone to Oregon to visit Aria during the summer. I called a few times, four tops, to check in. On my last call, Aria answered. She'd stolen Clara's phone to inform me that if I couldn't fuck off for the five days, she'd throw Clara's phone in the ocean.

And Clara thought we should attend a wedding together? That we could convince people we were a couple? Ludicrous. Aria and I would kill each other before the cocktail hour was over.

No, tonight I needed an ally by my side. Not a woman who thought I was a "demanding prick."

Maybe I did rely on Clara too much. That was Aria's hang-up. But Clara was the only person in this world I trusted. She was the only one I believed, without a shadow of a doubt, was on my side.

The employees at Carmichael Communications were loyal, but my grandmother emitted a strong sphere of influence.

Coreen was a master manipulator. She wove a dangerous web. Grandmother had a knack for making people feel special. Cherished. You trusted her faithfully, right up until that moment when she shoved a dagger between your ribs.

It was part of the reason I'd moved to Welcome: to escape Vegas and her pit of vipers. Here, I could do my work with minimal interference. On a good day, I spoke to her once. And here, I could run my own businesses, the ones she had no part in, while I bided my time.

Fifty-four weeks and three days.

Then I'd be thirty-five.

Then Carmichael would be mine.

When that day came, I needed Clara by my side. The last thing I needed was to strangle her sister at a wedding.

"I'm not taking Aria."

"Then I'll go." Clara sighed and stood.

"I'll go alone."

She walked to the door, ignoring me completely. "See you at five."

I waited until I heard the front door open and close. "No, you won't."

I'd leave here at four. By the time she wandered over, I'd be gone. And then she'd have no choice but to go home and rest.

It was just a wedding. I'd be fine alone, right?

This evening would be enough of a headache with my own family. I wasn't adding Clara's sister to the mix.

Fuck. Grandmother was a sick woman for making me go tonight. I rubbed a hand over my face and returned to the window.

And there she was. Aria. Still on the deck.

She'd traded her seat in the chair for a seat on the deck boards. Her legs were crossed as she and August bent over a toy. It looked like a car of some sort. Probably one of her presents. Gus loved remote-controlled toys so it wouldn't surprise me if he'd requested one from his aunt as a birthday gift.

I'd given him an actual ride-in Jeep. It always made me smile when I stood at the glass and watched him exploring his driveway and yard. There wasn't much for greenery around my house, but Clara's looked like a tropical paradise compared to the barren desert beyond the yard fence.

Aria's doing, no doubt. This morning, when I'd had my coffee, she'd been out with watering can and shears, pruning the pots and planters.

She was a gorgeous woman.

Much to my dismay, her looks always made my heart beat a bit faster. Just my type too. Beautiful. Obstinate. Bold. Aria's looks were different than Clara's, though they shared some features. The pretty bows of their lips. The tips of their noses. The same shining brown eyes flecked with gold. And a realism for life beyond their years.

Clara and Aria were four years my junior, having recently turned thirty, but they carried themselves with wisdom gained from experience, not age. Maybe that was why Aria disliked me so. On day one, she'd looked me up and down and found me lacking.

She wasn't alone.

Grandmother would probably love her. An image of them sitting together at the wedding popped into my head. They were laughing and drinking champagne as they kibitzed about my shortcomings and former vices. Women. Cars. Booze. Gambling.

Ten years ago, they would have been right. Ten years ago, I'd been young and impulsive. I'd thrown my money around like discount candy at a parade. But a lot had changed in a decade. I'd grown up. I'd made mistakes and learned from them. I'd been betrayed and learned from that too.

Still, when she looked at me, she saw my father.

Her son-in-law.

The man who'd corrupted her precious daughter. The man who'd spent her millions. The man who'd abandoned his own last name to assume hers.

At least he wouldn't be there tonight. Grandmother couldn't summon him or my mother from their graves. To this day I wasn't sure if she'd been hurt by their deaths or if she was simply mad that death had stolen her puppets.

Clara and Aria had lost their parents in a drunk driving accident. The same way I'd lost mine, only my parents had been the drunk drivers.

On the deck, Aria laughed, throwing her head to the sky as August shot to his feet, the car in his hand, and ran to the grass. He raced it in swerves and circles across the lawn while his aunt watched on, clapping and cheering.

A gorgeous woman.

Her hair was darker than Clara's. Both had dyed their natural dirty-blond shade. Clara had always gone for highlights, accentuating the blond. Aria's seemed to get darker with each visit to Arizona. Today it hung in chocolate waves, messy and sexy, down to the middle of her back.

Her arms were lean but strong, her legs long and firm. She had the body of a woman who knew how to work and wasn't afraid to meet the day head-on. There was no priss to Aria Saint-James. Nothing fake or plastic.

The exact opposite of every woman who'd be in attendance tonight. Especially the bride. I grinned, imagining Heather's face if I strolled into her wedding with a beautiful woman like Aria on my arm.

Revenge wasn't best served cold. It worked best when dripping with sex and superiority.

Maybe Clara had been on to something. Maybe—

No. Hell no.

Aria loathed my existence. And not even Clara held enough sway over her sister to get her to agree to be a wedding date.

Aria's gaze turned toward my house. The wind caught a lock of her hair and blew it into her mouth, so she tugged it away.

There was no way for her to see through the mirrored glass, but the way she stared, the way her eyes narrowed, was like she could see me watching. She wordlessly scolded me for intruding on her time with Gus.

So I backed away from the window and retreated to my desk, where I spent a few hours returning emails and phone calls, watching the clock tick down. The pit of dread in my gut grew deeper by the minute.

Jesus, I hated my family.

My grandmother. My brother. My soon-to-be sister-in-law. I hated them all. I hated their friends. I hated their colleagues. I hated that tonight they'd see me alone. Vulnerable.

Because besides my paid employee, who else did I have?

When time ran out, I hurried through a shower, then donned my best tuxedo, the black Italian fibers having been tailored specifically for my frame. I knotted a solid black tie at my neck and fastened my diamond cufflinks. And with my Patek Philippe watch around my wrist, I snagged the Jaguar's keys from the table beside the door and made my way to the driveway where my butler, Ron, had parked it this morning after having it detailed and waxed.

Stepping outside, I filled my lungs with the clear desert air. I wouldn't get another fresh breath until I returned home. Las Vegas would stick to me like gum under a shoe, unwelcome and a damn mess to clean.

The cooler temperatures of Arizona suited me fine. In the summer, it was warm. In the fall, the nights cooled and made life bearable.

My shoes clicked on the concrete as I made my way toward the driveway. The weight of the keys in my palm kept my hand from shaking. The other, I tucked into a pocket.

One night.

All I had to do was make it through this one night. Then one more year, two weeks, and three days.

Before Thanksgiving of next year, I'd be a free man. No longer bound by the wishes of a dead man. Trapped by the whims of his wife.

I sucked in one more fortifying breath and rounded the corner, only to stop short at the sight of my car.

And the woman standing beside it.

She huffed. "It's about damn time."

3

ARIA

"Thanks for opening the door," I deadpanned as Brody rounded the hood of his Jag. "Such a gentleman. Do you treat all your dates with such attention?"

"You're not my date."

"I didn't get dressed up for nothing." I motioned to the emerald gown Clara had conned me into earlier.

The dress was cut low in front, past my breastbone in a deep V. The back dipped beneath my shoulder blades. The satin clung to my torso before flaring out at the hips, billowing into a skirt that swished around my legs. For a woman who'd never had a prom, this dress was as fancy as I'd ever been.

Clara had taken one look and declared the dress had been made with me in mind. Then she'd watched me like a hawk from outside the bathroom, ensuring that I was doing my best primping work.

Her makeup stash had been properly raided and her curling iron thoroughly misused. My eyes were lined and my cheeks were rosy. My hair was curled and hung loosely down my back. She'd tucked a jeweled pin into one side, pulling a section away from my temple. The pin's stones matched the gown's color to perfection.

I'd spent more time on my appearance today than I had in the past year.

Brody shot me a look from over the top of the car, then he opened the driver's side door.

"Seriously? You're not even going to open my door." I gripped the handle and yanked it open with too much force.

"No." He shook his head. "You're not going."

"That gruff, bossy tone doesn't work on me." I gave him a saccharine smile. "I don't work for you."

"What did Clara tell you?"

I lifted a shoulder. "She begged me to be your date to some ostentatious wedding. She promised there'd be champagne. And she promised you'd be nice."

"He will be nice!" Clara shouted as she walked down the driveway with August at her side. The shout made her dissolve into a fit of coughs.

"You should be resting," Brody and I said at the same time.

I scowled at him, then turned it toward my sister. "Go inside."

She waved me off, coughing as she neared the car. "I'm fine. August is going to take care of me after you guys leave. Isn't that right, bud?"

His chest puffed up. "Yep. We're ordering pizza for dinner."

"Pizza," I moaned. I loved pizza. "There's no chance this wedding will be catered by Domino's, is there?"

Clara giggled. "None."

"Didn't think I'd get lucky."

"You can stay for pizza," Brody said. "Because you're not going."

If the man didn't want me along, fine. I wasn't going to force it. I'd already done my best by showing up, dressed to perfection and wearing a pair of toe-pinching heels. What more could I do? I knew when I wasn't welcome. And avoiding an evening with Brody was no hardship.

I opened my mouth, ready to accept defeat, but my beautiful, red-nosed and stuffed-up sister spoke first.

"She's going." Clara leveled her gaze on Brody. "Don't be an idiot. You and I both know this is the best option. Besides, look at her."

"What about me?" I dropped my gaze to my feet.

"You're beautiful," Brody admitted through clenched teeth. It sounded pained, like it was either admit that I looked good—because I looked *good* —or have a tooth pulled without anesthesia.

"Gee. Thanks." I rolled my eyes.

"Heather will hate it." Clara gave Brody an evil grin.

Who was Heather? My darling sister had skipped over some details in her rushed explanation as to why I was going. Because that gleam in her eyes was nothing more than petty spite.

I could get behind petty spite, as long as I knew who we were spiting.

Brody pondered her words, his jaw clenched and his stare impassive. "Shit."

"Brody said a bad word." August pointed at Brody and looked up to Clara, waiting for his mother to take action.

"Yes, he did." Clara cocked a hip and shot her boss a sideways look.

"Sorry. Dam-darn." He sighed and left the car, walking over to August. He dug in his pocket and came out with a quarter, handing it to my nephew. "Piggy bank."

"Yes." August fist-pumped and grinned at me.

I gave him a wink.

August had four piggy banks, more than any kid needed, but each had a purpose. One was for his birthday money. One was for money he found himself, like pennies and dimes discarded on sidewalks. The third was for his weekly allowance. Clara paid him five dollars a week to make his bed each morning and pick up his toys at night. And the fourth, the most recent addition, was for money he took off Brody and occasionally Clara when one of them slipped and swore in his presence.

Last night when he'd given me the full tour of his room, showing me everything new he'd acquired since my last visit, he'd made sure to give each of the banks a hefty shake.

The bad-word piggy had by far the most change.

"Okay, kid." Brody gave August a fist bump. "I'd better get out of here. I'm all out of quarters."

"Or you could stop saying bad words," I said.

That comment earned me a death glare over his shoulder, but when he touched the tip of August's nose, it was with a warm, genuine smile. Brody's affection for August was his only redeeming quality.

That, and the way he looked in a tux.

Even I had to admit he looked delicious. The suit wrapped around his broad shoulders and encased his strong arms. His slacks molded to his thick legs and muscled behind. The trimmed beard added a rough edge to his otherwise smooth, classy appearance. And the tie . . . I wasn't going to admit that I wanted to untie it with my teeth.

He was infuriating and arrogant. But damn . . . there were very adult words and scenarios running through my mind. If August had any clue what I was thinking, I'd fill that piggy bank to its ears.

My cheeks flushed. A flare of desire coursed through my veins. Any other man, and I'd be a puddle of lust by the end of the night. But this was Brody. All I had to do was wait until he opened his mouth to speak and he'd turn me off entirely.

"Have fun," Clara said as Brody returned to the driver's side of his car.

"Not likely," I muttered.

"Then have . . . er"—she looked between the two of us—"safe travels."

"Save me some pizza," I said when she came over for a hug.

Clara was a hugger. She hugged her hellos. She hugged her goodbyes. She hugged everything in between. When we'd split apart, it was the one thing I'd missed most. Conversations we could have over the phone, but they were no replacement for a rib-cracking hug.

I'd found myself giving more hugs when she wasn't around, simply because I'd missed them from her.

"Thank you for doing this," she whispered.

"For you? Anything." I let her go and waved goodbye to August.

I slid into the car, surprised to find the leather seat cool to the touch. Someone had come out here and started the engine to let the air-conditioning run. I rolled my eyes. It wasn't even that hot outside, but heaven forbid Brody break a sweat.

He climbed in behind the wheel, but he didn't pull out of the drive. "Why are you doing this?"

"Because Clara asked me to."

Beyond the windshield, my sister took August's hand and the two of them walked down the driveway toward their house. She was still in her sweats from this morning. Her hair was a mess and her eyes tired. But she hid it as best she could for her son. She smiled and swung his hand beside her hip, taking him home, where they'd probably cuddle on the couch watching cartoons until it was pizza time.

"You hate me," Brody said.

When I turned to face him, his green eyes were waiting.

Brody's eyes were the first thing I'd noticed about him years ago. They were disarming. They were almost too bright to be real. The green was a spiral of shades from lime to hunter. It was all held together by a ring of sable around the iris. They always reminded me of a patch of creeping Jenny snaking its way through moss on a summer day.

"Yes, I do." I hated Brody. I'd been hating him for years. "But I love Clara more than I hate you. Apparently, this wedding is important. And if I didn't go, she would have."

He blew out a deep breath, facing forward. "It is. Important."

"Then let's go."

He shoved the car in gear and roared down the asphalt, racing for the gate, like if he didn't get us off his property this instant, he'd change his mind.

I held my breath, fighting the urge to let my knees bounce. I'd seen plenty of weddings at The Gallaway. I often worked with florists in the area to tie the exterior flowers into centerpieces for the event. But this was different. I wasn't going to stay in my tennis shoes and tee, lurking in the dark corners and appreciating the show from a distance.

Tonight, I was a guest. I'd never been to a wedding as a guest. When I'd admitted that truth to Clara, she'd told me not to tell Brody.

No problem there. I doubted we'd share a lot of conversation.

I was arm candy, not entertainment.

The drive to the Welcome airport was uneventful. Silent. Though the air-conditioning was cranked, the heat won the battle. It seeped off Brody's large frame as tension radiated from his shoulders.

When he pulled into the airport, I expected him to park in the parking lot and lead me through the small terminal. Silly me. Brody was no mortal man. He drove straight for the runway. With the planes.

He parked beside a jet that gleamed silver and white under the Arizona sun. Its windows sparkled like those diamonds he had on his cuffs.

I'd never owned a diamond. Hell, I'd never even touched a diamond.

An attendant opened my door and extended a hand to help me from the car.

"Thanks," I breathed and steadied my feet.

The wealth was staggering. Maybe I'd gotten in a bit over my head because—*no freaking way*—there was a carpet leading to the plane. Gray, not red, but a freaking carpet nonetheless.

"Madam." The attendant bowed. He actually *bowed*.

He was older, likely in his fifties, with white streaked liberally through his blond hair. He carried a halo of sophistication, and even though his blue eyes were kind and welcoming, he knew I wasn't here by my own free will.

My sweet, sweet sister was going to owe me big-time.

I opened my mouth to tell him the bow wasn't necessary — I wasn't the queen — but he bowed again, this time to Brody.

"Sir. We're ready."

"Thank you, Ron." Brody tossed the man his keys, then strode toward the plane, taking the stairs without a backward glance my way.

"Oh, you're such a jackass," I muttered under my breath, glowering at Brody's shoulders. Then I hiked up my gown's billowing skirt and hurried to catch up. Stiletto heels were not my specialty and I teetered on the last step before emerging inside the airplane's cabin.

Leather and citrus filled my nose. Cool air rushed over my skin.

The plane was nothing but golden light and cream finish. Every surface was polished, every comfort ready at your fingertips. This plane cost more than my entire life. It wasn't the cold, modern style of Brody's home.

This was . . . lush.

No wonder Clara hadn't hesitated to tag along on a tropical vacation.

I'd always thought Mark Gallaway was the richest man I'd ever met. Clearly, I'd underestimated Brody. His house was enormous and state-of-the-art, but this was grand. This was affluence passed down from generation to generation. And the plane seemed more indicative of his wealth than his home or his car.

Had Brody been downplaying his money? That seemed so . . . unlike him. He'd always seemed like the type to flaunt his millions. He *did* flaunt his millions. Except maybe he'd been holding back.

Maybe millions were actually billions.

Brody was in a chair, sipping a glass of water with a lemon wedge, as his fingers flew across the screen of his phone. Probably texting Clara to tell her this was a horrible idea. I was going to do the same as soon as I pulled my phone from my black clutch.

"Madam." Another attendant appeared at my back, bowing again. This one was younger than Ron and his bow not quite as graceful or practiced.

"Aria. Not madam."

"Aria," he corrected with another bow. "May I get you a refreshment?"

"Water. Please."

"Of course."

Before I caught him in another bow, I walked down the aisle and took the seat across from Brody's. "Who's Heather?"

"My ex-fiancée." His attention stayed focused on the phone.

"Ahh. And she'll be at the wedding."

"Yes," he said flatly. "She's the bride."

"Oh," I murmured as the attendant appeared with my water glass balanced perfectly on a black tray. I took it, cringed at yet another bow — *please, stop bowing* — and waited until he'd disappeared behind a curtain toward the cockpit. "Tell me what I'm getting into here."

Brody scowled but tucked his phone into the jacket pocket of his tux. "My ex-fiancée, Heather, is marrying my brother, Alastair."

"Did she become his fiancée before or after she was no longer yours?"

"Before. During. Neither will admit they'd been fucking before the one time I caught them in the act, but I know Alastair and he's never been one to abstain."

"Alastair." My nose scrunched. "And I thought Broderick was pretentious."

"They are family names."

"Shocking." The word dripped with sarcasm.

That type of retort would normally incense Brody. It should have antagonized him into some verbal sparring. At the very least, that blatant censure should have earned me a glare and a jaw tic.

Instead . . . nothing. His gaze was unfocused as he stared ahead, like he'd missed my comment entirely. Brody's fingers tapped on his knee.

Was he nervous? The signs were subtle, so much so that most would probably miss them. But I knew Brody. He always fought for the last word. Always.

Like he always fought back.

"She left you for your brother, right? Heather?"

He nodded, his eyebrows coming together, but that gaze was still locked on some imaginary spot on the plane's wall.

Interesting. Clearly, I was along as revenge of sorts. Did he still love her? How painful would this be for him?

Or maybe his fears had nothing to do with the bride. Maybe his fears were because I was on his arm instead of my sister.

"I won't embarrass you," I promised.

Brody blinked and mentally replayed my words. And when his gaze met mine, it was softer than I'd ever seen it before. He looked at me the way he looked at Clara. With kindness. "That's not what I'm worried about."

"Are you sure?"

"My family is . . . difficult. I avoid them mostly. The last place I want to be is at this wedding, but I have no choice."

That was all the explanation I got. The attendant entered the cabin, his hands clasped behind his back. "We'll be leaving momentarily, sir."

"Very good," Brody said, dismissing him.

The pilot greeted us next, outlining the details of the flight and shaking Brody's hand. They all called him sir. Everywhere we'd gone tonight, he was *sir*.

It wasn't until we were in the air, the short forty-five-minute flight well underway, that I spoke again. "Clara doesn't call you sir."

"Why would she?"

"Everyone else does."

"Hmm." He hummed and drank the last swig of his water. "She's never called me sir."

Because Clara was different. His relationship with her was different.

And that relationship was the reason the man grated on my every nerve.

I'd first met Brody at his office in Las Vegas. Clara had been so proud of her new job and had wanted to show me her workspace. I'd been proud of her too. She'd built a career in no time flat. She'd climbed out of the junkyard and made something of her life.

Brody had been a budding entrepreneur, or so she'd called him. She'd gushed about his brilliance and creativity and drive. Maybe she'd set the bar too high.

Because the day she took me to the office, he was there too. Clara left me at her desk outside his office to run to the bathroom. The two of us had been guzzling water like thirsty camels after hitting an outlet mall before coming to the office.

Brody's office door was open and when he spotted me, the smug bastard told me that the cleaning staff was not to come in until after eight at night. When I corrected him, informing him that I was Clara's sister, he waved me away. He actually said *shoo*. What kind of asshole said *shoo*?

I stood fuming outside his door, listening as he picked up the phone and ordered someone to buy him a new car. A Ferrari. Whatever model was the most expensive.

By the time Clara returned from her pee break, I was disgusted. Brody then sent her home with a list of tasks to complete when he'd known damn well that she was on an approved vacation.

First impression? Mega douche.

Over the years, he'd done little to change my opinion. Mostly I hated how he spent money. He tossed it around like it was meaningless because Brody had never gone hungry.

Cars. Trips. Homes. Planes. Brody was rich. Did he appreciate it? Did he realize how lucky he was?

Clara promised he was a good man. Was he?

Brody doted on her. He provided for her because he wasn't stupid. He knew she was one of a kind. Clara was the fleck of true gold in a sea of pyrite.

I was the lesser twin, something he liked to remind me of as often as possible.

Once, he'd told Clara that the flowers beside her front door were gaudy and overgrown. I'd been standing right beside her.

For Clara. I was doing this for Clara. I'd fake a smile through this wedding. I'd drink a lot of champagne and enjoy what she promised would be a five-star meal. Then I'd climb back into my sweats and enjoy the next two weeks with family.

With any luck, Brody would hop back on this very plane and disappear for the rest of my vacation. We'd learned to avoid each other, mostly to spare Clara from being in the middle.

One night of pretending.

Then we'd go back to what we were good at.

Hating.

City lights twinkled in the distance, glowing outside the window. "Ugh. I hate Vegas."

"You and me both," Brody said, his gaze aimed out the small window. "When was the last time you were here?"

"When August was born. I came to help Clara. I offered to help her move too but you took care of that before I could get here."

"Are you really upset? I thought you would have wanted her away from *him*."

Him. Devan. August's father.

At the time, it had surprised me when Brody had asked Clara to accompany him to Welcome. Maybe he'd known how badly she'd needed to escape Vegas too.

"In that, we can agree. She's better off without Devan in their lives."

Clara had cut Devan loose when August had been a newborn. The two of them had dated for about a year when she'd gotten pregnant. It hadn't been planned. She'd tried to keep him involved, but by the third trimester, he'd already checked out. Knowing that he'd never make a good father—and knowing that she'd never succeed if she tried to change him—she'd given him an out.

He'd signed over his rights to August without hesitation.

Not long after, Brody had approached her with an offer that had been irresistible. A fresh start. A new town. All expenses paid.

"I wanted her to move to Oregon," I said. "I lobbied hard for it."

"Not hard enough." He gave me that smug, cunning grin. The one he always cast my way whenever he won.

"It's hard to compete against a free house, a free car and a free life."

"It's not free. Clara has earned it."

"Even Clara knows she hasn't."

"What do you mean?"

I rolled my eyes. "Why do you think she works so hard for you? Why do you think she would have come to this wedding tonight, sick as a dog?"

He blinked.

Yep. Clueless. "She's trying to balance the scales. You helped her out of a bad situation with Devan. She wanted to get out of Vegas and leave him behind. Then she came to Arizona and you'd gone so . . . overboard."

He lifted his chin. "I did what I would have done for any other employee."

"Bullshit. Be honest with yourself, Brody. You wouldn't have done that for any other employee. You treat her differently."

"No, I don't. I provide a life for Ron. He has a house on the property too."

"Okay, then why does Ron call you sir but Clara doesn't? I'm guessing she did once, a long time ago, and you told her not to. Because you treat her differently."

His forehead furrowed and there was that jaw tic.

Point for Aria. That round was mine. "There's a fine line between helping someone and making them feel like a charity."

"I don't pity Clara," Brody snapped. "And she knows it."

"Maybe. But the next time you tell her to jump, think about why she asks *how high*. Make sure you aren't taking advantage of my sister's work ethic and the fact that she'll bend over backward for you, all because what you've given her, she has no chance to repay."

He stared at me, shock etched on his handsome face. In his glass tower, he'd never stopped to ask himself *why*.

"We're beginning our descent, sir," the pilot said over the intercom, ending our conversation.

There was a wedding we had to attend.

There was a show for us to put on. Fitting that we were in Las Vegas.

As the plane dipped and headed for the runway, my nerves spiked. Adrenaline and anxiety grew. Rolling. Compounding. Like a snowball flying down a hill, getting bigger and bigger with each spin.

The plane's wheels skidded on the tarmac. The crew in the plane hurried to prepare for our departure, the crew outside for our arrival, red carpet included. When we stepped outside and into the Vegas heat, I groaned. There was no way I'd survive this sober.

"I'm going to need champagne," I told Brody as he led the way to a limo.

Lots and lots of champagne.

4

BRODY

"GOOD EVENING." The man stationed at the entrance nodded as we strolled through the door, following the line of guests filing into the reception hall.

Aria clutched my arm as her ankle rolled for the third time. Heels were not her forte, as she'd informed me in the limo. She'd threatened to chuck the shoes and go barefoot if I didn't have an arm available at all times to keep her steady.

"How long will this take?" Aria asked, casting a look over her shoulder to the exit.

"You know how these things drag."

"No, actually, I don't. Enlighten me."

"This is the reception. It will start with cocktails and hors d'oeuvres. Toasts. Then a dinner, likely five or six courses, so it won't be quick. Cake. Toasts. Dancing. More toasts." For each event, Heather would likely have a different dress. "If we're home before dawn, it will be a miracle."

"What about the actual wedding?"

"The ceremony is over." Thank God, I'd missed it. "Heather and Alastair had a private ceremony a few hours ago with close friends and family. Invite only. I didn't get one."

"You're his brother."

"Family doesn't mean the same thing in mine as it does in yours."

She hummed and gripped my arm tighter as we approached the ballroom doors. The pace slowed as people stood in the reception line. My stomach knotted tighter with each inch forward. Then there they were. The happy, cheating couple.

I'd avoided them since the day I'd caught them humping in Heather's apartment. I'd gone over to pick up a watch I'd left there the night before. Surprise. Engagement over.

That day, I'd gone back to work and assigned Clara the task of changing the locks to my penthouse. I'd also decided it was time to move while applauding my foresight to never let Heather move in. She probably would have screwed Alastair in my own damn bed.

Heather's billowing white gown caught my eye first. The cackle of her laugh stabbed my eardrums. Alastair looked so much like my father, there were times when it was difficult to look at his face. His dirty-blond hair was combed to precision, his nose straight and his dimpled chin raised.

He and Dad were alike in more than just looks. Alastair had inherited Dad's greed and gluttony and gullibility. Thankfully, I'd taken after Grandfather. I'd inherited his common sense and work ethic. His brain. Though Grandmother liked to remind me that I was more like my mother than I wanted to admit. Foolish. Impulsive. Driven by emotion.

After all, Mom's biggest weakness, my father, was the reason she was dead.

It was a blessing Mom wasn't here. Toward the end of her life, she'd hated these spectacles as much as I did. But oddly enough, seeing Heather and Alastair together didn't bother me like I'd expected. They deserved one another. When I looked at them, smiling and preening, I felt nothing other than annoyance because they'd ruined a perfectly good Saturday night.

"Her dress is gaudy and hideous," Aria said as we emerged through the threshold of the double doors.

The couple in front of us gaped and sent her horrified looks.

Aria simply smiled. "Hello."

I fought a laugh. It was . . . surprising. I hadn't thought I'd have to fight much other than my gag reflex tonight.

Gaudy was definitely Heather's style. The skirt of her dress ballooned to nearly four feet in diameter. Alastair had to stretch his arm over the skirts to touch his new bride's arm.

Golden light bathed us from head to toe as we shuffled deeper into the ballroom. Crystal sconces cast gleaming rays onto the blue and cream filigree–papered walls. My shoes sank into the lush navy carpet swirled with varying shades of sandstone, powder and ivory.

Islands of cocktail tables covered in white cloths filled the room. A string quartet was playing in the distant corner.

Ornately carved sills framed the windows that lined the room in steady succession. The domed ceiling was broken into sunken sections, each delimited by more carvings and accentuated with chandeliers. The circular ballroom provided a stunning view of the city lights beyond.

"Wow." Aria's eyes roved from wall to ceiling to floor to window. "Quite the place."

"It's something." When Heather had pitched it as the venue for our wedding, I'd nixed it immediately because this was most definitely not me.

"How do you want me to play this?" Aria whispered.

"I . . ." The words died on my tongue. I had no fucking clue. "You tell me. This is my first fake date."

"Same." She straightened. "Let's put on a good show."

This time, I let the smile go free. I glanced down and Aria's pretty brown eyes were waiting. They were flecked with honey and sangria. The reds and yellows were so slight, they swirled into the iris, mixing with the chocolate to give it fire. Aria's fire.

Did Clara have eyes like that? If she did, I hadn't noticed. Why hadn't I noticed? We'd spent more time together than I had with anyone else in a decade.

After only hours in Aria's company, I'd picked up details that I shouldn't have noticed. Like the pout of her lower lip. The delicate lobes of her ears. And now the mesmerizing color in her eyes.

It unnerved me more than seeing Heather and Alastair after all these years.

Aria gave me a small smile, but as we took another step, it changed. Twisted. The fire in her gaze sparked even brighter. The mischievous woman whose words cut like a samurai sword was ready for the show.

Her hand let go of my arm to slide down the sleeve of my tux jacket. Aria laced her fingers with mine as her other hand snaked up my chest. She inched so close that her scent, floral and sweet, filled my nose.

That intoxicating smell scrambled my brain and I couldn't tear my eyes away from the curls in her shiny hair. I wanted to twist them around my fingers, then take the strands in my fist and—

What. The. Fuck.

This was Aria. A woman who openly admitted she hated me the way I hated her. An enemy. My assistant's sister.

There'd be no fisting of her hair. No licking of her lips. No nibbling of her ears.

I tore my eyes away and looked up as we took the final step, just in time to see a different head of dark hair. Heather's hair was as rich and glossy as money could buy. Yet it dulled in comparison to Aria's.

Heather's smile tightened. "Brody."

"Heather." I nodded. "Congratulations."

"Thank you." Her gaze darted to Aria, who pressed deeper, almost indecently, into my side. "I don't believe we've met."

"This is Aria Saint-James," I said, not bothering with a bogus label. Girlfriend. Lover. Date. None were accurate and none mattered.

"Congratulations." Aria smiled at Heather, then at Alastair.

"Brody," Alastair greeted with a smug grin. It probably would have been worse had Aria not been on my arm.

My brother was a vain man. He always had his eyes set on whatever shiny toy I had in hand. Whatever I had, he wanted.

Probably why he'd seduced Heather. I highly doubted this was a love match.

"Congratulations." I reached out to shake his hand.

"We missed you at the ceremony." The asshole knew I hadn't been invited.

"That's my fault," Aria said before I could speak. "Brody is irresistible in a tux. It took me a moment to put myself back to rights and by the time we made it here, well . . . we really tried to make it on time."

The color drained from Heather's face and that grin of Alastair's faltered.

I bit back a laugh. God, Aria was something. Fearless. Bold. Unpredictable. Qualities that usually pissed me the fuck off, but tonight, she was on my side. And she was here to put on one hell of a show.

I'd play along.

Bending, I dipped close to her neck, nuzzling the sensitive skin with my nose as I dragged in a heady breath.

She giggled and swatted me away. "Brody, behave."

"With you? Never." I pulled myself away, something that took more effort than it should have, and I faced my brother again. "We're holding up the line. Again, congrats."

I whisked Aria away, not sparing a backward glance. "That went well, don't you think?"

She hummed as her heel twisted, but I kept my grip firm and she didn't stumble. "Damn heels."

"Don't worry. I won't let you fall."

"You do and you die. Now . . . let's find some champagne."

I raised a hand to signal one of the waiters carrying a tray full of flutes. "Pace yourself. This will be a marathon not a—"

"Broderick."

I cringed at my full name and the voice delivering it. *Christ*. Was it too much to ask for just one minute between confrontations? Yes. Grandmother wasn't one to give anyone a break, especially her eldest grandson.

She appeared in a flourish. Her jacquard dress and matching jacket were patterned with silver and pale green. Diamond earrings dripped from her ears. A matching pendant hung from her neck. Her white hair had been swept away from her face and twisted into an elegant knot.

"Grandmother." I let go of Aria to take Grandmother's hands in my own. Then I bent and brushed a kiss to her cheek.

"You missed the ceremony," she scolded, shaking her hands free from my grip.

"Apologies." Of course she didn't know I hadn't been invited. Alastair or Heather would have lied.

She tsked, her green eyes scrutinizing me from head to toe.

In my life, only two people had learned to rattle me with a single look. My grandfather. And my grandmother.

My skin itched and I struggled not to squirm as she stared. Then she whipped that cunning gaze to Aria.

I panicked. I should have warned Aria first. Clara knew about my grandmother, had put up with her for years, but this was all new to Aria.

"Who are you?" Grandmother's words were spoken with deliberate breaks, like there was a harsh period between the spaces.

"I am Aria Saint-James." Aria's tone matched Grandmother's, her enunciation nearly as precise and the tone as haughty.

And here I'd been worried for nothing. The knot in my gut eased. I should have expected Aria to meet attitude with attitude. She was not a woman to shrivel like so many dates had in the past under Grandmother's examination.

"You're not Clara," Grandmother declared.

"No, I'm not."

"Then *who* are you?"

"My date," I answered.

Grandmother frowned. "Your taste continues to worsen. Clara might be your employee, but at least the girl can stand up straight and doesn't need to drape herself all over you in public."

"Oh, Brody. You didn't tell me your grandmother was so charming and kind."

Grandmother harumphed. "And she's rude."

"Rude can't be helped." Aria shrugged. "When we drew straws in the womb, Clara picked the ones for poise and grace. That left me with sass and sarcasm."

"*You* are Clara's twin sister?" Grandmother's gaze moved to me. "Why would you bring her here?"

"Because Clara is sick. Aria volunteered to be my guest."

Aria fixed on a sweet smile. "Clara has been telling me for years about Brody's family. The stories seemed so cliché. I mean . . . certainly rich people couldn't really be that shallow. When she got sick, I figured I could come here and see for myself. Per her usual, my sister was right."

I choked on my own spit. *Oh, fuck.*

Grandmother's eyes widened into saucers. "Brody, you embarrass me by bringing a random stray to your brother's wedding."

Aria flinched at the word *stray*. It was small and thankfully Grandmother didn't notice how her word choice had hit a nerve.

Aria opened her mouth, probably to deliver another snarky retort, but I spoke first.

"Then I suppose we'll just be leaving." Maybe this evening would end much, much sooner than I'd planned. No disappointment here.

"You cannot leave." Grandmother frowned. "You know how that would look. Keep her quiet and well away from me. Tonight is not the night for an unseemly display."

"We're not sitting at the same table? Bummer." Aria's voice dripped that fake sugar I'd heard so many times.

For the first time, it tasted delicious.

Grandmother's eyes narrowed and I knew we'd be discussing this on Monday. Then without another word, she disappeared to mingle with her cronies. Namely, Heather's grandmother. Those two were the best of friends and had been for years. I think my broken engagement would have been upsetting if Heather hadn't traded one Carmichael male for the other.

"She's lovely," Aria deadpanned when Grandmother was out of earshot. "Thanks for jumping in there and coming to my rescue."

"You didn't need rescuing."

"True. Is your entire family that kind?"

"That is my entire family. You've met them all." Yes, I had some distant cousins and aunts and uncles, but I'd stopped communicating with them ages ago. When one of them contacted me, it was only for a loan they wouldn't repay. Why bother?

"It's only your brother and grandmother?" Aria asked.

I nodded. "My parents died years ago. In a car accident."

"Oh." The bravado on her face melted away. In its place, a deep sympathy. "I'm sorry."

The murmur of voices filled the ballroom as more people filed inside.

I took Aria's arm and guided her toward a hallway. "Come on."

"Where are we going?" She skipped to keep pace.

"This is where we'll have cocktails. Then we'll be shuffled into another space for dinner. And probably a third for cake and dancing."

"Okay," she drawled. "You didn't answer my question."

No, I didn't. She'd see soon enough.

The guests paid us no attention as we disappeared from view and slipped into the adjacent room. It was twice as grand as the space where we'd been.

A sea of tables covered in china and silver and enormous floral centerpieces filled the room. Golden lights hung from the ceiling. Archways of more flowers hugged the walls. Their perfume clung thick to the air as we weaved past chairs and empty tables.

I marched us straight for the front, to the row of tables closest to the head table.

It only took me one guess to find my tented place card. I picked it up, along with the one etched for my *guest*. "Be right back."

Aria leaned in to inspect the centerpiece, a tall bouquet of blooms that speared from a gold-dipped vase, while I jogged to the far end of the room and located the table closest to the exit. I searched for two place cards with the same last name. Finding them, I swapped them for my own, then rejoined Aria.

"What did you do?" she asked as I put the tented cards beside Grandmother's.

"Mr. and Mrs. Johnson just got a table upgrade." I held out my elbow for Aria's arm. "Come on."

"You're not worried they'll switch us right back?"

"And make a scene? Never." The wedding planner might be reprimanded for the blunder, but I suspected Alastair would know that I was responsible for the swap.

"You chose the table closest to the bar." Aria smiled as we walked past our new seating assignments. "Excellent choice."

"Thought you'd approve."

We slipped into the hallway, our steps unhurried as we meandered back to the cocktail room.

There were more people now, more waiters milling about with trays of food. I caught one with a tray of champagne and lifted two flutes, handing one to Aria as we settled next to a table conveniently close to the wall. Like the other tables, it held a floral bouquet.

"These are gorgeous." Aria touched the tip of a white rose. "This visit wasn't entirely wasted. I do love the floral arrangements."

She leaned in, drawing the flower's scent into her nose. Her eyes closed as she inhaled. Savored. The smoky shadow on her eyelids and the dark moons of her lashes were a beautiful sight. Different than her normal makeup-free look.

I stepped closer, close enough that anyone watching would think I was wooing my date. Really, I wanted to talk without prying ears, and if we looked like we were engaged in an intimate conversation, maybe people would leave us alone.

There were enough colleagues and acquaintances here, it wouldn't be long until I was inundated with business conversation. Before that happened, I wanted a quiet moment with Aria.

To apologize.

"And I'm sorry about my grandmother's comment."

"Which one?" she asked, moving away from the bouquet to sip her champagne.

"When she called you a stray."

"Oh." Aria's gaze dropped to the floor. "Does she know? How Clara and I grew up?"

"No, not to my knowledge."

"Then she was just lucky with her shot."

"Still, I apologize on her behalf."

"Don't. She doesn't deserve your grace."

Maybe that was true. But Aria hadn't deserved Grandmother's disdain.

"This is good." Aria raised her glass. "Keep 'em coming, Carmichael."

I chuckled, drinking from my own flute. Aria was right. This event wouldn't be a total bust. And having Aria in Clara's place had already been entertaining.

Clara wouldn't have given Grandmother grief. Clara wouldn't have looked this beautiful in the green dress. Clara wouldn't have pulled me in, closer and closer, until we touched.

Clara might have drawn plenty of eyes from the guests and other men in the room, but she wouldn't have drawn mine.

Clara wasn't Aria.

And Aria had my attention.

"How much do you know about my childhood?" she asked.

"Not much. Enough." Clara and Aria's parents had died in a car accident when they'd been only ten. A drunk driver had crossed the center line and smashed into their car, killing their parents on impact. Afterward, the sisters had gone to live with their uncle. "Clara told me that after you ran away from your uncle, you lived in a junkyard with four other kids."

"That about covers it."

"She said you lived in a van. A delivery van."

A faint smile whispered across Aria's lips. "The other kids, our friends, had their own places. Katherine and Gemma lived in a tent sort of thing, though it was more like a fort. Karson and Londyn lived in the Cadillac that I drove to Arizona. Obviously, it's been restored."

"How did you end up with it?"

"It's on its way across the country, starting in Boston. Clara is going to drive it to California."

"She is? When?"

Aria laughed. "I don't think she's planned it yet. Don't worry. I'm sure she'll plan her trip to coincide with your calendar and clear it first."

"If you actually think she'd ask me, then you don't know who's really in charge. Your sister is the boss. And if you tell her I said that, I'll deny it to the grave."

"My lips are sealed." She smiled, drawing a line across those lips. She hadn't gone for a dark lipstick. They were a natural rose, shiny with gloss.

Her tongue darted out to lick her bottom lip before she took another pull from her flute.

My mouth went dry. My focus was glued to the long, lickable column of her throat as she swallowed.

Back away. Join the crowd. Survive tonight and forget Aria Saint-James.

That was what I should have done.

Yet when she looked up at me, with those beautiful eyes and tempting lips, every reasonable thought went out the window.

"What would you say to stealing a tray of champagne and getting very, very drunk?" I asked.

Aria smiled. "I'd say you were reading my mind."

5

ARIA

"I CANNOT BELIEVE you stole those flowers."

I giggled and set the vase on Brody's kitchen counter, then touched the tip of a calla lily. "Look how beautiful they are. And they smell so good. I couldn't leave them behind to be tossed out."

"They'll die," Brody said.

"Eventually. But not tonight."

First, they'd brighten Brody's concrete home.

I'd been obsessed with the flowers at the reception. Whenever the party had shifted to a new ballroom, the centerpieces had changed to match the space. I'd dragged Brody from vase to vase so I could inspect the arrangements, smell their sweet perfumes and touch their silky petals.

On the way out, the temptation to swipe one had been too much. We'd been alone in the hallway and an elegant vase on one of the tables had called my name. So I'd carried it out the door.

Brody might tease, but I could have sworn I'd heard his kitchen whisper *thank you.*

The room was dim. When we'd come inside, Brody had only flipped on the blue-white lights beneath the cabinets. But it was enough to see that the inside of Brody's home matched the outside. Cold. Drab. Hard. Everything here was a shade of white or gray or black.

The cabinets were a modern style with sleek silver pulls. The floors were wood but the planks had been bleached so the grains and striations were muted. The windows were so clean that the black night seeped through their panes.

The only warmth came from my flowers, my green dress and Brody himself.

In my champagne haze, I studied him with a smile as he walked to the fridge. His polished shoes clicked on the floor and the stainless-steel door opened with a puff.

"We're in luck." He pulled out a bottle of champagne. The glass was a green so dark it was nearly black. The gold foil label screamed *expensive*. Not that I was a champagne connoisseur.

Though I suspected I'd consumed my annual salary's worth of bubbly tonight. The wedding had been an eye-opening study of extravagance. Not even the fanciest of weddings I'd seen at The Gallaway could compare.

The ballrooms alone had wowed. The flowers I'd taken were likely a thousand-dollar arrangement. It wasn't the season for peonies and tulips. And Juliet roses were pricey no matter the time of year.

There'd been hundreds. Thousands. The plates at dinner, all six varying sizes, had been trimmed in gold. Every glass had been crystal. The food itself had been delish, course after course, every bite decadent.

And the champagne had flowed in rivers. The servers, dressed in crisp white shirts and sharp black vests, had never let my flute go dry.

A dream wedding.

I was still dreaming. Because only in sleep could Brody be so . . . fun.

We'd laughed and talked and ignored the other guests at our table. He'd told me stories about people at the wedding. He'd entertained me with tales of blind dates with a few women in attendance. He'd laughed along as I'd impersonated his stuffy grandmother. And together, we'd heckled and teased every one of the toast makers. Twenty-eight in total. Why someone needed to have twenty-eight toasts at their wedding I would never comprehend.

Brody and I had been that couple, the annoying one who'd had fun despite being miserable, and yes, it had been at the expense of some others. I'd never see those people again and couldn't find the motivation to feel guilty.

The champagne bottle hissed before the cork loosened with a pop. It flew across the room and bounced off a wall. A spray of foam splattered the floor.

"Whoops." Brody ignored it and walked to a cabinet, opening it to pull out two flutes. They clinked on the silver-veined white granite counters. The champagne fizzed as he filled the glasses to nearly overflowing.

He handed me one, then lifted his own. "Cheers."

"Cheers." My cheeks pinched from so much smiling.

My head was fuzzy and tomorrow I'd have a bitch of a hangover. I drained my flute regardless. More alcohol wasn't the responsible choice, except it was delicious and I wasn't ready to go home yet.

Clara and August were asleep. By all rights, I should be dead on my bare feet—my shoes had lasted until the flight home, then I'd kicked them off and left them forgotten on the plane. Maybe Ron, the bowing butler, had picked them up when he'd collected us from the Welcome airport in a town car and driven us home.

It was two o'clock in the morning, well past my normal bedtime, but my body pulsed with restless energy. It was adrenaline from the party. A buzz from the champagne. And a high from Brody.

His aura was invigorating, his grin charming. His quick wit and dry sense of humor had kept a smile on my face all night. The brooding, grumpy billionaire would likely surface tomorrow, but tonight, I was enjoying this version of Brody. The version with a personality.

Maybe this was why Clara had worked for him after these many years. Maybe when Brody let his guard down, he was actually . . . nice.

"Thank you, Aria." He set his glass down and hopped up to sit on the edge of the massive island.

"You're welcome." I set my own flute on the counter at my back, planting my hands on the edge and hopping up too. The gown's skirt swished over my toes, the satin cool and smooth against my skin.

"Tonight was . . . unexpected." The rich baritone of his rugged voice warmed the lifeless room. It was as intoxicating as the champagne. More than once tonight, I'd let him lean in close and whisper in my ear.

More than once, I'd pretended the flirts were real. "Quite unexpected. And fun. Do you ever have fun?"

He chuckled and a shiver rolled down my spine. "Not often. I certainly hadn't planned on fun tonight."

"Does it bother you? Heather and Alastair?" I'd wanted to ask all night but had restrained myself until now. Did he still love her?

"Yes," he admitted. "But not for the reason you think. I don't like that Alastair won."

"Ah. Then it's a competition."

"Between us, yes." He lifted his glass to those soft lips for another sip. "We're not like you and Clara. We never have been. He's five years younger than I am, and I swear we've been battling since the day he was born."

Clara was my best friend. My confidant. My sister of blood and soul. Warring with a sibling seemed unnecessarily sad. "I'm sorry."

He shrugged, then he lifted a hand to touch the bouquet. "These are wasted on me. You should take them to Clara."

"No. Leave them here. This place is in desperate need of color." Even though the flowers were all pale shades of pink and peach and cream, at least they were warm.

"You don't like my house?"

"Not especially."

A grin spread across his handsome face. "What would you change?"

"Oh . . . everything. But mostly, I'd add some life. Color. Texture. You do know they make paint in actual shades besides greige, right?"

"Do they?" he teased. "I'll be sure to tell my interior designer. I bet your home is full of life."

"You'd hate it. There are colors everywhere. And plants. Lots and lots of plants."

He chuckled again, draining the rest of his glass. "Do you like your job?"

"I love my job. I like working with my hands and seeing things grow under my care. It's satisfying, seeing a flower blossom and knowing I'm the one who planted the seed."

"How did it start? How did you become interested in gardening?" He leaned forward, his gaze fixed on me. Brody had been like that all night. When I spoke, he listened. Intently. It had been unnerving at first. Now, I couldn't seem to stop myself from talking because his attention was addictive.

"It started at the junkyard. It was so . . . dead."

"Like my home."

I laughed. "Yes, but in a different shade. Dirt and rust. Everything had this reddish-orange tinge. I don't know why I got the impulse, but I was at the grocery store one day buying a loaf of bread, and beside the checkout stand, they had this display of packets. You know, the metal stand with all the seeds?"

He shook his head. "No, but I believe you."

"Have you ever been inside a grocery store?"

"Once or twice."

I shook my head and laughed. "God, our lives are different. Anyway, the packets were only thirty cents, so I bought three of them. I wanted to do something to make my little world prettier. I planted the seeds in an old egg carton and prayed they'd grow."

"You gave it life."

"I tried." I gave him a sad smile. "It was a hobby. Tending my plants and flowers gave me something to do. By the time I left, Lou had enough to start a greenhouse if he wanted."

"Lou?"

"The owner of the junkyard," I said. "He let us stay there."

"Right. The recluse. Clara never told me his name."

"Lou Miley. I think I only spoke to him once or twice during the years we were there. He let us be. We did the same for him. But there was a fondness there, even from a distance."

When Clara and I had left the junkyard, I'd replanted everything I'd grown and staged it closer to his home. I'd never forget the look on Lou's face when he spotted the pink flowers I'd left right outside his door. He gaped at them, shocked, and maybe a little bit proud.

I liked to think that he'd watered those flowers after I'd left. That he'd realized it had been the only thing I could give him as a token of my appreciation.

I'd given him the lives I'd grown as thanks for saving mine.

"Enough about that." I waved the topic away. I didn't think about the junkyard often or, even more rarely, the miserable years before. And tonight, I was enjoying myself too much to rehash the past.

Besides, it wasn't like Brody actually cared. I suspected this charm was his way of humoring me. His own token of appreciation for accompanying him tonight.

"You work at a hotel," he said.

"I do." I nodded. "The Gallaway. It's beautiful. Different than the hotel we were at tonight, but no less exquisite. It's right on the coast. I get to work with the ocean waves as my soundtrack and the smell of salt and sand in the air."

"You love your home. You love your job. What else should I know about you, Aria Saint-James?"

That maybe I don't hate you. "One day, I'd like to have a flower shop and a greenhouse of my own. I'd like to make bouquets like that one and keep growing plants."

It was a secret I hadn't told anyone, not even Clara. I didn't set many goals. I didn't think too far into the future. Because it was too easy for dreams to be stolen. Better they stay locked away.

"I don't know why I just told you that," I admitted.

"Probably the champagne."

I lifted my glass for another sip. "Probably. And tomorrow, I'll regret confiding in the enemy."

"I'm still the enemy?" he asked.

"Of course."

"Good." He grinned, hopping off the counter. "Come tomorrow, there will be no more need for a truce."

"Agreed." The word sounded breathy as he crossed the space between us.

There was hunger in his green eyes. It had been there for hours. If he pulled a mirror from his tux pocket, I'd likely see that same desire in my own gaze. He walked closer, his gait easy and confident. Each step was a seduction, like the one and only dance we'd shared at the wedding.

Brody had held me tight, his grip on my waist firm. And he'd given me that attention, that undivided attention. The spice of his cologne filled my nose as he closed the gap. With me seated on the counter, our eyes were nearly level. Not quite. He stood a few inches over six feet, and even with my perch, he had me beat.

His beard seemed thicker in the muted light and my fingers itched to touch the strands. His hair was combed so well, it needed a good tousle.

"What are you doing?" I asked as he inched closer, pressing into the skirt of my gown.

"I'm going to kiss you."

My heart skipped. *Yes.* That was the champagne talking. I didn't care. "What if I don't want you to kiss me?"

He leaned in close, the warmth of his breath caressing my cheek. "What if you do?"

What if I did?

I took his face in my hands, letting the scratch of his beard scrape against my palms, and I pulled his mouth down to mine.

Then *I* kissed *him*.

"Hey," Clara said, walking into the living room.

"Shhhh." I held up a finger from my spot on the couch. "Not so loud."

"Headache?"

I groaned. "I'll never drink champagne again."

She laughed and plopped down by my feet, taking my legs and pulling them over her lap. Then she massaged the arch of a foot. "How was it?"

"Fine." I closed my eyes and did my best to block out the image of last night. Not of the wedding.

Of Brody's bed.

God, what the hell had I been thinking? Why? Why had I slept with him? Sex with Clara's boss was the worst decision I'd made in years. Worse than the time I'd cut my own bangs seven years ago.

Brody was . . . irresistible. Damn him for being so. I didn't even like him. Did I?

He'd been out cold this morning when I'd woken up early. It was the lifelong habit of a groundskeeper to rise before dawn and prune and water before hotel guests made their way outside and tripped over my hoses.

So as he'd slumbered, I'd silently slipped out of his bed and into my dress, then raced from his bedroom. I'd hoped to save myself from the walk of shame, but butler Ron had been in the kitchen, washing last night's champagne flutes.

He'd given me another goddamn bow just before I'd made it to the door. Then I'd hustled to Clara's, hoping not to wake her or Gus as I'd showered, dressed in sweats and crashed here on the couch.

"Thank you for going," Clara said, her foot massage saving my life.

"Sure. How are you feeling?"

"Better."

"Good." I closed my eyes. Bad idea. The image of Brody's naked body —muscled arms, washboard abs, impressive arousal—popped into my mind.

I groaned. *Such. An. Idiot.* This was his fault. Why did he have to have such an amazing body? Why was he so handsome? Why did he have to be such a good kisser?

That first kiss had been my downfall. His tongue had slid between my teeth and goodbye common sense.

My body ached, not just from the hangover, but from being used. Incredibly, sinfully used. Brody Carmichael knew how to give a woman an orgasm. With his fingers. With his tongue. With his thick, long, talented—

I groaned again. *Curse you, Brody.* It would have been so much easier to keep hating him if he hadn't been so . . . perfect.

"Are you getting sick?" Clara asked. "Oh, no. I hope you don't have what I had."

"I'm sure it's just the hangover." The sex hangover.

"Tell me about the wedding."

"It was beautiful. Expensive. They spent more money on a party than I've made in three years. Or more."

"Strange, aren't they?" Clara asked. "Rich people."

"Strange what they think is important."

442

"Brody gets it," she said. "Even though he has more money than is healthy, he gets it."

Yesterday, I would have argued. Yesterday, I would have told her that when it came to her boss, she was delusional. But yesterday, I hadn't known Brody.

Or maybe that was just wishful thinking on my part. Maybe that was me wanting to believe that I hadn't let a rich jerk seduce me into a one-night stand.

I hated the idea that it all might have been a game. That he'd used me for sex. That I'd fallen for a trick.

"You aren't arguing with me," Clara said. "That means you really are hungover."

I forced a smile. "Do my other foot. And stop talking so loud."

She giggled and continued my massage.

We sat there, in comfortable companionship and quiet, until Gus woke up and, headache or not, I roused from the couch to spend time with my family.

We were outside on the front lawn when I heard a door close.

I looked down the driveway just in time to see Brody carry a duffel bag to his Jag.

He was wearing sunglasses. A suit, per usual. He looked striking and every bit a polished billionaire. The champagne didn't seem to have paled his skin like it had mine.

Brody got into his car and drove away without a word. Without a glance.

And two weeks later, when I returned home to Oregon, I reminded myself that Brody Carmichael was an asshole. My pride had kept me from asking Clara where he'd gone. It had also kept me from telling her that I'd fucked her boss.

Brody was the enemy. He was a one-night mistake and a man I didn't have to see again if I was lucky.

It didn't matter that he'd left Arizona, escaping my company. It didn't matter that I'd been just another willing body in his bedroom. It didn't matter that I'd fallen for him, just a little.

That night didn't matter.

And I'd forget about it soon enough anyway.

6

ARIA

I HATE BRODY CARMICHAEL.

"Oh, God." I slid to my butt on the bathroom floor, letting the cold from the tile seep into my jeans. My stomach churned and I rose up just in time to retch into the toilet. Again.

How much puking could a woman do when she hadn't eaten anything in twelve hours?

Apparently, a lot. This was the fourth time I'd had to rush to the bathroom this morning.

I wiped my mouth dry and waited, hovering beside the porcelain to make sure I was done. Then I glanced at my watch. Eleven o'clock. That was usually when the vomiting stopped.

Why? Why had I been so foolish? Why had I had so much champagne? Why had I let Clara talk me into going to that wedding two months ago?

And why had I slept with Brody?

That son of a bitch Carmichael got me pregnant.

Pregnant.

That word had been bouncing around in my brain for two days, ever since I'd held the positive test in my hand. *Pregnant.* Only reading the result a thousand times had helped it sink in.

When I'd missed my period, I'd fooled myself into thinking it was an anomaly. I'd chalked it up to exercise. After my trip to Arizona, I'd started working out hard at the gym in Heron Beach. They'd started a pre-holiday workout challenge, and after jumping and squatting and crunching, most nights I'd walked home like a limp noodle.

The class was a killer, but I had more muscle definition at thirty than I'd had at twenty. Women lost their periods from body fat changes all the time, right?

Denial was an evil bitch. She'd trick you into false securities. She'd

444

duped me into ignoring the real reason I hadn't bought my monthly supply of tampons. Then, after weeks of being my constant companion, she'd abandoned me.

My exhaustion hadn't faded, even after cutting time at the gym. My breasts were tender. My mind sluggish. And my stomach in a constant knot.

One week of morning sickness and the signs were all there, screaming at me to stop ignoring the truth.

Pregnant. I was going to become a mother.

And I had no idea what to do.

When Clara had realized she was pregnant with August, she'd called me crying from the bathroom in her Las Vegas apartment. She'd been hysterical. Her sobs had bounced off the walls.

What am I going to do? What am I going to do?

She'd asked me that question over and over. Once she'd calmed down, we'd spent hours talking it through. Her biggest fear had been telling Devan. Maybe because she'd known how he'd react.

Though handsome, Devan hadn't been the most loving of boyfriends. He was a narcissist. A child, even his own, would be competition for attention. There were times when he worshiped Clara, enough to make her stay. But a baby? Clara knew he was going to flip that her birth control hadn't worked. He proved predictable.

After breaking the news, she called me again, from the same bathroom, this time livid because Devan had accused her of doing it on purpose.

Would Brody do the same?

From what I could remember, he'd used condoms. Multiple condoms. One of them must have broken. And since I wasn't one to bring men to my bed, or sleep in theirs, I hadn't bothered with birth control. Sex for me was as rare as the steak tartare served at the wedding reception.

Stupid, Aria. Don't think about food.

My stomach rolled again, but being empty, nothing came up. That would change tomorrow morning when I'd repeat this blessed cycle again.

I shoved myself off the floor and out of the bathroom stall, then went to the sink to splash water on my face. The bottle of mouthwash in my purse was nearly empty but I had enough for a swish and spit.

When I chanced a look at my reflection, the mirror showed me that I looked the way I felt. Like shit.

My face was pale. The purple circles under my eyes were darker than they'd been yesterday. My shoulders slumped because the weight on them was so heavy I couldn't muster the strength to snap them straight.

Pregnancy had more of a greenish tinge than a glow.

What am I going to do?

Was I ready for this? I'd hoped kids would come after I'd found the man of my dreams. How was I going to do this on my own?

One day at a time. That's what I'd told Clara when she'd been the woman in the bathroom. I'd heed my own advice.

First things first, it was time to tell my sister. Two days, and this secret was barking to be let out of its cage. Clara had done this before. She'd navigated a pregnancy and faced single motherhood. Clara would make it all better—after she reamed my ass for sleeping with her boss.

"I'm going to tell her." I nodded to myself. "Today. As soon as I feel better."

Before my reflection could convince me one more day of secrecy wouldn't hurt, I walked away from the sink. The women's locker room at The Gallaway was empty. Most of the staff had already dropped off their personal belongings to start work for the day.

This time of year, the hotel wasn't as busy as it was during the warmer months. December's pace around the hotel was slower as the guest count dwindled. The housekeepers were less frantic. The grounds staff had been cut down to the bare minimum. Our seasonal workers would return in the spring.

With Christmas only five days away, this week would be one of the quietest all year. Though some families came to celebrate at The Gallaway, per their annual tradition. They'd be fussed over and given extra attention. Our chef was busy preparing for extravagant holiday meals.

Any other year and the kitchen would have been a regular stop on my daily rounds. But now, with the smells and my queasy stomach, I'd been avoiding that end of the hotel for the same reason I avoided marigolds in planters. They stank.

I wandered down the hallway, fighting to put on a happy face. I was five minutes late for a meeting with my boss, Andy, the new general manager.

Mark had hired Andy earlier this year, and the duties I'd covered as temporary GM had been handed over, but Andy insisted we continue this daily meeting. *I'm too tired for this.*

Regardless, I made my way to the lobby. Three Christmas trees decorated the vast space, each with golden lights and silver ribbons that had been wrapped in perfect spirals around the boughs. The crystal chandelier hanging low in the center of the space cast fractured beams across the marble floors.

The hotel looked magical, though I still preferred the spring and summer, when fresh flowers decorated the space and my plants greeted guests as they strolled through the wide front entrance.

I waved at the receptionist stationed at the desk, then disappeared through the door behind the counter marked for employees only. Then, using the last of my reserves, I trudged up the staircase to the second floor.

The corner office, Mark's, was dark. In the winter, he took Wednesdays off as personal days. His beachfront home was as impressive as his hotel, and if I owned it, I'd make it a point to spend time there too.

Beside Mark's was Andy's office. It wasn't quite as impressive as the corner, but with the view overlooking the ocean and the cliffs that gave way to the sandy beach, it sure didn't suck.

Forcing some pep into my expression, I knocked on Andy's door.

"Come in."

I turned the knob and entered. "Hey."

"Aria." He stood from his desk and straightened the lapel on his suit jacket. Then he smiled, a pleasant smile but one that betrayed his feelings.

Andy's crush on me was the worst-kept secret at The Gallaway.

"Please, allow me." He rounded his desk and pulled out the guest chair. "Have a seat."

"Thanks." I shied away as he lingered just a second too long beside the armrest.

Awkward and uncomfortable crush aside, Andy had proved to be a good boss in the months he'd been here. He treated the staff with kindness. He worked hard and had earned Mark's respect. But Andy was a single man in his midforties, and the affection he had for me was as obvious as the waves crashing onto the shore outside.

"Have you had lunch?" he asked, returning to his side of the desk.

Beyond him and through the windows, the winter sky was a lighter shade of gray than the ocean itself. Part of me wanted to find a quiet bench somewhere on the sprawling deck outside, curl up under a blanket and let the caw of the seagulls lull me to sleep.

How was I going to manage my job and a baby? It was possible. Deep down, I knew I'd figure it out, but the logistics escaped me at the moment. The idea of searching for daycare and babysitters was overwhelming. Today, this week, the future looked as hazy as the horizon outside where the sea met the clouds.

"Aria?"

"Huh?" I blinked, tearing my gaze away from the glass to focus on Andy's face. "Sorry. No, I haven't had lunch."

"Should I order something for us?" He gestured to the desk phone. "I heard the chef made a large pot of clam chowder today and it's delicious."

I gagged. "No. No lunch for me today."

"Oh." His face fell, but he recovered quickly with a smile. His blond hair was combed smartly at a part over his left eyebrow. His face was always clean shaven. Maybe in another life, Andy would have been a nice man to date.

I suspected he enjoyed long walks on the beach and romantic candlelit dinners. We'd never bicker or fight. Andy was much too polite for sarcasm.

Dating would soon become a distant memory, not that I'd dated much these past few years. Even Andy wouldn't want to get involved with a pregnant woman. Baggage might as well be my middle name.

"Sorry," I said. "It's not you. I'm just not feeling great today."

"Is there anything I can do?" The concern on his face was endearing. As a friend.

"I'll be fine." The new mantra. I'd be fine. *We'd* be fine. I fought the urge to press a hand to my belly. "My plan is to spend a few hours in the greenhouse. That always perks me up."

"Then don't let me keep you." He stood from his chair. "We can skip today's meeting. Catch up later."

"Are you sure?"

"Of course." He came to my chair, pulling it out for me as I stood. "We'll talk when you get back from Arizona."

Tomorrow, I was leaving to spend Christmas with Clara and August. My suitcase was packed and my flight booked.

Never in my life had I dreaded a trip to see my family.

"Merry Christmas and Happy New Year, Andy."

"Same to you, Aria."

I waved, then headed for the door. I didn't linger at the hotel. The fresh air outside beckoned, so I collected my jacket from the locker room and ducked out the employee exit. My condo wasn't far from the hotel, only blocks, and rather than drive, I walked to work most days.

Now that I'd left the Cadillac with Clara, I didn't have a vehicle. Not long before Katherine had come to Oregon with the Cadillac, I'd sold my old Jetta. It had been a piece of junk and prone to breakdowns and flat tires. I'd been searching for a replacement but then the Cadillac had magically appeared and voila. No more car shopping.

Besides, Heron Beach was a small town. Walking the streets was safe and the grocery store delivered.

The air wrapped around me cool and sharp, chasing the last dregs of nausea away. The Gallaway had golf carts for my staff to use for going back and forth between the off-site greenhouse and storage area five blocks away, but I hadn't climbed behind the wheel of one in ages.

Much like my journey to and from home, I preferred to hoof it.

The walk was invigorating, and by the time I made it to the greenhouse, my spirits had lifted. The future didn't seem quite as bleak. And though Clara was going to be surprised, maybe there'd be a little excitement there too.

I was having a baby.

My baby.

There'd never be a day when I was alone. There'd never be a day when I longed for a family. I was growing one. The life inside me deserved my best. He or she would have it. From now until my dying breath.

It was . . . exciting. Scary, but wonderful.

Digging the keys from my coat pocket, I unlocked the greenhouse door and stepped inside. Dirt and leaves and water. I breathed it all in, holding the air in my lungs for a moment.

"Better." I sighed, shrugging off my coat.

The greenhouse was my favorite place. A sanctuary. Here, we created life. We made messes. My staff all knew that when you were at The Gallaway, you smiled at guests but stayed in the periphery. The greenhouse was where we could all let loose and be ourselves.

Here, the world made sense. Here, I could figure this pregnancy thing out.

I meandered down the aisles between planting tables, my tennis shoes crunching on the gravel floor. There were a few poinsettias left that hadn't been perfect enough for the hotel. This morning, I'd earmarked each for my employees to take home. The seedling trays were mostly stacked and empty. We wouldn't fill and plant the majority of them until February or March, depending on the varietal. But the scent from the plants lingered year-round.

The small desk at the far end of the greenhouse was cluttered with papers. My laptop was collecting dust. Two forgotten water bottles joined the mess. The space served as my office, where I'd place supply orders and draft work schedules and answer the rare email.

When I'd worked as the temporary GM, I'd used Andy's office. The view was spectacular but spending my time there had been beautiful torture. I wasn't meant for a fancy office and paperwork. Though I'd muddled through fine, making sure that everyone had their duties covered, it had never fit. Not like the greenhouse. This was where I was most comfortable. This was where I was the most productive. This was where life made sense.

Most days.

I plopped into my black upholstered chair, spinning it to the desk and slouching down deep. Then I dug my phone from my pocket to make the call—or calls—that were two days overdue.

Clara answered on the second ring. "Hey. All set for tomorrow?"

"Yep." I sucked in a deep breath. I couldn't fly to Arizona and spend the day with her and August, waiting for him to go to bed, with this news hanging over my head. She'd know from the moment she picked me up at the airport that something was wrong. And this was not news I wanted to deliver with August in the car. "Got a second? I need to tell you something."

"I don't like that tone," she said. "What's wrong?"

I gulped. "I'm pregnant."

"W-what?"

"I'm pregnant."

"Oh." The silence dragged after that one pained syllable. "I, um . . . I didn't realize you were seeing someone."

"I'm not." God, this was hard. And about to get worse. "It was a one-time thing."

"Are you okay?"

"No," I admitted, tears welling in my eyes. "But I will be."

Tomorrow, when I could soak up one of her hugs, I'd tell her I was scared. I'd tell her I didn't know how to be a mother, not after we'd lost our own so young. I'd tell her that I didn't know how to fit an infant into my life, and I had no idea how to incorporate Brody into the mix.

"What can I do?" Clara asked.

My heart squeezed. "I'll be ready for a hug tomorrow."

"I'll have one waiting."

"And I need . . ." I closed my eyes. Damn it, this sucked.

"You need what?"

I swallowed down my fears and braced. "I need Brody's number."

"Why —" She gasped, putting the pieces together. "He's the father?"

I nodded.

"Aria?"

"Yes," I whispered. "It happened after the wedding."

"Um . . ." She trailed off and stayed quiet. Then she cleared her throat. "He's right here. Let me give him the phone."

"Wait. Clara —" Too late.

She'd taken the phone from her ear before I could tell her that I wasn't ready to talk to Brody yet. I wanted his number so I could call him before my flight tomorrow, but I hadn't worked out what to say yet.

Clara's voice echoed in the background as she spoke to Brody. "Phone call for you."

"Who is it?" His deep voice hit my ear and my panic spiked.

Tell him.

I was going to puke again. I'd survived plenty of hard moments in my life. The death of my parents. Living with my uncle. Running away at fifteen. But for some reason, this seemed like the hardest of them all.

My entire body trembled as I listened, waiting for Brody to get on the line.

Clara said my name, then there was a long pause.

"What?"

One word and all my fears disappeared. One bark from an arrogant jerk and I wasn't scared anymore. No, I was pissed. "Hello to you too."

"I'm busy, Aria."

"God, you are an asshole. I hope our baby gets his or her personality from me."

"W-what?"

So he wasn't a complete robot. I'd rattled him. *Good.* I was rattled too. "You heard me."

Brody went still. The air in the greenhouse swirled from the fans that we ran year-round. Their hum was the only noise. Not even his breath registered in my ear.

"Brody," I said.

No response, not even to ask me if I was sure he was the father.

"Brody."

Dead air.

I pulled the phone away from my ear and my mouth fell open. It was quiet because he'd hung up on me. "That son of a bitch."

Tossing the phone to the table, I shot out of my chair and stalked through the greenhouse. He'd hung up on me. He'd actually hung up on me. My fingers itched to strangle something — or someone, but that someone lived in Arizona.

"How dare he hang up on me? How fucking dare he?" My voice bounced around the empty room. "Grrr. I hate him."

I walked the length of the greenhouse twice, my anger growing with each step. Sitting at my desk would only make me crazy, so I grabbed a pair of leather gloves and got to work. I pulled a stool up to a table and began planting some seeds for the spring greenery. Million bells. Cosmos. Zinnias. It wasn't on the schedule to start them until January, but a few extra days wouldn't hurt.

I'd never been fancy with the varieties we planted. My predecessor and mentor hadn't been either. He'd taught me that sometimes the most amazing displays were nothing more than abundant color. I preferred hardy plants that would survive the regular touches from guests and the sniffs from pets and kids.

My anger at Brody kept me company while I lost myself in the dirt and seeds and quiet whirl of the greenhouse. Clara tried to call a few times but I pushed her to voicemail and sent her a text that I'd call later. I couldn't talk to her, not when she was so close to Brody. *Bastard*.

Hours later, well past the noon hour and close to dinner, my stomach growled so loudly the sound echoed in the greenhouse.

An enormous appetite came crashing down, and for the first time today, I was ravenous. The same had happened yesterday and the day before. My body didn't want a thing before four, then afterward, I'd eat and eat and eat until bedtime.

Quickly tidying up my workspace, I returned to my desk for my coat and keys. I jotted down a message on a sticky note for the staff to water the seed trays I'd planted while I was in Arizona for the holiday, though the note was unnecessary.

The winter grounds crew was the full-time crew. They were all at the hotel, completing the short to-do list I'd assigned this morning. If there was a snow flurry, they'd take care of the shoveling and plowing. They'd ice the sidewalks. And they'd water, inside the hotel and here too.

Today wasn't the first time I'd been in a mood that had resulted in new plants to tend.

With the greenhouse locked, I rushed along the sidewalk to The Gallaway, hoping the chef had something warm. The clam chowder would do. Or pasta. Or chowder *and* pasta. Maybe some bread too.

Could I eat clam chowder? I typed in a quick search on my phone. Soon, I'd have to find a doctor and learn the specifics. Clara had cut out certain things when she'd been pregnant with August, but since we hadn't lived together, I couldn't remember the exact items.

Today, all I cared about was that clam chowder was safe and so were carbs.

In the kitchen, the chef greeted me with a wide smile, as though he'd expected to see me. After only days, my odd eating schedule was becoming predictable. He whipped up a bowl of chowder and one of his fancy grilled cheese sandwiches. I devoured it all in the employee break room along with a cookie and a Coke from the vending machine.

With a full belly and a subdued temper, I pulled out my phone and called my sister.

"Hey," Clara answered. "You okay?"

"I don't know," I admitted.

"Brody is —"

"Don't. Please," I begged. "I don't want to talk about Brody. Not right now."

"Okay. Do you still want to come here tomorrow?"

"Yes." I wasn't letting Brody steal my Christmas. "I'll be there."

Maybe if I was lucky, he'd find somewhere else to spend the holidays. Yes, we had a lot to discuss and figure out, but it could wait. We had months, if Brody even wanted to be involved.

Would he want to be in our child's life? Or would he be like Devan and disappear? My heart sank. How was I going to explain to a kid that his father didn't want him? That her dad had abandoned her in favor of private jets and cold mansions?

Maybe Brody would surprise me. Maybe he'd stick. How were we going to raise a child from different states? How would we handle holidays? Would I only get to have my baby every other special occasion?

"There's so much to figure out," I whispered.

"You will."

"Yeah," I murmured. "We'll have lots to talk about tomorrow."

"Talking would be good."

"I'm sorry I didn't tell you about Brody."

"I understand." And the truth in her voice eased some of the guilt. We'd figure this out, like we had every hurdle life had put in our path. Together.

"I'll text you when I'm at the airport tomorrow."

"Love you," she said.

I smiled. "I love you too."

The next shift was due to start soon and one of the night-shift clerks came in to leave his dinner in the employee fridge. I waved, talked to him for a moment, then headed out to the lobby.

"Aria." Andy was at the receptionist counter and his entire face brightened when I walked through the door.

I forced a smile. "Hey."

"Feeling better?"

"I am, thanks." Surprisingly, much better. Now that I'd told Clara, I wasn't alone in this. Secrets had never been my thing and sharing the news that I was going to have a baby had lightened the load.

That was how it worked with Clara. We shared burdens.

Pregnancies. Brody.

If he abandoned our baby, at least I wouldn't have to convince Clara to quit and move to Oregon. There was no way she'd stay with him if he turned out to be a deadbeat dad.

"It's cold out." Andy nodded toward the french doors that opened to the deck on the ocean side of the hotel. In the summer, those doors were rarely closed. "I was just taking off for the day. Would you like a ride home?"

He was just so . . . clueless. And nice. Refusing him was not easy. When was he going to realize this was never going to happen?

I opened my mouth, my brain scrambling for a gentle rejection, when a flash of dark caught my eye over Andy's shoulder.

A man in a crisp black suit strode into the hotel, his green gaze locked on my face.

Brody.

7

BRODY

"WHAT ARE YOU DOING HERE?" Aria asked through a clenched jaw.

The guy beside her stepped closer, hovering beside her elbow. He lifted his hand, ready to touch her, but at my glare, he must have thought better of it and let his arm drop to his side.

I dismissed him and focused on the woman.

Aria's face was pale. The circles under her eyes looked more like bruises. And she'd lost weight — weight she hadn't had to lose.

"You look awful."

She crossed her arms over her chest. "You came all the way to Oregon to tell me I look awful."

The man stepped closer to Aria, positioning himself between us.

The look I sent him was the one I'd used countless times in the conference room. One I'd learned from Grandmother. People withered under the look. This guy did.

The only person who seemed immune was Aria.

Her scowl deepened, then vanished when she turned to him. "Andy, would you excuse me?"

"Is everything okay?" He touched her elbow.

I tensed.

Aria tensed. It was slight but visible. She gave *Andy* a tight smile. "All good. Thank you."

He reluctantly nodded and dropped his hand once more, but did he leave? Andy just stood there, staring at her like she was the sun and the moon and the stars.

Christ. I didn't have time to deal with a boyfriend. Was he her boyfriend? Because I wasn't okay with that. I wasn't okay with another man touching her. Kissing her. Definitely not sleeping with her.

My head, which had been spinning since her phone call earlier, was close to exploding. It was only by sheer force of will that I hadn't had a

454

complete and total mental breakdown—not that I'd ever had a breakdown.

But if there was a time, this was it.

The idea of this guy being in her life. Taking my place. *No. Fuck no.*

I was the father. This was my kid. Maybe. I hoped. Probably.

"Aria," I gritted out. Did she not see me coming out of my skin here?

Another glare for me. Another pained smile for Andy. "Have a merry Christmas."

"You too." Andy backed away and, finally, turned and disappeared down a hallway.

Leaving me and Aria in the middle of a hotel lobby to stare at one another.

She did look awful. Worse than awful.

And beautiful.

I'd had a hard time getting her off my mind since the wedding. For two months, I'd done my best to return to normal life. Work had been busy and I'd used it as an escape. But in the dark hours, when I was at home alone, I'd find myself in the kitchen, wishing those flowers she'd stolen hadn't died.

She'd been right. They had added some life to the house.

Her scent, floral and sweet, had disappeared from my bedroom the morning after she'd left. Ron was too good at his job at times and had washed my sheets while I'd been in the shower. But I could still picture Aria in my bed, sleeping soundly with the slightest smile on her face.

When I closed my eyes, her silky hair greeted me first. Then her eyes. Those molten, chocolate eyes with the fiery flecks. Next came her coy smile. The one she'd flashed me countless times at the wedding.

Aria Saint-James was impossible to escape.

And now she was pregnant. With my baby.

Pregnant.

I'd been playing that word in my head, over and over. Rolling it around. Testing its severity. For three hours during the flight, I'd mentally repeated it on loop. It was so . . . enormous. Eight letters that had changed my life.

The concept was too much. Too big. So I'd deal with a smaller one first. "Who is that?" I nodded in the direction where Andy had disappeared.

"Andy is my boss."

"He's in love with you."

"No, he isn't." She rolled her eyes. "He has a little crush on me. Nothing more. It's awkward but temporary."

Temporary. Clearly, she didn't realize the depth of Andy's feelings. Or that nothing about her rendered temporary. Aria had a lasting effect. She walked into your life and you struggled to remember what it had been like before you'd seen that first smile.

"Why did you come here, Brody?"

"You're . . ." I gulped.

"Pregnant."

That word was like a bullet racing out the barrel of a gun. By some miracle, my knees didn't buckle. Hearing it from her lips, watching them form the word, there was no denying it. That didn't stop me from asking a dumb question.

"You're sure?"

"Uh, yeah." Another eye roll. "Why would I lie?"

Because it wouldn't be the first time a woman had tried. But Aria had moral fiber. She wouldn't understand that a child with me meant the payday of a lifetime. "And it's—"

"If you ask me if it's yours, I will cut your balls off and string them on the Christmas tree."

I held up a hand. "That's not what I was going to say."

"Oh."

"It's okay? Healthy? You're okay?"

She dropped her gaze to the shiny marble floor. "I'm tired. I feel like shit. Probably why I look awful, as you so graciously pointed out."

"Sorry." I dragged a hand over my bearded jaw.

"What are you doing here, Brody?" she asked again.

"I'm in a little bit of shock. I had to make sure."

"A phone call would have sufficed. Or you could have not hung up on me in the first place."

Not an option. The moment her announcement had set in, I'd had to see her. In person. I'd had to watch with my own eyes as my ears heard the word come from her lips.

Aria was pregnant. The truth settled into my bones. The world that had been spinning in one direction suddenly shifted, spinning on an entirely different axis. One that was centered around the life growing inside her.

There was a lot of shit to figure out.

"Join me for dinner."

"I just ate."

I checked my watch. "At four o'clock?"

She shrugged. "I eat when I'm hungry. That doesn't happen all the time, so I take advantage."

"Coffee? Decaf. Please."

"What do you want, Brody?" Her frame slumped. Her voice held so much exhaustion, all I wanted was to scoop her up and tuck her into my bed for the rest of the week.

"To talk. I want to talk."

"Okay." She nodded. "I was just on my way home."

"Lead the way."

She gave me the side-eye, then shrugged on her coat. I followed close behind as she walked past me and out the front doors.

I fell into step beside her on the sidewalk, keeping up with her brisk pace. The cold air bit into my ears and nose. Where was her car?

Aria kept walking, following the curve of the street. I expected her to stop at one of the parking lots, but she kept on going.

Then we changed directions after a few blocks, starting up a side street.

Step by silent step, we made our way farther and farther from the hotel and the sound of the ocean.

She shouldn't be walking, not when she was this tired. Not at this hour. The sun was beginning to set. In an hour, it would be almost dark. Even now, the light was dim enough to mute the colors of the homes we passed.

The leaves had fallen from the trees, their limbs bare. The grassy lawns looked to have been frozen a time or twelve. It was just . . . cold. The damp chill from the humid air seeped through my suit coat and made me shiver. I clenched my teeth to keep them from chattering.

It was too cold for her to be walking every night. Alone.

"Why don't you have a car?"

"I haven't bought one since leaving the Cadillac with Clara. Besides, I like to walk."

I opened my mouth, ready to debate the safety merits of her preferred method of transportation, but I stopped myself first.

Aria would argue. I would argue. It was what we did. And tonight, with so many other important topics looming, this wasn't the argument we needed to have. So I closed my mouth and kept pace with her as she navigated us toward a two-story row of condos.

There was no need to ask which condo in the row was hers. Even in winter, she had plants on her porch while the other three condos had nothing surrounding their front doors.

Aria had two potted trees, their evergreen boughs trimmed precisely to a point. A row of red lights had been wrapped around them in a perfect spiral. Yellow lights, draped from the porch's beam, decorated the space. In the corner, a huge pot held a bush. Its red holly berries decorated the thick green leaves.

Aria slid her key in the door's lock and pushed inside. One step past the threshold and her scent enveloped me. Sweet flowers. A hint of vanilla. *Aria.* I dragged in a long breath and let the warmth of her home chase away the chill.

She shrugged off her coat, taking it into the living room and tossing it on the back of a cream couch. Inside was like stepping into another world. Sheer white curtains covered the dark windows. There were plants everywhere, most varying shades of green but some with flowers. Red and pink poinsettias decorated the dining table. A bouquet of yellow roses flourished on the kitchen counter. With the light walls and neutral furniture shades, it was like a bungalow tucked away on a quiet island.

Serene. There was no other way to describe it. She'd made herself a haven.

And I was going to beg her to give it all up.

"Would you like some water?" she asked.

"Please."

"Make yourself comfortable." She waved to the living room, then disappeared into the kitchen and turned on the faucet.

I paced in front of the couch, unable to sit. The flight to Oregon had been brutal enough, trapped in a seat, itching to get out. Not even a fifteen-hour flight to Australia had felt so long.

Clara had been texting me all afternoon. My phone buzzed in my pocket, but I ignored it. I hadn't told her where I was going when I'd rushed out of the office. We'd been in the middle of a weekly planning meeting when Aria had called. Clara didn't take many personal calls during our workday unless they came from August's school or her sister.

When Clara had handed me the phone, I'd thought Aria had finally decided to tell me what a prick I was for leaving after our night together. I'd been expecting it for months. I'd deserved it for months.

But pregnant? No. We'd used condoms. Multiple condoms.

I'd replayed our night together for two months. Never had it occurred to me that one of them had failed. Never. Or maybe I'd been too wrapped up in the woman to notice.

"Here." Aria came toward me, thrusting a glass of water in my hand.

I took it and gulped it to the bottom. "Thanks."

She sat down on the couch, her shoulders curling inward. "We used condoms."

"I was just thinking the same thing." I sighed, taking the chair across from her. "I didn't know that one had broken."

"This is a lot."

"Yeah."

"Not what you expected from a one-night stand, huh?"

I'd had one-night stands. My night with Aria didn't even come close to hitting that bucket. "Sorry. For leaving after the wedding."

"Why are you sorry? It was just a hookup."

Was it? Because it sure as hell didn't feel like a hookup. Definitely not with a baby on the way.

I'd been a coward for leaving without a word. She'd be right to call me on it. But I'd been scared. No woman in my life, not even Heather, had affected me like Aria. One night with her and I'd wanted more.

But this was not the time for a romantic entanglement. Certainly not a long-distance relationship. The company needed my focus if I was going to keep Grandmother from sinking the ship.

So I'd hopped on a plane the morning after Aria had snuck out of my bed—I'd woken up pissed that she'd already left—and flown back to Vegas, where I'd spent two weeks living in a hotel and working from dawn to dusk.

"Why did you come all the way here?" she asked.

"I own a plane. And I just . . . I couldn't stay in Arizona. I couldn't do this over the phone."

She tensed, studying my face. "I'm keeping this baby."

"Did you think I'd come here and ask you to have an abortion?"

"Yes."

I flinched. She might as well have slapped me. "I would never do that."

"I don't know you, Brody." Aria's voice gentled. "Not really. I just don't know what to expect from you. But I don't want to fight. I don't have the

458

energy for it. So please don't take offense. I honestly don't know why you're here."

That was the thing with Aria, the reason her company was so refreshing. She didn't want anything from me. She didn't care about my money. She didn't care about my business. She was simply honest. Sometimes, brutally so.

Honesty, I could deliver.

"I'm here because I want to be involved. With this—our, my—baby. I won't forsake my child."

Aria blinked, her eyebrows coming together. "Seriously?"

"Is that so hard to believe?" Did she really think I was such a cold monster? Probably. And I couldn't blame her for it.

"I don't know what to believe," she whispered.

"Believe that I see how hard Clara works to raise August on her own. Believe that I don't want my child growing up without me in his or her life. Please . . . don't shut me out from this."

Now it was her turn to flinch. An expression of sheer annoyance, distinctly Aria, added fire to those tired eyes. "I would never do that."

The tension eased from my shoulders. "On the way here, I had some time to think."

"I can already tell I'm not going to like this."

A grin tugged at my mouth. "Hear me out."

She leaned back, sagging into the couch. She yawned and covered it up with her hand. "I'm listening."

"You live in Oregon."

"I do?"

"Smart-ass," I muttered. "I live in Arizona. Traveling back and forth isn't going to work, for either of us. And I am guessing that you won't want to be away from the baby for extended stretches of time."

"No. I won't."

"Then one of us has to move."

"You mean me." She sat straight, her spine stiffening. "My life is here, Brody. My work. My home. I'm not giving it all up to live in the *desert*."

The way she spat the last word made me pause. "What's wrong with the desert?"

"It's a desert."

It was too much like California.

Clara had once told me the reason she suspected Aria had run from Vegas to Oregon hadn't been the fake people or the city life, but because she'd wanted to get away from anything that reminded her of life at the junkyard in Temecula.

"You move here," she said.

"I can't." I held up my hand when she opened her mouth. "I can't in the next year."

"After that?"

"It's a possibility."

"Why a year?"

I stood from the chair and stripped off my suit coat. If we were going to get into this, we might as well get comfortable. "Are you sure you don't want dinner?"

"I could eat. How about pizza?"

Pizza. Not exactly something I ate much of. Ron normally prepared all my meals, tailoring them to my personal trainer's specifications. Ron did not make pizza. And pizza sounded fucking awesome. "That would be great."

She pulled out her phone, quickly placing an order for delivery. Then she tucked it away and gave me her attention as I resumed my seat.

"In less than a year, I'll be thirty-five. My family's company, Carmichael Communications, will become mine."

"It isn't now?"

"Only partly. At the moment, the majority of my shares are governed by a trust. My grandmother is the executor and acting owner. But the stipulations on my trust disappear on my birthday in November. Until then, I have to play her game. Otherwise she'll sell the company from under me. She'll sell it before *I* can sell it."

"Wait." Aria held up a finger. "She wants to sell your company. But you want to sell your company. Spell it out for me, Carmichael. I'm too tired to read between the lines."

"It's complicated." In a word. "Grandmother likes control. Maybe she's bluffing but maybe she's not. Selling the company is her threat. It's the reason she can demand I show up at a wedding."

"Ahh." Aria nodded. "She'd sell it out of spite."

"Exactly. And in doing so, almost every employee would lose their job."

"They wouldn't if *you* sold it?"

I shook my head. "Not if I find the right buyer. Carmichael Communications is a small player in the scope of telecommunications companies, but that doesn't mean we don't have some pull. If I sold or partnered with a larger company, we could turn it into something that might change the world."

There were innovative companies looking to acquire resources like the ones we had at Carmichael. Our research and development team had made some amazing tech in the area of satellite communications and internet capabilities.

"How does all of this require you live in Arizona?"

"We have a small R&D office in Welcome along with a data warehouse. I've moved my best employees out of Vegas to Arizona, where I can focus our efforts on the developments that position us for the big sale. If I leave Welcome, my grandmother will insist we shut the site down and move it all back to Vegas. I don't want her to know what we're doing. So far, I've managed to keep it quiet. It works because I'm there. She trusts that my incentives are to make the company flourish. After all, I'm inheriting it. That's why my grandfather set it up that way in the first place."

Aria frowned. "Complicated. I'm not a fan of your grandmother."

"You and me both. But I have to play nice. It's a game I can't lose."

460

"I don't play games."

No, she didn't. "My grandmother is the most tenacious woman you'll ever meet. Her greatest pleasure is control. Like I said, maybe she's bluffing. But there are hundreds of employees, including your sister, who can't take the chance that she's not."

Aria closed her eyes. "What a mess."

"You have no idea."

"And your brother? Is he part of the mess too?"

"He's never worked at Carmichael. Probably because he never got along with my grandfather."

"But you did?"

"In a way." My relationship with Grandfather hadn't been one of love and loyalty. He had been just as ruthless as Grandmother, probably why their marriage had lasted. He hadn't liked Alastair because my brother was lazy and entitled.

Aria blew out a long breath. "Arizona."

"I know it's a lot to ask." I leaned my elbows on my knees. I'd drop to them if need be. "Please. Consider it. I don't . . . I don't want my—our—child hating me because I wasn't there."

There hadn't been many times in my life when I'd needed a parent—I'd always been fairly self-sufficient and, after all, I'd had employees as my keepers. But there'd been a handful of times when I'd wanted a parent sitting in the auditorium, like my high school and college graduations. To this day, I resented them for their absence.

I refused to be that kind of father.

Aria's gaze softened. Maybe she'd heard the truth in my words. She'd realized it was a confession of the life I'd lived. And there was sympathy in her eyes because her parents hadn't been there either.

"Let me think about it," she said. "Let me see what kind of work I can find."

"You don't—"

She held up a hand. "I have to work."

"Then how about you run my flower shop?" The words spewed out before I could catch them. *Jesus, Brody.* What the hell was I thinking? The lie spun in front of my eyes, like a spider weaving a strand of silk, its legs moving faster and faster. The idea formed like a web, ready to trap Aria. For her own good.

"What flower shop?" Her eyebrows creased together.

"I just bought the local flower shop when the owners retired." Lie. "I often buy businesses in Welcome." That was true at least. If she talked to Clara, her sister would confirm it.

When a local store was getting ready to close or the owners retire, as long as the finances made sense, I bought it. Not only were they usually good investments, but it ensured my town, my safe haven, thrived.

I employed a business manager to oversee them all and gladly stayed silent. I owned three restaurants, two bars, an insurance agency, a salon and a gym.

And now Welcome Floral.

Not that the owners of Welcome Floral knew this. Hopefully they'd be willing to sell it to me on short notice for a ridiculous price. If they didn't go for it, well . . . I'd think of something. As long as I got Aria to Welcome, the rest didn't matter.

"A year. Give me a year," I begged. "After my birthday and after the baby is born, we can come up with a new plan."

"I won't have this baby for months. Seven of them, I think. I haven't been to the doctor yet. By the time that's over and we get through a maternity leave, that should be close to your birthday. Why move? Why not just wait?"

"Because I'd miss the pregnancy."

She blinked. "I didn't think men cared about that."

"*Devan* didn't care about that." I spat the name. "I'm nothing like Devan."

"I guess not."

"Think about it. That's all I ask. Consider it." *Please.*

She nodded. "Okay."

"Thanks," I breathed and stood, pulling on my jacket. "I'll leave you to it."

"What about pizza?"

"I'll get dinner at the hotel." My stomach was in too much of a knot to eat, even though pizza sounded delicious. But if I stayed, chances were Aria and I would find something to fight about. Best I get out and end this conversation on a good note.

"You're staying?"

"Aren't you going to Arizona tomorrow for Christmas?"

"That was the plan."

"Might as well cancel your flight. There's no point in flying commercial when I'm going to the same place."

She frowned, like she wanted to argue, but she'd been on my plane. It was nothing like flying commercial. "What time are we leaving?"

"I'll pick you up at ten."

"No, don't. I'll come to the hotel."

"All right." I walked for the door, but before I touched the knob, I stopped and turned. "I know this probably seems strange, the urgency. Why I want to be there. I didn't have a good father. And I vowed a long time ago not to make the same mistakes that he made."

"You don't have to explain it to me, Brody."

"Yes, I do."

"Okay," she whispered. "Good night."

"Good night." I took one last look at her face, memorizing the contours of her cheeks and the shape of her mouth.

Her image had dulled some, since the wedding. Now it was fresh. Mesmerizing.

Fuck, but I'd missed it.

Without another word, I left, making it halfway down the block when I saw the pizza delivery car zooming up the road. As I strode down the sidewalk, I pulled out my phone and called Clara.

"Did she kick you out yet?" she asked.

"Not yet."

"What are you doing, Brody? You're freaking out, aren't you?"

"Yes."

She sighed. "Give it time to sink in. You two will figure it out. Long-distance parenting isn't ideal, but it's not impossible."

Long-distance parenting was not an option. "I need a favor. It's going to require you hide some details from your sister."

"I don't hide things from my sister."

"Do you want her to live in Arizona?"

"Well . . . yes."

"Then that's the price."

She hesitated. In the background, a cartoon played on the TV. "Tell me."

"Tomorrow morning, I need you to buy Welcome Floral."

"What? It's not for sale."

"Everything is for sale." A truth I believed to the marrow. "Make the Backers an offer they can't refuse."

8

ARIA

"You're joking," Mark said. "Right?"

"I'm not."

"No." His face fell. "You can't leave."

In all the years I'd known him, I'd never seen such sorrow on his face. And disappointment. I'd come in today to give my notice as head groundskeeper at The Gallaway. Mark had been in his office and I'd asked Andy if he had a moment. Better to tell them both at the same time.

"But . . . why?" Andy asked, standing beside Mark's desk. He had one hand on the surface, holding tight like he was about to faint.

Telling them the truth, that I was pregnant, wasn't an option. Not only did that seem cruel to Andy, but considering it was still early, I wasn't sure if it was smart to make the announcement.

Plus they'd ask questions about the father I wasn't ready to answer.

"I want to live closer to my sister and nephew. He's getting older and I want to be a part of his life. Both their lives." It wasn't a lie. It was just one slice of the truth pie.

Mark blinked, staring at me like this was some sort of hoax.

"But . . ." Andy shook his head, like he was trying to rewind the last ten minutes.

"I'm so grateful," I told Mark. "You've given me the career of my dreams. Please know that I'm so very grateful. But I need to be closer to family. I'm lonely."

Understanding crossed his features. Mark had been single for as long as I'd known him. Aside from the occasional girlfriend, he lived a solitary life. But he had family in the area and he often spent time with his parents. He knew I was alone here and that I was desperately close to Clara.

"How long can you stay?" he asked.

"Two months?" That was six weeks longer than the standard notice, but I owed them a lot. And two months here would give me time to pack my condo.

Last night, Brody had asked me for a year. Only a year. But in my heart, I felt the goodbye. When I left Oregon, I wouldn't be moving back.

"Could we work out an arrangement?" Andy asked. "More time off so you can travel. Expand your staff so you're not so tied here during the season. Before you quit, let's brainstorm."

I sighed. It came as no surprise that Andy had the energy for a debate, but I was simply too tired. And nauseous. Last night's pizza was churning in my stomach. I wouldn't make it through brainstorming without puking in Mark's trash can.

Mark and I had been through a lot over the years. We'd grown to know one another as friends, not just boss and employee. But puking in the owner and CEO's trash can was crossing a line. I had minutes, not hours, before I'd need to hightail it to the bathroom.

Besides, after staying up most of the night considering Brody's proposal, any negotiation would be pointless.

I'd made my decision.

Mark must have seen the conviction on my face because he held up a hand to silence Andy. Then he gave me a sad smile. "Two months is very generous. We'll take it."

"Thank you." My shoulders slumped. So did Andy's. "For everything. Thank you."

"You'll always have a place here," he said. "If Arizona doesn't work out, come back to us."

"I appreciate that. I'll put together a transition plan and make sure the staff is trained. We're in good shape at the greenhouse."

"Don't worry about that this week." Mark waved it off. "Go to Arizona. Enjoy Christmas. We'll plan when you return."

He really was the world's best boss's boss. I was going to miss Mark. I was going to miss The Gallaway. This job had been an anchor, keeping me grounded while I'd grown from a young woman into an adult.

And now I was going to become a mother.

I was to become the anchor.

God, I hoped I had the strength.

"Merry Christmas," I told them both, then left them alone. I closed the door behind me, but not soon enough to miss Andy release a pained groan.

Poor guy.

I breathed deeply, something I hadn't done all morning. Then the shaking set in and reality hit. It was done. I'd quit my job.

The urge to cry came on so strong I struggled to blink the tears away as I walked down the hallway, making my way to the main floor. But there wasn't time to cry. Because I had to puke.

After a quick stop at the bathroom—at least I was getting used to the retching—I went to the lobby. Mark and Andy had been my first stop of the day. Brody was the second.

465

"Hey," I greeted the receptionist. "Could you ring a guest room for me?"

"Sure. What's the name?"

"Bro—" The call wasn't necessary. As I glanced over my shoulder, I spotted him in the lobby. "Oh. Never mind."

Brody stood in the center of the room, dressed in the same suit he'd worn last night, talking on the phone. He looked rumpled. His hair was damp and finger combed. His suit wasn't its usual crisp. Still, he was the most handsome man to ever grace these halls.

He'd come here without a bag, hadn't he? The cold robot who loved money had cared enough and been freaked out enough to hop on a plane without so much as a toothbrush. He'd come here on a spur-of-the-moment decision because our lives were now different. Entwined.

He'd rushed to my side and begged me not to cut him out of our kid's life.

Brody never stopped surprising me.

It was endearing, seeing him as human, knowing he wasn't abandoning me to single parenthood. His apology for the morning after the wedding had helped too.

Hovering beside the reception counter, I waited until he hung up the phone. He let his arm drop, the device in his grip, but he stared at it like he wanted to throw it on the floor and walk away forever.

Brody dragged a hand through his hair, tucked the phone into his pocket and turned. He took one step before his chin lifted and he spotted me. Then he froze.

"Hi." I waved and crossed the lobby.

"Hi. How are you?" Brody towered over me, seeming taller than ever today, even disheveled.

Was it strange that I wanted him to hold me?

"Nauseated. Tired. Soon to be unemployed."

He blinked. "Unemployed."

I nodded toward the hallway. "Walk with me."

Without a protest, he fell into step at my side as I led him through the hotel, stopping by the locker room for my coat, then out an employee exit. Then we hoofed it in the chilly weather to the greenhouse.

Like yesterday, it was empty, most of the staff on vacation for the upcoming holiday. The ones working were at the hotel. We strolled past the long tables and into the area with the seedlings I'd planted yesterday. Someone had watered them this morning.

I pulled out a wooden stool and shrugged off my coat. Then I gestured for Brody to sit in the other stool. "I thought about what you had to say."

"And you quit your job."

"I don't know what I'm doing," I confessed. "I'm winging it and picking the option that feels right. This, moving to Arizona, seems less scary than raising a baby here alone. And I'm tired of feeling lonely."

That was the second time I'd admitted it today. Now that the word *lonely* was out there, I was having a hard time hiding from it.

"I don't want this baby to be lonely," I said. "Family is important and living close to Clara and August has been something on my mind for a while now. I'd hoped to convince her to move here but . . . we'll try Arizona."

Brody's entire face changed. Gone was the fear and worry. Gone was the stoic, stony gaze. Everything melted. His eyes. The hold of those soft lips. His shoulders dropped from his ears. He almost looked . . . happy. He looked like the man who'd charmed me at a wedding.

"Thank you."

"I can't promise it's forever. But I can give you the year."

He took one of my hands in both of his, his palms warming my skin. He pressed it, my hand sandwiched between his, and he dropped his chin. "Thank you."

"What did you expect me to say?"

"No. I thought you'd say no."

"I almost did," I admitted. "Last night, I thought about what you said. And I thought about what I wanted. Arizona is not what I want."

I wanted to live here in my cozy condo. I wanted to keep my job at The Gallaway because it was dependable. I wanted to avoid turning my life upside down. But if I'd wanted all that, then I shouldn't have had sex with Brody.

If only he'd been resistible.

"But it's not about me. And it's not about you," I said, splaying my free hand over my belly. "It's about this baby. I don't want our child to feel torn between two worlds."

Brody had the right to be included in this baby's life. He was as much a part of this as I was.

"I promised my boss two months. I'd like to give them a chance for a smooth transition, and I need to pack up my life here."

Brody stared at me, my hand still tight between his. The shock on his face was much like Mark's. Apparently, I was surprising the men in my life today.

"Is that okay?"

He dropped my hand and, in a flash, those warm palms were on my face, pulling me off my stool. Brody's lips crushed mine, sending a zing down my spine. God, his lips were soft. The texture from his beard tickled my chin, and when his tongue darted out to lick the seam of my mouth, a whole new flutter rocked my stomach. This one the good kind.

A gasp escaped when he licked my lips again. His eyes opened.

And we stared at one another, our lips still locked. His hands still firm on my face.

As quickly as it happened, Brody must have realized what he'd done. He let me go and backed away, clearing his throat. "I, uh . . . Thank you."

Disappointment rolled over me in a wave, sending me back to my seat.

There was no reason to be upset, right? It was just a grateful kiss. Nothing romantic. The two of us would be lucky to survive parenthood together. A romantic relationship? Never. We really shouldn't be kissing.

"You're welcome. Maybe we shouldn't make a habit of kissing one another."

He chuckled. "Sorry. I was excited. But you're right. Let's think of this as business."

"Business." I truly hated that word. People tossed it out there as an excuse to be cold and impersonal. "This is not a business arrangement."

"Of course it is."

My mouth dropped. "Seriously?"

"You'll be running my new flower shop. That's business. I mean, it's not like we're friends."

My jaw dropped. "So you think of me like an employee?" Oh, hell. Maybe I'd quit The Gallaway too soon. Mark and Andy would hire me back, right?

Brody frowned. "You say that like being an employee of mine is a nightmare. I doubt your sister would agree."

"I am not your employee."

"I know that but—"

"No buts. We are equals, Brody. You're the father. I'm the mother. I don't need your goddamn flower shop. I can find another job. Any other job." My temperature began to rise and I slid off my stool, pacing beside the table.

"Aria, I'm just being pragmatic. Please don't take offense. I have a flower shop that needs a manager. You're qualified."

"Qualified. I'm qualified." My molars ground together. When had this become a job interview? "I won't work for you."

"Why not?"

"Because that makes this entire thing weird." I threw up my hands. Couldn't he imagine payday? *Here's your check, Aria. Thanks for your hard work. And thanks for growing my baby in your uterus.*

"If you don't like the term 'employee,' then fine. I'll deed the place over to you."

"A gift. You'd give me a flower shop." My hands dove into my hair. "Who does that?"

We weren't even friends. We'd slept together once and were having a kid. Normal people didn't gift flower shops.

He lifted a shoulder. "You're moving. Consider it a relocation present. And it's not like I can't afford it."

"There." I pointed to the arrogant jerk's face. "That, right there."

"What, right there?" He rubbed the tip of his nose, checking his fingers to see if there was something on them.

"That, right there, is the reason I hate you. You throw money around like it's meaningless. Don't try to buy me."

"I'm not trying to buy you." He frowned. "I'm trying to make this easy on you. On both of us. If you want the flower shop, it's yours."

"What if . . ." I snapped my fingers. "What if I bought it from you?"

"It's unnecessary."

"How much did you pay for it?"

His jaw ticked, the hold on his patience slipping. "Why does it matter?"

"How. Much?"

"One hundred and twenty-five thousand dollars."

Well, shit. I didn't have anywhere near that much in savings. But maybe I had enough for a down payment.

I held out my hand. "Deal."

"What deal?"

"The flower shop. I'll buy it from you. If you will accept monthly payments."

Brody shook his head. "That's not the point of this. I came here to ask you to move. I'm not going to put you in debt because of it."

"Then we'll make the monthly payments manageable." I wiggled the fingers of my outstretched hand, waiting for him to accept.

"Aria—"

"I won't budge on this. I won't be a charity case."

He sighed. "It's not charity."

"It feels like it to me."

Brody's mouth flattened because I'd just won. "I won't have the monthly payment become a burden. This cannot be something that causes you stress."

"Life is stressful."

"But it shouldn't be for you."

The gentleness in his voice tempered my anger. "Okay."

He took my hand in his, sealing the deal.

I'd bought a flower shop. *Oh my God.* I'd just bought a flower shop.

The dream. It was my dream. And my head was spinning so fast I wasn't sure if I should cry or laugh. It was too much, all of these changes were too much. I was in the middle of an ocean during a hurricane, and the seasickness was overwhelming.

If I looked too far into the future, the uncertainty would crumple me to my knees.

One day at a time. That's all I had in me at the moment. One moment. One step. One day at a time.

I was moving to Arizona. I was buying a flower shop. I was becoming a mother.

I'd tackle them each, starting with the first, but not today.

"Now what?" Brody asked, seeming as lost as I was.

I shrugged. "How about that ride to Arizona? I have some Christmas presents to deliver."

9

BRODY

"WHERE IS SHE?" I checked my phone for the tenth time.

"You're worse than August," Clara muttered.

Not quite. August was outside, bundled in a coat and hat for the cooler February weather, driving his child-size Jeep around the driveway. Circle after circle, his eyes were locked on the entry gate.

Mine were too.

We were both anxious for her to arrive.

I paced in front of the window. "This is fucking ridiculous."

"So you've said." Clara sat on the couch in my living room, her eyes locked on her phone. She'd been pinning recipes and baby outfits on Pinterest—I'd asked what had her so enraptured when she should be worrying about Aria.

Aria, the obstinate, exasperating woman who had refused to let me hire her a moving company. Aria, my pregnant—*friend? associate? acquaintance?* —someone, who had insisted on packing her own belongings and loading them into a U-Haul to drive from Oregon to Arizona.

Would she let me fly up to help her? No.

Would she let me hire someone to drive the truck so she could fly here on my jet? No.

Would she listen to reason that a pregnant woman should not be lifting boxes and hefting houseplants? No.

Aria hadn't even let her sister come to Oregon and help when Clara had offered.

There wasn't a more stubborn woman on planet Earth than Aria Saint-James. In the past two months, she'd pushed me to the brink of sanity.

"Never in my life have I met a person so inflexible as your sister."

Clara scoffed. "Then you need to look in the mirror."

"What?" I spun away from the glass. "I'm not inflexible."

That earned me an eye roll. "If it's not your way, then it's the wrong

470

way. Did you ever think that maybe Aria needed to do this herself? That she needed some time on the road to say goodbye to her old life? She loves surprises and spontaneity, but that doesn't mean she hasn't let her roots grow deep."

"If she needed time, I would have given her time. All I asked is that she not drive a rental truck from Heron Beach to Welcome by herself."

"We lived in a junkyard, Brody. We were fifteen. Alone. Broke. Aria's not scared of a two-day drive."

I opened my mouth to argue but clamped it shut. Maybe I didn't give Aria enough credit.

It was her beauty that made me forget about their childhood and all she'd endured. When she smiled and laughed, it was like she'd lived the happiest life in the world. Aria was strong, I knew that. So was Clara. Still . . . "I just want to help her. Make this easier."

I had the means to make her life simpler. She'd called it charity. Why couldn't she see it as generosity? What the fuck else was I supposed to spend my money on if not the woman who was carrying my child? How was offering to find her work and a home charity? I'd be an asshole if I let her fend for herself.

"You didn't tell her about the flower shop, right?" I asked.

"No," Clara said. "My answer hasn't changed since you asked me yesterday. And the day before that. And for all the days before that over the past two months."

I frowned. "I know you don't like to keep secrets from her."

"When she finds out, she'll be furious. At both of us."

"*If* she finds out."

Clara laughed. "You don't know Aria very well. I promised you I wouldn't tell her but that doesn't mean she won't find out. She has a way of sniffing out secrets."

"She can't find out." The contract had a nondisclosure clause in place to ensure my secret was safe. And the previous owners were in Hawaii. Gone for good, so the chances of it slipping were slim to none.

Welcome Floral hadn't cost me one hundred and twenty-five thousand dollars like I'd told Aria. No, the flower shop had cost me four hundred and eighty thousand dollars. Nearly half a million.

I had to hand it to the previous owners, the ruthless bastards. Ned and Stephanie Backer had smelled my desperation and pounced like lions on a wounded gazelle. But my payment had meant they could retire in Hawaii, far from Aria's prying ears.

It would take Aria a lifetime to pay for the floral shop at the Backers' price tag. Hell, even with the *discount* price I'd quoted her it would be a lot. I'd seen the financial statements from the flower shop and Aria had some work to do if she wanted to turn a larger monthly profit.

But it was a solid business. She'd own the building downtown, and I hoped that after a year in Welcome, she'd realize my small town wasn't without its charms.

I'd meant what I'd told her. After my birthday, I'd consider moving.

But I also liked it here in Arizona. I loved this lifeless house. It was safe. Comfortable. Ron had his bungalow on the property. Clara had her house. One day, I wanted to see my child outside playing in the driveway.

If Aria insisted on moving, I'd move. But I had nearly a year to get those roots of hers to sink into the desert sand.

I checked my watch again, wondering for the thousandth time where she was. Aria had promised to be here no later than two, so where the hell was she? It was two thirty, and if she didn't get here within the next fifteen minutes, I was going out to search.

The text message I'd sent her had gone unanswered.

Aria and I hadn't spoken much over the past two months. Most of our communication either went through Clara or was via text. How we were going to live together was a mystery.

It was the one thing about this move — other than the destination — Aria had conceded without a fight. She was moving into my house.

Clara had offered her guest room but Aria had told me during a rare phone conversation that she didn't want to invade her sister's life. When I'd offered her my place, a stone's throw from Clara and August plus more space than she'd find in a local rental, she'd shocked me by agreeing.

It would be the first time I'd lived with a woman. Not even Heather had occupied my space. I'd never invited her to move in. The weekends when she'd slept over had been bad enough. Makeup all over the bathroom counter. Clothes strewn on the floor for the housekeeper to pick up. Yes, I paid my staff to do that very thing, but for fuck's sake, the laundry basket had been twenty feet away in the closet.

Thankfully this house was much larger than my Vegas penthouse, and I wouldn't be sharing a bed. Aria would occupy one end of the house with me in the opposite. If she was sloppy or loud, I'd be too far away to notice.

"I'm going to wait outside," Clara said. "Your pacing is making me nervous."

Was I pacing? I stopped midstride. "Fifteen minutes and I'm going to go look for her."

Clara shook her head. "I'm going to give you some unsolicited advice about Aria."

"Okay," I drawled. For the most part, other than playing messenger for logistical details, Clara had stayed far away from the mess that was Aria and me. Though I wasn't foolish enough to think that if push came to shove, she'd choose me over her sister.

But when we spoke of Aria, Clara maintained a neutral stance. She relayed facts. She let me rant without much commentary. And she didn't offer more than a shred of insight into the mysterious woman who had consumed my waking thoughts. Until now.

"Aria needs control in her life. After Mom and Dad died, she became the sister in charge. I didn't . . . She didn't fall apart. I did."

My heart twisted as I stood frozen, watching her struggle with whatever she was going to say. Clara didn't speak much about that time. Or about her time in the junkyard. She'd told me the big picture, but any details had been glossed over. Clara had told me facts. Dates. Nothing more.

And the cold asshole that I was, I had never asked how she'd actually felt.

Now, with Aria coming here, I wanted to know. To truly know what their youth had been like. We were a family of sorts, tied together by this unexpected baby.

"It was Aria's idea to run away from our uncle's home."

"Why?" What had happened with her uncle that had been so terrible that a desolate life in a junkyard had been the better option? "What happened?"

Something crossed Clara's gaze, a sadness deeper than anything I'd ever seen before. "You'll have to ask Aria."

I frowned. "If you won't tell me, she certainly won't."

"Give it time." She gave me a watery smile. "Don't take her freedom, Brody. Don't take her control."

"I'm trying to help."

"No, you're keeping *your* control. You need to find a way where you can both have it."

"Share," I grumbled. I'd hated the word *share* since kindergarten.

"Yes." She laughed. "You have to share."

I turned my back to her, facing the glass. When she walked outside to join her son, I resumed my pacing. It was the only way to keep my vibrating nerves from shaking my bones loose. This restless energy had plagued me since Aria had told me she was pregnant. I'd paced a lot since.

I was becoming a father.

Christ. What had I gotten myself into? It would be easy to blame it on the champagne. I didn't drink often, certainly not like I had at the wedding. But it hadn't been a drunken haze. It had been Aria.

Sitting on my counter in that stunning green dress, her feet bare, she'd rendered me helpless. One kiss and I'd been lost.

Lost in her mouth, her hands, her taste. Four months later and I couldn't get that night out of my head. Her body, sleek and tight, had been a dream. Moving inside her, hovering above her, had been the best sex of my life.

"Don't," I told myself. It had been a constant reminder over the past couple months.

Sex could not, would not, enter into this arrangement. Aria and I had a tumultuous relationship at best. Somehow, we had to forge a truce. A friendship would be ideal, but I'd settle for civility.

I just wanted my kid to know me. That was it. Simple. I didn't need love and adoration. I just wanted knowledge.

Liar. I couldn't even fool myself.

I wanted love. I wanted my son or daughter to think I was the best man in the world. There was no way I'd pull it off. But that wouldn't stop me from trying. How was I supposed to be a good father? There hadn't been a kind and gentle male influence in my life. What did I know about raising a child?

I breathed and swallowed the fears. The insecurities would attack later. Probably for the rest of my life.

Down the driveway, something flickered. I stood straighter, leaning closer to the glass as a white and orange truck emerged. My heart leapt into my throat as I rushed from the window, jogging for the front door. I flung it open and hurried outside, joining Clara in the driveway. August was racing down the concrete, his arms waving as he screeched, "Aunt Aria!"

She honked, the noise more of a muted bark than a blare. Her smile beamed from behind the wheel as she eased the truck to a stop with an ear-splitting squeal of its brakes.

"*That* is the truck she rented?"

"Shut it." Clara elbowed me in the ribs, then rushed for the driver's side door as Aria shoved it open.

Her feet had barely hit the ground before Clara had her in a hug. The two of them held on to one another as August crashed into their sides.

And I stood back, watching.

I wanted to be in that hug. I wanted to be included. Where had that longing come from? It niggled but I shoved it away. When had I turned into such a damn sap? Carmichaels didn't hug.

Aria let Clara go and turned my way. "Hi."

"Hi." I cleared my throat. "You're late."

The woman had the gall to laugh. Then she slammed the door shut on the U-Haul and moseyed my way. Her dark hair was lighter than it had been at Christmas. She'd added streaks of a dark blond that highlighted the flecks of gold in her eyes. The dark circles under her eyes were gone. The rosy color in her cheeks matched the pink pout of her mouth.

A surge of lust shot straight to my groin. *Fuck.* This was not the time.

"Be grumpy later," she said, patting my stomach as she marched past me for the house. "We have work to do."

Clara pulled in her lips to hide a smile as she passed me, following her sister.

I looked to the blue sky and dragged in a deep breath. If they knew why I was *grumpy*, they'd have an entirely different reaction. Getting a grip on this attraction to Aria was taking more effort than I'd expected.

August raced past me, following his mother and aunt. "Come on, Brody!"

"Coming," I muttered, taking a moment with my back turned to adjust my swelling cock. Then I turned and met them in the house.

Aria was looking around, surveying the space. "It's bigger than I remember."

"Are you feeling okay?"

She dropped her gaze and smiled. "I'm good. Much better. The morning sickness has pretty much disappeared now."

"Good. Can I get you some water or juice or—"

"Here you are, sir." Ron appeared, carrying a tray from the kitchen filled with glasses of ice and sparkling water, each with a lemon wedge on the rim.

"Thank you, Ron." I took a glass, then handed one to both Aria and Clara. August received a juice box.

"Cheers." Clara raised her glass. "To a new adventure."

"Cheers." Aria clinked glasses with her sister, then with mine before taking a long drink. If she felt uncomfortable about being here, it didn't show. This was the woman who'd waltzed into a wedding full of strangers and held her chin high the entire time.

"The crew will be here in fifteen minutes," Ron said.

"Excellent. I—"

"Crew. What crew?" Aria asked.

"The crew to unpack."

"Oh, we don't need a crew. I don't have much. You can just cancel them."

"But—" One pointed look from Clara and I cut myself off. Control. Aria needed control. It went against my nature, but I could let this one go. "All right. Cancel them, Ron."

"Yes, sir." He tucked his now-empty tray under an arm and disappeared.

"Let me show you around." I gestured for them to follow me deeper into the house, toward the wing that would become Aria's. "I don't spend much time in these rooms. I stick to my office, bedroom and the gym, so I won't bother you. You've got complete run of the place. Please make this your home."

"I don't need much space."

She'd have it regardless.

We walked down a hallway that led toward the back of the house. Windows made up the exterior walls, as they did in the entire place. She'd have a view of the desert property that surrounded us on all sides.

This side of the house had five bedrooms. There was an office for her on the second floor as well as a sitting room with a fireplace. I escorted her to the largest bedroom first, opening the door to the room. Along one wall was a king-sized bed with a white canopy and ivory quilt. I'd had the gossamer draping added just last week.

The walls, once midnight blue, had been repainted a soft cream. The hardwood floors had been refinished and restained from the pale gray she'd objected to the night of the wedding. Their honey-colored grains emitted a warm glow in the space. The fawn and mushroom area rug beneath the bed was so plush that even I'd tried it beneath my bare feet— then I'd ordered one for my own bedroom.

At Christmas, we hadn't broached the topic of where she'd live. That vacation had been awkward at best. Aria and Clara had invited me over for Christmas dinner, and the moment the meal had finished, I'd retreated to my office. The evening had been pleasant, but Aria had left me unsettled.

Her stare from across the table had been unnerving, like she'd seen my fears about the pregnancy.

Like she'd seen the restraint it had taken to keep from touching her shiny hair and caressing her pretty skin.

Insecurity wasn't in the Carmichael gene pool. At least, I hadn't thought so until Aria and this baby had proved me wrong.

After Christmas, she'd returned to Oregon and I'd hired a designer to rework the bedrooms. They now had the light, bright and airy feel that I'd seen in her condo. The only things missing were the plants.

No doubt those were in the U-Haul.

"Um . . . this is not what I expected." Aria blinked, her eyes wide as she stepped into the space. She had her own walk-in closet. An en suite bathroom. And a pair of french doors that opened to the pool outside.

"Brody had it redesigned," Clara announced.

Aria looked all around the room, her eyes landing on me. "You didn't have to do this."

"It was no trouble. I want you to be comfortable. If you don't like it, we can—"

"I love it." She smiled, and if I'd thought the room was bright before, I'd been entirely mistaken. Her smile was luminescent.

A flutter rippled through my chest, odd and unfamiliar. Must be heartburn. "If you need anything at all, there's a call system in each room that rings directly to Ron."

"I'm fairly self-sufficient," she said.

"Just in case." I nodded toward the door. "Let me show you the rest, then we'll get the truck unloaded."

The tour took another twenty minutes. We didn't linger in the other bedrooms, one of which I'd earmarked for a nursery. Aria had instantly agreed since it was adjacent to hers. She'd taken one look at the gym and told me she wouldn't be spending much time there. Then she claimed the theater room as her own.

"I'll get changed," I said. "Meet you outside."

Aria and Clara were too busy picking out lounge chairs in front of the massive projector screen to notice when I disappeared to the opposite end of the house to change out of the navy slacks and starched white shirt I'd pulled on this morning.

When I went outside to find them, Clara met me on the sidewalk carrying a box. August trailed behind her, his arms wrapped tightly around a potted fern twice the size of his face.

Aria was in the back of the U-Haul, loosening a strap she'd used to secure boxes.

"This is it?" I counted twenty, maybe thirty boxes in total. They were all stacked to one side while the rest of the floor had plants. "What about furniture?"

"I made an agreement with my landlord to leave it furnished for a free month's rent." She shrugged, rolling the strap into a coil. "I didn't think there'd be much point trying to load up furniture myself and haul it down here when I assumed you had everything here already."

"That's why you refused a moving company."

She grinned, walking to the end of the box, towering over me. "The heaviest thing in here is a box of books. Those are marked and waiting just for you."

"Here." I held out my hands to help her down.

She grabbed them, jumping to the ground. Then she cocked her head to the side, looking me up and down.

"What?"

"You're in jeans."

I dropped my gaze to my dark-wash jeans and simple white thermal. "What's wrong with them?"

"Nothing." Her eyes twinkled. "I've just never seen you in anything but a suit."

"You've seen me naked."

"This is true." Her cheeks flushed and she pulled her bottom lip between her teeth.

Why the hell had I brought up being naked? Now all I could picture was her flawless skin when I'd stripped her of that green gown.

Aria had perfect skin, smooth and supple. It had been like silk against my palms. Her hair had threaded through my fingers like strands of the finest satin.

I raised a hand, ready to tuck a lock of hair behind her ear, then realized I'd almost touched her and froze.

Her gaze darted to my hand, stuck in midair.

An impulse. When it came to Aria, I seemed to have them constantly, like that kiss at the greenhouse. I'd never in my life kissed a woman so blindly. It hadn't been sexual or foreplay. She'd made me so happy that I'd just . . . kissed her.

Maybe I'd kiss her again. The idea should have scared the hell out of me, enough to have me racing into the house and telling Ron he had book box duty. Instead, I inched closer.

Aria's chin lifted so she could keep my gaze.

And the stray lock of hair was mine. One sweep around the shell of her ear and Aria's breath hitched.

"Aunt Aria! I'm ready for another plant!"

She jerked.

I stepped away as August rounded the corner of the truck, his arms outstretched.

"Great. Good job." She smiled at him and kept her gaze anywhere other than me. Then she found the smallest pot she could within reach and loaded it into her nephew's grip.

I ran a hand over my beard and willed my body to cool. *Get it together, Brody.* What was wrong with me today?

Aria was off-limits. A hard no. Why couldn't I seem to grasp that concept? Maybe because I didn't like the word *no*, even when I issued it myself.

I put my head down and went to work unloading the truck. The sooner I got away from Aria, the better. She'd be busy unpacking today, and I could get some space. Yes, she was beautiful. Yes, she smelled like a dream.

But she was carrying my child.

That was where this relationship had to end.

It only took an hour to empty the moving truck. While Aria, Clara and August went to return it to the local drop-off, I locked myself in my office, where I spent the remainder of the afternoon and evening.

This was the only way it would work. Aria had her half of the house. I had mine. Not wanting to risk an encounter, I had Ron deliver dinner to my desk. Not that it mattered. He informed me that Aria had gone to Clara's.

When night fell and darkness came, I finally ventured out of my office at close to midnight for some fresh air. I went to the kitchen for a glass of water, then slipped outside. The light from Aria's bedroom was off. The blue glow from the pool lit up the patio.

I padded, barefoot, to one of the chairs, hoping to spend a quiet moment looking at the stars. But that plan went to hell with a splash of water.

"Do you always work so late on a Saturday?" Aria was seated at the edge of the pool. She'd rolled up her own jeans to her knees. Her feet and calves dangled in the warm water.

"I didn't see you."

"Obviously." She laughed. "Are you done avoiding me?"

"I wasn't—" *Shit.* "Yes."

She patted the concrete space at her side. "I won't bite."

I opened my mouth to correct her, because she most definitely did bite. I'd had the mark to prove it for two days after the wedding. But I caught myself and blocked out all memories of that night.

"Brody. Sit down."

I unglued my feet and crossed to the pool, bending to cuff my own jeans before putting my feet in the water beside hers.

Aria kicked her legs and wiggled her toes, then leaned back, using her arms as a brace, as she looked up at the sky.

Diamonds studded the endless night. The white haze of the Milky Way threaded through the stars' glowing beams.

"I used to climb on top of the delivery van at the junkyard and look up at the stars. It's better than TV, don't you think?"

"Yes, I do." I leaned back too, taking my first deep breath. "What kind of delivery van?"

"It wasn't entirely different than the one I drove down here, though the one at the junkyard hadn't worked in years. It had gotten into an accident. The front end was all smashed and crumpled. But the box had a fairly solid floor. There were a few jagged tears and holes from the accident, but we found some plastic to cover them up. It let the sunshine in and kept the rain out. And the rodents."

I grimaced. It physically pained me to think of Aria and Clara living with mice and rats. When I'd been fifteen, I'd lived at a private school in New Hampshire. My biggest fear hadn't been vermin or scrounging up enough money to buy a loaf of bread. I'd concerned myself with more trivial matters, like teenaged girls and acne.

"I don't like that you had to go through that."

"Me neither," she admitted. "But it wasn't that bad. I learned how to grow plants there. Clara made us these little bedrolls and shelves out of yellowed and torn books she bought for a dime at the thrift store. It became home."

And now my home was her home. "Thank you, Aria."

"You keep saying that."

"Because it deserves to be said more than once."

"You're welcome." She pressed a hand to her belly. The gray sweater she was wearing was loose and had been draped over her midsection earlier. But now that she was leaning back, I could see the faintest swell to her belly.

That was my baby in there. Mine.

"Think we'll survive this?" she asked. "Living together. Having a baby."

I took in her profile, studying the tip of her nose and the pout of her lips. Yeah, we'd survive it. If I could find a way to keep from screwing it up. Namely, by dragging her back to my bed.

Survive it?

"I hope so."

10

ARIA

WELCOME FLORAL.

The letters etched in gold on the door's glass panel smiled at me as Brody twisted the key in the lock and we stepped inside. Above our heads, a bronze bell shaped like a lily of the valley bloom dinged.

"First impression?" Brody asked quietly.

"Not bad, Carmichael. Not bad."

The air, infused with a clean floral fragrance, wrapped me in a warm hug as the door closed behind us. The humid air plumped my dry skin. The greenery and bright colors were like taking in a long-lost friend.

I'd bought this place.

Welcome Floral.

This was mine. Or would be one day after a string of payments to Brody.

"You really like it?" he asked at my side. There was a wary look on his face, like he was scared I'd hate it and call this entire thing off.

But I wasn't a quitter.

And Welcome Floral was my dream come true.

"It's charming."

The garden gnomes beside a large potted hosta had smiles and pink cheeks. One winked at me. Another showed me his butt cheeks. The glass display case was filled with arrangements and bouquets. I preferred clean, tight bundles to wild sprays and billowing greens, but while they weren't exactly my style, they were tasteful and bright and balanced.

An old window with foggy glass panes and a chipped frame hung above the display table to my right. A rusty bicycle dangled above the table to my left. Tin cans surrounded table legs. An antique chair held a bouquet of peach roses. The walkways were narrow and curved, forming a maze through the shop.

Shabby chic. That was the only way to describe the eclectic style. It was cute. Maybe a little cluttered, but as I'd told Brody, charming.

He checked his watch. "Marty should be here any minute."

"Okay." My nerves spiked.

Marty was the manager here. He'd worked for the previous owners for years, and during the negotiations, they'd asked Brody to keep him on.

"This is your business," he reminded me for the third time today. "You can do whatever you want."

Meaning I was free to let Marty go if we didn't get along.

But I wanted us to get along. I'd need an experienced manager when this baby came. And from what Brody had told me, Marty was not only experienced, he was affordable. This meeting had to go well.

I hummed and walked away, letting those words sink in as I touched the tip of an Easter lily.

This was my business.

My business.

My training was geared toward landscaping and growing stock in a greenhouse. In Oregon. Now I was the owner of a floral shop in a desert. Clueless was the word that popped into mind.

My business needed a Marty.

I needed an ally.

Because so far, my few interactions with Brody had been . . . strained.

Even after our conversation by the pool, Brody had avoided me most of the day yesterday. I'd had plenty to keep busy. All of the boxes I'd brought from Oregon had been unpacked. I'd spent a nice chunk of time with Clara and August. The only time I'd seen him had been at dinner.

Brody had been seated alone at the dining room table, his meal before him, his attention on his phone. We'd exchanged a glance. I'd smiled. He'd nodded and asked me how I was feeling. Then I'd retreated to my room to sleep.

This morning I'd woken up at five. With nothing to do and my anxiety about today's visit to the shop going at full steam, I wandered around the house, trying to rid myself of nervous energy while getting oriented with the different hallways and rooms.

The noise of leather smacking leather and a few sharp breaths had stopped my feet. I'd entered Brody's part of the house. He'd been in his home gym, a space twice as large as my Oregon condo.

He'd been at a punching bag, beating the hell out of the swinging cylinder, wearing only a pair of shorts. His back and shoulders had glistened with sweat. His tennis-shoe-clad feet had skipped, light and fast like grasshoppers, over the red cushioned mat.

I'd stayed at the doorway, watching him until he'd finally dropped his gloved hands. Before he could catch me spying, I'd ducked out of sight. But not before catching a glimpse of those washboard abs in the wall of mirrors.

The man's body was a work of art. Chiseled and powerful. Graceful

481

and strong. Brody was incredible in a suit. Truly mouthwatering. But this morning, barely clothed, I'd nearly orgasmed from the sight alone.

Pregnancy hormones were going to be a bitch.

An hour later, he'd found me in the kitchen, eating at the island. Ron, who doubled as butler and chef, had cooked me a feast. Spinach and egg white omelet. Fruit and yogurt parfait. Fresh squeezed orange juice and a homemade bran muffin.

Brody had shown up—protein shake in hand—with a set of keys and a folder full of codes and passwords. The garage, the internet, the security system. After giving me the rundown, he'd disappeared.

An hour ago, he'd summoned me to his office via text, where he'd had the official buy-sell agreement for the floral shop waiting. Clara had been there, smiling on, as I'd signed on the bottom line.

Then she'd stayed home to wait for August to get done with school for the day, while Brody had brought me here.

Welcome Floral was closed on Mondays, something I'd be changing soon enough. But today, I was glad for it. I didn't need a customer coming in during my initial meet and greet with Marty.

The door chimed behind us, and a man in his fifties with a bald head and tortoiseshell glasses perched on his freckled nose walked inside. His green, short-sleeved button-down was undone nearly to his sternum. Whatever hair he lacked on his head he made up for with curly grays peeking out from above his heart.

"Marty." Brody extended his hand. "Good afternoon."

"Afternoon." Marty's gaze traveled my way. He looked me up and down, taking in my black skinny jeans and white Adidas shoes.

The pants I couldn't button anymore, but I'd secured the button to its hole with an elastic hair tie. My flowy white tee was covered with a thick cream cardigan because Welcome was cold today. To my delight, my winter wardrobe, sans snow boots, wouldn't be completely pointless in Arizona.

"Hi." I crossed the space for the door, my hand outstretched for Marty. "I'm Aria Saint-James."

"Marty Mathers." He shook my hand, then straightened his shoulders. "I've worked here for seven years. I specialize in floral design, but I also take care of the ordering. I'm willing to do delivery if necessary, though there's a young lady who's been doing it for the past year and she'd like to keep her job. So would I."

"This isn't an interview." I gave Marty my warmest smile. "Well, maybe it is. I guess I assumed today you'd interview me and decide if you wanted to stick around and help me get my feet wet."

Marty blinked. "Oh."

Time would tell if Marty was the right fit for my long-term vision. But I'd be stupid to let him go. If the previous owners had trusted him and he'd run this place for Brody since the business had shifted hands, that was good enough for me.

"I'd like that," Marty said, relief washing over his face.

482

"Good."

"Water?" He pointed toward the far wall. "My throat is a little dry."

"Please and thank you."

He smiled, revealing a little gap between his front teeth, then he moved past me and disappeared into the shop.

"Phew." I blew out a long breath and pressed a hand to my heart. "That went okay."

"Marty's a good guy. At least, that's what my business manager said. She's been working with him, checking in and such, during the transition. Marty pretty much does it all around here. I think you two will get along."

"I hope so."

"I'll leave you two to get acquainted," Brody said, taking his phone from his pocket. "I'll be in the car. Take your time."

"Thanks." I nodded as he walked out the door, giving his backside a thorough inspection.

Broad shoulders. Long, powerful legs. His suit jacket covered his ass. *Damn.* But at least I had this morning's mental image to call up and appreciate.

"He's something, isn't he?"

I jumped at Marty's voice. While I'd been ogling Brody, he'd returned with two mugs. Both brimmed with water. "Pardon?"

"Here." Marty handed me my cup. It was white and hand painted with small, bright flowers. I'd noticed the same on a display table, each selling for fifteen dollars. "He's something. Brody."

"Oh." *Busted.* "He's . . . handsome enough."

"You were undressing him with your eyes, my darling. I get it." Marty laughed. "My husband and I both have him on our cheat list."

"You have a cheat list?"

"Of course. Why would you not have a cheat list? We know Brody's straight but my mother always said I had a penchant for grand delusions."

I giggled. "Good to know."

"Now come on back to the table so we can sit down. Then you're going to tell me all about yourself, Aria Saint-James."

"I'd like that."

Two hours later, I walked out of the floral shop with a beaming smile.

The moment he spotted me, Brody hopped out of his car and rounded the hood, meeting me at the passenger door. "How'd it go?"

"Great." I was so happy I could cry. "I love Marty."

Time had flown talking to him. Hilarious and honest and dedicated to the shop and our customers, Marty was exactly the kind of person I needed by my side. When I'd told him I was pregnant, he'd immediately assured me I could count on him to run the shop during my maternity leave. Then he'd listened intently and followed me around the shop as I'd rambled ideas.

"And the shop?" Brody asked. "Do you like it?"

"I must be insane. I bought a flower shop without ever setting foot inside."

"We can rip up the paperwork."

I shook my head. "It's perfect. I want to put my own mark on it. Change the style a bit. But I want it."

"Then it's yours." He opened the car door for me, something he'd done earlier today when we'd left the house.

"You wouldn't open the door for me before the wedding, when I was in death heels, but now that I'm in tennis shoes, you do."

"Forgive me." He feigned a dramatic bow as I took my seat. "I hadn't appreciated the precious cargo."

My cheeks flushed as he shut the door and walked to the driver's seat, getting behind the wheel. He'd been teasing too, but the comment still tasted sweet.

"You didn't need to drive me. I could have come down myself."

"In what car?" Brody asked, driving us through downtown Welcome.

"The Cadillac." It was currently parked in Clara's garage, collecting dust.

As much as she loved the idea of the handoffs, she'd stalled planning her trip to California. I hadn't asked her why. I didn't need to.

Returning to California would bring back a barrage of emotions, and she was psyching herself up for it.

"Tomorrow you'll be on your own," Brody said. "Today, I wanted to come along and make the introductions."

"Thank you." It had been nice to have him at my side, to not do this alone. And though we were still adjusting to sharing a roof, I wouldn't have wanted anyone else at my side, not even Clara. Brody's confidence was contagious, and it had given me that extra boost to dive in. "I think this is a record, Carmichael. We've managed to get along for nearly two days."

"Give it time. I'm sure you'll do something soon to piss me off."

I fought a smile. "Count on it."

Brody rolled down the road, taking every block deliberately, like he was giving me time to inspect each and every storefront.

The coffee shop three doors down from Welcome Floral had green metal tables on the sidewalk and a chalk sandwich board that boasted the daily latte special. An attorney's office had silver letters stenciled on a large plate-glass window. Brian's Pub had an orange neon sign that glowed even in broad daylight.

The black streetlamps stood tall, hoisting their clear glass globes. The brick storefronts alternated in shades of classic burnt red and limestone cream. They reminded me of the desert rocks along Route 66, faded and worn but unique.

"It's real here," I said. "Every street."

"Refreshing, isn't it?"

"In Heron Beach, the local neighborhoods were real. You could count on your neighbor for more than just a cup of sugar. But everyone catered to the tourists. You wore a smile at all times. You put on your best show. I never minded because I genuinely enjoyed what I was doing. It's easy to smile when you like your job. But I always made sure to wash my hands

484

before going inside the hotel and clean dirt from my cuticles. I'd tuck in my T-shirt and wipe clean my shoes. I won't have to do that here."

"No. What matters here is who you are."

"Then why do you dress in a suit every day?" I shifted in my seat for a better view of his face. I'd always wanted to know why he dressed so impeccably, especially after seeing him in jeans on Saturday. The image of those long legs in denim was as fresh as the mental picture of him at the gym this morning.

They'd been nice jeans, more expensive than any pair I'd owned in my lifetime, but they'd fit Brody so perfectly. Loose, but not baggy. Fitted, but not tight. They'd showcased his strong thighs and narrow waist.

Unbuttoned, the man was irresistible. If he had leaned in the other night at the pool, I probably would have kissed him.

"I have a meeting with my grandmother," he said.

"Oh, is she here? Because if she is, I'm going to hide at Clara's."

Brody chuckled. "No, she's in Vegas. The meeting is virtual."

"Oh. Do you have meetings with her every day?" It wouldn't surprise me at all if Coreen required he be in a suit.

"Not daily, but often enough."

"But you still wear a suit every day."

"This is really bugging you, isn't it?" The corner of his mouth turned up. "My suits?"

Yes, it was. Because when it came to Brody Carmichael, my curiosity was piqued. "Humor me."

"It's something I started doing years ago. Any day that I'm working, I wear a suit. And I work every day. People expect a certain image from their leader."

"Not Clara. You don't need to dress up for her."

"Yes, I do. She deserves me at my best. All of my employees do. It was something my grandfather always did. He wore a suit every day. He showed up for his company every day."

"And you're showing up too." I took in his handsome profile and the strong cut of his jaw. "You wore jeans on Saturday."

"That was different."

"Why?" Because we were hauling boxes?

"Because that was for you."

One sentence. One answer.

And the world fell away from my feet.

Did he realize what he'd just confessed? Did he realize how special he'd just made me feel?

I was the exception to his rules.

One sentence, one answer, and we were back to that night. He was in a tux. I was in a green gown. And electricity sparked between us.

Brody's hands tightened on the wheel as he picked up speed, racing down the highway toward his house.

Maybe he hadn't meant to let it slip, but it was too late. It was out there, living and breathing and changing everything.

What did this mean? Did he want a relationship? Did I?

I'd been so absorbed in this pregnancy, I hadn't let myself consider my feelings for Brody. I hadn't realized until just this moment that there were even feelings there.

Feelings more than the obvious sexual attraction, because Brody was gorgeous, and I wasn't blind. I *liked* the man behind the suit. I *liked* the man who showed up for his people every day. I *liked* the man who let down his guard just for me.

God, this was so messed up. Any other guy and we'd date. Any other guy and we'd have sex and fun and see if this was the lasting sort of fling.

The baby changed everything.

My mind spun as fast as the Jaguar's wheels. When Brody slowed to open the gate and ease down the driveway, I still hadn't figured out what to say, probably because I didn't know him. I was walking on eggshells around Brody because he was practically a stranger.

And that was a problem we were going to fix.

"Would you make me a deal?" I asked.

"Depends on the deal." He kept his eyes focused on the road. His spine was ramrod straight. He'd shown me a hint of vulnerability and now he was erecting those walls.

"Have dinner with me. Every night."

"Why?"

"We should know each other. I'd like to know you, Brody."

He glanced over, and in those green eyes, I could so easily lose myself. Brody gave me a single nod, then returned his gaze to the road.

"Thank—" My mouth closed at the black SUV parked in front of the house. "Company?"

He shook his head and parked the car in the driveway.

Ron, who I was convinced had magical powers, appeared out of nowhere to open my door. "Miss Aria."

"Don't bow." I got out and shook my head. "Ron, if we're going to get along, you have to stop bowing like I'm Queen Elizabeth."

The corner of his mouth turned up. Then the wiseass bowed. "Very well, miss."

"You're as insufferable as that one." I hooked a thumb toward Brody.

Ron retrieved a set of keys from his pocket and took them to Brody. Then with a nod, he disappeared inside the house.

"Here." Brody walked over and took my hand in his, pressing the cold metal keys into my palm. "For you."

"For me what?" I jiggled the keys.

"The car. It's for you."

My jaw dropped. "You bought me a car. A BMW. Without asking me about it first."

"Yes. Is that a problem?"

And just like that, our two-day no-fighting streak came to an end.

11

BRODY

HER LAUGHTER GREETED me when the flower shop's door chime faded. I followed the musical sound toward the back of the shop, expecting to find her at the long wooden counter that held the cash register and a fresh bundle of blue hydrangeas. The only reason I knew they were hydrangeas was because of the little chalkboard sign beside it.

Hydrangeas $15/Bunch

There was a metal bell beside the mason jar of pens, and I tapped the plunger, then held my breath.

Marty came out first. The smile on his face dropped, something I'd never seen before because the guy always had a smile for me. "If you're not here to grovel, I'd head to the door before she sees you."

"I'm here to grovel."

"Good." He nodded. "Head on back."

"Thanks." I rounded the counter for the door, ducking into the workroom.

Aria's smile, like Marty's, dropped when she looked past the arrangement she was making. "Are you here to buy me a pony? An island? An island of ponies?"

"Not today."

She picked up a rose from the metal table and stabbed it into the vase she was filling. Her hair was braided over one shoulder with wisps loose around her ears. Her brown eyes sparkled—angry, but I did love their fire. Her cheeks held a pink flush.

Aria was more beautiful than any flower in the world. Even mad, she was lovelier than any rose.

This was the first time I'd seen her in three days, other than small glimpses of her coming and going from Clara's place or this shop. I took her in like a thirsty man standing before a clear mountain stream.

Three days. I'd finally cracked, said to hell with my pride and driven to the flower shop for just one drink.

Aria looked at ease and comfortable here. This was her domain. In just days, she'd made it her own. When I walked into a room, I could usually tell who was in charge. Last month, the shop had been run by Marty. Aria held the power now. And Christ, it was sexy as fuck.

She ignored me and kept working on the arrangement.

Plastic industrial buckets dotted the floor. Some had flowers. Most held discarded stems and leaves. The walls were lined with shelves, each crammed with empty vases in varying shapes and sizes. The long counter that ran the length of the room was littered with scissors and knives and twine and ribbon. Behind Aria, there was an opening to the cool room. The doorway didn't have an actual door, just strips of thick plastic that draped from the frame to the concrete floor.

It was as messy and unorganized as it had been when I'd come down to finalize the purchase with the Backers. We'd sat at that very table, Clara at my side, and signed papers for this shop.

An hour later, while they'd probably been planning their retirement in Hawaii, my lawyer had been busy drawing up a different set of papers. An agreement between Aria and me, one that would ensure she'd never know exactly how much I'd paid for this shop.

"What are you doing here?" She took the scissors in her hand and cut the stem of a rose. The snap rang through the workroom like a sharp bite.

"You've been avoiding me for three days."

"Tell me something I don't know."

I frowned. "I thought you wanted to have dinners together."

"Then you bought me a car without asking."

A car that had been in the exact same place since Monday. The Cadillac, red and gleaming, was what she'd been driving. It was currently parked diagonally on the street outside the shop beside my Jaguar.

Yesterday, I'd asked Clara what it would take to just buy the Cadillac. She'd informed me that their friend Londyn owned it and Londyn would never sell. *Not everything has a price, Brody.*

The car was a lot like Aria in that regard.

"I wanted you to have a vehicle. Something safe." The BMW I'd bought her came with one of the highest safety ratings available for SUVs.

"People don't just buy other people cars without asking."

"You're right. I should have asked." That way she could have picked the color and style.

"And?" She crossed her arms over her chest.

"And, what?"

Her nostrils flared. "You suck at apologies."

"I'm sorry." I meant it.

"And?"

"And . . . you can have a different car if you want."

Her mouth pursed in a thin line. "And you won't do it again."

"Oh."

"Yeah, oh," she mimicked. "No more buying me stuff."

"Define stuff."

"Anything with a price tag."

I frowned. "That seems extreme."

"You're an extreme sort of man. I trust you can figure this out."

For the sake of ending her cold war, I let it go. Would I stop buying her things? Absolutely not. Especially when the baby came. But for today, I'd change the subject.

I took the envelope from under my arm and set it on the table. "I wanted to bring this by."

"What is it?" She stood, walking closer to flip open the folder.

"It's the deed to the flower shop and the executed contract."

"Oh. Okay." She picked up the papers, running a hand over the first page. "This makes it official."

"It is official."

She stared at the page, not speaking, as a crease formed between her eyebrows.

"What's wrong?"

"I've never owned anything before. Nothing like this." The fear in her voice pierced my heart. "What if I screw it up?"

"You won't." I put a hand on her shoulder, nudging her to turn. When her eyes tipped up to meet mine, the worry in her gaze made it hard to breathe.

She shouldn't worry. She shouldn't have fears. Aria deserved an easy life. I'd make sure of it, if she'd just let me.

"I won't let you fall."

"You say that and it's sweet. But you don't get it."

"Get what?"

"I need to do this on my own."

"Understandable. Think of me as the safety net."

"I've never had a safety net."

"You do now."

Without thinking, I brushed a stray hair away from her temple. One touch and my heart galloped. Aria had said on Monday that she wanted to know me. I wanted to know her too, inside and out. Again and again.

Her eyes searched mine. Her breaths shortened.

It was her lips that drew me in. Before I could rationalize what I was doing, my mouth was on hers and my arms banded around her back.

She let out a small whimper, a mewl, as I dragged my tongue across her lower lip. Then her mouth opened, and I swept inside, savoring the heat of her mouth. Aria gripped the lapels of my jacket, clutching me as her tongue tangled with mine.

Fuck, but she tasted good. Sweet and warm like melted honey.

She molded to my body as I held her close, soaking her in. My pulse pounded and I slid my hands down, fitting my palms to the curve of her ass as I pulled her into my arousal.

Aria moaned, holding me closer, as I swallowed the sound down my throat.

The distant sound of a bell chimed. The front door. The flower shop.

Marty's voice carried to the back room as he greeted the customer. "Hello there. What can I help you with today?"

We snapped to reality and tore our lips apart. Aria blinked rapidly, clearing the fog. I ran a hand over my damp lips.

Then she was gone, stepping away and retreating to the other side of the table. She palmed her forehead, her eyes wide. "That was . . ."

"Sorry."

She waved it off. "It's fine."

Was it fine? Because it felt right. So fucking right. Like we should have been kissing all along. Every day.

"Aria." Marty poked his head around the corner. "Miss Julia from the diner is here. She was hoping to meet you."

"Okay." Aria put on a smile. "Be right there."

"I'll see you at home," I said after Marty disappeared.

Aria nodded, her eyes fixed on a rose. She didn't look up as I turned to leave. The color had drained from her face. Her hand rested on the swell of her belly. She looked . . . petrified.

Damn it.

What the actual fuck had I been thinking?

"Oh my God." Aria gasped as light flooded the kitchen. Her hand was pressed to her heart. "You scared me."

"Sorry," I said from my seat at the island.

"What are you doing?"

"You asked for dinner together."

"On Monday." She walked into the room, wrapping her arms around her middle. "That was three days ago. And it's nine o'clock."

I shrugged. The stool was hard and my ass had gone numb hours ago. As darkness had settled outside, I hadn't been able to bring myself to move.

"You didn't eat?"

"I was waiting." And thinking. And kicking myself in the ass for kissing her earlier.

Aria's shoulders fell and her arms dropped to her sides. She was wearing a baggy sweatshirt that hit her midthigh. Her toned legs were encased in black leggings. Her feet were bare and her toes painted a sexy hot pink.

Maybe waiting, hoping she'd show, had been a bad idea. I'd wanted to apologize and work this out. But now, seeing her relaxed and at home here, well . . . now I wanted to kiss her again.

"I'm sorry about the kiss," I said. "When it comes to you, I can't seem to help myself."

She padded to the seat beside mine.

I pulled it out for her, waiting until she sat. Then I twisted, leaning an elbow on the counter. I'd discarded my navy pinstripe jacket in my bedroom. I'd rolled up my baby-blue shirtsleeves and undone the top two buttons. Even my tie was gone.

"What are we doing, Brody?" she asked, her voice no louder than a whisper.

"No idea."

"What do you want?"

You. To be a good father. "A healthy baby."

"Then that's our common ground. It has to be our common ground."

I nodded. "Agreed."

"But—"

"Please, don't leave," I blurted. That was all I could think about tonight. That my kiss in the shop earlier would drive her away.

She put her hand on my arm. "I'm not going to leave over a kiss."

The air rushed from my lungs. "Okay."

"I'm starving. I came in to scrounge for a snack." She hopped off her stool and went to the fridge, opening the door. "Did you eat?"

"No."

She glanced over her shoulder. "Because you were waiting."

"I was waiting."

"I'll make us something."

"Ron has leftovers. Enchiladas. Pasta pomodoro. Roasted chicken and vegetables."

"Wow." She whistled. "Go Ron. What do you feel like?"

"Food."

Aria laughed and pulled out the container on the middle shelf. Then she went about warming up our plates. Enchiladas. When she settled in beside me, we both tore into the meal.

"Didn't you eat dinner?" I asked.

"Yes, I did. But I get hungry at night." She put her hand on her belly. "This kid is going to be a night owl."

"I'm excited," I admitted. "I get more anxious every day to meet him or her. To learn what he or she will be like."

"So do I." Aria's eyes softened. "I'm really excited."

The giddiness on her face was a rush. A comfort. Who else could I share that with but her?

"I haven't told anyone," I admitted. "Except Ron."

"I didn't have many people to tell but Clara and the girls from the junkyard."

"What did they say?"

She smiled. "They're happy for me. Gemma just had a baby. Katherine is pregnant. Londyn has a little girl and a baby too. Clara has August. It's been fun to share this with them. To have that in common."

"I'm glad."

She ate a few bites, then set her fork down. "Why haven't you told anyone?"

I sighed. "Because my family has a way of ruining the good things in my life. I won't let them ruin this."

"That's understandable. I can't see your grandmother doing cartwheels over the fact that this *stray* is pregnant." Aria rolled her eyes. "But eventually, you'll have to tell them."

"Eventually. Like when he or she graduates from high school."

Aria giggled. "Do you want to find out if we're having a boy or a girl?"

"Yes. No. I don't know. Do you?"

"No." She grinned. "I like surprises."

"Then a surprise it is." I nodded and took another bite. "This is good."

"Ron is quite the chef."

"Yes, but that's not what I meant. This, the conversation, is good. I almost enjoy your presence when you're not snapping at me," I teased.

She huffed. "Well, you haven't tried to buy me anything in the past fifteen minutes, so it makes me less snappy."

I chuckled. "Then we'll avoid all discussion of material things."

"Can I ask you something?"

"Of course."

"You rarely talk about your parents. What happened to them? I only ask because I'd like to know. One day, this kid is going to ask the same question. It would be nice to know the answer before then."

"Fair enough." I set my fork down and wiped my mouth with a cloth napkin. "My mother is Coreen's daughter. She got pregnant with me when she was seventeen. Needless to say, that didn't go over well."

Aria cringed. "I can't see your grandmother happy. Ever. But especially with a teen pregnancy."

"Mom didn't go to college like her parents had planned. She didn't go to work for Carmichael Communications like they'd planned. She didn't give me up for adoption like they'd insisted."

"How do you even know that? It seems cruel."

"That's my family." I lifted a shoulder. "My grandfather was brutally forthcoming. When I was ten, he sat me down, and instead of telling me about the birds and the bees, he laid out exactly what my mother had done to disappoint him. And he did it in a way that I knew I had no choice but to fall in line. He assumed the role of my father that day."

"And that didn't bother your dad?"

"No, because my father would never argue or go against Grandfather's wishes. My father married my mother and ditched his own last name for Carmichael. He saw my grandparents as his meal ticket, and if that meant giving up a kid, so be it."

"You were only ten." She gave me a sad smile. "I guess both of our lives changed at ten."

"I guess they did."

"I'm sorry."

"Don't be. I look at Alastair and think I got the better end of the deal. My grandparents, despite all their threats, never cut my mother off. They bought her a house and provided a life for her and my father. Neither of my parents ever had a job. They never had responsibility. They remained teenagers in a sense because my grandparents enabled them. I went to live with my grandparents at ten, Alastair was only five. He stayed with our parents. And they spoiled him rotten."

"That's . . . sad." She scrunched up her nose. "I don't like Alastair and you're making me feel bad for him."

"Don't." I chuckled. "Maybe as a kid he couldn't help himself, but he's an adult and his choices are his own. He's a dick because he wants to be a dick."

"You said it." She picked up her water and raised it to her lips. I stared, blatantly, as she drank, jealous of a glass because it got to touch her mouth. "So you moved in with your grandparents."

"Technically. Though they sent me away to private schools, so I was rarely in their home. Only on school breaks and holidays."

"And your parents? Did you see them?"

"At times. It became harder and harder to be around them as I got older. They were never going to grow up. They were never going to stop spending money and feeding bad habits. Especially Dad."

"What habits?"

"The wrong ones." Drugs. Booze. Women. "My parents died in a car accident."

"You told me."

"Dad was driving. He was high and drunk on their way to a casino. He veered off the road, lost control and slammed their vehicle into a tree going seventy miles per hour."

Aria winced and closed her eyes. "God."

"At least they didn't hit another car." Like a car carrying parents. "That was seven years ago."

"Brody." She stretched her hand out and covered my wrist. "I'm sorry."

I put my palm over her knuckles. "I'm sorry too."

It had taken me a long time not to feel like the cause of my mother's downfall. It had taken me well into adulthood to realize that she'd made her own choices. Still, at a young age, I'd seen the mess that was her life. I'd recognized the difference in my mother's lifestyle compared to mothers of friends from school. And I'd felt responsible. My birth had been the trigger.

But I hadn't been the one holding the gun.

She'd made her choices. She'd died because of them.

"Thank you for telling me," Aria said.

"You're welcome. One day, I'd like to know your story too. If you'll share it with me."

Aria dipped her chin. "I will. But not tonight."

"There's no rush. I'll be here when you're ready." I stood and took our empty dishes to the sink, rinsing them out and putting them in the dishwasher.

When I was done, I turned, just as Aria's gaze flicked up. She'd been staring at my ass. And the lust in her eyes was unmistakable.

"You can't look at me like that," I pleaded.

She swallowed hard. "I can't help it."

I knew the feeling.

My feet carried me across the kitchen, right to her space. I stood above her, staring down into those beautiful brown eyes, and let myself drown.

"I told myself earlier I wasn't going to make this a habit. That I couldn't let you kiss me again." Her hand snaked up my stomach, her palm rising to where my heart was beating out of my chest. "But what if we did?"

A pained groan escaped my throat. "I want you. I fucking crave you, Aria."

She flipped open a button on my shirt. "Then you'd better kiss me again."

12

ARIA

HOLY SWEET JESUS, this man could kiss.

Brody swept me off the stool the moment his lips seared mine. The energy, the anticipation, the longing was like climbing to the top of a peak and jumping off into the abyss.

Was this a mistake? Was this reckless? Yes, on both counts, but I wasn't going to stop, and as Brody carried me from the kitchen, I knew he wasn't going to either.

"God, you taste good." He latched on to my pulse, licking and sucking the skin at my throat.

I held on to his shoulders and closed my eyes, savoring the wet heat of his tongue as his strides hastened toward the staircase. Since moving in, I hadn't ventured to the second floor much. I'd done my best not to snoop more than once or twice on his side of the house, deciding it was best to stay away from that invisible boundary.

Brody crashed right through it and, much like the night of the wedding, carried me toward his bedroom.

His hands held me tight with a grip under my ass. He peppered my jaw with a trail of kisses before breaking away to climb the steps. His green eyes were dark with hunger. His face was like granite, nearly unreadable. Except I'd seen this look before. The last time he'd carted me to his bed.

This was Brody on a mission. He was all business. Serious. Stoic. I grinned, because I also knew how quickly he'd flip the switch and become the sensual lover. Last time, it had happened before my dress had pooled to the floor.

Brody took the stairs two at a time, even with my legs wrapped tightly around his hips.

My chest heaved as I tried to regain my breath. The heat between us was like standing in the middle of an active volcano.

We reached the landing and Brody jostled me, hoisting me higher so that my center pressed against his zipper. A whimper escaped my throat. My core was drenched and aching. The throb in my body vibrated from my bones, shaking me from skull to toe.

Brody stormed through his open bedroom door, then he had me on the bed, setting me down and covering me with his weight. His lips slammed down on mine, his tongue plunging deep.

I moaned and threaded my fingers through his hair, letting the short strands at the nape tickle my palms. The longer strands were like silk against my fingertips as Brody ravaged my mouth, exploring every corner.

When had a kiss been so erotic? Not even the night of the wedding had I been this close to an orgasm from a kiss alone. Thank you, hormones.

I spread my legs, making room to cradle Brody's hips with mine. The steel rod behind his slacks rubbed against the thin fabric of my leggings.

"Yes," I moaned when he rocked against me, his lips trailing down my throat.

He found my pulse again and sucked. "I want to taste you."

I gulped. "Yes."

His hands dove under the hem of my sweatshirt, sliding up my ribs. When he found that I wasn't wearing a bra, his entire body froze. Those green eyes whipped to mine.

"Spoiler alert." I winked. "I'm not wearing panties either."

A slow grin spread across his face as he pulled away and stood from the bed. "Next time don't tell me. I like surprises too."

Next time.

I wanted a next time. We hadn't even gotten to the good stuff tonight and I was already looking forward to doing it again.

And again.

And again.

Brody's long fingers slipped into the waistband of my leggings. He tugged, stripping them over my hips. When my bare mound came into view, his eyes flared, and he ran his tongue over his bottom lip. *Ravenous.* He was ravenous for me.

I squirmed, hoping he'd ditch the leggings and get down to business. But he took his time, pulling them inch by inch, collecting the stretchy cotton in his hands as he worked lower and lower.

Finally, he pulled them off my feet and tossed them over a shoulder.

"Christ, you're beautiful." He knelt at the foot of the bed, hooking his hands behind my knees. Then with a fast tug, he had me splayed before him.

Brody didn't linger. He dove in, flattening his tongue as he tasted my glistening folds. When he reached my clit, I nearly came off the bed.

"Oh my God." I writhed, shaking and trembling for more.

He licked me again. "You taste fucking incredible."

My hands found their way into his hair, gripping it as he feasted. The torture was pure ecstasy and I succumbed to the build. It came in a rush, hard and fast. My toes curled as the sensation swallowed me whole and I orgasmed on Brody's lips, moaning his name and praising the angel who'd blessed him with such a gifted tongue.

The aftershocks shook my limbs as he stood but the sound of his belt buckle loosening snapped me out of my sated stupor. I cracked my eyes open and propped up on an elbow as he worked the buttons on his shirt with practiced efficiency. He tugged it free from his slacks and whipped it off his arms.

Brody's body was mouthwatering. I hadn't appreciated it enough the night of the wedding. His stomach was made of perfect squares, the definition between them crisp and lickable. His arms were honed to perfection, muscle upon muscle. The veins beneath his skin bulged. I'd be tracing those little lines later with my tongue.

My eyes drifted lower, taking his body in with a slow perusal.

"Sweatshirt." He jerked his chin. "Off."

I sat up and stripped it as fast as I could, not wanting to miss the show as he shoved down his pants and the white boxer briefs beneath. They slid off his thick legs, the muscles as defined on his lower half as they were the top. I'd study them later because right now, my gaze was fixed on his swollen cock. The velvet shaft was hard and long, the tip decorated with a pearled drop.

Brody came into the bed, taking me deeper into the pillows. Then he dropped his mouth to my throat, his breath fluttering there before he took a deep inhale.

"You smell like flowers."

I hummed, closing my eyes as the heat from his bare skin warmed mine. Brody smelled like spice and earth. It was a clean scent, rich and robust, like the man himself. A scent I missed when I went too long without a pull.

He was an addiction. I'd had no trouble giving up wine or lunch meat or soft cheese during this pregnancy. But if someone asked me to give up Brody's scent, I wouldn't be able to do it.

In all these months, I hadn't let myself believe that the night of the wedding had been anything more than sex. A one-night stand. Except it had meant more, hadn't it? Not just because of the baby, but because Brody was . . . special. Lasting.

"Will this be okay?" He leaned back with concern in his eyes. "Sex?"

"For the baby?"

He nodded.

"It's fine." I wrapped my legs around his ass, raising my hips to brush my soaking center against his erection.

Brody hissed, his jaw flexing as he closed his eyes. "If I hurt you —"

"You won't." I urged him closer. "Come inside."

That sharp jaw flexed again, like he was fighting for control, then he positioned himself at my entrance and slid deep.

My breath hitched when the root of his cock pressed against my clit. My back arched off the plush bed and my fingertips dug into the skin at his shoulders.

"Fuck, you feel good." He dropped a line of open-mouthed kisses across my chest, right along the swell of my breasts. "So good."

"Move." I gripped his arms, holding tight as he slid out and rocked us together again.

The night of the wedding, he'd fucked me. Hard. The next morning my core had ached from the power of his thrusts. But tonight would be different. We both needed it easy. With the baby, this wasn't a rough and rowdy tumble in his sheets. This was the slow savor. The steady climb.

Stroke after stroke, Brody glided us together. He never gave me all his weight, careful to hover above my body. His thrusts were full of the same grace he held in every movement. The roll of his hips. The firm press.

My God, he knew how to give pleasure. My breaths turned to pants. My toes dug into the comforter. My hands gripped its gray cotton, squeezing it as my inner walls fluttered around Brody.

"Aria," he whispered into my ear. One of his hands dropped to mine, threading his fingers between mine and raising it above my head. He pinned it to the headboard, then did the same with the other.

"You're so tight. So wet." His hands held my arms there, his fingers tight to mine. "Come, baby. Come for me. Come while I fuck you."

The naughty words shot straight to my pussy and I exploded, crying his name as I lost control. White spots exploded in my vision. My legs shook and my arms, still locked above my head, pulled hard against Brody's locked grip. Through my release, his hips never slowed, and when I dared open my eyes and return to earth, his green gaze was waiting.

"That was . . ." Brody's throat bobbed. "Beautiful. God, you are beautiful."

I tipped my hips, drawing him deeper into my body. "Your turn."

He moved, faster and faster, still using care. Then his lips crashed down on mine, my taste lingering on his tongue, and he kissed me until his release came over him and he poured himself into my body.

"Fuck," he groaned, dropping his forehead to mine as he came down from the rush. Then he twisted, rolling to his back and taking me with him.

I collapsed on his chest, struggling to regain my breath.

A lock of hair was in my face but my arms were too weak to push it away. I huffed a breath, trying to blow it free. When that didn't work, Brody tucked it behind an ear for me.

"Should we talk about this?" he asked.

I shook my head. "No. We should sleep."

Tomorrow there would be time to talk. Tonight, I only wanted to rest.

And not think about the fact that we might have just ruined everything.

"OH MY GOD."

The words woke me from a dreamless sleep.

I sat up, remembering just in time that I was naked in Brody's bedroom. I clutched the sheet to my chest and blinked the fog from my

498

eyes. Then I squinted at my sister, who stood in the doorway to Brody's bedroom.

"Clara?" My voice was groggy and my head fuzzy. I glanced at the clock on the nightstand, doing a double take at the time. *Eight thirteen.* When was the last time I'd slept past five?

"I was just looking for Brody." Her eyes stayed fixed on the floor. "We always meet at eight. I didn't see him in the office and the door was open so . . ."

Beside me, Brody stirred. "Bump it to nine."

"Okay." She spun around too fast, nearly colliding with the doorframe as she scurried down the hall.

I fell back onto a pillow. Brody's was the most comfortable bed I'd slept on in my life. Maybe that was why my internal alarm clock had taken the day off, even though I couldn't.

I was due at the flower shop to meet Marty when it opened at ten. It was taking some getting used to, not arriving at work before dawn. The hours would get longer as I learned more, but for the first week, I was easing into my new routine.

Today, he was introducing me to the bookkeeper who'd come on to do the accounting after Brody had purchased the shop. Then we were going to do a walk-through of the store and prioritize redecoration.

But first . . . there was a man in my bed.

Or I was in his.

"Now should we talk about this?" Brody asked. His eyes were still closed, and he was hugging his pillow. The sheet had fallen low, nearly to his ass, and the strong, wide plane of his back was on full display.

The responsible decision would be to discuss this and agree on how sex would or would not fit into our relationship.

"No." I whipped the covers off and kicked my legs over the bed. Then I stood, hurrying to tug on my sweatshirt and pull on my leggings. "Later. I need to get ready for work."

And I needed to think this through.

Without another word, I tucked my bedhead hair behind my ears and aimed my feet at the door.

"Aria." Brody's voice stopped me before I could disappear.

"Yeah?" I turned.

He'd sat up. His hair was mussed, his face sleepy. But his eyes were alert and commanding. "See you at dinner."

I nodded, then ran.

By a miracle, I managed to avoid Ron when I walked through the kitchen but the smell of bacon told me he was close. Escaping to my side of the house, I thought I was home-free when my bedroom door came into view — until I walked in and found my sister sitting on the bed with a smirk on her pretty face.

My face flushed and I kicked the door closed behind me. "Don't look at me like that."

She raised an eyebrow. "Like what?"

"You're all . . . smug."

"I'm not smug."

"Then you need a mirror." I walked to the bed, plopping down beside her. Then I covered my face in my hands. "This is a disaster."

She giggled. "Dramatic much?"

"I had sex with Brody."

"Duh. You're pregnant."

"Last night, Clara."

"I'll repeat. Duh."

I swatted at her as she laughed. "You're not helping."

"What do you want me to say? I love you. I love Brody. When you two are in the same room, the sexual tension is so thick I've nearly choked on it for the past ten years."

"What?" I sat up. "Nu-uh."

"Please." She rolled her eyes. "It was only a matter of time before you realized you don't really hate him the way you want to hate him."

I frowned. "You're a pain in my ass."

"And you love me too. This could be a good thing. You're having a baby."

"Exactly!" I threw my hands in the air. "What if we try this and fail? What if we truly end up hating one another? I don't want my child in the middle of that."

"But what if it works? What if . . . what if you can give your child the life that I can never give August?"

My heart twisted. "Clara, you're a good mom. The best."

"And you will be too. Even if it doesn't work, Brody is a good man. You can navigate this."

I blew out a deep breath, leaning into her side. "I don't know what I'm doing. With men. I haven't had many in my life. And any guy I've slept with was a guy I dated. Brody was my first hookup."

There were reasons why I was so selective when it came to lovers. Reasons why I was careful with who I let touch my body. Reasons I wouldn't let myself think of today or talk about with Clara.

I wouldn't drag her back to that place.

Four lovers. That was the extent of my experience. My first had been a man I'd dated in Vegas. He'd taken me on eight dates before I'd given him my virginity. I'd dumped him before date number nine because I'd been so mortified by my fears during sex.

As different boyfriends had come and gone, I'd worked through many of those fears, but they still lingered. It was difficult for me to give up control of my body. To surrender it to a man.

Until Brody.

Brody beat back the anxiety when it came to sex. There were no insecurities with him. He made it easy to relax and enjoy. Maybe because he oozed confidence and authority. Every touch was deliberate. Every caress solid. There was no fumbling, and in that surety, he made me feel safe.

500

Last night, and the night of the wedding, he'd given me everything I'd needed to shut out the noise and just . . . be.

"He's not who I thought he was," I whispered. Beneath the cement and glass exterior, there was a big, beating, beautiful heart. "What would you do?"

"Trust him," she answered without hesitation. "Give him time. He's learning too."

Trust him. At least Brody had always been honest with me. There were no secrets. No lies.

I could trust him.

Clara and I sat together in silence until she had to go meet Brody for her meeting and I had to shower before going to the shop.

I drove the Cadillac into town, not ready yet to concede that the BMW Brody had bought was a really nice car. After a fun day with Marty, soaking in his wisdom and imparting some of my own, I returned home.

It hadn't been easy to ignore thoughts of Brody at work, but I'd tried. When I walked in the house and his smell hit my nose, I knew with one breath I was in trouble.

So instead of meeting him for dinner like he'd expected, I stayed in my bedroom, watching the clock tick away until dinner. My stomach growled but I didn't move. Cowardice was a different look for me and one I suspected wasn't all that becoming.

What did I say? Did I want a relationship? Did I have the energy to nourish this baby and give attention to anyone else? What if Brody thought it best we return to platonic cohabitation?

The last question scared me the most.

Because it would hurt. More than I wanted to admit. If Brody rejected me, that was going to freaking sting.

An hour passed as I lay on my bed, my eyes trained on the ceiling as the anxieties flourished like a freshly watered tulip. The sun was setting outside, casting the pool with its glow.

Shifting one ear into a pillow, I studied the colors as they faded. Blue to yellow. Yellow to orange. Pink to red. I did love desert sunsets. Bright and beautiful, I found myself on the back patio often, watching the colors shift over the dusty horizon.

In the mornings, I'd venture outside to watch the desert bloom. Years of visiting Clara and I hadn't timed a trip in the early spring, probably because March was always a hectic time at The Gallaway, planting for the season. Boy, had I missed out.

It was just beginning, but soon, the wildflower super bloom would carpet the rugged landscapes in pinks and yellows and purples. Clara had told me it was beautiful, but even now, at the beginning, words hadn't done the spectacle justice.

The spring desert was truly breathtaking, and it was only the start.

When I'd stopped wanting to hate it here, I'd fallen in love.

"You missed dinner."

I flinched, sitting up with a jolt.

Brody stood in the doorway with one ankle crossed over the other. His feet were bare, his jacket and tie gone. His shirtsleeves were rolled up and the buttons at his throat were undone. Just like last night. And just like last night, I couldn't take my eyes off him.

"I wasn't sure if dinner was a good idea," I confessed. "I wasn't sure what to say."

He pushed off the door and walked into the room. Then he climbed on the bed, lying at my side. "I'm not sure what to say either."

"Really?" I propped up on an elbow. "You always seem sure."

"Not always. Do we have to decide now?"

Clara's advice had been to give him time. And here he was, asking for it too.

So instead of worrying, I leaned closer and brushed his lips with mine.

"No. I guess we don't."

13

BRODY

"I HAVE TO GO." I kissed Aria's bare shoulder as she combed her wet hair. She wore the towel she'd wrapped around her body after her shower. A shower I'd missed because I'd been in my own bathroom preparing for what would likely be an exhausting day.

"Have a safe trip."

"I will." I kissed her shoulder again, then took a long look at her in the mirror.

My God, she was gorgeous. If we had a girl, I hoped she looked exactly like Aria. If we had a boy, I wanted him to have her bewitching eyes.

"I think I'll tell her."

The comb in Aria's hand froze. "Are you sure?"

"Would you mind?"

She shook her head. "We can't keep this a secret forever."

"All right. Then I'll do it today." It would be better to tell Grandmother about the baby in person.

I was flying to Vegas today for a string of meetings, but I had an hour carved out after lunch to catch up with Grandmother. She wasn't going to like this—the baby or Aria—and I didn't give a single fuck.

This was my child and I was excited. The fear of fatherhood was there, a constant worry at the back of my mind, and I suspected it'd be there for the remainder of my life. But excitement had taken center stage, especially now that Aria and I had started . . .

Sleeping together? Dating? I hadn't dated since college. Since Aria and I rarely went anywhere outside the home, I doubted this would qualify.

Maybe I should change that.

"Tomorrow night, I'd like to take you out to dinner."

Aria returned to her brushing. "Okay. I've been craving a burger from the diner ever since Marty and I ordered in lunch from there last week."

"The diner it is." I drew a circle on her shoulder with my finger, then reluctantly stepped away. It was nearly impossible to keep my hands to myself when she was within reach. And if I kept touching her, that towel would hit the floor and I'd be late for my flight.

"Don't work too hard. No lifting heavy arrangements."

"Yes, sir." A smile toyed at her mouth.

She'd started teasing me lately, calling me sir. The three-letter word sent a rush of heat to my groin.

"You're evil." I didn't hide the adjustment I made to my hardening dick.

Her smile widened. "I know."

I chuckled and walked out of the bathroom while I still could, then headed to the garage. I pulled off the property and onto the highway. Within a mile, I missed home. I missed her.

I wasn't exactly a homebody. Clara called me an introvert, but mostly, I didn't like many people. Many people didn't like me. With so much work to be done, why make friends when I didn't have time to give them? Why date a woman who would only demand attention I didn't have to spare?

Aria was the exception.

When it came to her, none of my rules applied. She had my focus. She had my free moments. She had my nights.

It had been two weeks since the night Aria had told me to kiss her in the kitchen. Two weeks and we hadn't spent a night apart. There were some evenings when I had to work late and I'd find her in her room, tucked into bed, reading a book. Other nights, we'd eat dinner together before I'd start the process of giving her as many orgasms as I could until she passed out.

Those were the best nights.

We slept in her room. My room. Wherever we landed. And never had my house felt so much like a home.

She'd bring home flowers from the shop. They'd sit on the kitchen counter, brightening it for the weekend. The arrangement she'd brought five days ago had started to droop and I suspected there'd be a new one tonight when I got home from Vegas.

My flight left on time. My morning meetings went off without a hitch. And when it was time to meet with Grandmother and tell her the news, her initial reaction was exactly as I'd expected. A double blink. A demand to repeat myself. Then the fury set in.

"How could you be so foolish?" she snapped, her face as red as I'd seen in a year.

"It wasn't intentional."

"Maybe for you. That woman is trash. She did this on purpose."

"I can assure you, Aria was just as surprised as I was."

"Then she should be an actress." Grandmother scoffed. "Because that woman only wants your money."

If she only knew how wrong she was. Aria still hadn't so much as touched the keys for the BMW I'd bought her. She'd made her first monthly payment on the flower shop even when I'd tried once more to tell her it was unnecessary. Three days ago, I'd heard her tell Ron that whether

504

he liked it or not, she was picking up some groceries on the way home. He was smarter than I was and chose not to argue and had reluctantly handed over his list.

"Whether you like her or not, Aria is in my life," I said. "I won't forsake my child. Or my child's mother."

"Then you prove my point. You were an easy target."

I pinched the bridge of my nose. "Please. Can you just be happy for me? I want this."

"Then you're as foolish as your mother."

My jaw clenched. "I guess I am."

"You will get a nanny. You will find someone suitable to raise that baby so he doesn't turn out like his mother."

"I have a nanny." I sighed.

Or I would have a nanny. Ron had already begun lining up interviews. We'd likely hire someone outside of Welcome, meaning we'd build another home on the property. There was time.

"Unbelievable." Grandmother sat rigid behind her desk, her entire frame locked tight.

"Aria is a kind, loving person. I realize you two didn't start off on the right foot. Ironically, she has as much tenacity as you. If you give her a chance, I'm sure you'll get along."

"She is trash, Broderick. Trash." She made the statement sound like fact. *The sky is blue. The oceans are deep. She is trash.*

Except Aria Saint-James was not trash.

Nothing I said would convince Grandmother otherwise, so why was I here wasting my breath on a woman who was never going to change her mind?

I wouldn't let her steal this joy.

"We're done here." I stood from the chair and walked to the door.

"Get back here. Immediately. I am not done speaking."

I kept walking.

"Broderick."

Aria had been right. My full name really was pretentious. Grandmother knew I preferred Brody.

"Broderick! I will sell this company. If you don't deal with this woman and find a way to get her out of our lives, I will sell this company."

I stopped walking and turned. "Aria is the mother of my child. She is in our lives whether you like it or not."

"Get rid of her. Pay her to disappear."

"No."

"Don't push me. I will sell."

"No, you won't." For too long, she'd made that threat.

It was time to call her bluff.

"You won't sell this company. You won't sell Grandfather's legacy. And you won't threaten me with it again. This is *my* company."

"Not yet, it isn't. I'll sell."

"You can make that decision, but I truly hope you don't. I hope you care about me and my future enough to give me the opportunity to prove myself."

A flicker of guilt crossed her gaze.

Grandfather had stipulated she receive a monthly stipend as the executor of my trust. Knowing him, it had been a heavy sum, enough to tie her to his company. And she'd also receive a sum when her time as trustee ran out. Maybe he'd worried that she'd sell after his death.

I'd assumed that she didn't need the stipend. And that if she sold, she'd receive more money for her own shares than the stipend and lump sum together. But maybe Grandmother's personal finances weren't as strong as they once were. Or maybe the offers for Carmichael that she'd bragged about had been greatly exaggerated.

Whatever her motives, I wasn't going to stick around and listen to her shred Aria.

"Have a nice day, Grandmother."

"Broderick."

"I'm sure we'll talk soon."

"Broderick!"

Grandmother was still yelling as I shoved open the door and disappeared to my own office. I slammed the door shut and went to the windows overlooking the city.

God, she made life difficult. After my birthday, after she was out of Carmichael, I suspected Grandmother would mostly disappear from my life.

I just had to endure until my birthday.

What if I didn't?

What if I walked away? What if I let it all go? The years and years of work I'd put into this place. Was it even worth it?

Yes. My vision was worth fighting for. So were the employees.

I could lead them and this company into a bright future. Just yesterday, I'd had a call with the CEO of a large communications corporation in California. It had been a casual visit, but we'd danced around a potential deal in the future.

So I'd deal with Grandmother's dramatics and barked orders. I'd do it for employees like Erika, the head of human resources, who'd been working at Carmichael for twenty-eight years. She was eighteen months from retirement, and if the company dissolved before then, she'd lose the twenty-five-thousand-dollar bonus Grandfather had set up for employees who'd worked here for thirty years. That bonus meant Erika could move to Idaho and live closer to her son and grandkids.

I'd endure for Joshua, the head of security who'd started here as a custodian. He was a single father whose daughter was in college. He was determined to pay for her education and his job was the key to that dream.

I would deal with Grandmother for Matt because that poor guy was her third personal assistant this year. He'd just graduated from college and this was his first job. I'd asked him once, after witnessing Grandmother tear into him for getting her coffee order wrong, why he wanted to work at

Carmichael. He'd told me his young wife was undergoing chemotherapy and no other job he could find offered such comprehensive health insurance.

Erika, Joshua, Matt. They were all trapped in their jobs.

And I'd stay trapped in mine.

"Brody?" A knock came at the door and I turned from the window as Laney, my second assistant, walked into the room with a stack of papers in her hand. "Your two o'clock is early. Would you like me to show him to a conference room to wait? Or would you like to get started early?"

"I'm ready. Send him in. And let's see if we can move up or cancel my last meeting. I'd like to get home before dark."

"Of course." She smiled, more brightly than normal. Probably because I'd told her this morning that I was going to be a father. She'd been especially smiley since.

I wasn't close to Laney like I was Clara. She lived in Vegas, so we didn't see each other as often. I'd never consider her a personal friend, but she was a nice woman and a fantastic employee. She had two young kids who attended our onsite daycare for employees.

The remainder of my meetings went quickly, and I was able to get out of Vegas an hour earlier than planned. When the plane's wheels touched down in Welcome, I breathed and unknotted my tie.

I'd stripped it off completely, along with my jacket, by the time I parked in the garage at home. Ready for dinner and a long night worshiping Aria's body, I opened the door to a loud crash.

"Aria." I ran toward the source of the noise.

Another crash. "Shit."

"Aria!" A cold gust of air hit me as I rounded the corner and rushed toward her bedroom.

The patio doors were open. Beyond them, the pool shimmered in the March evening light. The sunsets had been beautiful, and two nights ago, Aria had insisted on sitting out by the pool, bundled in a sweater and wool socks, to watch the colorful show.

Her room was cold and empty. I checked the bathroom, where I'd left her this morning, but it was dark. Another crash echoed from the hallway and I jogged to the room next door.

And there she was, standing in the middle of a mess. Boxes were strewn across the floor. A crate had been ripped open with the hammer and pry bar clutched in her hands. The crate's paper stuffing had exploded through the room.

"What's going on?"

Aria whirled, the hand with the hammer ready to strike. "Don't sneak up on me."

"I called for you." I walked into the room as her arm dropped to her side. But the look of fury on her face didn't fade.

"You ordered a cradle?" She pointed the tool at the crate where the soft wooden edge of the cradle peeked out from the packing paper straws.

"Yes."

"And what's in that one?" She glared at the crate in the corner.

"A rocking chair."

Aria's nostrils flared. "You didn't think I'd want to have some input?"

"No." *Shit.* "I figured if you didn't like them, we could send them back and get something else."

"When did you order them?"

"Months ago. They were both custom-made and I knew it would take time."

She crossed her arms, her grip on both tools tightening. "And what about the nanny? I got home from work and Ron was escorting his top candidate out. He wanted to make sure I could meet her before he gave you the final recommendation."

My stomach dropped. This wasn't about the cradle or the chair. This was about the nanny. "It's just an idea."

"A nanny? You think I want a nanny?"

"Well . . . yes."

She threw the tools to the floor of the crate with a clank and thud. "Stop doing this."

"I'm trying to help."

"You're not helping!" The flush rose in her cheeks.

"Aria, this isn't a big deal. Calm down."

"Calm down? No. And this is a big deal." She shook her head. "First it's the car. Then it's the cradle. Then it's the nanny. You make these decisions, these important decisions, without talking to me."

Christ. "I'm sorry."

"Then stop doing it." Her shoulders fell. "Don't make decisions *for* me. Ask me. Share with me. Talk to me."

"Like you talk to me?"

"I talk to you." She planted her hands on her hips. It was then that I noticed her feet were bare amidst wood splinters and metal staples.

I shook my head and turned, stalking away. Knowing she'd follow because Aria didn't let battles go unfought.

She caught up to me in my bedroom, where I was stowing my cufflinks.

"What was that supposed to mean?" she snapped.

I didn't answer.

Instead, I went to work on my shirt's buttons, stripping it off and tossing it in the hamper. Then I pulled a black T-shirt from a drawer and tugged it on. My slacks got traded for the jeans Aria loved so much. And I put on some tennis shoes so I could wade into the mess she'd made in the nursery because she was pissed.

Well, I was pissed too. More than I'd realized.

I was trying to help. Maybe I'd fucked it up. I should have told her about the nanny but I hadn't expected Ron to work so quickly. I certainly hadn't expected him to have an interviewee here at the house.

Why couldn't Aria give me a little credit? And a little slack? I was trying to make her life easier. Why wouldn't she let me?

None of those thoughts were voiced. They stayed trapped in my head as I stalked back to the nursery.

Aria followed, silently fuming. She leaned against the doorjamb as I took the cradle from the box, then unpacked the rocking chair. And once they were out of the way, I went about cleaning up the mess on the floor.

She didn't say a word. Neither did I.

Aria stared. I worked.

Carrying the last piece of the dismantled crates to the garage, I returned to the nursery to find Aria gone. Along with the cradle.

"Damn it, woman." I marched out of the nursery and to her bedroom.

She'd dragged the cradle to the foot of the bed where she sat, rocking it gently.

The cradle was wooden with sleek lines, simple but stylish. I thought she'd be proud that I'd picked something in a warm shade, especially when white and gray had been options.

"This is pretty," she whispered.

"If you want something else, we can get something else."

She shook her head and looked up to meet my gaze. All of the anger she'd been wearing earlier had disappeared. Somewhere during my trips to and from the garage, the fight had gone out of her.

I realized as I crossed the room to sit beside her that my anger had deflated too. "I'm sorry. I said it earlier. I meant it."

"I know. You don't say things you don't mean." She leaned into my side, her hair tickling my bare forearm. "I don't want a nanny. I want to be the one to change diapers and puree baby food and get up in the middle of the night."

"Are you sure?"

She nodded. "No nanny. I'm going to be selfish and keep all of my baby's moments for myself."

"Just share some with me, okay?"

"You can have the poopy diapers."

I chuckled. "So generous."

"And I want a will. I want one ready the day he or she is born. If something happens to us, no matter what, Clara gets custody."

My insides clenched. Just the idea that she—we—might not be there to see our child grow up made me sick. But Aria was right. This was important. "I'll have my attorney draft it up tomorrow."

She sat statue still, staring at the crib with her temple on my shoulder. "My parents didn't have a will. To this day, it's the one thing I haven't been able to forgive them for. It wouldn't have taken more than an hour or two. A phone call to a lawyer. But they put it off and then . . . they were gone."

"We'll have one," I promised, then did my best not to tense because I didn't want her to stop talking.

I knew only pieces of her history, the parts Clara had trusted me with over the years. But I wanted the full story and I wanted it from Aria. I wanted her to trust me with her past, like I'd trusted her with mine.

"Since they didn't have a will, Clara and I became wards of the state while their estate was settled. We spent four weeks in foster care, waiting for family services to sort out where to stick us."

"You ended up with an uncle, right?"

"Uncle Craig." She shivered. "My mom's stepbrother. They were estranged. My grandmother had been a single mom. She'd had Mom young. Then later she'd remarried a man a few years older, with a son. Her husband died but my grandma kept Craig. It was his senior year, I think. I didn't know my grandma well. She died when Clara and I were babies. My dad's parents were living in a retirement village outside of Phoenix, of all places. Not that far from here."

"And you didn't go with them?"

She shook her head. "I'm sure that's what Mom and Dad had expected to happen. But when my uncle offered to take us, family services thought it was for the best. He was younger and lived in Temecula too, so we wouldn't have to move to a different town. And my dad's parents didn't put up a fight. They didn't want us, not really."

It broke my heart that she'd felt unwanted. That she'd been at the mercy of the adults in her life. I could relate. It had been crushing to feel like a pawn and a burden rather than a child.

"I will never go back to California." Her voice turned cold like the air drifting in from the open patio doors. "Clara wants to go back. She'll take the Cadillac and return because she needs that closure."

"And what do you need?" I'd give it to her. Without question.

"I need that son of a bitch to rot in hell for the rest of eternity."

I twisted, forcing her to sit straight, because I had to see her face. "Did he . . ." I gulped, not even able to choke out the words.

"There was a reason he and my mother were estranged. I'll never know if he did something to her. But . . . it isn't hard to guess. Not after what he did to me."

"Tell me," I gritted out.

She stared at the floor, unblinking. "He took everything. Our house. Our things. Anything of value he sold and kept every dime for himself, pissing it away. And we moved into this shitty trailer where Clara and I shared a bedroom and a bathroom, both with doors that didn't lock."

My spine went rigid and my heart pounded. "Aria, I won't make you go through this. If you don't want to talk about it —"

"No. You were right. And you should know."

"Are you sure?"

She gave me a sad smile. "I haven't told this to anyone. Ever. Only Clara knows."

They'd survived it together.

"It was fairly miserable for five years. That's about how long it took Craig to run out of money. He literally just . . . spent it. He gambled. He quit his job. He threw parties while Clara and I hid in our room and prayed no one came in. He was such a loser, but there was always food and he normally left us alone."

"You were ten."

She lifted a shoulder. "Old enough to care for ourselves and get to school."

Meanwhile at ten I'd had a full staff of private teachers at my disposal. And parents and grandparents. Yes, they'd been on the opposite side of the country, but had I called, they would have sent a plane.

"By the time we turned fourteen, things started to get strange. Craig would look at us. He'd lick his lips and there'd be this gleam in his eyes as we started to develop breasts. Girls know when a man is staring. One night, Clara woke up to see him standing over her bed. After that, we hung a can on the door so we'd hear if he came in. After about a year, it became so bad—the looks and long touches—that we started packing."

"To run away."

She nodded. "There was this girl who lived in the trailer park, two trailers down. Londyn."

"Cadillac Londyn?"

"The same. Her parents had been junkies, so she was on her own too. One day she was just gone. We started asking around at school and the pizza parlor where she worked. No one knew she was living in the junkyard, just that she was hanging out there. But we figured that was where she was staying too. And if it was good enough for her, it was good enough for us."

A junkyard wasn't good enough for her, but it was better than the alternative.

"We didn't leave right away," she said. "We stole some money from Craig and bought the biggest backpacks we could find. Then we filled them to the brim with clothes and food and cash and Tylenol. We'd planned to take twice as much as we actually did but things . . . well, things got out of hand."

My pulse pounded at my temples, fury coming on before she could explain.

I knew what was next. The question was, just how out of hand had it gotten?

"We waited one night too many," she whispered. "I was in the kitchen, making dinner. Macaroni and cheese. I didn't even know he was home, but then I felt him. He came up behind me and . . ."

I took her hand.

She laced her fingers through mine and held tight. "He touched me."

With her free hand, Aria touched her breast. Then lower.

I wanted to scream. I wanted to punch the wall and kill a man in Temecula, California. But I sat still and let her squeeze my hand so hard that my fingertips turned white. Tomorrow, I'd take it out on my heavy bag, but tonight I was here for Aria.

"He kept touching me. He ripped my shirt. He got my pants open. I fought, hard, and stomped on his foot. It was enough to squirm away and run to our room. It happened so fast, Clara barely registered what was happening when I came racing down the hall. After that, we barricaded ourselves in the bedroom. We sat against the door, wedging ourselves between it and one of the beds. He beat on that door for hours, until our legs were so weak they shook and the tears had dried on our cheeks."

At fifteen. *Fuck*. They had to have been terrified.

"We waited for hours after his footsteps retreated from the door, just in case. Then when we were sure he was gone, we pushed every piece of furniture against the door. By morning, we'd shoved the backpacks and supplies out of the tiny bedroom window, then squeezed out ourselves."

All these years I'd known Aria. All these years I'd worked with Clara. And I hadn't really known them at all.

Aria's strength was humbling.

"Clara and I walked hand in hand to the junkyard, and that was it," she said. "We found the delivery truck and made it our home. We did what we could for money until we were old enough to get jobs. We stayed far away from the school and the trailer park. If we saw someone we knew, we didn't tell them where we were living because we were all scared the cops might stumble upon our makeshift home and take us away. By some miracle, it worked. We survived. Together. The six of us leaned on each other. And we survived."

Aria. Clara. I'd underestimated them both.

Later, when my temper had cooled, I'd find out about the uncle. I'd find out if he was still alive. I wasn't going to ask if she'd kept tabs on the motherfucker.

"I'm sorry." I kissed her knuckles. "I don't . . . I don't know what else to say."

"There's nothing to say. It's in the past. I want it to stay in the past."

"Then we won't talk about it again."

"Brody . . . the cradle. The nanny. You do it because you want to help. But I need to earn things. I need to know they are mine."

"They are yours."

"No, they're not. They're gifts."

"What's wrong with gifts?"

She stared at me, searching for the right words. When she found them, her gaze softened. "I went for so long wondering what was going to happen. I have spent so long relying only on myself."

"And now you have me."

"Brody, I know this seems strange. I know Clara can take a gift and say thank you. I can't."

"Why?"

"Because tomorrow it might be gone. If I earn it myself, then maybe it won't disappear."

In that single sentence, it all made sense. She was protecting herself. She was insulating herself from heartbreak. If she counted on me and I left her . . . "I won't leave you, Aria."

"You might."

"Never."

Not when I was falling for her.

She closed her eyes and collapsed into my chest.

512

I wrapped my arms around her and kissed the top of her hair. "I'll always take care of you. Let me. Please."

"Make me a part of it. Share it. Please?"

"Okay." I kissed her hair again, holding her for a few precious minutes. Then I stood from the bed, her dainty hand tucked firmly in my grasp. "Come on."

Aria stood too. "Where are we going?"

"Dinner. Bed."

"Not yet." She dropped my hand to snake her arms around my waist. Her fingers dove into the back pockets of my jeans and she squeezed my ass. Hard. "Did you wear these jeans because you thought it would make me less angry at you?"

"Maybe. Did it work?"

She stood on her toes and her lips whispered across mine. "I guess you'll find out when you take them off."

14

ARIA

"COURTLAND."

"I will never, ever name my child Courtland."

Brody frowned. "That was my great-uncle's name."

"Did you love and admire this uncle?"

"I didn't really know him."

"Then it's a no." I took a bite of my cheeseburger and scrolled down the list of names I'd been collecting on my phone. "Parry. Spelled with an *a*."

"Meh."

That made five in a row he'd nixed with a *meh*. Ben. David. Steven. Jacob. They'd been too plain. And now Parry. "Fine. Your turn."

Brody and I had been making lists of baby names. We'd collect favorites throughout the week, then have lunch at the flower shop on Fridays to pitch them to each other. Today he'd come bearing cheeseburgers from the diner because it was the one craving I'd had consistently during the transition from the second trimester to the third.

In the past month, ever since I'd confided in Brody about my past, the two of us had settled into little routines, like this one. Dinner every evening. Breakfast after he'd worked out in the morning. Texts throughout the day to check in. Saturday night dates in the theater room. Anything to spend time together.

Today we were debating boy names. Next week, we'd start tackling the girl list.

"Adler," he said.

I scrunched up my nose. "Adler?"

"It was my grandfather's name."

"It's not awful. But it's . . ."

"Pretentious?" Brody finished.

I pointed a finger at him. "Now you're learning."

He chuckled and wadded up the paper wrapper from his meal. "What if we can't agree?"

"We have three months. I'm sure we'll find one boy name and one girl name that we both like."

"I think you underestimate our natural tendency to disagree."

I giggled and tossed my napkin at his face.

The smile on his made my heart flip.

I'd seen that smile more in the past month than in all the years I'd known Brody. Even Clara had commented on how happy he was.

How happy we both were.

We bickered endlessly about stupid topics like nursery purchases and the BMW I wouldn't drive. Every time I lifted an object weighing more than two pounds, Brody would scold me for five solid minutes.

The arguments, I was learning, were foreplay. Because by the time each day closed, we would be together, either in his bed or mine, and there was never any argument about ending the night naked and wrapped in each other's arms.

"I brought cookies too." Brody pulled another to-go container from the white paper sack on the table.

Before he'd arrived at noon, I'd cleared away the floral petals, leaves and discarded stems from the bouquet Marty had made for one of five deliveries we had today.

"Can I run an idea by you?"

"Of course," he said.

"You have to promise not to run out and spend a bunch of money."

He frowned. "Have I bought you anything extravagant lately?"

I tore off a chunk of cookie and popped it into my mouth. "This cookie is fairly extraordinary."

He grinned. "Your idea."

"Someday, in the distant future when I'm ready, I want to build a greenhouse. I love working with the flowers and making bouquets. It's been an exciting change from what I did in Oregon, but I miss playing in the dirt. I can grow houseplants for the shop and maybe even expand to have annuals and perennials available to customers."

"I like it. Whatever you set your mind to, I have complete faith you'll make it a success."

"Thank you." I blushed and tore into the chocolate chip cookie, moaning as the sugary, buttery confection melted on my tongue. The greenhouse idea wouldn't be anytime soon. I needed to save some money and get the shop turning a bigger profit, but someday, I wanted both.

"Marty's going to have to run the shop this afternoon," I said, devouring my cookie. "I'm going to be in a food coma."

"I heard that." Marty walked into the room with a grin on his face. "And I'll allow an afternoon nap if you agree to call the Friday promotion Fresh Flower Friday."

"Done." I clapped. "Easy."

That was my favorite name out of the options anyway. But if I could get a nap in on the gold velvet couch in the office, I was taking it.

"See how easily some people can agree on names?" I shot Brody a smirk.

He simply shook his head. "Eat your cookie."

"Yes, sir." I winked and took a huge bite to polish it off.

Fresh Flower Friday was going to be a new addition to Welcome Floral. We were going to rearrange a wall just inside the door. We'd add shelves to hold tin buckets. Then each Friday, we'd fill them with bundles of fresh flowers and offer them at cost.

The goal was to get people into the shop. For too long, Welcome Floral had survived on deliveries to area residents. That would always be our core business, but to expand, we needed foot traffic.

When John Doe drove home from work, we wanted him to stop here and grab a bundle for his wife, Jane, who'd had a long week. We wanted Jane to then come in and shop for a birthday gift for her mother.

Over the past month, we'd rearranged the shop. The tables had a better configuration to showcase not only the floral arrangements, but also the houseplants and knickknacks and gifts. The shabby-chic style had been toned down, the clutter cleared and the lights brightened to give the shop a clean and open look.

It still had charm and character. But individual pieces were given space so they could breathe. The layout didn't overwhelm the eye, but showcased items so customers could appreciate the beauty of a clay planter or a lawn ornament or a succulent terrarium.

The door dinged, and when I made a move to stand, Marty held up a hand. "Sit. I've got the shop."

"Thanks." I smiled at his back as he disappeared from the workroom. Then I rubbed my belly. I might have gone too far with lunch. I was stretched tight. "Ready?"

Brody inched closer, putting both hands on my rounded stomach. After every meal, the baby would kick for a few minutes, sometimes longer. Brody was on a mission to feel as many as he could.

The black-and-white-striped tank top I'd worn this morning stretched tight across my abdomen. I'd finally had to give in and buy maternity jeans. Today I'd rolled up a dove-gray sweater and knotted it at my ribs, over the bump.

Brody and I were color coordinated today, him in a light-gray suit. He'd even traded his normal dress shoes for sneakers. They were new and perfectly white, but they were casual. And he'd left his normal tie at home.

"Come on, little one," I whispered. "Kick Daddy for wanting to name you Adler and Courtland."

Brody laughed and leaned in to kiss my forehead. "You're such a smart-ass."

"You like it."

"You're right." He put his forehead to mine and we both waited, our breaths held, until one tiny baby foot slammed into Brody's palm. "That never gets old."

"No, it doesn't."

"I've got to get back to work."

I'd see him in hours, but I always hated to watch him walk away. "I know."

I was so in love with him.

The realization had snuck up on me this morning when he'd curled his strong, tall body around mine. He'd held me and I'd realized that the soul-deep loneliness I'd felt for years had truly vanished. Not even Clara's hugs or August's cheek smooches had chased it completely away.

Only Brody.

And our baby.

I loved him, more than I'd ever known it was possible to love another person.

Soon, I'd find a way to say the words. But in this moment, as the three of us huddled together in a bubble away from the real world, I closed my eyes and savored the moment. The peace.

The bubble popped before I was ready.

"Sorry to interrupt." Marty poked his head into the room. He was grinning from ear to ear. "We've got some guests. Friends. I'd like you to meet them."

"I better get back to work anyway." Brody lifted his hands and framed my face. Then he dropped a soft kiss to my lips. "Don't work too hard."

"I won't." I slid off my stool and took his hand. "Will you take a plant with you? We got the coolest snake plant in this morning and I decided to steal it for the entryway."

"There are already seven pots in the entryway."

"Your point?"

He fought a smile, then looked to Marty. "Don't let her lift anything heavy. Yesterday, I caught her trying to move a—what kind of plant was that?"

"A fiddle-leaf fig tree."

"A tree. She was trying to move a tree."

"It wasn't heavy."

Brody's expression flattened. "Ask Marty for help."

"She won't have to," Marty declared. "I won't let her out of my sight."

"Good." Brody took my hand and together we followed Marty into the shop. The easy grin on his face faltered and his feet skidded to a halt when he spotted the older couple inspecting the shop.

"Ned. Stephanie. I'd like you to meet Aria Saint-James." Marty introduced me to the couple. "Aria, Ned and Stephanie Backer. Former owners of Welcome Floral."

"Oh." I stood a little taller and extended a hand. "Hello. It's so nice to meet you."

Because Brody had bought the shop from them, I'd never known their first names. Marty didn't talk about them much, but when he had, he'd referred to them as the Backers. Never Ned and Stephanie.

517

"You too." Ned took my hand, shaking it with gusto. "It's just a pleasure."

Stephanie simply smiled, her eyes wandering around the room. "You've made a lot of changes."

"We have." I held my breath, hoping they wouldn't take offense. "I truly love this space."

Ned turned to Brody and extended a hand. "Mr. Carmichael. Nice to see you again."

"A pleasure." The easy posture from lunch was gone. Brody stood stiff, his face drawn tight.

"What brings you to town?" Marty asked, leaning against one of the display tables. "Judging by your Instagram photos, I figured we'd never get you back from Hawaii."

Stephanie laughed. "We love living there. It's so green and wonderfully humid. My skin has never felt better."

"We're back for John Miller's sixtieth birthday," Ned said. "Then we'll fly home."

"It's been lovely to see you." Brody gestured for the door. "May I escort you out? We'll let Aria and Marty get back to work."

The smiles on Ned's and Stephanie's faces dropped.

I shot Brody a scowl. Why was he being rude? "No, please. Stay. We're not that busy. And you should catch up with Marty."

"Are you sure?" Stephanie asked me, giving Brody a cautious glance.

"Yes, it would be wonderful. Please."

"Thanks." She relaxed, taking another gander around the room. "We've missed this place. We ran this shop for twelve years. It was sort of like our third child."

"A third child who actually made us money." Ned barked a laugh. "I don't see Suzie or MJ selling for four hundred and eighty thousand dollars. Not that we'd ever sell our kids."

Stephanie laughed. Marty laughed.

Brody tensed.

And my jaw dropped.

Four hundred and eighty thousand dollars.

It was tacky as hell for Ned to announce that number.

And enlightening.

"You said one hundred and twenty-five," I whispered, looking up at Brody.

His eyes were on the door, like he wanted Ned and Stephanie gone. Now I knew why he was so eager to shove them onto the sidewalk.

Except the damage was done. They'd spilled his secret.

"You said one hundred and twenty-five," I repeated, crossing my arms over my chest.

He dropped his gaze to meet mine and there wasn't an apology on his face. No, there was only guilt.

Tension settled like a black cloud in the room, thickening the air so much it was hard to breathe.

518

"Say something," I demanded.

He blinked, then looked over my head at Marty. "Would you please excuse us?"

Brody didn't wait for Marty's reply. He gripped my elbow and led me back through the workroom and into the adjoining office, closing the door behind us. It was a small room, taken up mostly by the wooden desk and couch. But there was just enough floor space for me to put a good three feet between us.

"How could you?"

"Aria, let me explain."

"Why? It seems fairly clear. You bought the flower shop for a half a million dollars—"

"Not quite that much."

"Details," I hissed. "Half a million dollars, then lied to me about the price. Why?"

"Because there's no need for you to be saddled with an enormous debt. Not when I can afford it."

"It's not about the money!" I shouted, my voice bouncing off the walls. "You came to Oregon and told me you had a flower shop. Did you?"

His silence was the only answer I needed.

It slashed through my heart. It nearly dropped me to my knees.

All this time and I'd had such faith that Brody had always been honest. What else had he lied to me about?

"You lied to me."

"I had to."

I shook my head. "No, you didn't. I would have moved. Without the flower shop, I still would have moved."

"I couldn't take that chance." He waved to my belly. "I needed you here."

And I would have been here. Simply because he'd asked to be involved in our child's life. But he hadn't given me that chance. He hadn't given me his trust or his faith.

My chin began to quiver as my eyes flooded with hot, angry tears. Goddamn hormones. They were stealing my edge. "I am so mad at you right now. You don't get to decide the course of my life. You don't get to keep secrets from me. You've had months to tell me the truth. Months."

"We didn't think it was worth upset—"

"We?"

Brody flinched, realizing he'd just fucked up.

"Clara. She knew."

He closed his eyes and nodded.

"Get out." I turned my back to him before he could see the first tear fall.

"Aria—"

"I said get out."

He stood there, for minutes, waiting. But when I didn't turn, he blew out a long breath and left.

It wasn't until the door's bell jingled that I breathed. Then I let myself cry the unshed tears, for just a moment, before pulling myself together and wiping my face dry.

Nothing good came from crying. I'd learned that after my parents had died. Clara and I had been ten when our parents had been stolen from us. The pain never did go away. It had dulled with time, but like the junkyard, it was unforgettable.

Rivers of tears hadn't brought them back to life. Rivers of tears hadn't kept my uncle away. Rivers of tears hadn't saved me from living in a junkyard at fifteen.

Tears were pointless.

Tears wouldn't make Brody change.

Dirt. "I need dirt."

I needed work. So I stormed out of the office to find Marty alone in the shop, a look of worry etched on his face.

"Are you—"

"I'm fine." I marched to one of the pots that we'd ordered a few weeks ago. I'd left it empty because it would need the right plant. Well, that snake plant was it.

There was no use taking it to Brody's home. There was no use making myself comfortable there when I couldn't possibly stay. Not now. I'd let myself get swept away with the idea of *what if*.

This baby didn't need a mother with her head stuck in romance novels. It was time for a reality check.

I wouldn't stay with a man who refused to *listen* to me. I wouldn't live with a man who didn't *respect* why I needed to control my own destiny.

After all I'd confided in him, all the pain I'd dredged up so he could understand. He still hadn't told me the truth.

That hurt the worst. In all the nights he'd held me in his arms, he hadn't found the courage to admit he'd lied.

The tears threatened to return but I blinked them away. Then I crouched, ready to haul the pot to the back room, when a sharp zing raced through my abdomen.

"Ow!" I cried, letting go of the pot as I clung to my belly.

"What?" Marty was at my side in a flash.

"I don't know." I gripped his arm, using him for balance. "It hurts. Just . . . give me a second."

"What are you doing lifting that?"

"It's not heavy." It wasn't heavy. Maybe ten pounds. I'd put it in this very spot just three days ago. "It's not heavy."

"Breathe." He clutched my arm, just as another pang raced through my side. The pain was so sharp, it was like someone had hold of my stomach and was ripping it in two.

"Ah!" I gasped, dragging in some air. *Please, let the baby be okay. Please. Please. Please.*

"Aria, what do I do?"

I met his worried gaze. "Take me to the hospital."

15

BRODY

"Aria Saint-James." I braced my hands on the counter as the nurse behind it looked over the rim of her clear-framed glasses.

"She's my sister," Clara blurted from beside me. "We're family."

The nurse opened her mouth, but before she could speak, Marty rushed to my side.

"Brody." His face was pale. A sheen of sweat clung to his bald head. "She's down here."

Clara and I followed him, the three of us jogging down the hospital hallway, dodging carts pushed against the walls and a wheelchair outside of an open door.

When Marty reached Aria's room, he stood aside and let us rush in first.

Aria was in the narrow bed, her hair draped over her shoulders. Her hands rubbed circles on her belly, and when she spotted Clara, the worry lines on her forehead relaxed. She spared me a brief glance.

She was pissed. She had a right to be. But I didn't care.

I rushed to her side and took her hand.

She ripped it free.

"Are you okay?" I asked.

"I'm okay."

"The baby?"

"Fine." She sighed and focused on her sister as Clara sat on the opposite side.

"What happened?"

"I was at the shop and I bent to pick up a pot."

"You should have let Marty—"

She shot me a glare so pointed that it shut me up. "It wasn't heavy. I lifted it three days ago."

521

I would still be having a word with Marty about what Aria lifted at work.

"I got these sharp pains." She ran a hand over her stomach, indicating the spot. "It freaked me out, so I had Marty bring me here. The doctor said it was round ligament pain."

"Is it serious?" I asked.

Aria shook her head. "No, it's normal. The round ligament just got stretched too far and too fast when I moved."

"Good." Clara sighed. "When Marty called . . . God, you had us worried."

When Marty had called, I'd nearly come out of my skin. I'd never driven so fast in my life. Clara had barely hopped into the passenger seat before I'd sped away from the house.

I'd gone home after Aria had kicked me out of the shop. Work had been pointless, and what I should have done was stay there and watch over her.

"How long do you need to stay?" I asked.

"The doctor said I could go home soon. The nurse was here a few minutes ago. She said they're getting my discharge papers ready."

"Okay. Then what?"

"Rest." She lifted a shoulder. "It will go away. If it doesn't, then I need to come back."

Clara leaned in and pulled Aria into a hug. "Are you okay?"

"I'm okay." Aria closed her eyes and wrapped her arms around Clara. "It scared me."

Scared was too mild a word. Terrified. Panicked. Those weren't right either.

Never in my life had I felt such a deep, endless fear. If Aria had been hurt. If the baby . . .

They were my life. Both of them.

Aria was my heart.

"Can we have a minute?" I asked as Clara let Aria go.

"Sure." She gave me a sad smile, then kissed her sister's forehead. "I love you."

"Love you too. Later we're going to talk about you keeping secrets from me. You know, like how much the flower shop actually cost."

Clara cringed. "You found out."

"I found out."

"Sorry. You can yell at me later. For now, I just want you out of this hospital."

"You and me both," I muttered.

Clara slipped into the hallway where Marty hovered. When the door closed, I sank to the edge of the bed.

Aria turned her gaze to the wall.

"I'm sorry." I clutched her hand with both of mine. "I'm sorry, baby."

"You should have told me about the shop."

"Yes, I should have told you."

She slumped deeper into the bed. "We can't keep doing this. Having the same argument. My heart can't take it, Brody. I think . . . maybe this was never going to work."

"Don't."

"This was about the baby. You know that if I wasn't pregnant, we never would have gotten together. I think we need to call this what it is. We're trying to make something that isn't meant to be."

Aria was giving up on me.

She was giving up on us.

But there was so much to fight for. Too much to lose the battle of my lifetime.

I refused to let her give up.

"I met Heather at a party."

That won her attention. She turned away from the wall to face me.

"It was a company Christmas party. She came as the date of one of our employees. She left with me." Maybe that was why I hadn't been truly shocked when she cheated with Alastair.

"Why are you telling me this?"

So she'd understand something I'd realized earlier today when she'd kicked me out of her flower shop. Something I suspected Clara had figured out a long, long time ago and was the reason she'd never objected to my gifts.

She'd known why.

"Heather and I dated for a while, then she started to hint at wanting a ring. I bought one. I gave it to her. I didn't even ask. One day, she didn't have a ring. The next, she did and she could tell everyone she was engaged to Brody Carmichael. That's all she'd really wanted. Bragging rights."

Heather had cared more for my name than she had for me. And I hadn't really cared at all. She'd been a companion. I hadn't had to search for dates for company functions or business meetings. She was beautiful and absent.

That was what I'd liked best about Heather. She'd left me alone to do my work. She hadn't bulldozed her way past my guards like Aria, not that Heather would have stood a chance.

She wasn't Aria.

"I didn't buy her things," I said. "Yeah, I got her birthday and Christmas gifts. I'd pay for a vacation. But otherwise, she was on her own."

Heather had begun to resent me when I hadn't let her move into my place. While the rest of her friends who'd landed rich fiancés had been able to quit their jobs, Heather had needed to keep working.

When Alastair came around, she must have seen him as her ticket to financial freedom.

All she'd had to do was time it so that I'd catch the two of them in bed. Heather had to have known that Alastair would want her simply because it had been another way to one-up me.

"I don't understand," Aria said. "You didn't buy her things?"

I shook my head. "No."

523

"Why?"

"Because I didn't love her."

Aria's mouth fell open. "What?"

"My parents. My grandparents. They didn't hug me. They didn't tell me they loved me. I watch you and Clara together and it's . . . I never had that. When I was a kid, my birthday meant a mountain of gifts, all wrapped and purchased by my mom's assistant. The nanny watched me open them. When I turned sixteen, my grandfather had a car sent to my school. They bought me things."

"That's not love, Brody."

"Isn't it? Because that's the only kind of love I know."

Aria shifted, sitting up straighter. "Not anymore."

"No." Not anymore. I tucked a lock of hair behind her ear. "I love you. Damn, but I love you, woman."

"And that's why you buy me things."

I nodded. "That's why I'll try to stop."

She stared at me, those mesmerizing eyes glassy with tears. "I love you too."

I closed my eyes and let the words sink past the skin and into my heart. Had anyone ever told me they loved me? I think Heather had, probably before she'd asked for something. Maybe my mother, a long, long time ago.

They'd been empty words.

From Aria, they were magic. They were the future.

I leaned down, dropping my forehead to hers. "It was never about the baby."

"Sure it was."

"No." I shook my head. "I fell in love with you the moment you stole that vase of flowers."

"They were really pretty flowers." She let out a quiet laugh and the sound filled my chest so full I could barely breathe.

"I love you," I whispered.

"You said that already."

"It's worth repeating."

She took my face in her hands, her thumbs stroking my beard. Then she pulled my lips down to hers, kissing me with so much tenderness and promise, I knew that for the rest of my life, I'd hold on to her. Above all else, Aria was the endgame.

"Take me home," she said against my mouth.

"I'll go find the doctor."

An hour later, after one last check from the doctor and a string of nurses bearing pamphlets on pregnancy—the Welcome hospital was nothing if not thorough—Aria was home. Clara had ridden to the shop with Marty to pick up the Cadillac.

"I think I'm going to lie down." Aria yawned as I led her inside.

"Good idea. Your bed? Or mine?"

"Mine's closer."

"How about tomorrow we pick one and just call it ours?"

524

"Deal. As long as you let me pay for the entire flower shop."

"No." I shook my head as we walked into the bedroom. "It's not worth that price."

"But you paid it anyway."

"For you? I'd buy the moon."

"Brody, this is . . . it's too much. You know why it bugs me."

I led her to the bed and pulled back the covers. Then after she slid beneath the sheet, I settled in behind her, holding her close. My hands rested on her belly, hoping to feel the baby kick just to be sure he or she was okay.

A little tap. That's all I got. But it was enough.

"I'm not going anywhere, Aria. I have all this money. What's the point of it if that means we struggle?"

"The struggle is what affirms you're alive. Without it, the bright moments don't shine."

"How about a compromise?"

She twisted to look at me. "I'm listening."

"You'll pay the one twenty-five for the shop. And you agree to drive the BMW. It's safer than the Cadillac."

"Do you actually understand what compromise means?"

I chuckled. "Shh. Listen. I'm getting to the part you're going to like. In exchange for that, I won't buy you anything new for six months."

"Twelve."

"Nine."

"Twelve. And once that time is up, we'll put a limit on the size of future gifts."

"Christ, you are stubborn."

"Then it's agreed." She gave me a smug grin. "A year. And a limit."

"A year," I conceded. "And a limit. But items for the baby don't count."

"Agreed." She nodded and snuggled deeper, then drifted off to sleep.

I waited for an hour or so, watching before slipping out of the room. When I went to my office, it was no surprise to find Clara there. She'd canceled my last meeting of the day and rescheduled those I'd missed.

"I'm just about done here," she said. "I need to get August from preschool. Do you need anything before I go?"

"No. I'm not doing much." My concentration was shit and I wanted to be close when Aria woke up. "I'm not working tomorrow. Or Sunday. You should take them off too."

"That's the plan. I've got a date with my main man for a bike ride and picnic."

August was a lucky kid to have her as a mom. And my child would be lucky to have her as an aunt.

"I'm not good with sentiment."

"Really?" she deadpanned.

"Your sarcasm has really blossomed since Aria moved here."

She laughed. "What can I say? She brings out the best in people."

"She really does. I just . . . I wanted you to know that you don't owe me anything. For the house here or anything. I didn't buy them out of charity. I don't want you to feel obligated or indebted or—"

"Brody." She cut me off and smiled. "I know. This isn't necessary."

"You work hard."

"I'm grateful for all you've done for August and me. But that's not why I work hard."

"You're sure?"

"I promise."

I sighed. "I'm glad I'll have you as my sister."

Her eyebrows rose. "Sister?"

"If she'll have me."

Clara rushed me for a hug. It was short but strong, and when she stepped back, she pressed a hand to her heart as her eyes lit up. "Thank you for loving Aria."

"I will until the day I die."

"I know." Tears flooded her eyes as she waved goodbye, leaving me alone in the office.

After an hour of returning emails, I went to see if Aria was still asleep, but when I walked into the room, the bed was empty and the patio doors open.

"There you are." I found her wrapped in a blanket, standing beside the pool. Her eyes were cast to the horizon. "What are you doing out here?"

The sun was slowly setting and the temperature dropping. Even though it was spring, the nights were cool.

"I like the sunsets here." She leaned into my side. "In a way, they remind me of the sunsets we used to watch at the junkyard. When you don't have TV or video games or smart phones, you look to the world for something to watch. I've missed that since leaving. I haven't appreciated the world enough."

I guess that was true for all of us. So we stood together, watching as the colors shifted. When a layer of orange coated the sky, I dug the ring that I'd pulled from the safe earlier out of my pocket.

"Aria Saint-James?"

"Yes, Brody Carmichael?"

I grinned and turned her to face me. Then I dropped to a knee, the ring in hand. "Marry me."

"W-what?" She did a double take at the five-carat Harry Winston.

"Will you marry me?"

"Seriously? You just promised two hours ago not to buy me anything for a year."

"I said anything new. This isn't new. I've had it for a week."

She blinked. "You have?"

"Can we focus, please? I asked you a question."

"I kind of like seeing you on your knees."

I shook my head and the ring. "You're impossible."

"Someone has to keep your ego in check."

I chuckled. "You're doing a damn fine job at the moment. You're shredding it to pieces here, baby."

"We can't have that." She touched a fingertip to the ring and smiled. "Yes. I'll marry you."

I surged to my feet and sealed it, crushing her to my chest as I swept my tongue into her mouth. Mine. She was mine. From now until forever, the one thing in this world not for sale was the best gift of my life.

She laughed, breaking the kiss. "That ring is too big."

"You'll get used to it."

Aria leaned into me. "I love you."

"I love you too." I kept her in my arms as we faced the sunset again. "What do you think? Want to stay in Arizona? Or go back to Oregon?"

"Arizona is growing on me. And besides, it's where the Cadillac brought me."

"So?"

She tipped her chin up and smiled. "You can't argue with that Cadillac."

EPILOGUE

ARIA

Three months later . . .

"Drive safely."

Clara nodded and slammed the trunk of the Cadillac. "I will."

August was buckled into his car seat, his legs bouncing wildly as he waited for them to get on the road.

"Call when you get to Phoenix." I pulled her in for a hug.

"Okay. We're going to swim and relax tonight. Then Elyria tomorrow." Her voice shook as she clutched me tight.

"Are you sure about this?"

She let me go and squared her shoulders. "I need to do this. And it's my turn in the Cadillac."

The car gleamed cherry red under the bright and beautiful Arizona sun. I'd miss it. That car had brought me to the home I hadn't realized I'd needed.

"Be careful," Brody told her.

"We will." Clara stepped closer, giving him a sideways hug as she touched the baby's foot. "You two try and rest. I know it's hard when they are so little. Take naps whenever you can."

Here she was worried about Brody, me and our five-day-old newborn son. We'd be fine. Tired, but fine. It was her I was worried about.

Clara had finally planned her trip to California. She'd waited until the baby was born and probably would have waited longer, but with August on summer break, it made sense for her to go while things at work were quiet. Brody's paternity leave meant Clara wasn't needed in the office all day.

And when she'd asked Brody for a week off, he'd encouraged her to go. We both had. My sister needed this trip, not only for a vacation with her son, but also because the longer she waited, the longer the car sat in her garage, the more anxious she became.

528

After twelve years away, Clara was facing old demons. At least she'd have August, her little pillar of strength, with her on the way. And the car. There was courage in that car.

The Cadillac was finally returning to California.

To Karson.

"We'll be back soon." She forced a smile and went to the driver's side door. She patted her pocket where she'd tucked a note with Karson's address.

Years ago, before she'd started her own journey in the Cadillac, Gemma had hired a private investigator to track all of us from the junkyard down. When we'd had our latest book club virtual chat, she'd told us that she'd had the PI confirm Karson's address, not wanting to send Clara to the wrong place. It was a good thing too since Karson had moved to a new town.

Elyria, California. A small town on the coast known for its surfing and loving community. Elyria.

All of us—Londyn, Gemma, Katherine, me—were excited for Clara. Karson had been the glue who'd held us together at the junkyard. He'd discovered it, made it a home, and kept that home safe for the rest of us. If he wasn't doing well, if his life had fallen apart . . .

It would break our hearts.

Clara's especially.

I'd cautioned her to expect anything, to be prepared for the worst, but she'd insisted it would be fine. She was eager to see him for herself.

"Bye." She pulled me into one last hug, then got in the Cadillac.

My heart crept into my throat as the engine rumbled to a start and the wheels inched forward, picking up speed as she drove down the lane.

"She'll be okay." Brody put his free arm around my shoulders and tucked me into his side.

"I hope so." As the Cadillac disappeared, I leaned into Brody's strong body, using it for support. And yawned.

"What about Danny?" he asked.

"Boring." I yawned again.

"What about Adl—"

"If you suggest Adler one more time, I'm going to the courthouse tomorrow and putting Parry, with an *a*, on his birth certificate."

Brody frowned and let me go. Then he retreated with the baby into the house, passing the plethora of plants I'd added to the entryway. After some paint and colorful toss pillows and throws, this concrete house was coming to life. He carried the baby into the bedroom and carefully set him in the cradle at the foot of our bed.

"He's five days old," he said. "My son needs a name. Adler's not that bad."

"Look at him." I tossed up a hand. "Does he look like an *Adler*?"

The name made me cringe. Probably because Brody kept suggesting it. If I actually thought he loved the name and was paying homage to his late grandfather, I would have caved. But even he didn't like it much. It was just at the top of his mind.

Much like Parry, with an *a*.

Neither of them was the right name. None of the countless other options we'd debated were either. The baby name book that rested on my nightstand had a hundred pages dog-eared, but no matter what we threw out there, nothing fit.

Our son had arrived five days ago after thirteen hours of labor. He had gray eyes that I hoped would become Brody's green. He had a mat of dark hair and the cutest nose on earth. He was the center of our universe.

And damn it, he had to have the perfect name.

"Come on." Brody took my hand and pulled me to the bed. "We're exhausted. Let's just . . . lie down for a few minutes."

"Why does he only sleep during the day?" I collapsed onto the mattress.

Brody did the same, facing me as we both relaxed into our pillows. He stretched one hand across the tiny space between us and took mine, bringing it to his lips before closing his eyes.

The black T-shirt stretched across his broad chest was fresh, as were his gray sweats. It wasn't entirely fair that he looked gorgeous after a ten-minute shower. Meanwhile I'd taken a thirty-minute bath and blow-dried my hair in an attempt to feel human again but still looked like I'd been trampled over by a herd of dirty zebras.

"Brody?"

"Hmm."

"I love you."

"I love you too, baby." Those words never got old. "Rest."

I closed my eyes but my mind refused to shut down. This was the most exhausted I'd ever been in my life, but there was daylight beyond the blinds and my brain wouldn't shut the hell up.

Name. We needed a name.

What kind of mother couldn't think of a name for her baby? We'd run through the entire list of family names on Brody's side and mine. None fit. Clara had already named August after our dad so that wasn't an option.

Why couldn't we come up with something? Why wasn't it bothering Brody more? Didn't he care about our baby? Didn't he want to get this right? Clearly not if he could just lie there and fall asleep in five seconds flat.

"Brody."

He didn't stir.

"Brody."

Nothing.

"Brody." I yanked my hand from his grip and poked him in the ribs.

He gasped awake, snapping up to look at the baby. "What? What's wrong?"

"We need a name."

He groaned and face-planted into his pillow. "Aria, he doesn't need a name this second."

"What kind of parents are we that we can't give him a name?"

"The indecisive kind." Brody reached for me, inching close. Then with my hand firmly in his once more, he held it to his heart. "We're the kind of parents who love him so much that we're not rushing a decision he'll live with his entire life."

I sighed. "I hate it when you win our fights."

"Were we fighting?"

"In my head."

He chuckled and scooched close to kiss my forehead. "Sleep. I don't want you worn out."

"Too late."

"Close your eyes." The command was meant for me, but he obeyed it himself. Those eyelashes fluttered shut.

I counted sixty-three sheep and still hadn't drifted off. "Brody."

He answered with a snore.

"Brody," I whispered.

Brody.

Like the man, I loved the name. It was pretentious and arrogant. It fit him perfectly because he was both of those things. And loving. Generous. Kind.

Never in my life had I felt so cherished than when I was with my husband.

Brody and I were married not long after he'd proposed. We didn't invite anyone but Clara and Marty. August was Brody's best man. Ron, a man who never stopped surprising me with his hidden talents, performed the ceremony on the patio at sunset.

No fuss. No party. No expenses besides my dress, and since Brody hadn't been able to buy it for me thanks to our purchasing armistice, I'd bought it myself. A long-sleeve, ivory tulle gown with lace on the bodice and wrists. The empire waist had showcased my belly, not hidden it away. Three hundred bucks and a floral arrangement from my own shop.

With the sunset at our backs and Brody impeccable in a tux, it was the second most special day of my life, eclipsed only by the day our son was born.

Brody.

That was his name. Brody. After a father who had been fighting for him since the beginning. After a father who'd rather die than miss a day of his life. After a father who loved him and his mother with every beat of his heart.

"Brody." I poked him again.

This time he just opened his eyes and glared. "Sleep."

"I want to name him Brody, after you."

He blinked, coming awake and shoving up to his elbow. "After me?"

"Yes. Brody Carmichael Jr."

"Actually. He'd be the third. Dad's name was Broderick."

"It was?"

He nodded and yawned. "His family might not be as wealthy, but they are just as pretentious."

Brody didn't speak much of his parents. Of any of his family, really. Alastair hadn't contacted him once, not even bothering to reply to Brody's email that we'd gotten married. Coreen had done her best to disown Brody and would have if not for business. She was still throwing a tantrum and making threats to sell Carmichael Communications, but Brody had called her bluff and she hadn't had the gall to see it through.

He was simply enduring her fits until his birthday this fall.

Then he would be free.

Once he was in control of Carmichael Communications, he'd pursue the best deal possible to sell the company. There were already options being discussed in secret, but at the moment, everything work related was on pause while we adjusted to life as parents.

"Brody Carmichael the Third." I smiled at the rush of adrenaline that shot through my veins. *Brody Carmichael the Third.* "I don't hate it."

"Me neither." He grinned. "We could call him Trace."

"For the Third." *Yes. Yes. Yes.* "That's it. Trace."

"Trace." Brody's smile widened. "We'll go to the courthouse tomorrow. Now will you go to sleep?"

"Yes, sir." I closed my eyes and snuggled into his arms. Thirty seconds later, a whimper came from the cradle. The baby was hungry. Nap time was over.

So Brody and I both roused.

And introduced our son to his name.

Dotted Lines

1

CLARA

"What are the yellow lines for?"

"They're dotted lines," I answered.

"But they aren't dots." August sent me his famous look through the rearview mirror. The look that said I was wrong, and he was skeptical of everything I'd taught him in the five, nearly six, years of his life. He'd picked up that suspicion toward the end of his kindergarten year, and I'd been getting the look a lot this summer.

"No, they aren't dots. But when you go fast enough, they sort of look like dots."

"Why aren't they called stripes?"

"I think some people might call them striped lines."

"That's what I'm calling them." He dipped his chin in a single, committed nod. Decision made. "What do they mean?"

"It means that if you get behind someone going slower than you, and as long as there isn't someone else coming in the opposite direction and the road is clear, you can pass the slower driver."

August let my explanation sink in, and when he didn't ask another follow-up question, I knew I'd satisfied his curiosity. For one topic.

One. Two. Three.

"Mom?"

I smiled. "Yes."

"How much does the ocean weigh?"

Now there was a whopper. But my son's endless questions never disappointed to entertain. I'd lost count of how many topics we'd covered on this trip alone. August was nothing if not inquisitive. I couldn't wait to see what he'd do with all the facts he was storing in his head for later.

"With or without the whales?" I asked.

"With the whales."

"With or without the yellow fish?"

"With them."

"And the blue fish?"

"Yes. All the fish."

"Even the starfish?"

"Mom," he groaned. "How much?"

I laughed, glancing at the backseat, then turned back to the road. "The ocean, with the whales and the fish and the starfish, weighs more than the moon and less than Jupiter."

His little forehead furrowed as he rolled that one around. "That's a lot."

"It sure is." My cheeks pinched from smiling, but that was the case with August. When he was younger, I'd told him he had magical powers. That if he smiled, I smiled. Every time. That was his magic, and he used it often.

I adjusted my grip on the steering wheel as the tires whirred over the pavement. The Cadillac floated down the road more than it rolled. In a way, it was like we were flying, skimming just above the asphalt as we soared toward California.

August stared out his window, his legs kicking. He was already restless to get out of the car even though we'd just started today's journey, navigating the roads of Phoenix as we headed toward the interstate.

We were halfway through our two-day journey from our home in Welcome, Arizona, to Elyria, California.

In total, the trip was only eight hours, but I'd split it up, not wanting to torture my son with an entire day strapped in a car seat. Last night, we'd stopped in Phoenix and had a nice evening at the hotel. August had spent the hours after dinner doing enough cannon balls into the pool to sink a pirate ship. Then he'd passed out beside me in bed while I'd read a book for a few hours of distraction.

This morning, after a continental breakfast of pastries and juice, we'd loaded up the Cadillac and hit the road.

"Mom?"

"August?"

"Do you like this car?"

"I love this car," I answered without hesitation. Even though I hadn't spent enough hours behind the wheel to consider it mine, I loved this car. For reasons that would be lost on my son.

"But there's no movie player," he argued. It was the third time he'd reminded me that the Cadillac didn't have a video console like my Volkswagen Atlas.

"Remember what I told you. This car is a classic."

He huffed and sank deeper into his car seat, totally unimpressed. "How much longer?"

"We've got a while." I stretched a hand to the backseat, palm up.

He might not be having the time of his life in the car, but he was still my best pal. With a crack, he slapped his hand to mine for a high-five.

"Love you, Gus."

"Love you too."

538

I returned my hand to the wheel and relaxed into the buttery leather seat.

Yes, I loved this car, even if it wasn't mine to keep. The 1964 Cadillac DeVille had once been a heap of rust and dented metal. The car had rested on flat tires in a junkyard in Temecula, California, home to bugs. Probably a mouse. And two runaway teens.

The on-ramp for the interstate approached and I took it, my heart galloping as I pressed the accelerator.

Today was the day. Today I was returning this Cadillac to one of those runaway teens. Today, after more than a decade away, I was going to see Karson.

My stomach twisted. If not for my firm grip on the wheel, my hands would shake. Twelve, almost thirteen years ago, I'd left California. I'd left the junkyard that six of us had called home for a time.

My twin sister—Aria—and me.

Londyn, Gemma and Katherine.

And Karson.

He'd been our protector. The one to make us laugh. The shoulder to cry on. He'd made a bad situation bearable. An adventure. We'd survived the junkyard because of Karson.

And the Cadillac was his, a gift from Londyn. I was simply the delivery girl.

In another lifetime, Londyn and Karson had made this Cadillac their home, back in the days when it didn't have glossy, cherry-red paint or a working engine. But Londyn had hauled the Cadillac out of the junkyard and had it completely restored. She'd kept it herself for a time, then set out to give it to Karson.

Her trip from Boston to California had only made it to West Virginia. From there, Gemma had taken the Cadillac to Montana. Katherine had been the third behind the wheel, driving it to Aria in Oregon. Then my sister had brought it to me in Arizona.

Ready or not, it was time to finish what Londyn had started. I'd put off this trip long enough. But it was time to make the handoff, to take the last leg of the journey.

The final trip.

It wasn't the hours on the highway or the destination that had kept my heart racing since we'd left home yesterday. It was the man waiting, unsuspecting, at the end of the road.

Had Karson found whatever it was he'd been searching for? Had he built a good life? Was he happy? Did he remember our moments together in vivid clarity like I did? Did he replay them during the long nights when sleep was lost?

Will he recognize me?

"Mom?"

I shook off the anxiety. "Yeah?"

"How much longer till we get there? Exactly?"

"About four and a half hours."

He groaned and flopped his back. "That's gonna take *forever*."

"You could take a nap. That will make the trip go by faster."

August sat up straight and sent me a look of pure poison through the mirror. "It's morning."

I pulled in my lips to hide my smile. "How about some music?"

"Can I play a game on your phone?"

"Sure." I rifled through my purse in the passenger seat, finding my phone. Then I handed it back to him.

August unlocked the screen with the code, though his face worked at times too.

I'd be forever grateful to Devan, August's father, for helping me create this magnificent boy. But I was also forever grateful that August looked exactly like me. He had my blond hair, though his had been lightened by the Arizona summer sun, whereas I got mine highlighted at the salon. We shared the same nose and the same brown eyes. August's second toe was longer than his big toe, something he'd also inherited from me.

He was mine.

Mine alone. The lawyer I'd hired when August was a newborn had assured me that once Devan had signed his rights away, Gus was mine.

It wasn't the life I'd wanted for my son, to grow up without a father, but it was better this way. Devan hadn't wanted a child and no amount of coercion would have turned him into a decent parent.

So I showered my son with love and attention. I would, shamelessly, for the rest of his life.

Good luck to any girlfriend he brought home. Fathers were allowed to put boyfriends through an interrogation. Well, this mother was taking that liberty too.

The sound of a math game drifted through the cab as August played on my phone. The dings and chimes of the app mixed with the hum from the wheels on the road.

And I breathed as the miles toward California whipped by.

It was only a state. Only a name. But somewhere along the way after we'd left Temecula, California had become synonymous with the past.

California meant hungry days. California meant dark nights. California meant death.

It was the reason Aria wouldn't go back. Same with Katherine. Neither of them had any desire to set foot in California again. Maybe, if I'd begged, Aria would have come with me, but I wouldn't have asked that from her. Besides, she'd just had a baby and was in no shape for a road trip.

Aria and Brody were currently enduring the sleepless, grueling nights as parents of a newborn. Logistically, it made sense for me to take this trip now. Brody was both brother-in-law and boss, so while he was taking time to spend with Aria and the baby, there was a lull in work to do as his assistant. With August on summer break from school, this was the window.

Or maybe I knew that if I kept avoiding the trip, I'd never take it.

I could do this.

I have to do this.

540

Because for twelve years, I'd been holding on to a hope. A distant hope, but one powerful enough that it had kept me from letting go and moving forward.

It was time.

After only thirty minutes, August gave up on his math game. He asked me another long string of questions, and then by some miracle, he fell asleep. Swimming at the hotel last night must have worn him out.

He was drooped in his chair, his head hanging down at an angle that would have given me a neck kink, when we approached the California border. Elyria sat on the coast, north of San Diego, and we still had hours to drive, but crossing the border was a hurdle of its own.

I'd opted for a southern route through Arizona, wanting to avoid Los Angeles traffic. And Temecula.

Visiting California was enough for one weekend. Returning to the town where we'd spent our childhood was an entirely different matter. Temecula had happy memories from the early years, from the happy lives Aria and I had lived before our parents had been killed in a car accident when we were ten. After that, I could count the number of happy memories on one hand. Temecula was full of ghosts, and though they still called to me at times, I wouldn't go there even with August as my steadfast companion.

This trip was about closure. It was about Karson. That was plenty.

I gripped the wheel, my heart in my throat, as I passed the sign at the state border. *California.*

My stomach rolled and sweat beaded at my temple. I sucked in a long breath, dragging it through my nose to then push out my mouth. *In and out. In and out, Clara.* Just like Karson had taught me years ago when he'd witnessed one of my panic attacks.

I hadn't had one in years.

My hands were trembling when my phone rang. I stretched for it in the passenger seat, checking that August was still asleep. It always amazed me that he could sleep through about anything.

"Hey," I answered, not at all surprised that my sister was calling. Whether it was a twin thing or a sister thing, we usually had a good pulse on each other's moods, even thousands of miles apart.

"Hi." Aria yawned. "Are you okay?"

"No," I admitted. "This is harder than I thought it would be."

"Are you in California?"

"Yes." I blew out a trembling breath. "I can do this, right?"

"You can do this. You're the bravest person I know."

"No, you are."

Aria had brought us both through the hardest time in our lives. While I'd fallen apart after our parents' deaths, she'd kept us moving. Ten-year-old me had gone comatose for a few weeks, mostly from the shock. What kid wouldn't buckle under that much heartbreak? *Aria.* Maybe it was because I'd needed her and she'd stayed strong. She'd kept me going through the motions until the fog of grief had cleared.

Then I'd vowed never to fall apart again. As a child, I'd made good on that promise to myself. As an adult and parent, failing was not an option.

Aria thought I could make this trip and she was right. I could do this.

Granted, she didn't know what had happened with Karson. Maybe if she knew the truth, she would have given me different advice.

"How are you doing? How's Trace?" I asked, needing a different topic to focus on.

"We're both good." There was a smile in her voice and a tiny squeak hit my ear. "He's nursing. I think he likes his name."

"Because it's perfect." Broderick Carmichael the Third. *Trace*. It had taken them over five days to give the baby a name, but when I'd called to check in last night from the hotel, Aria and Brody had proudly announced Trace.

"How is the drive?" Aria asked.

"It's fine. Taking *forever* according to August."

Aria laughed and yawned again.

"I'll let you go. Take a nap if you can, okay?"

"That's the plan. Brody fell asleep about an hour ago. Once he wakes up, we're switching."

I was glad she had him. I was glad he had her.

Maybe it had been watching my sister fall in love with my friend that had been the final push to send me on this trip. Someday, maybe, I wanted love. I wanted a man to hold me at night. I wanted a man who'd be a good role model to August. I wanted a man who made me feel cherished.

Until I confronted the past, I'd always wonder. I'd always compare.

I'd always think of Karson.

"Call me when you get there," Aria said.

"I will."

"Take a picture of Karson with the car if you can. I think Londyn would like to see that."

"Good idea. I think she would too," I said. "Love you."

"Love you. Bye."

When I ended the call, the anxiety from earlier had lessened. That was the way with my sister. On a bad day, we had each other. It had been that way our entire lives.

There was a good chance—better than good—that I'd return home with a bit of a bruised heart. And she'd be there to help it heal.

I can do this.

There was no turning back now. The Cadillac had sat in my garage for too long as it was. Maybe it would have been easier if not for the track record with these handoffs. For every trip this Cadillac had taken, one of my friends had found love.

Londyn had met Brooks in West Virginia, thanks to a flat tire.

Gemma had returned to Montana and found Easton waiting.

Katherine and Cash had fallen in love on the sleepy highways between Montana and Oregon.

542

Aria had come to Arizona and realized the hate she'd harbored for Brody had actually been affection.

I had no delusions that this trip would result in a major life change. I fully expected to be the one woman who returned home single. Months of preparing myself for that reality hadn't made it easier to swallow.

Yet there was that glimmer of hope I'd buried deep. It mingled with the fear because, unlike my friends, I hadn't set out into the unknown unsuspecting.

I knew exactly who I was seeking.

Had his smile changed? Did he grin like he used to? God, I hoped so.

I hoped that whatever had happened to Karson in the past twelve years, his smile hadn't dulled. Because on my darkest nights, when the ghosts escaped their confines at the California border and drifted into Arizona, it was the memory of Karson's smile that chased them away.

That, and my son.

August stirred, blinking heavy eyelids as he came awake.

"Hey, bud."

"Are we there yet?"

I gave him a sad smile. "No, not yet. But we're getting closer."

He sagged in his seat, his eyes still sleepy and his cheeks flushed. "Mommy?"

"Yeah?" My heart squeezed each time he slipped and called me Mommy. One of his friends at school last year had told August that he called his mom *Mom* and not *Mommy*. From that day forward, I'd been Mom except for the rare moments when he was still my baby boy.

"Do you think we can go swimming as soon as we get there?" he asked.

"Probably not right away," I said. "First we need to stop by my friend's house. Remember?"

"Oh, yeah. Is it going to take a long time?"

"No, not too long."

"Then we can see the ocean, right?"

"Yes, then we'll see the ocean."

August yawned but sat straighter. His eyes lost their sleepy haze and his gaze flicked out his window, chasing the sage brush and sand that bordered the interstate. "What do you think is more scary, a shark or a lion?"

This boy would never know how grateful I was for his questions. He'd never know that he kept me grounded. He kept me sane. He kept me going. "That depends. Is it a hammerhead shark or a tiger shark?"

"Hammerhead."

"A lion."

He nodded. "Me too."

The questions continued until the open road clogged with vehicles and the Cadillac was swallowed up in traffic. August was about to come out of his skin by the time we made it to the outskirts of San Diego.

We stopped for lunch and August devoured a well-earned Happy Meal at McDonald's. Then after a refill at a gas station, we loaded up once more for the drive along the coast. After we passed the city, the Sunday traffic moved in the opposite direction, most people returning home after a weekend trip.

Thirty miles outside of Elyria, the ocean came into view, and I decided to pop off the interstate for a quieter highway that hugged the coast. August's eyes were wide as he stared at blue water and the waves glittering under the bright July sun.

"Let's do something fun," I told August, touching the brake to ease us into a turnout along the road.

"What?" He bounced in his chair, then his jaw dropped when I moved to put the convertible top down. "Cool!"

We both laughed as I pulled onto the road. August's hands shot into the air, his hair, in need of a cut, tousling in the salt-tinged wind.

He needed sunscreen. He should be wearing sunglasses. But for thirty miles, fun was more important than being the responsible mother every moment of every day. That and I didn't want to do anything to ruin that smile on his face.

I needed that smile as the nerves crept in, twisting up my insides and making it hard to breathe. So I braced my knee against the wheel and raised my arms. "Woohoo!"

"Woohoo!" August cheered with me.

His laughter was the balm to my soul, and I soaked it in, reminding myself that this was August's trip too. This was his summer vacation to the ocean, something he could brag about on his first day of first grade this fall.

Vacation. We'd explore the oceanside. We'd shop for souvenirs we didn't need and eat too much ice cream. We'd have a fun trip, then go home. Brody had volunteered his jet to save August from a two-day return trip in a rental car.

The speed limit dropped as we passed a sign welcoming us to Elyria.

I gulped.

My phone chimed with directions through town toward the address I'd entered days ago. Brightly colored shops lined the main road. A couple crossed the road ahead, each carrying surf boards. Signs for parking areas sprang up every few blocks, directing people toward the beach.

Later I'd explore this charming town, but at the moment I kept my focus forward, listening intently to the navigation. When I turned down a side street, I was so anxious I didn't bother taking in the neighborhood around us.

Then we were there. Karson's address. The destination was on our left.

I slowed the Cadillac to a crawl in front of a white stucco house with arched windows and a terra-cotta roof. The tiled walkway to the front door was the same rich, caramel brown as the clay. Two baby palm trees towered over the green yard, and off to the side of the house was a garage.

I pulled around the corner, parking in the driveway. The thunder of my heart was so loud I barely registered August's question.

"Mom, is this it?"

I managed a nod as I turned off the car and unbuckled my seat belt.

Then I stared at the house. How would I make it to the front door? Maybe I should have called first. Karson might not even be home. If not, I guess we'd come back later.

But this was definitely his house. I double-checked the number beside the garage door.

"Can I get out?" August asked, already unbuckling his harness.

"Sure." I'd need him with me for this.

I climbed out of the car, walking on unsteady legs to his side to help him out. Then with my son's hand in mine, I stood in the driveway and let the sun warm my face. The sound of the ocean was a gentle whisper on the air. The scent of salt and sea hit my nose.

Aria had lived on the Oregon coast for years, and though the smell was similar, there was something sweeter in the Elyria air.

Karson had always said he wanted to be close to the ocean. He'd wanted to learn how to surf. I was glad he'd gotten that wish.

The sound of a door opening caught my attention and I turned, just in time to watch a tall man with dark hair step outside. A short-trimmed beard shaded his sculpted jaw. He was wearing a pair of khaki cargo shorts slung low on his narrow hips. His green T-shirt stretched over his broad chest and clung to the strength in his biceps. His feet were bare.

Karson.

My heart skipped.

He'd grown up. Gone were the lanky arms and legs. Gone was the shaggy hair in need of a cut. Gone was the youth from his face.

This was Karson Avery, a man who stole my breath. But he'd done that at nineteen too.

Those beautiful hazel eyes studied me, then darted to the car as he came toward us. A crease formed between his eyebrows as he took it in. Then they moved to me and that crease deepened.

My stomach did a cartwheel. *Please recognize me.*

If he didn't . . . I clung to August's hand, drawing strength from his fingers. It would break my heart if Karson had forgotten me. Because in all these years, he'd never been far from my mind.

Karson's feet stopped abruptly and his entire body froze. Then he blinked and shook his head. "Clara?"

Oh, thank God. I swallowed the lump in my throat. "Hi, Karson."

"I can't believe it." He shook his head again, then his gaze shifted to August. "Hi there."

August clutched me tighter and murmured, "Hi."

"Is it really you?"

"It's me."

"It's really you." A slow smile spread across his face, wider and wider.

It hadn't changed. There, on the face of a man, was the smile from the boy I'd loved.

The boy I'd loved before his life had gone one direction and mine had gone the other.

And between us streaked those dotted lines.

2

CLARA

TWELVE YEARS EARLIER...

"Here." Aria tossed me the dry-erase marker.

I caught it and rubbed my fist on the van's wall, erasing yesterday's number. Then, popping the cap, I wrote today's number in blue. The sharp scent of the marker had become the smell of hope.

Sixty-one.

We had sixty-one days until our eighteenth birthday. Sixty-one days until we could leave the junkyard as legal adults and get on with our lives. After three years of living in this van without electricity or heat or air conditioning, our time here was coming to a close.

I'd thought as the days had ticked away, I'd be more excited to say goodbye to this shitty old van. I guess leaving any home was hard, even a dirty one. Even my uncle's. Though any shithole was better than living under that bastard's roof.

"Are you sure you don't want to go to Montana?" Aria asked from her bedroll where she was bent, tying her shoes.

The laces had been white at one point, just like the laces on mine. But after nearly three years, they were permanently a brownish red—the color of the dirt outside that we did our best to keep from tracking in.

"I don't know." I shrugged. "That's where Londyn, Gemma and Katherine went."

"Exactly my point."

"Don't you think we should, like, find our own place?"

"Yeah," she muttered. "I guess so. Then where?"

"LA?"

"Hell to the no." She stood up and plucked her favorite black hoodie from the backpack that was her closet. "I want out of California. Forever."

"I just want out of this freaking town." I took one long look at the number on the metal wall, then recapped the marker and tossed it into my wooden crate.

Sixty-one.

The excitement would come. Eventually. Right?

"Will you water my plants for me today?" Aria asked.

"Sure." I had nothing else to do.

On the days when I wasn't working, life in the junkyard was boring. The day would stretch without TV or a phone or . . . anything. So I'd water her plants. I'd sweep out the van with the handheld broom I'd gotten from the dollar store a couple years ago. Both chores would take an hour total. Then I'd have to find something else to do.

"What do you want me to bring you back from the restaurant?" she asked.

"Food."

My answer was the same as always. Just like Aria's answer on the days when she was stuck here and I went to work at a truck-stop diner. I washed dishes for six dollars an hour. It was below minimum wage but since the owner paid me in cash under the table and didn't ask questions about why I hadn't been in school all last year, it was worth the cut.

Staying off the grid was the only way we'd made this living arrangement work.

For sixty-one more days, Clara Saint-James was a ghost.

Then Aria and I would leave here and rejoin society with a real address and social security numbers and birth certificates—the documents tucked away beneath my bedroll in a plastic bag. We'd made sure to take them from our uncle before we'd run away.

Maybe when we got out of here, we'd actually get driver's licenses. A credit card. A bank account.

"Any requests?" Aria asked. She worked as a dishwasher too at a greasy spoon about a thirty-minute walk from here. The owner of her restaurant had actually asked for an application.

Aria had listed me as her mother's name, the junkyard as our address. Thankfully, they hadn't tried to call the fake phone number she'd put on the application. Or if they had, they hadn't asked why the call hadn't gone through.

Like me, she was paid under the table, so why her boss had needed an application, I wasn't sure. Whatever the reason, all that mattered was that we both worked in restaurants. The food was worth more than the hourly wage.

On the days we worked, neither of us had to worry about a meal. And normally, there'd be enough left in the kitchen for an extra sandwich or two to bring home.

"Ham and cheese," I said. It was Karson's favorite, not that I'd tell Aria that was the reason I always asked for it.

"'Kay. I'm out." She stood at the mouth of the van, waiting.

I walked over and wrapped my arms around her.

The night our parents had died, I hadn't wanted to give my mom or dad a hug good night. I'd been in the middle of a game of Fallout on my Play-Station. I'd gotten to level eight and the blocks had been falling so fast. My fingers had flown over the control. And when my parents had kissed me goodbye, when they'd told me to have fun and be good for our babysitter, I'd dismissed them with a grunt.

Hours later, on their way home, a drunk driver had crossed the center line and crashed into their car.

Ten-year-old me hadn't understood that life was short. I'd been so worried about a stupid video game that I hadn't hugged my parents goodbye.

I wouldn't make that mistake again.

"Be careful." I let Aria go and watched as she hopped out of the van.

When her shoes hit the dirt, she looked up at me and waved. "Bye. Have a good day."

"You too."

I didn't like the days when we walked into town alone. Yes, we'd been doing it for nearly three years, but that didn't mean it was safe. Until we were gone, until we left Temecula and turned eighteen, we would never be safe. Not until we had control over our own lives.

Aria didn't head for the small gate in the junkyard fence that served as our own personal door. Instead, she rushed over to Lou's shop, disappearing into the bathroom.

I stayed standing at the end of the van, waiting until she came out. Then with another wave, she disappeared through the rusted cars and stacks of metal parts.

I sighed, scanning my rust-colored world. Everything here was tinged orange-brown. Some of the old cars still had flecks of paint—teal or black or red. This van had once been white. But with every passing day, the colors disintegrated, little by little. Chip by chip. It was a losing battle against the wind and the sun and the rain and the dust.

The only bright, fresh color came from Aria's plants. She'd been growing more and more this year, ever since the girls had left.

I think she missed Londyn and Gemma and Katherine more than I did. Not that I didn't miss them. I did. I missed our friends. It was just . . . easier with them gone.

I didn't have to work so hard to hide my crush on Karson.

Instead of masking it from five people, I only had to hide my true feelings from two—my sister and Karson himself.

Easy when I was here alone.

The sun would be warm today, perfect for growing, so I hopped down from the truck and found the old coffee can that Aria used to water her plants. It rested by one of the truck's flat wheels.

Our home wasn't fancy but it kept the rain out, mostly. And the mice. It was an old delivery vehicle, the back a rectangular metal box. It had gotten into an accident at some point, hence its lifetime membership in this grave-yard with the other broken-down heaps.

The front end was smashed. The hood was a crumpled piece of metal, and wherever the engine was, I doubted it had survived. But the box was mostly solid. The few jagged holes in the metal siding let in some natural light. We'd covered them with plastic shower curtains to keep out the wind and water and bugs.

It was time to replace the curtains. They were tinged with dirt and film. But with only sixty-one days to go, I didn't see the point in wasting the money.

Inside the truck, Aria had her side and I had mine. At the foot of each of our bedrolls rested our backpacks. By my pillow, I kept neat stacks of tattered romance novels I'd bought for a dime at the thrift store. Most I'd read ten or eleven times.

The books formed a little shelf of sorts to hold a bottle of water, a flashlight and my battery-powered alarm clock. At night, that shelf also held the foldable knife I'd stolen from Uncle Craig.

I patted it in my pocket, feeling its weight against my hip. That knife went with me everywhere, even in the junkyard.

Taking the can, I walked toward the shop. It was one of two buildings in the junkyard, the other a shack where the owner, Lou Miley, lived.

Lou's windows were arguably dirtier than my windows, but at night, they let out enough of a glow that we knew Lou was inside. In the winter, a steady plume of smoke would stream from his metal chimney and the scent of a campfire would fill the air. Lou was a recluse most days. He'd venture outside only when necessary to run the yard.

I cast a quick glance at his shack, sniffing bacon in the air. The kitchen window was cracked and Lou must have had a nice breakfast.

My stomach growled. The granola bar I'd scarfed earlier would have to do until Aria came home from work. We needed to get to the grocery store and pick up some more bread and peanut butter, but I didn't get paid until Friday.

And I refused to raid our savings.

Alongside the plastic bag of legal documents under my bedroll was another full of cash. Half of everything Aria and I made went into that pouch. It was our future, and we'd built it with sheer determination and discipline.

We were saving up to get out of here. That money was going to be the foundation for the days when we could afford bacon for breakfast.

And a stove.

And a refrigerator.

Shoving the hunger aside, I walked to the shop. It stood nearly three times as tall as Lou's shack, tall enough that all of his equipment could fit inside.

I slipped in through the metal side door and flicked on the row of lights. The smell of grease and oil and gasoline hit my nose as I weaved past the machinery. An excavator with a claw on its arm. A tractor with a large bucket. A forklift crowding the doorway to the shop's bathroom.

The florescent light above the cracked mirror flickered, giving me an instant headache. I went to the deep white sink, stained from years of dirty hands and not enough bleach, and twisted on the faucet to fill the can.

It might not be the biggest or brightest bathroom, but it was better than nothing. And we'd cleaned it enough that I didn't have any issue walking around in my bare feet.

Lou allowed us to use this bathroom. It still smelled like Aria's shampoo and conditioner from her morning shower. The floral scent clung to the air and I breathed it in as the can filled.

The shower stall was just large enough to stand in and wash under the silver head. There wasn't even a curtain to separate it from the rest of the bathroom. But a shower every day made this place livable. It kept the dirt from building up. It kept my honey-blond hair from hanging limp to my waist.

Most days, I braided it to keep it out of my face, but at night, when I lay down on my pillow, it was a comfort to know that at least my hair was clean.

With the can filled, I left the bathroom, shutting off the light behind me. Then I retreated through the shop toward the door, only to have it whip open just as I reached for the handle.

Water sloshed out of the watering can, soaking the toes of my shoes.

"Shit. Sorry." Karson stepped back, holding the door for me. "I didn't know you were in there."

"That's okay." My heart raced and my voice was breathy. Because, holy abs, he was shirtless.

No shirt. None. I was staring at a bare chest, naked arms and a fantastic belly button, which wasn't actually all that interesting, but beneath it a line of dark hair disappeared beneath the gray towel wrapped around his waist. The whole image was . . . *wow*.

Don't stare. Don't stare.

My mantra this year.

I dropped my gaze, pretending to inspect my wet shoe.

This wasn't entirely new. I'd seen Karson without a shirt on before, but it hadn't been for a while. And back then, he'd belonged to Londyn. It had been easier to pretend I wasn't head over heels for the guy when his girl-friend had always been nearby.

Now it was impossible.

He was lean, we were all lean, but Karson was cut too. His chest was broad, his stomach hard and flat. There was a V just where the terry cloth circled his hips.

My mouth went dry thinking about the slight bulge beneath that towel. The flush in my cheeks felt hot and red.

Oh my God. I sucked at this. How was I supposed to hide my crush on Karson when he walked around in nothing but a towel?

"I . . ." I swallowed hard and stepped through the open door, moving past him, careful to keep a wide berth. "I'll get out of your way."

"You're not in my way."

I gave him a small smile, then dropped my chin to my chest and watched every one of my steps as I scurried away, only daring to look back when I heard the shop door close.

"Ugh," I groaned, looking up to the blue sky. "What is wrong with me?"

Karson was never going to like me. Ever. He was in love with Londyn. The two of them had lived together in the Cadillac for years. She might have left for Montana with Gemma and Katherine, but that didn't mean Karson would ever want me instead.

Londyn, with her silky blond hair three shades lighter than my own. Londyn, with her pretty smile and rich green eyes. Karson and Londyn. He loved her. He'd had sex with her. I'd heard them once, giggling and kissing. Then the Cadillac had started to rock, and I'd had to sleep with the pillow over my face to block out the noise and hide my tears from Aria.

He wanted Londyn, not me.

The only reason Karson was still here at the junkyard was because he saw Aria and me as little sisters. He'd stayed to watch out for us even though he'd just turned nineteen and by all rights should have left over a year ago.

Like Londyn, Gemma and Katherine.

The girls had done exactly what Aria and I would be doing in sixty-one days. The day they were all eighteen, they'd hopped on a bus destined for Montana. Katherine had found them housekeeping jobs at a resort or ranch or something.

But Karson had stayed, saying it wasn't safe for Aria and me to be here alone.

He wasn't wrong.

It would just be easier if I didn't have this epic, ridiculous crush on a guy who was never, ever, ever going to like me. Karson probably thought I was a freak. As the months went on, it got harder and harder to make eye contact as we talked. Then there were the times that I stuttered like a moron. Example: today.

"Great, Clara. Just great," I huffed as I reached the truck and Aria's plants.

Whereas I'd spent my extra change on books, Aria had splurged on a hand trowel and seed packets. How she got anything to grow in the dry, hard-packed dirt of the junkyard was a mystery, but the greenery proved it possible.

She'd planted cosmos and morning glories. She had Shasta daisies and sweet potato vines. I'd water them all, grateful for their color to brighten our temporary home.

The watering can was empty too soon, and I'd need to take a few more trips to the bathroom for refills, but I climbed into the truck instead. Once Karson was showered and dressed, I'd venture out. In the meantime, I'd spend my morning studying.

And do my best to forget about the definition in Karson's arms and the gold and green sparkle in his hazel eyes.

I kicked off my shoes, leaving them by the sliding door we left up most days to let in the fresh air. Then I made myself comfortable on my bedroll, which was just a sleeping bag that had lost most of its fluff over the years. It was still warm, combined with the fleece blanket I draped on top, but even the foam cushion under the covers didn't hide the fact that we were sleeping on a metal floor.

My GED study guide rested on top of the wheel well. I grabbed it, cracking it to the section where I'd left off last, and began hammering through practice questions.

I was in the middle of a language arts section when a knock came on the wall.

"Hey." Karson vaulted into the truck, fully clothed.

I forced a smile to hide my disappointment.

"Brought you a banana," he said. "I just bought a bunch yesterday. Thought you might want one."

"Thanks." I took it as he handed it over.

"You're welcome." He sat down across from me on Aria's bed, his long legs eating up the floor space between us. "How's studying going?"

"Okay." I ran my hand over the guidebook's page.

Karson had gotten me this book. I'd told him that I wanted to get my GED after we left the junkyard and two days later, he'd brought this home. It was new, unlike the used books I could afford. The cover was glossy. The page corners were crisp and square, meaning it hadn't been cheap.

We spent our money on necessities. Food. Clothing. Blankets. Toiletries. Not GED study guides.

I knew he'd stolen it. He hadn't admitted it, but there'd been no receipt and it hadn't come in a plastic sack. It wasn't the first time he'd stolen, and I doubted it would be the last. I'd never forget the first time I'd watched him palm an apple from the grocery store and start eating it in the aisles. He'd dropped the core into a garbage can before we'd gone through check-out, no one the wiser.

Sure, it bugged me a little. Aria and I didn't steal. There was a pinprick of guilt when I cracked the book's pages, but it was also a gift. A gift from Karson for my future. I'd been so touched by his thoughtfulness that I'd cried after he'd dropped it off—that was before I'd realized it had likely been shoplifted.

We all did what we had to do.

I shut the book and ripped open the banana's peel. I was hungry and wouldn't turn down food, but someday, I would never eat a banana again. The same was true for granola bars and canned green beans. Peanut butter and honey sandwiches too.

When Londyn had lived here, she'd worked at a pizza place. It was the only thing we'd eaten a lot of that I hadn't completely lost the taste for. Though I never craved it.

"What are you doing today?" I asked as I chewed.

"Nothing. I'm bored. Are you working?"

"Nope." I took another bite and almost gagged. Freaking bananas. I hadn't liked them before coming here either.

"Want to play cards?" he asked.

I shrugged, trying to hide my excitement at time alone with Karson. "Sure."

An hour later, we'd moved from my place to his, and I was kicking his ass at gin rummy. "Gin."

"Gah." He tossed his cards onto the discard pile. "We need a new game."

I giggled and collected the deck. The edges were worn and gray. The nine of clubs had a noticeable bend. "Poker?"

"Yeah." He stood and disappeared into the other section of the tent, returning with a little cup of toothpicks. We didn't have money to gamble or actual poker chips, but toothpicks worked fine.

After Gemma and Katherine had left, their tent slash fort had been unoccupied. The structure was a collection of metal sheets and tarps that Gemma had engineered into a shelter.

For a guy who stood over six feet tall, it made sense for Karson to get out of the cramped backseat of the Cadillac. He'd moved in here, taking up Gemma's old room. The common area had lost some of its life without the girls here. Katherine's tiny paintings on the wall weren't as bright as they used to be.

"What do you think will happen to this place when we all leave?" I asked Karson, shuffling the cards.

He resumed his seat across from me, leaning against one of the makeshift walls. "I don't know. Probably nothing, knowing Lou."

Lou had sectioned off the junkyard. His house, the shop and the area where we lived was off-limits to customers. Whether it had always been like that I wasn't sure, but from the time Karson had come here, Lou had all but given us free rein of our small portion of the yard.

Beyond his shack swam a sea of rusted cars and old parts. People would come in during the day and rummage through the piles. Lou would emerge to show them around, always careful to keep them away from our area.

"What do you think will happen to Lou?"

Karson lifted a shoulder. "I don't know that either."

"Will you come back here? After you leave?"

"Maybe. You?"

"Maybe." *Maybe not.*

Karson pulled a toothpick from the cup and rolled it between his fingers. The movement was mesmerizing, much like his face. He'd shaved today. The dark stubble that matched the color of his hair was gone from his cheeks and jaw. It made his lips seem softer. His smile wider.

I caught myself staring and tore my eyes away to focus on the cards. "Five-card draw? Or hold 'em?"

"Hold 'em."

We used to have poker tournaments in this room, when the girls were here. "Do you miss them? Londyn and Gemma and Katherine."

"Sure." He counted toothpicks, handing me a handful of twenty. "Don't you?"

"Yeah, I do." I didn't miss seeing him kiss Londyn, but otherwise, yes.

They were my friends. Londyn was the reason we'd found the junkyard in the first place. We'd lived in the same trailer park and after she'd run away from her junkie parents, we'd tracked her down. A couple of the kids who'd worked with her at a pizza parlor had known that she'd been hanging out at the junkyard during the day, ditching school. Though they hadn't known she'd been living here too.

"Do you think we'll ever see them again?" I asked.

"Honestly? No." He looked up and the gentle smile he gave me nearly broke my heart. "I mean, maybe someday. But I doubt it."

"Even Londyn?" The question slipped out before I could swallow the words. I knew they'd broken up. Clean. As friends. But maybe he hoped to see her again one day. Maybe he'd continue on to Montana when our sixty-one days were up.

"Yeah. Londyn too." Karson gave me another smile. One that made me want to scream. It wasn't his playful smirk or his wide grin when he thought something was funny. It was the sweet smile, for a little sister.

Kill me now.

I dealt the cards and focused on the game, winning the first five hands in a row. When Karson was down to three toothpicks, he went all in on a bluff. I called it.

Game over.

"Damn." He laughed. "Not my day for cards. Let's do something else."

"Okay. What?"

"Feel like going for a walk? I wouldn't mind stretching my legs."

I pushed up off the ground, brushing off my jeans. Then I followed him outside and through the junkyard, toward the ten-foot chain-link fence that had a row of barbed wire on top.

Lou didn't like people in his space. He'd erected the fence to keep them out.

We were the exception.

The main entrance had two large gates set on wheels. Lou kept a chain and padlock around them unless he was expecting a customer. The *PRIVATE PROPERTY* sign hung below another that read *MUST CALL FIRST.*

But there was another entrance, a small gate that was hidden from the road and bordered by an old car. Karson had discovered it his first night at the junkyard years ago. To anyone passing by, it looked blocked. But the gate opened enough for us to squeeze in and out. Some days, we strolled through the main entrance if Lou had gotten up and unchained the lock. But mostly, we used the side gate.

Once on the road to town, we settled into an easy pace on the asphalt. There were no sidewalks bordering the one-mile stretch of pavement. Or what we assumed was one mile. None of us knew for sure, but before Karson had dropped out of school and run away, he'd been able to run a mile in under six minutes. One day, bored, he'd run the road as a test.

The junkyard was on the outskirts of Temecula, lending it privacy. The closest neighbor was halfway down the road and even then, the overgrown trees and tall fence hid the house and its occupants from view. Or maybe . . .

"Do you think they planted all the trees in an attempt to block out the junkyard?" I asked Karson as we walked past the house.

He chuckled. "Definitely. Wouldn't you?"

"Totally." I laughed. "So where are we going?"

"Where do you want to go?"

Anywhere with you. "I don't care. I'm up for whatever."

"How about the movie theater?"

"Last time we tried to sneak in we got caught. And you got into a fight."

"That guy was a fucking asshole, Clara. He shouldn't have grabbed you like that."

It hadn't been a big deal. The theater manager had taken my arm and pulled me toward the exit. He'd literally been trying to throw me out.

Except the moment he'd touched me, Karson had exploded. He'd punched the manager so fast I'd barely registered his fist flying through the air before the loud crack of knuckles hitting jawbone.

As the manager had collapsed onto the floor, another employee, a tall, lanky kid, had rushed Karson. Those two had shoved and grappled and traded a couple of hits until Karson had landed another solid punch to the nose—I'd never seen a nose gush so much blood. But it had been enough for us to get away before the cops had shown up.

Karson's eye had been bruised for a couple of days. It wasn't the first black eye he'd gotten, and again, I doubted it would be the last. I worried most about the fights he got into when none of us were there to drag him home.

He protected us. But who protected him?

"We'll go to another theater," he said.

"That's a long walk."

"We've got nothing else to do. Besides . . ." Karson reached into his pocket and pulled out a wad of cash. "This time we'll pay."

"No, don't waste it." I pushed at his arm, urging him to put the cash away. I didn't want to risk anyone seeing it and coming after him. Not that there was anyone around to see. The two of us were alone on the road.

"It's settled. We'll go to a movie. And I'll have the prettiest girl in the universe in the seat beside me."

I blushed and elbowed him in the ribs. "Flirt."

"With you? Always."

If only that flirting meant something.

It was pointless to argue—and I really wanted to see a movie—so I let Karson treat me to an afternoon of fun. Of normalcy.

In a dark theater, we weren't a couple of runaway teens who ate popcorn by the fistful because at our home there was no such thing as a microwave. Or asked for extra ice in our shared Coke because both ice and Coke were scarcities.

We were just Karson and Clara. A hot guy. And the girl who wished he saw her as more than a friend.

Still, by the time we left the theater, my smile felt permanent.

We talked about the movie the entire way home, our favorite lines and the twist at the end that Karson had seen coming but I hadn't. Evening was upon us by the time the junkyard came into view, which was good since I liked to be back by dark. So did Aria. Unless it was absolutely necessary, we didn't take late shifts and were home before sunset.

"That was fun," Karson said as we walked through the gate.

"Thank you." I smiled up at him and soaked in that handsome face. The strong jaw. The straight nose. The high cheekbones. In my romance novels, the heroes always had those traits, and Karson was most definitely my kind of hero.

"Thanks for hanging with me today." He nudged his arm against mine, escorting me to the truck. "Even if I let you win at cards."

"Whatever." I swatted him back.

He chuckled.

The noise must have drawn Aria's attention because she poked her head out of the truck. "There you are. You didn't leave a note."

"Shoot. Sorry." I winced. We always left notes if our plans changed. It wasn't like we could text on our nonexistent phones.

"You suck. I was worried." Then she disappeared, probably sulking on her bed.

"Oops." Guilt hit hard. Aria was my number one. I should have remembered a note. "I'm a bad sister."

"No, you're not." Karson put his hand on my shoulder. "Better go apologize."

"Yeah." I took a step away but stopped and turned back. "Thank you."

"You already said that."

"I know." My cheeks blushed as he stared at me so intently, as if waiting on my every word. If only that were the case. "Sweet dreams, Karson."

"Then I'll have to dream of you."

I rolled my eyes, covering up the fact that a cheesy line sent a swarm of butterflies fluttering in my belly. "Flirt."

He winked. "With you? Always."

3

CLARA

"Forty-seven," Aria said as she wrote it on the wall.

That should have been cause for celebration. We were only forty-seven days from freedom. Why the freaking hell wasn't I more excited? I mean . . . there was a little bit of anticipation. A lot of nerves. And mostly dread that seemed to grow faster than Aria's plants as the number ticked lower.

Because in forty-seven days, Karson would be a memory.

He didn't think we'd ever see the girls again, and what scared me the most was that he didn't seem to mind never seeing three people that we'd lived and survived alongside. When Aria and I left, would he feel the same?

He'd stayed here for us. He clearly cared, right? Maybe we were different. Maybe . . .

"I was thinking of asking Karson to go with us." I blurted the thought that had been in the back of my mind for two weeks. "Wherever we go. If you don't care. I just don't want him to be alone."

"That's cool. I don't think he will, but I don't care if you ask." Aria put the marker away and scooped her hair into a ponytail.

Even though my sister and I were fraternal twins, we had similar features. Our mouths. Our noses. Our brown eyes. And our hair.

Or . . . we used to have the same hair.

Aria had come home with a dye box from the grocery store yesterday. Every week we kept five dollars out of our pay to use on whatever our hearts desired. Mine was normally spent on books or a tabloid magazine—another attempt to be like normal girls my age and fawn over the latest Hollywood heartthrob. Aria had spent hers this week to become a brunette.

"It's going to take me a while to get used to seeing you with brown hair."

557

She smiled and stroked her chocolate strands. "Me too. But I love it."

If I ever dyed my hair, I was going lighter. Like Londyn. I wanted hair like sunshine.

"Okay." She sighed, letting her shoulders sag. "We'd better go."

I stood from my bedroll and followed her out of the truck. We were both working today and even though my shift started an hour after hers did, we were walking into town together. Then she would come to the diner and hang out until I was finished so we could walk home.

The two of us had just started down the path toward the gate when the creak of hinges echoed across the junkyard from Lou's shack.

Aria and I both looked over as he shuffled out, heading for the fence with a ring of keys in one hand.

We slowed, waiting and watching, as Lou unlocked the padlock on the chain wrapped around the fence's posts. He hadn't noticed us yet. Or maybe he had but was just ignoring us. When it came to Lou, I wasn't sure how much attention he paid to his teenage squatters.

Lou was wearing a white T-shirt, the cotton thin and dingy. Like everything around here, dirt had become a part of its fibers. Aria and I didn't own a light color, not anymore. Anything we'd brought with us that had been white or a pale shade had been ruined early on. Even with a weekly trip to the laundromat, it was simply too hard to keep whites bright.

Lou's jeans bagged and sagged on his frame, the faded red suspenders he wore at all times the only thing keeping them up. He was a big man, taller even than Karson.

He would have been a mountain if he had stood straight and pulled his shoulders back. As it was, they were always hunched and curled forward. The gray scruff on Lou's face covered his jaw. The white hair on his head was oily and stuck up in all directions.

Lou finished with the padlock and shoved the fence open a few feet. Then he turned and trudged back to his shack, not sparing us a glance.

"See?" Aria shot me a smirk as she continued on to the fence. "Told you he loves us."

"Maybe he has a customer coming."

"He totally opened the gate for us so we didn't have to squeeze through the little one today. Because he loves us."

I laughed. "You're delusional."

"You know I'm right."

Aria wanted to believe there was an adult in this world who looked out for us. Maybe she was right and Lou did care. Part of me wanted to believe it too because we'd never really know.

Lou had hardly spoken to us in years and with just weeks left to go, I doubted we'd ever know the man. Not one of us had set foot inside his shack, even Karson.

Following Aria through the gate, I cast a backward glance over my shoulder to Karson's tent, but there was no sign of him. I hadn't seen him in two days.

That time seemed precious now.

I just hoped he hadn't gotten into any trouble.

"How about Florida?" Aria asked as we started down the road toward town.

"Too far away."

"But it's so green and there's the ocean. I think I'd like the ocean."

"It's on the exact opposite side of the country. Traveling that far is going to cost too much. Besides, if you want the ocean, we can just find another place in California."

"No. Never. I want out of here." She spoke in a way that said she wouldn't be back either.

"Um . . . how about Vegas?" I held my breath, hoping she didn't immediately nix the other idea I'd been toying with lately.

Aria looked at me like I'd grown another arm. "Seriously?"

"It's not that far away. There are tons of hotels where we could work as housekeepers or whatever. And there's money there, Aria. It's *Vegas*."

"True," she muttered, thinking it over for a few moments. "I guess if we didn't like it, we could leave."

"Exactly." A rush of excitement swelled, exactly what I'd been searching for.

We walked a few more steps until she nodded and said, "Okay. Vegas."

I smiled and did a fist pump with the hand she couldn't see. I'd thought it would take more convincing. One of the line cooks at the diner had visited Vegas a couple of weeks ago and had told me he was getting ready to move there. He'd spent an entire shift telling me about the Strip and the hotels and how he'd already lined up another job.

The way he'd described the neon lights of the casinos had been so vivid that I'd wanted to see them for myself. There was no way I'd go without Aria. Since I'd convinced her so easily, maybe I could convince Karson too.

He wasn't set on a certain place, at least not one that he'd told me about. So why not Vegas? The three of us could find a place to rent, an actual apartment with a roof and bedrooms and a bathroom.

Hope for that future blossomed as we walked. Visions of a living room filled with Aria's plants and a TV for Karson to watch swirled in my mind. Maybe one day, Karson would be watching a movie on that TV and I'd be curled into his side on the couch that we'd picked out together.

"What the hell?" Aria whispered.

"What?"

"Her." She nodded down the road where a woman was jogging our way.

Any normal kid might not wonder about a woman running on a quiet road, but Aria and I were far from normal.

"Have you ever seen her before?" I asked.

"No. You?"

"Never." In the nearly three years we'd been living in the junkyard, not once had we encountered a jogger or pedestrian of any sort on this road.

Not once. People didn't walk around here. And there were many, many roads to run on that were better than ours.

One neighbor, farthest from the junkyard, had five pit bulls. They were contained by the thick fence that surrounded their property, but those dogs loved to bark. The ruckus they could create still startled me at times.

Then there was the neighbor who'd planted the jungle to block out the world. Because the trees and shrubs were so overgrown, walking past the mouth of their driveway was borderline creepy, so we always walked on the opposite side of the street.

The junkyard itself had enough *KEEP OUT* signs to shingle a mansion's roof.

Nothing about this road was welcoming. It screamed *go away*. And this woman running did not belong.

Her dark hair was trapped under a headband that was as electric blue as her leggings. The white of her shirt was nearly blinding under the morning sun. Her fuchsia shoes crunched on the rocks that littered the pavement. Not even the city's street sweepers came this way.

She was too clean. Too colorful. Too happy.

"Morning." The woman smiled and waved as she passed us.

Aria and I didn't respond. We stared at her, our necks twisting to keep her in view as she jogged on by.

"Think she's lost?" I asked.

"I don't know," Aria muttered, her legs moving faster. "It's weird, right? Or am I just getting paranoid?"

"Then I'm paranoid too."

Maybe other seventeen-year-old kids didn't get gut feelings, but my sister and I had learned a long time ago to trust our instincts.

"Maybe she just got turned around," Aria said. "One jog down our road and she'll never be back."

"Yeah."

On cue, the dogs started howling and snapping at the chain link. Aria and I both paused enough to glance back.

The woman yelped and leapt away from the fence. Her hand pressed against her heart. Yet she didn't turn back. She kept on running, getting closer and closer to the junkyard with each step.

"Come on." I took Aria's arm. "You'll be late."

She checked her black wristwatch, one that matched mine. "What are you going to do before your shift?"

"I'm going to hit the store. Get some bread and maybe applesauce or something. We're almost out of peanut butter too."

"We need cat food."

"Okay."

When Katherine had lived with us, she'd adopted this stray cat. The beast was unfriendly to everyone but her, but when she'd left, she'd begged us to keep feeding it. So Aria and I bought the damn thing food, feeding it enough to survive but not so much that it would lose the incentive to hunt mice.

We reached the edge of town and walked past two industrial buildings, then turned down the block that would lead us to an arterial. When we got to the first stoplight, I hugged her goodbye. "Have fun at work."

"You too. See you later."

She went one way and I went the other, making my way the seven blocks to the closest grocery store. My shopping didn't take long. I didn't have the money to fill a cart or the means to get it home, so I picked out the few items on my list, made it through checkout and found a bench outside to load my haul into my backpack.

I was just zipping it up when a flash of electric blue caught my eye.

The jogger.

I stood straight and faced her.

She was staring at me, hovering beside the store's brick wall. Her face wasn't red. Her chest was dry, not even a sheen of sweat above her breasts. No way this lady had gone for a strenuous run.

The hairs on the nape of my neck stood on end. With a fast swoop, I swung my bag over a shoulder and scurried away, dodging the few people going in and coming out of the grocery store.

I didn't look back to see if she'd followed as I hurried to the diner, where I ducked in the rear employee entrance and let the door shut with a slam.

"Hey." One of the cooks spotted me as he came out of the walk-in refrigerator.

"Hey." I forced a shaky smile, hovering by the door until he left. Then, when I was alone, I cracked the door open and scanned the alley. The dumpster was overflowing and due to be picked up today. The cars parked next to the building all belonged to the staff.

Besides a crow pecking at a clump of dry grass, the alley was devoid of any life. No lady in electric blue.

"You're early."

I jumped at my boss's voice and let the door close again, turning to face her. "Yes, ma'am."

"Dishes are waiting."

I nodded and got to work, stowing my backpack in a small cubby. Then I tied on a grease-stained apron and took my place at the restaurant-grade dishwasher, spending my day scrubbing away syrup and ketchup from thick, heavy ceramic plates.

When Aria arrived an hour before my shift ended, she poked her head in to say hello before retreating into the diner to wait at a small table and drink a Dr. Pepper. The waitresses were supposed to charge for soda and refills, but they never made Aria pay.

The hour she waited was the longest of the day. All I wanted to do was tell her about the creeptastic jogger, and by the time my shift ended, the nervous energy was making my bones rattle. The second we stepped outside, I told her the whole story.

"Do you think she's a cop?" I asked. "Like, maybe undercover or something. Or a private investigator? Maybe the sick fucker hired her to find us."

The sick fucker. Our uncle. Aria and I referred to him with a variety of expletives, only speaking his name when necessary.

"Do you think he's been looking all this time?"

"I don't know." The worry on her face made the knot in my stomach bunch tighter. "He's crazy."

And after all he'd done—to us, to her—there was no telling how psycho he'd gone after we'd run away. "Let's just . . . get home."

Home to the junkyard, where there was a padlock to keep people out. Where there was a maze of scrap metal and broken cars to hide in.

Where there was Karson.

We walked so fast that both Aria and I were panting as we squeezed through the side gate. Between the two of us, we'd kept a constant eye behind us. There'd been no sight of the woman in blue in town, and when we'd hit the road to the junkyard, there'd been no sign of anyone. Even the dogs were absent, probably down for an afternoon nap or snack inside with their owners.

"Tomorrow, we should go in even earlier. Like, mix up our routine," Aria said as we unloaded our things into the truck.

"Yeah. Good idea. And maybe we don't walk home right after work. We could go to a park or something."

She nodded and kicked off her shoes. Then she plucked my newest book off the stack. "Can I read this?"

"Sure. I'm going to go say hi to Karson. Tell him about the jogger."

"'Kay." Aria settled on her bed and opened the book to the first page.

She'd be lost in the first chapter before I returned. It was a really good book, maybe good enough to make the take-to-Vegas pile.

I'd take them all if weight and space were unlimited, but I had to pack my entire life's possessions into bags I could carry. Everything else in the truck would be left behind, because when we left here, I was beginning to realize, we wouldn't be coming back.

Climbing down from the back of the truck, I made my way to Karson's tent. When I passed Londyn's Cadillac, I ran a hand over the top. A twinge of longing and guilt made me pull my hand away. Londyn had been my friend and I had a major crush on her boyfriend—ex-boyfriend.

Not that it mattered. Karson didn't like me that way.

When I reached the tent, I drew in a steadying breath. *Be cool. Don't smile too much. Don't stare. Just be cool.* Then I rapped my knuckles on the metal siding beside the tarp that was the door.

"Karson?" I called when he didn't answer.

A groan caught my ear. I hesitated, waiting, then peeled away the tarp to poke my head inside. "Karson?"

"Yeah," he grunted from his bedroom.

"Are you okay?" I dropped my gaze to my feet. He was a boy—man. My mind immediately went to Karson naked and . . . doing things. To himself.

562

Freaking romance novels.

"Can I come in?" I asked, squeezing my eyes shut to block out the image of a naked Karson.

"Yeah."

I shoved the tarp aside and stepped inside, giving myself a minute to adjust to the dim light. He was lying on his sleeping bag in the fetal position. "Oh my God. Are you sick?"

He hummed his agreement.

I rushed to his side and pressed a palm over his forehead. "You're burning up."

"I'll be okay. Just need to rest."

No. This was bad. It was rare that any of us got sick, but it was terrifying when we did. There were no moms here who knew what to do. No doctors to call and ask for advice.

I shoved off the floor and raced out of the tent, running to the truck. "Aria, Karson's sick."

"What?" She flew off her bed, the book tossed aside as I vaulted inside.

"Where's the first aid kit?" I asked even though I was already rushing for the backpack where we kept the small plastic box.

Gemma had gotten sick a couple years ago. It had scared Karson enough that he'd gone to Lou, who'd given him a bottle of Tylenol. After Gemma had left for Montana, the medicine had been given to us in case of emergency.

Today was that emergency.

I ripped the first aid kit open and grabbed the Tylenol, then scanned the truck for the fresh bottle of water I'd bought at the store earlier. From my clean clothes stack, I plucked the last washcloth. Aria and I were planning to go to the laundromat tomorrow so I could wash the others.

"I'm going to stay with him," I said, jumping down to the dirt.

"Want me to come too?"

I shook my head. "We can't all get sick."

She sighed, crossing her arms. "I hate this."

"Me too. Lock yourself in tonight. I'll sleep in the tent."

"Be careful. Yell if you need me."

"I will." I rushed back to Karson, finding him exactly where I'd left him.

His entire body was trembling and his face ashen.

"Here." I cracked the water bottle, then popped the lid on the medicine. "Can you sit up?"

It took him a moment, but he opened his eyes and shoved up on an elbow to take the pills from my hand and chase them down with a sip of water.

"More." I tipped the bottle back to his lips.

He shook his head.

"More," I insisted and only when he swallowed a long gulp did I let him lie back down. I dumped some of the water onto the washcloth. It wasn't cold, but it was cool. Then I laid it across his brow.

"Thanks," he murmured and opened his eyes to scan the space. "Where's my blanket?"

"Here." It was tucked against the wall beside his feet. I grabbed it and shook it out, making sure there wasn't a spider or another bug between the folds. Then I laid it over Karson, watching as he clutched it to his heart.

I sat back, watching. Was the Tylenol working? What if it didn't? "I think I should get Lou."

"No." Karson reached for me and took my hand, tucking it to his chin.

The whiskers on his jaw tickled my knuckles, but even past them, his skin felt too warm. "Karson, I should get Lou."

"I'll be okay. Just . . . sit with me."

"Okay," I agreed, but if he didn't stop shivering soon, I was getting Lou.

I inched closer, crisscrossing my legs. Then I slipped my hand free of his and pulled the cloth from his forehead, folding and refolding it so it would feel cool.

"Lou gave me this blanket. Did I tell you that?" Karson's eyes drifted shut. His words were hushed and slurred.

"Yeah."

We all knew this blanket was special.

Maybe Aria was right after all and Lou did love us.

After Karson ran away from home, he'd wandered around Temecula for a while. Somehow, he'd chanced upon the road to the junkyard, hoping to find a spot to sleep, like on a bench or under a tree.

He'd come toward the junkyard and spotted a fire. Lou had been burning wood scraps in a metal barrel. Or maybe it had been trash. Lou burned most of his garbage, even though Karson had told me it was illegal. Lou just put wood on top to hide the garbage.

The light from the fire had caught Karson's attention, illuminating the side gate. After Lou had gone inside, Karson had shoved it open and snuck in. Then he'd camped out on an old truck's bench seat in the yard.

He kept coming back for a month, nearly every night.

"Scared me to death," Karson murmured. "That night he came out with the blanket. I thought I was so clever, coming in and out under his notice. Then he tossed the blanket on me, and I realized he'd known all along."

I gave him a sad smile. "Aria thinks he loves us."

"He does. In his own way." Karson's shivering became violent. Sweat sheened his cheeks and his breaths were coming in shaky pants.

"Karson, I think—"

"Stay. I'm fine. Don't leave, Clara. Promise."

Ugh. This was stupid, but that didn't stop me from whispering, "Promise."

And I stayed. All night. Until dawn cracked the horizon and the sun's rays bled through the gaps in the tent's walls. Until Karson's fever broke.

I stayed until he opened his eyes and smiled. "I had the sweetest dream."

564

"About what?"

"You."

I sighed, relief coursing through my veins. He was okay.

"Flirt."

4

CLARA

"CLARA." A hand touched my shoulder, shaking me awake.

I flinched, sitting up on my bed in a jolt. My fingers scrambled for the knife by my side and I gripped the hilt, ready to slash and cut.

"Whoa." Karson held up his hands and backed away. "Clara, it's me."

"Oh." My heart climbed back down my throat and I blinked rapidly, clearing the sleep haze. "Sorry."

"You sleep with a knife?" His gaze darted between my face and the weapon.

I shrugged as embarrassment crept into my cheeks. God, I'd almost slashed at Karson. *Smooth, Clara.* "It's, um, just in case, you know?"

A crease formed between his eyes. "Yeah."

I shoved the hair off my forehead and slumped against the truck's wall. It was bright out and the heat was beginning to seep inside like it did every afternoon. My midmorning nap must have lasted longer than I'd planned.

"Are you feeling okay?" Karson asked.

"Yeah." I yawned. Staying up beside him while he'd sweated through his fever had worn me out. "Just tired."

"Thanks. For last night."

"Sure." I shrugged. "How are you feeling?"

"Better. I was just getting ready to head into work. My shift starts at two."

"Are you sure you should be working?"

"I'll be fine. It's only for a few hours to cover for one of the guys until close."

He didn't look fine. His skin was pale, and his hazel eyes were missing their usual mischievous glint. Whatever bug he'd caught had wiped him out.

Karson needed to rest, but instead, he'd walk to town and go to the car wash. There was no such thing as a sick day in our life. We worked rain or shine.

So this afternoon he'd run the sprayer for any of the vehicles that came through, and by the time he was done, his jeans would be nearly soaked. Karson always joked that he didn't need to do laundry, even though he still took his clothes to the laundromat anyway. In this heat, those jeans would be dry, though stiff, by the time he made it back.

"I'll come to town with you." I shifted and picked up my shoes that I'd kicked off earlier.

"You don't have to."

I smiled. "I don't have anything else to do today. Besides, it'll be unbearable in here soon."

By early evening, the truck would be sweltering. I tucked my knife into my jeans pocket, then slipped on a shoe. When I looked up, Karson's eyes were on the pocket.

"You sleep with it."

I dropped my gaze. "Yeah."

"How long?"

"Always." Since we'd run away. Aria had stolen one from our uncle too.

We'd added the knives to our collection of backpacks and flashlights and raincoats. We hadn't stolen those from our uncle, though we certainly had stolen the money to buy them with. When we'd dragged our haul to the cash register at the sporting goods store and handed over a fistful of cash, the clerk had looked at us funny.

But since Craig had stolen everything from us, everything from our parents, that money had been ours to spend.

"Ready?" I asked Karson when my other shoe was on.

Karson nodded, but he didn't move from the floor. "Do you, um . . . the knife. Is it because of Lou? Or . . . me?"

"What? No! Of course not." I hated that he'd think I was scared of him. Or Lou.

"Then why?"

In the years that we'd lived here, I'd never shared the nasty details about why we'd left our uncle's. Aria and I had skimmed over the real story.

We'd told Karson and the girls that our parents had died in a car accident. We'd told them that we'd been sent to live with our uncle. And we'd told them that he'd been a bastard who'd made living under his roof impossible, so we'd run away.

End of story.

None of them had asked questions because they'd all had their own stories. Their own skeletons and demons.

The only ones who'd realized that Uncle Craig had been a pervert were Londyn and Gemma.

Londyn, because she'd lived two trailers down from ours and had seen Craig around. And Gemma, from her one trip to the trailer park with my sister.

Aria had decided to go back and rescue my bike. She'd wanted to surprise me—or she'd known I would have said hell no—so instead of taking me, she'd taken Gemma.

Uncle Craig had been there, though he hadn't seen them. But Gemma had spotted Craig. When she'd told me about the bike fiasco, she'd shivered and commented how his beady eyes had freaked her out.

I had nightmares about those beady eyes.

So did Aria.

That was the extent of what we'd shared. After the bike, which was parked beside a pile of junk because it had two flat tires we couldn't afford to fix, Aria and I hadn't returned to our former neighborhood.

Our friends here had no idea that Craig used to watch us in our sleep. That three times I'd come out of the shower to find him in the bathroom, waiting with my towel pressed to his nose.

Craig was the reason we carried the knives. Because if he ever found our junkyard home, I'd kill him before living under his roof again.

"Just . . . in case," I told Karson. Maybe someday I'd tell him more, but today was not that day.

"All right." He pushed up to his feet and led the way outside.

I closed the sliding door on the truck, bathing my belongings in darkness. With the door closed, it would be stuffy, but I'd take some stale air over a swarm of bugs.

"Short shift today, huh?" I asked as I followed Karson out of the yard for the street.

"Yeah. One of the guys needed to leave early. A doctor's appointment for his kid or something. So I said I'd come in and take the rest of his shift. It's money."

We didn't turn down money.

After Karson's eighteenth birthday, he'd gone to his boss at the car wash and told him he was going to find a better-paying job. To Karson's surprise, his boss had asked him to stay and given him a raise.

He was a real employee now, with a job application and tax withholdings. Karson had even gone to a local bank and opened a checking account, using the junkyard's address as his own. Whenever Lou got the mail, anything addressed to us kids was left in the shop's bathroom for us to find.

I hoped that once Karson built up a little in his checking account, he'd stop stealing.

"Have you and Aria decided where you'll go?" Karson asked as we set out down the road.

I nodded. "We were actually thinking Las Vegas."

"Sin City. I like it."

He liked it? Really? *Ask. Just ask.* I took a deep breath, listening to our footsteps on the pavement. "Would you, um . . . would you want to come with us? Because that would be cool. If you want."

"Thanks, but actually, I think I'm going to explore for a while."

No. My heart crashed to the street, splattering blood over my dirty

568

shoes. But I forced a smile. "E-exploring sounds fun. Are you going to Montana?"

Would he go after Londyn? Did he still love her? I couldn't blame him if he did. Londyn was amazing and smart and funny and sweet. Of course he loved her. We all loved her.

"Nah." Karson shook his head. "I think I'll head toward the coast. I'd like to hit the ocean, breathe some clean air for a while. Learn to surf."

Part of me was overjoyed that he wasn't chasing his ex. The other part was still devastated because I would lose him soon.

"The ocean sounds fun," I lied. The ocean sounded lame and not nearly as fun as Las Vegas. I still had forty-six days. Maybe I could change his mind. "Don't get eaten by a shark."

Karson chuckled. "I'll do my best."

"Maybe you can come and visit us. In Vegas."

He looked down and grinned. It was a grin that made my insides go fuzzy and the heart that had fallen only a minute ago do a tiny flip. "I'd like that."

I smiled. "Me too."

He stared at my mouth for a moment and the crease between his eyebrows came back.

"What?"

"Nothing." He shook his head and faced forward. "So what are you going to do while I'm at work?"

"Maybe go to the library. Or the thrift store."

"Getting another one of your books?" He nudged his elbow with mine. "A little Fabio action?"

"Whatever." I bumped his arm with my shoulder. "You just wish you looked like Fabio."

"Fabio wishes he looked like me." Karson pretended to flick his hair. The dark locks had grown longer this year. It had been a while since he'd gone to get it cut. It curled at the nape of his neck and bangs draped over his forehead.

Last night, when he'd been asleep, temptation and concern had gotten the best of me, and I'd run my hands through his hair. It was as silky and soft as I'd expected.

Lucky for me, Karson would never know. That touch, along with my epic crush, would be my secret. Not even Aria knew how I felt about Karson.

It was probably for the best that we were going our separate ways, right? *Ugh. No.*

I mean . . . we'd have a lot to do in Vegas. Karson sort of distracted me. Without him around, I'd probably stay more focused.

Aria and I would need to find a place to live. We'd need to get jobs. As soon as I could get signed up for the test, I was going to earn my GED. I didn't need a boyfriend distracting me from building a life. It was almost time to become an adult, right?

Ugh. No, again. Having Karson with us would just make it all better.

"Want to hear something strange?" I asked, ready for a new topic.

"Duh."

"Yesterday, Aria and I saw this lady jogging toward the junkyard."

"Jogging?"

"Yup. Seriously, have you ever seen a jogger on this road?"

"No. Never."

"Strange, right?"

Karson nodded. "Yeah."

"Oh, it gets worse. Aria and I split up at the stoplight so she could go to work. I went to the store to get a few things and I was outside, packing up my bag, and the jogger was there. She was, like, watching me."

Karson slowed his steps and his forehead furrowed. "Are you sure?"

I nodded. "For sure. I think she followed me."

"Have you ever seen her before?"

"No. Neither had Aria."

He frowned and glanced around, but as usual, we were alone on the road. "Could just be a coincidence."

"Maybe. Probably."

"Keep an eye out. Watch for her."

"Aria and I thought we should mix up our schedule a little. She left for work earlier this morning than normal. I'll do the same tomorrow when I go in."

"We should all start walking together. I'll come in with you both. Even on the days when I'm not working."

"You don't have to do that."

He winked. "I want to."

God, it was hot when he winked. He had this sexy grin afterward that made me want to melt. "Thanks." I bit my lower lip to hide a goofy smile.

"Always." He slung a hand around my shoulders and pulled me into a sideways hug.

I tensed, unsure of what to do, but since he kept walking, so did I. One foot in front of the other, like everything was normal. Like it was no freaking huge deal that Karson's arm was around my shoulders.

Why wasn't he letting go? What did this mean? Karson didn't hug me, like . . . ever. He'd elbow me or poke me or flick the end of my hair. But a hug? Did this even count?

Was this just a guy slinging his arm around the shoulder of his friend? When he'd hug Londyn, he'd wrap both arms around her. Normally his hands would dive into the back pockets of her jeans.

That was a hug. A lover's hug. This was . . . what the hell was this?

I held my shoulders as still as possible. I barely let my hands swing at my sides. If this was the only hug I got from Karson Avery, then I was making it last as long as I could.

The sun beat down on us, the afternoon rays growing stronger with every passing minute. I struggled to take a deep breath, my heart racing like a Ferrari in my chest.

Karson was relaxed. Content to leave his arm around me. His side was pressed to mine, his hand draped over my shoulder, his wrist relaxed.

He looked casual. This was a casual hug, right?

But what if I was wrong? What if this was Karson's way of testing the waters? What if he liked me? *Liked* me, liked me. What if this hug was his way of breaking past the friend zone?

Before I could make sense of my thoughts, his arm was gone and we were in town, cars whizzing by us on the street.

"What time does Aria get off work?" he asked at the stoplight.

I glanced down the road in the direction she'd walk to her restaurant. "Five."

"I'm done at six. Before the end of her shift, why don't you go to the restaurant and get her? Then come back to the car wash so we can all walk home together."

"Sure." I glanced up at his handsome profile, hoping for a sign that his hug had been . . . more.

Karson must have felt my stare. He looked down to me and those hazel eyes held me captive. My romance novels were always describing the hero holding the heroine captive with his gaze.

Totally got that one now.

Because I was pinned to the sidewalk. The air had vanished from my lungs. I was at Karson's mercy, waiting with every beat of my heart for his next move.

The breeze caught a lock of hair and blew it into my face.

Karson pulled it free from my cheek, tucking it behind my ear. His fingers skimmed the shell, sending a tickle over my skin. He swallowed hard, his Adam's apple bobbing. "I, um . . ."

Love you? Please, please let the rest of that sentence be that he loved me.

The beep of the crosswalk sounded beside us. Karson looked away, facing the street, and dropped his hand. Then he took a step forward and the moment was gone.

Stupid freaking crosswalk.

I kicked at an invisible clump of dirt, then trudged after him, hating every step that took us closer and closer to the car wash. When the sign came into view, I covered up a groan with a fake cough.

"Thrift store?" he asked.

"Yeah." I shrugged. "I guess. There's a dime in my pocket and I've got a date with Fabio."

"Need some money for a coffee or something?"

"No, thanks." While he'd swipe things here and there, he knew I wouldn't steal. He'd spent too much money on me already.

Besides, on Friday afternoons, the closest café was always packed with high school girls. They'd taken over since summer break. It was impossible to sit in there and not get overwhelmed with conversations of college and cars and clothes.

I didn't hate my life. It wasn't ideal, but I didn't hate our situation. Aria and I had our freedom and that was priceless. Living at the junkyard was better than where we'd been.

Still, listening to normal girls was painfully hard. Because if our parents hadn't died, that would have been Aria and me. We would have been the girls at a coffee shop who'd never wondered where their next meal would come from. Who didn't fear police cars that might drag them back to hell.

"I'm going to go get my new book and then find a park or something," I told Karson.

"Stay in public where people can hear you, okay?"

"I will." Other than the junkyard, I didn't go to places where someone couldn't hear me scream.

"Have fun working."

"Oh, yeah. Washing cars is my dream," he deadpanned.

I giggled and it made him smile.

He smiled so wide and bright, I refused to blink. I had to memorize that smile in the next forty-six days so that when we left California, I could take it with me.

Standing on the sidewalk, I waved and watched as he walked away. About ten feet away, he spun and grinned, giving me a mock salute. I laughed, watching his long strides and the way he walked with such grace.

Then he was gone and I left for the thrift store, taking my time over the ten-block route. There were no new additions to their very limited book supply, so next was an extra thirteen blocks to the closest library.

Not that I checked out books. I'd need a library card for that and requesting a fake one had seemed like an unnecessary risk. But I came to the library often, never speaking to the librarians, simply walking through the stacks.

There was adventure here. There was hope. There were imaginary worlds behind each dust jacket and hard spine, ready to swallow the reader whole. The smell of paper and books infused the air. The quiet whispers of patrons reminded me of fall leaves rustling on the grass.

Finally, after I'd killed another hour, I began the slow journey to Aria's restaurant. She wouldn't be ready to leave yet, but I didn't want to risk not catching her. And I hoped I could beg a lemonade with extra ice from the waitress.

She gave me two while I waited for my sister.

Aria laughed after I explained to her what was happening. "Don't you think Karson's gotten more protective lately? Do you think all big brothers are like that?"

Eww. Karson was *not* my big brother. "I don't know. Maybe."

Overprotective or not, I liked that Karson cared about our well-being. It was the one gesture that set him apart from most of the people in our lives.

"We still have an hour before he's ready," Aria said, checking the clock in the restaurant as she slung her backpack on. "Want to go somewhere?"

"Not really. I've been walking all afternoon. What if we just went and hung out at the car wash?"

"Fine by me." She said her goodbyes to her coworkers, then we made the trek to Karson's work.

There was a concrete ledge behind the row of vacuums, and Aria and I made ourselves comfortable under the shade of a tree.

I had the perfect view of Karson standing inside the metal shed with a pressure spray wand in his grip. Some days, he washed the cars. Others, he was outside, polishing the wax or running a vacuum.

It was difficult to stop myself from staring. His jeans were wet, like usual. So was his gray T-shirt. It stuck to his flat stomach. Every time he moved, the fabric seemed to stretch tighter over his shoulders and arms.

Stop staring. I had to force my eyes away, locking them on Aria, even though in my head all I could picture was Karson shirtless, wearing that towel.

Aria was telling me about her day while I fantasized about Karson. I hadn't heard a word she'd said because I was an awful sister. But then a familiar voice barked and jerked me out of my stupor.

"Stay away from me." Karson's voice filled the air.

"What the hell?" Aria muttered, twisting. Then we were both on our feet.

"That's her." I reached for my sister's arm. "Aria, that's her, isn't it?"

She took my hand, her eyes narrowing. "I don't know. Is it?"

"Yes." It was her.

The jogger from yesterday was inside the car wash, clearly ignoring the *Employees Only* sign. She was talking to Karson, waving her hands wildly as he lifted an arm and pointed toward the exit.

"Go. Away." Another shout that carried our way.

The woman didn't budge. She crossed her arms over her chest, planting her legs wide.

Karson clenched his jaw, then stormed into the office and slammed the door behind him.

The woman didn't notice us watching. She scowled and marched to her car. With a snap of her fingers, she ordered away the guy drying it with a towel. Then she was behind the wheel and on the road, her tires squealing as she raced onto the street.

I didn't wait for my sister as I rushed to the office, almost at the door when it flew open and Karson stalked outside.

He spotted me and changed direction. "Hey."

"Karson, that was her. The jogger."

"What?"

"Yes, that was her. I'm sure."

"Fuck."

"Who is that woman?" I asked as Aria joined us.

Karson gritted his teeth and stared at the road where she'd disappeared. "My mother."

5

CLARA

"HEY." I smiled at Karson as he came striding my way. I was outside the van, shaking the remainder of the cat food from the bag into a bowl for the stray.

The bag that I'd bought over a month and a half ago, the day we'd seen Karson's mother jogging down our road, had lasted a long time. Too long. Katherine's cat hadn't been coming around much, probably because Katherine wasn't here.

"Hey," he said. "Where's Aria?"

"Shower." I crumpled the bag into a ball for Lou's metal trash can. "She's been working on her plants all day, getting them ready for when we go. She wants to stage them around Lou's place as a goodbye present."

Karson nodded and sank onto an old car hood. It rested on top of a heap of large metal scraps and a rusted wheel well. The hood was our equivalent of a living room chair.

"How was work?" I asked. While Aria and I hadn't had to work today, he'd gone in for an eight-hour shift at the car wash.

"Work." He shrugged, but the lines on his forehead spoke volumes about his day.

And who'd paid him a visit.

"She was there again, wasn't she?"

"Yeah," he muttered. "Came right before I clocked out."

In the time since Karson's mother had made her first appearance at the car wash, she'd continued to confront him at least once a week.

"What did she want?"

He lifted a shoulder. "Didn't let her catch me. The second I saw her car, I shut myself in the office."

"Does your boss care?"

"I mean, he doesn't like it. But he gets it."

I gave him a sad smile. "Sorry."

"Yeah. Whatever. She can fuck off."

Karson hadn't spoken about his mother. Not since her first visit and not before. In all the years that we'd lived together, he hadn't elaborated. Just like me. What I knew of his past were bits and pieces. Karson's mother had been an alcoholic. Maybe she still was. And she'd been a bitch, according to her son. That obviously hadn't changed. But I didn't know exactly what had happened to make him run away.

The best decision of my life. A phrase he'd repeated countless times.

"Anyway"—he stood—"wanted to let you know I was back."

"Oh, okay."

He walked away, his shoulders tight and his hands shoved into his jeans pockets.

Karson had withdrawn from me over the past month and a half. Every visit from his mother sent him deeper and deeper into himself. He rarely ate with us these days. He walked us to and from town, but the trips were quiet and tense.

Gone was the playful Karson who'd tease and flirt. Gone was the Karson who'd put his arm around my shoulders. Gone was the Karson who'd looked at me at the stoplight like maybe he wanted to kiss me.

I was losing him.

And there were only three days left.

The hope I had of seeing him again after we left this place was dwindling like the numbers on the truck's wall.

I struggled to find any excitement at all for Las Vegas. For the first time, I didn't want to go. I didn't want to leave here and leave him.

Regardless, I'd packed. Aria and I were both preparing to leave. Ready or not, time was running out, and I had to move on with my life. Most of what we'd done today had been to organize our belongings.

We'd be taking a bus to Vegas. Four days ago, we'd gone to the station to ask about tickets and get the schedule. There would be room enough for us to each take two backpacks. Today, I'd packed the keepers and set out the clothes I was leaving behind. I'd be wearing them for the next three days, like my shirt today. It was a favorite but the hem was frayed and there was a hole in the armpit. Aria and I had decided that wrinkled jeans and tattered shirts were worth wearing now, so that when the time came, we were loaded to leave with our best stuff.

"Come smell me." Aria emerged from the maze, her hair wet and a towel looped over her arm.

"Why am I smelling you?"

"Because I smell awesome." She smiled and came close, putting an arm around my shoulders.

I scrunched up my nose. "You did use soap, didn't you?"

"Huh?" She stepped back and sniffed her underarm.

I giggled. "Kidding. You smell great."

"It's that new shampoo I got at the dollar store. I love that it smells like a flower. From now on, that's going to be my smell."

"Flowers?"

She nodded. "Yup."

"Good choice." My favorite smell was orange and vanilla. It reminded me of Creamsicles, the ones Dad used to buy us on hot summer days from an ice cream truck. But I still hadn't found a soap that smelled just right. Probably because there were only so many options at the dollar store. Maybe when I had a job and some money, I could go to a beauty store and buy my smell.

"What do you want to do for dinner?" Aria asked, hanging up her towel on our "hook." It was just a hinge in the truck door, but it worked.

"Should we have peanut butter and honey sandwiches? Or honey and peanut butter sandwiches?"

"Hmm." She tapped her chin. "Peanut butter and honey is fancier than honey and peanut butter, and I'm feeling fancy tonight."

"Then allow me to cook for you, madam."

"And fetch me our best champagne."

"But of course." I feigned a bow and hopped into the truck, going to the food stash. With our one and only butter knife, I made us each a sandwich.

"Is Karson back?" Aria asked, taking a bite after handing me a bottle of lukewarm water.

"Yeah. He came over when you were in the shower. She was there again today."

"Bitch," she muttered.

"Has he said anything to you?"

Aria shook her head. "No. But he doesn't talk to me like he talks to you."

"I might make him a sandwich. See if he's okay."

"Fine by me. This bread is about done anyway." There was no mold, but the crust was hard and dry.

We ate in comfortable silence and when I was done, I made Karson's sandwich. When I left, Aria was settled on her bed with a book on her lap, braiding her hair into a long rope.

A nervous flutter settled in my belly as I walked toward Karson's tent. The flap on the door was open but I knocked on the wall anyway. "Hey. It's me."

"Hey." Karson sat in the main room with a deck of cards spread out in a game of solitaire.

The sight of him playing alone broke my heart.

Karson had been alone a lot this past year. When Londyn had lived here, she'd been his constant companion. Best friends. And though Aria and I were here, it wasn't the same.

I'd always be grateful to my parents that I'd been born with my best friend. Even on the darkest days, I was never alone. I always had Aria.

"Want to play a game?" I settled across from him on the floor.

"Sure."

"Here." I handed him the sandwich. "Dinner."

"Thanks." He took it and chomped a huge bite. "Mmm. Peanut butter and honey. I haven't had this in *so* long."

I laughed. "Like a day?"

"Two." He chewed, a grin forming on his lips.

"What are we playing?" I asked, scooping up the cards.

"You beat me at both gin and poker last time, so a rematch of either would be good."

"Gin." I dealt the cards.

He swiped his hands clean after demolishing the sandwich, then picked up his hand. "One of the guys at work bought me beer."

I blinked, stunned by the admission. "Really?"

"It's not the first time."

"Oh." How had I missed that? "Do you, um . . . drink a lot?"

"Nah. I am not about becoming my mother."

Right. He'd mentioned once that she'd get really nasty after too many vodkas.

"I brought the six-pack home with me. Want one?"

"Um . . ." Why did this feel like breaking the rules? *Because it was.* Despite my current living situation and the fact that we were basically trespassing, I still tried to follow the rules. Even in the beginning when we hadn't been able to get good jobs, Aria and I had never stolen food like he did. "I've never had a drink before."

"You don't have to." Karson stretched behind him, reaching past the partition to his room. Then he lifted the six-pack and set it down at his side.

The cans were white with red letters. The tops were a shade of brassy gold. Karson plucked one from the plastic rings and the top hissed as he popped it.

"I guess . . . I'll try it." My voice cracked a little with the thrill.

He handed over the can, then opened his own to raise in the air. "Cheers."

"Cheers." I tipped the can to my lips and sipped. And gagged. "Gross."

He chuckled, swallowing his own gulp. "It's different."

"If different and horrible mean the same thing, then yes, it's different."

The smile that stretched across Karson's face was worth the nasty beer. His laugh boomed through the tent, drowning the fears I'd had of losing him.

"You haven't smiled much lately," I said.

He sighed and took another drink. "No, I haven't."

"Are you okay? This thing with your mom . . ."

"I don't understand why she can't let me go. She didn't want me years ago when I actually needed her. Now she comes looking for me? Now? What the fuck? Why?"

"Maybe you need to hear her out."

He scowled as he took another drink.

Okay. Bad suggestion. I sipped from my own can, the second taste not as bitter and startling as the first. "Sorry."

"It's not your fault. I'm being a dick. Sorry. I just don't want anything to do with her."

"You never talk about your home with her."

"You never talk about yours either." Karson's hazel gaze locked on mine. In it, the silent plea to trust him broke any resolve I'd had to keep my past hidden.

So I took another drink, and told him the story that only Aria knew.

"Our uncle is a sick son of a bitch. After our parents died, we went into foster care for a while, waiting until they could figure out what to do with us. My parents didn't have a plan for us."

Parents did that for their kids, right? Planned for the worst? I'd heard our social worker say a few times that our parents hadn't had a will. They should have.

"We ended up with our uncle. He was Mom's stepbrother. I didn't even know we had an uncle until after Mom and Dad . . ." I didn't like to say it. Seven years later and I didn't like to say that they'd died.

"Maybe we shouldn't talk about this. I don't want it to hurt you, Clara."

I met his worried gaze. "If there's anyone I'd want to tell for the first time, it's you."

"Okay." He nodded toward my beer.

I took another drink, letting the carbonation tickle my tongue. "My grandma had Mom before she married Craig's dad. I guess that made him my grandpa too, not that I knew him. He died before I met him. My grandma too, when I was a baby. I only remember her face from pictures."

And even then, the pictures were fading. Some nights I'd wake up in a cold sweat because I couldn't remember what Mom and Dad had looked like either. What their laughs had sounded like. Aria and I had a few pictures, but even with them, the memories were fuzzy.

"My dad's parents, my other grandparents, live outside of Phoenix. They have a pool we played in whenever we visited. Before."

"Why didn't you go live with them?" Karson asked.

"They didn't want us. Craig did. I don't think my grandparents knew about him. What he was."

Craig had been a different guy then. Kind. Gentle. Fake. I remembered him meeting us, crouching down and shaking our hands. I remembered him saying how pretty we were and how much we reminded him of Mom. He'd given us stuffed teddy bears that day and a pack of M&M's to split.

"He'd put on a good show for the social workers. They believed it. He was younger than my grandparents, and since he lived here in Temecula, I guess all the adults thought it made sense not to move us."

"Stupid fuckers."

"Yeah." I huffed, taking another drink. Warmth spread through my chest, making it easier to talk. Maybe it was the beer. Or maybe it was just Karson. "He just wanted their money. Mom and Dad's. He took everything. The house. The furniture. Our toys. If he could sell it, he did. Then he moved us into that shitty trailer and kept the money for himself. By the time we ran away, it was pretty much gone."

"What did he do with it? Drugs?"

I lifted a shoulder. "Maybe. I know he gambled because one night this guy showed up and broke down the front door. He had a gun and told Craig that if he didn't pay his gambling debt, he was dead."

Part of me still wished it had ended that night. That Craig had had a roll of cash in his pocket and that guy had fired the gun.

"He used to throw parties while Aria and I hid out in our room. We couldn't even lock the door because it was broken. And I think . . ." I took in a deep breath, bracing myself for the realization it had taken me a while to understand. "I think there was a reason Mom didn't let us see Craig. That she didn't talk about him."

Karson's spine stiffened. "What?"

"He was a jerk and didn't give a shit about us most of the time. But since there was food and Aria and I could take care of ourselves, it didn't matter. Then it got creepy. We turned fourteen and got, um . . . boobs." I grimaced, not wanting to say that word to Karson. "He stared at us. A lot. He'd touch us too much."

A chill crept over my skin. A sour taste spread across my mouth, so I chased it down with another gulp of beer.

"Eventually it was so disgusting that we started packing. We knew Londyn had run away. Why not us too?"

"She was here then, right?"

I nodded. "Yeah. We were trying to save up as much as we could first, not sure what kind of jobs we'd be able to get since we were only fifteen. But then he came after Aria."

The tent went eerily still. Karson sat like a rock but the fury pulsing off his body was like a heat wave.

"He didn't, like . . ." *Rape*. I couldn't say that word either. "He touched her. He ripped her shirt. He got her pants open. I didn't even know it was happening. I was in the bathroom but then I heard her scream and by the time I came running out, she'd already fought her way free."

I closed my eyes and heard the echo of her scream. It haunted me. I expected it always would.

"I'll fucking kill him." Karson moved so fast, I blinked and he was out the tent's door.

"No!" I scrambled to my feet, running to catch up. "Karson, stop."

"He's dead."

"Karson." I caught up to him by the small gate, grabbing his elbow with both of my hands. "Don't. If you go there, what are you going to do?"

"Kill him."

"And then who will be here with us?" I asked gently. Karson would go kill Craig. He had that sort of rage inside of him.

His body tensed but he stopped fighting my grip.

"It was a long time ago," I said.

"Doesn't make it fucking right."

I sighed. "I know. But if you go there and do something reckless, he wins. Please, please don't."

He seethed for a full minute before he backed away from the fence. Then he faced me, planting his hands on his hips. "Did he touch you too?"

"No. We ran and shut ourselves in the bedroom. He pounded on the door for hours, but we held him off." Aria and I had braced our backs against the door and our feet against a bed, then pushed with all our might. By the time the pounding and Craig's bellowing had stopped, my legs had lost all their strength. Well, nearly all.

Never in my life had I wished so hard for my parents. I'd silently begged Mom and Dad to appear, for us to wake up from the nightmare and be home in our beds with them sleeping down the hallway.

I wished for them a lot, during the hard days. Aria seemed so angry at them sometimes. She never said it, but I could tell she was mad at them for leaving us—for leaving us vulnerable to a man like Craig.

She had a right to be angry, and there were times when I felt that too. But mostly . . . I just missed Mom's smile and gentle voice. I missed Dad's loud laugh and how he'd scoop us into his arms every evening when he'd come home from work.

I wished for them even though I knew that wish wouldn't come true.

"Then what?" Karson asked.

"Craig gave up eventually. And when he did, we climbed out the window before dawn with our backpacks and supplies, then came here."

"Clara." The pain on his handsome face broke my heart.

"I'm okay, Karson."

Without warning, he pulled me into his chest, wrapping his arms around me tight. "I fucking hate him."

"Me too." I dragged in a long breath of his shirt. He smelled of soap and earth and Karson. My Karson. My arms snaked around his waist, and I hugged him. A real hug, with his cheek resting on my hair.

Until he loosened his hold and tipped my chin up to his face. "I'm sorry."

"Don't be."

"I shouldn't have brought it up. We should have just played cards and had fun."

"We can still do that. If you want." I hooked a thumb toward the tent. "Your beer is growing on me."

"Only you could make me smile right now." He chuckled and put an arm around my shoulders, then he steered me for the tent.

We played gin and pretended we weren't living in a junkyard. We drank beers like other teenaged kids did to break the rules and push the boundaries.

"My lips are numb." I dabbed my lower lip, flicking it with my index finger.

Karson laughed. "I don't feel anything yet."

"Really?" Was I slurring? "I feel . . . good. Aria is going to be mad that we left her out."

"She can have the rest of mine." He shrugged and surged to his feet.

But he'd forgotten that he couldn't stand in the center of the tent and he wacked his head on the roof. "Ow."

I burst out laughing. "I thought you weren't feeling anything."

"I guess I am now." He swayed on his feet. While I'd only had a beer and a half, Karson had nearly gone through the other four.

"She's probably asleep." I got to my feet, extending my arms like an airplane to find my balance. When one of my hands landed on Karson's hot skin, I clung to his forearm, not shy about touching him. Not tonight.

What did they call alcohol? Liquid courage? I got that reference now.

My smile pinched my cheeks as I tugged Karson out of the tent. The air outside was still warm, even as the sun dipped below the horizon. The stars were just beginning to show in the royal blue sky.

"Want to watch for shooting stars?" I asked, walking toward the Cadillac. "We can make a game out of it. First one to three wins."

"What about Aria?"

No light was coming from inside the truck. She'd always been an early riser and tended to go to bed before dark. That or she was hunkered under a blanket, consuming her book by flashlight. "She's probably asleep."

"'Kay. Stargazing it is." Karson climbed onto the Cadillac's wide hood, leaning so his back was against the windshield. Then he raised his arms and placed them beneath his head.

I scrambled to his side, settling against the metal. My jeans and shirt were going to be filthy, but in my happily beer-buzzed state, I didn't care. These were short-term clothes anyway.

"I can't believe you suck so much at gin *and* poker." I barely got the sentence out before I broke into a fit of giggles.

"You should be saying thank you."

"For what?"

"For letting you win."

I scoffed. "You did not let me win."

He stayed quiet, his gaze on the sky.

"Did you let me win?"

Still, no response.

I shifted, pushing up on an arm to look down at him. "Karson."

"Clara."

"Did you let me win?"

He looked over and winked. "You'll never know."

"Jerk!" I poked him in the side, then lay down again, my smile wider now than it had been all night.

He chuckled. If that was what I could do for him, make him laugh, then I was calling tonight a success. And maybe I needed a laugh too.

I was lighter, having told him my story. The fear that came with it had eased. Maybe I should have told him a long time ago.

"I know it's not ideal, but I'm going to miss these starry nights," Karson said.

"Me too."

The junkyard was far enough from the center of town that the glow from the city's lights didn't completely obscure the night sky. The stars would come out and on clear nights like this, they were little blips of hope, twinkles of joy that promised life wouldn't always be this hard. They were there, watching over us. Maybe the stars were the lost souls of the ones we'd loved.

Maybe two of those stars were for my parents.

I hoped at this very moment, with me lying beside the boy I really liked, Dad wasn't watching.

"I'm not going to miss the dirt," he said.

"Same. And I'm not going to miss the tight spaces. Sleeping in an over-sized coffin. Someday, I want a house with lots of windows. So that even when I'm inside, it feels open and airy."

"I just want four walls. Four real walls. A fridge. A microwave."

I snuck a glance at Karson's profile. It was perfection. His nose was straight. His jaw strong and dusted with stubble. His lips soft.

"I'm going to miss you." The words came out before I could stop them.

When he faced me, his hazel eyes had that captivating edge again. The same one he'd given me the day of the stoplight. "I'm going to miss you too."

My breath caught in my throat.

"Clara . . ."

"Yeah?"

Karson didn't answer. He turned to the sky and my heart sank. I was imagining this. It had to be the beer. It had to be —

I didn't get to finish that thought. Because one moment, my eyes were glued to the darkening night sky.

The next, Karson was there.

And his lips came crashing down on mine.

6

CLARA

THE RATTLE of metal on metal woke me from sleep.

I blinked, wincing at the ache pounding in my temples. God, it was hot. Why was it so hot?

A weight rested on my side, and behind me, there was a furnace. A hard, strong furnace.

No, a body.

I gasped and sat up, scrambling out of Karson's hold. *Tent.* We were in the tent. We were in his . . . bed.

He stirred, cracking open his eyes. Then he stretched an arm over his head and the movement caused his shirt to ride up, revealing a peek at those washboard abs. "Morning."

"Morning." I gulped and looked down at myself. Still clothed. Then last night came rushing back.

The Cadillac. The stars. The beers.

The kiss.

We'd come back to the tent after Karson had kissed me.

Oh my God. Karson had kissed me. A lot. He'd kissed me a lot, *a lot.*

My fingertips drifted to my swollen lips. *Holy. Shit.*

Karson Avery had kissed me. I held back a squeal.

The shock on my face must have woken Karson up completely because he sat up, his eyes on alert. "Clara."

"You kissed me."

He nodded. "That's all that happened."

That's all? It was a kiss. A freaking kiss. Something I'd wanted for months and months and months. "I remember."

"Are you—"

"Good. Great! I'm great. Except I have a headache." Though I couldn't tell if the spinning was because I was experiencing my first hangover or because of the kiss.

"Yeah." He ran a hand through his hair. "I do too."

What did we do now? There was no way I'd be kissing him again until I brushed my teeth. My mouth was dry and tasted . . . blech. Beer breath was awful. Though I didn't have a mirror, my hair was most certainly a mess.

Aria was going to take one look at me and . . . know. *Oh my God.* My stomach pitched. She was going to know. There was no way I'd be able to hide my puffy lips and this perma-grin from my sister. My secret crush was about to be the talk of the junkyard.

My head throbbed as I forced myself to unsteady feet. "I'd better go."

"Clara, wait."

I didn't stop moving. "Thanks for the, um . . . see ya."

Leaving him in the tent, I hurried outside and into the bright morning sun. I winced as my temples pounded but dragged in some air and put one foot in front of the other. When I passed the Cadillac, I kept my gaze on the path, refusing to let myself look at the hood.

The hood where Karson had kissed me.

What did this mean? This was a good thing, right? Karson. Avery. Kissed. Me.

Except at the moment, I kind of wanted to hurl. Pressing a hand to my stomach, I hustled to the truck, hopped in and gathered my towel and shower supplies.

"Morning." Aria was on her bed with the novel she'd had last night.

"Hi. Sorry. I was in the tent. I, uh, fell asleep."

She shrugged. "I figured. I crashed early. This book wasn't good enough to stay up late with."

I ducked my chin, hoping to keep my face hidden until I could assess the damage. Luckily, my hair was hanging everywhere like a curtain. "I'm taking a shower."

"'Kay."

Before she could say anything else, I disappeared, rushing for the shop. The smell of grease and gasoline made me gag, but I locked myself in the bathroom and cranked the shower on hot. Then as steam flooded the room, I faced the mirror.

Yep. Swollen lips.

A laugh escaped as I leaned closer, taking them in. Karson had kissed me. I had kissed him. We'd had a full-on make-out session on the Cadillac. Londyn's Cadillac.

Would she hate me for it? Would she hate me for loving Karson? A wave of guilt swept over my shoulders, but I shook it away.

"She'll never know," I whispered, then went for my toothbrush, scrubbing my mouth until all I tasted was mint.

The mirror began to fog so I stripped off yesterday's clothes and stepped into the shower stall. I lingered, soaking in the warmth and letting it chase away the hangover. At least . . . I assumed it was a hangover. By the time I stepped out, my headache wasn't as bad and my mind was clear.

I'd need a clear head. Because I'd bolted on Karson and we had to talk about the kissing.

Would he want to do it again? Or would he say it was a mistake? I was fairly certain I'd die if he told me I was a mistake.

We only had two days left until our birthday. They'd be the longest two days of my life if Karson rejected me now.

Aria was dressed and eating a rice cake when I returned to the truck. She was sitting on the end, kicking her legs.

"I tried beer," I blurted, climbing inside. I put my soap and shampoo away, then hung up my towel. Then I sat beside her and let my head rest on her shoulder. "Beer is really bad."

She laughed. "Where'd you get beer?"

"Karson. Some guy at his work bought him a six-pack."

"Ahh." She nodded. "Was that why you fell asleep in the tent?"

"Yeah." I sighed, holding back the rest of the story. I wasn't ready to admit my feelings. I wasn't ready to admit that I'd betrayed Londyn by falling in love with her boyfriend—ex-boyfriend.

"I thought maybe you and Karson . . ."

"Huh?" My heart dropped as I feigned confusion.

"Do you like him?"

"We're friends." I sat up straight. Not a complete lie. Then I stood and walked to the truck's wall, picking up the dry-erase marker to write today's number.

Two.

Only two days left and I'd say goodbye to Karson. Kiss or not, we were going our separate ways. Maybe his kiss had been a farewell.

"What time do you want to head in for work?" I asked after swallowing the lump in my throat.

"About an hour. But you don't have to come with me. I doubt Karson's mother wants anything to do with us. I think she was just looking for him."

"Yeah." We'd explained that much to Karson, but he still insisted on escorting us into town.

"I'm actually going to head out when he's not looking." She smirked. "See you later."

"Be careful." Before she could jump down, I went and wrapped my arms around her. "Love you."

"Love you too. Enjoy your day off. Will you—"

"Water your plants? Of course."

She snatched her empty backpack, then jumped down and scanned the plant buckets that surrounded the truck. The happy smile on her face disappeared as she took in the flowers and green leaves.

Those were her babies and there was no way for them to come to Vegas. They'd probably die before fall—never something I'd say aloud. But Lou wasn't going to care for them.

The man only had so much to give, though what he'd given us had been enough.

"Bye." She waved, then headed out, hooking the pack's straps on her shoulders as she walked.

"Turkey if you bring home a sandwich," I called to her back.

She lifted a hand with a thumb up.

Two days, then there'd be no more scrap sandwiches. Well, after we got on our feet.

Aria and I weren't delusional about what waited for us at the end of our countdown. The days were likely to get harder for a while as we started a new life. Without jobs or a home, I imagined we'd be spending a week or two in a sleezy motel with bedbugs and cockroaches.

But that was what we'd been saving for. We had enough money to afford a cheap room while we got an apartment lined up. Neither of us wanted to be living on the streets, especially in Las Vegas.

The sudden urge to count our savings stash came over me, and I hurried to my bed, taking it out and separating the cash into piles.

Two thousand three hundred and fifty dollars. Exactly what had been there the last time Aria and I had counted it out. Nearly three years of peanut butter and honey sandwiches, eating whatever our respective restaurants would give us and spending next to nothing, all so we could have a decent shot at a future.

Please, let it be enough.

I returned the money to the bag and stowed it in its hiding place. My stomach growled, driving me to the foodstuffs. Bent over the supplies, I was debating my limited options when Karson knocked on the truck. "Hey."

"Hi." I blushed.

He held up two rolled tortillas, probably with peanut butter and banana inside. That was a staple breakfast around here. "Since you brought me dinner."

"Thanks."

He hopped into the truck, handing one of the rollups over, then we sat down and ate.

Meals here were without fanfare and took only moments. I wished there was more to do because by the time I'd chewed the last bite, I still didn't know what to say.

"Where's Aria?" he asked.

"Work. She left." Probably while he'd been in the shower. The strands of his dark hair were damp and finger combed.

"She should have waited."

"She'll be fine." I waved it off. "Why would your mom want anything to do with us?"

"Who knows?" He frowned. "But she's fucking crazy, so . . ."

I waited for more, but he let that sentence hang, and with it my hopes that he'd tell me about his past. I'd confided in him. Would he ever trust me with his story?

"I need to head in and grab my paycheck. Cash it at the bank. Want to come?" he asked.

"Sure. But I'd better water Aria's plants first."

"'Kay." He stood up. "I'll help."

Thirty minutes later, after working and most definitely *not* talking about the kiss, Karson and I were on the road to town.

"Want a coffee or something?" he asked. "My treat. I'm definitely getting one because my head goddamn hurts. Fucking beer."

I giggled. "Should have stuck to two, like me."

"How are you feeling?"

Confused. Happy. Anxious. Sad. Take your pick. "Fine. Better after my shower."

"That's good."

And that was the end of our conversation about last night, apparently. The only sound between us was the smack of our shoes on the street and sidewalk. When we got to the nearest café, Karson led the way inside, going to the counter, where a display case flaunted baked goods.

"Two black coffees," he ordered. "To go."

The waitress nodded, quickly filled a pair of white paper cups and pressed on black plastic lids. Then we got out of there before the smell of sugar and butter and muffins and cookies became too tempting.

He groaned as we walked out the door. "God, those cookies smelled good. I almost swiped two. Proud of me for not stealing?"

"Very." I nodded. "I want to learn how to bake one day. When I have a kitchen. I remember my mom baked a lot. Aria and I would help her in the kitchen by dumping ingredients into the bowl after she'd measure them out."

"What's your favorite type of cookie?" Karson sipped his coffee.

"Ginger molasses. Or pumpkin chocolate chip."

"I don't think I've ever had those."

"Seriously?"

He shrugged. "My mom wasn't much for baking. Or cooking. Or doing anything but drowning in a bottle of vodka."

"Sorry."

He waved it off and took another sip.

I took a drink, cringing at the bitter flavor. Coffee had never appealed. Maybe it would as I got older, but I'd still drink it because Karson had spent a dollar. And because it gave me something to do.

I was coming out of my skin here. How could he be so calm? So normal? Was this how he wanted to act? Like nothing had happened? Maybe pretend it was just nothing?

My insides clenched. He regretted it. That had to be the answer. He regretted the kiss. I was a mistake.

Ugh. I was blaming beer for this.

I bit my lip as we walked, determined not to cry. We made our way toward the car wash but when we passed a small park, Karson nodded for me to follow him across the grass toward a bench. "Let's sit. Drink our coffee."

The park was empty, probably because it was still early. In the afternoons, there were always mothers pushing kids on the swing set and watching as they zoomed down the slide.

Karson and I sat on the bench, a visible space between us. "Guess we should probably talk about last night."

"Yeah?" I held my breath.

"I'm not going to apologize for kissing you."

The air rushed from my lungs. "I wasn't sure if you might, um . . . regret it, maybe?"

"What? Never. Do you?"

My heart skipped and I shook my head. "Never."

"Good." His shoulders relaxed and he lifted his cup to his lips.

"But . . ." The cup froze in midair. "Is this, like, a rebound thing?"

It had taken every ounce of courage I had to ask that question.

Karson shifted to face me as he set his coffee on the ground. Then he moved, closing the gap between us, until his thigh brushed mine. His arm went to the back of the bench. "No. Definitely not a rebound."

"Are you sure? You and Londyn were together for a long time."

"I'm sure. Londyn and I were better friends than we were a couple. It was over the day she left." Karson raised his hand and his fingers sifted into my hair, brushing it away from my ear.

My breath hitched.

Then his mouth was there, hovering over mine. Karson brushed his lips across mine, teasing, and then he pressed in deep, his arms wrapping around my shoulders.

My cup of coffee fell out of my hand, landing on the grass beside our feet. I didn't care. I didn't think. Like last night, I just let Karson kiss me.

His tongue ran across my lower lip, and I opened so he could sweep inside. Karson pressed closer, the heat from his body soaking into mine. Our tongues tangled and twisted. Every breathless second was bliss and when he finally broke away, I was lost in the darkened green and gold swirls of his eyes.

Karson wanted me. Me.

"Why?" I hadn't meant to voice my insecurity, but that damn word had slipped out.

"Why what?"

I closed my eyes and braced. "Are you kissing me because we only have two days left?"

"Clara, look at me." His fingers tugged on a strand of hair that hung between us. He twirled it around his index finger as I lifted my lashes. "I'm kissing you, wishing I had kissed you *two hundred* and two days ago."

I practically slid off the bench as I melted. If not for his arms still around me, I would have joined my coffee as a puddle in the grass. "Really?"

He leaned in and brushed his lips across mine, whispering, "Really."

The next kiss was a lot like I'd remembered from last night. Fumbling hands. Wet lips. Tentative nips and licks as I learned more about what he liked. What I liked. His coffee was forgotten as we clung to each other, sitting on the park bench, kissing like we were the only people in the world. It was only when the shout of a child rang through the air that we broke apart.

My lips were raw and puffy again. Karson inched away, drawing in a few pained breaths. I ducked my chin to hide a smile because there was a noticeable bulge beneath his jeans.

"Need to go anywhere else?" Karson asked, finally standing from the bench.

"No." I took his outstretched hand and stood, letting him lace our fingers together. Then we walked, our arms swinging between us, to the car wash. "Do you think all beer tastes like that stuff last night?"

Karson laughed. "Probably."

"Yuck." I faked a gag as we rounded the block. "I'll stick with lemonade, thanks."

"Same here. With ice. Lots and lots of ice."

"And ice cream."

"With chocolate syr—" Karson froze, his tennis shoes slapping to a stop.

"What?" I followed his gaze to the car wash's parking lot.

And there she was. His mother.

She was in jeans and a gray button-down shirt. Her hands waved in the air as she spoke to Karson's boss, who stood with his arms crossed over his chest and his mouth glued shut.

But it wasn't Karson's mother or his boss that sent a jolt of panic through my veins.

It was the uniformed police officer standing between them who sent my heart into my throat.

The officer looked up and spotted us. He narrowed his gaze and cocked his head. The movement caused Karson's mother to stop speaking. She turned and her eyes widened. Then her hand was in the air, shaking a pointed finger.

Karson kept a firm hold on my hand as he took a step backward.

"Run."

7

CLARA

"DO YOU THINK THEY FOLLOWED US?" I panted. There was a kink in my neck from constantly checking over my shoulder as we'd raced home.

Karson had led the way. He'd taken us in circles around the blocks surrounding the car wash. Then we'd jogged down alleyways and cut through unfenced yards. Finally, after an hour, we'd decided to head to Aria's work and wait until the end of her shift.

After she'd clocked out, we'd given her a fast explanation that Karson's mother had brought in the police.

"I don't think so." Aria's cheeks were flushed, and her forehead was covered in sweat as she cast one last look down the road toward town. Then she stepped through the gate with us and into the safety of the junkyard.

"Why would she talk to the cops?" I asked Karson.

He kicked at the dirt. "Fuck."

"Karson, why?"

He didn't answer me.

Adrenaline had been coursing through my system for hours and suddenly, it felt like my legs were too weak to hold me up. My head started swimming. My chest felt too tight.

"Clara." My sister put her hand on my shoulder. "Are you okay?"

I shook my head. "Can't breathe."

"Hey." Karson put his hand on my other shoulder. "In and out. Do it. Breathe in."

I obeyed.

"And out."

I followed his order again but still felt like crashing.

"Do it again. In and out, Clara. In and out."

I closed my eyes and listened to his voice, letting it soothe the panic. It had been a long time since I'd freaked out like this. The last time had been after our parents' accident.

When the ground beneath my feet no longer felt like it was giving way, I cracked my eyelids.

"You okay?" Aria asked.

"Yeah. Sorry."

"Don't be." She took my hand in hers, then shot a scowl at Karson. "What is going on with your mother?"

He sighed, let me go and jerked his chin to the tent.

Aria and I followed as he walked away, the three of us congregating in his place.

Karson dragged a hand through his hair. "She wants me to come home."

"But why?" I asked.

He shrugged. "Because she's fucking crazy? I don't know. The last time she came to work, she begged me to come home."

"You're nineteen." I tossed out a hand. "Isn't she, like, three years too late?"

He scoffed. "She doesn't want me to come home so she can act like a mother. She wants me to come home because I *am* nineteen and can get a decent job. She wants me to be her paycheck."

"She said that?" Aria asked.

Karson shook his head. "She didn't have to. I know her well enough to understand how she operates. It's all lies and manipulations. The second time she stopped by, she'd promised that she'd stopped drinking and wanted to make amends. The next visit, I could smell the booze on her breath when she asked me for a loan. She's never been able to hold down a job, and she's desperate. Somehow she stumbled onto where I work so she's out to make my life hell."

"But she has a nice car," I said. "Those jogging clothes were fancy."

"My guess? After I ran away, she found a guy to take care of her. Gave him some sob story or something. She was always good at that. Making men feel like they could rescue her. He probably tossed her and now she's looking for the next fucking idiot to leech from. That idiot just isn't going to be me."

That was more than he'd ever told us. Karson's words were so bitter. Pain and anger infused his tone and made me ache.

"You're sure?" Aria asked.

He shrugged. "No, but it's an educated guess. She's been doing shit like this my whole life."

"Okay, what now?" I asked. "She came jogging down our road. She has to know that you're living here."

"Maybe. But if she knew, Lou's fence and padlock wouldn't stop her. My guess is she heard a rumor I was here but doesn't know for sure. And the car wash is open to the public."

Not surrounded by chain link and razor wire.

"She saw us together today. She saw me walking. It doesn't take much to know we're together and living around here."

He dropped his gaze to the floor and nodded. "We could be at any of the houses on this road. But it doesn't matter. There's nothing she can do. Eventually, she'll realize that I'm not playing her fucked-up games and move on."

"There's nothing she can do to *you*," Aria said. "You're nineteen. But we're seventeen."

"Only for a couple days."

"Two days. Two years. It doesn't matter." She held up her chin. "If the cops find us, they'll send us back to our uncle's house and I won't go back. Not for two seconds."

I took Aria's hand and squeezed it tight. "We're not going back."

"She'll go away," Karson promised. "Two more days."

That number should have brought me comfort, but instead, my heart lurched. Two more days, forty-eight hours, and we'd go our separate ways.

"Well, I'm going to take a shower." Aria stood up. "I stink like grease."

I stayed on the floor, waiting until she left us alone, then I put my hand on Karson's forearm. "Are you okay?"

"I'm pissed." His jaw clenched. "I hate her. I fucking hate her, Clara."

"Want to talk about it?" I held my breath, hoping he'd open up.

He picked up my hand, but not to shrug off my touch. He played with my fingers, tracing them with his own. He pressed our palms together. He circled our thumbs. "She's a pathological liar. She's a drunk. She hates me."

"I'm sorry."

"But it's nothing, you know? Nothing compared to what the rest of you had to live with."

Oh my God. It suddenly made sense. "That's why you don't talk about it? Because you think it's not bad enough?"

"I brought a lot of trouble onto myself. It's not the same. Londyn's parents were junkies. Gemma's mother did some fucked-up shit to her. Katherine's too. What your uncle did to you and Aria is sick. You guys . . . you survived so much."

"So did you."

"No." He caressed my knuckles with the pad of his thumb. "Nothing like that."

"I'd like to know what happened with your mom. If you want to talk."

His frame deflated. "She's a drunk. She hides it from boyfriends so she can use them for whatever she needs. She's got a fake face for the world but the real one comes out behind closed doors. I got the real one."

"Did she hurt you?"

"She didn't give a fuck about me. She'd cook me a meal and tell me I didn't deserve to eat it. She'd see me watching TV and tell me she hated the sight of me in her house. When I was little, I did everything to please her. I'd clean. I'd get good grades. I'd help her to bed when she was piss drunk. And the whole time, she'd tell me I was dog shit."

"Karson." Oh my God. How could he think what he'd been through wasn't horrific?

"You know what though, I am a screwup."

"What are you talking about? Of course you're not."

"No, she was right about one thing. I fuck up everything I touch."

My jaw dropped. "What are you talking about?"

"A lot of her problems are because of me."

"How?"

He rubbed at an invisible spot on his jeans, hesitating long enough that I held my breath, worried about what he'd say. "A while back, before I ran away, I got into some trouble. Me and some friends went out one night. We'd been drinking and smoking pot. We found this old warehouse, not that far from here actually. One of the guys had a can of spray paint. He drew a dick on the wall. Me and the others found some rocks and threw them through the windows."

I bit my tongue. I wanted so badly not to picture him there. To see him doing those things. But Karson had always had a reckless edge. There was anger in him and defiance. Most of the time he kept it hidden, especially when we were here and it was just us. But outside this chain-link fence, he rebelled by stealing food. By getting into fights.

"What happened?"

"Got caught," he said. "Cops arrested me. I called Mom to get me out of jail. On the way to pick me up, she got pulled over. She was drunk so we both spent the night in jail. It never would have happened if I'd just stayed home."

"She was drunk. She was driving drunk." I gaped at him as my temper bubbled. "Drunk drivers *murder* innocent people, Karson."

"I know that. Don't you think I know that?" His voice cracked. "She could have killed someone else's parents and it would have been my fault."

"No, it would have been her fault."

He shook his head. "Mine, Clara. I fucked up. And it wasn't the first or last time."

"What else happened?"

"Fights, mostly. Got suspended from school three times. I beat the shit out of one of her boyfriends with a baseball bat because he tried to have sex with her when she was practically unconscious. Turns out, she didn't care. When she sobered up, it was my fault that he left her. He had money too. He'd been paying for our food. And I chased him away. We didn't eat for a week. I never asked how she finally got money. My guess is she went out and found a new guy. I did that. I made her whore herself out because I couldn't control my temper."

Was he even listening to his own words? "You were trying to protect her."

"She didn't see it that way."

"You can't be serious." His mother was a bitch. She could have gotten a job. She could have provided for her son instead of blaming him for her problems.

Karson shrugged. "After sixteen years of her reminding me every damn day that I was worthless, of her telling me that I'd ruined her life, I decided it was enough. If I was ruining her life, why stay?"

Oh, God. My heart cracked. He was so good. So incredible. How could his own mother not see that? How could he have this so wrong? "No, Karson. It's not you."

"She loved my father. Maybe the only person in her life that she actually loved more than herself. I don't think she was a drunk back then. But he split two weeks after I was born."

"That's not your fault." He'd been born to shitty parents.

"It is and it isn't. That's just my life."

"Karson, you did not ruin her life."

He didn't say a word.

He didn't believe me.

"Karson. That's not on you."

Again, silence. No matter what I said, he didn't see it. Why? How? There was no way he should carry all of this on his shoulders. "You really think you ruined her life."

He looked up and the raw honesty in his eyes broke my heart. "I think we ruined each other. I think there are toxic people in this world and maybe I'm one of them."

"You're not," I insisted, clenching my jaw so I wouldn't scream. "You're not toxic."

"I was for her. And maybe others."

He didn't mean me, did he? He couldn't. No way. Karson was the foundation to our lives here. He'd been there for all of us.

"I don't know what to say," I whispered.

He shrugged. "Nothing to say."

"I'm sorry." Yes, Craig had been a nightmare, but our parents had loved us. That was the one thing Aria and I had always held tight to. Our parents had loved us.

It set us apart from the others in the junkyard.

No matter how many times I saw it, how many of my friends had gone through it, I still couldn't understand how a mother or father couldn't love their children.

"She's wrong." I twisted my hand and threaded my fingers through Karson's. "You have to know that. She's so wrong. You're amazing. You're the best guy I've ever known."

He stared at our fingers but didn't reply.

"Karson."

No response.

He didn't believe me. I could sit here and scream it into his face, but he was not hearing my words. Whatever that bitch of a mother had done to him had slashed deep. He covered it up with that dreamy smile and easy charm, but there were wounds hidden beneath.

"Why did she go to the cops?" I asked. "Why would she bring them to the car wash?"

594

"Desperation? Before I ran away, I stole a bunch of jewelry from her. I pawned it ages ago, but maybe she thinks I still have it. That she can blackmail me into coming home. Who knows? She's crazy, remember?"

"It's not like they can do anything to you. They can't prove you pawned it, though, can they?"

"Maybe. That was a long time ago but . . . they'll believe her over me," he muttered. "They'll want to know where I'm living and search my things."

"Can they do that?"

"They're the cops."

And if they came here, we were in trouble. "Lou wouldn't let them in."

"He won't have a choice."

"Why would she think that getting the cops involved would make you go home? Or talk to her?"

He circled a finger around his temple. "You're thinking rationally now. Nothing she does is rational. But she can cry on cue. She'll give you these eyes that make you feel bad for her. It's all a trap. She needs money and at first, she must have thought she could guilt me into being her meal ticket. Now she's going for blackmail."

And she seemed determined. His mother would come here eventually. Of that, I had no doubt. She'd find a way to torment him until . . .

Until he was gone.

My heart ached. I knew what I had to say, and I knew the words would taste like acid on my tongue. "You should go. Leave early. Start exploring the world and live your life."

Karson's gaze met mine and softened, then he let go of my hand to cup my cheek. "I'm not ready to leave you yet."

I leaned into his touch as my heart flipped. "I'm not ready either."

Not when I'd just found him. There was so little time left. I didn't want to cut it short.

A muted curse came from beyond the tent's walls. Karson pulled his hand away and I inched backward, putting space between us, right before Aria poked her head inside. "I stubbed my toe."

"No shower?"

She lifted the soap, towel and washcloth in her hand. "I decided to water my plants again first. It was hot today. And I was just thinking that maybe we should tell Lou. Warn him about your mom and the cops."

"Yeah," Karson mumbled. "Probably a good idea. I'll tell him in the morning. He's better in the mornings."

Lou rarely came outside in the afternoons or evenings. It was something I hadn't noticed for a long time, not until Gemma had pointed it out.

"Okay. I'm dealing with the stink that is me," Aria said.

"I'm going to hang out here for a while."

She nodded, then left us alone with a wave.

I turned to Karson, waiting until her footsteps disappeared. Then he was there, kissing me. His hands framed my face and his lips consumed mine. I melted into him, shifting closer to wrap my arms around his waist.

God, I wasn't ready to say goodbye.

I wanted time. I wanted more kisses. I wanted . . . Karson. I wanted him to be the one.

A whimper escaped my throat as Karson dragged his lips away. I opened my eyes to find his hazel irises waiting and full of lust.

"Did you tell Aria?"

I shook my head, breathing, "No. I wasn't sure what we were."

"I get it." He dropped his forehead to mine. "We'd better slow down."

"Yeah," I muttered.

Aria would know if I showed up at the truck with swollen lips and flushed cheeks. I loved my sister, but Karson was mine, and I didn't want to share. Just this one thing I wanted as my own.

I didn't want to hear her warnings. I didn't want to answer her questions.

How long? What about Londyn? Do you love him?

"I better go," I breathed.

He nodded and let me go, his Adam's apple bobbing as he swallowed. If there were time, if I were braver, I'd lick the column of that throat. I'd taste the saltiness of his skin, like so many of the characters did in my books.

I stood and walked to the doorway on shaky legs. Walking away from Karson was like waking from a dream. I longed to go back, to kiss him again. Because with him, I could get lost in another world. A world without junkyards and dead parents and peanut butter and honey sandwiches.

How was I supposed to leave him for Las Vegas? How was I supposed to walk away from the only person who could make reality disappear?

I couldn't. He had to come with us. If he tried Vegas, he might like it.

"Karson—"

"Come back tonight."

We spoke in unison.

"Okay," I agreed. Tonight, I'd ask him again tonight. I'd beg if I had to. But he had to come with us.

With my fingertips pressed to my lips, I returned to the truck, where I sat on my bed and did my best to look normal by the time Aria arrived from her shower. Then we busied ourselves by dividing up the books, each deciding which three we'd bring along.

I loved time with my sister, but every minute dragged until finally, she yawned as darkness crept over the junkyard.

"I'm going to bed."

A wave of excitement stirred in my belly. "Oh. Already? I'm not tired."

She stripped off her jeans and pulled on the ratty sleep shorts she'd had for years. It was a good thing neither of us had bloomed early. Though my pants were snug in the hips and shirts stretched across my breasts, our bodies hadn't changed so much that we'd had to buy completely new clothes over the years.

But someday. Someday I would wear clothing without a single tear or frayed hem.

"Are you going to read?" She yawned again as she climbed into her sleeping bag.

"Actually, I might see if Karson wants to play cards or something. We were in a poker game last night."

"Okay." She snuggled with her pillow.

"I'll close this door. In case I just crash there again. In Katherine's room." Before Aria could say anything else, I scurried from the truck, closing the back so she was safe inside.

Karson was outside the tent, standing with his face turned toward the stars.

"Hey," I said, slowing my footsteps even though my heart was pounding.

He looked down and the wide smile he gave me caused tingles to skate across my skin. "Hey."

"What are you looking at?" I searched the sky but there weren't many stars out yet.

"Nothing. Just waiting for you."

"So, um, what do you want to do? Play cards?"

He shook his head.

"Talk?"

He shook his head again, and in one stride he was in my space. His hands came to my face, tilting my chin so he could smash his lips on mine.

I let out a mewl as his arms banded around me, pulling me flush against the hard lines of his tall body. Then he swept me off my feet, my toes skimming across the dirt as he carried me to the tent.

Karson ducked inside, breaking away from my mouth, but his arms never loosened their hold until we were both on our knees in the center of the room.

Our lips were fused together. Our tongues glided and stroked and dived in for more. His hands skimmed over my ribs and down my hips. Then he cupped my breasts and the intimate touch startled a gasp.

"You okay?"

I nodded. "Yeah."

"Did I go too far?"

"No." I leaned into his touch, my nipples hardening. "It's okay."

But even with the assurance, Karson pulled his hands away. He inched backward on his knees. "We'd better slow down."

"Oh." The disappointment in my tone filled the space.

"I don't want to rush this."

"We only have two days left."

"Clara, I want you. God, I want you. But . . ." He ran a hand over his jaw. "Maybe you should go."

Because he wouldn't want to stop.

I didn't want him to stop.

Maybe if my life had been normal. If I were the girl who'd crushed on the boy in school. If we had had weeks of flirting beside lockers and going on dates, then I would have slowed this down.

But we only had two days. And if I couldn't convince him to come to Vegas, then I'd lose him.

"I don't want to go." I squared my shoulders, feigning more confidence than I actually felt.

Karson let out a pained groan. "Clara."

"I want you to be the one," I whispered.

His eyes locked on mine and whatever restraint he'd been holding onto shredded. He came at me, strong and sure, and kissed me until I was breathless. Then he took me to his room, laying me on the bed that I'd slept on with him just last night.

Karson's kisses were tender and soft as he settled on his side, careful not to crush me under his weight. "Tell me to stop and I'll stop."

"Don't stop." I closed my eyes and arched into his lips as they trailed down my neck.

One of his hands was on my breast, the other in my hair.

When his fingers drifted to the waistband of my jeans, I ached in places I hadn't ached before. A throb boomed in my core.

Karson never pushed too fast. He looked at me before every touch, waiting for that nod to continue. He let me conquer the fears, one by one. He let me know with his kiss and his touch and those gorgeous hazel eyes that I was in control.

And when we were both naked, our clothes piled beside us, he settled into the cradle of my hips and brushed his thumb across my cheek.

"Clara." He whispered my name like a prayer.

I ran my fingers across his collarbone. I fit my palm to the hard muscle of his bicep. Then I gave him the nod that brought us together as one.

Later, after he'd made me see a different kind of stars, we curled together, our legs tangled and his arms encircling mine. I fell asleep with a smile.

Karson didn't know it, but he'd just given me something I'd never had before.

A dream come true.

8

CLARA

THE MURMUR of voices woke me from sleep. "Who is tha—"

"Shh." Karson's arms squeezed around me as he whispered in my ear. Then he let me go and silently slipped from beneath his blankets, swiping up his jeans from the floor. He tugged them on and tiptoed, barefoot, toward the opening of the tent. With a glance over his shoulder, he pressed a finger to his lips and crept outside.

I scrambled to get dressed, strapping on my bra first, then rifling through the clothes scattered around me for my panties. With them on, I yanked on my jeans and shirt, then followed Karson outside. Crouching low as I walked, I weaved through the piles of junk around the tent, finding him ducked behind an old truck.

Aria was by his side.

They were both staring at Lou, who stood beside the gate.

Talking to two police officers.

Their voices echoed across the yard.

Lou's was gruff and raspy as he thrust a photo back at one of the cops. "Never seen him."

"Are you sure?" The officer took the photo, looking at it himself. "This is an outdated photo. Maybe you could look again."

Lou scowled. "Never seen that kid."

The officers shared a look. "Sir, we have reason to believe this young man is living here. In your junkyard. On your property."

"Not here."

"Mr. Miley, if we could just take a look around—"

"No," Lou barked. "There's no kid here. Don't you think I'd know if a damn kid was living at my place?"

"There are a lot of places where a person could hide." One officer scanned the junkyard. When his face shifted our way, all three of us hit the dirt.

599

Aria's face was pale. She sat unmoving other than the short, fast breaths that made her chest rise and fall. They matched mine.

Karson's jaw was clenched tight and his fists balled at his sides.

His mother had done this. She'd sent the police here and given them that photo.

"There's no one here but me," Lou repeated, agitation tainting his words.

Maybe I heard the lie because I knew the truth. But if I didn't believe Lou, the cops might not either.

"We believe he's involved in a breaking and entering," one of the officers said. "He's been stealing from his mother for years now. Family heirlooms and such. She's finally decided to get the authorities involved."

"Fuck," Karson muttered.

So his mother had decided to blackmail him.

The three of us shifted again, daring another glance at the officers. Thankfully, neither was looking our way. They were focused on Lou, who seemed to be getting more frazzled every second. He shifted his weight from foot to foot. He rattled the ring of keys in his hand.

Even when he had customers come to the yard, he'd point them in the right direction, then send them on their way. He never played tour guide. If a mechanic or antique hunter came here searching for spare parts, they were left on their own, given clear directions where they could and could not search. And Lou never haggled. He had signs around the shack saying as much.

It was all so he didn't have to prolong human interaction.

"Would you call us if you see anyone?" one of the officers asked, handing over a card.

Lou nodded and took the paper, shoving it into the pocket of his baggy jeans. Then, without waiting for the cops to leave, he turned and disappeared into his shack, slamming the door behind him.

The officers shared a look of disbelief, then walked to the street, where their cruiser was parked. As they rolled down the road, Karson, Aria and I stayed hidden, waiting until the only sound was the soft breeze through the drying summer grasses around the property.

Karson was the first to stand, shaking his head as he marched to the tent.

Aria stood and sighed. "Shit."

"This is bad." I got to my bare feet and pinched the bridge of my nose. "This is very bad. He told me a little about her last night. His mother. From the sound of it, she's a manipulative, lying bitch."

"He should leave."

The twist in my chest was so tight I struggled to breathe. She was right. The best thing was for Karson to move on. But I wasn't ready to give him up. Not yet. Not after last night.

"You slept in the tent again," she said.

"We played cards pretty late. I didn't want to wake you," I lied.

Today was not the day to tell Aria I'd given Karson my virginity.

600

The sound of a slamming door echoed across the yard. Aria and I both turned toward the shop door, recognizing the sound.

Karson had disappeared to the bathroom.

"I'm going to go get my shoes." I left Aria's side and hurried to the tent, scanning around Karson's bed for anything I might have left behind. Only my shoes and socks remained. The condom he'd worn last night was gone, along with the wrapper.

I blushed and took a moment to breathe before I had to face my sister again.

Should I tell her? It would make it all easier if she knew what had happened, right? There'd be no sneaking around. Right. I'd just tell her. Decision made, I stepped into my shoes and found her in the truck. I climbed inside as she was making her bed.

"I, um . . ." *Tell her.*

The words clogged my throat.

Why was I so scared to confess that I'd been with Karson? I was in love with him. People in love had sex. But I couldn't get my mouth to form the sentence.

"Um, what?"

"Nothing." I swallowed hard. "Once Karson is done, I'm going to take a shower too. Then we should talk."

"I'm just glad I showered before the cops showed up." She plopped down on her bed. "They totally would have seen me coming out of the shop."

"Maybe we should start showering at night."

"Maybe." Her gaze was focused on the truck wall, her forehead furrowed. She was staring at today's number.

One.

It wouldn't matter when we showered because today was our last day.

Tonight was our last night.

The urge to cry came on so strong I almost dropped to my knees.

The shop door slammed again, this time not as loud. I blinked the tears away and collected my soap and towel, then went to the shop, finally breathing when I was under the warm spray.

I hated the idea of washing away Karson's kisses. His touches. My body was sore in places I'd never been sore before, and the tenderness between my legs was going to make work difficult today. It was my last shift at the diner.

Still, despite the ache, a smile toyed at my lips as I toweled off.

Karson and I had had sex. We'd been as intimate as two people could get.

Would he change his mind about Vegas now? Did he feel the same way about me that I felt about him?

Dressed in fresh clothes and smelling like my soap, I hurried to the truck, finding Karson already there, waiting with Aria.

"Hey." I gave him a tiny smile.

With his back to Aria, he winked at me. "Hey."

"So what do we do?" Aria hopped out of the truck to pace beside her buckets of plants.

Karson dropped to the truck's edge, sitting so his legs could hang over the end.

And I took the space by his side, careful not to get too close. What I wanted to do was pull him aside, to see if we were okay. To let him kiss me again. But not until we talked.

"I don't understand why she's doing this," I said. "Your mom. Why couldn't she just let you go? You ran away. You're done with her."

Karson scoffed. "Like I told you last night. She's crazy and desperate. Her life's mission is to make mine hell."

"I hate her," I spat, fury racing through my veins.

"Join the club," he mumbled. "She won't stop. And I don't like that look the cops had when they left. I think they knew Lou was lying."

"If they come here again, they'll find us." Aria waved to our home. "Three teenagers are sort of hard to miss."

Karson nodded and turned to face me. *No.* The look in his eyes made me want to scream.

I knew before he opened his mouth what he was going to say. "We're leaving tomorrow anyway."

"Yeah." Aria ran her hands over a pink bloom from a bucket. "We'll be gone first thing in the morning."

My heart was breaking.

This had always been the plan. Always.

"Come with us." My plea escaped before I could stop it. "You could come with us."

The look Karson gave me was so gentle and kind, I wanted to die.

Because in that look was his answer.

No. He wouldn't come to Vegas with us.

"It's okay." I waved it off so he wouldn't have to come up with an explanation.

"Clara."

"It was just an idea." I got to my feet and went into the truck, folding up the clothes I'd worn last night. They were trash. I'd leave them behind. Still, I folded.

"What time are you going to work?" Aria joined me in the truck.

I glanced at my little clock. "I'd better leave soon."

When I turned to Karson, he was staring at the number on the truck's wall.

One.

Time was up. We'd just started this. And now it was ending.

Without so much as a glance in my direction, Karson jumped down and vanished.

I wanted to cry. I wanted to yell. I wanted to beg him not to leave us.

Instead, I blinked away the threat of tears.

And went to work.

"HEY." Karson knocked on the side of the truck.

I tensed as he hopped inside. "Hey."

"How's it going? It looks different in here."

"Yeah."

After my shift had ended, Aria and I had spent the afternoon and early evening organizing. The items that were coming with us were stowed in our backpacks, ready for tomorrow. Everything else we'd moved to the front of the truck. The bedding. The books. The clothes. The forgotten pieces that would probably remain in this truck until the end of the junkyard's days.

"Where's Aria?" he asked.

"Moving her plants. She's staging them beside Lou's."

"Does she need help?"

I shook my head. "I think she wanted to be alone for a while. She was going to write him a note."

"Clara, about Vegas."

"You don't have to explain. I get it. You've done your duty and stayed to watch us. You don't deserve to be chained to us anymore."

"Is that how you think I feel? Chained?"

I lifted a shoulder. "I wouldn't blame you if you did."

"Well, I don't."

"Then why?" I asked even though I knew the answer. My voice was too loud and it bounced off the metal walls.

The emotion was bubbling up and I was about to lose it, so I gave him my back, not wanting him to see me cry. I'd had to take three breaks from the dishwasher today to run to the bathroom and cry. When my boss had given me my final pay, I think she'd thought the tears in my eyes had been because I was leaving.

"Because you shouldn't be chained *to me*." His hand came to my shoulder and his thumb circled the bare skin of my neck. "Would you look at me?"

"I can't." My voice cracked.

"Clara, you deserve this fresh start. I won't risk ruining it for you. What if I got caught stealing? What if I got into another fight? What if someone asked when we started having sex and then I got put away for statutory rape?"

My hands fisted at my sides. He could stop stealing. He could stop fighting. "I would never tell."

"I'm not going to make you lie for me. I won't ruin you too."

"You wouldn't."

"I might. I don't want to take that chance."

My throat burned. "Even for me?"

"Especially for you. We all deserve to be set free."

Yes, he did. Karson deserved to be set free.

No matter what I said, he truly thought of himself as a toxic person.

Maybe if I'd seen it sooner, years ago, I could have convinced him of the truth. But after weeks, I couldn't even persuade him to go exploring with me in Vegas. How was I supposed to convince him that he was not the person his mother had spent sixteen years telling him he was?

I didn't have sixteen years to fix this. I only had a day.

It was too late. I was too late.

Tears flooded my eyes as I spun around to face him. I'd worked so hard today to keep them at bay and hide my emotions from my coworkers and Aria. But there was no hiding from Karson, not anymore.

He stepped closer and caught the first tear as it dropped down my cheek. "Don't cry."

"I don't want to say goodbye."

"Then we won't."

A sob escaped right as he pulled me into his arms, holding me close as I cried. More footsteps sounded in the truck and when one of Karson's arms loosened, it was only to make room for Aria to join our huddle.

The three of us clung to one another, and when Karson finally let us go, my tears had soaked his shirt and Aria was sniffling.

"Where will you go?" she asked him.

"Exploring," Karson and I answered in unison, then laughed.

"Out of Temecula, that's for sure," he said, then looked to me. "And maybe someday, to visit you two in Vegas. I expect you'll be running the town by then."

I forced a smile. "That's the plan."

"What time are you leaving?" Aria asked.

"Early. You?"

"We'll go to the bus station first thing," I said. "The bus to Vegas leaves at nine. But we'll be early, just in case."

"So this is it. The last night. Calls for a celebration."

"Like what?" I followed him as he walked to the end of the truck to look out at the junkyard.

"Peanut butter and honey sandwiches, of course."

HOURS LATER, after the sun had set and Aria had fallen asleep, I snuck out of the truck, careful not to wake her, and I made my way to the tent.

Karson's lantern was on. His bags were packed beside the door and he was sitting on his bed.

Waiting for me.

Neither of us spoke as he took me in his arms and kissed me breathless. Or as he stripped off my clothes and his own. Or as he made love to me, one last time, holding me tight until morning.

I refused to fall asleep when he drifted off. Instead, I clung to him until the first rays of dawn lit the sky, and I snuck to the shop for a shower before he or Aria woke up.

While Aria was in the bathroom, I found the small notebook and pen

Aria kept in her pack and tore out a page. Then I wrote Lou a note, leaving it at the base of his front door.

I LOVE YOU, Lou. Thank you.
   Clara

"GOODBYE, LOU," I whispered to his shack. "Take care of yourself."

Aria had done her farewell yesterday. Never before had her plants looked so green and her flowers so bold as they did around his shack. She'd staged them so artfully, I doubted even a professional gardener would have done such a nice job.

While she collected her things, I set out a bowl of cat food for Katherine's cat. Then I took the half-empty bag of food to the shop, leaving it beside the door where Lou would find it.

"I didn't think I'd be sad," Aria said as we both stood outside the truck.

I had. I'd known this would hurt.

We each wore a backpack on our shoulders and held another in our hands. On the wall, I'd erased yesterday's number, but I hadn't written anything in its place.

"Thank you," I said to the truck, my chin quivering. *Thank you for being our home. Thank you for being our refuge. Thank you for keeping us safe.*

With tears in my eyes, I took Aria's hand. Then, like the day we'd come here, we walked, together, toward the gate.

I didn't look at the Cadillac. I didn't look at the tent.

I knew it would be empty.

I kept my face forward and my feet moving until we journeyed down our road one last time. Until we were at the station with bus tickets in our pockets. And as I settled into my seat on the bus that would take us to Vegas, I replayed the last words we'd said to each other before he'd fallen asleep.

"Happy Birthday, Clara."
"Will I ever see you again?"
"I hope so. I really hope so."

9

KARSON

TWELVE YEARS LATER . . .

"It's really you."

Clara Saint-James.

There she was, standing in my driveway, and all I could do was grin at her like a fool. She looked beautiful. More beautiful than I'd ever imagined.

"It's really me." She smiled and my heart fluttered. Her smile had always hit me dead center.

The boy at her side stared up at me. Other than a quick glance, I hadn't paid him much attention, because it was impossible to tear my eyes away from Clara for long.

God, I'd imagined this. I'd hoped for this. Just to see her again, in the flesh, and know that she was safe. Know that she'd found a new life. Know that she was happy.

"What are you doing here?"

"It's a long story." She waved a hand toward her car.

I followed the movement, taking in the classic Cadillac. It was a stunner, but nothing like Clara. The hood ornament, a V embossed with red and gold and silver, glinted under the sun. It looked familiar. Too familiar.

I knew that ornament.

I knew that car.

"Wait. Is this . . ."

Clara nodded. "Looks a little different than it did back in the day, huh?"

"What? How?" My jaw dropped as I rushed to the car, splaying my hands on the cherry-red hood, the metal still warm. I walked along the Cadillac's side, inspecting and savoring every inch. "I can't believe it. I can't believe this is the same car. It's incredible."

The Cadillac was a dream. It looked nothing like the rusted heap it had been so many years ago. The interior was refinished in a white, soft leather. The dash, which had been cracked and busted, was new. The polished chrome accents sparkled.

I had no idea what had brought this car and Clara to California, but what a Sunday surprise.

Skimming my fingers over a rear fin that bordered the broad trunk, I touched the car again just to prove it was real. "I bet I won't find peanut butter and honey stashed in here like we used to."

She scoffed. "Most definitely not."

"How?" Clara was the best of this surprise visit, but the car was the literal red cherry on top.

"Londyn," she said.

"Londyn." I nodded, rounding the trunk. "Before Lou died, he told me that she'd called and bought the car. But I didn't expect to see it again. How do you have it?"

"Kind of a long story." She looked down at the boy and smiled. "We surprised you today. Want to meet for dinner or something? If you're free?"

"I'm free now." There was no way I was letting her out of my sight. Not yet. I glanced down at the boy who watched my every step as I approached. I crouched down in front of him and held out a hand for a shake. "But how about some introductions first? I'm Karson. What's your name?"

"August." He looked at my hand, then slapped his to mine, grabbing it tighter than I would have expected for a young kid. One hard shake and he looked up at Clara and smiled.

She winked down at him.

"Quite a grip." I shook out my hand, pretending it hurt. "You're pretty strong for a—what, four-year-old?"

"I'm five. Almost six."

"Ah. Still, you're pretty strong." I grinned at him as he puffed up his chest, then stood and motioned toward my home. "Did you ever learn to like coffee?"

"I can't believe you remember that." Clara's pretty brown eyes softened, and I was whisked away to the past. To a junkyard where I'd once fallen for a girl with pretty brown eyes. This girl.

"Coffee became a necessity because of this guy." Clara ruffled August's hair. "He loves to torment his mother in the middle of the night."

"Nu-uh," he argued.

"Yes-huh."

His mother. Clara was a mother. I'd already known. One look at them and it was no secret. The resemblance, along with the onslaught of surprises in the past five minutes, was enough to keep my head spinning.

The boy looked just like her. They had the same mouth and nose. They had the same sparkling eyes with flecks of gold. His hair was the color of honey, like hers was in my memory.

A twist pinched in my gut. Clara was a mother. Where was the father?

Why hadn't he come along? I had no right to be jealous, but as sure as a Cadillac from over a decade ago was parked in my driveway, envy took up the free space in my chest.

My eyes flew to her left hand. Other than the stack of bracelets on her wrist, there was no other jewelry. Was she divorced then?

Maybe if I stopped gawking at her and invited her inside, she'd answer those questions.

"Coffee." I cleared my throat and extended a hand toward the house.

"Want to grab your Nintendo?" Clara asked August.

He answered by sprinting to the car and vaulting over the side wall for the seat in the back, rifling through a bag. He emerged with a handheld game and a smile.

They had the same smile too. Bright. Cheerful. Honest.

"God, it's good to see you." The words spilled out.

A flush crept into her cheeks. "I wasn't sure you'd remember me."

"What?"

"It was a long time ago."

"It could have been fifty years. A hundred. I will always know you."

Clara swallowed hard and pressed a hand to her heart. "It's good to see you too."

Bubbly music chimed between us. August was already playing his game, concentration scrunching his face.

"Come on in." I jerked my chin for the house.

"Hit pause, bud," Clara said, then gripped August's hand as they followed me to the door. "This is a beautiful home."

"Thanks. I got it for a steal." A three-million-dollar steal. Homes in this neighborhood of Elyria didn't come cheap. I walked to the living room, gesturing to the caramel leather couches. "Make yourself at home. I'll get coffee. And for August?"

"Water's fine," Clara said, taking a seat on the love seat.

August plopped down beside her, his thumbs on the Nintendo's controllers and his eyes glued to the game as the music started up again.

"Ever wish we'd had those things?"

Clara laughed. "Then I would have had another game to beat you at."

"Please." I scoffed. "I let you win, remember?"

"I remember too." Her smile turned bittersweet.

"Be back." I disappeared into the kitchen and took a moment to collect myself.

Holy fuck. That was not who I'd expected to see in the driveway today. And with that car. And alone with her son.

Clara Saint-James.

My Clara.

She hadn't been mine for a long time. My mind acknowledged that truth. But in my heart . . . she'd always felt like mine.

I shook my head, focusing on the coffee pot. I'd brewed a large pot today because I'd slept like shit last night. Though I always slept like shit.

Waking at three or four in the morning had become normal over the past decade. If I got five hours sleep, that was a good night.

There was just too much on my mind. Too much to shut down.

Too many thoughts.

Clara was one of them.

How had she found me? How had Londyn's car found its way to Clara? And what about the others? Had she heard from them? The questions seemed endless. I swiped a bottle of water from the fridge and carried the coffee mugs to the living room.

Clara was bent over her son, watching along as he played with more animation than the game characters themselves.

"Here you go." I handed her a mug, then took the couch opposite hers, setting my coffee on a coaster so it could cool.

"Thanks." She did the same, then touched some buttons on August's game, turning the volume down.

He shot her a scowl but didn't argue.

"Your home is gorgeous," she said, taking in the room's white walls and plethora of windows.

"I wanted something bright. Airy. I like to be able to see outside."

"Mine's got more of a modern style, but lots of windows too."

"Where do you live?"

"Welcome, Arizona. It's a little town on old Route 66. I moved there five years ago, when August was a baby." She toyed with his hair, brushing it off his forehead as he played.

"You like it there?"

She nodded. "I do. It's quiet and safe. Good schools. The desert is truly beautiful in the spring, when the wildflowers bloom. Though at the moment, it's hot. Aria just moved there."

"Aria." I smiled at the name. A name I hadn't said aloud for years. I hadn't spoken any of their names in longer than I could remember. "How is she?"

"Great. She just had a baby. She's married to my boss, Brody. They live next door so we can invade each other's privacy on a regular basis."

"Good for her." I leaned forward and put my elbows to my knees. "Okay, I was going to go for small talk, but the curiosity is killing me. How are you here?"

She stretched for her coffee mug. "Like I said. Londyn. That's the short answer."

"Londyn." Another name. Another memory. "I'm going to need more than that."

Clara laughed and shifted in her seat, crossing a leg over the other. She moved with such elegance. It was something I'd always noticed. She was graceful, like a dancer who'd missed out on dance lessons, but the talent didn't need instruction because it was in her bones. If anything, time seemed to have only accentuated her poise.

"Londyn hauled the car to Boston and had it restored," she said.

"But she didn't keep it?"

Clara shook her head. "She wants you to have it."

"Me?" My jaw hit the area rug beneath the couch. "Seriously? Why?"

"Because it was yours too. That was the reason she gave me. But I think because she doesn't need it anymore. She found what she was looking for."

"Is she happy?"

Clara smiled. "She is. She lives in West Virginia with her husband. Has a couple of cute little kids."

Something inside me clicked. A piece snapped into place. A worry disappeared. For many, many years I'd wondered what had happened to Londyn. To Clara. To the rest of our junkyard crew. I hadn't had the courage to seek them out. Maybe I'd been too afraid of what I'd find. But knowing Londyn was happy was a balm to the soul.

"Good. You've seen her?"

"Just on our virtual chats. We have them every month or so. It started as a book club but we rarely discuss books. Mostly we talk. Catch up on the years we missed. The chats are a fairly recent thing. Ever since the Cadillac started its trip across the country."

Another string of questions zipped through my mind but rather than blurt them in rapid succession, I picked up my coffee and settled into the couch. "I think you'd better give me the long answer now."

She laughed. "We might need more coffee."

"For you? I'll make all the pots in the world. I also have lemonade with lots and lots of ice."

"You remember that too?"

Everything. "I remember everything."

AN HOUR LATER, I stared at Clara in amazement. There was no other word for her story. It was simply amazing.

"Handoffs. That's . . . damn, that's cool."

"Right?" She'd been smiling for nearly the entire hour we'd talked. With every twist and turn of the Cadillac's journey across the country, her smile seemed to widen.

And I kept on drowning, sinking deeper and deeper into those twinkling eyes and breathtaking smile.

"So Londyn's in West Virginia," I said. "Gemma and Kat in Montana. And you and Aria in Arizona."

"Yep." She nodded. "I don't know if we would have come together again without that Cadillac. Maybe. I guess I like to hope so. But it's been the catalyst. All because Londyn wants you to have it."

"But I can't take it." I shook my head. "That car must have cost her a small fortune."

"She doesn't care about the money. She wants you to have it. You deserve that car. You were the one who made it safe for us to live at Lou's. You stayed. You protected us."

"It's too much."

"No, it's not enough." She shook her head. "Besides, I'm not taking it with me when we go home. And after you spend an hour or two behind the wheel, you'll never let it go."

I chuckled. "Should we go for a drive?"

"I was hoping you'd say that." Clara nudged August away from the game. "Gus, time for a break."

"Okay, Mom." He looked up at her with so much love and admiration. That kid worshiped his mother. *Lucky guy.* All kids deserved to have a mother like Clara.

We hadn't gotten into much of her story yet. Or his. I hoped we would on the drive because while my curiosity was sated for the moment, the hunger to know everything about her would return.

I stood from the couch and collected her empty coffee mug. We'd been so into the story, I hadn't needed a refill. I'd been glued to her every word. "Let me put these in the sink. I'll meet you outside."

With flip-flops on my feet and my wallet tucked into a pocket of my shorts, I found them in the driveway. August was already buckled into his car seat while Clara stood beside the passenger door. Her green shorts left her long, tanned legs on display. A white tee draped over her trim frame.

Beautiful. She'd only grown more beautiful.

She tossed me the keys with a smirk and popped open her door.

It was strange, getting behind the wheel of a car I'd once slept in for months. One glance at the backseat and I didn't see white leather or August, but Londyn lounging against one side while I was against the other, our legs tangled.

Clara followed my gaze. "It's hard not to see her back there, isn't it?"

"We had a lot of good times in this car."

"What's that saying? You never forget your first love."

My gaze shifted to her face.

Londyn hadn't been mine. I was sure that Clara thought so, but Londyn had been a great girlfriend. A best friend. My first love? No. I'd thought so at the time but now, years later, after growing up, I knew the difference between affection and love.

"No, you don't forget."

When she turned my way, something crossed her face. Shock, maybe. Or was she back there with me, at the junkyard when we'd lain on the hood of this car to count shooting stars?

"Where are we going?" August asked.

I tore my eyes away from Clara's soft lips and put the key into the ignition.

Clara cleared her throat. "Um, just for a drive."

"Another drive," he groaned. "For how long?"

"Short." I turned and gave him a wink. "Promise."

"I bet we could drive by the ocean again," Clara said.

"Sure thing." I started the engine, feeling the rumble and vibration of

611

what had to be a state-of-the-art engine. "Ahh. She purrs. Like she always should have."

"And she floats." Clara dug a pair of sunglasses from her purse and slid them on, covering up those sparkling irises.

I fought the urge to take them from her face. I fought the swell in my chest—and behind my zipper.

Get your shit together, Avery. This should not be my reaction. It had to be history, right? Shock? That was the only explanation for why my head and my body were having such a hard time distinguishing the Clara from my memory and the Clara riding shotgun.

Shaking it off, I put the Cadillac in reverse and backed out of the driveway. I drove us to the highway, and as my foot pressed the gas pedal, I couldn't help but smile. "Oh, yeah, she floats."

"Told you."

"Londyn's never getting this car back."

Clara giggled. "She thought you might say that."

"I feel like an asshole for not keeping in touch." Though I'd had my reasons. Or excuses.

"He said a bad word." August sat up straight in his seat, but instead of a glare or scowl, he was grinning eagerly.

"Sorry." I gave Clara an exaggerated frown.

"You owe him a quarter. He's going to fund his college tuition off the bad language of the adults in his life, aren't you, Gus?"

"Yep. I have three hundred twenty-seven dollars and fifty cents."

"Wow." I shifted in my seat, keeping one hand on the wheel so I could dig my wallet out of my shorts pocket with the other. By some miracle, there were three quarters inside the main fold. I plucked them out and passed them all back. "This is in case you bust me later today."

"That's what Uncle Brody does too. He calls it paying in advance."

"Brody has supplied the bulk of that three hundred and twenty-seven dollars," Clara said.

We drove for a few miles, letting the wind blow past us, but curiosity kept gnawing at me.

Where was August's father? Why didn't Clara have a ring on her finger? Had they met in Vegas? How long had she worked there? Why had she left? When?

Damn it, I shouldn't have looked her up all those years ago. One ten-minute glimpse into her life on Facebook, and I'd been haunted by a string of pictures ever since. Those photos had taken on a life of their own in my imagination. I'd seen her with him. I'd seen her happy and free.

I'd lived with them and the envy that tainted them because in my mind, Clara had been happy. She was happy, right? She looked happy. So why were she and August here alone?

Maybe I shouldn't have let those pictures scare me away.

I glanced at Clara, memorizing the small smile on her mouth. Not that I needed to. I'd memorized that look years ago. August's attention was rapt on the passing buildings and the ocean beyond.

612

"Been to the beach yet?" I asked Clara, keeping my voice low.

"Not yet. We came straight to your house."

I grinned at her, then pushed down the blinker and drove to my favorite spot. When I pulled into the parking lot, August's excitement was palpable. His legs kicked and he bounced in the confines of his seat's harness.

"Can we go swimming?" he asked, nodding like he could influence his mother's answer.

"Uh, not yet. But later we'll go swimming. After we get checked into the hotel."

"How long are you staying?" I unbuckled as she climbed out and helped August out of the car.

"Two nights."

Two nights. Not enough. "What hotel?"

"The Kate Sperry Inn. It's a local spot, I guess." She shrugged. "The ratings were good."

"It's very nice." The place was a four-star hotel that cared more about quality than quantity. She'd have access to the beach and a pool.

"Mom, can I—" He tugged on her arm.

"Go ahead. Only go into the water as far as your ankles." She laughed as he raced away, stumbling a bit on that first footstep into the sand. But he righted himself quickly and threw his arms in the air as he ran.

"I did the exact same thing when I came here." I chuckled and led Clara to the beach. Our pace slowed as we joined August at the water's edge. He dipped a toe in, then dropped to put his hands in the foam.

"I hope you don't feel like we invaded today," she said.

"Not at all. It's a Sunday. I don't do much on Sundays except come to the beach. Surf if I'm feeling it. Today, I didn't have to come alone."

She tipped her head to the sky, letting the sunshine light the fine contours of her cheeks. Her every movement had my focus. It had always been like that, hadn't it? Even when it shouldn't have been. Even when I'd had to hide it from everyone else.

Clara had always held a special place in my life. She was sweet. She was strong. She made me laugh.

She made me feel like I could move mountains. Like I could swim across the ocean and back. She was . . . she was my Clara.

Maybe that was why it had been so easy to fall for her, even when I'd known I shouldn't.

Twelve years ago. Today. Here I was, still hanging on her every step. Clinging to every word. Every smile.

Even when I knew I shouldn't.

10

KARSON

"AUGUST LOVES PIZZA," Clara said, digging a fork into her salad. "I'll eat it every now and then but rarely."

"Same." I twirled a twist of spaghetti around my fork. "I haven't had peanut butter since."

"Me neither. Gus didn't even know what a peanut butter and jelly sandwich was until he started kindergarten last year. He thinks they are the best things ever."

August was sitting behind a plastic steering wheel with his eyes glued to a video game screen where a race was about to start. The arcade room of the restaurant had been a hit. His foot slammed into the gas pedal and he shifted his body with every turn of the wheel.

After spending the afternoon at the beach, mostly watching August and the ocean, I'd taken them to get checked in to their hotel. Then we'd watched August swim for an hour.

Clara and I had talked poolside, mostly reminiscing about old times. She'd filled me in on the lives of the others and shown me pictures on her phone of Aria and her newborn baby.

The longer the day went on, the more and more I'd resented the noticeable lack of detail about *her* life in our conversation.

So I'd insisted on dinner. I wasn't ready to say goodbye until I knew more of her story.

Around us, the sounds of arcade games filled the air with beeps and bells. Most of the tables were full of parents visiting. Like Clara, they seemed to keep one eye on their children, ready to dole out more quarters when needed.

Garlic and tomato and cheese scents infused the air. The owners of this little Italian restaurant had been brilliant to bring in the games for kids because it brought families here to savor their delicious food. The kids had the games. The parents, the wine selection.

"August is a great kid," I said, smiling as he shot both hands in the air, game won.

"He's my whole world." Clara's eyes lit up when they landed on her son. It reminded me so much of the past. She'd had that same look when we'd stood in line at the movie theater for tickets. Or the day I'd brought her that GED study guide, even though I'd stolen it. Or when she'd beat me at cards.

When I'd teased her that I'd let her win, when really, she'd kicked my ass.

"I keep getting this feeling like no time at all has passed," I confessed. "Then I blink and remember how long it's been."

"I was thinking the same thing when we were on the beach today. Weird, right?"

"Weird."

Wonderful, heartbreaking, beautiful misery.

I was so damn glad to be sitting across from her. And so fucking sad that I'd missed so much when maybe . . .

Maybe I hadn't had to miss it.

Clara set her fork down and gave me a sad smile. "When you never came to see us in Vegas, I thought maybe . . . oh, never mind."

"Thought what?"

"That you'd forgotten about us. That maybe we weren't as good of friends as I'd built up in my head."

Friends. That word rang through the air like a gunshot. Pain speared my chest. Direct hit.

Was that all she'd thought we were? Friends? Clara had to know that she'd meant so much more. And because of what she'd meant, it was the reason I hadn't gone to Vegas with her in the first place.

I'd had to get my shit together. I'd had to realize that the words she'd once told me were true—that I wasn't toxic to the people in my life. I'd had to grow up. Too bad it'd taken me so damn long.

By then, it had been too late.

"I never forgot about you. You know why I didn't come with you to Vegas after the junkyard. I didn't want to taint your life. I might have run away from my mother, but that didn't mean her words hadn't come to the junkyard with me. It took me a long time to erase them from the back of my mind. To move past them. You were right, what you told me. Wish I had listened. But I needed to figure it out on my own, you know?"

Understanding crossed her face. "Karson."

"It wasn't that I didn't want to go with you. I just didn't want to bring my bullshit into your new life. And by the time I realized it was just that— bullshit—well, a lot of years had passed."

"I get it," she said. "It's the same reason all of us lost touch for so long. We all needed that time to put the past away."

"Exactly."

What I was never good at articulating, Clara could voice perfectly.

There was no person on earth who'd gotten me like she always had. She knew it had been my mountain to climb.

God, how I had missed her.

"Thank fuck for that goddamn Cadillac."

She laughed and the sound was a blast to the past. Sweet. Musical. Sincere. Clara's face was like a shooting star when she laughed. You didn't want to blink and miss a second of the show.

A soul-shattering shake ran through my entire body. The same feeling that had come over me years and years ago while I'd been by her side, staring up at the stars from a rusted Cadillac.

I wanted to kiss her. In this moment, I wanted to take her cheeks in my hands and kiss her until I forgot my own name.

Goddamn it. Why? Why now? Why hadn't she come a year ago?

When I was nineteen and after Londyn and I had broken up, I'd known my time with Clara was short. Hell, for the longest time, I hadn't realized she'd liked me that way. I'd done so well at keeping her as a friend and nothing more. Then I'd felt that shake and my willpower had shattered.

That had been the best damn kiss of my life.

But I wasn't nineteen anymore.

Tearing my eyes away, I focused on my food, finishing the last few bites of my pasta. August had decimated his slice of pizza in record time because Clara had promised he could play games but only after eating dinner.

"We've talked so much about the past today," she said, going back to her salad. "I'd like to hear more about you. What do you do for work?"

"I'm a realtor." I put my fork down and found August changing games. This time he was at the Big Game Hunter. To Clara, it probably looked like I was checking on her kid. Really, I just needed a minute before I faced her again.

I needed to fortify the walls.

Not that it did any damn good. When I turned to her, my heart skipped. So I focused on answering her question. Maybe then she'd answer more of mine.

"I got started about seven years ago. In Temecula, actually."

"I'm surprised you went back."

"For a while." But that was not a story for tonight. "The market was booming, and a friend was working construction for a builder who could barely keep up. The builder had a broker selling all his homes, so I went to work with my friend one day and met the agent. Talked to her for about three hours and decided to get licensed. She sponsored me and I worked for her for a few years. Then I decided to branch out on my own when I moved to Elyria."

"I'm not at all surprised you're successful. Do you like it?"

I nodded. "I do. I work hard. Have some flexibility in my schedule, which I appreciate, and it pays the bills."

"Gemma was in real estate for a while. Before she started her companies and skyrocketed through the stratosphere."

"Sounds like Gemma."

"She hasn't changed." A smile toyed on Clara's pretty mouth. "None of us have, really. We just grew up."

Yes, she'd grown up. And no, she hadn't changed. Thank God for that.

Clara had this ageless wisdom, this realistic vision of the world. She wasn't bitter or harsh or jaded, she just knew that life wasn't fair. And she smiled through it anyway.

"Do you mind that Gemma hired a PI to find you?" she asked.

I shook my head. "Nah. You?"

"No. I'm glad." She collected plates, stacking them and shoving them to the side. Then she rested her forearms on the table with a quick glance at August to make sure his pocket was still bulging with unspent quarters. "Tell me all about exploring."

"Exploring was fun. Really fun." I grinned and draped an arm over the back of my booth.

Clara was still leaning forward, and I ignored the magnetic pull to lean in closer. Clara considered us friends. We were friends. Two old acquaintances swapping stories over a meal. Nothing more.

"I went to LA first. Hated it. Stayed for about a week, then kept going south. Sometimes I hitchhiked. But I walked a lot. Walked until I got to San Diego." The miles had been healing. They'd given me time to reflect and think about where I was going and what I wanted in my life.

At the top of the list had been stability. For that, I'd needed money.

"I stayed in San Diego for about eighteen months. Moved on right before my twenty-first birthday."

"To where?" She propped her chin in a hand, listening. I'd always loved how Clara listened, not just with her ears but her entire body.

"Houston. I stayed there for about three years, working mostly. I took a page from the Clara Saint-James playbook and got my GED."

"I still have that book you gave me. I couldn't throw it out." She smiled. "What did you do there?"

"Worked two jobs, one as a bouncer at a nightclub and another as a caddy at a golf course. I saw a lot of rich people at both places and I decided that I didn't need to be rich, but I sure as hell wasn't going to be poor."

"Amen to that. What made you leave Houston?"

"Mostly, I was restless," I admitted. "That last year, I took a few trips with some buddies I worked with at the club. We went to New Orleans for Mardi Gras. Dallas and San Antonio for a weekend here and there just to break things up. After the last trip, I realized it was time for a change of scenery."

"What made you come back to California?"

"The ocean. The sunshine. The air. Those days I walked to San Diego were some of the best. I'd camp out where I could and wake up to the sound of breaking waves. Even when I got there, I didn't have money for an apartment right away, so I slept on the beaches and did my best to avoid cops. So I went back to San Diego for a couple of years. Decided I hated the city. Realized I didn't have time to surf when I worked eighty hours a week. That's when I went back to Temecula."

It was part of the truth. The other part was not something I felt like sharing.

"After I had my bearings as a realtor, I started looking for another town again." And because for the first time, there had been nothing tying me to Temecula.

"Still restless?" Clara smirked.

I chuckled. "Something like that."

"How'd you find Elyria?"

"From all that walking I did from LA to San Diego. Most of my trip was just about getting from one point to another, but the night I stayed here, I actually paid attention to the town. I slept on the same beach we went to today. Never forgot it. There was this restaurant close by that served the best chips and salsa I'd ever had. After Temecula, I decided to come and see if that restaurant was still in business. It was. So I moved here so I could eat there every day if I wanted."

"And you didn't take us there tonight for chips and salsa?" she asked, pretending to be offended.

"Tomorrow. We'll go there tomorrow." If all I had was two days with her, I was going to take them.

August slammed into the table, his hands cupped and ready to receive some change. "Mom, can I have more quarters?"

Clara checked the time on her phone. "No, sorry, bud. I think we'd better get going."

"Not yet," he pleaded.

"Did you want to swim before bed?"

He thought it over, his mind visibly weighing the options. Then with a nod, he said, "Swimming."

I raised my hand for the waitress and the check. Then I left some cash on the table to pay our tab and escorted Clara and August to the Cadillac.

"Are you sure you want to go swimming?" I asked August. "Because I know this ice cream spot on the beach and —"

"Ice cream!" He jumped. "I want ice cream."

"Probably should have asked you first," I told Clara.

She waved it off. "I never say no to ice cream."

"Neither do I." I grinned as we all climbed into the car and set off down the road.

Even for a Sunday evening, the beach was full of people walking. The line at the ice cream hut was twenty deep. We debated the best flavor as we waited our turn to get waffle cones and set out for an evening stroll across the sand.

August ate his kid's cone faster than I'd ever seen a human consume ice cream before. Then he looked to his mother for permission to chase the seagulls.

"Not too far, okay?"

"Okay." He handed her a wadded-up, sticky napkin, then took off running.

"Maybe he'll burn off some sugar before bed." She frowned at the napkin, then shoved it into a pocket of her shorts.

August chased a bird, then spun around and raced toward us, only to turn around and find another distraction. But he stayed within shouting distance.

"It's your turn," I said as we settled into an easy pace. "How was Vegas?"

"Vegas was exciting. For a time. Aria hated it. She only lasted a month."

My footsteps stuttered. "You were there alone?"

I should have gone with her. *Son of a bitch.* I should have gone to Vegas. But never, in my wildest dreams, had I imagined Aria would leave her sister. And vice versa. Those two did everything together.

"Sort of." She shrugged. "But I was busy. I got my GED. A driver's license. We found an apartment in a not-so-great neighborhood, but the rent was cheap enough for me to afford on my own. I worked hard and things fell into place. Aria did the same, just in Oregon. We talked on the phone a few times a day. So not really alone, but on my own—if the difference makes sense."

"Yeah," I muttered. It made sense. But I still didn't like it.

She shouldn't have been alone. Clearly, she'd survived and thrived but that was not what I'd wanted for her. Clara was tough, but she'd had it hard enough.

"How'd you come to work for Brody?" I asked.

"Aria went into hospitality. There were so many hotels with tons of jobs to choose from and the pay was better than anything we'd had before. I didn't want to clean rooms, so I waited tables to start with until I got my GED. Not long after, Brody's company, Carmichael Communications, hired me as a receptionist."

I could see her doing that, being the smile that greeted people when they walked through a door. A damn fine greeting.

"I didn't start working for Brody right away," she said. "I sat at the front desk for a while and as new positions opened up, I'd apply. Then when Brody's personal assistant quit, I put my name in for that too. I've been working for him ever since. When he decided to move from Vegas to Arizona, he asked me to come along. It was time for a change, so that's where we've been since."

"Ah." I nodded. "And that's how Aria met him?"

"Yes, but they hated each other." She laughed. "Last year, I was supposed to go to a wedding as Brody's plus-one, but I got this nasty cold, so Aria went in my place. It wasn't until then that they'd managed a civil conversation. Even afterward, things were dicey for a while. But the baby brought them together. Trace. They just named him the other day."

"Trace. Cool name."

August came racing in our direction with a shell in his hand. He held it up, just long enough to get a smile and a wave from Clara, then he tucked it into the pocket of his shorts and raced away.

"He turns six next month. I feel like I woke up one day and he was this little boy. My baby vanished before my eyes."

"And his father?"

Clara took a few steps, not answering. Her shoulders were stiff. Her smile gone.

"Forget it. I'm prying."

"No, it's just . . . it didn't work out. He's not involved in August's life and I prefer it that way."

What the hell? When? I opened my mouth to tell her never mind, I *was* going to pry, but she took off, jogging to catch up to August.

Well, shit.

For most people, I would have let it go. It wasn't any of my business. But this was Clara. Years apart, and she was still . . . mine. My business.

I hustled to catch up, and now that Clara was with August, her smile had returned, as gorgeous as ever.

She bent to inspect another shell, then when she spotted me, gestured to the parking lot. "Let's head back. Maybe you can still get some swimming in, bud."

"Yes." He fist pumped and ran in the direction of the car.

"I'm sorry," I said as we walked.

"It's fine." She waved it off. "It's in the past. As long as August is happy, I'm happy."

"He's a good kid. You're a good mom."

She looked up at me and smiled. "Thanks. That means a lot."

I nudged her elbow with mine. "It's good to see you."

"Same here." A lock of hair flew into her face.

Instead of tucking it behind an ear like I wanted to, I shoved my hands in my pockets. "I get you tomorrow, right?"

She nodded. "Our schedule is wide open."

"Good." The back of my hand brushed against hers, and for a second, I nearly took her hand.

She hadn't hugged me today. She used to hug. A jolt of electricity zinged to my elbow. Maybe it was the waves, but I swore I heard her breath hitch.

I inched away. I put space between us and did my best not to think of the last time I'd touched Clara.

It had been the night before we'd left the junkyard. She'd been in my arms after we'd had sex. There'd been no fumbling touches like our first time. There'd been no fear or worry. We'd come together like two people who'd been lovers for years, not a day.

A night I'd never forget.

"August!" she called, waving him back to us.

Yeah. Let's keep August here. Maybe with the kid close, these very intimate, very sexual, very naked thoughts about his mother would stop.

Christ, I was a fucking asshole.

"You should take the Cadillac," I said as we hit the lot. "Keep it while you're here."

"You don't mind?"

I shook my head. "Not at all. Still doesn't feel like my car."

"Okay. Thanks. That will make life a little easier for us to get around town tomorrow."

We all climbed in the car and I aimed us toward my house. "I've got some work to do tomorrow, but if you're up for it, I'd like to see you again for dinner. Chips and salsa?"

"We're up for it."

"And swimming in the ocean," August said.

Clara laughed. "You got it, bud."

The drive to my place was short, too short. The day had gone by too fast. I had this niggling fear that once Clara left California, I wouldn't see her again.

For years, I'd held on to hope that since she hadn't said the word *goodbye*, it hadn't been goodbye. Even after I'd looked her up and seen her with him. Foolish hope had stuck to me like grains of sand between my toes.

This time around, I doubted it would turn out the same. Though maybe it was for the best if I didn't see her again given the circumstances.

Why hadn't she come a year ago?

The sun was only beginning to go down as we parked in front of my garage. Orange tinged the horizon.

"Catch the sunset from your hotel if you can. They've been pretty lately."

Clara nodded and got out of the Cadillac, meeting me in front of the hood. "Thank you for dinner. And today."

"No thanks needed. It was, well . . . my head is still spinning. I look at you and can't believe you're here."

The color crept into her cheeks as another tendril of hair blew across her mouth. And damn it, my hands weren't in my pockets. They acted of their own accord, lifting to brush the blond strands away.

Clara's eyes were waiting as my hand fell away. And the look she gave me, the longing, twisted me into a knot.

"Clara, I—"

The door to the house opened and Holly emerged, walking down the sidewalk to the driveway. She was still in her baby blue scrubs from work and her dark hair was tied up. "Hey, baby. There you are. I texted you when I got here."

"Hey. Sorry. I haven't checked my phone."

"That's all right. Who's this?"

I couldn't look at Clara as Holly came to my side, standing on her toes to brush a kiss to my bearded jaw. "I want you to meet someone."

"Okay." Holly smiled at Clara, then glanced at the car. When she spotted August, she lifted her hand and waved.

I couldn't avoid Clara's gaze any longer. Anyone else would have just seen her smile. But I wasn't anyone. I'd learned to read her a long time ago and there was pain there. Hurt that was totally my fucking fault.

"Holly, this is Clara Saint-James." I swallowed hard, making the most painful introduction of my life. "Clara's an old friend. She lived with me at the junkyard."

Holly gasped, then lunged to take Clara's hand and shake it. "What? Oh my goodness. It's so nice to meet you."

"You too." Clara's smile widened. Too wide. She looked to me for an explanation.

I only had one to give.

"Clara, this is Holly Fallon. My girlfriend."

11

KARSON

"And their tongues weigh as much as an elephant."

"That's a big tongue," I said.

August nodded, barely taking a breath between facts. "And you can tell how old they are from their ear wax."

"No kidding." I glanced at Clara, hoping to catch her gaze, but she was staring at her son. Just like she had been the entire meal. Eye contact had been fleeting at best.

"You sure know a lot about blue whales," Holly said, leaning into my side.

Gus beamed. "We learnded about them in school."

"Learned," Clara corrected.

"That's what I said."

She shook her head and smiled, then focused on the restaurant, taking in the colorful décor and other patrons. Again, looking everywhere but at me.

Holly and I were on one side of the booth, August and Clara the opposite. Only a basket of chips and two bowls of salsa separated us, but for the tension between Clara and me, it might as well have been the Grand Canyon.

Thankfully, Holly hadn't seemed to notice. Neither had August. Clara had smiled politely as we'd gathered at the hostess station, just like last night when she'd shaken Holly's hand.

Maybe I was making too much out of this. Clara seemed . . . fine. She was laughing with her son and had gushed over her first chip and salsa bite. Was it just me?

She hadn't flirted with me yesterday. She hadn't acted strangely. Maybe it was my own bullshit making this weird.

How could it not be weird? I was attracted to Clara. I doubted there were many men on the planet who wouldn't find her alluring. Add that to the emotional connection I'd had with her years ago and I was as enchanted by her as I had been as a kid.

For that, the guilt was eating me alive.

I hadn't slept much last night. Holly had stayed over like she did most nights lately. Never in my life had I been so glad for a period week. I hadn't had to come up with a reason to skip sex. I just . . . it didn't feel right. I didn't feel right.

Holly and I had been dating for a year but she kept her own place. We'd talked about her moving in after her lease expired, but I hadn't insisted on it. She had a key. She knew she was welcome anytime.

The only night it had ever bothered me was last night. She'd curled into my side and I'd felt like a total fucking son of a bitch because while I'd been in bed with one woman, I hadn't been able to get my mind off another.

After tossing and turning for a few hours, I'd finally given up and disappeared into my office. Hours of sifting through paperwork and emails hadn't done anything but give me a headache.

I just . . . I needed a sign from Clara that we were good. That we were friends and whatever I'd been feeling yesterday was one-sided. *Look at me.*

She wiped a bit of salsa from the corner of August's mouth.

Look at me.

She plucked another chip from the basket.

Clara, look at me.

She brushed a crumb from her lap, then locked her attention on her son.

Goddamn it.

August was the true champ tonight. That kid had filled every second with all the facts stored in his little head.

"We learnded about skeletons too," he said.

"I like skeletons." Holly leaned forward. "I'm a nurse so I know lots about skeletons."

"Did you know the femur is the largest bone in your body?"

She nodded. "I did know that."

"The smallest bone is in your ear. It's the . . ." His forehead furrowed. "I can't remember the name."

"Stapes."

"Yeah, yeah." His eyes lit up. "The stapes."

"What was your favorite thing about kindergarten?" I asked.

"Recess."

I chuckled. "I liked recess too."

"Karson said you guys live in Arizona." Holly sipped from her margarita. "He actually told me about all of it. The Cadillac and how you came to bring it here. It's so fantastic. The whole trip across the country. Truly . . . wow."

"It's been incredible to connect with everyone again." Clara smiled and lifted her own drink, sparing me just a quick look over the rim. "I sent the girls a text last night. They all wanted me to tell you hello. And Londyn said she's sending you the title to the car before you try to do something stupid like return it."

I chuckled. "I'll have to get her number from you."

Somehow, I knew it wouldn't be strange talking to Londyn again. And somehow, I knew the feeling I'd had yesterday with Clara, that longing, wouldn't be there with my former girlfriend. Londyn and I would talk as old friends because that door had closed a long, long time ago.

No way could I say the same about Clara.

I took a chip, scooped some salsa and chomped it with fury. What the hell was wrong with me? Clara was an old friend too. We were history. So why couldn't I shake the feeling from yesterday? Why did it feel like I was on the wrong goddamn side of this booth?

Holly deserved better than this.

I just had to get through today and life would go back to normal. Clara was leaving tomorrow, and I'd put the memories in the past. Move forward.

"What did you guys do today?" I asked, eating another chip.

Clara glanced up, then her eyes skidded away.

Yeah, this hadn't been one-sided. I could fool myself all I wanted but she'd felt that spark yesterday too.

Fuck. I was such a prick.

"We spent most of the day at the beach," she said.

"I built a sandcastle," August said proudly, shifting to his knees so he could bend down and gulp his lemonade from the cup's straw.

"And we took one last drive in the Cadillac." Clara's eyes softened and she looked at me, really looked at me, for the first time this evening. "I hope you don't mind a few extra miles on her."

"Not at all."

"It's too bad you're leaving so soon," Holly said. "It would be fun to hear more stories about the junkyard. Karson rarely talks about it."

Because it wasn't a time I wanted to relive. I'd been angry and channeling a lot of false confidence. The stealing and the fights . . . I wasn't particularly proud of myself at that age.

"What's a junkyard?" August asked. The kid didn't miss much. Obviously, it wasn't something Clara had spoken to him about either. I doubted she would until he was older.

"It's a place where they take old cars and trucks that are broken," I answered.

"Do they get fixed?"

"No, not usually," Clara said. "They call it a junkyard because most of it becomes junk."

"Like garbage?"

She nodded. "Like garbage."

"What about the Cadillac then? It's not garbage."

"Sometimes, the best cars get rescued," I said. "That's what happened to the Cadillac."

"Oh. Sort of like my puppy stuffy that got ripped but Mom fixed it so we didn't have to throw it away."

I grinned. "Exactly."

August snatched a chip from the basket, content with the explanation. His curiosity was infectious, but the questions I wanted answers to weren't ones I could ask today. Mostly, I wanted to know about his father. Yesterday's attempt to broach the subject had backfired.

"Did you tell her about the junkyard?" Holly nudged my elbow.

"No. It, uh, didn't come up yesterday."

Holly thought the junkyard was an interesting piece of my history. Like most people, unless they'd lived it, she didn't realize how hard it had been. How close I'd been to breaking so many times.

Maybe it was my fault for not explaining it to her. But why would I want to rehash the struggles? She'd gotten the glossed-over version of the past. To her, it had sounded like an adventure. Again, probably my fault for not painting it in a dirty, rust-tinged light.

That was part of why talking with Clara had been so easy yesterday. She understood. She'd always understood.

"What about the junkyard?" Clara asked.

Before I could answer, the waitress appeared with our meals. Even with the few minutes it took to get August settled with his quesadilla, when Clara looked at me for an answer, I still hadn't figured out exactly how to say it.

"The junkyard is . . . well, it's mine."

"Yours?"

I nodded. "Yeah. I own it."

"Did you buy it?" She set down her fork. "When you lived in Temecula?"

"No, I didn't buy it." I gave her a sad smile. "Lou left it to me. In his will."

"Oh." Her gaze dropped.

"Who's Lou?" August asked, his cheeks bulging with food.

"An old friend." Clara touched his hair, then focused on her plate. Though her fork only poked at her enchiladas.

"Are we gonna see him too?"

She shook her head. "No, bud. He . . . died."

"Oh." August looked down. "How?"

"In his sleep," I answered. "Surrounded by his collections."

The sadness in Clara's eyes broke my heart. "Did you see him often?"

"No. You know Lou."

"Yeah."

Lou didn't like visitors, even me. The few times I'd visited, I'd made sure to call ahead first. I'd gone in the morning. And only on the last visit had he actually invited me inside his shack.

The inside of Lou's home had looked much like the yard. There'd been piles stacked in hallways. There'd been shelves overloaded with books and boxes and binders. The kitchen counters had been so cluttered that the only free surfaces had been the sink and stove.

He'd led me through the maze and we'd sat at a small table, surrounded by his possessions. That was when he'd told me about Londyn and how she'd called for the Cadillac. How two days after that call, a fancy truck had shown up to haul it away.

I'd debated walking through the yard, but fear had stopped me, and instead, I'd left Lou to his solitude. I'd given him my card and told him to call me if he ever needed anything. That I'd stop by again.

He'd died before I'd had the chance.

Three months after the Cadillac had disappeared from the yard, so had Lou.

When his lawyer had called to break the news, and to inform me that Lou had bequeathed me all of his belongings, I'd nearly fallen out of my chair.

"I went to his funeral," I said. "I met his sister."

"He had a sister?" Clara asked.

"And two nieces. They were nice. Kind. They arranged for him to be buried beside his wife."

Clara's eyes bulged. "Lou had a wife?"

"She died young. In childbirth. Lou had been a mechanic back then. The junkyard had been in his family. After his wife and baby . . . he gave up his shop and moved to the shack."

"Lou." Clara pressed a hand to her heart.

"We didn't really know him, did we?"

"No, we didn't," she whispered, her eyes glassy.

August looked up at Clara with worry on his face. "Mom?"

"I'm okay." She shook away the sadness and smiled. "How's your quesadilla?"

"Good." He shrugged and took another large bite.

Holly leaned in closer, her hand finding my leg under the table. When I looked down, her brown eyes were waiting. They were the color of coffee, rich and warm. But they weren't as pretty as Clara's.

And I was a son of a bitch for making the comparison. *Fuck.*

"Maybe you should ask . . ." Holly nodded at Clara.

I gave her a slight headshake.

Either she missed it or ignored it, but when she turned to Clara and opened her mouth, it wasn't to eat. "Karson has been putting off going back to Temecula, but he finally is. On Wednesday."

"Seriously?" Clara's face whipped to me. "This Wednesday?"

"In two days." I lifted a shoulder. "Your timing is ironic. My plan was to go there tomorrow and check the place out before my meeting."

"What meeting?" she asked.

"There's a developer in Temecula who's trying to reclaim the area. He's building a housing development and wants to buy the junkyard. I agreed to meet him on Wednesday."

"Maybe you could go too," Holly suggested. "If you wanted to see it again and if you don't have to hurry home. I think it would be cool to go back to a place like that. See if it's changed. I work Wednesday through Sunday at the hospital, otherwise I'd go along. I've been wanting to see this junkyard since Karson told me about it."

Which was the reason I'd scheduled the meeting for a Wednesday. Holly was a supportive girlfriend, but this trip wasn't for her.

"Uh . . . no." Clara shook her head. "I don't think . . . no."

I nudged Holly, and this time, my headshake wasn't to be ignored.

She didn't know what she was suggesting. She didn't know the pain it could cause Clara to go back to that place.

Holly didn't even know the specifics of my childhood, let alone Clara's. All I'd told her about my past was that I'd had a bad relationship with my mother and run away at sixteen.

Dinner conversation was nonexistent after that. At least, between the adults. August came to the rescue once more, providing the entertainment with tales of kindergarten and a long list of his favorite toys. When the waitress came with the check, Clara insisted on paying the bill.

"You brought me a car," I said as we all walked outside. "You didn't need to buy dinner."

"I'm happy to. It was lovely to meet you, Holly."

"You too." Holly smiled. "I hope you keep in touch. Does Karson have your number?"

"I don't." I pulled my phone from my pocket, and when Clara recited hers, I sent her a text.

It dinged in her purse as she reached in to pull out the Cadillac's keys. Clara turned them over in her palm, holding them for one long moment, then she handed them over. "She's all yours."

"Thank you." The weight of the keys was too heavy. It wasn't just handing over a car, it was the end.

This was goodbye.

"I'll see you at home." Holly gave my arm a gentle squeeze. Then she gave August a fist bump and walked to my Audi, the two of us having driven it here to meet Clara tonight.

I'd drive her to the hotel. Then go home.

To Holly.

We loaded up and I pulled away from the restaurant, finding it hard to meet even the minimum speed limit. Cars began to pile up behind us but I couldn't press my foot into the gas pedal.

"Sorry. About Holly," I told Clara. "She doesn't understand."

"No apologies needed. Most people don't."

The air was warm as it rushed past our faces. August seemed so content in this car. One of his hands rested on the door as he took in the world around him.

The Cadillac made too short a trip and as I parked in front of the entrance to the hotel, my lungs wouldn't hold any air. The pain in my chest was crushing.

628

Clara was out the door the moment the tires stopped moving. She seemed in a rush to get August out of his seat and unclip the seat belt that had held it in place.

I got out, taking it from her to set it aside. "I could take you to the airport tomorrow."

"No, that's okay. We'll get an Uber."

"Mom, can we go swimming?"

"Sure, bud. Can you say goodbye to Karson?"

I knelt in front of him and held out my hand. "It was nice to meet you, August."

He grinned as he shook it.

"Ouch." I flexed my fingers after he let go. "Pretty strong kid you've got, Clara."

She put her hand around his shoulders, pulling him into her legs as I stood.

Then I memorized her face, one last time. The pink bow of her lips. The golden flecks in her eyes. The smile that woke me from my dreams. The breeze picked up her scent and carried it closer. Oranges and vanilla. Sweet. *Clara*.

"It was good to see you." My throat burned and the words came out in a rasp.

"You too."

I waited, wanting that hug. Clara had always hugged goodbye.

Instead, I got a wave and a small smile. "Take care of yourself, Karson."

"Yeah."

Then she was gone, ushering August inside with one hand while she carried his seat with the other.

She left me standing beside a Cadillac with a hole in my chest.

I stood there for a few minutes, staring through the glass doors to the lobby, hoping and wishing maybe she'd come back. But when the desk clerk gave me the fifth strange look, I unglued my feet.

This was the end.

"Goodbye, Clara."

The drive home was a blur, and when I walked through the door to find Holly in the living room with a book in her lap, for the first time, the sight didn't make me smile.

"Hey." She closed the book. "How'd it go?"

"Fine."

"Do you want to—"

"I'm going to go for a run." I walked away, but not fast enough to miss her startled expression.

I kept walking, disappearing to the bedroom to change. Then I was out the door, my feet pounding on the sidewalk to the beat of the music in my earbuds as I ran the couple blocks to the beach. When I hit the sand, I pushed harder. Faster. With every step, I willed Clara out of my mind.

There was a woman in my house who loved me. A woman who made me laugh. A woman who I cared for.

Holly didn't deserve this from me. I would do better.

Tomorrow, I vowed to do better.

Clara was returning to Arizona, and I would forget about her.

Or . . . try. I would try.

I pushed myself until my legs were burning and my lungs were on fire. Sweat dripped down my face and over my bare chest. I hadn't bothered with a shirt, I rarely did.

Three miles from home, I stopped and collapsed on the sand, resting my forearms on my knees until I regained my breath. Then I sat there for hours, watching as the sunlight faded from the sky.

Tonight. I'd give myself tonight to mourn the loss of Clara again.

Then tomorrow I'd let her go. For good this time.

Lost in my own head, I jumped when my phone rang, the jogging earbuds I wore still locked in place. When I tugged the phone from my shorts pocket, I expected to see Holly's name on the screen.

But it was an out-of-state number. A number I'd memorized the same moment I'd typed it in earlier tonight.

"Hi," I answered.

"Hi," Clara said, her voice low. August must have fallen asleep. "Are you busy?"

"No." My heart raced faster now than when I'd been running.

"I was thinking about what Holly said. About Wednesday."

"Come with me." The plea in my voice was unmistakable. "I don't want to go alone. And I don't want to take Holly. She's the best. It's just that . . ."

"She doesn't get it."

I shook my head. "No one does."

"Okay," she whispered.

"Okay, you'll go?"

"I'll go."

I closed my eyes as a wave of relief crashed over my body. She was coming. Tonight hadn't been goodbye. "I'll pick you up around ten tomorrow."

The plan was to stay at a hotel tomorrow night before the meeting Wednesday. The drive back to Elyria wasn't long, but my meeting with the developer was at eight. With the regular morning traffic, it didn't seem worth the rushed commute.

"We'll be ready," she said.

I breathed. "Good night."

"Karson?" she whispered before I could hang up.

"Yeah?"

The other end of the line was silent other than her breathing.

"Clara?"

"Was it real?"

I closed my eyes. "It was real."

"It's been a long time, and I worried that maybe you were just a teenage boy and I was just a teenage girl and sex was . . . sex. Please don't take offense at that. We were young and I wouldn't blame you but —"

"It was real."

She went quiet again.

"You still there?"

"Yeah. Sweet dreams, Karson."

Then I'll dream of you. "Good night, Clara."

12

KARSON

"What made you change your mind?" I asked Clara. "About coming along."

"Aria." She glanced over from the passenger side as we rolled down the highway. "She asked me if I'd regret it in ten years. At first, I said no. But it nagged at me and I realized I need this closure."

"I can relate." I needed this closure too.

With Temecula. With the junkyard.

With Clara.

The top was up today to keep the wind and sun from August's face. And the exhaust. The trip from Elyria to Temecula was about an hour but if we hit traffic, it could take considerably longer.

So far, the road hadn't been too crowded, likely because it was midmorning on a weekday.

August was playing his Nintendo, something that must be a treat because his eyes had gone wide when Clara had handed it to him. I suspected that Gus had been given a lot more video game time on this trip simply so the adults could talk without interruption.

"I think a part of me wants to go back just to remind myself of how far I've come," she said. "Or to remind myself that I won't ever have to go back."

"I felt the same when I moved to Temecula. It took me weeks to work up the nerve to drive to that side of town and when I did, it was at night. I parked outside the gate and just stared inside. Told myself I never had to survive those kinds of days again. So I get it."

She looked over again and smiled. "I know. Aria told me that if there was any time to go, it would be with you. She didn't want me going alone."

"Truth? That's why I've been avoiding this meeting. It was hard enough going back when Lou was there. Since he died, I only went once. And that was after his lawyer told me about his will. I drove up, left the car running, went to the gate and put a new padlock on the chain. Didn't even go in."

"So no one has been there in years?"

"No." I sighed. "I pay the electric bill every month. That's it."

"You said you went into his shack. Did you ever go look through the yard?"

I squirmed in my seat, not wanting to admit this was a weakness. That a place full of rusted cars and metal parts had so far gotten the better of me. "Couldn't do it."

"Then we'll go together."

Was that why I'd never gone back? Because I'd been waiting for Clara to come with me?

She looked beautiful this morning. Her blond hair was pulled back into a braid that hung down her spine. The sheer cream blouse she wore was embroidered with lacey flowers. Beneath, a silky camisole clung to her frame. With a pair of jean shorts, she looked casual. Comfortable. *Sexy.*

I hated how the last word popped into my head with one glance at her toned legs. I hated how she'd walked out of the hotel lobby this morning and my heart had stopped. I hated that what I wanted most was to take her hand just to see if her fingers still fit between mine like they had when we were younger.

I hated myself for the thoughts running through my mind.

How fucked up was it that Holly had been the one to suggest this trip? While she was at work today, I'd been struggling to keep my mind off Clara.

Good thing was, the junkyard would be a distraction. Just setting foot in Temecula was sure to be strange for Clara again. Hell, it was still strange for me and I'd lived there as an adult.

Clara's phone rang in the purse at her feet. She bent to pluck the phone out and smiled at the screen. Then she held it up for me to see.

Londyn.

"Want to say hi?" she asked.

"Yeah."

Clara hit the screen, putting it on speaker, then held it up between us and let me answer.

"Hey, Lonny."

"Oh my God." She gasped at my voice. "Karson?"

My heart twisted. "It's me."

"It's you. I can't believe it." Her voice trembled. "Clara? Are you there too?"

"I'm here." She smiled, shifting sideways. "We're in the Cadillac. Karson is driving us to Temecula."

"Temecula? I thought you were going home today. I was calling to get the full scoop on Karson."

"Little change of vacation plans," Clara said. "First Temecula. Then we'll go home. Want me to call you later?"

"No way. I can't wait that long. It's been torture for the past two days. Tell me everything about Karson."

"Uh . . . I'm still here," I said.

"Good," Londyn said. "Fill in any blanks. And keep your eyes on the road. That car is nearly as precious as your passengers."

I chuckled. "I see you still love bossing me around."

"Hey, when you're good at something, why quit?"

Clara giggled. "Okay, what do you want to know about Karson?"

"Is he still handsome?"

"Yes." Clara's eyes darted to the seat, but I caught the flush rising in her cheeks. "He looks like Karson, just all grown up. He's got a short beard."

"A beard." Londyn groaned. "No. Not you too."

"What do you mean, not me too?" I asked.

"Brooks grew one and I hate it. Which I made the mistake of saying, so now he won't shave. He likes it because when he kisses Ellie it makes her giggle. But he has such a sexy jaw I hate that it's covered up with all that hair."

"In my defense, my beard usually only lasts a month, then I shave." I chuckled. Hearing her talk about her husband and daughter made my heart swell. "Are you happy, Lonny?"

"So, so happy." The smile in her voice filled the car. "Clara, what's his house like?"

"It's beautiful. It's white with warm touches. It's close to the beach. And clean, obviously. This is Karson we're talking about."

I barked a laugh. The girls always teased me for being the cleanest one in the junkyard. Not that they were messy, but I think they'd thought the token male would have left his things lying around. Except when you were living in dirt, the least you could do to take care of it was to put it away.

"Were you surprised? By the Cadillac?" Londyn asked.

"You could have knocked me over with a feather," I answered. "What you did is nothing short of a miracle. But this car is too much."

"Shush. It was as much yours as it was mine."

"You put a lot of money into it. Let me pay for it."

"Never."

"Londyn—"

"Oh, look at the time. Gotta go. Drive safe. Clara, call me when you get home."

Clara giggled. "I will."

"It was good to hear your voice, Karson," Londyn said. "Expect a phone call from time to time."

"I look forward to it. And Lonny? Thanks. I'm not sure what I did to deserve this car I'm driving."

"You were the rock." Clara spoke for Londyn. "You were the glue. You saved us all when you found that junkyard."

"And that's why I want you to have that car," Londyn added. "Because if it makes you smile every time you get behind the wheel, then maybe

634

you'll remember that you made me—us—smile through the hardest days. You deserve a lifetime of smiles. So take that car, drive it, and be happy."

My throat burned as Clara ended the call. She dabbed the corners of her eyes, then, as I'd expected, she twisted to look at her son.

August looked up and smiled before going right back to his game.

She drew strength from him. He rooted her. She anchored him. They relied on each other.

Once upon a time, she'd been a constant for me too.

My North Star.

"I'll have to get everyone's contact info from you," I said. "Now that I got to talk to Londyn, I'd like to say hi to Gemma, Kat and Aria too."

She nodded, her fingers flying over the phone's screen. "I'll text you their numbers."

Clara had been right about driving the Cadillac. It was a dream and every minute behind the wheel made me love it more. The hum of the engine and the gentle whisper of the wind took the place of any conversation as the miles disappeared beneath the tires.

Neither Clara nor I spoke of the question she'd asked me last night.

Was it real?

For twelve years she'd doubted the answer. Was it real?

Clara had been as real as the stars in the sky and the dirt below my feet. But at nineteen, I hadn't realized how much she'd meant. As a friend. As a lover. The sex had been incredible. Maybe I'd blown it up in my head because I *had* been nineteen and a guy and, well . . . it was sex. That had been fairly top of mind at that age.

When I'd walked away from the junkyard, I'd had no idea that Clara would stick with me. I guess I'd thought it would be like my breakup with Londyn. Just time to move on. But Clara had always been different, hadn't she? She'd always been there, like a quieter version of my conscience.

When I'd stop to catch a pretty sunset, I'd wonder if she was watching it too. When I'd sell a house, I'd hear her applause. When it was time to move on to a new town, I'd hope beyond all reason that I'd bump into her at the grocery store.

Now here she was.

If this was the universe's idea of ironic timing, it was a sick fucking joke.

Why now? When I'd finally decided to let go of the past. When I'd finally settled down in the town I planned to live in for the rest of my life. When I'd found Holly, the first long-term girlfriend I'd had in over a decade.

Time always seemed to be working against Clara and me.

As we reached the outskirts of Temecula, my hands tightened on the wheel. Tension crept up my spine, stiffening my shoulders and arms.

Clara fidgeted in her seat. Every minute she'd shift, tucking a hand under a leg or twisting to stare in a different direction.

Our exit approached and I dragged in a long breath, then hit the turn signal. *Here goes.*

"You okay?" I asked as I eased off the freeway.

"I don't know yet. Ask me later."

There was so much worry in her face, not even the large sunglasses could disguise it. Coming back here was always hard, especially after moving away. But my own anxieties vanished at the fear on her face.

I'd been here before. I'd lived here again. This trip was for Clara, and like Aria had said, she shouldn't do this alone.

"Where do you want to go first?" I asked. "Hotel? Or junkyard?"

"You said you wanted to check on the junkyard before your meeting tomorrow."

"Yeah, but we don't need to go there right away. We can get settled first at the hotel. Ease into this."

How people did this commute every day, driving in and out of California cities, was not for me. Most of the properties I sold in Elyria were for people who worked one, sometimes two hours away.

"I think . . ." Clara clasped her hands on her lap. "I think let's go to the junkyard before I chicken out."

"I'll be right here with you."

She looked over and some of the worry lessened. "I know."

I aimed the car in that direction. The hotel I'd booked was on the opposite end of town, next to the parks where they often launched hot air balloons. Maybe August would get to see one today or tomorrow.

Clara's nervous energy was palpable, growing with every block. Maybe August felt it too because he put his game down.

"Where are we going?" he asked, his eyes tracking my every turn of the wheel.

"To a place where Karson and I used to li—visit. A place we used to visit when we were younger."

"As kids?"

"No." She glanced behind us, giving him a soft smile. "Not as kids."

Adults would have called us kids. To August, a kid was probably someone his age. And the moment we'd run away, we'd stopped being kids.

"Is it a playground?"

"It's the junkyard."

"Oooh." He nodded. "With the broken stuff."

"With the broken stuff," she whispered.

Beyond the worry in her expression there was pain. Pain for the loss of her parents. Pain for the life she and Aria had lived.

Pain from being part of the broken.

The moment I pulled onto the road, Clara wrapped her arms around her middle, sitting stiff and rigid. Her eyes darted everywhere, taking it all in. "It looks different."

"The developer," I explained.

Gone were the other run down homes on this deserted road. No more fences to contain barking dogs. No more overgrown bushes. The street we'd traversed countless times was now a collection of barren lots. There was a spec home in the middle of construction, the crew pounding at nails

636

on the roof. Side streets were being added to separate the land into square blocks.

A blank slate.

And at the end, the place we'd called home.

"I wondered if this road would ever change," Clara said. "There were days when I wished it would be swallowed in an earthquake. Others when I hoped it looked exactly the same just in case I ever needed it again."

I lifted a hand from the wheel, wanting to take hers, but I stopped myself and raked that hand through my hair instead.

Then, before either of us was ready, we were there.

The grasses around the junkyard's fence were as thick and unruly as ever. It looked unchanged from the day I'd left it behind. My heartbeat pounded in my ears as I slowed. Clara had her hand on the door, gripping it tight, like she wanted to keep it closed.

I did a quick U-turn so we could park on the same side of the street. Then I stopped us in front of the gate and put the Cadillac in park.

Clara stared out her window, seeing past the rusted chain and padlock to the mess beyond.

"We—"

She was out of the car before I could tell her we didn't have to go in.

I stayed in my seat and looked back at August.

His eyes were glued to the window. To his mother. "What's she doing?"

"Just looking."

Clara walked to the gate. She put her hands to the chain link, her fingers splaying between the holes. She stood there, her spine straight. Then she shoved away, and as quickly as she'd gotten out of the car, she was back in it, shaking her head. "This was a bad idea. I can't . . ."

"It's okay. Let's go to the hotel."

Her chin fell. "I'm sorry."

"Don't be. We'll come back tomorrow. And if you don't want to, that's fine too."

Clara nodded as her shoulders curled forward.

I put both hands on the wheel, holding it so I wouldn't hold her, and got us the fuck away from the junkyard.

———

"I'M SORRY ABOUT EARLIER." Clara pushed her sunglasses into her hair and turned to face me. "I didn't expect to feel so much. I thought once I saw it that I'd want to go inside."

"No need to apologize."

She gave me a sad smile. "I didn't expect it to hurt so much. Not having Lou there. Isn't that crazy? We didn't even know the man."

"Yeah, we did. We knew what mattered."

Lou had cared for us in the only way he'd been able. He'd given us a shelter. He'd given us protection. And he'd given us his secrecy. I couldn't have asked more from the man.

"Mom! Watch this one!" August jumped with all his might from the edge of the pool and did a spin before splashing into the water.

"We're in that stage. The *watch me* stage." Clara smiled and clapped for her son as he surfaced in the pool. "He'd live in the pool if he could."

"All right, I'm going in." An hour in the heat and I was ready for a swim.

I stood up from the lounge chair and stripped off my T-shirt. I tossed it away, glancing at Clara only to find her attention was on my torso. My chest. My arms. My abs. Unless I'd forgotten how to read attraction, there was lust in her eyes.

Christ. She wasn't making this easy on me.

Like she'd heard my thought, she ripped her eyes away, dropping her focus to her lap.

That was my cue to get the hell in the water. In three long strides I was at the pool's edge. I dove in, giving a long kick as I surfaced beside August.

He laughed, his arms spread wide with his water wings on his biceps helping to keep him afloat.

"Want to play a game?" I asked.

"Okay!"

Then I spent the next hour launching him into the air and crashing into the water. He laughed, we both did, every time.

Clara never moved from her chair. She stayed, watching. At first, she'd done it with a smile, but as the afternoon went on, the happy look on her face vanished. She almost looked . . . sad. Why would me playing with her kid make her look miserable?

Finally, after his fingers were pruney and the sunscreen Clara had smeared on him had most certainly worn off, she dragged her son to their hotel room to shower and get dressed for dinner.

They had a suite with a couple of bedrooms. My single was across the hall and we met in the lobby an hour later.

Much like last night at the restaurant in Elyria, August stole the show. He told me all of the things he wanted for his upcoming birthday and how he was having a pool party at Brody and Aria's house with six friends from his school. The kid was an exceptional buffer.

Every time I looked at Clara, every time my gaze lingered on the long line of her neck or the pretty shape of her ears, August would demand my attention.

Bless that kid.

And fuck my life.

When dinner ended and we walked back to the hotel, I was strung tight, ready to say good night and hit the pavement for another punishing run.

"Temecula is nice," Clara said as we reached the hotel lobby.

"Huh?" I'd been too busy staring at her ass in those goddamn shorts because I was an asshole. A complete motherfucking asshole.

"The city. It's nice," she said as August pushed the button to call the elevator. "You get away from the shi—bad neighborhoods where we grew up and it's actually sort of charming with the Old Town wineries and hot air balloons."

We'd seen three balloons over the course of the day and each had enamored Gus.

"In another life, I would have stayed here," I said. "It is a nice town." But history tainted even the best of places.

"What made you leave? You said you always remembered Elyria. Was that why you moved?"

"No. I left because I didn't have to stay anymore."

"Have to?"

I gave her a sad smile as we stepped into the elevator. "For my mom."

"Oh."

"That's another discussion." I nodded at Gus. He didn't need to hear the gory details about the end of my mother's life.

The elevator carried us to the fourth floor and we all stopped in the hallway outside our rooms. Clara opened her door, letting August inside. "Thanks for dinner. And for your patience today."

"Do you want to go with me tomorrow? No judgment if you don't."

"Yeah." She seemed steadier now, like she'd conquered her fears. "I'd like to go tomorrow."

"Okay. Meet you in the lobby at about seven."

"Perfect. Good night, Karson." She turned to disappear into her room but the curiosity from earlier at the pool came rushing back and I shot out an arm, brushing my fingers along her elbow.

The shiver running down her body was visible.

The fire racing through mine was not.

"Why didn't it work out with August's dad?"

Clara's eyes closed. Her chin dropped. For the second time I'd pushed this subject. When was I going to learn to let it go?

"Sorry. I'll leave it alone. Good night, Clara." I dug the key from my pocket and unlocked my door. It was only after I'd taken one step inside that she whispered my name. When I turned, she had tears in those beautiful brown eyes.

"He wasn't you."

One sentence and she destroyed me. Then she rushed into her room, leaving me with the answer that I'd wanted to hear.

And the answer I had to forget.

13

KARSON

"I know I don't really understand what it was like for you back then, but I just wanted to tell you that I'm here if you need to talk," Holly said.

Because she was a good woman. And I didn't deserve her. "Thanks, babe."

"Call me later? After your meeting?"

"Yeah."

"Are you coming home tonight?"

I glanced over at Clara and August, standing beside the Cadillac. "I don't know. I was thinking I might stay another night, hang out, then take them to the airport."

"You should. Spend time with them. Relax. You've been working so hard. And we don't know when you'll see them again."

If only she knew what she was suggesting.

But I couldn't go home. Not yet. Not after Clara's confession last night. Today was likely my last chance to get some answers, and I couldn't let her go, leaving me to wonder for the rest of my life.

"I'll let you know," I said.

"Okay. I love you." Holly had been saying *I love you* for months.

I hadn't said it back.

Maybe because I needed this closure with Clara. If I was going to move forward, I had to let this part of my life go.

"Have a good day at work. Bye."

"Bye." There was a hint of hurt in her voice. I suspected she'd cover it up with a smile, like she normally did whenever I didn't reciprocate those three words.

I raked a hand through my hair and over my bearded jaw, then shoved my phone away and walked to the car.

"Was that Holly?" Clara asked.

I nodded. "She just wanted to check in."

"She's very nice."

"Yes, she is."

I had a nice girlfriend. And because of it, my soul felt like it was being ripped in two. But now was not the time to deal with this. First, we had a job to do.

"All good?" I motioned toward the yard.

"I'm ready." Clara nodded and followed me to the gate.

The air was cool this morning as I unlocked the heavy chain. A breeze lifted the scent of rusted metal to my nose as I shoved the gate open wide enough to walk inside.

Clara followed close behind with August in tow. Her shoulders were pinned straight. There was determination in her gaze—yesterday's fears weren't going to stop her.

"This is a junkyard?" August shook his hand loose of hers and walked ahead of us both, turning in a circle to take it all in. Then he shrugged. "It's dirty."

I chuckled. Leave it to Gus to break the ice.

"Wow. Look at that." Clara walked past us, heading toward the side of Lou's shack. Her focus was on the green vines creeping along the exterior wall. "I didn't notice it yesterday."

The plant's roots stemmed from a black five-gallon bucket. A bucket I'd helped Aria fill with dirt years ago. Whatever vine she'd planted had not only survived under Lou's care, but it was growing wild. The far wall of his shack was nearly covered.

The plants had been here when I'd visited Lou, but over the past couple of years, they'd taken on a life of their own. With Clara running a fingertip over a leaf, it was beauty amidst the chaos.

"I'll be damned."

"Quarter." August marched up to me, hand out.

Digging a dollar bill from my pocket, I smacked it in his palm. Just yesterday he'd earned another one from me. I didn't realize how much I cussed until there was a kid to collect on every swear word.

"Aria is going to freak." Clara took her phone from her pocket and snapped a string of pictures. Then she held out a hand for August. "Your aunt Aria planted this a long, long time ago."

"She's a good planter."

"Yes, she absolutely is." Clara giggled, and with that musical sound, I was blasted twelve, nearly thirteen years into the past, when living in this junkyard had been hard. But damn, it had been good too.

Whatever tension I'd felt this morning after another sleepless night melted away. We could do this today because we were together.

I could do this today because Clara was here.

"Shall we?" I jerked my chin toward our end of the junkyard.

She nodded, giving August a smile, and then the three of us set off on a path that had once been as familiar as walking down the hallway in my own home. There was the large stack of old hoods that we passed first.

Then a line of engine blocks that Lou had arranged by size. Then two stacks of tires, three rusted trucks to round and then . . .

"It's still there," Clara whispered.

The tent that Gemma had built was nearly unchanged.

The canvas tarp that had acted like the front door was pooled on the dirt, dusty and matted from years of enduring the elements. But the walls were intact. The sheets of metal and the tarp roof were still pitched together and solid.

"Wow." Clara surprised me, taking the lead and rushing for the doorway.

"What's in there?" August asked, dashing around her.

His curiosity lightened the mood. He saw it like a child, as a fort and an adventure. He saw it for what we'd once seen it for too.

Clara was close behind him as he ducked his head through the door. She nudged his shoulder and the two of them bent to step inside. I crouched and joined them, dropping to a knee to take a look around.

The air was stale and smelled of earth. The common room was the same. The paintings that Katherine had done in her bedroom were there, nearly as perfect as they had been because the walls had protected them from rain.

Clara took a picture of them too. "I don't know if she'll want to see them, but just in case."

She didn't take a photo of Gemma's room—the space that I'd taken after the girls had set out for Montana. The room where Clara had been mine. She wouldn't even look there. She wouldn't look at me either.

Was she thinking about those precious nights? Was she remembering? They were as fresh in my mind as yesterday. The softness of her lips. The sweet scent of her hair. The delicate touch of her hands.

No. Stop, damn it. Stop remembering. I shot to my feet and went outside, shaking the past away. These fucking memories were killing me.

So were the words she'd said to me last night in the hallway.

We hadn't talked about it this morning. We'd spoken politely over breakfast, both of us counting on August to carry the conversation. Then we'd driven here in silence, and I'd stepped away to take a call from Holly.

"Now where?" August asked, bursting out of the tent.

Clara didn't answer her son. She just took off on the narrow path to where the Cadillac had once rested.

The hole where it had been was noticeable. Other parts and pieces had been pushed aside, probably to make room for the crew to haul it out of here.

I studied Clara's expression as she stared at the space. I'd give anything to know what she was thinking. To know if she was picturing two teenage kids staring up at the stars.

She gave me no insight before continuing down the path, her graceful steps a sharp contrast to the wreckage around us. Clara had always been too good for this place, but today, she especially stood out. Maybe it was the white dress she'd worn. Or the colorful flowers embroidered on the front that trailed from the neck to the hem that hit midthigh.

Did she always wear white? Since she'd come here, I'd only seen her in light colors.

I lingered behind her and August as they made their way down the path. I knew exactly where she was headed, and I didn't want her to feel rushed because I was crowding her.

Funny how I'd needed her to come inside this place. But now that she was here, she didn't really need me. Not when she had August.

I'd never seen a mother-son duo like theirs. Maybe it was because she was his only parent—I assumed she was his only parent—but they had this bond. It was like a string tied between them, visible if you looked hard enough.

When I caught up to them, Clara was standing at the back of the delivery van, staring at the closed door.

August had left her side and was bent over the rusted can that Aria had once used to water her plants.

"Want me to open it?" I asked.

She sucked in a deep breath, nodding as she blew it out. "Yes."

The latch was rusted and stiff but after a hard tug, it sprang free. The scrape of metal on metal echoed across the yard along with an ear-splitting squeak as I lifted the door.

I hopped up into the back, surveying the space. Then I held out a hand to help Clara up so she wouldn't get that dress dirty.

She didn't let my hand go as she looked around. Her grip tightened when she saw the wreckage of old books and blankets shoved against the far wall.

An animal had gotten in here at one point and had turned the pages and cloths into shreds. A bed of its own.

Clara bent down, picking up something from the floor. The dry-erase marker. The one they'd used to track their countdown on the wall. She held it up, inspecting it for a moment, then tossed it into the mess. "It's small."

"It all feels small."

A place that had once felt so vast, like a continent of its own, had been reduced to its three acres by time and age and reality.

"I'm not taking a picture of this." She spun away, ripped her hand free and was on the ground before I could blink.

I took one last glance, wishing it hadn't been like this for Clara's sake, and left it behind, not bothering to close the door. Then I jogged to catch them on their way to the shop since I had the keys.

Going in first, I flipped on the lights. "I'm surprised so many work."

The smell of gasoline and oil was thick from years of sitting. I had no idea if the equipment would work, but I'd let someone else deal with that.

I checked my watch. It was nearly eight. "I'd better head out front to meet the developer."

"We'll come with you." Clara backed away from the shop and we all walked toward Lou's front door. "Did you decide what you want to do with it?"

"Sell it." Now that I'd come here and seen it again, there was no reason to hold on to an old junkyard. "I'd like to go through Lou's shack. Make sure there isn't anything inside to keep. But there's nothing for me here."

"Not quite." Clara looked up at me with a sad smile. "There was something here. I think that's why Lou left it to you. Because he knew that you needed to come here and be the one to put it to rest."

I almost tripped over my own damn feet. "How do you do that?"

"Do what?"

"Say what I'm feeling but haven't figured out how to articulate."

Her eyes softened. "I'm glad we came here."

"Me too."

We rounded the corner just as a large white truck pulled up behind the Cadillac. A man in a nice pair of jeans and a button-down shirt hopped out, raising one hand to wave while he held a notebook in the other.

"Would you mind if I went into Lou's?" Clara asked.

"Not at all." I handed her the keys, then winked at August before going to shake the developer's hand.

I spent the next thirty minutes taking him on a tour of the junkyard. He told me about his plans for the neighborhood and the park he'd be adding on this section of land. Maybe it wouldn't happen, but I liked the idea of this being a place for kids to play. A safe place for future generations, like it had been for me.

"There's a lot here," I told him as we walked back to his truck. "I don't have the time or energy to sift through it all. So I'll sell it to you, as-is."

"How much?"

"Make me a fair offer based on the valuation of the land."

He nodded. "I'll have my realtor draw it up today."

"Great." I shook his hand once more, waited until he was gone, then headed for the shack.

August was sitting at the same table where I'd once sat with Lou. He looked bored out of his mind with one hand holding up his head. When he spotted me, he sat up straight. "Can we go now?"

"Soon," I promised. "Where's your mom?"

"Back here," Clara called.

I found her in what had been Lou's office. Or library. Or notebook-hoarding room. "Um . . . whoa."

There were spiral-bound notebooks stacked against the walls in towering columns. Some almost as tall as me. Three bookshelves against the wall were so overloaded with books and binders that the shelves sagged in the middle beneath the weight.

"What's in these?" I slid a notebook off the top of a stack and opened it to the first page. It was a series of numbers on the left side with a sketch of a car's grill that took up the center. It had the make, model and year of the car it would have belonged to. At the bottom was a location. *Zone 4.*

"I think he had this entire place cataloged." Clara had a few notebooks open on Lou's desk, flipping through them. Page after page was more of the same. "I bet he knew what and where every single piece was. These were his treasures."

I shook my head, unable to believe all that I was seeing. Lou must have spent years in here, detailing every scrap and every part on this property. I put the notebook back on the stack, then left the office, wandering deeper into the shack. Lou's bedroom was at the rear of the building, and unlike the rest of his home, it was clutter-free.

Everything was filmed with dust, but the emptiness of the room was utterly shocking.

A bed rested in the center of the space, pushed against the far wall. On either side were two nightstands. One held a box. The other a framed photograph. The picture drew me in, and I skirted the bed to get a closer look.

It was of Lou, barely recognizable as a younger man, seated with a woman wearing a yellow polka-dot dress. *His wife.* He had a smile on his face. He looked happy. He'd been a different man.

In a different life.

"When he lost her, he lost his way." Clara had snuck up on me and was peeking past my shoulder. With a sad smile, she went to the other nightstand, running her fingertips over the dusty box. Then she flipped the clasp to lift the lid and gasped at whatever was inside. "Karson."

"What?" I rounded the bed to her side, the photograph of Lou and his wife still in my grip. There wasn't much to save here but this picture was definitely coming home.

"It's a letter. To you." She lifted it out, then narrowed her gaze at whatever else was in the box. "Wait. There are more."

She pulled out a stack of letters, sifting through them. Each had one of our names on top. Six letters for the six kids who'd lived here. There was more in the box, but my focus was on Lou's neat and tidy script and the envelopes in Clara's hands.

"Oh my God." She rifled through the stack again.

"I can't believe it."

She nodded. "He even spelled Londyn's name right. With a *y*. I didn't know he actually knew our names."

I blinked, unable to process what I was seeing.

"He left them for you to find," she said. "He put all of his stuff in the other rooms, but this one was clean because he wanted you to see this box and that photo."

Lou. I wished I'd known him better. I wished I'd come back again before he'd passed. "He noticed more than he let on, didn't he?"

"I think he noticed everything."

I tore my eyes away from the letters and met Clara's gaze. We were close. Too close. My chest brushed against her arm. Her hair, left long, draped between us and the ends tickled my forearms.

God, she was beautiful. Her tender heart. Her unwavering strength. I soaked her in, giving myself a moment to swim in those chocolate eyes.

My hand lifted, my fingertips desperate to trace the soft line of her jaw, when little feet pounded at our backs.

"Mom!"

She jerked, dropping her gaze. Then she inched away, as far as she could toward the nightstand, and cleared her throat. "In here."

"Can we go now?" August begged.

"Yeah." I took a step away from his mother. "We'd better go."

They'd better go.

For the first time since Clara had surprised me with the Cadillac, I was ready to send her back to Arizona.

Maybe if she was five hundred miles away, I'd actually be able to resist her.

14

KARSON

"How do you feel?" Clara asked as we drove away from the junkyard.

"Lighter. You?"

"Free."

Free. Not quite. But almost.

I wouldn't be free until I could let Clara go.

But for the moment, I was content.

We'd put the top down to get some fresh air. I drew in a long breath, holding it in my lungs. In the back of my mind, I heard the click of a door. The turn of a page.

A chapter had ended, and it was time to move on.

August was in his seat, playing with some metal rings he'd found at Lou's and had asked to keep. Beside him was the box that contained Lou's letters and whatever items he'd stored beneath.

Clara and I hadn't spent time looking through them. Gus had been antsy to get out of there and since he'd been such a trooper all morning, we'd locked everything up and left.

"Think you'll come back here in twenty years?" Clara asked as we rolled down the road and put the junkyard in the rearview. "See what it's like?"

"Maybe. You?"

She shook her head. "Probably not. I'm glad I got to see it again. I feel like that door is closed now."

"I was just thinking the same damn thing."

"It's a good reminder of how far we've come and why I'm working so hard to make sure August never has that sort of life."

"You're a good mom, Clara."

"That's the best compliment you've ever given me."

"Ever? What about the time I told you that you were the prettiest girl in the universe?"

"That was because you were a shameless flirt."

"With you?"

"Always," we said in unison.

Clara closed her eyes, scrunching up her nose.

I cringed.

Back to awkward then. Because I couldn't seem to help myself.

Why couldn't I just see her as my friend? Completely platonic. Why? The answer was buried deep and at the moment, I was not going to acknowledge it. I *couldn't* acknowledge it.

The trip to the junkyard had been another distraction to shove it all away, but now that the meeting was over, the nagging guilt came rushing back.

"Sorry." I ran a palm over my chin.

Maybe it was time to shave. Holly would hate it. She loved the beard. Did Clara? *It doesn't matter, asshole. She's not your girlfriend.*

"I'd better get some gas," I said, needing a task and a moment to pull my shit together. We were in the middle of town and I stopped at the next station. When I pulled in beside the pump, I got out and stayed out, hovering beside the tank, letting the guzzling sound from the nozzle block out Clara's muted conversation with Gus.

One more night.

I'd swim with August this afternoon. We'd have a nice dinner. Then tomorrow I'd take Clara to the airport and put this behind me. For good.

Holly deserved better.

And fuck, so did Clara. She needed to find a man who was free.

The tank was nearly full when a door opened and Clara stepped out of the Cadillac, her wallet in hand. "August earned a treat for being so good this morning. Want anything?"

"Nah. Thanks."

She gave me a small smile and turned, but instead of walking across the lot, she froze. Her entire body turned to stone.

"Clara."

She didn't answer. Instead, she stared forward at the convenience store where an older man had just come out the door with a plastic sack in his hand.

Abandoning the gas pump, I rounded the trunk and went to her side. "Hey. What's wrong?"

She gulped and nodded at the man. "That's him."

The man had thinning brown hair and a splotchy pallor to his face. He pulled a cigarette from his pocket and placed it between his lips. His frame was thin beneath his shirt, the bones of his shoulders trying to cut through the cotton.

When he glanced our way and those beady eyes narrowed on Clara, her body flinched.

"Your uncle," I guessed.

I hadn't seen the guy before, not that I'd needed to. There wasn't a person on earth who was likely to get this reaction from Clara. And

Gemma had seen him once, ages ago, and the way she'd described him fit this man perfectly. A total fucking creep. That hadn't changed.

And the rage I'd felt toward that man hadn't dulled either.

My fists balled at my sides. When Clara had told me about her uncle, I'd wanted to kill the bastard. The anger was still there, an inferno churning in my veins. Hungry for a victim.

I took a step forward, ready to walk over and make that son of a bitch pay for all that he'd done to them, but before I could take my second step, Clara's hand slipped into mine.

She clutched it, not holding me back, just holding on.

Her gaze was still glued to him as he stared back. She kept her shoulders straight, her chin held high. She didn't cower. And the glare she sent him was nothing short of murderous.

A swell of pride mixed with my rage. Good for her. Damn, but she was strong.

It took a moment, but he recognized her. His bony frame tensed. He gave her a sideways look, and then he was gone, scurrying to his nineties-model Honda Civic, the tires squealing as he raced out of the station's lot.

And Clara just held on, staring at the spot where he'd been.

"He tried but he didn't ruin us," she whispered.

"No, he didn't."

"He knew who I was."

"Yes, he did."

"We were scared of him as kids. We knew it was wrong but not how to fix it. We should have turned him in."

"You still can. You have the power here, Clara."

Her head tilted to the side. "You're right. We should have. I didn't get that as a kid but we're not those scared girls anymore. And we've been ignoring it, burying it. He deserves to pay. To be registered as a sex offender at least. When we get home, I'll talk to Aria. We'll do what we can and then never think of him again."

"Good for you."

"Thank you," she whispered. Then she closed her eyes and finally, her shoulders sagged. "I really hoped that he was dead."

"Me too." Without hesitating, I spun her toward me and hauled her into a hug, wrapping her in my arms and feeling her cheek press against my heart.

Clara snaked her hands around me, and as tightly as I held her, she clung to me.

"I'm sorry," I said into her hair.

"They should have made a better plan. My parents. They let us down."

I stayed quiet. My hatred was aimed at her uncle, but there was resentment for her parents too. Resentment I hadn't understood as a teenager. Her mom and dad had let their daughters down by not having a better plan in case of their deaths.

Clara and Aria never should have been given to their uncle.

"What can I do?" I asked.

"You're doing it." She relaxed, giving me her weight.

The scent of orange and vanilla filled my nose as I rested my chin on her head. Having her in my embrace felt so familiar. So . . . right.

I should let her go. *Let her go.*

I didn't move.

"Do you still hug everyone goodbye?" I asked.

"Yes."

"Then why not me?" I remembered that so clearly from our time at the junkyard. Whether it had been in town when she'd go one way and I'd go the other, or even when she caught me at the junkyard before I'd leave for the day. Every goodbye had come with a hug. Most hellos too.

Until now. Last night, there'd been no hug.

Not once since she'd come to Elyria had she touched me.

Clara loosened her grip on me and slid her arms free. Then, too soon, she was gone and there was a gulf between us.

I'd asked the question.

But she didn't answer.

We both knew the answer would only make this worse.

"I'd better get August his treat." She pointed to the store, but the crease between her eyebrows told me she didn't want to go inside.

"What does he want? I'll grab it."

She opened her wallet, but I waved it off. "I've got it. I'm going to get some water too."

"Skittles or Swedish Fish or Starbursts or Twizzlers. He loves fruity candy."

"Got it." Then I got the hell away.

Fuck. Maybe we should say our goodbyes tonight and I should go home. That would be the smart thing to do. Call it over and done with.

Instead, I bought August's candy and listened to him tell me about which color combinations of Skittles were the best as we drove to the hotel. Then we went swimming for a few hours while Clara looked on from a lounge chair.

Entertainment at dinner was once again provided by the five-year-old, and when we returned to the hotel, I had this sinking feeling that I wasn't going to see him again. In just a few days, August had made a lasting impression.

I'd miss dinners without a nonstop stream of interesting facts that he learned at school. I'd miss the excitement that seemed to pour from every word.

But if I couldn't control these feelings about Clara, then I had to cut off contact. I'd done it for twelve years, so what was a lifetime more?

No Clara meant no Gus. I'd miss out on seeing him as a teenager. A young man. An adult. There was a twinge in my chest as he pushed the elevator button. I couldn't tear my eyes away from his smile and his small hands and the slight waves in his dark-blond hair.

Was this why Clara was always looking to him? Because she knew how fast he would change?

My throat was dry as we stepped into the elevator and rode to our floor. As Gus raced down the hallway toward the room, my steps dragged like I was wearing lead-filled shoes.

Clara's steps seemed even shorter and heavier than mine.

This was goodbye. There was the trip to the airport in the morning, but that would be full of logistics, baggage and a rushed farewell.

"Can we rent a movie?" August asked, standing beside their door.

"Sure." Clara nodded.

"Want to watch with us?" he asked me.

I opened my mouth to let him down gently, but then Clara answered for me. "Yeah. Watch with us."

"Okay." Reckless, but that was my defining trait this week.

So we went inside her room, the three of us settling on the couch in the common room in her suite, with August in the middle, and rented a movie.

Gus fell asleep halfway through the musical cartoon.

"This is more excitement than he's used to," Clara said, turning down the volume on the TV.

"He's such a great kid. Maybe the best I've ever met."

She smiled down at him as he slumped into her side. "He's pretty fantastic, isn't he?"

"I have to tell you something," I said. "Probably should have admitted it sooner."

"What?"

"I looked you up on Facebook."

Her eyes widened. "You did? When?"

"About six years ago. I was curious. Temptation got the better of me and I wanted to know that you were okay. You didn't have much posted but a few pictures. I saw one of you and him together. You looked happy. In love. It was hard to see."

So I hadn't looked her up again. Clara or Londyn or Gemma or Katherine. I'd taken it as a sign to move forward. Easier said than done.

"I assume the guy was Gus's father. What happened?"

She sighed. "About what I said last night. I'm sorry. I shouldn't have. I know it put you in an uncomfortable position with Holly and . . . I'm sorry."

"It's okay." If only she knew the real reason that I was uncomfortable had nothing to do with her words, but the words I wanted to say back.

"I met Devan in Las Vegas." She stared at the TV as she spoke. "I'd been living there for years and work was mostly my life. It was rare that I did anything exciting, but one weekend some friends dragged me to a nightclub. That's where I met him."

Green crept under my skin but I stayed expressionless, listening. "How long were you together?"

"About a year. I should have ended it long before that. But Devan had his moments when he was wonderful and funny and loving. Whatever pictures you saw were probably from those times. But the longer we were together, the more I realized that those good moments were only because he knew I was about to call it off. Then he'd charm me, and I'd fall for it. I'd forget that he was a narcissist, and I was only a beautiful decoration in a world that revolved around him."

How could anyone in Clara's presence not want to fall into *her* orbit? This guy Devan must have been blind.

"I got pregnant. Obviously. It hadn't been planned, but he accused me of doing it on purpose even though I'd been on birth control."

"Seriously?"

She shrugged. "A baby meant Devan wouldn't be the center of attention. To this day, I don't know if he ever believed that it was an accident. We'd fight about it. I'd tell him we were done. He'd apologize and we'd be good for a week. Until we weren't. It was this sick, unhealthy cycle, but I didn't want to let him go. Not for me, but for August. I was sure that if I could just get Devan through the pregnancy, he'd meet our son and realize that love wasn't a competition. That there was enough for him and a baby."

"Did he?"

"No." She tore her eyes away from the wall, dropping them to August. "By my third trimester, he was already checked out. I suspected he'd already found another woman who'd worship him. I was an afterthought by then. When August was a newborn, I told him we were done. He didn't argue."

"Has he been involved at all?"

"No. Devan was never going to change. He was never going to make a good father. I didn't want to put August through any disappointment when Devan made a promise he couldn't keep. So I gave him an out. I wouldn't ask for any money or support if he signed over all of his parental rights. Ask me if he put up a fight."

Of course he hadn't, the dumb son of a bitch. "I'm sorry you went through all that alone."

"Don't be. I had Aria. And Brody. Not long after that, Brody told me he was moving to Welcome, Arizona, and asked if I wanted to come along. A new town. A fresh start. It was a no-brainer."

Had Brody always planned on offering Clara the opportunity in Arizona? Or had he offered after the fallout with Devan? I had a feeling I wasn't the only man who did what he could to protect her.

Regardless, Clara and Aria were good allies to have in your corner. Brody was a lucky man to have them both.

Clara blew out a long breath. "After I broke it off with Devan, I'd go through these days when I was so mad at myself for not seeing through his façade. He was . . . attractive. I'm not proud to say that I let his looks cloud my judgment. But when August was a baby, one day I just stopped being mad. At myself. At Devan. I got the best part of him and he was too self-absorbed to realize that when I left Vegas, I took that piece with me."

"I like the name August."

She gave me a sad smile. "That was my dad's name. Did I ever tell you that?"

"No."

"If I'd had a girl, I would have named her after Mom. Hopefully Aria will have another baby one day and if it's a girl, she can take that name. Millie. That was her name."

"Pretty name."

"I like it too." She shifted, turning slightly sideways on the couch so August's head rested in her lap.

The muted light from the TV cast a light glow over the room. They caught the gold flecks in her gaze, making them dance.

How could he have let her go?

How could *I* have let her go?

Two stupid men.

"I should have come to you anyway. Despite the Facebook pictures. I assumed you were happy and had moved on, but I should have come to find you."

"Except then I wouldn't have August." She gave me a sad smile. "Timing was never on our side, was it?"

"No, it wasn't." If I had looked her up a year later, after Devan had been out of the picture, or if she had come here a year earlier, before Holly . . .

Or if at nineteen, I hadn't been so wrapped up in my mother's words.

You're a piece of shit, Karson. You're worthless.

Get out of my sight. I hate you. I hate looking at you.

You are nothing. A disgrace. You're a fuckup.

"My mom died," I blurted.

Clara tensed. "When?"

"Not long before I moved to Elyria. After she died, I wanted to get out of Temecula for good."

"Is that why you came back here? When Gemma hired the PI the first time, he'd said you were here. That always seemed so crazy to me. I figured you'd be long gone like the rest of us."

"Yeah." I sighed. "I got a call one day when I was living in San Diego the second time from a police officer here in Temecula. Mom had been in a car accident and was in a coma."

"Karson, I'm so sorry."

"Should I tell you this? It might be hard to hear."

"Drunk driver?" she guessed. Her own parents had been killed by a drunk driver, and the last thing I wanted was to cause her any pain.

"Yeah." I nodded. "I'd expected the drunk to be her, but it wasn't. I think that's the only reason I came back. If she had hurt someone . . . well, there's a lot I struggle to forgive my mother for. That would have been a deal breaker."

"You came back to take care of her, didn't you?"

"She probably didn't deserve it. But I did it anyway." I lifted a shoulder. "It took me a long time to learn that she was sick. That she hated herself so much that it was all she knew. That her taking that hate out on me was because I was the only person she had. And it took me a long time to let go of her ghost. To realize I was not the person she told me I was."

"You're a good man, Karson Avery."

I dropped my eyes to August, curled up between us. This kid didn't even know how lucky he was to have a mother like Clara.

"After she passed, I felt like I could leave it all behind. That's when I moved to Elyria."

"Your fresh start."

I nodded. "We all needed them, didn't we?"

"We did." Clara gave me a sad smile. August squirmed on the couch, an arm flailing in the other direction. Clara scooped him into her arms and pushed up off the couch, carrying him to the adjoining room. The rustle of clothes and the thud of shoes dropping to the floor was my hint to leave.

It was time. It was time to say goodbye. To get back to life in Elyria.

To Holly.

She and I had a shot. We had a chance at a future. I hadn't felt like that about any woman I'd dated before, not Londyn. Not even Clara. Not the women I'd met along my way. Mostly because I'd been too young, but with Holly, there was a real chance.

Like Clara said herself, timing had never been on our side. Maybe that was for a reason.

I waited for Clara to finish with August. She emerged, closing his bedroom door. Then I spoke the words I'd been dreading all evening. "It's been so great to see you. To meet August."

"You too."

"Good night, Clara." I spun for the door, ready to make my escape, when she stopped me.

"Wait. What about the box?" Clara went to the small table where we'd left Lou's box and letters.

The box. Damn it.

"Oh, I forgot about it." In an effort to get out of here while I still could, before I said or did something that would tarnish these days with Clara, I'd completely forgotten about the box.

The door would have to wait.

She took a chair on one side of the table while I sat in the other. Then she lifted out the box's contents. Other boxes, all small. "These are jewelry boxes."

Six in total, in varying colors and sizes. And each of them had a small piece of paper taped to the underside.

"Here you go," she said, passing over my letter and the navy velvet ring box with my name on it.

I opened the envelope first, pulling out a crisp piece of ecru paper and unfolding it.

KARSON,

These were my wife's rings. She couldn't wear them when she was pregnant with our baby because her fingers swelled up like sausages. That's what she called them. Sausage fingers.

654

By rights, I should have buried her with them. But that was a hard time. I'm ashamed to admit that I didn't realize she hadn't been wearing the rings in her coffin until I found them in her jewelry box a few weeks later.

Now that she's gone and I'm not long to follow, I'd like you to have them.

Give them to a woman like my Hope. She was smart and brave. She laughed through the good times and made me laugh through the bad. She was the soul on earth I was made to find.

I left a picture of her beside my bed. Wasn't she a beauty? One look at her and the world made sense.

Take care of yourself. And I'll thank you in advance for taking care of these for Hope. I trust you'll give them to someone special. You always had good taste in girls. I suspect that won't change.

Lou

I READ IT TWICE. Three times. And my heart ached so badly I could barely breathe.

It was an elegant letter for a man who'd mostly spoken in grunts. Refolding the paper, I returned it to the envelope, tucking it carefully inside. Then I took the box and pried the lid open.

The center jewel on the engagement ring was a deep grayish blue, the color of the ocean on a stormy day. It was accented by tiny diamonds on each side. The white jewels were arranged without a pattern, like leaves beneath a flower. The white gold band was smooth and shiny. It matched the simple wedding ring beneath.

"Damn, Lou." I pulled the ring from the box, holding it up to catch the light. "This was his wife's ring."

Clara didn't respond. She was too busy staring at the ring pinched between her own fingers.

It was Lou's wedding band. I didn't have to ask to know. And I suspected Clara's letter was also about Hope.

A tear dripped down her cheek, snapping her out of her trance. She blinked her eyes clear and swiped at her face. Then she refolded her letter and put it away. "I'll send the others their letters and boxes when I get home."

"Thanks." I put Hope's ring away, then shoved the box into my pocket. Then I took the letter and stood, needing a minute to let Lou's words sink in.

The timing of this had me reeling. Two months ago, that letter would have meant something else entirely.

"I'm going to go," I said. "Good night."

"Good night," she whispered.

I was almost to the door when she stopped me again.

"Does Holly know about us? About what happened in the past?"

My shoulders fell and I turned. "No."

She got up from the table and walked closer. "Aria never knew about us either. I always wondered if she did, but she never said anything."

"You didn't tell her? Why?"

"Because you were mine. You were the one thing I didn't want to share. With anyone." Her confession rocked me to my heels. "Why didn't you tell Holly?"

"Because I fucked up," I admitted, the weight of Lou's letter settling on my shoulders.

"What do you mean?"

"I should have gone with you to Las Vegas."

A fresh sheen of tears flooded her eyes. "Sweet dreams, Karson."

"Then I'll dream of you."

I shouldn't have said it, but the words were unstoppable.

When I left, she let me go.

When the door closed, there was no turning back.

I drove the Cadillac home.

15

KARSON

"It's Clara, isn't it?" There were tears in Holly's eyes. "When you wake up in the middle of the night, it's because of her."

"Yes, it is."

Years of sleepless nights and it was almost always because of Clara. I'd dream that she was hurt. I'd dream that she was calling my name, begging for help. I'd dream that she was drowning in the ocean or standing in the middle of a freeway, stuck between racing cars.

Other nights I'd simply hear her voice. I'd hear her laugh and kiss another man. And the fear that drove me awake was not that she was in danger. The fear was that I'd lost her to someone else.

For too long, I'd ignored it and hidden in work or travel or relocating to new cities. For a time, I'd been busy caring for my mother, who never had woken up from her coma. I'd gone to visit her in hospice nearly every day, speaking to the shell she'd once been.

No matter the current focus of my life, I'd kept Clara's memory tucked into the quiet corners of my heart.

"Nothing happened," I promised Holly.

The problem was that I wanted it to happen. I wanted Clara. No amount of time or distance would change those feelings. And Lou's words had confirmed it all. With every sentence, I'd known the right choice. He'd entrusted Hope's rings to my care, and they belonged to Clara.

Holly deserved the truth.

After I'd left Clara's room, I'd called Holly and told her I was coming home. I'd asked her to wait up. Maybe she'd heard the breakup in my voice because when I'd come through the door, she'd been in the living room. Her backpack had been beside the door, closed and full. I suspected that the toothbrush she'd left here and the extra clothes were inside.

"I'm sorry, Holly."

She sniffled and swallowed hard. "Is there anything I could have done?"

Christ, I hated this. I hated seeing hurt on her beautiful face, but she deserved to find the man who saw her and only her. "No."

"Ouch. I thought . . . I thought we had a chance."

I opened my mouth to apologize again, but she was already gone, standing from the couch and hurrying across the living room.

I followed, standing by as she picked up her backpack and purse. Then she closed the distance between us, raised up on her toes to kiss my cheek. "Goodbye, Karson."

"Goodbye, Holly."

She slipped out of the door without a backward glance.

I didn't move until the lights from her headlights had vanished. Then I bolted for the door myself, flinging it open and whipping it closed behind me as I ran for the Cadillac.

The roads to Temecula were nearly deserted as I raced to my Clara.

The hotel lobby was empty and dark. The front desk clerk side-eyed me as I jogged through the lobby for the elevator. The slow ride to our floor was torture.

It had been over three hours since I'd bid Clara good night. Was she still awake? I checked the time on my phone as I strode down the hallway toward her room. It was after midnight. She was probably asleep behind that closed door, but there was no way I was waiting until morning. "Fuck it."

I knocked lightly, waiting. If she didn't answer, I'd call. I shifted from one foot to the other, my breath lodged in my chest.

Then there was a click and the slide of a chain. Clara opened the door, wearing a pale pink silk camisole and matching sleep shorts with a lace hem. Her hair was loose, draped over her bare shoulders. But she hadn't been sleeping. There was red rimming her eyes and her cheeks were splotchy.

She'd been crying.

Lou's words clicked into place.

One look at her and the world made sense.

"I love you."

Clara gasped, her body tensing. "W-what?"

Smooth, Karson. I hadn't meant to just blurt those three words but now that they were out there, I might as well just go with it. "I love you."

She blinked, clearly confused. "What about Holly?"

"I just got back from Elyria."

"Oh." Her eyes widened. "Why?"

Why? My stomach dropped. Had I read this wrong? Did she not feel the same? *No.* No goddamn way. "Because she wasn't you."

Her chin began to quiver. "You love me?"

"I—"

"I love you too." The moment she spoke, she dropped her face into her

658

hands. Her shoulders began to shake and I crossed the distance between us, urging her into the room before easing the door closed.

Why was she crying?

"Clara, I—"

Before I could finish my sentence, she surged, throwing her arms around my shoulders. Then there was no more talking. Her lips found mine and a bolt of lightning shot through my body, fusing me to her. We were a mess of fumbling hands and wet lips.

The urgency of her mouth. The desperation of mine. She opened for me and I dove in, my tongue tangling with hers as my arms engulfed her.

Never in my life had a kiss meant so much. I gave in, surrendering to this woman's soft lips and the slick of her tongue against mine. She clung to me as I clung to her, the softness of her body pressed into my hard lines.

This was her. This was my Clara.

And I'd kiss her every day for the rest of my life.

I scooped her up so her toes were dangling above the carpet, then I walked us to her bedroom, laying her on the bed. Covering her with my body.

Her hands came to my face, holding me to her lips, as my hands roamed down the silk of her top and shorts to the bare skin of her legs. I kneaded the flesh of her toned thighs. I drew my fingers along the back of her knee in a featherlight touch.

When she began to tremble, I forced myself to break away, going to the door and closing it quietly before flipping the lock. The sight that greeted me on the bed when I turned sent all my blood rushing to my groin.

Clara was seated on the edge of the bed. The lust in her eyes darkened them to chocolate pools. The faint light from the street outside seeped through the sheer curtains, acting like moonlight on her flawless skin.

She reached for the hem of her shirt, slowly gathering it in her hands. Then she dragged it over her head, tossing it to the floor.

My mouth went dry. Her rosy nipples were peaked and the desperation to feel them under my palms sent me flying across the room, dropping to my knees before her.

"You are beautiful. So fucking beautiful." I slid my hands up her ribs, savoring the moan that escaped her lips. Then I found her breasts in my palms, letting them fill my hands as I raked my thumbs over her nipples.

Clara's back arched, pressing herself further into my touch. The silk of her skin was intoxicating, and tonight, I'd touch every inch. I'd lick and worship because she was mine.

"Say it again," I said, urging her down to the mattress. When that hair was splayed beneath her, I ran my hands down the swell of her hips, hooking my fingers into the shorts and the panties beneath. Then I pulled them from her legs, inch by torturous inch.

Her breath hitched when they landed on the floor. She lay bare and perfect, her gaze locked on mine.

I swallowed a groan. "Say it again."

"I love you."

"One more time."

The corner of her mouth turned up as she pushed up on her elbows, moving backward until she reached the pillows. Then she crooked a finger, beckoning me to the bed. Did she have any idea the power she had over me?

I reached behind me to yank my T-shirt over my head. My flip-flops crashed to the carpet as Clara's gaze dropped down my stomach to the hem of my jeans. I flipped open the button, then dragged down the zipper. I shoved the pants and my black boxer briefs over my thighs, my erection bobbing free. Then I wrapped a fist around my shaft.

Clara watched as I gave it a long stroke, her eyes glued to my cock. Her cheeks were pink, her breaths heavy. "Karson."

I stayed at the foot of the bed.

"I don't have a condom." It was a fucking shame because what I wanted most was to sink inside her. To forget where I started and she began. But I'd make her come tonight, with my fingers and my tongue. "I've always used one. Always."

"I, um . . . not since Devan."

Fuck me. I didn't like that son of a bitch's name anywhere near a naked Clara, but knowing that she'd been without a man since was a damn rush because I'd be the last lover in her life.

"You sure?"

"I don't want to wait." She gave me a sheepish smile. "But I'm not on birth control."

Fuck, but she was shredding me here. "Your call, baby."

"I don't want to wait."

I crawled to her, hovering above her body. The intensity of her gaze was nearly my undoing as her hips cradled mine and my cock rested against her center.

"I want you to have my kids." Apparently, I had no filter tonight. Confession after confession streamed out.

Her eyes flared.

"I'm not going to hold back. I'm not going to take this slow. I've missed too many years with you, and I am not going to waste another second. You're mine. August is mine."

Her hand came to my cheek as another wash of tears flooded her eyes. There was so much emotion there. Regret for the missed years. Hope for the future.

What she felt, I felt too.

"Karson . . ."

"I know." I dropped a soft kiss to her mouth, running my tongue over the bottom swell of her parted lips. I deepened the kiss, treasuring her sweet taste and the feel of her bare chest against my own as I nudged against her center.

Clara locked her eyes with mine, her hands trailing down my spine toward my ass. Then I inched forward, catching her mewl with another kiss.

660

I rocked us together, deliberately, until I was rooted deep. "You feel so fucking good."

"Move." She hummed and locked her legs around my hips, shifting me deeper.

Ruined. I was ruined. And I relished every damn second of it.

I eased out and slid back inside her tight, wet heat. Over and over, I brought us together as her hips moved to match my rhythm. We were hushed whispers and swallowed moans. We were lost lovers making up for missed days and nights.

By the time her eyes drifted shut and her inner walls fluttered around me, the build in my lower spine was punishing. The pressure to pour myself into her was almost impossible to keep at bay.

Clara's back arched, her entire body shuddering as she held back a cry and pulsed around me. She came so hard, so strong, that I went over with her, letting the stars break across my vision and succumbing to my release.

We panted, holding tight to each other's sweaty bodies, until finally I eased away and rolled her atop my chest.

Our breaths mingled. Her ear was pressed against my heart.

"Wow."

"Holy fucking shit."

She giggled and propped her chin on my pec. "How long?"

"How long for what?"

She gave me a wicked grin. "How long until we can go again?"

I flipped her in a flash, so she was on her stomach. Then I dropped a trail of kisses over her shoulders, reaching between her legs and finding her swollen clit.

She gasped. "Already?"

"For you?" I moved up, using my free hand to pull her hair away from her face. Then I whispered in her ear. "Always."

"So ARE you going to be my dad?" August had never looked so serious. Gone was the boy. Instead, I was crouched beside a warrior.

A warrior who'd spend his entire life looking out for his mother.

From now on, he'd have company on the battlefield.

"I'd like to be your dad. If that's okay with you."

He looked to the sand beneath his bare feet. He squished some between his toes, then he looked over to where Clara was seated on a large blanket.

She caught his gaze and waved with one hand while the other held her phone to an ear. When we'd gotten to the beach, I'd taken August to the water while she'd called to check in with Aria.

Clara looked magnificent under the sun and on the sand. She was wearing a simple teal bikini, sexy and tempting as hell. When she'd walked out of the bedroom this morning wearing it and a sheer coverup, I'd almost lost my damn head.

It had been two days since Temecula, and I'd done exactly as I'd promised.

I hadn't gone slow.

I hadn't held back.

We'd returned to Elyria and there'd been no hotel. I'd brought Clara to my home and set her and August up in the guest bedroom.

She snuck into my room after he fell asleep each night and we spent the midnight hours exploring each other's bodies. With her by my side, I'd slept better than I had in years. So much so that when my alarm had gone off at five this morning, I'd been totally dead to the world.

If she thought I was sleeping without her again, she was dreaming.

During the day and when August was in the room, I pulled Clara in for a hug. For a kiss. Gus had been watching. Closely. Clara had sat him down for a one-on-one, but it hadn't erased all of the wariness in his gaze.

We just needed time. Thankfully, we had it.

Clara had called Aria on the way back to Elyria and told her about us. There hadn't been a lot of surprise in Aria's voice. Just a smile as she'd talked to us both on speaker.

I wondered about you two back then.

Then Aria had laughed and handed the phone to Brody.

The great thing about a boss slash brother-in-law who owned a private plane was that Clara had no pressure to rush home to Arizona. Which was good because we had some details to figure out first.

"I don't have a dad," August whispered.

There was such longing in his voice I nearly toppled over on my ass. Kids his age started to know what made them different. For August, it was that other kids had two parents. Clara was the best mother in the world, but her days of walking alone were over.

"You do now." I put my hand on his shoulder and the smile that played on his mouth stole my heart. "I'm going to need your help."

"With what?"

I winked. "We need to find two sticks."

The light in his eyes was so much like Clara's that when I stood, I couldn't help but drop a kiss to the top of his head.

When I glanced over, Clara was watching with a hand pressed to her heart.

I waved and mouthed, "I love you."

She blew me a kiss and went back to her call.

Then August and I went exploring for our sticks. By the time we were done with our job, I went to Clara, leaving Gus to splash on the surf with his promise not to go past his knees.

"Hi." I collapsed on the blanket beside her and kissed her shoulder.

"Hi." She leaned into me. "What were you guys doing?"

"Just playing," I lied. "How's Aria?"

"Good. She asked me if I was moving here."

"Do you want to move here?" I took her hand and laced our fingers together.

"I don't know." She sighed. "I love Welcome. But I like it here too and your job is here."

"My job is flexible, baby. How's the real estate market in Welcome?"

"Probably not as exciting as it is in California." She ran her fingers through my hair. "You'd move? Really?"

"I got an email from that developer in Temecula this morning."

She sat up straighter. "And?"

"Sold. Half a million bucks, which is more than the land is worth, but he thinks there's value in the parts. So I figure that sale plus the equity I have in my house here should be plenty to set us up wherever you want to live."

"I have a house but it's on Brody and Aria's property. I love them both, but I want our own space."

"Same here." I wanted a home we chose together, where we could raise Gus and any other kids who came along.

"Do I have to decide today?"

"Yes."

She looked at me, startled for a moment, until she realized I was teasing and burst out laughing.

My God, she was beautiful when she laughed. I lunged for her, tackling her to the towel and pinning her down with a leg. Then I took her hands, raising them above her head so she was completely at my mercy. "I love you."

"I have an idea."

"What's that?"

"Let's go to your place. Give August his Nintendo and we can take a shower."

I swelled instantly, pressing the bulge against her hip. "Good idea."

She lifted her head, her lips seeking mine, but as fast as I'd pinned her, I was on my feet, bringing her with me.

"Can't leave yet."

"Why?"

I put two fingers to my lips and whistled.

August heard it, his head snapping up from where he'd been beside the water. Then he tore off, running for the spot where we'd prepared our surprise.

"Come on." I took Clara's hand, threading our fingers together, and willed my heart not to explode.

We caught up to August, who stood proudly by our creation.

"What's—" Clara's breath hitched when she saw the words we'd written in the sand. From the towel, she had been too far away to read them, but not so far that others on the beach might have ruined them.

I stepped in front of her and dropped to a knee. Then I fished the ring Lou had given me out of my shorts pocket and slid it onto her finger. "Marry me."

The words etched in the sand said the same.

Clara wouldn't have been the woman she was if her gaze hadn't shifted away from mine to August.

Behind me, August had a beaming smile on his face as he nodded.

"Yes." She crashed to her knees and framed my face with her hands.

I kissed her, lingering long enough to elicit an *eww* from August. Then I tackled Clara to the sand, getting her good and dirty as she laughed, before carrying her into the ocean and dunking us both in the water.

Needed to justify that shower.

Later that night, after we'd celebrated and decided that I had yet another move to make—we were starting our next chapter in Welcome—I found Clara at the living room window, staring at the Cadillac in the driveway.

"I'll always be grateful for that car," she whispered, then raised her hand to look at the ring. "This was his wife's, right?"

"Yeah. That was Hope's ring."

"Hope." She leaned into my chest as I wrapped her in my arms. "I like that name."

WHEN OUR DAUGHTER was born nine months later, we named her Hope.

Two years after that, we named our son Lou.

It didn't take me long to realize that no amount of exploring the world would ever be as thrilling as the adventure of living life by Clara's side.

She was the soul on earth I was made to find.

EPILOGUE
CLARA

TWENTY-THREE YEARS LATER . . .

"Have you ever seen so many stars?" I whispered.

It was like someone had shattered a diamond on a blanket of the deepest blue velvet. The white whisps and swirls of the Milky Way streaked between them like dust.

This wasn't our first trip to Montana, but the clear mountain nights never failed to take my breath away.

Karson circled his arms around me, pulling me closer as I snuggled on his lap with my eyes to the sky. "It's something, isn't it?"

"Maybe we should move to Montana."

Aria laughed from her camp chair beside ours and shared a smirk with Brody at her side. "You wouldn't make it one winter."

"True." I laughed with her, tearing my eyes from the heavens.

We were circled around a bonfire, the light from the flames flickering over familiar faces.

Londyn and Brooks.

Gemma and Easton.

Katherine and Cash.

Aria and Brody.

Me and Karson.

My friends. My family.

"When we were in high school, we'd come out here to party," Cash said, tossing another log on the bonfire before he settled into his chair beside Katherine's. "Sneak beer and girls onto the ranch."

"Ugly girls, right?" Kat asked.

"Friends. Just friends." Cash leaned over to brush a kiss to her mouth.

"And I'm sure our parents knew we were out here, just like we knew every time the kids thought they were fooling us." Easton chuckled. "Jake built a fire so big one time his senior year we could see it from the house miles away."

Gemma smiled from her husband's lap, because like me, I'd opted for a warm embrace instead of a chair of my own. "When I told him we were coming to his party spot tonight, you should have seen the look on his face. Even though he's an adult, it's fun to remind him every now and then that his mother wasn't oblivious during his teenage years."

Their son was the spitting image of Easton. Jake had grown into a tall, strong man much like his father. Their daughter, on the other hand, looked a lot like Gemma. Hailey was beautiful, elegant and witty.

Lou had a massive crush on her, something he tried so hard to hide. But my youngest son hadn't yet realized that *his* mother wasn't oblivious either.

"Ellie's boyfriend seems nice," I told Londyn.

Brooks grumbled. "He's too nice. I don't trust him."

Londyn rolled her eyes. "*Someone* is having a hard time accepting that his three children are no longer children."

"Grandpa Brooks," Gemma teased. "Wyatt's twins sure are growing up fast. It feels like just yesterday they were three and we were giving them pony rides around the arena."

"It was yesterday." He chuckled. "Where is time going? When did we get old?"

"You're not the only one struggling," Brody said, sharing a look with Aria. "Trace told us on the trip up that he was offered a job in Dublin and is thinking of taking it."

"Dublin." I pressed a hand to my heart and looked to my sister. "That's an ocean away."

She shrugged, but the worry line between her eyebrows deepened. "Good thing we own an airplane."

And I doubted Millie would ever stray far from her parents, especially now that she'd graduated from college and taken a job with Brody's company. After he'd inherited Carmichael Communications from his family, he'd sold it and made a fortune. Then he'd turned around and started another mega-successful company with Millie under his wing. She was Aria's best friend and worshiped her dad.

"Who needs another beer?" Katherine asked. Her chair was closest to the cooler we'd brought out. When hands lifted, she popped up and hurried to deliver frosty bottles. Cash put his hand on her thigh when she returned to her seat, drawing circles on her jeans with his thumb to show her his love. And to trap her in the chair.

I'd give it five minutes before she was up again, finding something else to busy herself with. Katherine was coping with her emotions through perpetual motion.

"Good thing we snagged that cooler when we did," Easton said. "All the kids were congregating at the lodge and I saw the beginning of a party starting."

That was typical. Years ago, the parties had been sleeping bags and hot

666

cocoa and popcorn from the floor while they watched a movie projected onto a white wall. Then later, the parties had been games and teenage jokes until three in the morning. Maybe a kiss snuck here and there.

Our kids had grown up together. We lived in our own worlds and different towns, but at least once a year for the past twenty-three years, we'd come to Montana and spent a week at the Greer Ranch and Mountain Resort.

Now that our kids were out of the house, Karson and I came to Montana every few months. Arizona was home base, where we worked and lived, but the travel bug—Karson's love of exploring—had infected us both.

We went to Elyria a few times a year. We loved Hawaii and New York and London and Melbourne. Though most of our trips were to see the kids.

Hope had moved to Phoenix after graduating from college to work as a trainer for the Arizona Cardinals football franchise. Lou still had a year left at Stanford and then he was planning on law school. He'd mentioned a few schools on the East Coast, and I'd bitten my tongue before I could protest.

Like Aria had said, they owned a plane, one that they insisted Karson and I use often.

That plane had taken numerous trips to Montana, and not just for the annual summer reunion.

August had decided to go to Montana State for college, and I'd known his freshman year we'd lost him to the mountains.

Then we'd lost him to Delilah.

Not that I was complaining, because I loved her too. I'd loved her since she was a baby.

This year's trip to Montana wasn't just the yearly get-together. This year's trip was special.

In two days, August was marrying Cash and Katherine's oldest daughter.

It would be a wonderful spectacle compared to the courthouse ceremony Karson and I'd had at the Welcome courthouse, when I'd been a month pregnant with Hope.

August and Delilah's wedding promised to be a fancy affair. Hundreds of guests. A white gown. Five tiers of cake and a live band for the reception after the three-course meal.

Since we'd arrived earlier in the week, it had been nothing but wedding madness. August and Delilah were getting married in a meadow on the ranch. Cash and Easton had been working hard to get the field mowed and free of cowpies. Katherine, Gemma and the entire Greer family had spent months planning and preparing for the reception in the lodge.

It was all coming together but there had been plenty of work to do this week, leading up to the big day.

Tonight was the first time since we'd arrived that there hadn't been a planned function. It was the first time we'd gathered, just us. The runaways and our loves.

667

"Let's ask them now," I whispered into my husband's ear.

"Okay." He kissed my cheek.

I took a fortifying breath, then looked around our circle. "We wanted to run something by you guys."

"For the wedding?" Kat asked, sitting straighter.

"Sort of." I laced my fingers through Karson's, silently telling him to take over.

Like Katherine, I was a bundle of emotion this week. While she buried hers in activity, I'd resorted to what seemed like an endless stream of near-tear moments.

I was so happy for Gus. I was so proud of the man he'd become. And he loved Delilah with every cell in his body, treating her with such adoration and respect. I'd told him as much in another mess of tears a few days ago. Gus had hugged me and said he'd learned that from watching Karson. His dad.

But happy and proud, I still felt like I was losing my baby boy. So I'd been leaning on my husband, like tonight, to speak up for me when I couldn't get the words past the lump in my throat.

"We drove the Cadillac up here," Karson said. "As you know."

The day we'd pulled into the lodge's parking lot, everyone else had already been here. They'd descended on the car, greeting it like an old friend. This wasn't the first trip to Montana that we'd brought the car, and like past times, having it here gave everyone the chance to drive it again.

Gemma and Katherine had taken it to town on grocery store runs. Londyn and Brooks had spent a few hours getting lost on the Montana highways. Then Aria and Brody had done the same.

"We want to give it to August and Delilah," Karson said. "As a wedding present. But we wanted to check with you guys first."

The crackle of the fire was the only sound.

Then Londyn nodded and the smile that stretched across her face was brighter than the flames. "Yes. Absolutely."

"Best idea ever." Gemma nodded.

Cash shook his head in disbelief. "Are you sure?"

"It's time for that car to go to the next generation," Karson answered. "Your daughter. My son. I can't think of a better pair. And maybe someday, they'll continue the tradition. Send it down the road with someone else who needs it."

Katherine buried her face in her hands, her shoulders shaking. Cash stood and scooped her up, settling her on his lap. She took a moment, then sniffled and looked up, drying her eyes. "Sorry. I'm a wreck this week. Who needs another beer?"

Cash trapped her before she could stand. "No one needs another beer, sweetheart."

"Let's have a toast." Aria raised her beer bottle into the air. "To the original Lou."

I smiled. She'd deemed one Lou the original and the other Lou—my son—*the famous Lou*. "To the original Lou."

The circle cheered.

Lou usually got a toast at these functions. He'd stuck with us all, decades later, especially since every woman in the circle was wearing a piece of his jewelry. Lou had gifted Hope's jewelry to us all, along with our own respective letters.

Well, except for me.

Over the years, we'd shared the contents of those letters with each other. Mostly, Lou had written about his wife. Combined, those letters had given us a glimpse of his love for Hope, and wearing something of hers was an honor.

To Londyn, he'd gifted a gold locket. To Gemma, an opal pendant necklace. To Katherine, a pair of ruby stud earrings. To Aria, a ring adorned with tiny gold roses. I wore Hope's wedding rings as my own. And Karson wore Lou's wedding band, the piece Lou had gifted to me.

It was almost like he'd known that the man it was destined for was Karson. I liked to think so.

I dropped my forehead to Karson's, closing my eyes. "I love you."

"Love you too, baby." He cupped my cheek, tipping my face so he could cover my lips with his. We kissed like we had in the beginning. We kissed like we hadn't kissed for twenty-three years. We kissed like two people who had never taken our days for granted.

After I pulled my lips away from Karson's, I sat up straighter. "One more toast. To the junkyard."

It had long been demolished, but it lived in our hearts.

"To the junkyard," nine other voices said in unison.

To the place where our stories had started and the place we'd found a family.

To the place where I'd found the love of my life.

To the place that would bind us together forever.

ACKNOWLEDGMENTS

Thank you for reading *The Runaways*! These stories hold a special place in my heart and was a passion project of mine, inspired by a daydream I had one day when organizing my bookshelf.

When I was a kid, I loved reading. My favorite "chapter books" were The Boxcar Children. Over the years, I've been collecting them, hoping one day my own kids would love them as much as I did. One day I was in my office, staring at my bookshelf and lost in thought, when I spotted the spines for that series and wondered what happened to those kids as adults. From there, the junkyard and these characters were born.

Special thanks to Elizabeth Nover, Julie Deaton, Judy Zweifel, Sarah Hansen, Nina Grinstead, Logan Chisholm and Vicki Valente.

ABOUT THE AUTHOR

Devney Perry is a *Wall Street Journal, USA Today* and *#1 Amazon* bestselling author of over forty romance novels. After working in the technology industry for a decade, she abandoned conference calls and project schedules to pursue her passion for writing. She was born and raised in Montana and now lives in Washington with her husband and two sons.

Don't miss out on Devney's latest book news.
Subscribe to her newsletter!
www.devneyperry.com

Made in United States
North Haven, CT
01 August 2023

39813537R00407